My Little Pony
Friendship is Magic

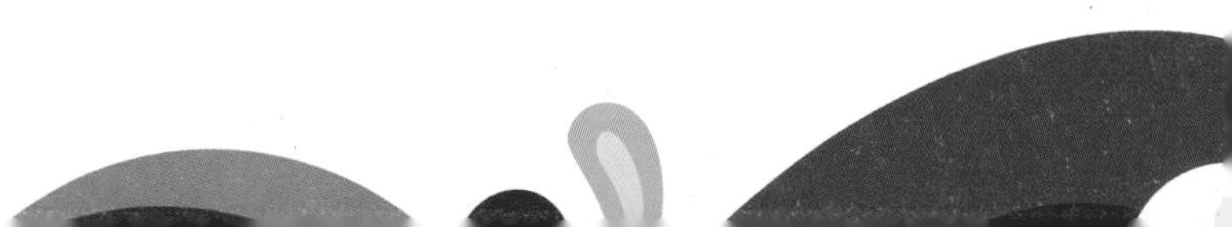

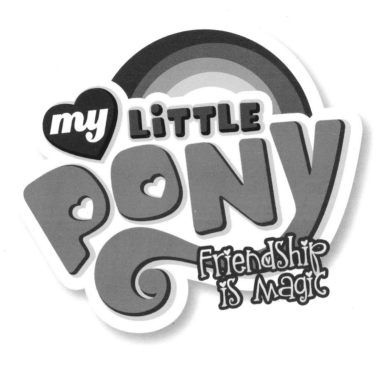

Become our fan on Facebook **facebook.com/idwpublishing**
Follow us on Twitter **@idwpublishing**
Subscribe to us on YouTube **youtube.com/idwpublishing**
See what's new on Tumblr **tumblr.idwpublishing.com**
Check us out on Instagram **instagram.com/idwpublishing**

Licensed By:

978-1-63140-140-4   23 22 21 20   6 7 8 9

COVER BY
AGNES GARBOWSKA

COLLECTION EDITS BY
JUSTIN EISINGER
AND ALONZO SIMON

COLLECTION DESIGN BY
GILBERTO LAZCANO

Jerry Bennington, President
Nachie Marsham, Publisher
Cara Morrison, Chief Financial Officer
Matthew Ruzicka, Chief Accounting Officer
Rebekah Cahalin, EVP of Operations
John Barber, Editor-in-Chief
Justin Eisinger, Editorial Director, Graphic Novels and Collections
Scott Dunbier, Director, Special Projects
Blake Kobashigawa, VP of Sales
Lorelei Bunjes, VP of Technology & Information Services
Anna Morrow, Sr Marketing Director
Tara McCrillis, Director of Design & Production
Mike Ford, Director of Operations
Shauna Monteforte, Manufacturing Operations Director

Ted Adams and Robbie Robbins, IDW Founders

For international rights, please
contact licensing@idwpublishing.com

written by
Katie Cook
& Heather Nuhfer

art by
Andy Price
& Amy Mebberson

colors by
Heather Breckel

lettered by
Neil Uyetake
& Robbie Robbins

series edits by
Bobby Curnow

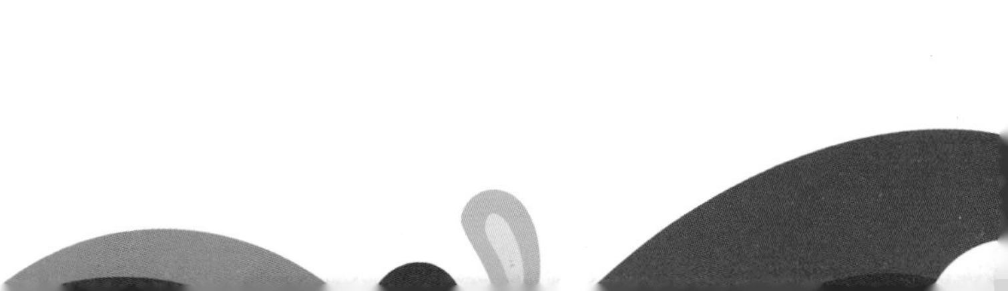

Twilight Sparkle

Twilight Sparkle is a unicorn with a big heart. Even though she prefers to have her muzzle stuck in a book, she's always willing to put her work aside to help her friends! She's also one of the most magically gifted unicorns there is, thanks to her studies and the personal guidance of Princess Celestia.

Rarity

Rarity is a unicorn who has dedicated her life to making beautiful things... she's a fashion designer in Ponyville and has aspirations to be "the biggest thing in Equestria." She has big dreams, but she's very dedicated to her Ponyville friends who have always been there for her.

Fluttershy

Fluttershy is a shy pegasus with a gentle hoof. Her love and understanding of animals is almost legendary to the ponies around her. She's calm and collected, even when faced with some of the scariest beings in the Everfree Forest!

Applejack

Applejack is a pony you can trust. She's the hardest worker in all of Ponyville and will always be there to lend a helping hoof! She and her family run Sweet Apple Acres, the foremost place to acquire apples and apple-related goodies in Ponyville.

Pinkie Pie

Pinkie Pie is a pony that likes to PAR-TAY. Friendly, funny... and maybe a little weird, Pinkie Pie is always on hoof for a celebration for any occasion! She's always there with a smile and an elaborate cake, even if she's just saying "thanks for pet-sitting my alligator."

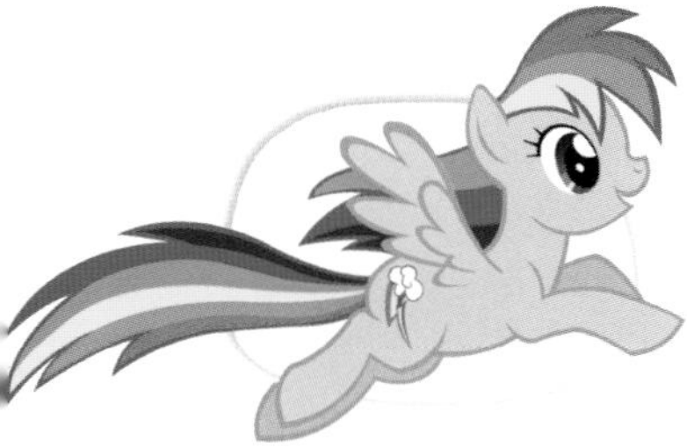

Rainbow Dash

Rainbow Dash is the fastest pegasus around… and she KNOWS it! Never one to turn down a challenge, she's always ready to seize the day (in the spirit of friendly competition of course!).

Spike

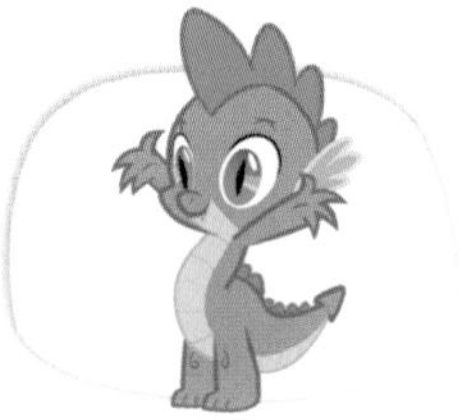

Spike the Dragon is the pint-sized assistant to Twilight Sparkle. Besides helping her out in the Ponyville library, he helps her practice spells and the duties of her daily life… he may be in the designated role of "helper," but he's also her dear friend.

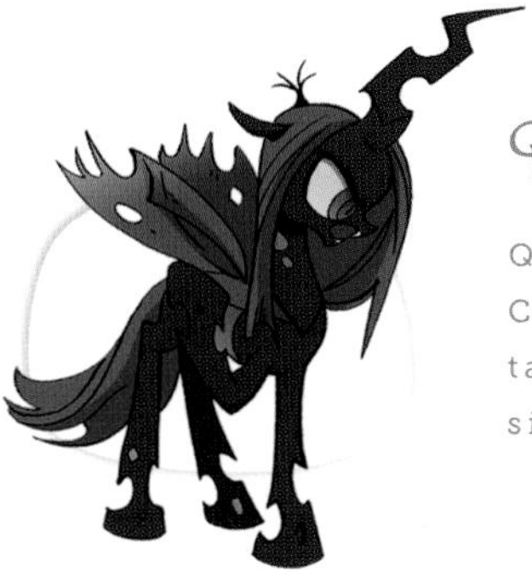

Queen Chrysalis

Queen Chrysalis is the Queen of the Changelings. After a failed attempt to take over Equestria, she now has her sights set on Twilight and her friends.

Princess Celestia

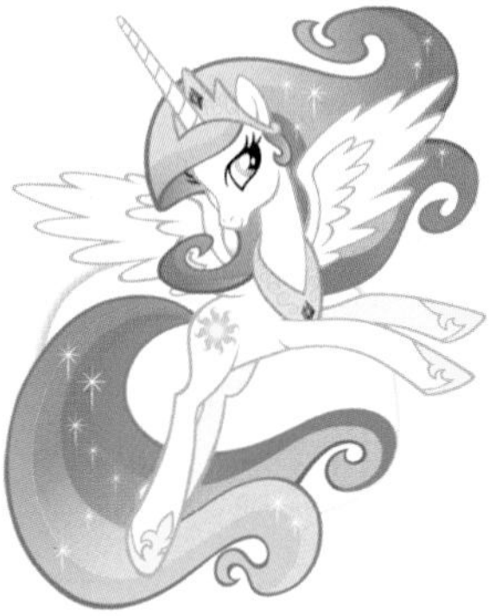

Princess Celestia is the ruler of Equestria and Twilight Sparkle's mentor. Princess Celestia is kind, gentle, and powerful… everything she needs to be to rule and protect her kingdom.

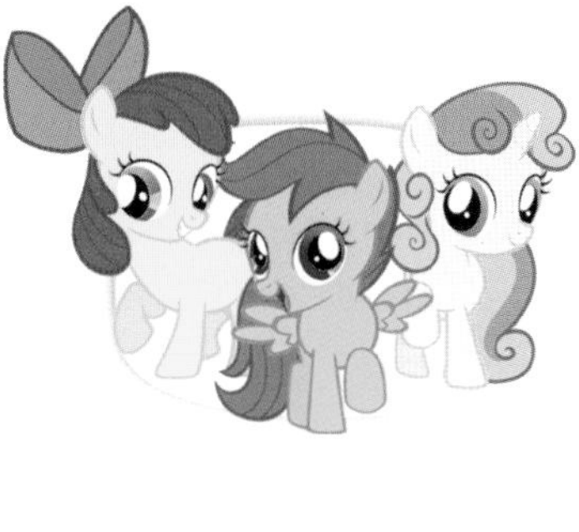

The Cutie Mark Crusaders

The Cutie Mark Crusaders are comprised of Sweetie Belle, Apple Bloom, and Scootaloo. These young fillies have yet to earn their cutie marks (the image on a pony's flank depicting their special talent!) and they are dashing through task after task together with the sole purpose of finding what makes them unique.

Art by
Stephanie Buscema

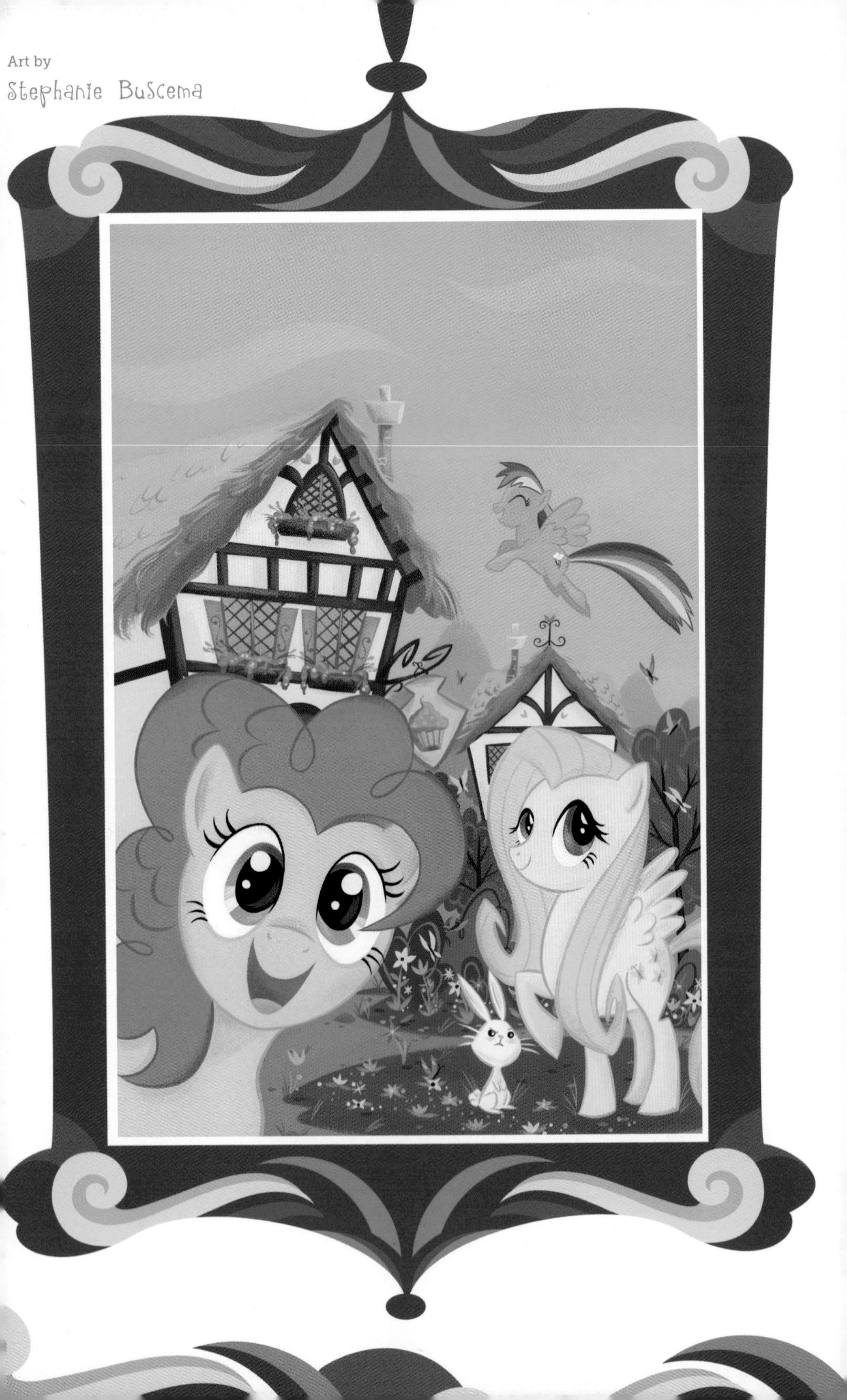

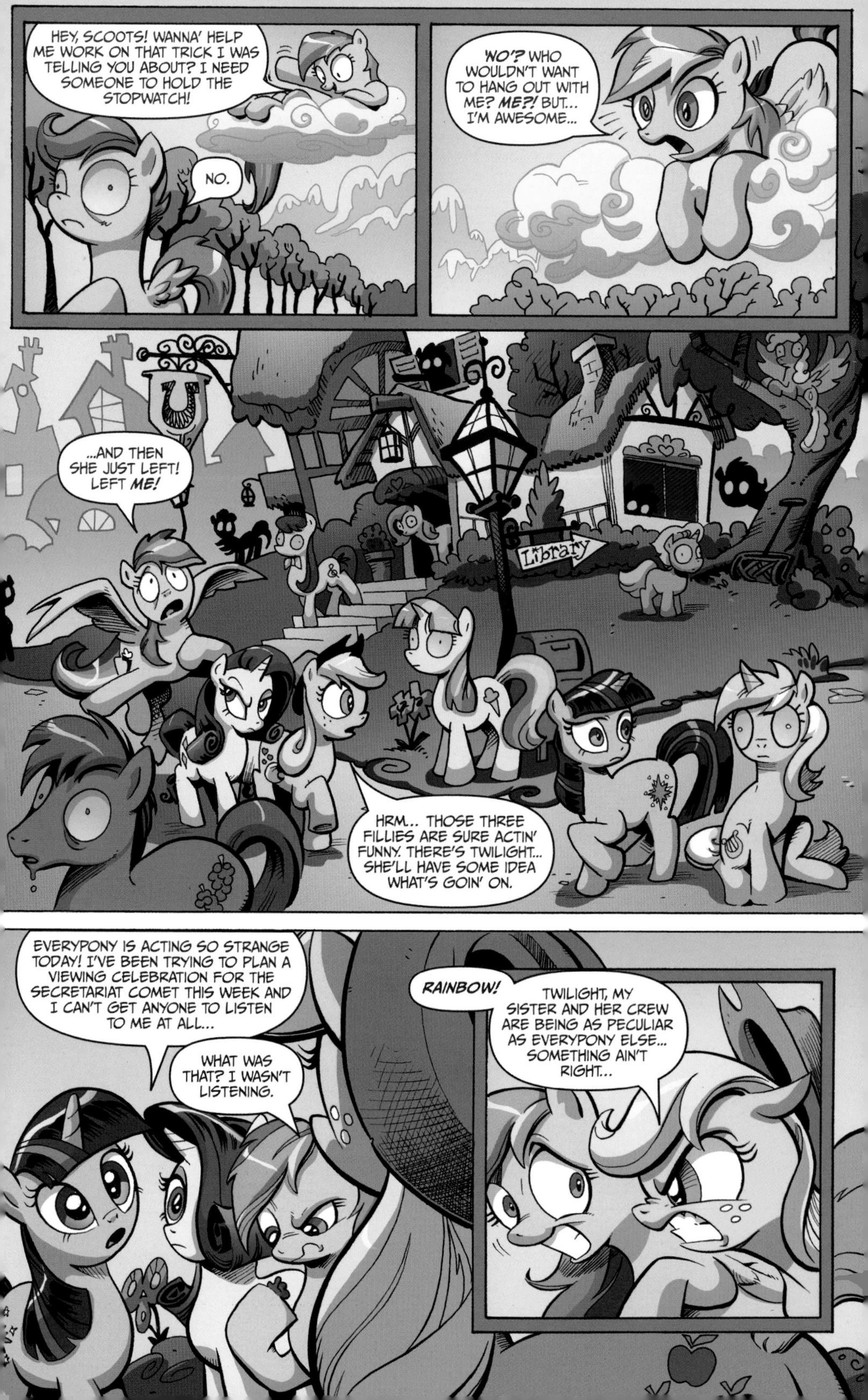
HEY, SCOOTS! WANNA' HELP ME WORK ON THAT TRICK I WAS TELLING YOU ABOUT? I NEED SOMEONE TO HOLD THE STOPWATCH!
NO.
'NO'? WHO WOULDN'T WANT TO HANG OUT WITH ME? ME?! BUT... I'M AWESOME...
...AND THEN SHE JUST LEFT! LEFT ME!
Library
HRM... THOSE THREE FILLIES ARE SURE ACTIN' FUNNY. THERE'S TWILIGHT... SHE'LL HAVE SOME IDEA WHAT'S GOIN' ON.
EVERYPONY IS ACTING SO STRANGE TODAY! I'VE BEEN TRYING TO PLAN A VIEWING CELEBRATION FOR THE SECRETARIAT COMET THIS WEEK AND I CAN'T GET ANYONE TO LISTEN TO ME AT ALL...
WHAT WAS THAT? I WASN'T LISTENING.
RAINBOW!
TWILIGHT, MY SISTER AND HER CREW ARE BEING AS PECULIAR AS EVERYPONY ELSE... SOMETHING AIN'T RIGHT...

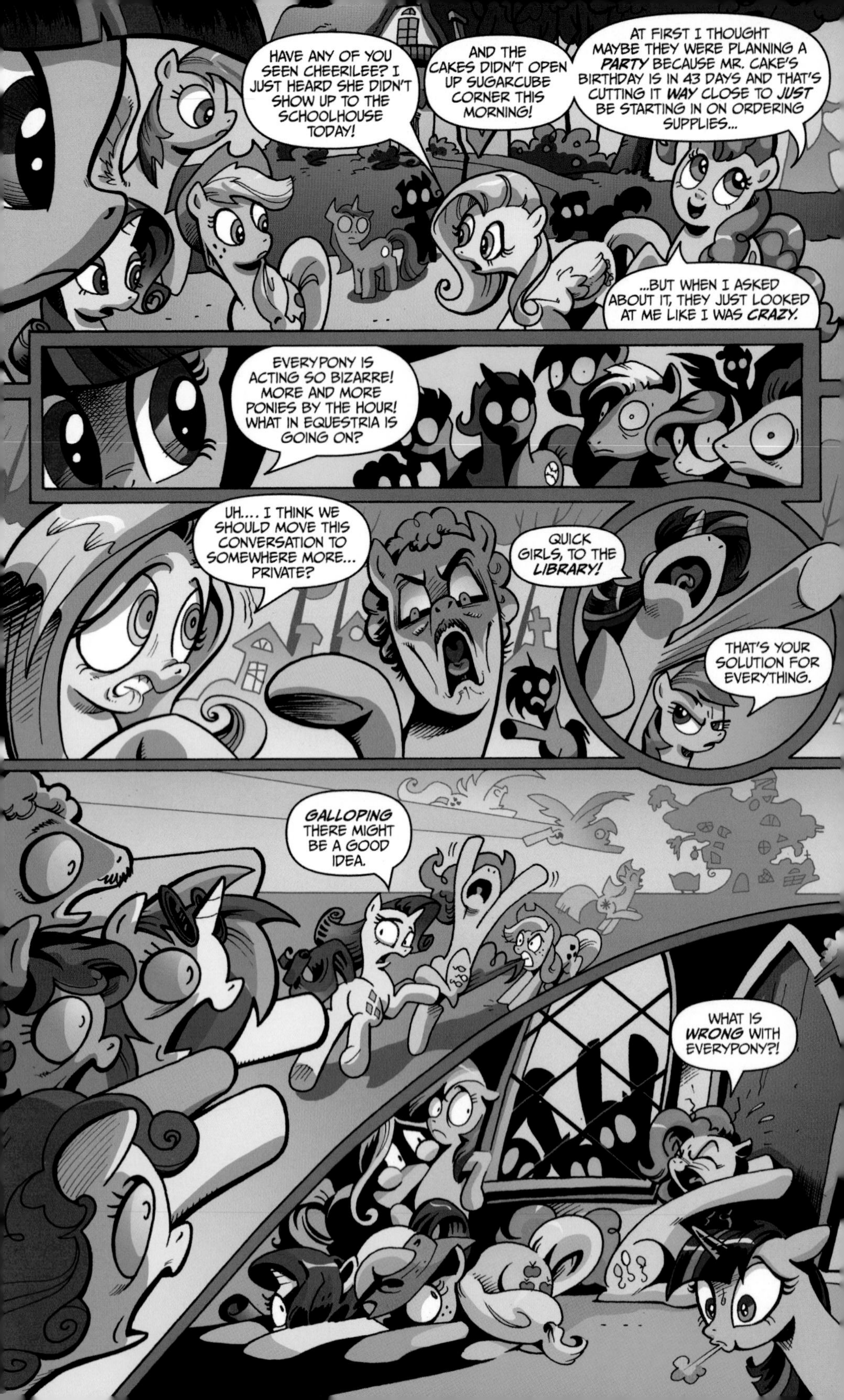
HAVE ANY OF YOU SEEN CHEERILEE? I JUST HEARD SHE DIDN'T SHOW UP TO THE SCHOOLHOUSE TODAY!
AND THE CAKES DIDN'T OPEN UP SUGARCUBE CORNER THIS MORNING!
AT FIRST I THOUGHT MAYBE THEY WERE PLANNING A *PARTY* BECAUSE MR. CAKE'S BIRTHDAY IS IN 43 DAYS AND THAT'S CUTTING IT *WAY* CLOSE TO *JUST* BE STARTING IN ON ORDERING SUPPLIES...
...BUT WHEN I ASKED ABOUT IT, THEY JUST LOOKED AT ME LIKE I WAS *CRAZY.*
EVERYPONY IS ACTING SO BIZARRE! MORE AND MORE PONIES BY THE HOUR! WHAT IN EQUESTRIA IS GOING ON?
UH.... I THINK WE SHOULD MOVE THIS CONVERSATION TO SOMEWHERE MORE... PRIVATE?
QUICK GIRLS, TO THE *LIBRARY!*
THAT'S YOUR SOLUTION FOR EVERYTHING.
GALLOPING THERE MIGHT BE A GOOD IDEA.
WHAT IS *WRONG* WITH EVERYPONY?!

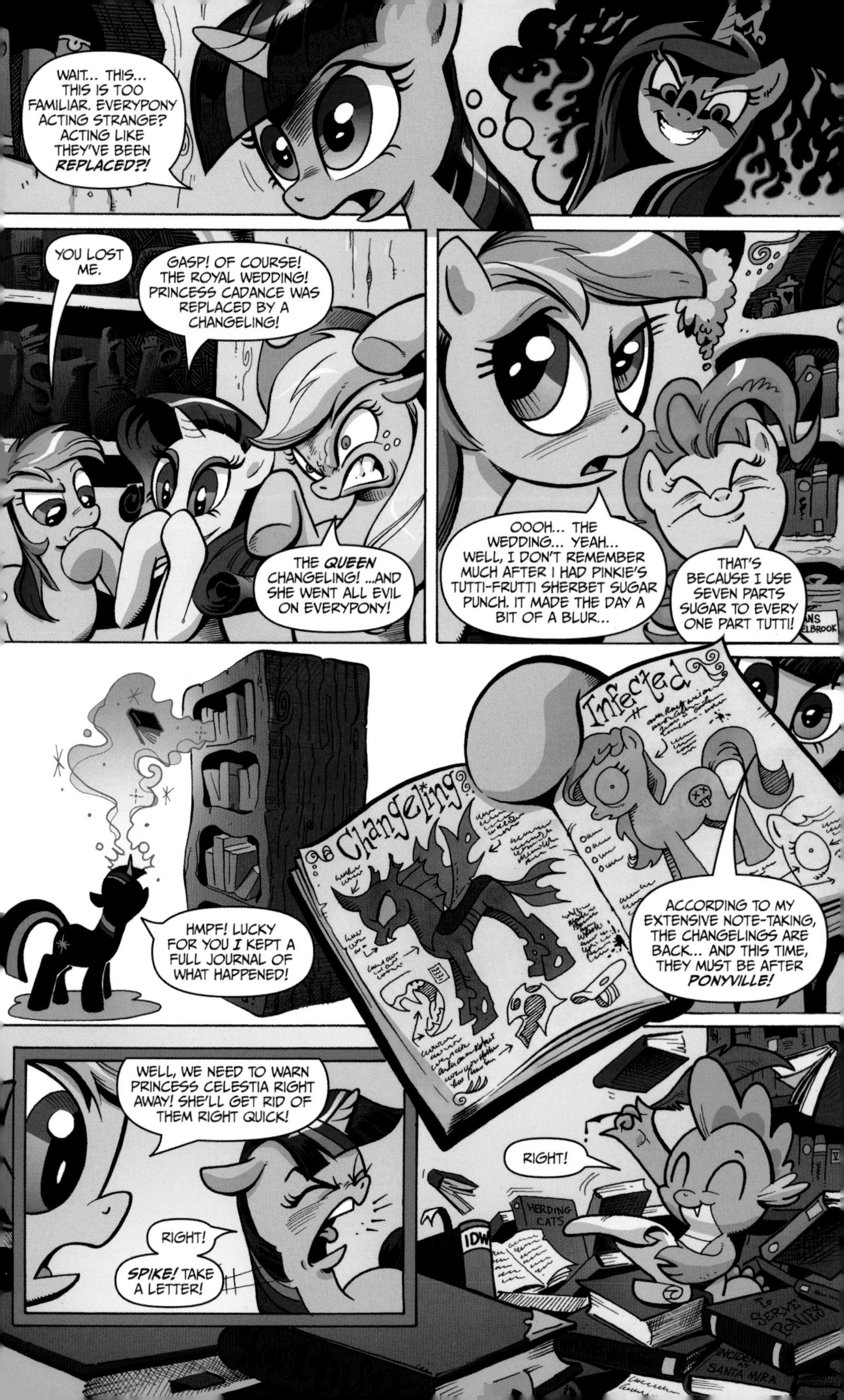

WAIT... THIS... THIS IS TOO FAMILIAR. EVERYPONY ACTING STRANGE? ACTING LIKE THEY'VE BEEN *REPLACED?!*
YOU LOST ME.
GASP! OF COURSE! THE ROYAL WEDDING! PRINCESS CADANCE WAS REPLACED BY A CHANGELING!
THE *QUEEN* CHANGELING! ...AND SHE WENT ALL EVIL ON EVERYPONY!
OOOH... THE WEDDING... YEAH... WELL, I DON'T REMEMBER MUCH AFTER I HAD PINKIE'S TUTTI-FRUTTI SHERBET SUGAR PUNCH. IT MADE THE DAY A BIT OF A BLUR...
THAT'S BECAUSE I USE SEVEN PARTS SUGAR TO EVERY ONE PART TUTTI!
HMPF! LUCKY FOR YOU *I* KEPT A FULL JOURNAL OF WHAT HAPPENED!
Changeling
Infected
ACCORDING TO MY EXTENSIVE NOTE-TAKING, THE CHANGELINGS ARE BACK... AND THIS TIME, THEY MUST BE AFTER *PONYVILLE!*
WELL, WE NEED TO WARN PRINCESS CELESTIA RIGHT AWAY! SHE'LL GET RID OF THEM RIGHT QUICK!
RIGHT!
SPIKE! TAKE A LETTER!
RIGHT!
HERDING CATS
IDW
TO SERVE PONIES
INCIDENT AT SANTA MIRA

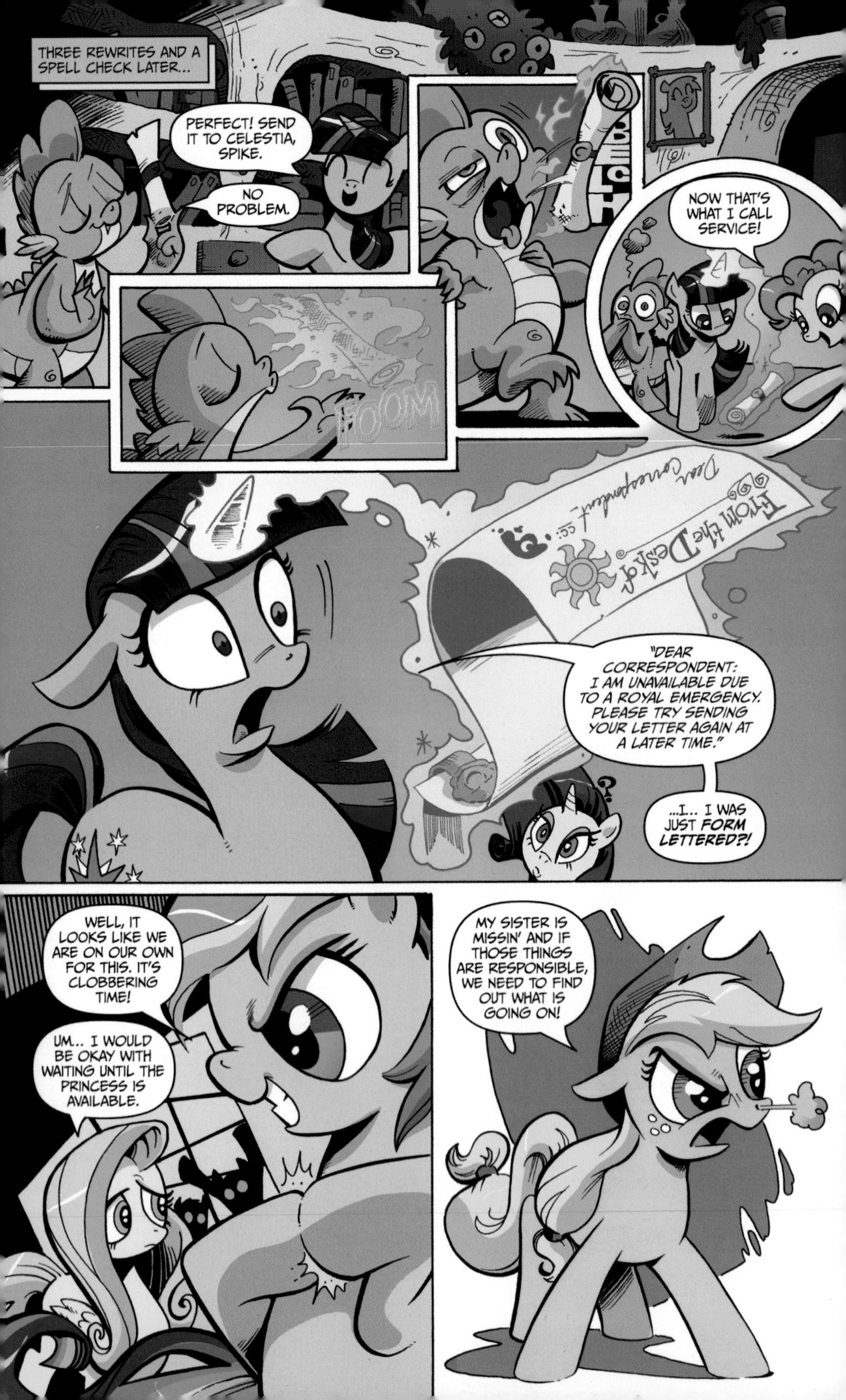
THREE REWRITES AND A SPELL CHECK LATER...
PERFECT! SEND IT TO CELESTIA, SPIKE.
NO PROBLEM.
FOOM
BELCH
NOW THAT'S WHAT I CALL SERVICE!
From the Desk of
Dear correspondent,
"DEAR CORRESPONDENT: I AM UNAVAILABLE DUE TO A ROYAL EMERGENCY. PLEASE TRY SENDING YOUR LETTER AGAIN AT A LATER TIME."
...I... I WAS JUST FORM LETTERED?!
WELL, IT LOOKS LIKE WE ARE ON OUR OWN FOR THIS. IT'S CLOBBERING TIME!
UM... I WOULD BE OKAY WITH WAITING UNTIL THE PRINCESS IS AVAILABLE.
MY SISTER IS MISSIN' AND IF THOSE THINGS ARE RESPONSIBLE, WE NEED TO FIND OUT WHAT IS GOING ON!

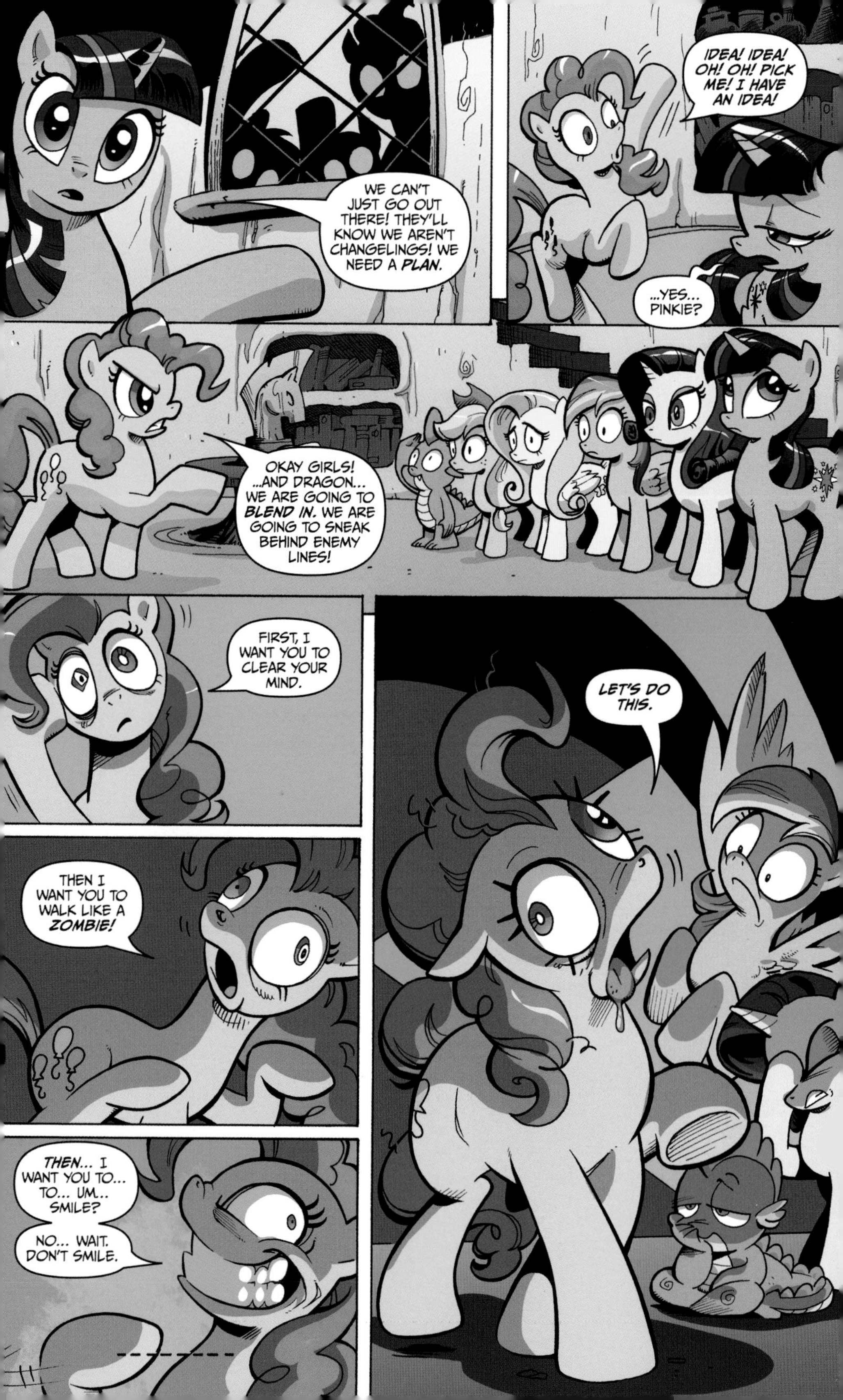
WE CAN'T JUST GO OUT THERE! THEY'LL KNOW WE AREN'T CHANGELINGS! WE NEED A PLAN.
IDEA! IDEA! OH! OH! PICK ME! I HAVE AN IDEA!
...YES... PINKIE?
OKAY GIRLS! ...AND DRAGON... WE ARE GOING TO BLEND IN. WE ARE GOING TO SNEAK BEHIND ENEMY LINES!
FIRST, I WANT YOU TO CLEAR YOUR MIND.
THEN I WANT YOU TO WALK LIKE A ZOMBIE!
THEN... I WANT YOU TO... TO... UM... SMILE?
NO... WAIT. DON'T SMILE.
LET'S DO THIS.

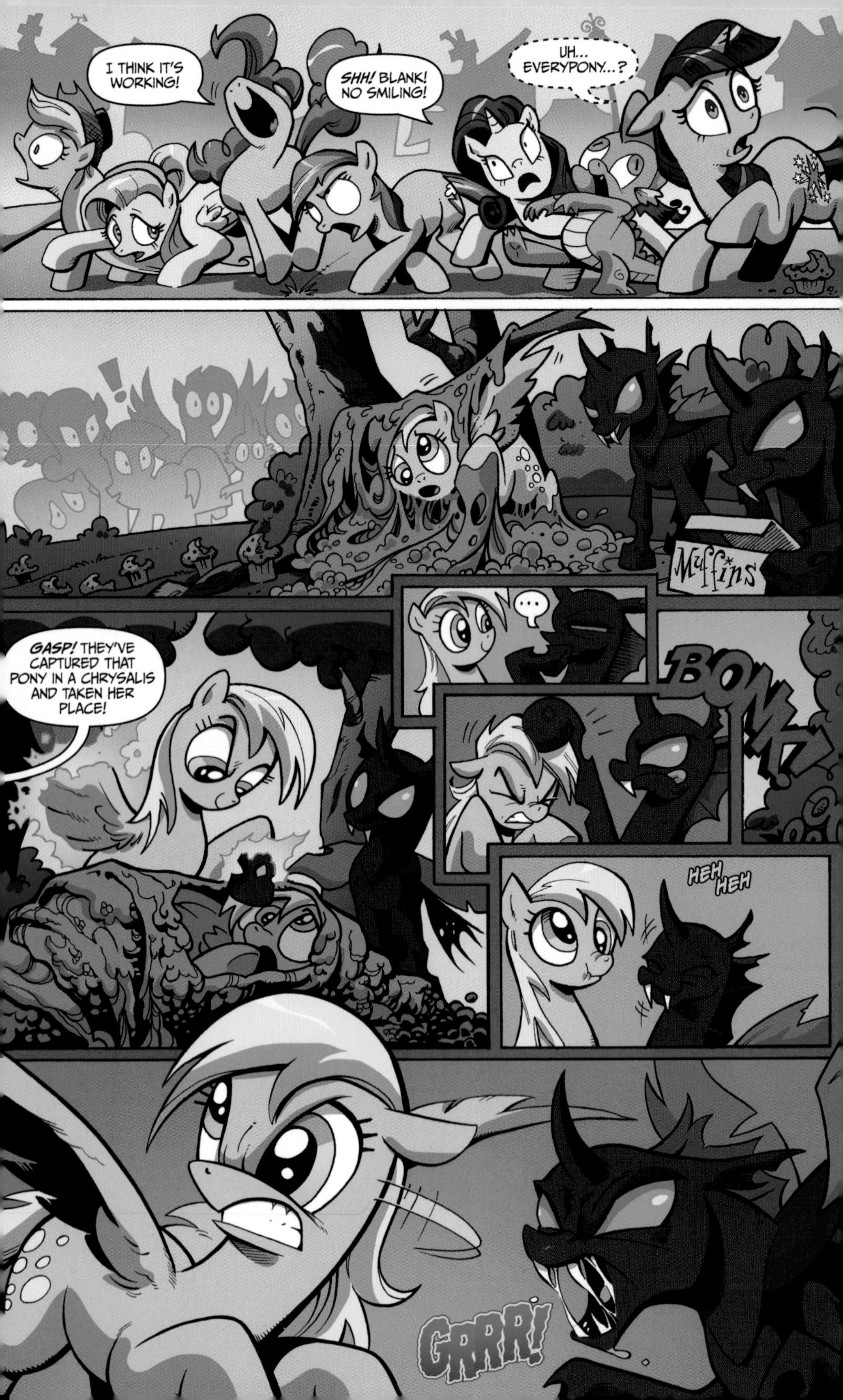

I THINK IT'S WORKING!
SHH! BLANK! NO SMILING!
UH... EVERYPONY...?
Muffins
GASP! THEY'VE CAPTURED THAT PONY IN A CHRYSALIS AND TAKEN HER PLACE!
...
BONK!
HEH HEH
GRRR!

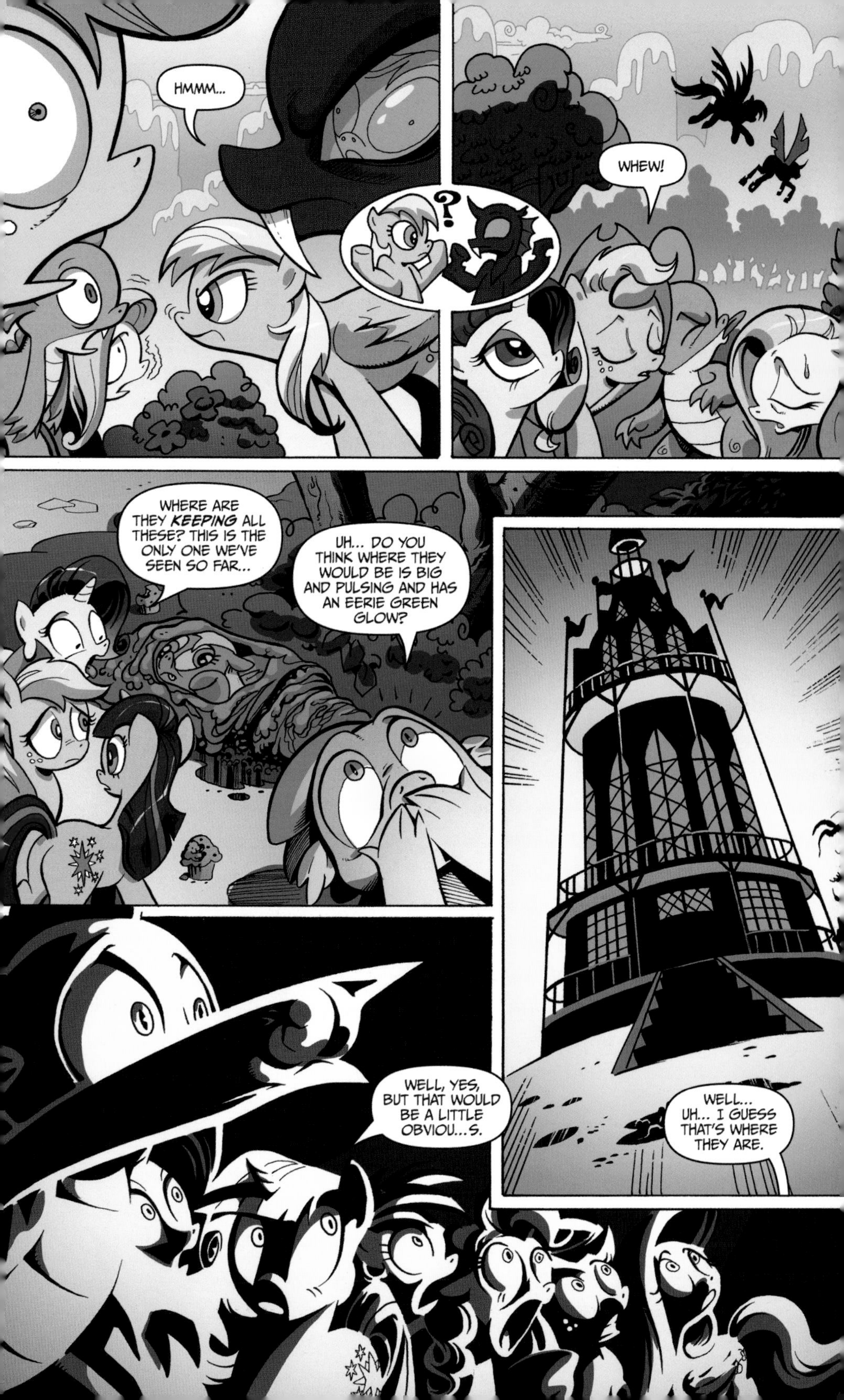
HMMM...
?
WHEW!
WHERE ARE THEY *KEEPING* ALL THESE? THIS IS THE ONLY ONE WE'VE SEEN SO FAR...
UH... DO YOU THINK WHERE THEY WOULD BE IS BIG AND PULSING AND HAS AN EERIE GREEN GLOW?
WELL, YES, BUT THAT WOULD BE A LITTLE OBVIOU...S.
WELL... UH... I GUESS THAT'S WHERE THEY ARE.

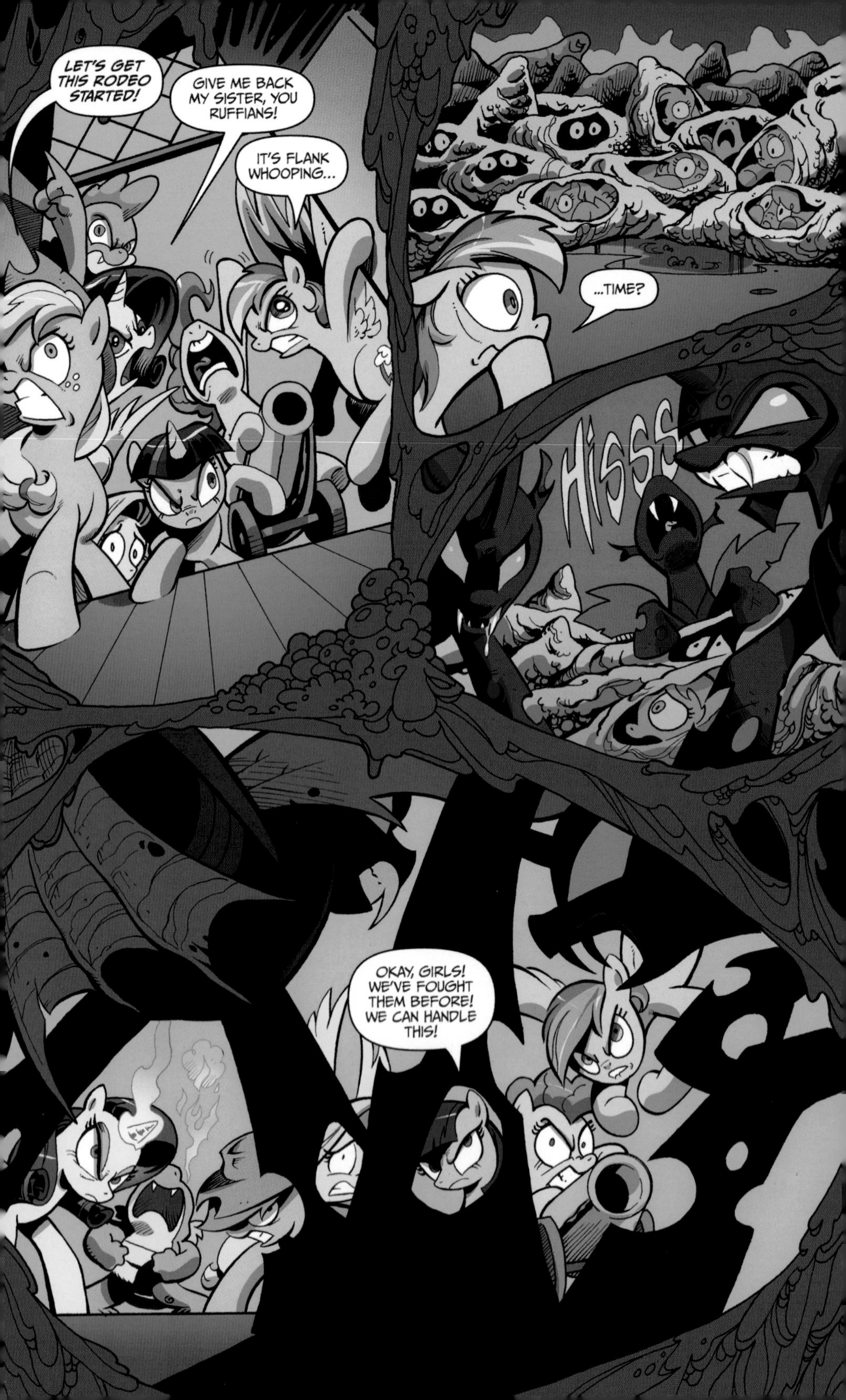
LET'S GET THIS RODEO STARTED!
GIVE ME BACK MY SISTER, YOU RUFFIANS!
IT'S FLANK WHOOPING...
...TIME?
HISSS
OKAY, GIRLS! WE'VE FOUGHT THEM BEFORE! WE CAN HANDLE THIS!

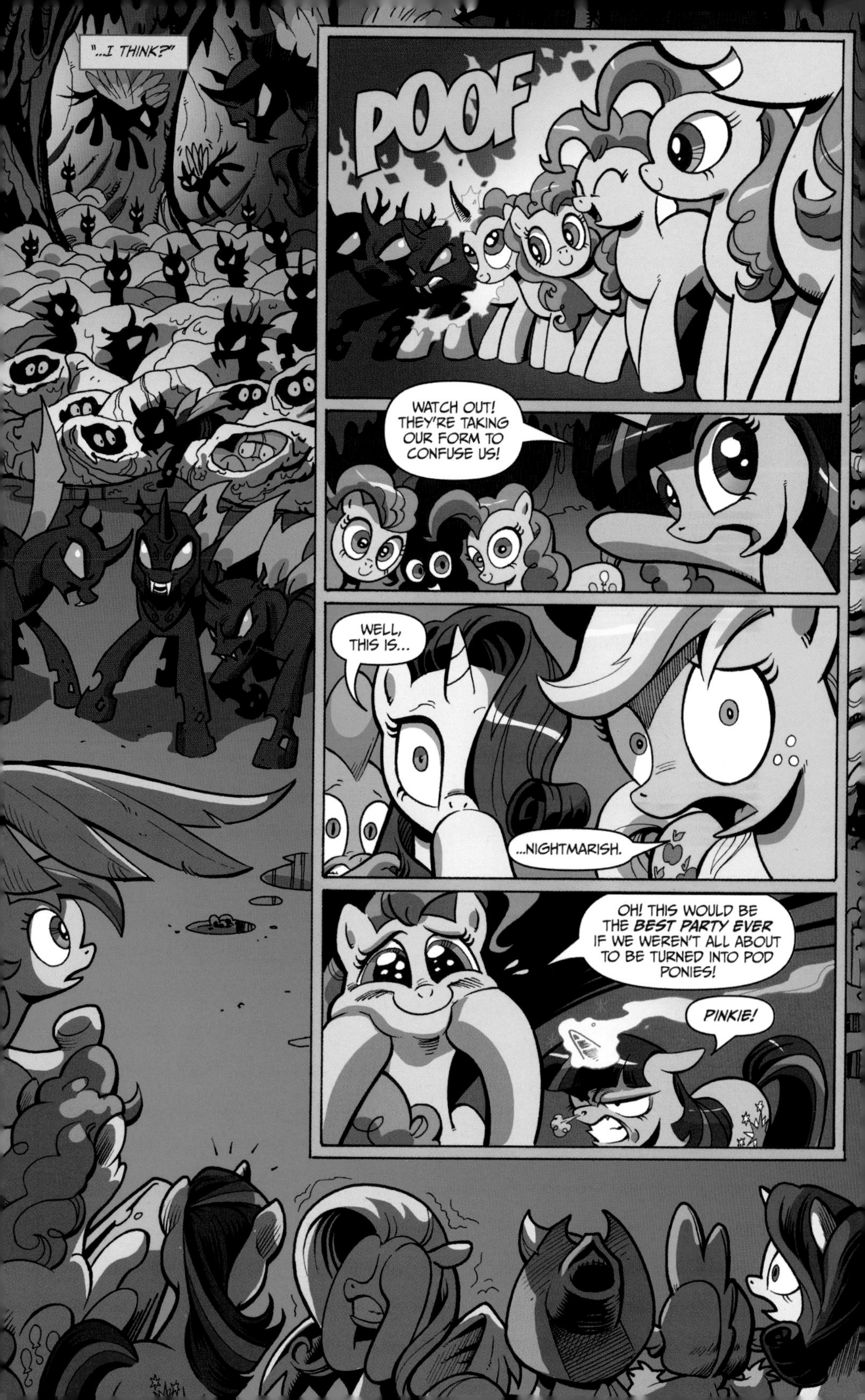
"...I THINK?"
POOF
WATCH OUT! THEY'RE TAKING OUR FORM TO CONFUSE US!
WELL, THIS IS...
...NIGHTMARISH.
OH! THIS WOULD BE THE ***BEST PARTY EVER*** IF WE WEREN'T ALL ABOUT TO BE TURNED INTO POD PONIES!
PINKIE!

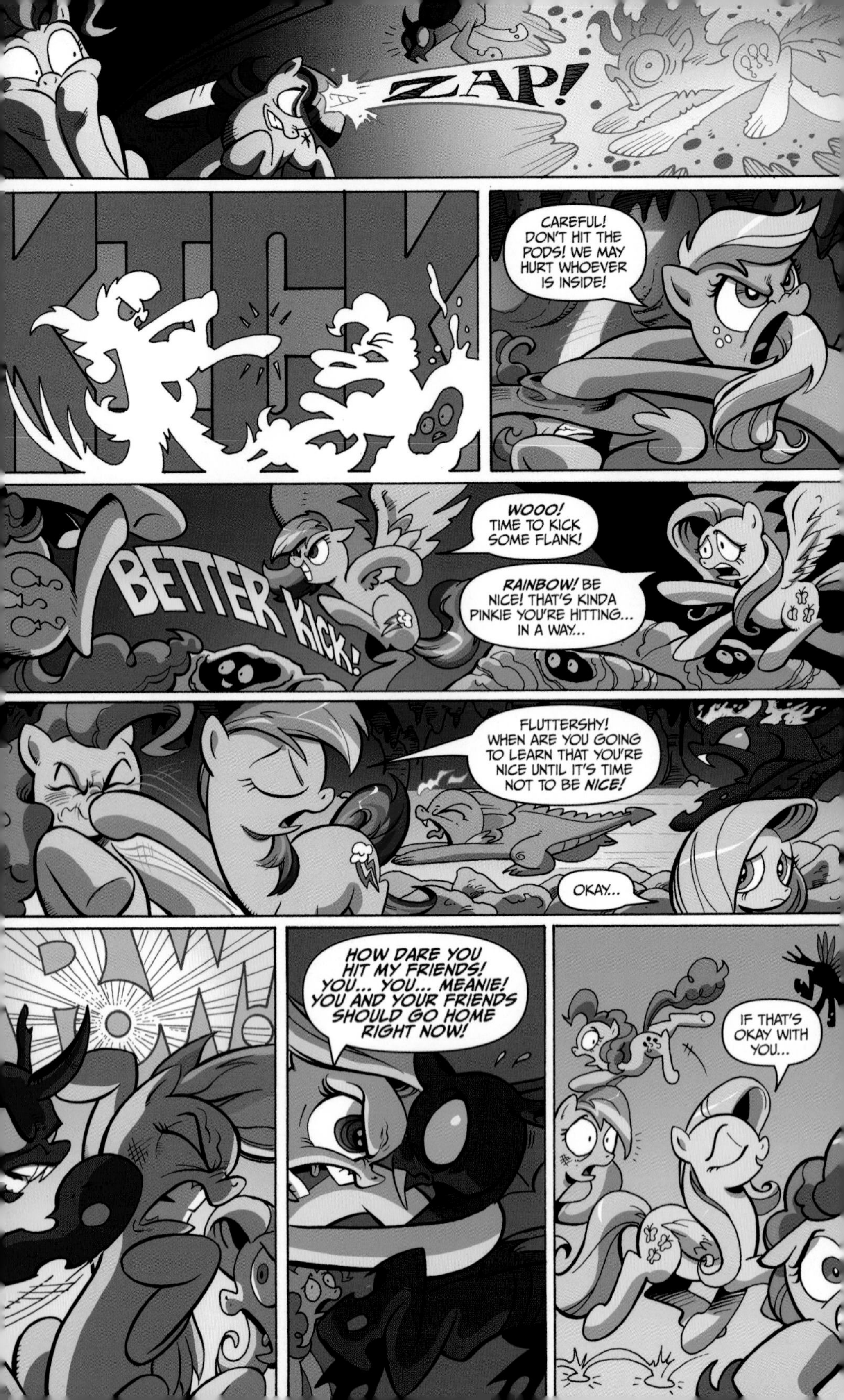
ZAP!
CAREFUL! DON'T HIT THE PODS! WE MAY HURT WHOEVER IS INSIDE!
WOOO! TIME TO KICK SOME FLANK!
BETTER KICK!
RAINBOW! BE NICE! THAT'S KINDA PINKIE YOU'RE HITTING... IN A WAY...
FLUTTERSHY! WHEN ARE YOU GOING TO LEARN THAT YOU'RE NICE UNTIL IT'S TIME NOT TO BE NICE!
OKAY...
HOW DARE YOU HIT MY FRIENDS! YOU... YOU... MEANIE! YOU AND YOUR FRIENDS SHOULD GO HOME RIGHT NOW!
IF THAT'S OKAY WITH YOU...

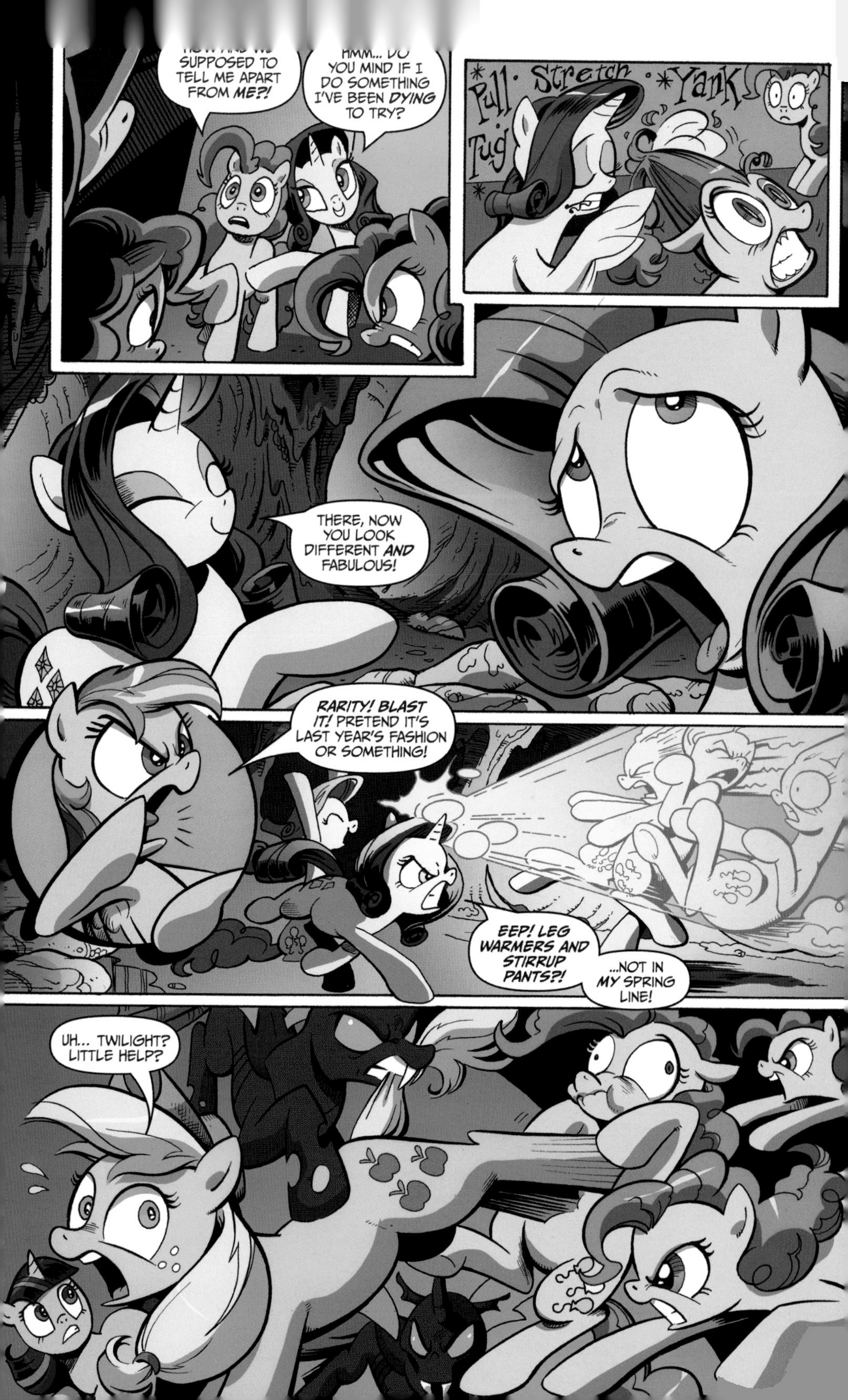

SUPPOSED TO TELL ME APART FROM ME?!
HMM... DO YOU MIND IF I DO SOMETHING I'VE BEEN DYING TO TRY?
Pull · Stretch · Yank!
Tug
THERE, NOW YOU LOOK DIFFERENT AND FABULOUS!
RARITY! BLAST IT! PRETEND IT'S LAST YEAR'S FASHION OR SOMETHING!
EEP! LEG WARMERS AND STIRRUP PANTS?!
...NOT IN MY SPRING LINE!
UH... TWILIGHT? LITTLE HELP?

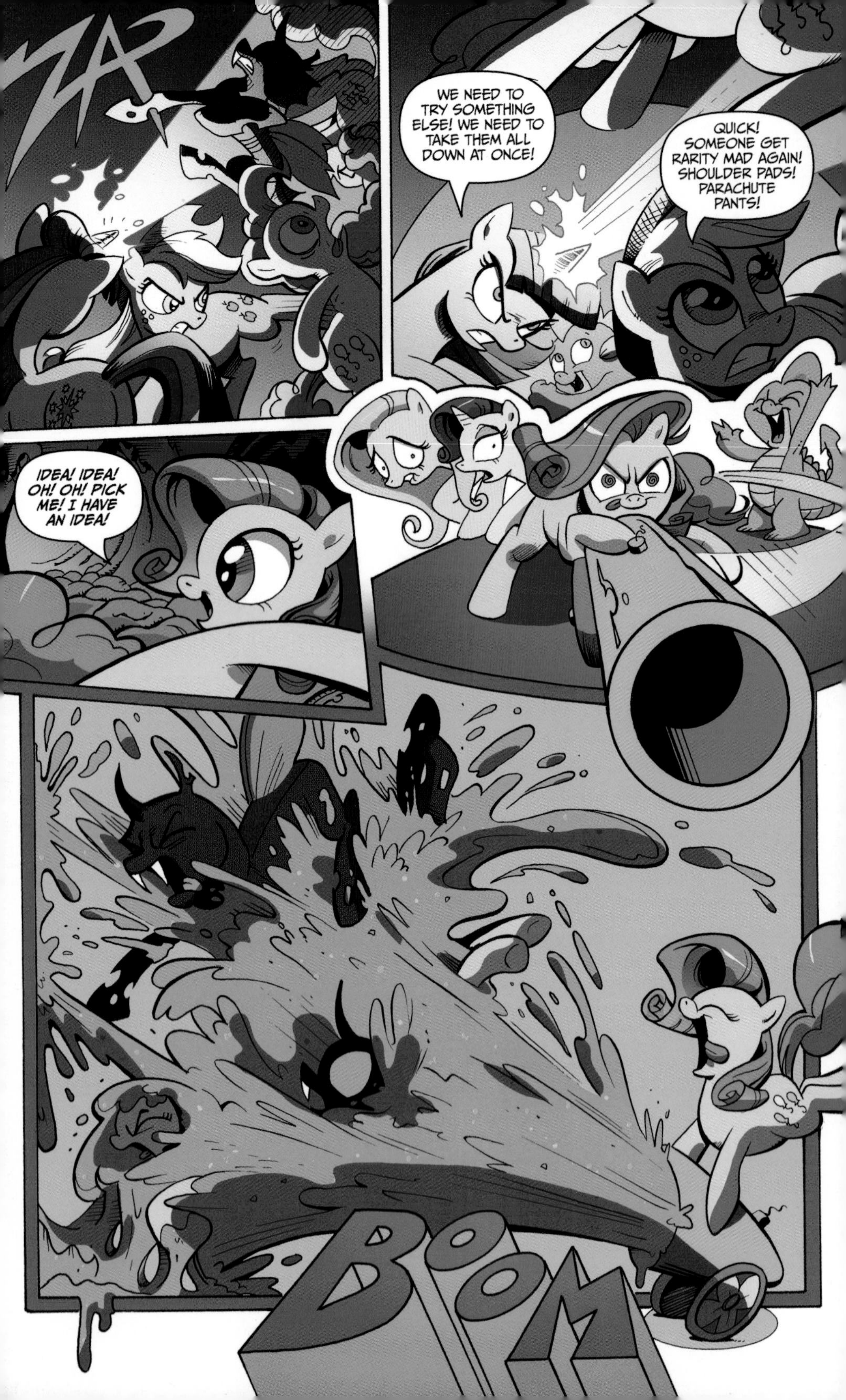
ZAP
WE NEED TO TRY SOMETHING ELSE! WE NEED TO TAKE THEM ALL DOWN AT ONCE!
QUICK! SOMEONE GET RARITY MAD AGAIN! SHOULDER PADS! PARACHUTE PANTS!
IDEA! IDEA! OH! OH! PICK ME! I HAVE AN IDEA!
BOOM

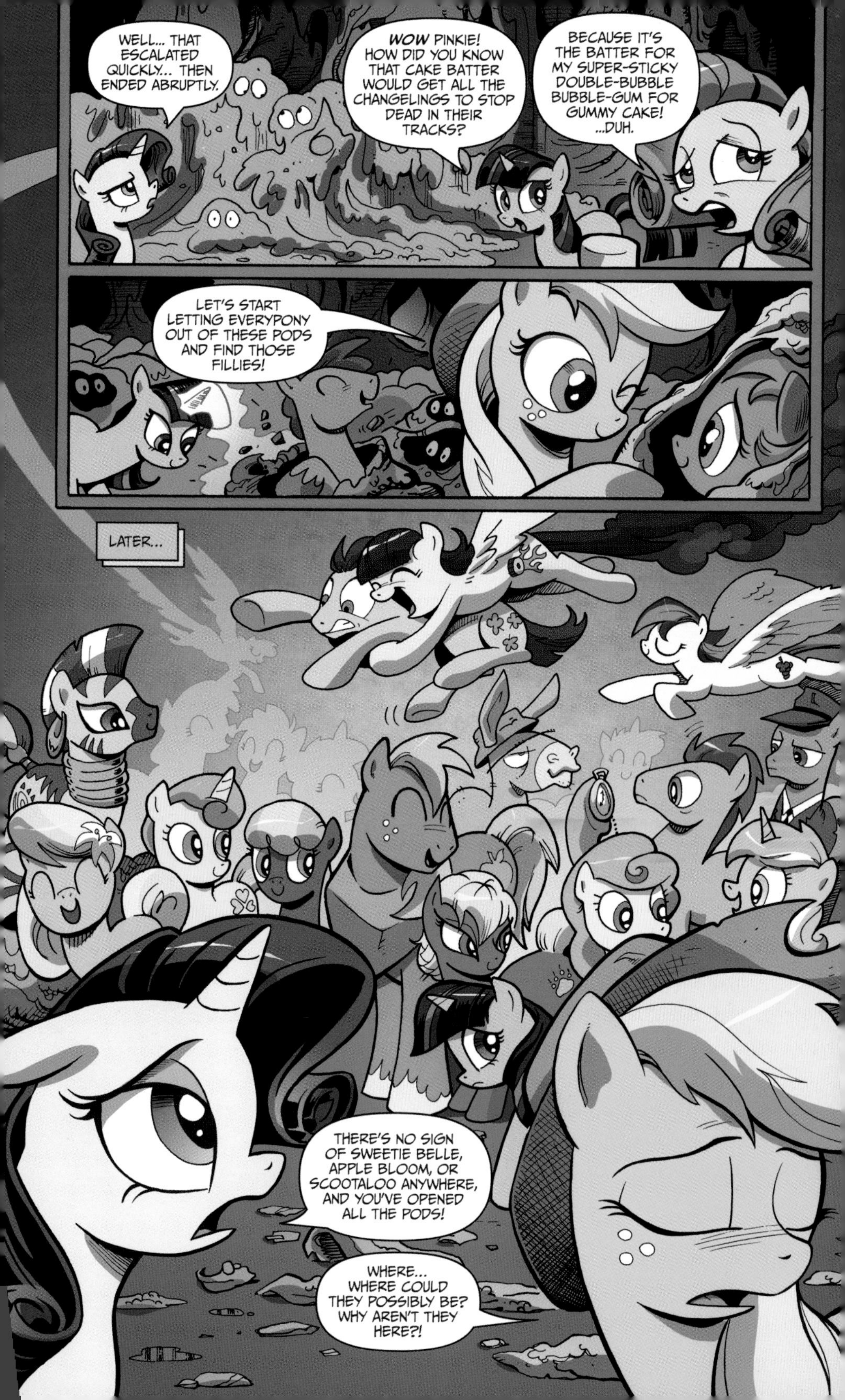
WELL... THAT ESCALATED QUICKLY... THEN ENDED ABRUPTLY.
WOW PINKIE! HOW DID YOU KNOW THAT CAKE BATTER WOULD GET ALL THE CHANGELINGS TO STOP DEAD IN THEIR TRACKS?
BECAUSE IT'S THE BATTER FOR MY SUPER-STICKY DOUBLE-BUBBLE BUBBLE-GUM FOR GUMMY CAKE! ...DUH.
LET'S START LETTING EVERYPONY OUT OF THESE PODS AND FIND THOSE FILLIES!
LATER...
THERE'S NO SIGN OF SWEETIE BELLE, APPLE BLOOM, OR SCOOTALOO ANYWHERE, AND YOU'VE OPENED ALL THE PODS!
WHERE... WHERE COULD THEY POSSIBLY BE? WHY AREN'T THEY HERE?!

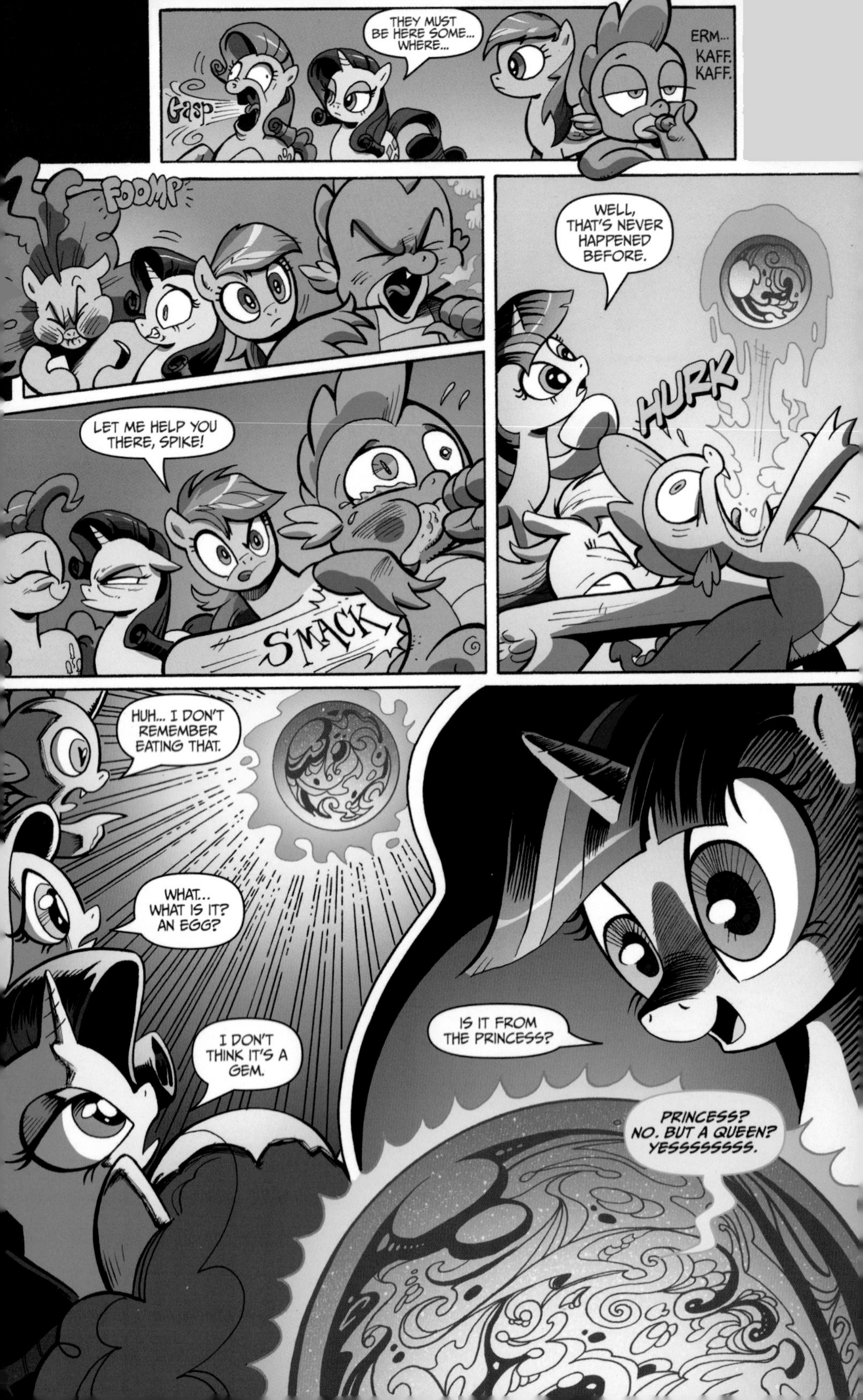
GASP
THEY MUST BE HERE SOME... WHERE...
ERM... KAFF. KAFF.
FOOMP
WELL, THAT'S NEVER HAPPENED BEFORE.
LET ME HELP YOU THERE, SPIKE!
SMACK
HURK
HUH... I DON'T REMEMBER EATING THAT.
WHAT... WHAT IS IT? AN EGG?
I DON'T THINK IT'S A GEM.
IS IT FROM THE PRINCESS?
PRINCESS? NO. BUT A QUEEN? YESSSSSSSS.

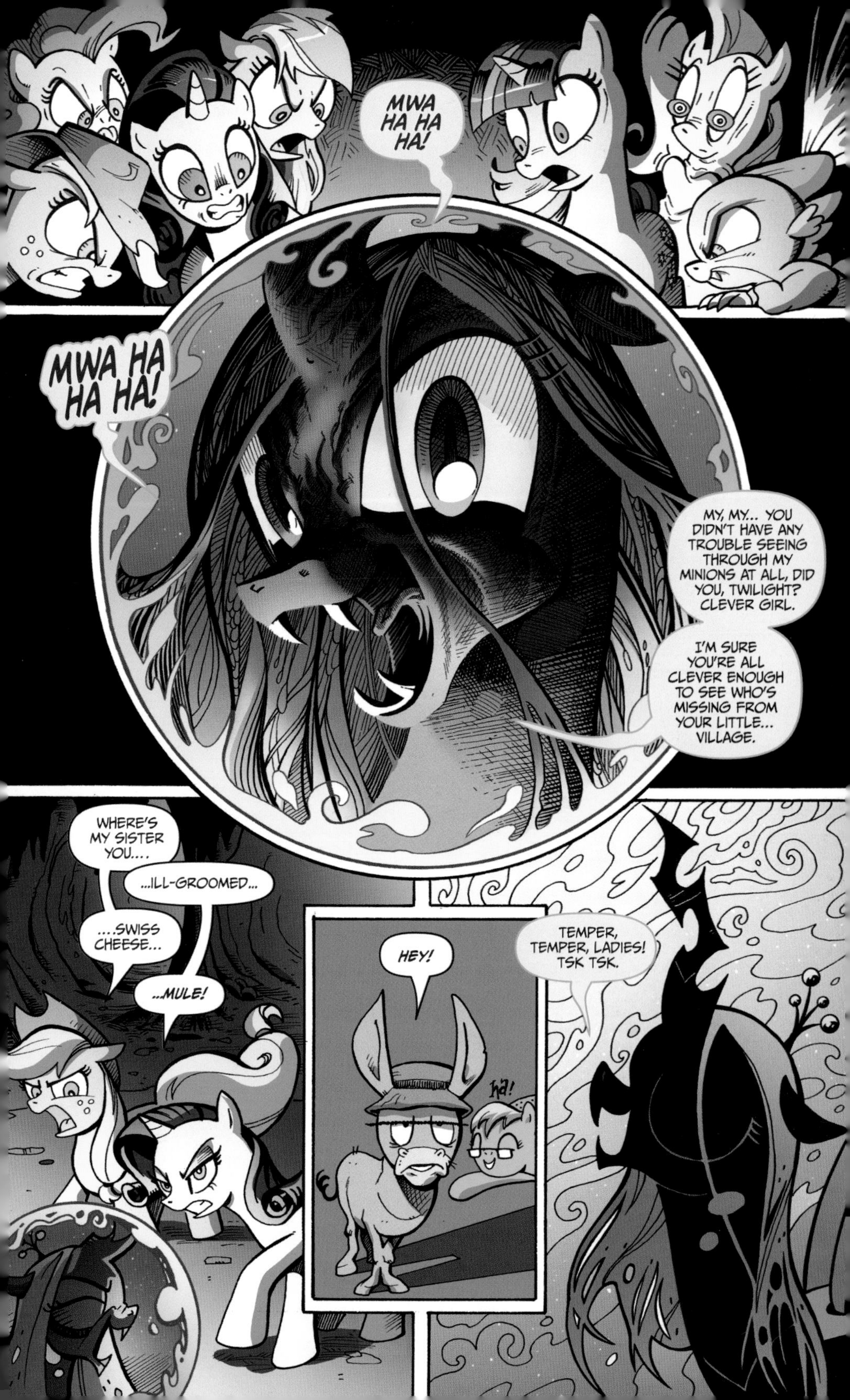
MWA HA HA HA!
MWA HA HA HA!
MY, MY... YOU DIDN'T HAVE ANY TROUBLE SEEING THROUGH MY MINIONS AT ALL, DID YOU, TWILIGHT? CLEVER GIRL.
I'M SURE YOU'RE ALL CLEVER ENOUGH TO SEE WHO'S MISSING FROM YOUR LITTLE... VILLAGE.
WHERE'S MY SISTER YOU....
...ILL-GROOMED...
....SWISS CHEESE...
...MULE!
HEY!
HA!
TEMPER, TEMPER, LADIES! TSK TSK.

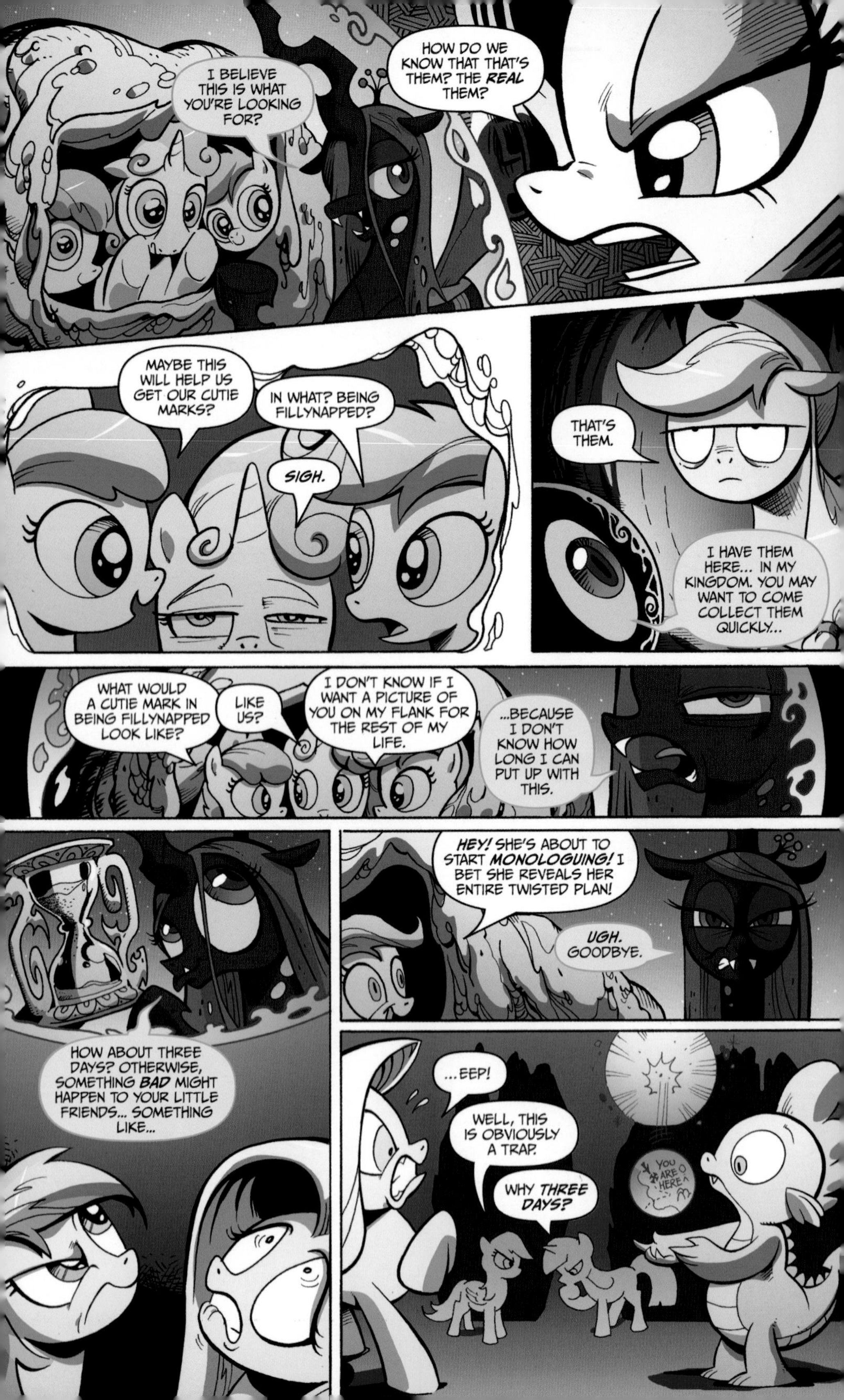
I BELIEVE THIS IS WHAT YOU'RE LOOKING FOR?
HOW DO WE KNOW THAT THAT'S THEM? THE REAL THEM?
MAYBE THIS WILL HELP US GET OUR CUTIE MARKS?
IN WHAT? BEING FILLYNAPPED?
SIGH.
THAT'S THEM.
I HAVE THEM HERE... IN MY KINGDOM. YOU MAY WANT TO COME COLLECT THEM QUICKLY...
WHAT WOULD A CUTIE MARK IN BEING FILLYNAPPED LOOK LIKE?
LIKE US?
I DON'T KNOW IF I WANT A PICTURE OF YOU ON MY FLANK FOR THE REST OF MY LIFE.
...BECAUSE I DON'T KNOW HOW LONG I CAN PUT UP WITH THIS.
HEY! SHE'S ABOUT TO START MONOLOGUING! I BET SHE REVEALS HER ENTIRE TWISTED PLAN!
UGH. GOODBYE.
HOW ABOUT THREE DAYS? OTHERWISE, SOMETHING BAD MIGHT HAPPEN TO YOUR LITTLE FRIENDS... SOMETHING LIKE...
...EEP!
WELL, THIS IS OBVIOUSLY A TRAP.
WHY THREE DAYS?
YOU ARE HERE

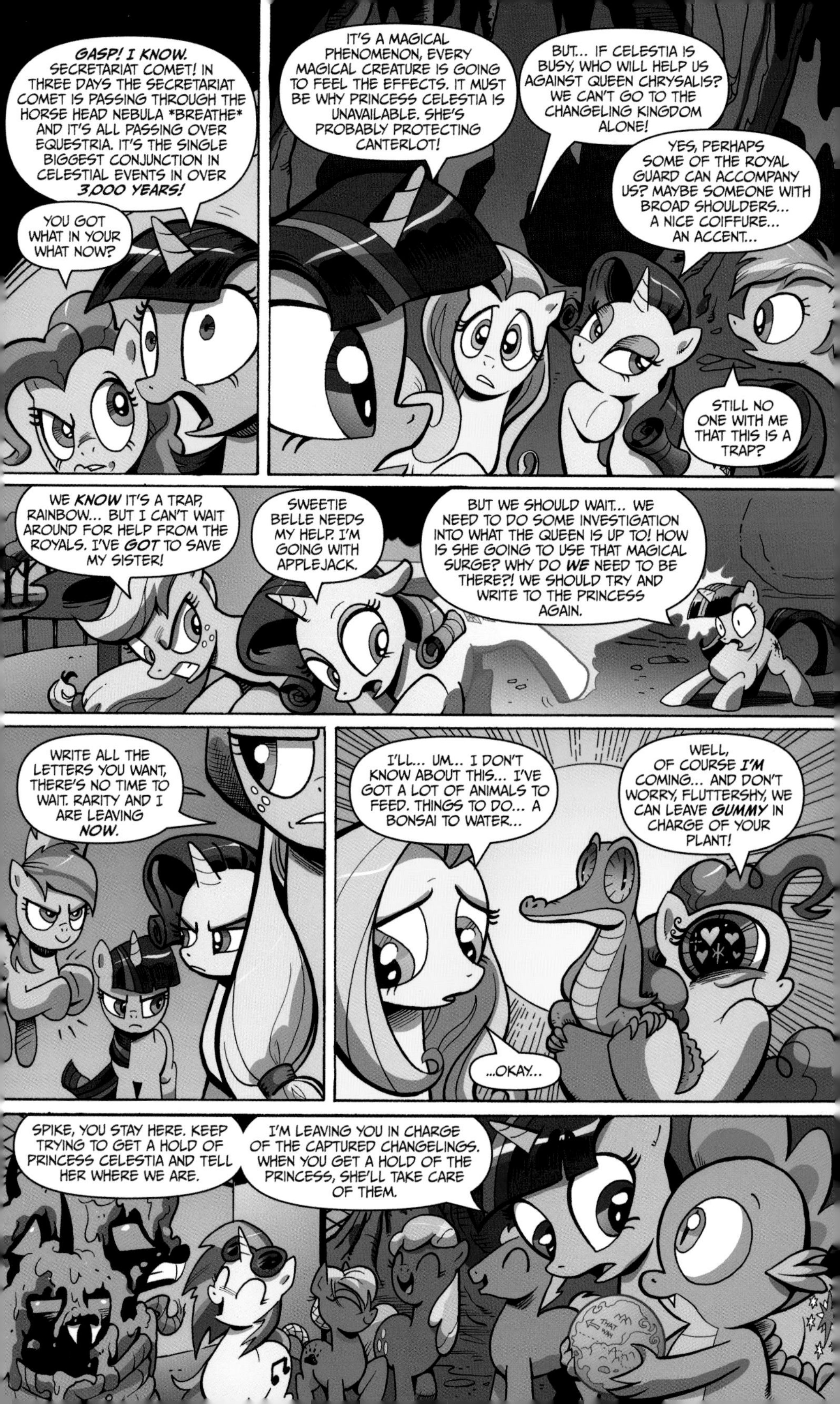

GASP! I KNOW. SECRETARIAT COMET! IN THREE DAYS THE SECRETARIAT COMET IS PASSING THROUGH THE HORSE HEAD NEBULA *BREATHE* AND IT'S ALL PASSING OVER EQUESTRIA. IT'S THE SINGLE BIGGEST CONJUNCTION IN CELESTIAL EVENTS IN OVER 3,000 YEARS!
YOU GOT WHAT IN YOUR WHAT NOW?
IT'S A MAGICAL PHENOMENON, EVERY MAGICAL CREATURE IS GOING TO FEEL THE EFFECTS. IT MUST BE WHY PRINCESS CELESTIA IS UNAVAILABLE. SHE'S PROBABLY PROTECTING CANTERLOT!
BUT... IF CELESTIA IS BUSY, WHO WILL HELP US AGAINST QUEEN CHRYSALIS? WE CAN'T GO TO THE CHANGELING KINGDOM ALONE!
YES, PERHAPS SOME OF THE ROYAL GUARD CAN ACCOMPANY US? MAYBE SOMEONE WITH BROAD SHOULDERS... A NICE COIFFURE... AN ACCENT...
STILL NO ONE WITH ME THAT THIS IS A TRAP?
WE KNOW IT'S A TRAP, RAINBOW... BUT I CAN'T WAIT AROUND FOR HELP FROM THE ROYALS. I'VE GOT TO SAVE MY SISTER!
SWEETIE BELLE NEEDS MY HELP. I'M GOING WITH APPLEJACK.
BUT WE SHOULD WAIT... WE NEED TO DO SOME INVESTIGATION INTO WHAT THE QUEEN IS UP TO! HOW IS SHE GOING TO USE THAT MAGICAL SURGE? WHY DO WE NEED TO BE THERE?! WE SHOULD TRY AND WRITE TO THE PRINCESS AGAIN.
WRITE ALL THE LETTERS YOU WANT, THERE'S NO TIME TO WAIT. RARITY AND I ARE LEAVING NOW.
I'LL... UM... I DON'T KNOW ABOUT THIS... I'VE GOT A LOT OF ANIMALS TO FEED. THINGS TO DO... A BONSAI TO WATER...
WELL, OF COURSE I'M COMING... AND DON'T WORRY, FLUTTERSHY, WE CAN LEAVE GUMMY IN CHARGE OF YOUR PLANT!
...OKAY...
SPIKE, YOU STAY HERE. KEEP TRYING TO GET A HOLD OF PRINCESS CELESTIA AND TELL HER WHERE WE ARE.
I'M LEAVING YOU IN CHARGE OF THE CAPTURED CHANGELINGS. WHEN YOU GET A HOLD OF THE PRINCESS, SHE'LL TAKE CARE OF THEM.
THAT WAY

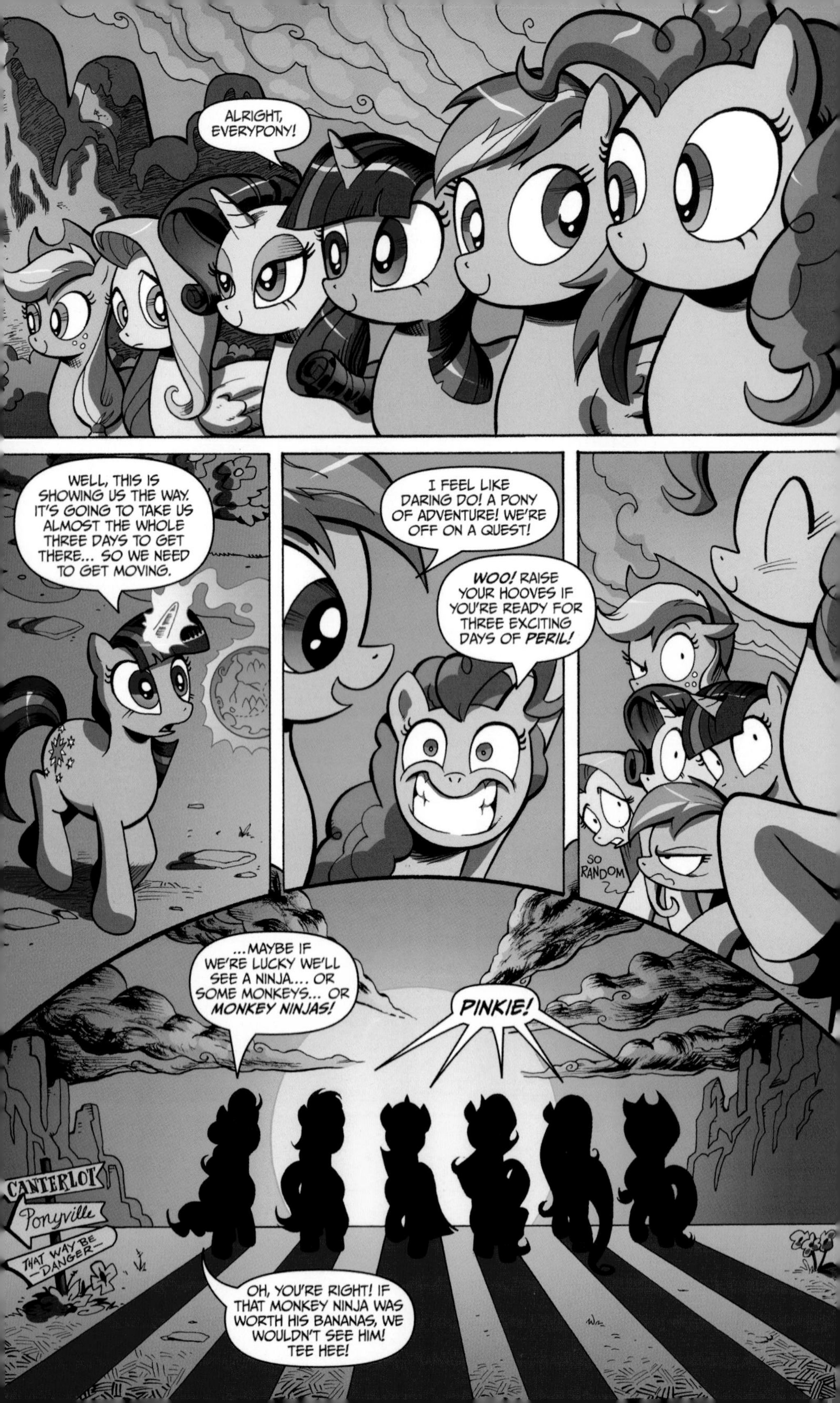
ALRIGHT, EVERYPONY!
WELL, THIS IS SHOWING US THE WAY. IT'S GOING TO TAKE US ALMOST THE WHOLE THREE DAYS TO GET THERE... SO WE NEED TO GET MOVING.
I FEEL LIKE DARING DO! A PONY OF ADVENTURE! WE'RE OFF ON A QUEST!
WOO! RAISE YOUR HOOVES IF YOU'RE READY FOR THREE EXCITING DAYS OF PERIL!
SO RANDOM
...MAYBE IF WE'RE LUCKY WE'LL SEE A NINJA.... OR SOME MONKEYS... OR MONKEY NINJAS!
PINKIE!
CANTERLOT
Ponyville
THAT WAY BE —DANGER—
OH, YOU'RE RIGHT! IF THAT MONKEY NINJA WAS WORTH HIS BANANAS, WE WOULDN'T SEE HIM! TEE HEE!

Art by
Katie Cook

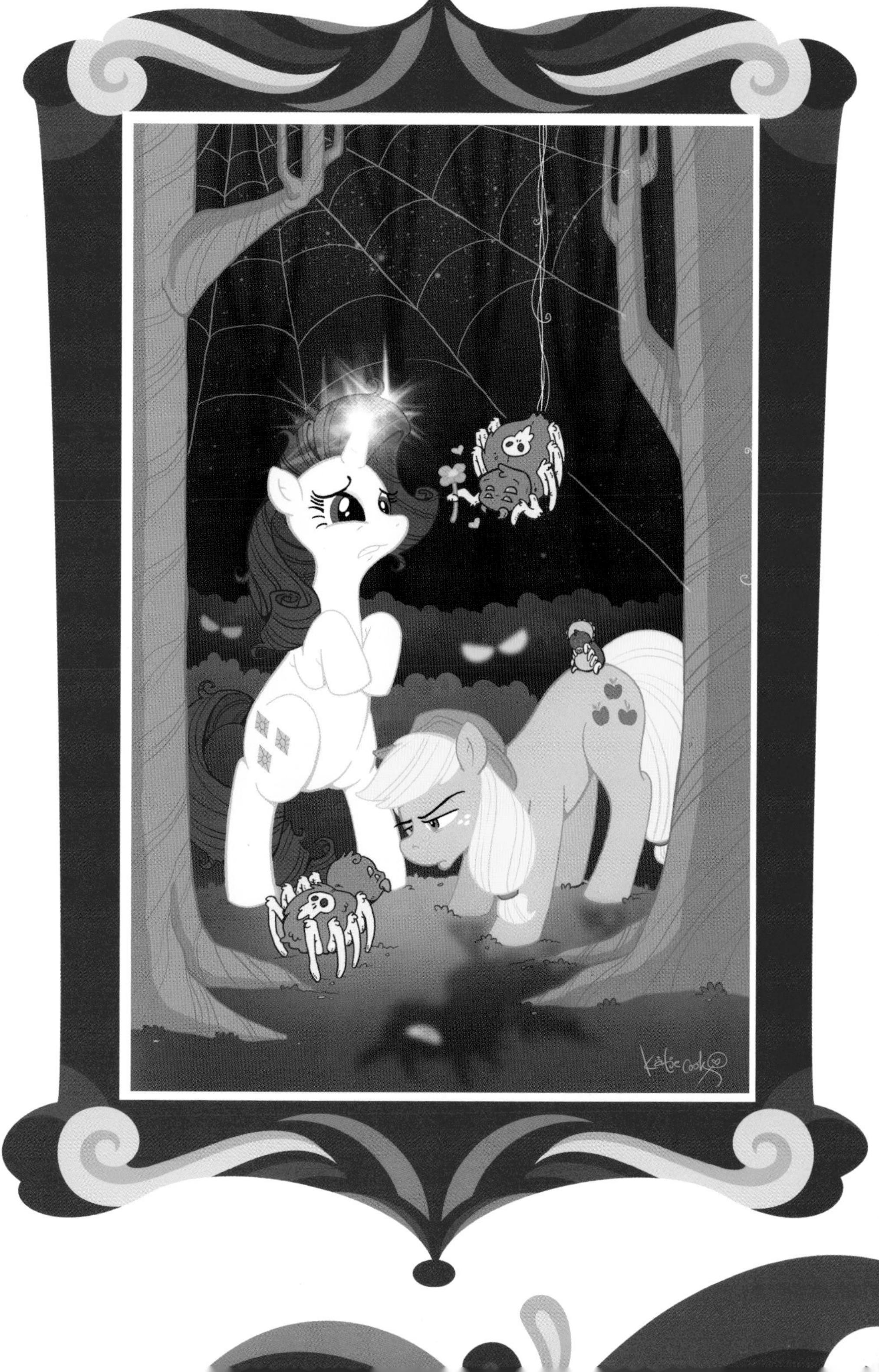

Art by
Stephanie Buscema

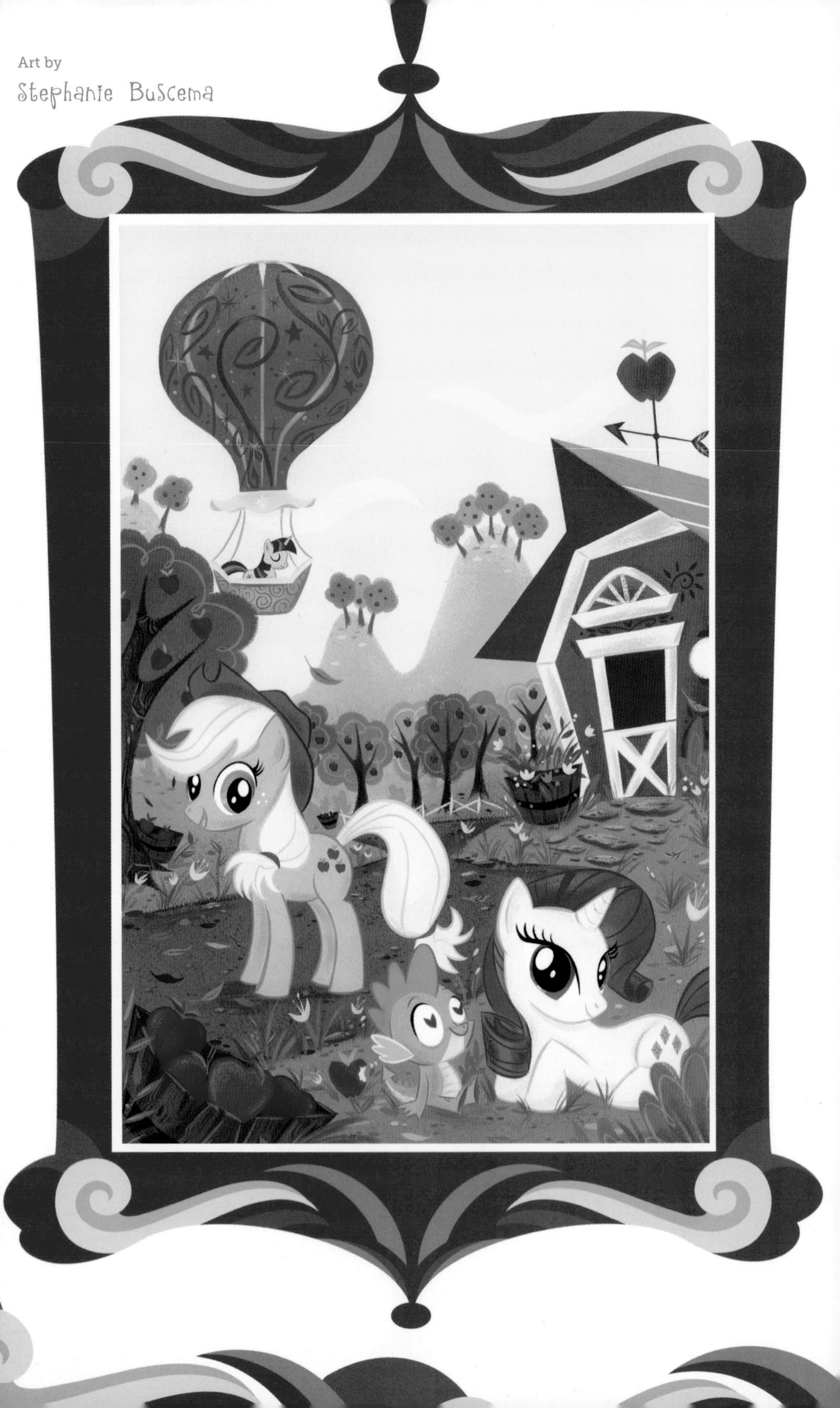

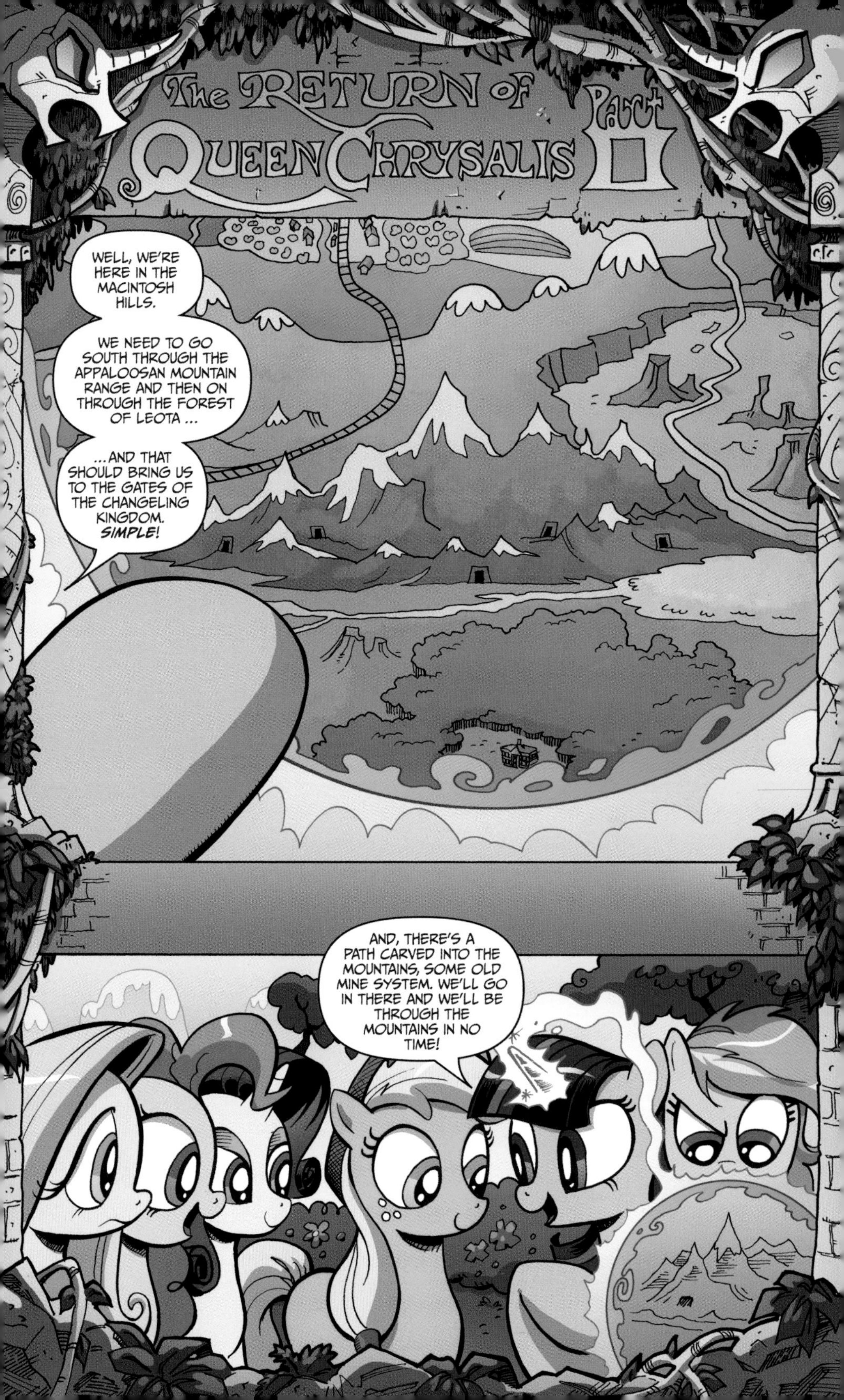
The RETURN of QUEEN CHRYSALIS Part II
WELL, WE'RE HERE IN THE MACINTOSH HILLS.
WE NEED TO GO SOUTH THROUGH THE APPALOOSAN MOUNTAIN RANGE AND THEN ON THROUGH THE FOREST OF LEOTA ...
...AND THAT SHOULD BRING US TO THE GATES OF THE CHANGELING KINGDOM. *SIMPLE!*
AND, THERE'S A PATH CARVED INTO THE MOUNTAINS, SOME OLD MINE SYSTEM. WE'LL GO IN THERE AND WE'LL BE THROUGH THE MOUNTAINS IN NO TIME!

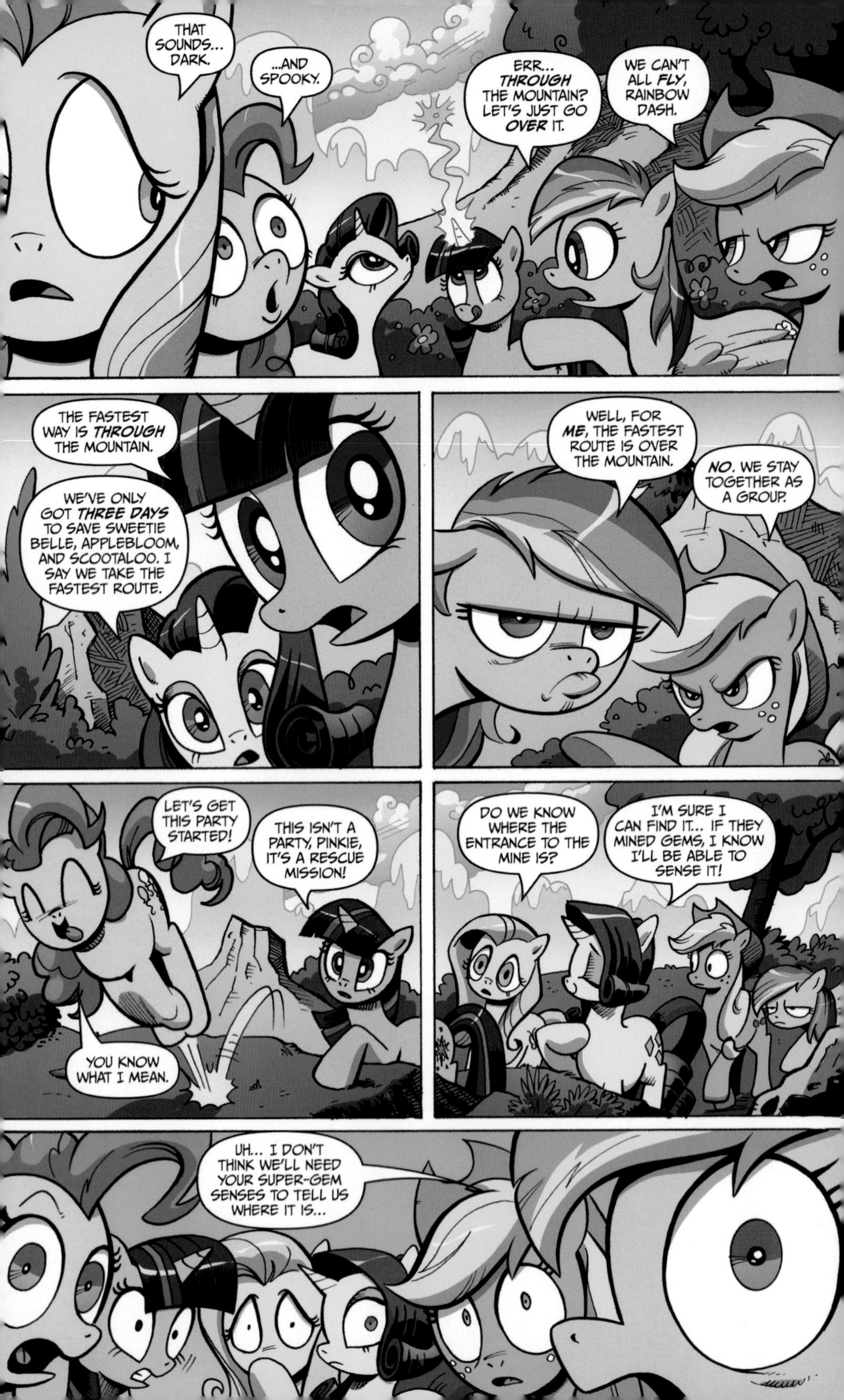
THAT SOUNDS... DARK.
...AND SPOOKY.
ERR... THROUGH THE MOUNTAIN? LET'S JUST GO OVER IT.
WE CAN'T ALL FLY, RAINBOW DASH.
THE FASTEST WAY IS THROUGH THE MOUNTAIN.
WE'VE ONLY GOT THREE DAYS TO SAVE SWEETIE BELLE, APPLEBLOOM, AND SCOOTALOO. I SAY WE TAKE THE FASTEST ROUTE.
WELL, FOR ME, THE FASTEST ROUTE IS OVER THE MOUNTAIN.
NO. WE STAY TOGETHER AS A GROUP.
LET'S GET THIS PARTY STARTED!
THIS ISN'T A PARTY, PINKIE, IT'S A RESCUE MISSION!
YOU KNOW WHAT I MEAN.
DO WE KNOW WHERE THE ENTRANCE TO THE MINE IS?
I'M SURE I CAN FIND IT... IF THEY MINED GEMS, I KNOW I'LL BE ABLE TO SENSE IT!
UH... I DON'T THINK WE'LL NEED YOUR SUPER-GEM SENSES TO TELL US WHERE IT IS...

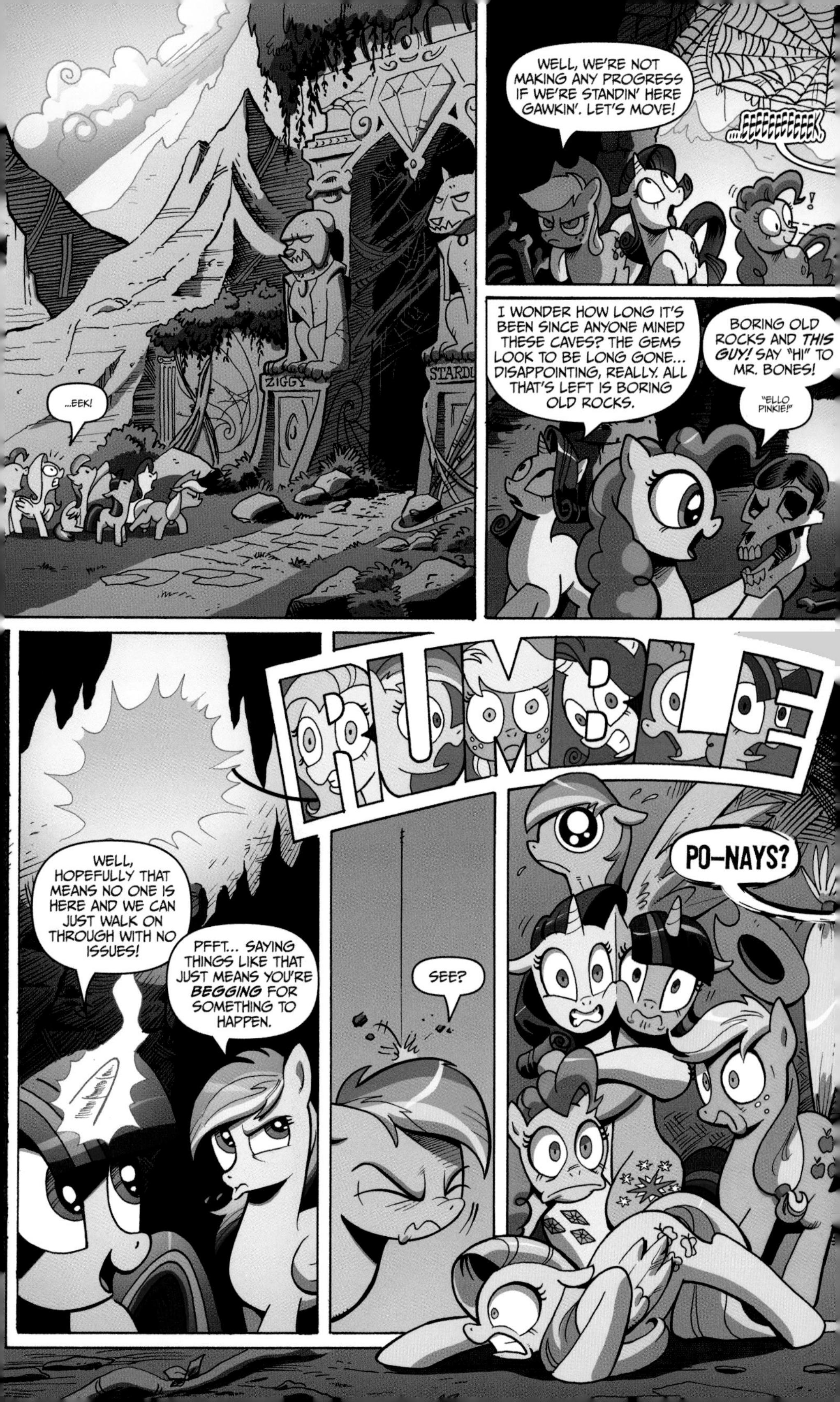
...EEK!
ZIGGY
STARDU
WELL, WE'RE NOT MAKING ANY PROGRESS IF WE'RE STANDIN' HERE GAWKIN'. LET'S MOVE!
...EEEEEEEEEEEK!
!
I WONDER HOW LONG IT'S BEEN SINCE ANYONE MINED THESE CAVES? THE GEMS LOOK TO BE LONG GONE... DISAPPOINTING, REALLY. ALL THAT'S LEFT IS BORING OLD ROCKS.
BORING OLD ROCKS AND THIS GUY! SAY "HI" TO MR. BONES!
"ELLO PINKIE!"
RUMBLE
WELL, HOPEFULLY THAT MEANS NO ONE IS HERE AND WE CAN JUST WALK ON THROUGH WITH NO ISSUES!
PFFT... SAYING THINGS LIKE THAT JUST MEANS YOU'RE BEGGING FOR SOMETHING TO HAPPEN.
SEE?
PO-NAYS?

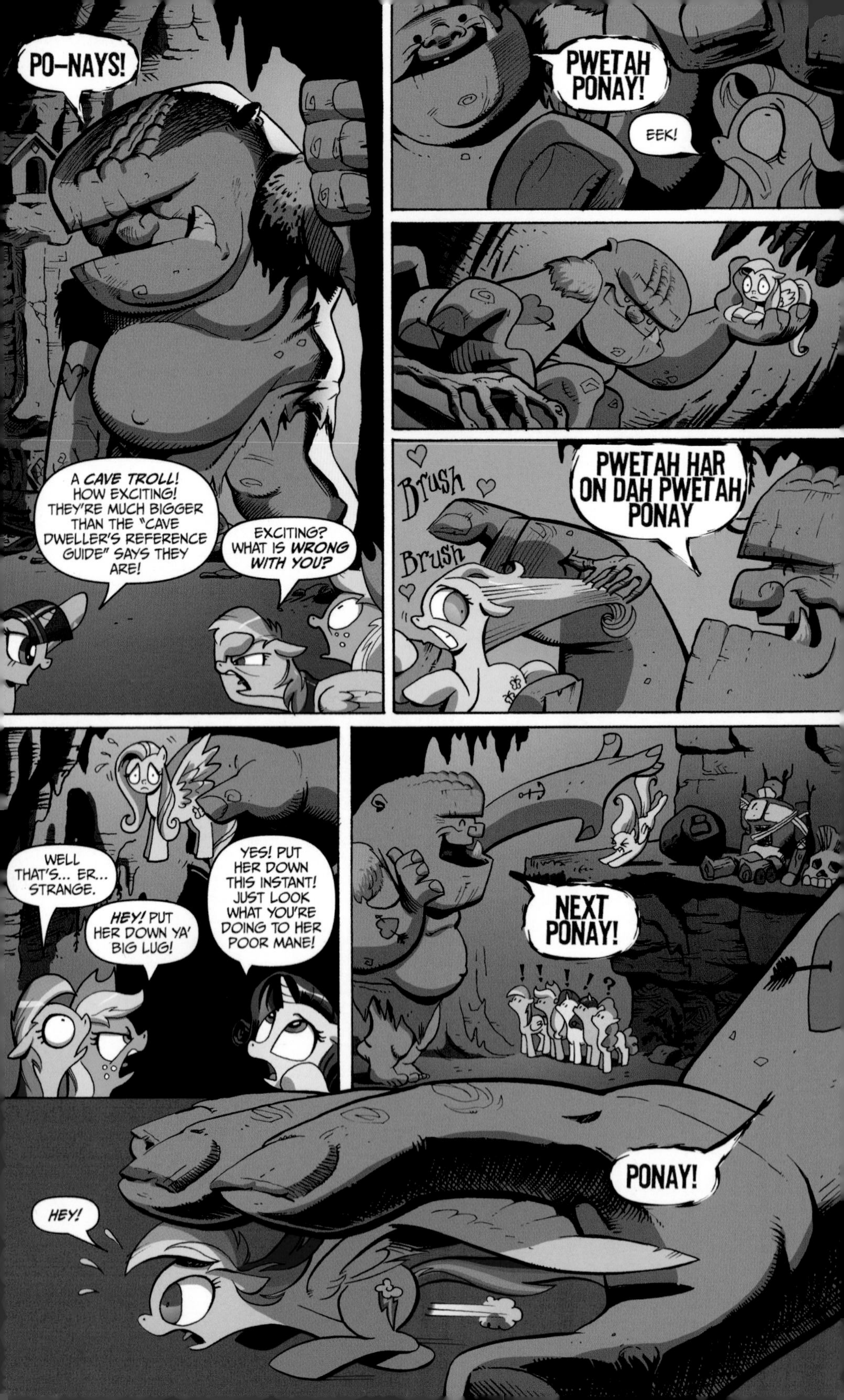
PO-NAYS!
PWETAH PONAY!
EEK!
A CAVE TROLL! HOW EXCITING! THEY'RE MUCH BIGGER THAN THE "CAVE DWELLER'S REFERENCE GUIDE" SAYS THEY ARE!
EXCITING? WHAT IS WRONG WITH YOU?
Brush
Brush
PWETAH HAR ON DAH PWETAH PONAY
WELL THAT'S... ER... STRANGE.
HEY! PUT HER DOWN YA' BIG LUG!
YES! PUT HER DOWN THIS INSTANT! JUST LOOK WHAT YOU'RE DOING TO HER POOR MANE!
NEXT PONAY!
PONAY!
HEY!

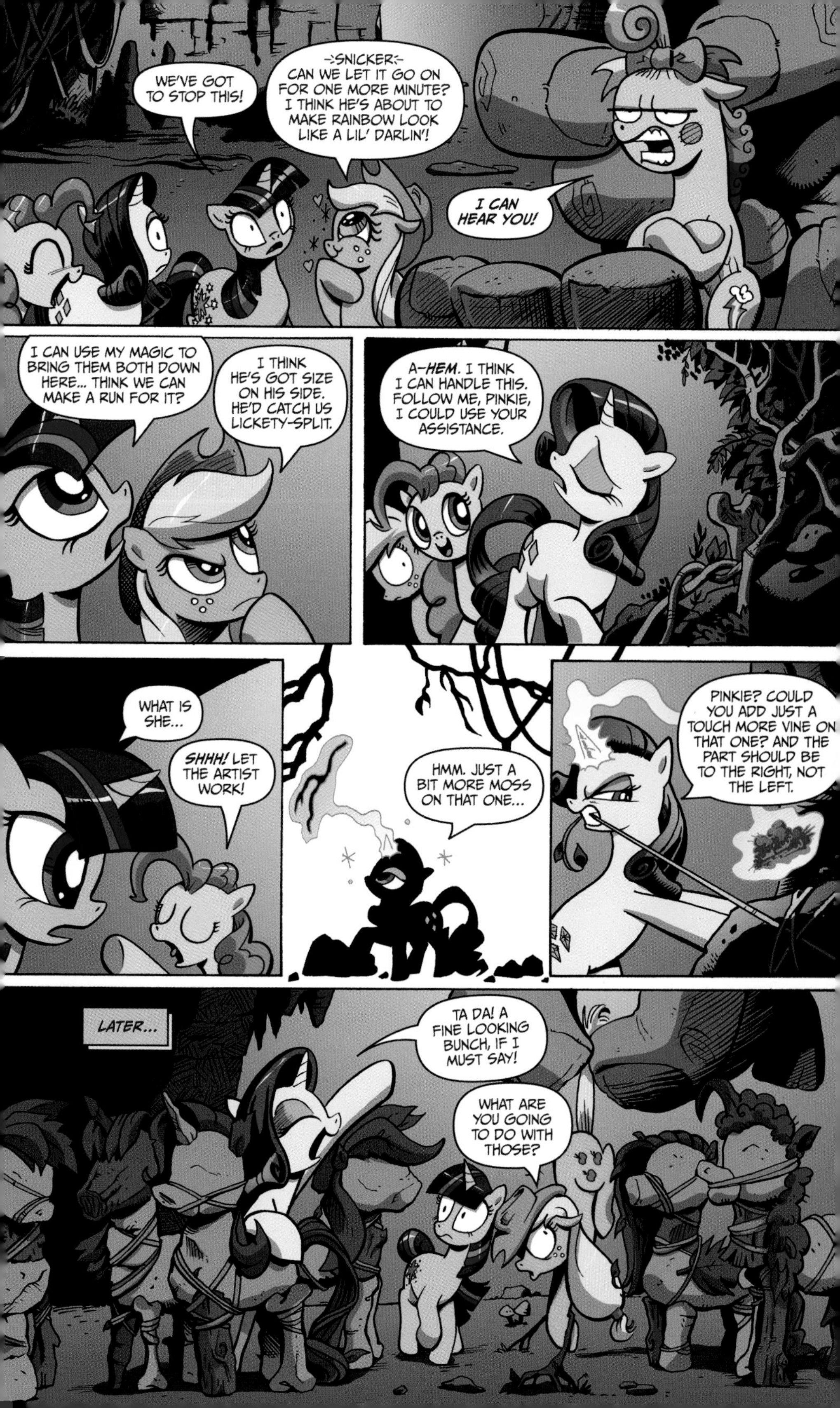
WE'VE GOT TO STOP THIS!
-SNICKER- CAN WE LET IT GO ON FOR ONE MORE MINUTE? I THINK HE'S ABOUT TO MAKE RAINBOW LOOK LIKE A LIL' DARLIN'!
I CAN HEAR YOU!
I CAN USE MY MAGIC TO BRING THEM BOTH DOWN HERE... THINK WE CAN MAKE A RUN FOR IT?
I THINK HE'S GOT SIZE ON HIS SIDE. HE'D CATCH US LICKETY-SPLIT.
A-HEM. I THINK I CAN HANDLE THIS. FOLLOW ME, PINKIE, I COULD USE YOUR ASSISTANCE.
WHAT IS SHE...
SHHH! LET THE ARTIST WORK!
HMM. JUST A BIT MORE MOSS ON THAT ONE...
PINKIE? COULD YOU ADD JUST A TOUCH MORE VINE ON THAT ONE? AND THE PART SHOULD BE TO THE RIGHT, NOT THE LEFT.
LATER...
TA DA! A FINE LOOKING BUNCH, IF I MUST SAY!
WHAT ARE YOU GOING TO DO WITH THOSE?

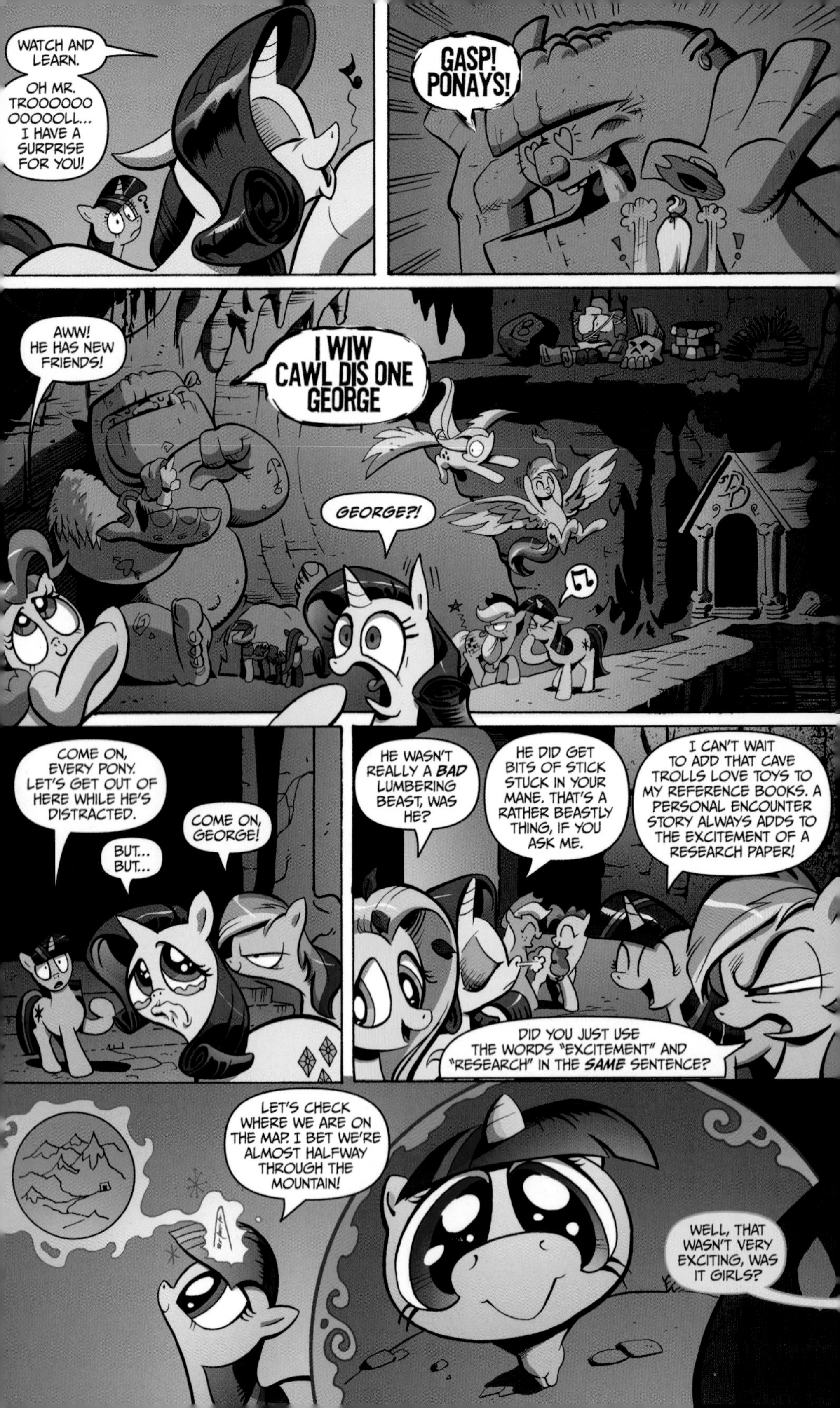

WATCH AND LEARN.
OH MR. TROOOOOO OOOOOLL... I HAVE A SURPRISE FOR YOU!
GASP! PONAYS!
AWW! HE HAS NEW FRIENDS!
I WIW CAWL DIS ONE GEORGE
GEORGE?!
COME ON, EVERY PONY. LET'S GET OUT OF HERE WHILE HE'S DISTRACTED.
BUT... BUT...
COME ON, GEORGE!
HE WASN'T REALLY A BAD LUMBERING BEAST, WAS HE?
HE DID GET BITS OF STICK STUCK IN YOUR MANE. THAT'S A RATHER BEASTLY THING, IF YOU ASK ME.
I CAN'T WAIT TO ADD THAT CAVE TROLLS LOVE TOYS TO MY REFERENCE BOOKS. A PERSONAL ENCOUNTER STORY ALWAYS ADDS TO THE EXCITEMENT OF A RESEARCH PAPER!
DID YOU JUST USE THE WORDS "EXCITEMENT" AND "RESEARCH" IN THE SAME SENTENCE?
LET'S CHECK WHERE WE ARE ON THE MAP. I BET WE'RE ALMOST HALFWAY THROUGH THE MOUNTAIN!
WELL, THAT WASN'T VERY EXCITING, WAS IT GIRLS?

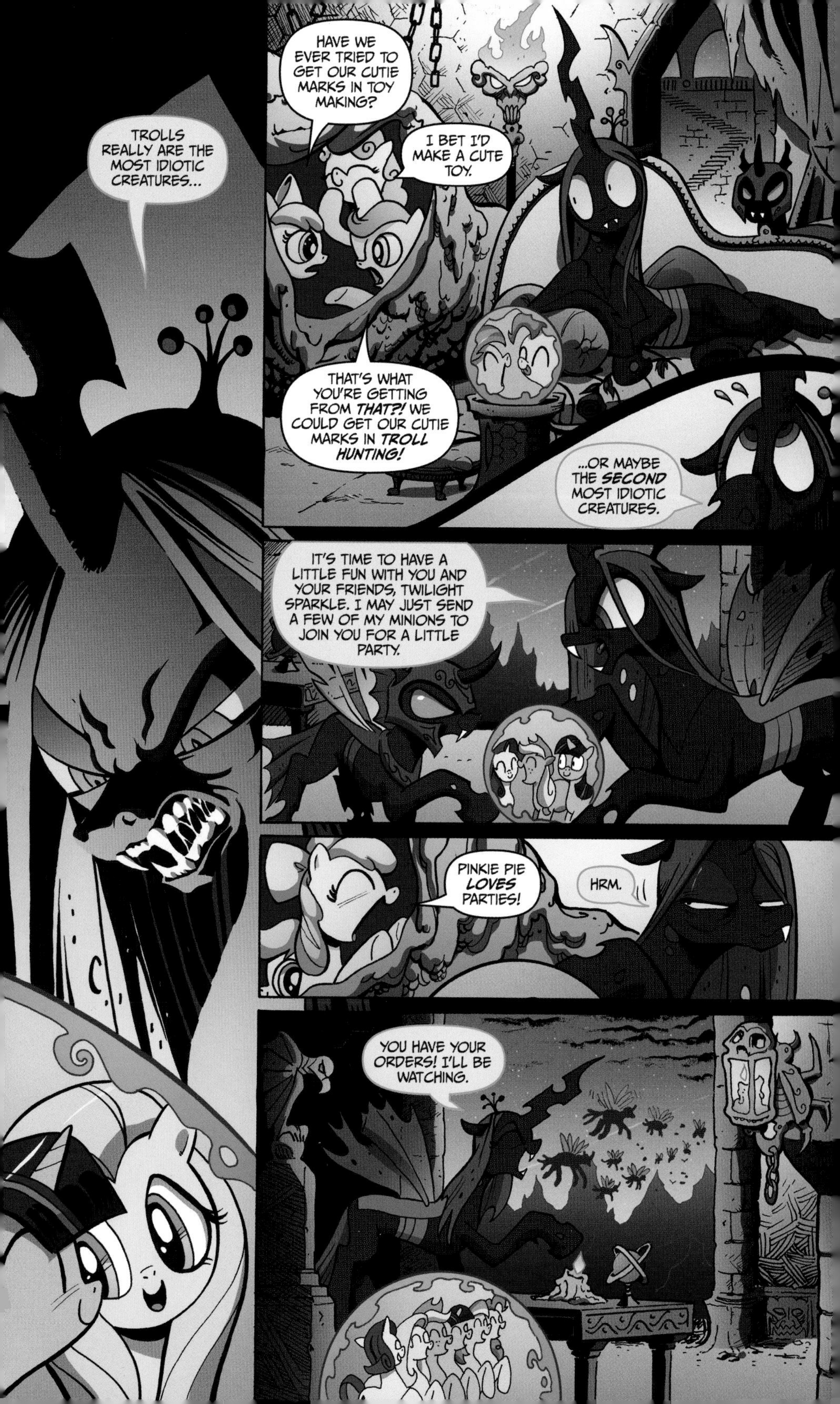
HAVE WE EVER TRIED TO GET OUR CUTIE MARKS IN TOY MAKING?
I BET I'D MAKE A CUTE TOY.
TROLLS REALLY ARE THE MOST IDIOTIC CREATURES...
THAT'S WHAT YOU'RE GETTING FROM THAT?! WE COULD GET OUR CUTIE MARKS IN TROLL HUNTING!
...OR MAYBE THE SECOND MOST IDIOTIC CREATURES.
IT'S TIME TO HAVE A LITTLE FUN WITH YOU AND YOUR FRIENDS, TWILIGHT SPARKLE. I MAY JUST SEND A FEW OF MY MINIONS TO JOIN YOU FOR A LITTLE PARTY.
PINKIE PIE LOVES PARTIES!
HRM.
YOU HAVE YOUR ORDERS! I'LL BE WATCHING.

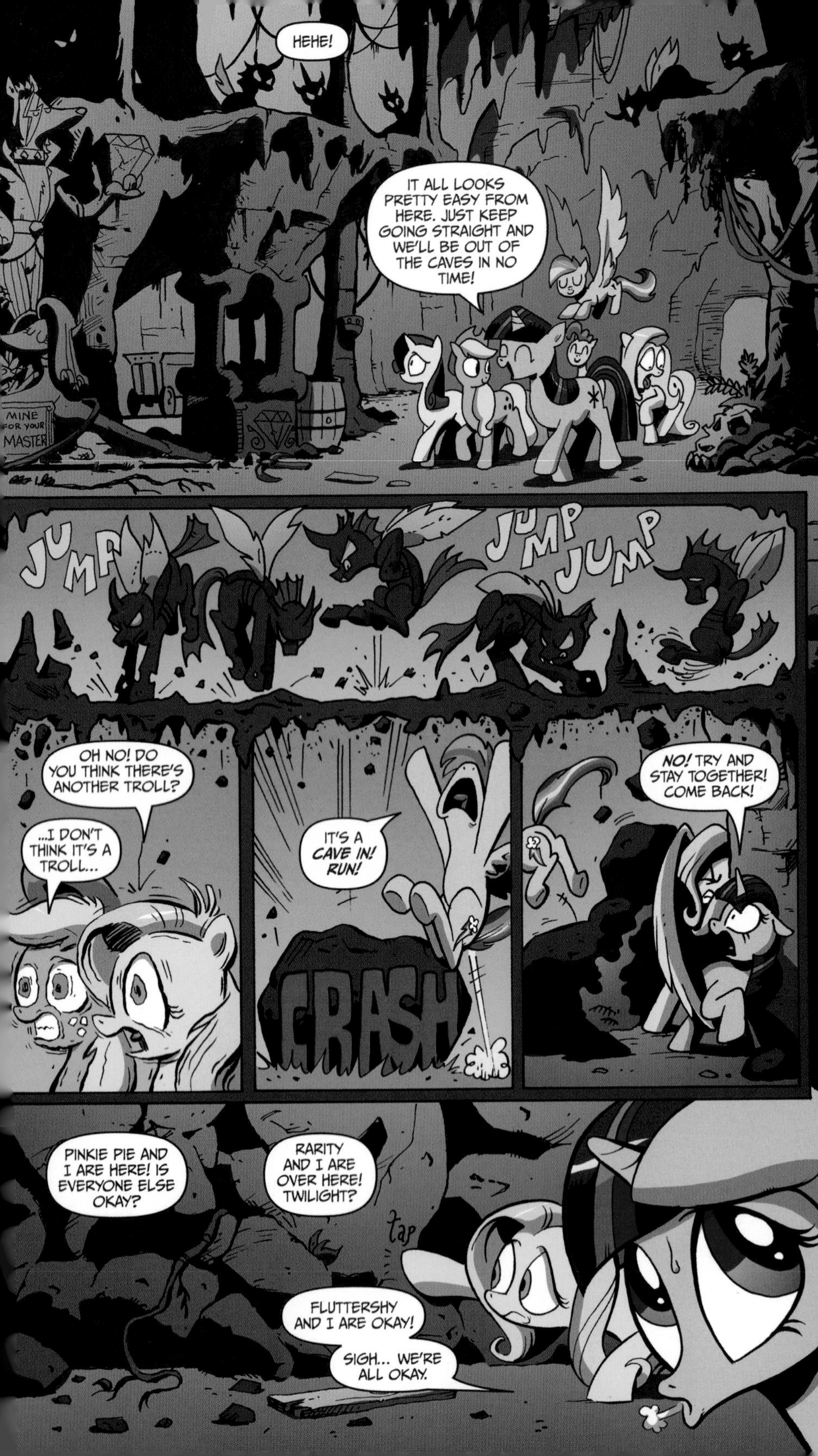
HEHE!
IT ALL LOOKS PRETTY EASY FROM HERE. JUST KEEP GOING STRAIGHT AND WE'LL BE OUT OF THE CAVES IN NO TIME!
MINE FOR YOUR MASTER
JUMP
JUMP JUMP
OH NO! DO YOU THINK THERE'S ANOTHER TROLL?
...I DON'T THINK IT'S A TROLL...
IT'S A CAVE IN! RUN!
CRASH
NO! TRY AND STAY TOGETHER! COME BACK!
PINKIE PIE AND I ARE HERE! IS EVERYONE ELSE OKAY?
RARITY AND I ARE OVER HERE! TWILIGHT?
tap
FLUTTERSHY AND I ARE OKAY!
SIGH... WE'RE ALL OKAY.

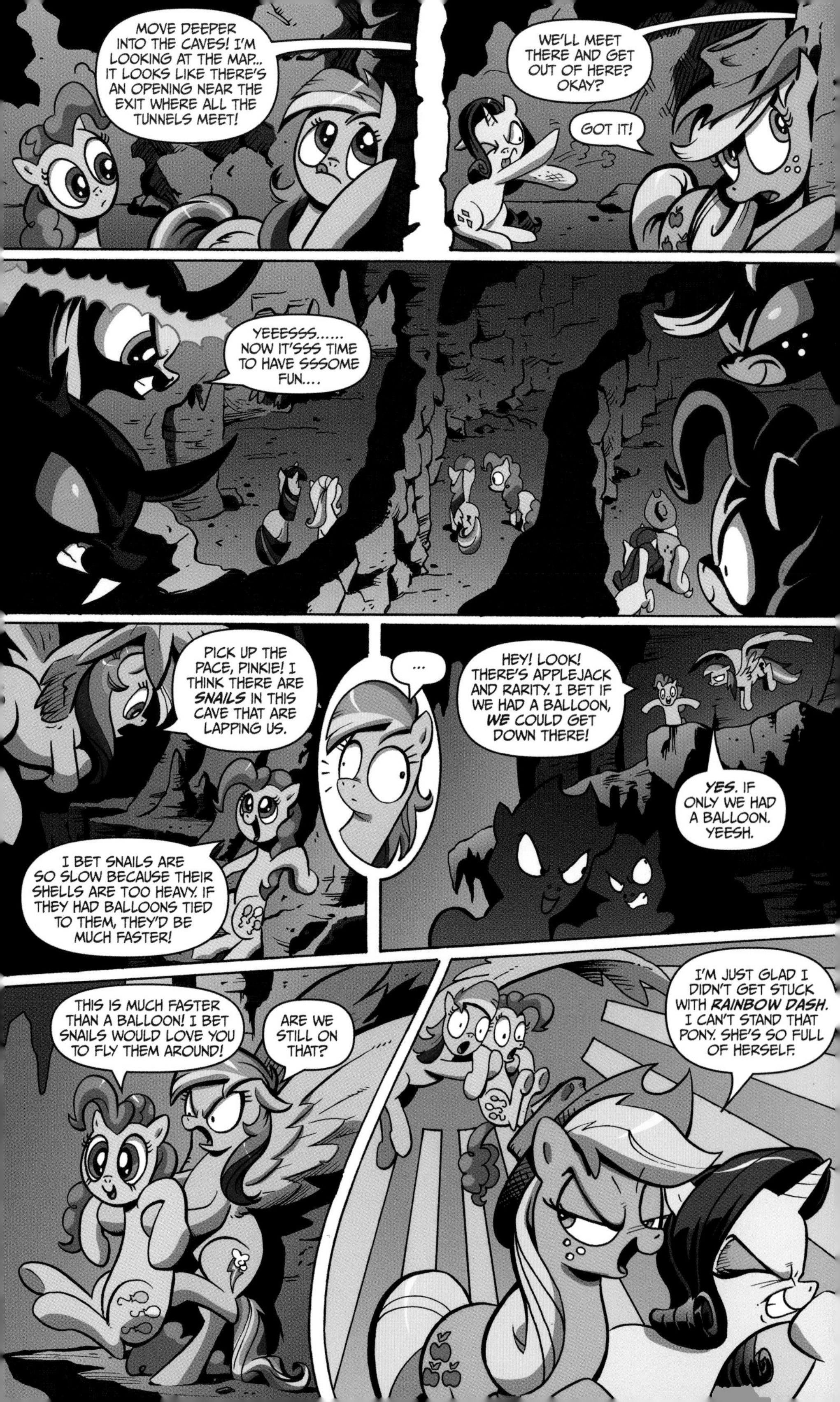
MOVE DEEPER INTO THE CAVES! I'M LOOKING AT THE MAP... IT LOOKS LIKE THERE'S AN OPENING NEAR THE EXIT WHERE ALL THE TUNNELS MEET!
WE'LL MEET THERE AND GET OUT OF HERE? OKAY?
GOT IT!
YEEESSS...... NOW IT'SSS TIME TO HAVE SSSOME FUN....
PICK UP THE PACE, PINKIE! I THINK THERE ARE SNAILS IN THIS CAVE THAT ARE LAPPING US.
I BET SNAILS ARE SO SLOW BECAUSE THEIR SHELLS ARE TOO HEAVY. IF THEY HAD BALLOONS TIED TO THEM, THEY'D BE MUCH FASTER!
...
HEY! LOOK! THERE'S APPLEJACK AND RARITY. I BET IF WE HAD A BALLOON, WE COULD GET DOWN THERE!
YES. IF ONLY WE HAD A BALLOON. YEESH.
THIS IS MUCH FASTER THAN A BALLOON! I BET SNAILS WOULD LOVE YOU TO FLY THEM AROUND!
ARE WE STILL ON THAT?
I'M JUST GLAD I DIDN'T GET STUCK WITH RAINBOW DASH. I CAN'T STAND THAT PONY. SHE'S SO FULL OF HERSELF.

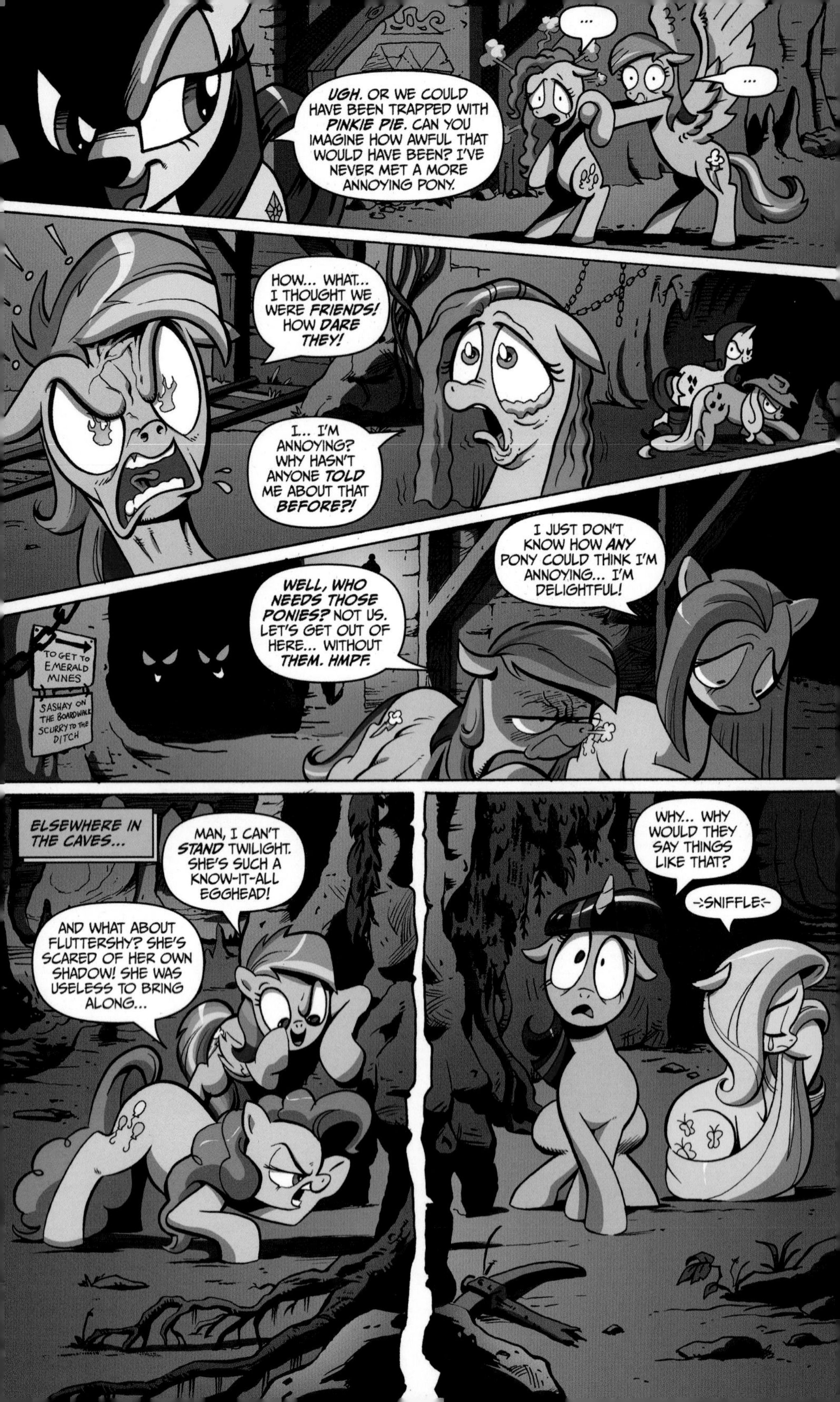
UGH. OR WE COULD HAVE BEEN TRAPPED WITH PINKIE PIE. CAN YOU IMAGINE HOW AWFUL THAT WOULD HAVE BEEN? I'VE NEVER MET A MORE ANNOYING PONY.
...
...
!
HOW... WHAT... I THOUGHT WE WERE FRIENDS! HOW DARE THEY!
I... I'M ANNOYING? WHY HASN'T ANYONE TOLD ME ABOUT THAT BEFORE?!
TO GET TO EMERALD MINES
SASHAY ON THE BOARDWALK SCURRY TO THE DITCH
WELL, WHO NEEDS THOSE PONIES? NOT US. LET'S GET OUT OF HERE... WITHOUT THEM. HMPF.
I JUST DON'T KNOW HOW ANY PONY COULD THINK I'M ANNOYING... I'M DELIGHTFUL!
ELSEWHERE IN THE CAVES...
MAN, I CAN'T STAND TWILIGHT. SHE'S SUCH A KNOW-IT-ALL EGGHEAD!
AND WHAT ABOUT FLUTTERSHY? SHE'S SCARED OF HER OWN SHADOW! SHE WAS USELESS TO BRING ALONG...
WHY... WHY WOULD THEY SAY THINGS LIKE THAT?
SNIFFLE

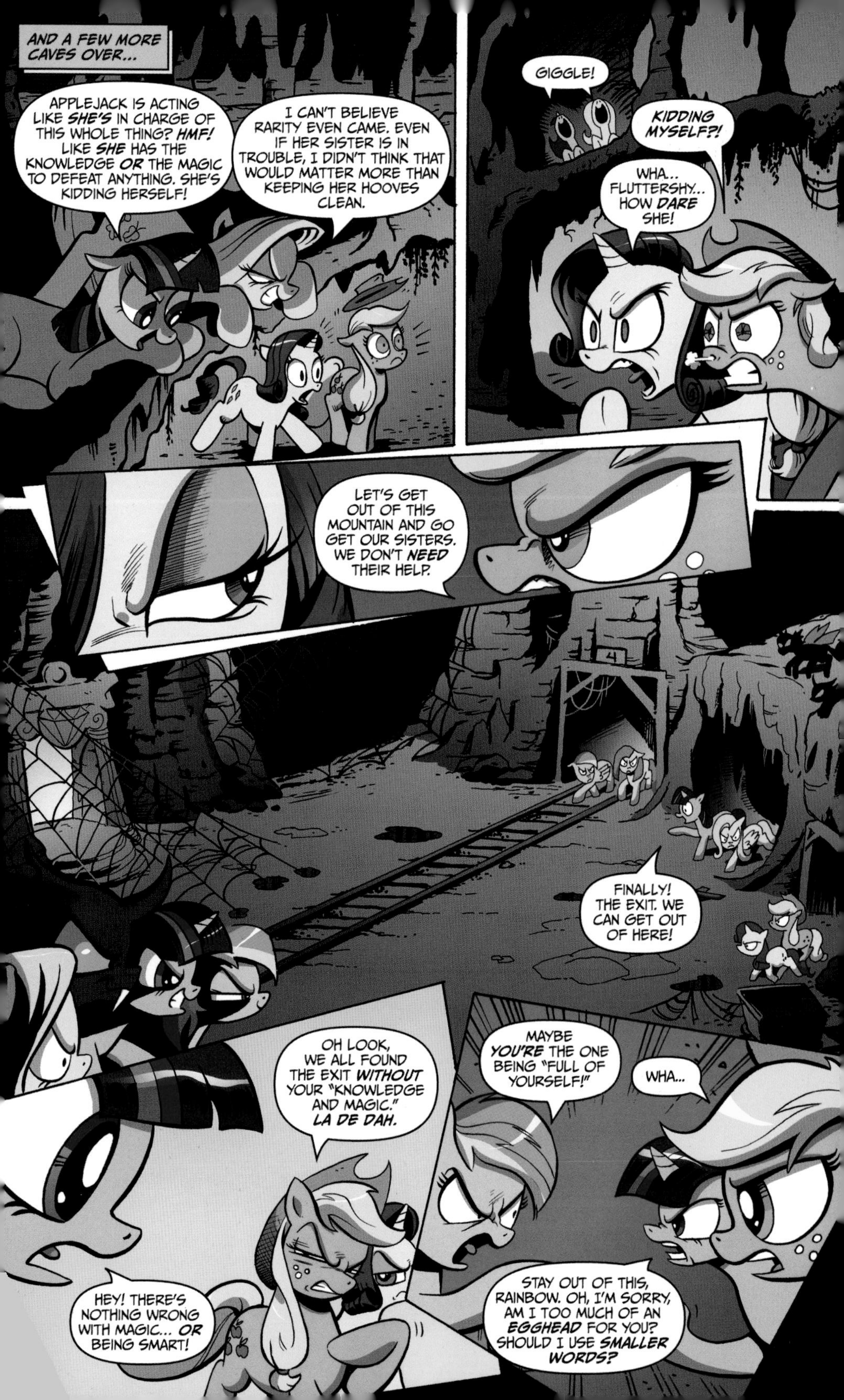
AND A FEW MORE CAVES OVER...
APPLEJACK IS ACTING LIKE SHE'S IN CHARGE OF THIS WHOLE THING? HMF! LIKE SHE HAS THE KNOWLEDGE OR THE MAGIC TO DEFEAT ANYTHING. SHE'S KIDDING HERSELF!
I CAN'T BELIEVE RARITY EVEN CAME. EVEN IF HER SISTER IS IN TROUBLE, I DIDN'T THINK THAT WOULD MATTER MORE THAN KEEPING HER HOOVES CLEAN.
GIGGLE!
KIDDING MYSELF?!
WHA... FLUTTERSHY... HOW DARE SHE!
LET'S GET OUT OF THIS MOUNTAIN AND GO GET OUR SISTERS. WE DON'T NEED THEIR HELP.
FINALLY! THE EXIT. WE CAN GET OUT OF HERE!
OH LOOK, WE ALL FOUND THE EXIT WITHOUT YOUR "KNOWLEDGE AND MAGIC." LA DE DAH.
MAYBE YOU'RE THE ONE BEING "FULL OF YOURSELF!"
WHA...
HEY! THERE'S NOTHING WRONG WITH MAGIC... OR BEING SMART!
STAY OUT OF THIS, RAINBOW. OH, I'M SORRY, AM I TOO MUCH OF AN EGGHEAD FOR YOU? SHOULD I USE SMALLER WORDS?

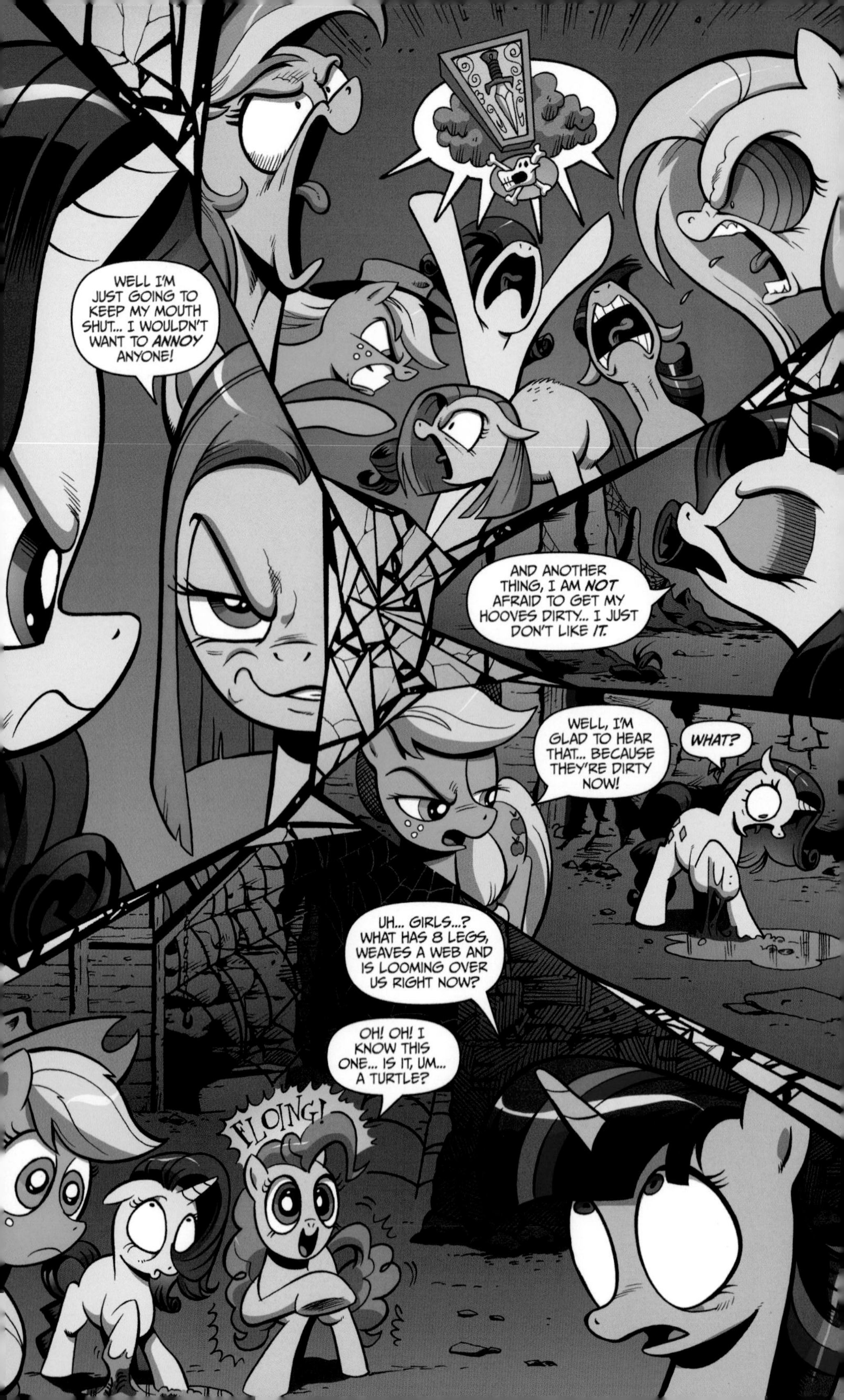

WELL I'M JUST GOING TO KEEP MY MOUTH SHUT... I WOULDN'T WANT TO *ANNOY* ANYONE!
AND ANOTHER THING, I AM *NOT* AFRAID TO GET MY HOOVES DIRTY... I JUST DON'T LIKE *IT.*
WELL, I'M GLAD TO HEAR THAT... BECAUSE THEY'RE DIRTY NOW!
WHAT?
UH... GIRLS...? WHAT HAS 8 LEGS, WEAVES A WEB AND IS LOOMING OVER US RIGHT NOW?
OH! OH! I KNOW THIS ONE... IS IT, UM... A TURTLE?
FLOING!

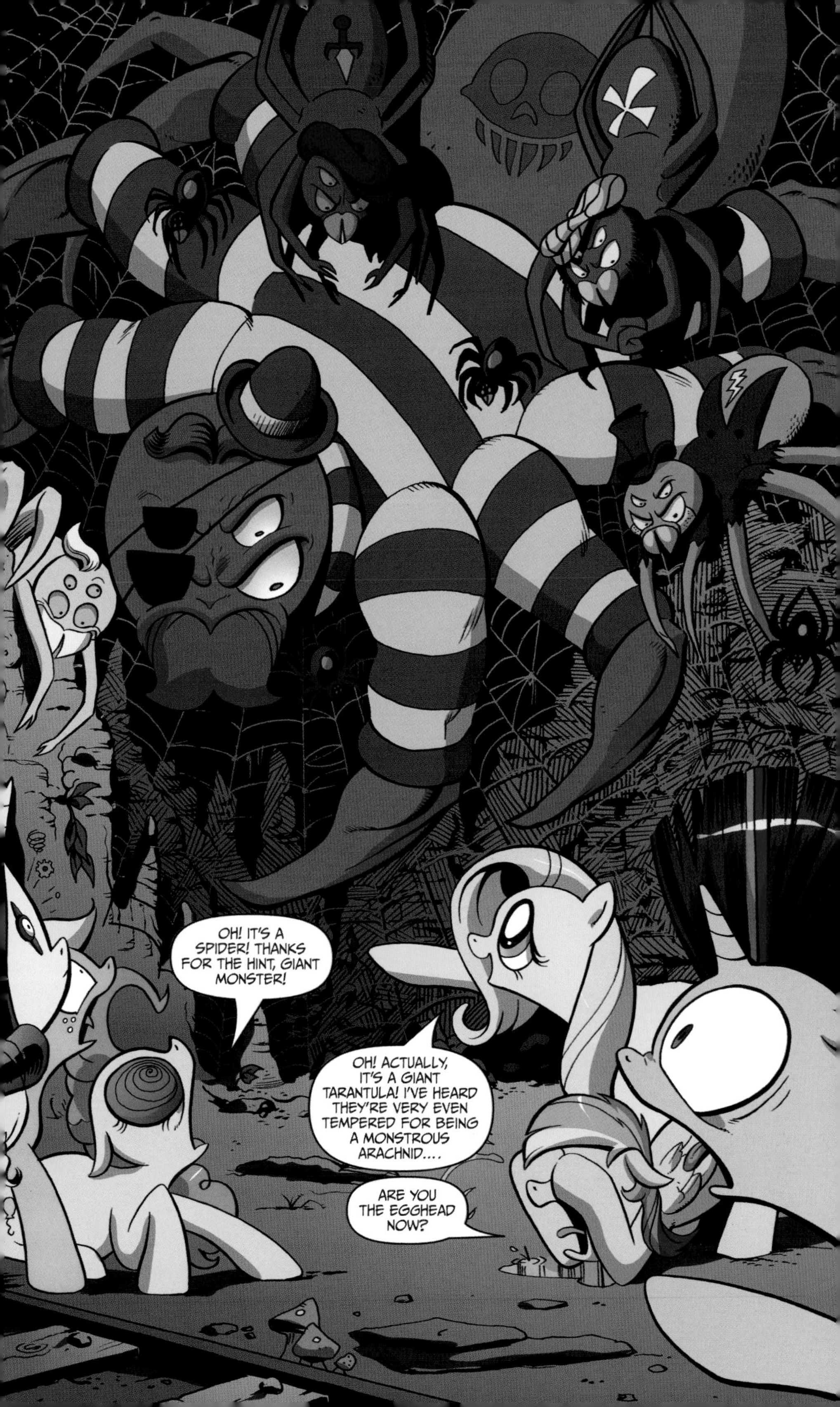
OH! IT'S A SPIDER! THANKS FOR THE HINT, GIANT MONSTER!
OH! ACTUALLY, IT'S A GIANT TARANTULA! I'VE HEARD THEY'RE VERY EVEN TEMPERED FOR BEING A MONSTROUS ARACHNID....
ARE YOU THE EGGHEAD NOW?

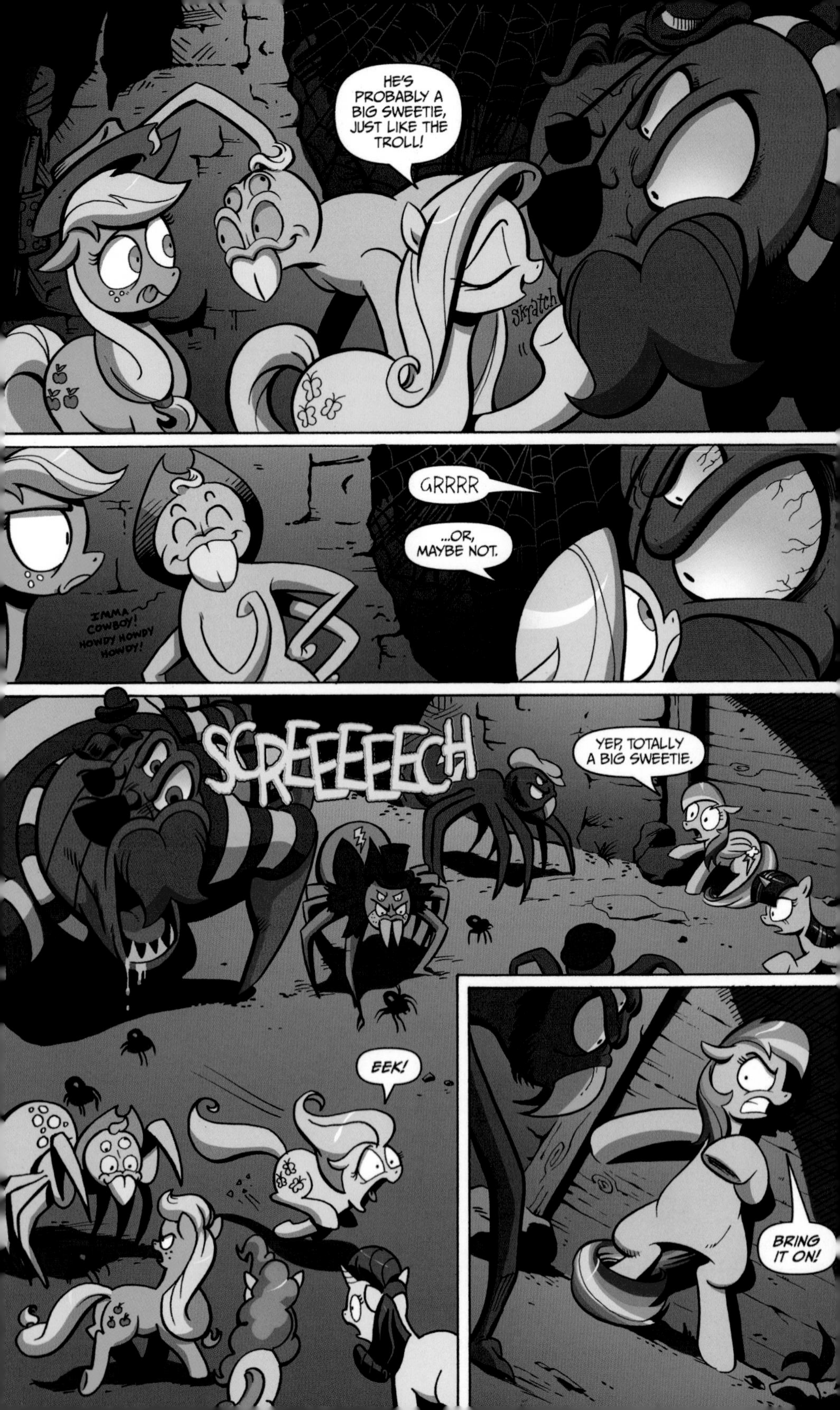
HE'S PROBABLY A BIG SWEETIE, JUST LIKE THE TROLL!
SKRATCH
GRRRR
...OR, MAYBE NOT.
IMMA COWBOY! HOWDY HOWDY HOWDY!
SCREEEEECH
YEP, TOTALLY A BIG SWEETIE.
EEK!
BRING IT ON!

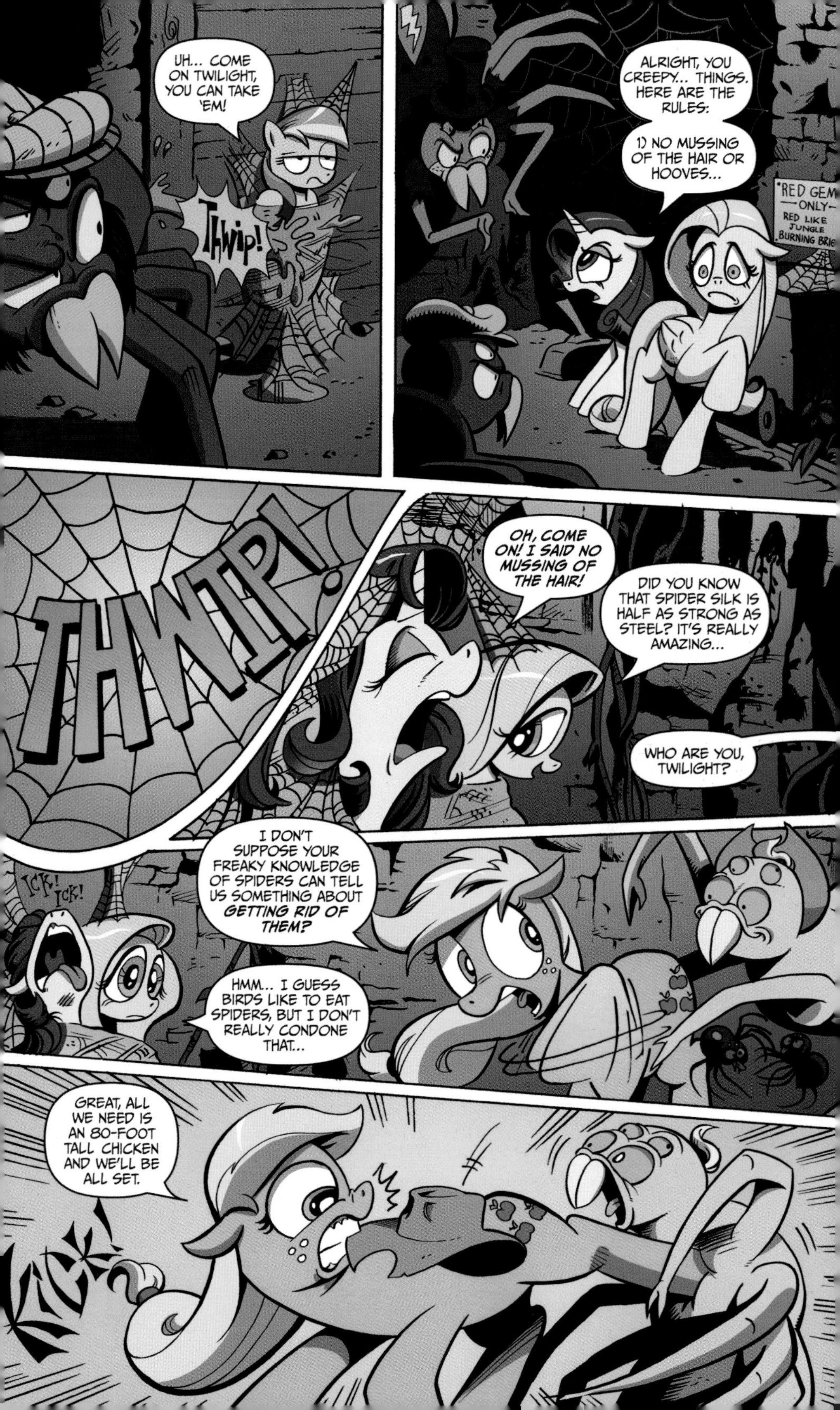
UH... COME ON TWILIGHT, YOU CAN TAKE 'EM!
THWIP!
ALRIGHT, YOU CREEPY... THINGS. HERE ARE THE RULES:
1) NO MUSSING OF THE HAIR OR HOOVES...
RED GEM ONLY
RED LIKE JUNGLE BURNING BRI
THWIP!
OH, COME ON! I SAID NO MUSSING OF THE HAIR!
DID YOU KNOW THAT SPIDER SILK IS HALF AS STRONG AS STEEL? IT'S REALLY AMAZING...
WHO ARE YOU, TWILIGHT?
ICK! ICK!
I DON'T SUPPOSE YOUR FREAKY KNOWLEDGE OF SPIDERS CAN TELL US SOMETHING ABOUT GETTING RID OF THEM?
HMM... I GUESS BIRDS LIKE TO EAT SPIDERS, BUT I DON'T REALLY CONDONE THAT...
GREAT, ALL WE NEED IS AN 80-FOOT TALL CHICKEN AND WE'LL BE ALL SET.
KICK!

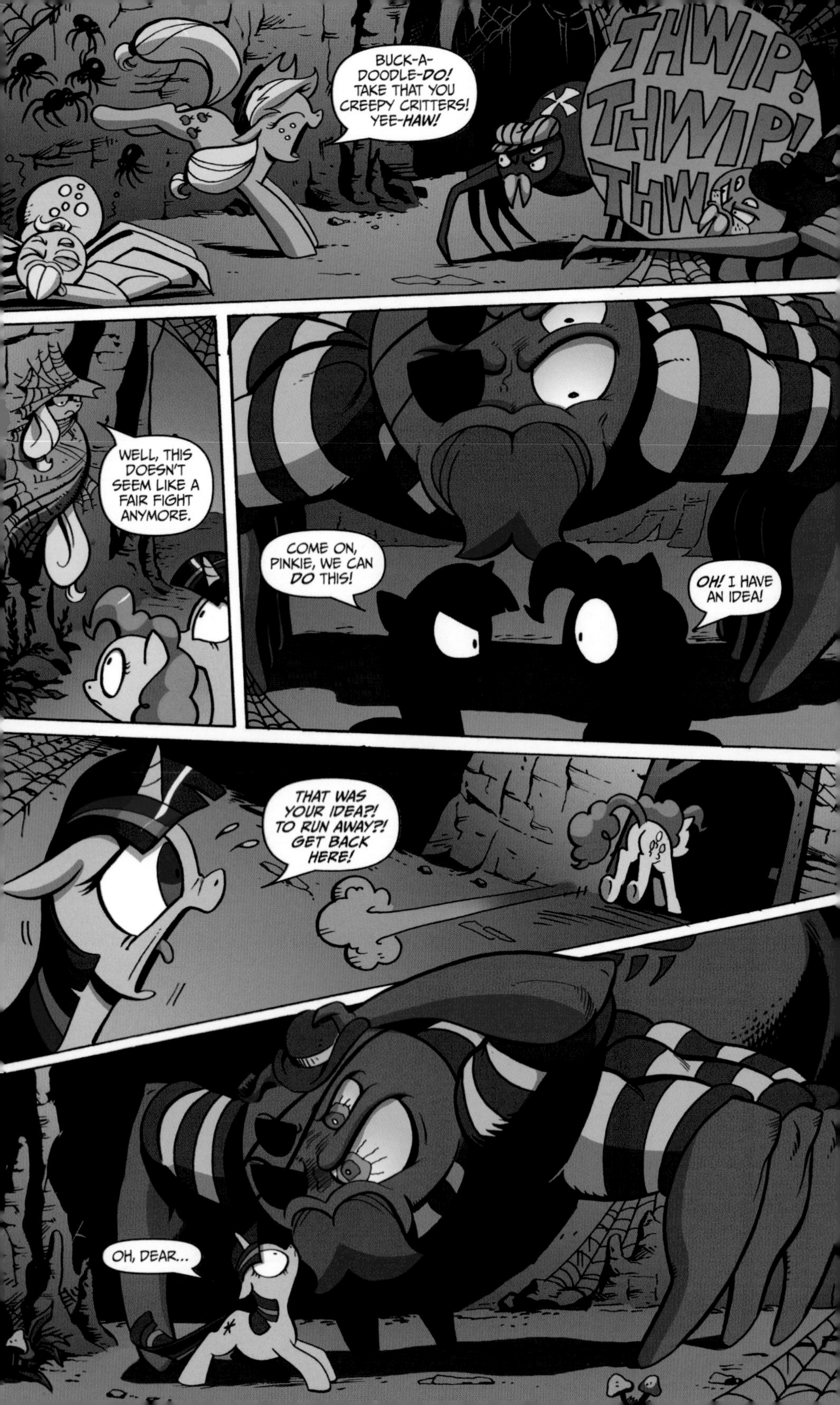
BUCK-A-DOODLE-DO! TAKE THAT YOU CREEPY CRITTERS! YEE-HAW!
THWIP! THWIP! THW
WELL, THIS DOESN'T SEEM LIKE A FAIR FIGHT ANYMORE.
COME ON, PINKIE, WE CAN DO THIS!
OH! I HAVE AN IDEA!
THAT WAS YOUR IDEA?! TO RUN AWAY?! GET BACK HERE!
OH, DEAR...

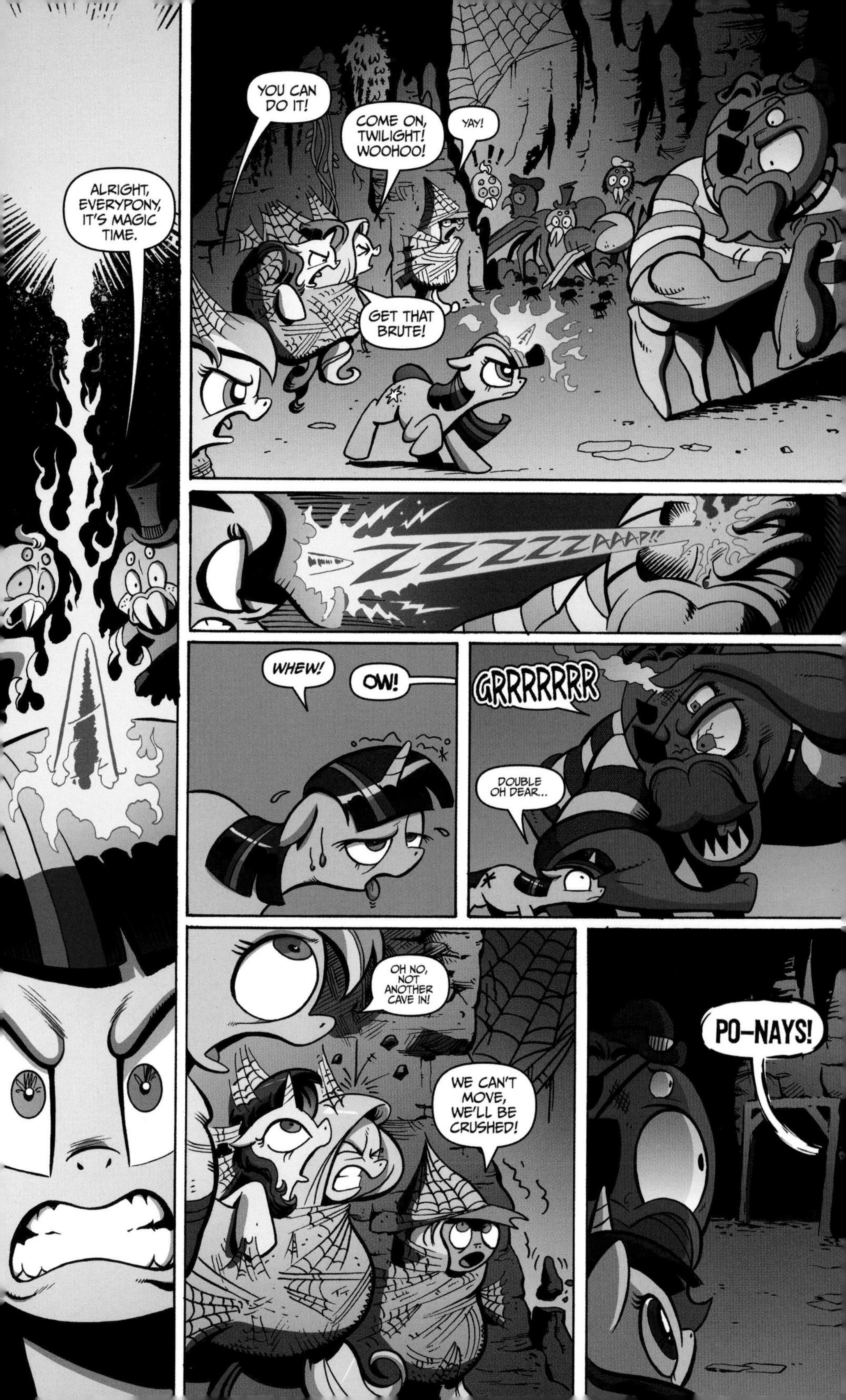
ALRIGHT, EVERYPONY, IT'S MAGIC TIME.
YOU CAN DO IT!
COME ON, TWILIGHT! WOOHOO!
YAY!
GET THAT BRUTE!
ZZZZZZZAAAP!!
WHEW!
OW!
GRRRRRRR
DOUBLE OH DEAR...
OH NO, NOT ANOTHER CAVE IN!
WE CAN'T MOVE, WE'LL BE CRUSHED!
PO-NAYS!

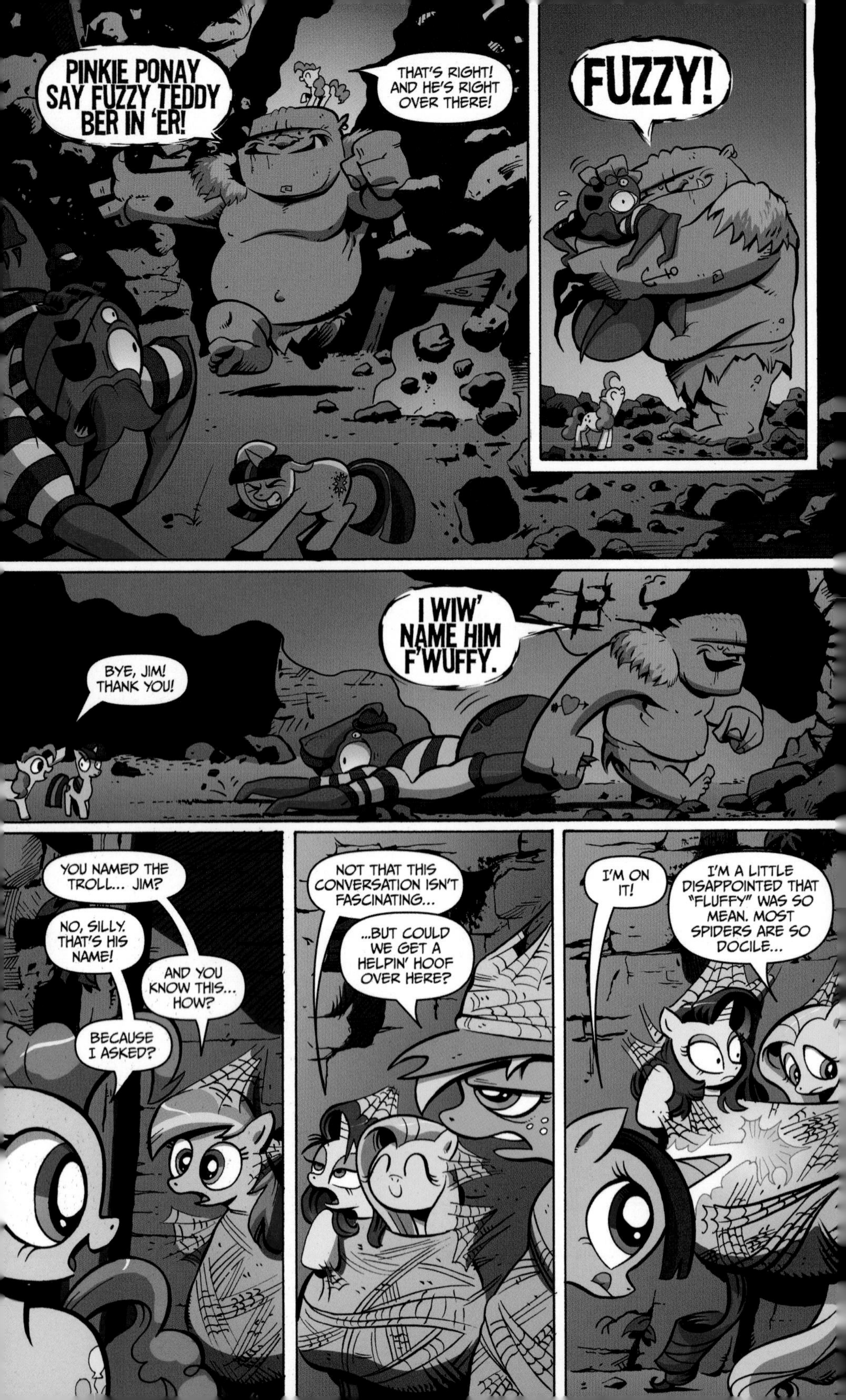
PINKIE PONAY SAY FUZZY TEDDY BER IN 'ER!
THAT'S RIGHT! AND HE'S RIGHT OVER THERE!
FUZZY!
I WIW' NAME HIM F'WUFFY.
BYE, JIM! THANK YOU!
YOU NAMED THE TROLL... JIM?
NO, SILLY. THAT'S HIS NAME!
AND YOU KNOW THIS... HOW?
BECAUSE I ASKED?
NOT THAT THIS CONVERSATION ISN'T FASCINATING...
...BUT COULD WE GET A HELPIN' HOOF OVER HERE?
I'M ON IT!
I'M A LITTLE DISAPPOINTED THAT "FLUFFY" WAS SO MEAN. MOST SPIDERS ARE SO DOCILE...

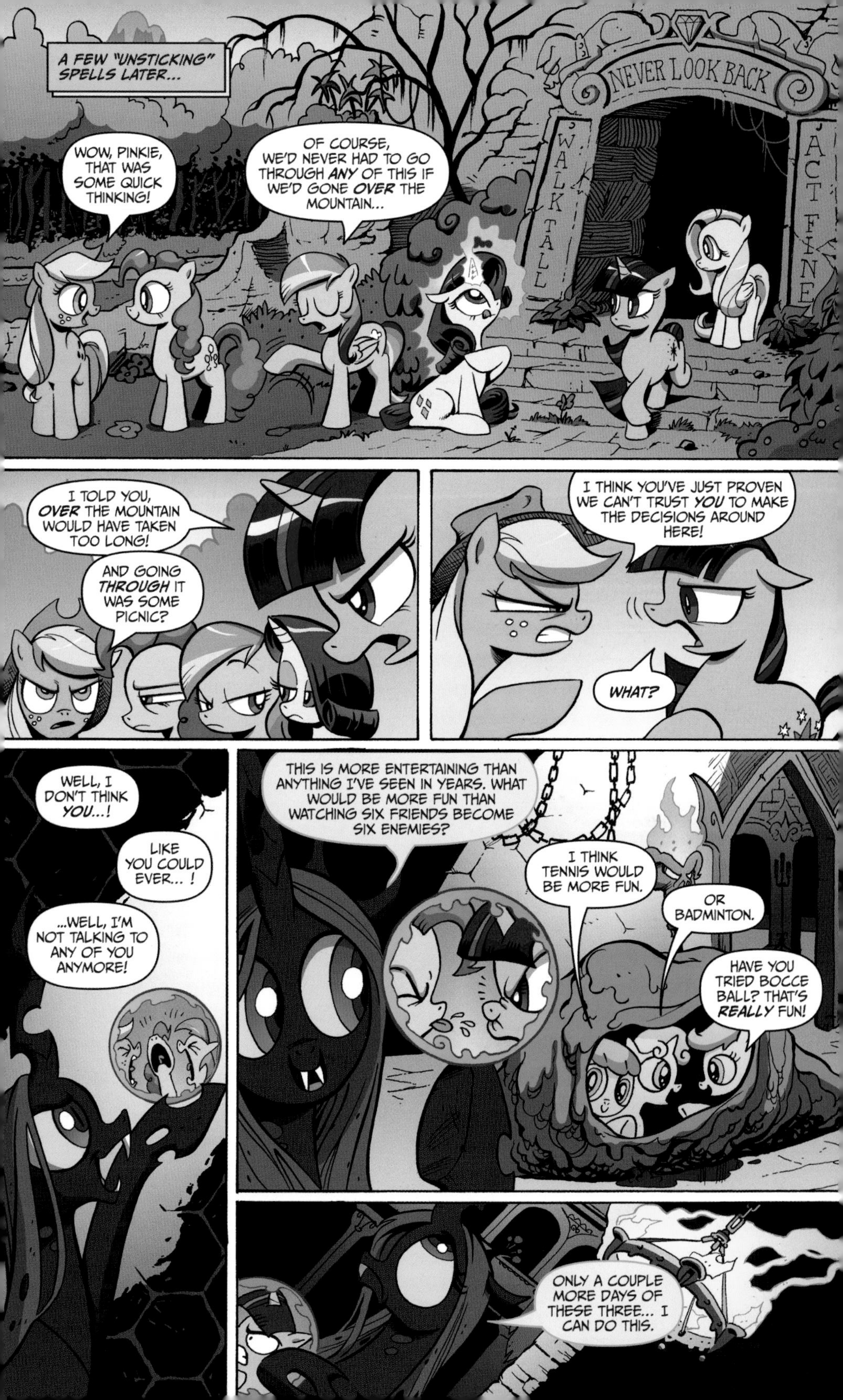

A FEW "UNSTICKING" SPELLS LATER...
NEVER LOOK BACK
WALK TALL
ACT FINE
WOW, PINKIE, THAT WAS SOME QUICK THINKING!
OF COURSE, WE'D NEVER HAD TO GO THROUGH ANY OF THIS IF WE'D GONE OVER THE MOUNTAIN...
I TOLD YOU, OVER THE MOUNTAIN WOULD HAVE TAKEN TOO LONG!
AND GOING THROUGH IT WAS SOME PICNIC?
I THINK YOU'VE JUST PROVEN WE CAN'T TRUST YOU TO MAKE THE DECISIONS AROUND HERE!
WHAT?
WELL, I DON'T THINK YOU...!
LIKE YOU COULD EVER... !
...WELL, I'M NOT TALKING TO ANY OF YOU ANYMORE!
THIS IS MORE ENTERTAINING THAN ANYTHING I'VE SEEN IN YEARS. WHAT WOULD BE MORE FUN THAN WATCHING SIX FRIENDS BECOME SIX ENEMIES?
I THINK TENNIS WOULD BE MORE FUN.
OR BADMINTON.
HAVE YOU TRIED BOCCE BALL? THAT'S REALLY FUN!
ONLY A COUPLE MORE DAYS OF THESE THREE... I CAN DO THIS.

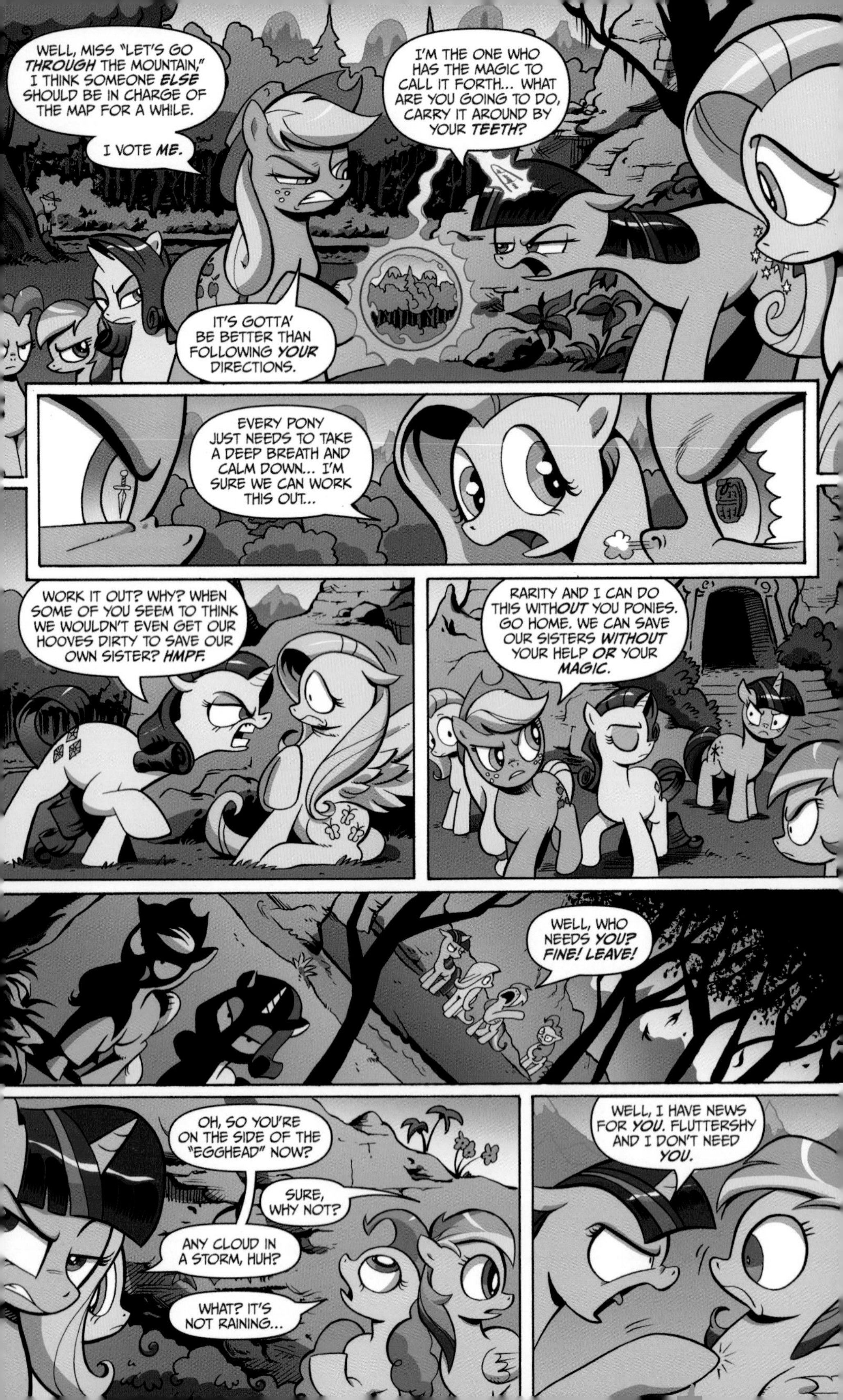
WELL, MISS "LET'S GO THROUGH THE MOUNTAIN," I THINK SOMEONE ELSE SHOULD BE IN CHARGE OF THE MAP FOR A WHILE.
I VOTE ME.
I'M THE ONE WHO HAS THE MAGIC TO CALL IT FORTH... WHAT ARE YOU GOING TO DO, CARRY IT AROUND BY YOUR TEETH?
IT'S GOTTA' BE BETTER THAN FOLLOWING YOUR DIRECTIONS.
EVERY PONY JUST NEEDS TO TAKE A DEEP BREATH AND CALM DOWN... I'M SURE WE CAN WORK THIS OUT...
WORK IT OUT? WHY? WHEN SOME OF YOU SEEM TO THINK WE WOULDN'T EVEN GET OUR HOOVES DIRTY TO SAVE OUR OWN SISTER? HMPF.
RARITY AND I CAN DO THIS WITHOUT YOU PONIES. GO HOME. WE CAN SAVE OUR SISTERS WITHOUT YOUR HELP OR YOUR MAGIC.
WELL, WHO NEEDS YOU? FINE! LEAVE!
OH, SO YOU'RE ON THE SIDE OF THE "EGGHEAD" NOW?
SURE, WHY NOT?
ANY CLOUD IN A STORM, HUH?
WHAT? IT'S NOT RAINING...
WELL, I HAVE NEWS FOR YOU. FLUTTERSHY AND I DON'T NEED YOU.

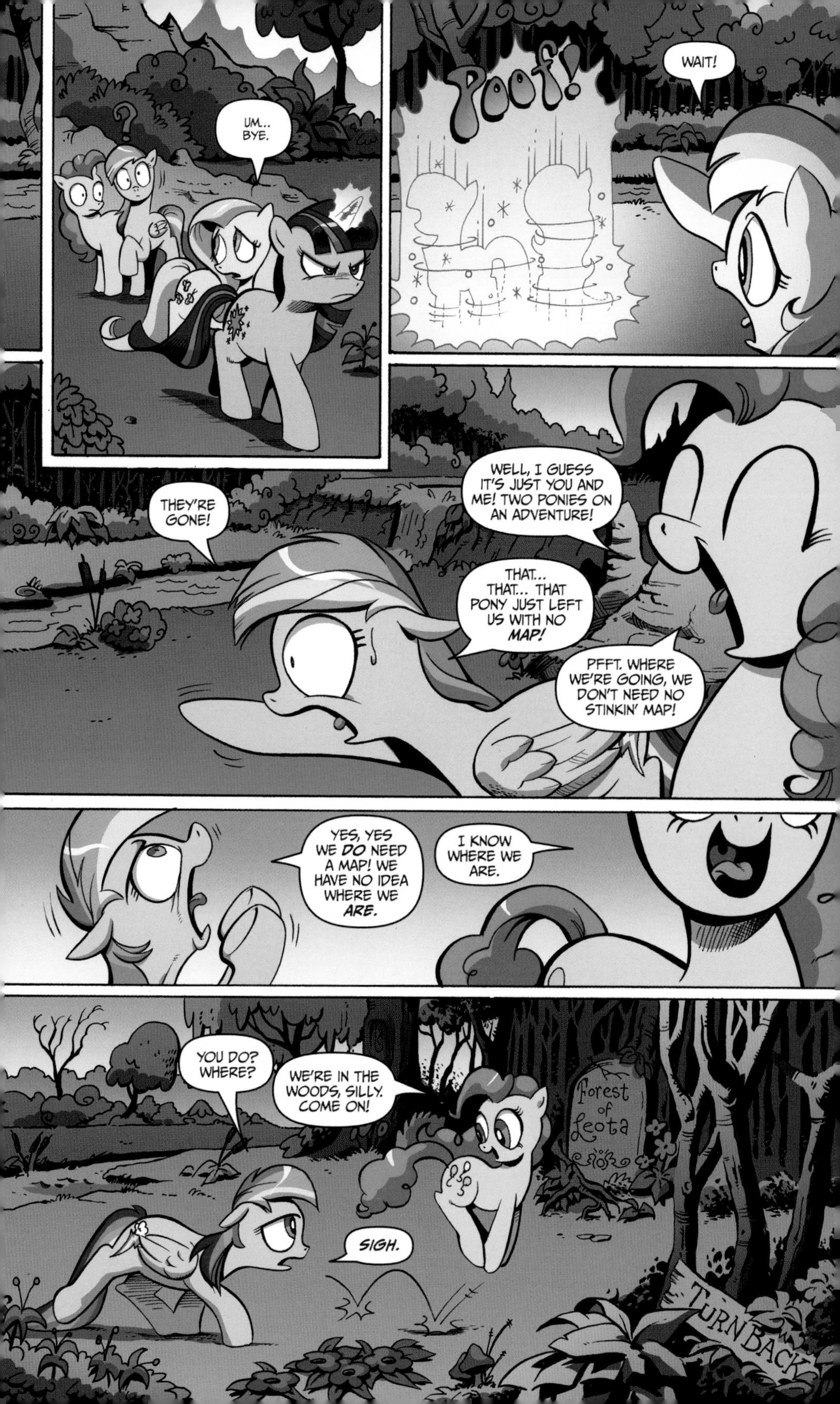
UM.. BYE.
POOF!
WAIT!
THEY'RE GONE!
WELL, I GUESS IT'S JUST YOU AND ME! TWO PONIES ON AN ADVENTURE!
THAT... THAT... THAT PONY JUST LEFT US WITH NO MAP!
PFFT. WHERE WE'RE GOING, WE DON'T NEED NO STINKIN' MAP!
YES, YES WE DO NEED A MAP! WE HAVE NO IDEA WHERE WE ARE.
I KNOW WHERE WE ARE.
YOU DO? WHERE?
WE'RE IN THE WOODS, SILLY. COME ON!
Forest of Leota
SIGH.
TURNBACK

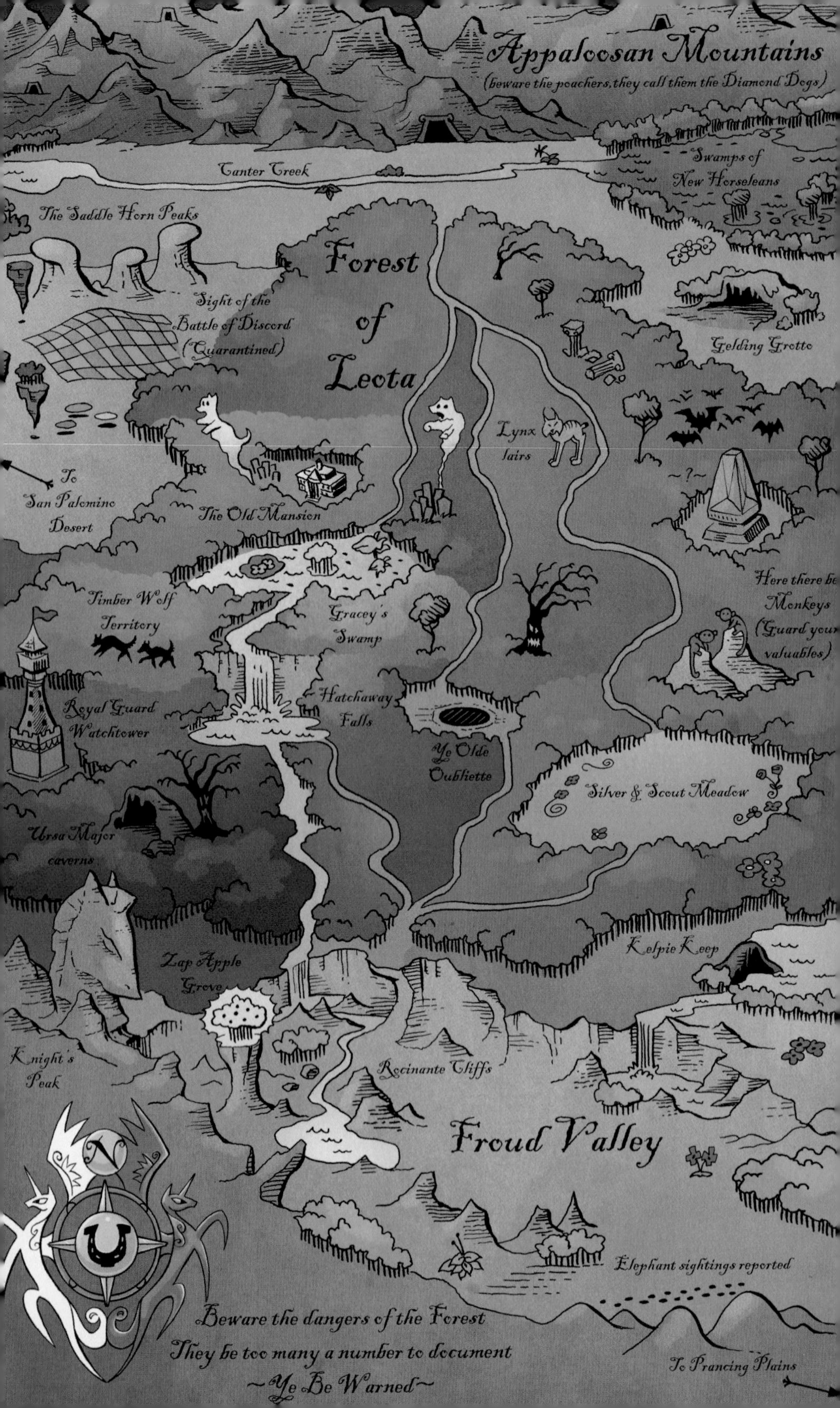
Appaloosan Mountains
(beware the poachers, they call them the Diamond Dogs)
Canter Creek
Swamps of New Horseleans
The Saddle Horn Peaks
Forest of Leota
Sight of the Battle of Discord (Quarantined)
Gelding Grotto
Lynx lairs
To San Palomino Desert
The Old Mansion
~?~
Here there be Monkeys (Guard your valuables)
Timber Wolf Territory
Gracey's Swamp
Royal Guard Watchtower
Hatchaway Falls
Ye Olde Oubliette
Silver & Scout Meadow
Ursa Major caverns
Kelpie Keep
Zap Apple Grove
Knight's Peak
Rocinante Cliffs
Froud Valley
N
Elephant sightings reported
Beware the dangers of the Forest
They be too many a number to document
~Ye Be Warned~
To Prancing Plains

Art by
Stephanie Buscema

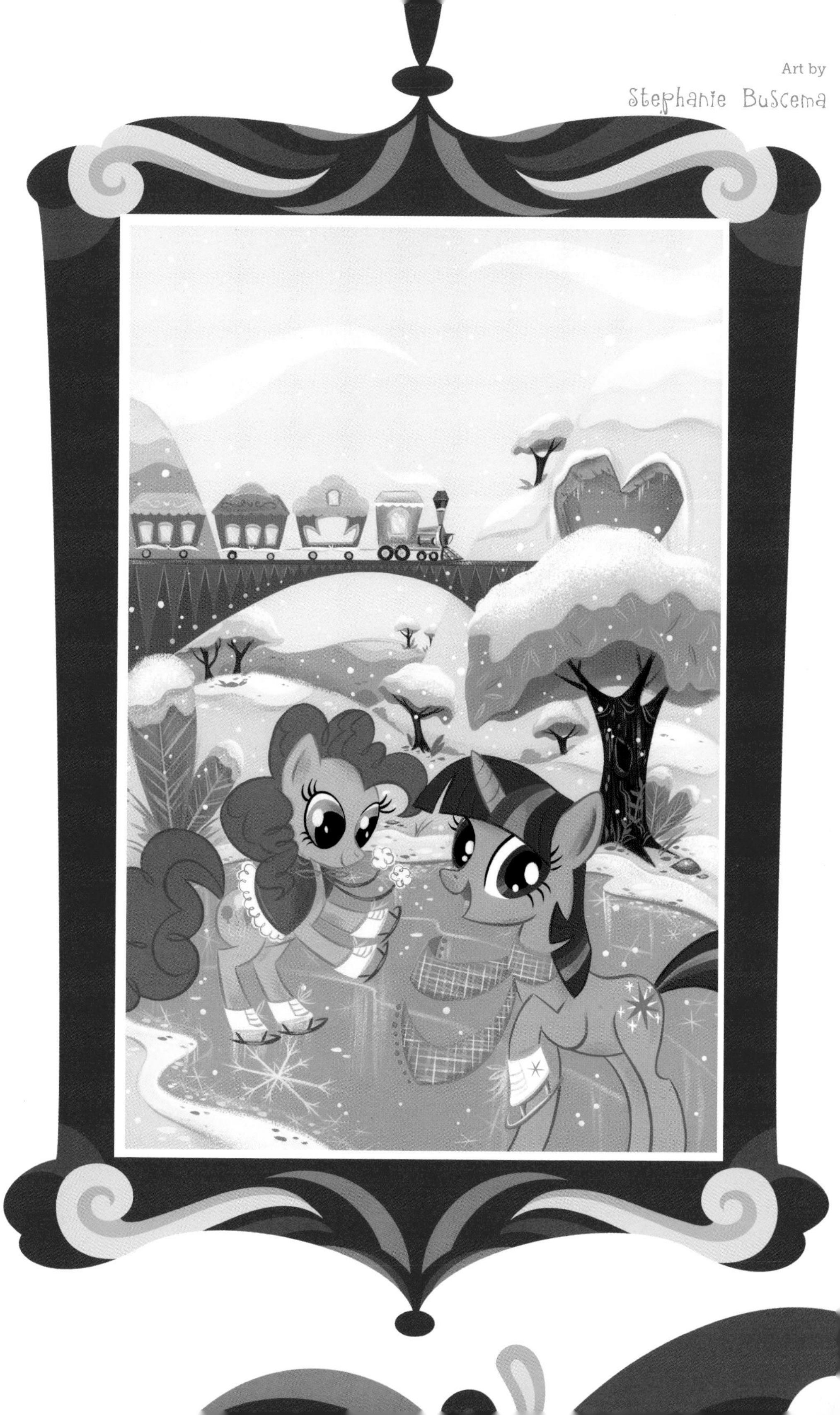

Art by
J. Scott Campbell

Colors by
Nei Ruffino

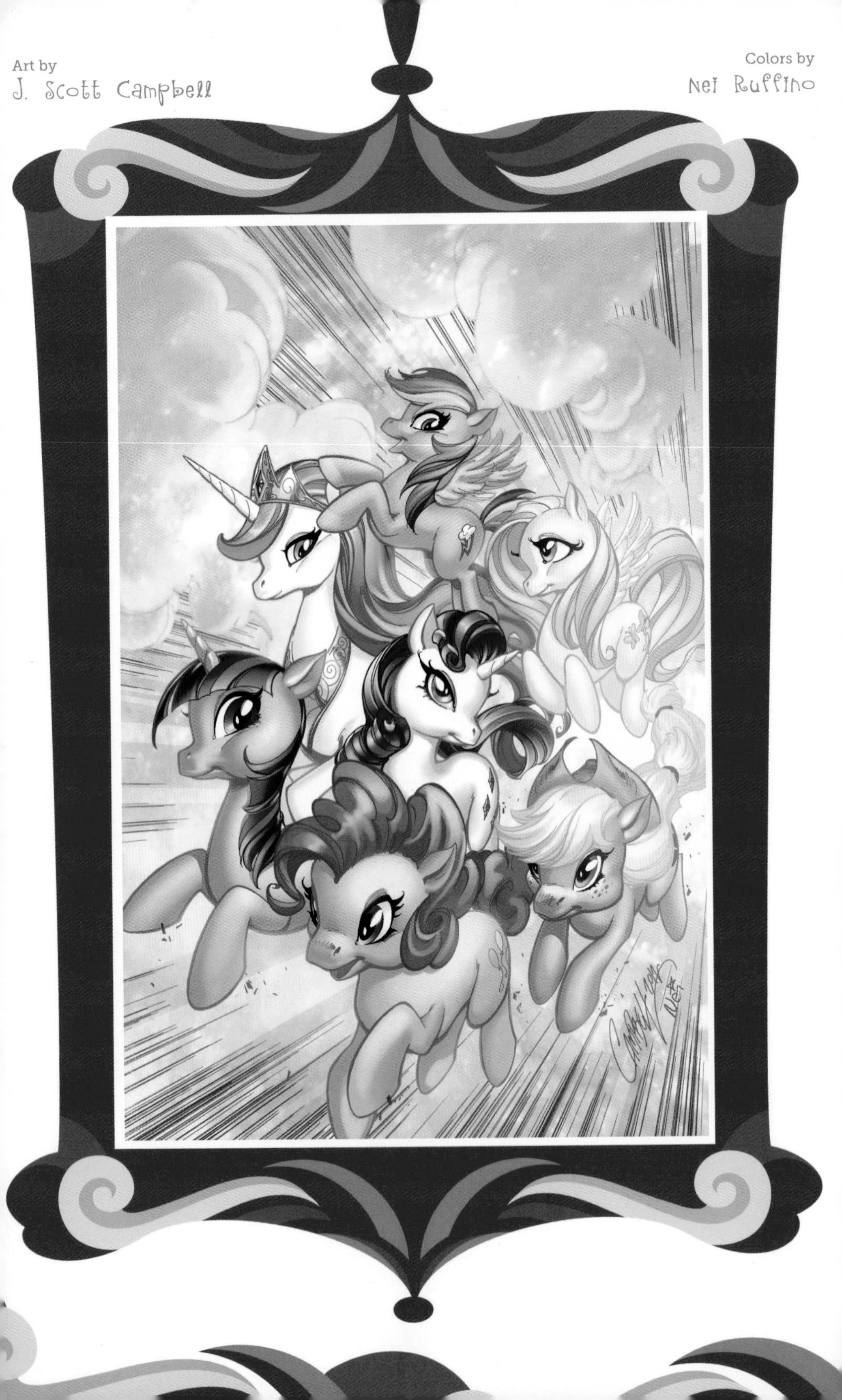

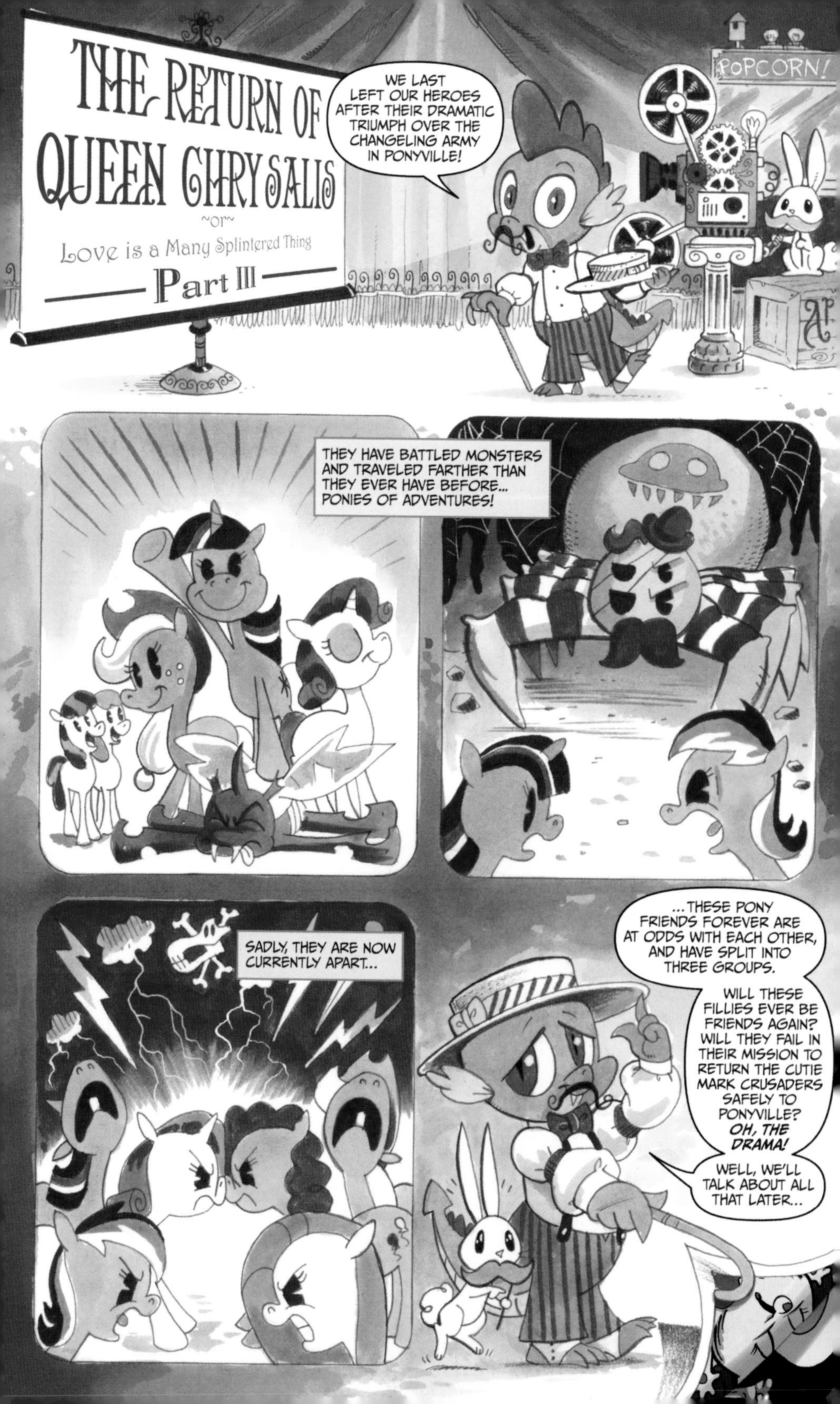

THE RETURN OF QUEEN CHRYSALIS
~or~
Love is a Many Splintered Thing
Part III
WE LAST LEFT OUR HEROES AFTER THEIR DRAMATIC TRIUMPH OVER THE CHANGELING ARMY IN PONYVILLE!
POPCORN!
THEY HAVE BATTLED MONSTERS AND TRAVELED FARTHER THAN THEY EVER HAVE BEFORE... PONIES OF ADVENTURES!
SADLY, THEY ARE NOW CURRENTLY APART...
...THESE PONY FRIENDS FOREVER ARE AT ODDS WITH EACH OTHER, AND HAVE SPLIT INTO THREE GROUPS.
WILL THESE FILLIES EVER BE FRIENDS AGAIN? WILL THEY FAIL IN THEIR MISSION TO RETURN THE CUTIE MARK CRUSADERS SAFELY TO PONYVILLE? *OH, THE DRAMA!*
WELL, WE'LL TALK ABOUT ALL THAT LATER...

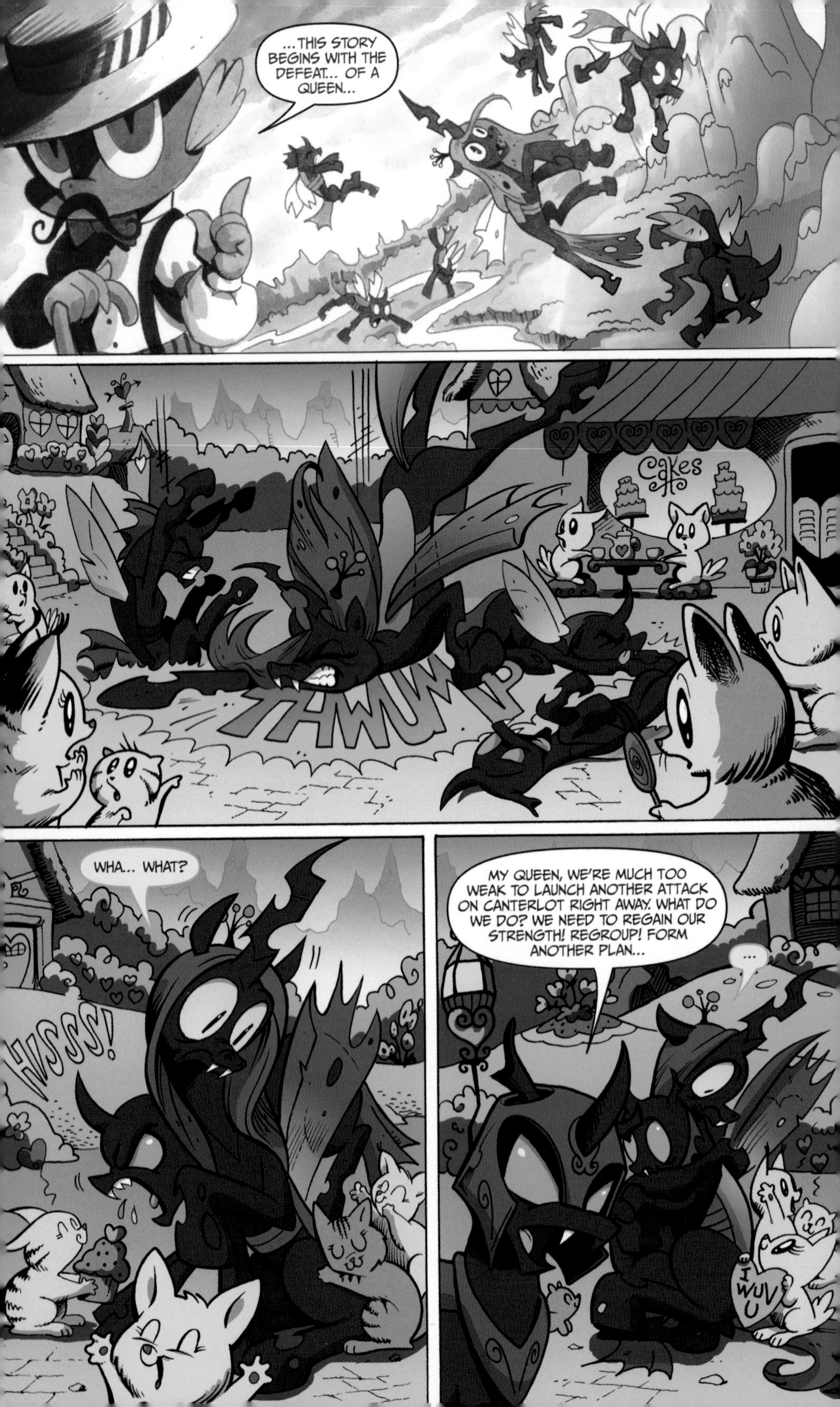
...THIS STORY BEGINS WITH THE DEFEAT... OF A QUEEN...
Cakes
THWUMP
WHA... WHAT?
HSSS!
MY QUEEN, WE'RE MUCH TOO WEAK TO LAUNCH ANOTHER ATTACK ON CANTERLOT RIGHT AWAY. WHAT DO WE DO? WE NEED TO REGAIN OUR STRENGTH! REGROUP! FORM ANOTHER PLAN...
...
I WUV U

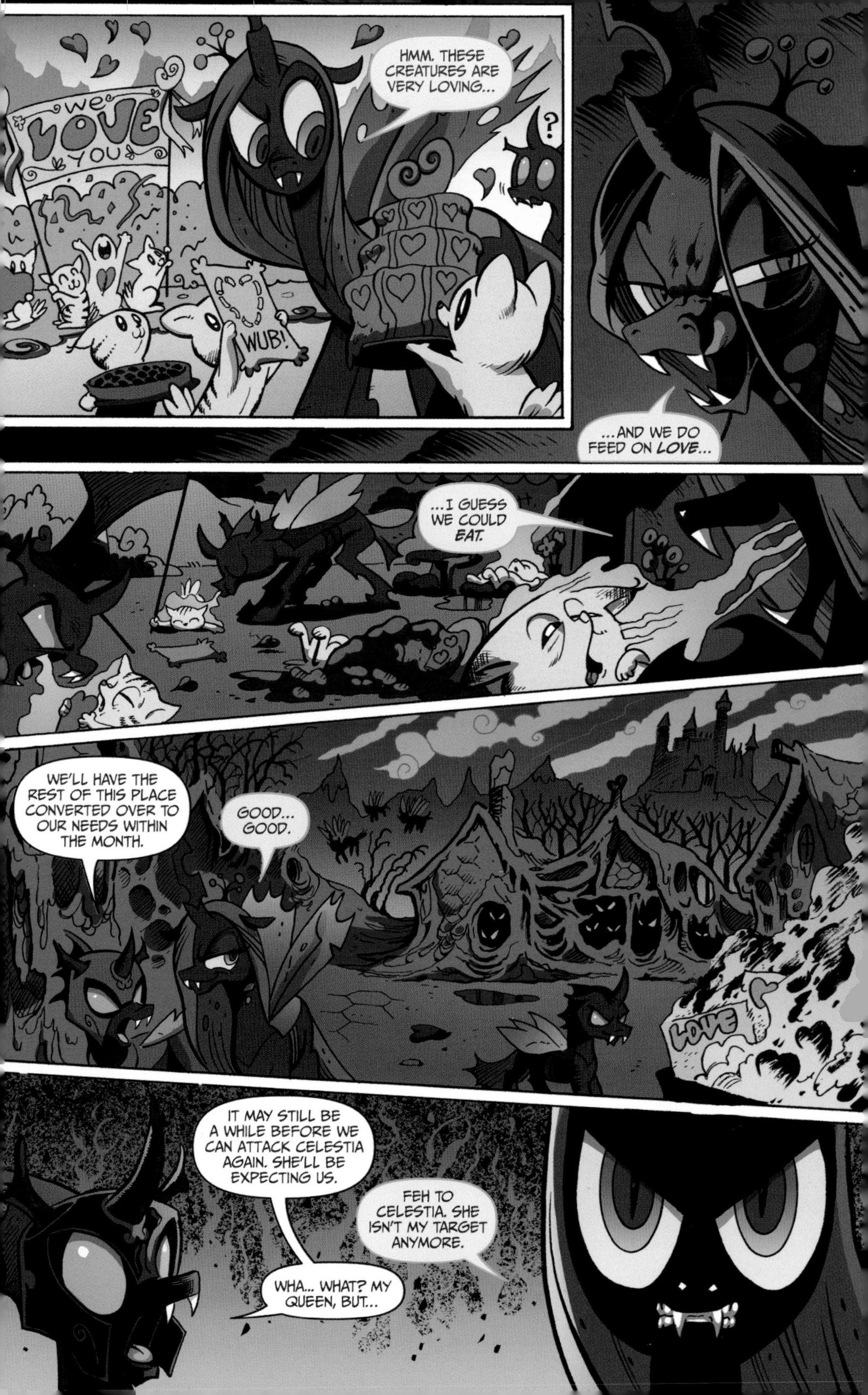

WE LOVE YOU
WUB!
HMM. THESE CREATURES ARE VERY LOVING...
?
...AND WE DO FEED ON LOVE...
...I GUESS WE COULD EAT.
WE'LL HAVE THE REST OF THIS PLACE CONVERTED OVER TO OUR NEEDS WITHIN THE MONTH.
GOOD... GOOD.
LOVE
IT MAY STILL BE A WHILE BEFORE WE CAN ATTACK CELESTIA AGAIN. SHE'LL BE EXPECTING US.
FEH TO CELESTIA. SHE ISN'T MY TARGET ANYMORE.
WHA... WHAT? MY QUEEN, BUT...

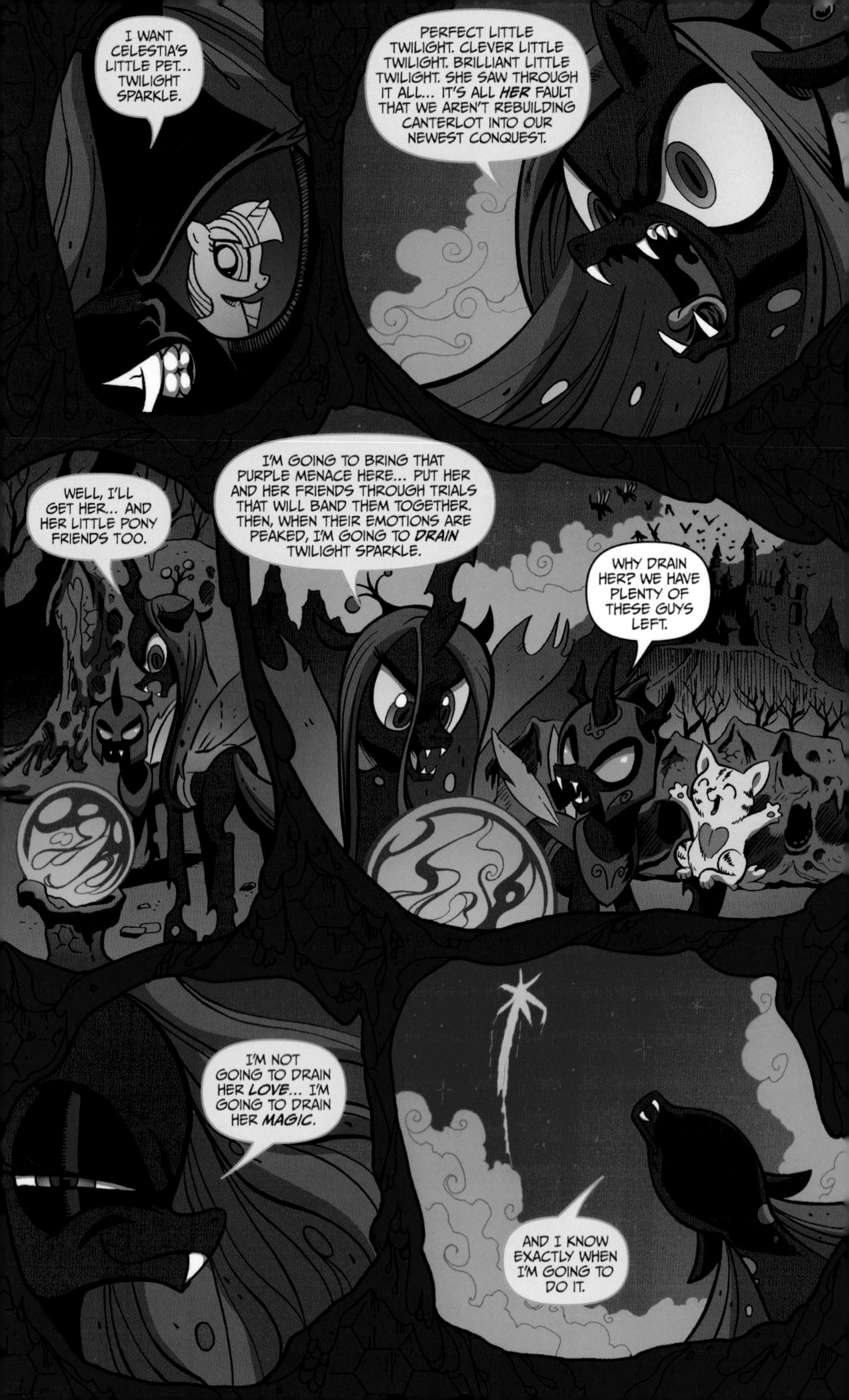
I WANT CELESTIA'S LITTLE PET... TWILIGHT SPARKLE.
PERFECT LITTLE TWILIGHT. CLEVER LITTLE TWILIGHT. BRILLIANT LITTLE TWILIGHT. SHE SAW THROUGH IT ALL... IT'S ALL *HER* FAULT THAT WE AREN'T REBUILDING CANTERLOT INTO OUR NEWEST CONQUEST.
WELL, I'LL GET HER... AND HER LITTLE PONY FRIENDS TOO.
I'M GOING TO BRING THAT PURPLE MENACE HERE... PUT HER AND HER FRIENDS THROUGH TRIALS THAT WILL BAND THEM TOGETHER. THEN, WHEN THEIR EMOTIONS ARE PEAKED, I'M GOING TO *DRAIN* TWILIGHT SPARKLE.
WHY DRAIN HER? WE HAVE PLENTY OF THESE GUYS LEFT.
I'M NOT GOING TO DRAIN HER *LOVE*... I'M GOING TO DRAIN HER *MAGIC*.
AND I KNOW EXACTLY WHEN I'M GOING TO DO IT.

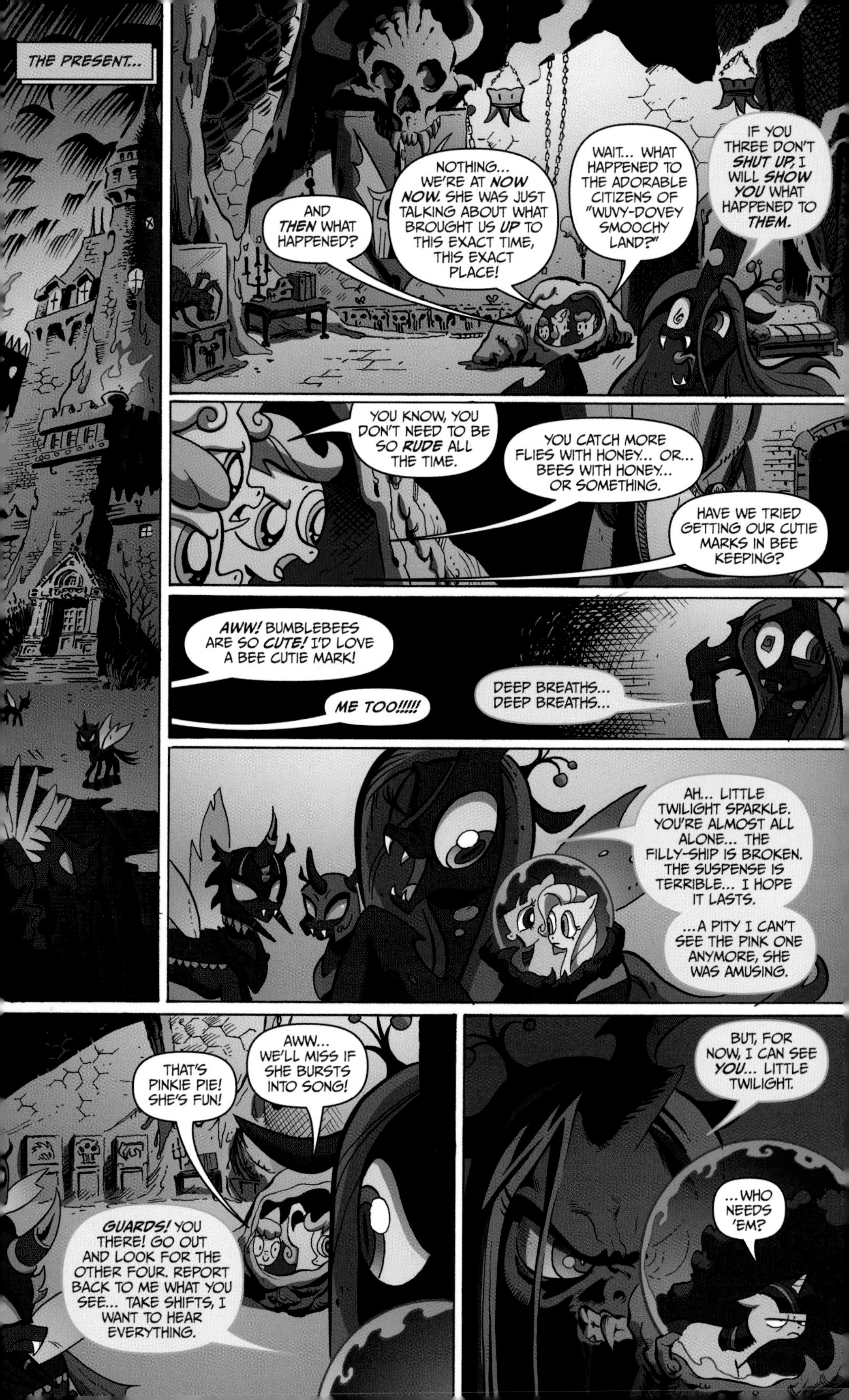
THE PRESENT...
AND THEN WHAT HAPPENED?
NOTHING... WE'RE AT NOW NOW. SHE WAS JUST TALKING ABOUT WHAT BROUGHT US UP TO THIS EXACT TIME, THIS EXACT PLACE!
WAIT... WHAT HAPPENED TO THE ADORABLE CITIZENS OF "WUVY-DOVEY SMOOCHY LAND?"
IF YOU THREE DON'T SHUT UP, I WILL SHOW YOU WHAT HAPPENED TO THEM.
YOU KNOW, YOU DON'T NEED TO BE SO RUDE ALL THE TIME.
YOU CATCH MORE FLIES WITH HONEY... OR... BEES WITH HONEY... OR SOMETHING.
HAVE WE TRIED GETTING OUR CUTIE MARKS IN BEE KEEPING?
AWW! BUMBLEBEES ARE SO CUTE! I'D LOVE A BEE CUTIE MARK!
ME TOO!!!!!
DEEP BREATHS... DEEP BREATHS...
AH... LITTLE TWILIGHT SPARKLE. YOU'RE ALMOST ALL ALONE... THE FILLY-SHIP IS BROKEN. THE SUSPENSE IS TERRIBLE... I HOPE IT LASTS.
...A PITY I CAN'T SEE THE PINK ONE ANYMORE, SHE WAS AMUSING.
THAT'S PINKIE PIE! SHE'S FUN!
AWW... WE'LL MISS IF SHE BURSTS INTO SONG!
GUARDS! YOU THERE! GO OUT AND LOOK FOR THE OTHER FOUR. REPORT BACK TO ME WHAT YOU SEE... TAKE SHIFTS, I WANT TO HEAR EVERYTHING.
BUT, FOR NOW, I CAN SEE YOU... LITTLE TWILIGHT.
...WHO NEEDS 'EM?

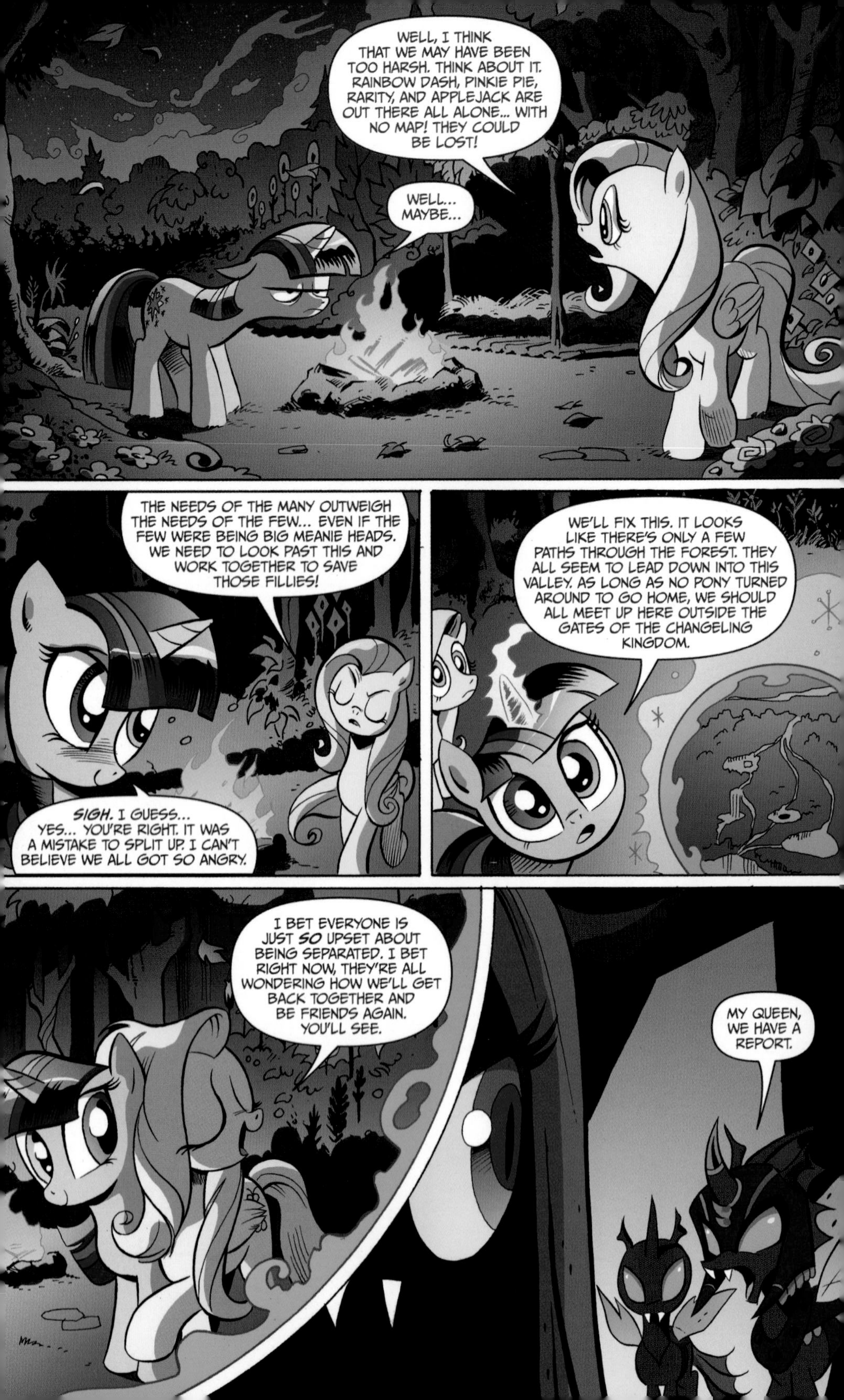
WELL, I THINK THAT WE MAY HAVE BEEN TOO HARSH. THINK ABOUT IT. RAINBOW DASH, PINKIE PIE, RARITY, AND APPLEJACK ARE OUT THERE ALL ALONE... WITH NO MAP! THEY COULD BE LOST!
WELL... MAYBE...
THE NEEDS OF THE MANY OUTWEIGH THE NEEDS OF THE FEW... EVEN IF THE FEW WERE BEING BIG MEANIE HEADS. WE NEED TO LOOK PAST THIS AND WORK TOGETHER TO SAVE THOSE FILLIES!
SIGH. I GUESS... YES... YOU'RE RIGHT. IT WAS A MISTAKE TO SPLIT UP. I CAN'T BELIEVE WE ALL GOT SO ANGRY.
WE'LL FIX THIS. IT LOOKS LIKE THERE'S ONLY A FEW PATHS THROUGH THE FOREST. THEY ALL SEEM TO LEAD DOWN INTO THIS VALLEY. AS LONG AS NO PONY TURNED AROUND TO GO HOME, WE SHOULD ALL MEET UP HERE OUTSIDE THE GATES OF THE CHANGELING KINGDOM.
I BET EVERYONE IS JUST SO UPSET ABOUT BEING SEPARATED. I BET RIGHT NOW, THEY'RE ALL WONDERING HOW WE'LL GET BACK TOGETHER AND BE FRIENDS AGAIN. YOU'LL SEE.
MY QUEEN, WE HAVE A REPORT.

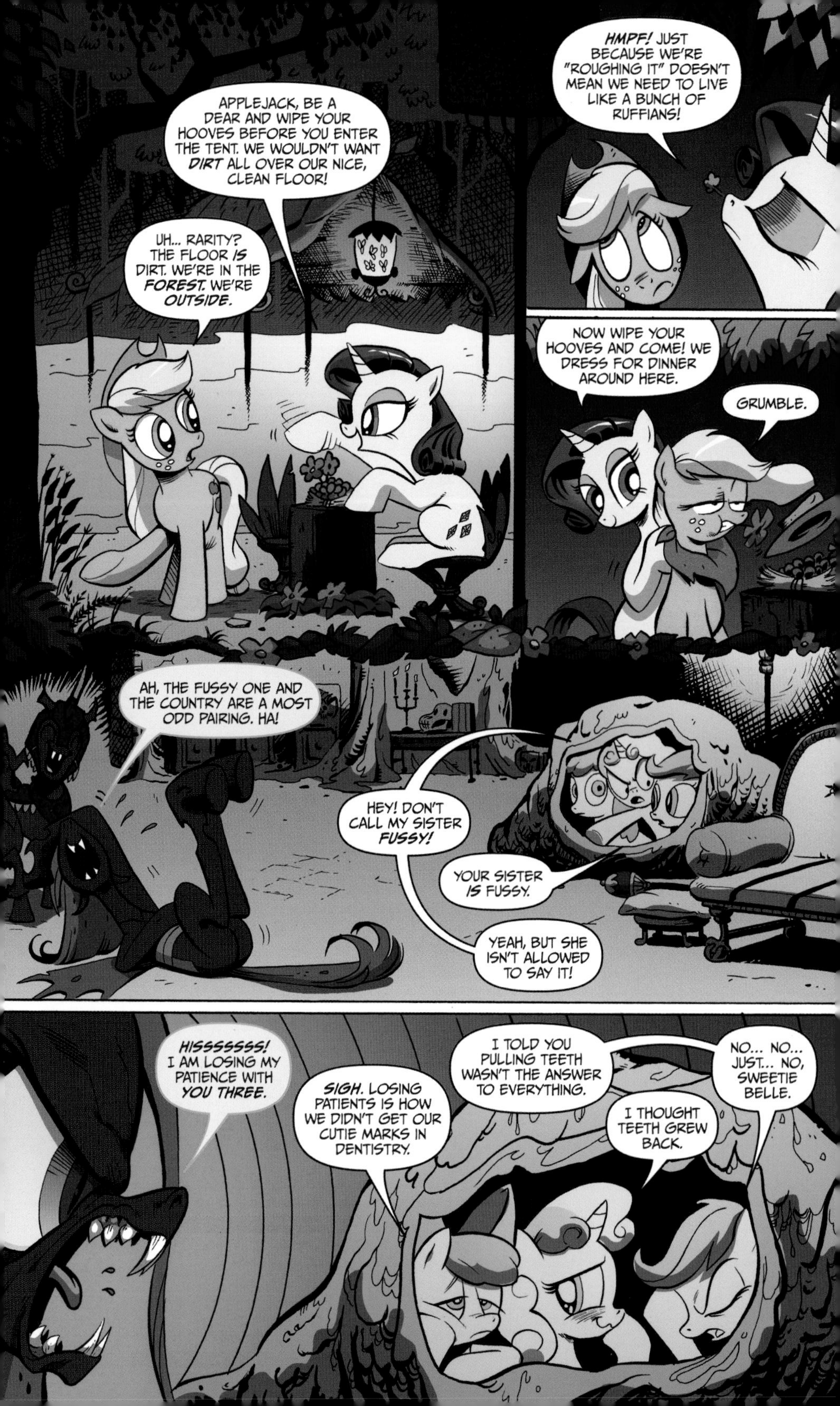
APPLEJACK, BE A DEAR AND WIPE YOUR HOOVES BEFORE YOU ENTER THE TENT. WE WOULDN'T WANT DIRT ALL OVER OUR NICE, CLEAN FLOOR!
UH... RARITY? THE FLOOR IS DIRT. WE'RE IN THE FOREST. WE'RE OUTSIDE.
HMPF! JUST BECAUSE WE'RE "ROUGHING IT" DOESN'T MEAN WE NEED TO LIVE LIKE A BUNCH OF RUFFIANS!
NOW WIPE YOUR HOOVES AND COME! WE DRESS FOR DINNER AROUND HERE.
GRUMBLE.
AH, THE FUSSY ONE AND THE COUNTRY ARE A MOST ODD PAIRING. HA!
HEY! DON'T CALL MY SISTER FUSSY!
YOUR SISTER IS FUSSY.
YEAH, BUT SHE ISN'T ALLOWED TO SAY IT!
HISSSSSSS! I AM LOSING MY PATIENCE WITH YOU THREE.
SIGH. LOSING PATIENTS IS HOW WE DIDN'T GET OUR CUTIE MARKS IN DENTISTRY.
I TOLD YOU PULLING TEETH WASN'T THE ANSWER TO EVERYTHING.
I THOUGHT TEETH GREW BACK.
NO... NO... JUST... NO, SWEETIE BELLE.

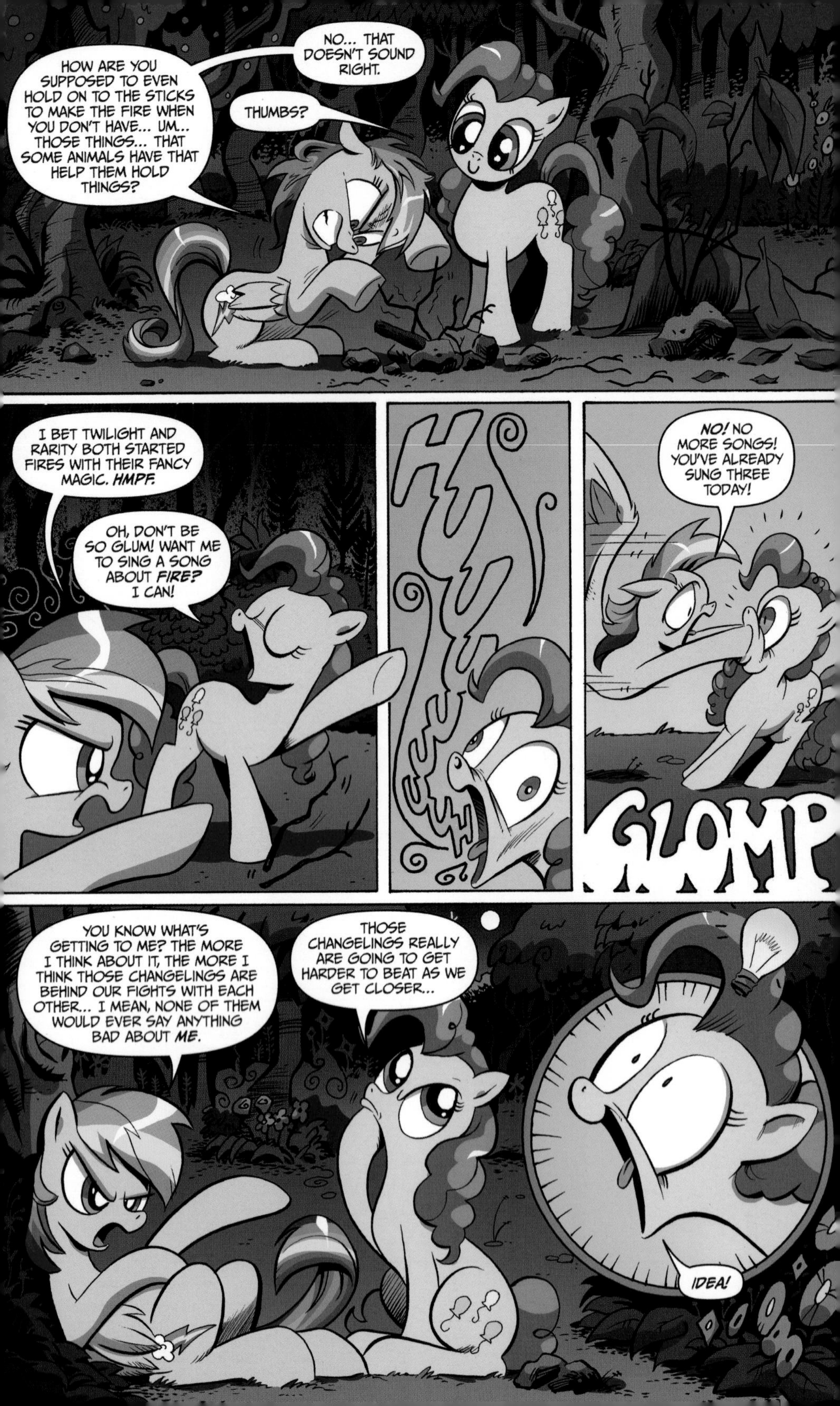

HOW ARE YOU SUPPOSED TO EVEN HOLD ON TO THE STICKS TO MAKE THE FIRE WHEN YOU DON'T HAVE... UM... THOSE THINGS... THAT SOME ANIMALS HAVE THAT HELP THEM HOLD THINGS?
THUMBS?
NO... THAT DOESN'T SOUND RIGHT.
I BET TWILIGHT AND RARITY BOTH STARTED FIRES WITH THEIR FANCY MAGIC. *HMPF.*
OH, DON'T BE SO GLUM! WANT ME TO SING A SONG ABOUT *FIRE?* I CAN!
HUUUUH
NO! NO MORE SONGS! YOU'VE ALREADY SUNG THREE TODAY!
GLOMP
YOU KNOW WHAT'S GETTING TO ME? THE MORE I THINK ABOUT IT, THE MORE I THINK THOSE CHANGELINGS ARE BEHIND OUR FIGHTS WITH EACH OTHER... I MEAN, NONE OF THEM WOULD EVER SAY ANYTHING BAD ABOUT *ME*.
THOSE CHANGELINGS REALLY ARE GOING TO GET HARDER TO BEAT AS WE GET CLOSER...
IDEA!

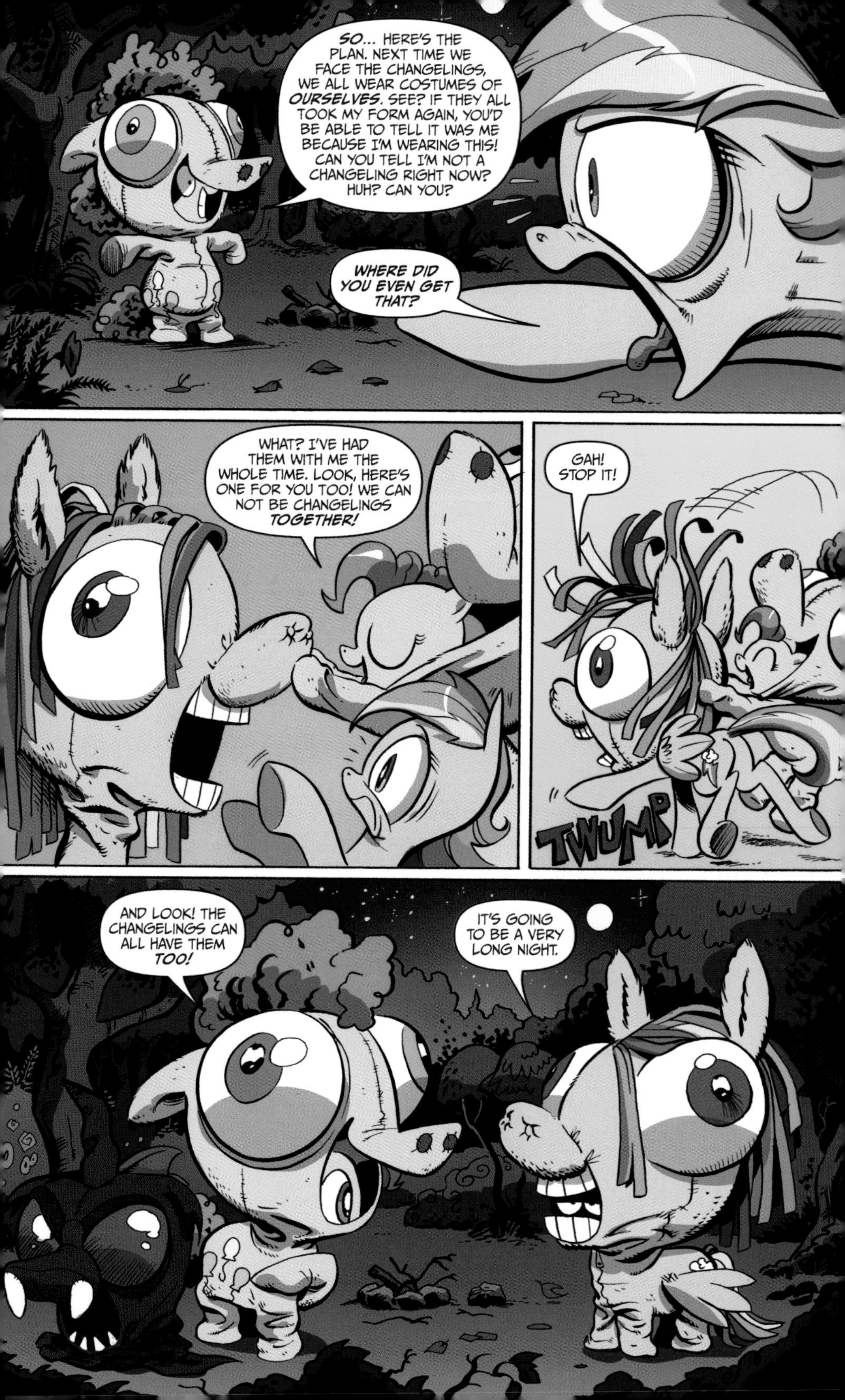
SO... HERE'S THE PLAN. NEXT TIME WE FACE THE CHANGELINGS, WE ALL WEAR COSTUMES OF OURSELVES. SEE? IF THEY ALL TOOK MY FORM AGAIN, YOU'D BE ABLE TO TELL IT WAS ME BECAUSE I'M WEARING THIS! CAN YOU TELL I'M NOT A CHANGELING RIGHT NOW? HUH? CAN YOU?
WHERE DID YOU EVEN GET THAT?
WHAT? I'VE HAD THEM WITH ME THE WHOLE TIME. LOOK, HERE'S ONE FOR YOU TOO! WE CAN NOT BE CHANGELINGS TOGETHER!
GAH! STOP IT!
TWUMP
AND LOOK! THE CHANGELINGS CAN ALL HAVE THEM TOO!
IT'S GOING TO BE A VERY LONG NIGHT.

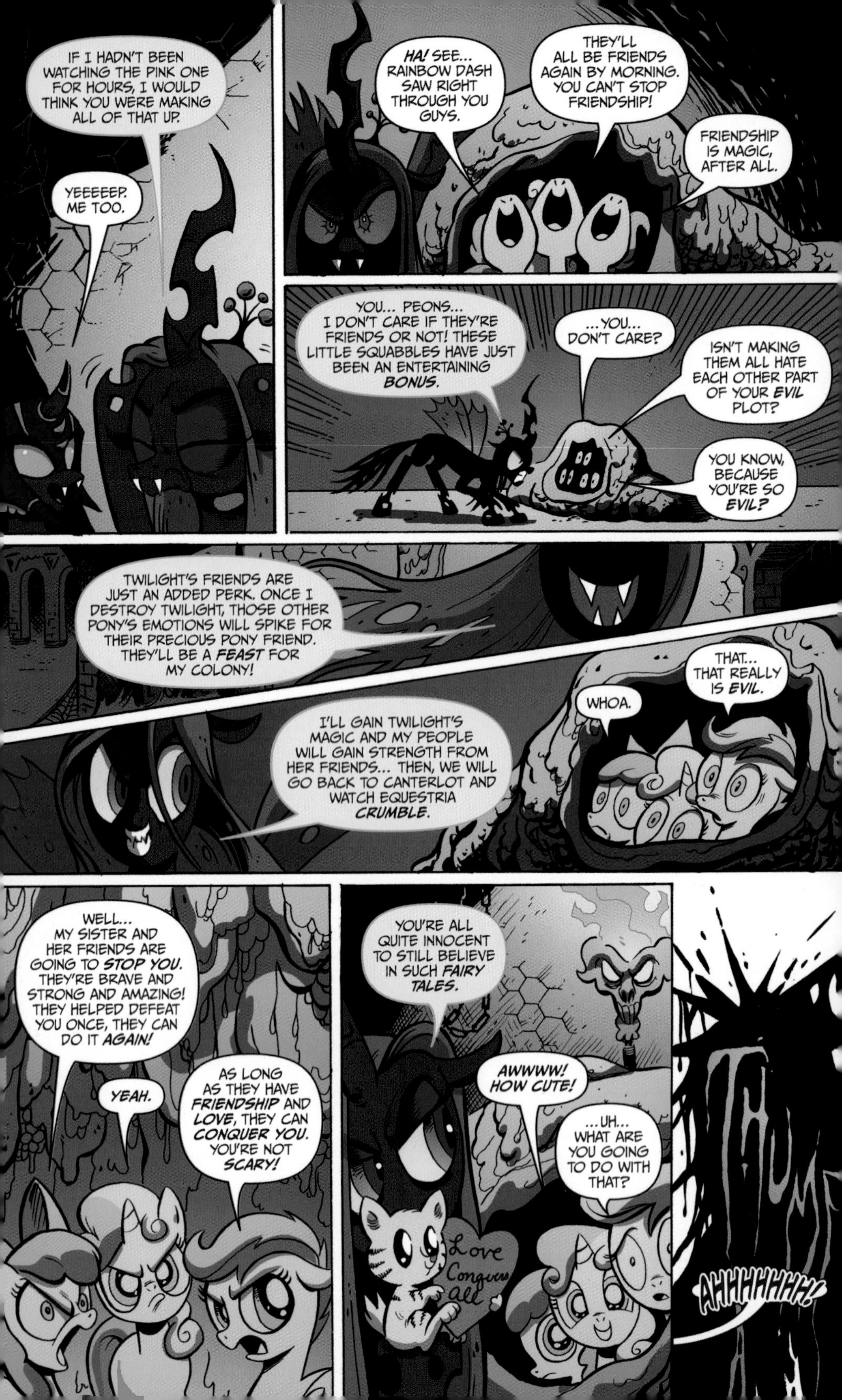
IF I HADN'T BEEN WATCHING THE PINK ONE FOR HOURS, I WOULD THINK YOU WERE MAKING ALL OF THAT UP.
YEEEEEP. ME TOO.
HA! SEE... RAINBOW DASH SAW RIGHT THROUGH YOU GUYS.
THEY'LL ALL BE FRIENDS AGAIN BY MORNING. YOU CAN'T STOP FRIENDSHIP!
FRIENDSHIP IS MAGIC, AFTER ALL.
YOU... PEONS... I DON'T CARE IF THEY'RE FRIENDS OR NOT! THESE LITTLE SQUABBLES HAVE JUST BEEN AN ENTERTAINING BONUS.
...YOU... DON'T CARE?
ISN'T MAKING THEM ALL HATE EACH OTHER PART OF YOUR EVIL PLOT?
YOU KNOW, BECAUSE YOU'RE SO EVIL?
TWILIGHT'S FRIENDS ARE JUST AN ADDED PERK. ONCE I DESTROY TWILIGHT, THOSE OTHER PONY'S EMOTIONS WILL SPIKE FOR THEIR PRECIOUS PONY FRIEND. THEY'LL BE A FEAST FOR MY COLONY!
WHOA.
THAT... THAT REALLY IS EVIL.
I'LL GAIN TWILIGHT'S MAGIC AND MY PEOPLE WILL GAIN STRENGTH FROM HER FRIENDS... THEN, WE WILL GO BACK TO CANTERLOT AND WATCH EQUESTRIA CRUMBLE.
WELL... MY SISTER AND HER FRIENDS ARE GOING TO STOP YOU. THEY'RE BRAVE AND STRONG AND AMAZING! THEY HELPED DEFEAT YOU ONCE, THEY CAN DO IT AGAIN!
YEAH.
AS LONG AS THEY HAVE FRIENDSHIP AND LOVE, THEY CAN CONQUER YOU. YOU'RE NOT SCARY!
YOU'RE ALL QUITE INNOCENT TO STILL BELIEVE IN SUCH FAIRY TALES.
AWWWW! HOW CUTE!
...UH... WHAT ARE YOU GOING TO DO WITH THAT?
Love Conquers All
AHHHHHHH!

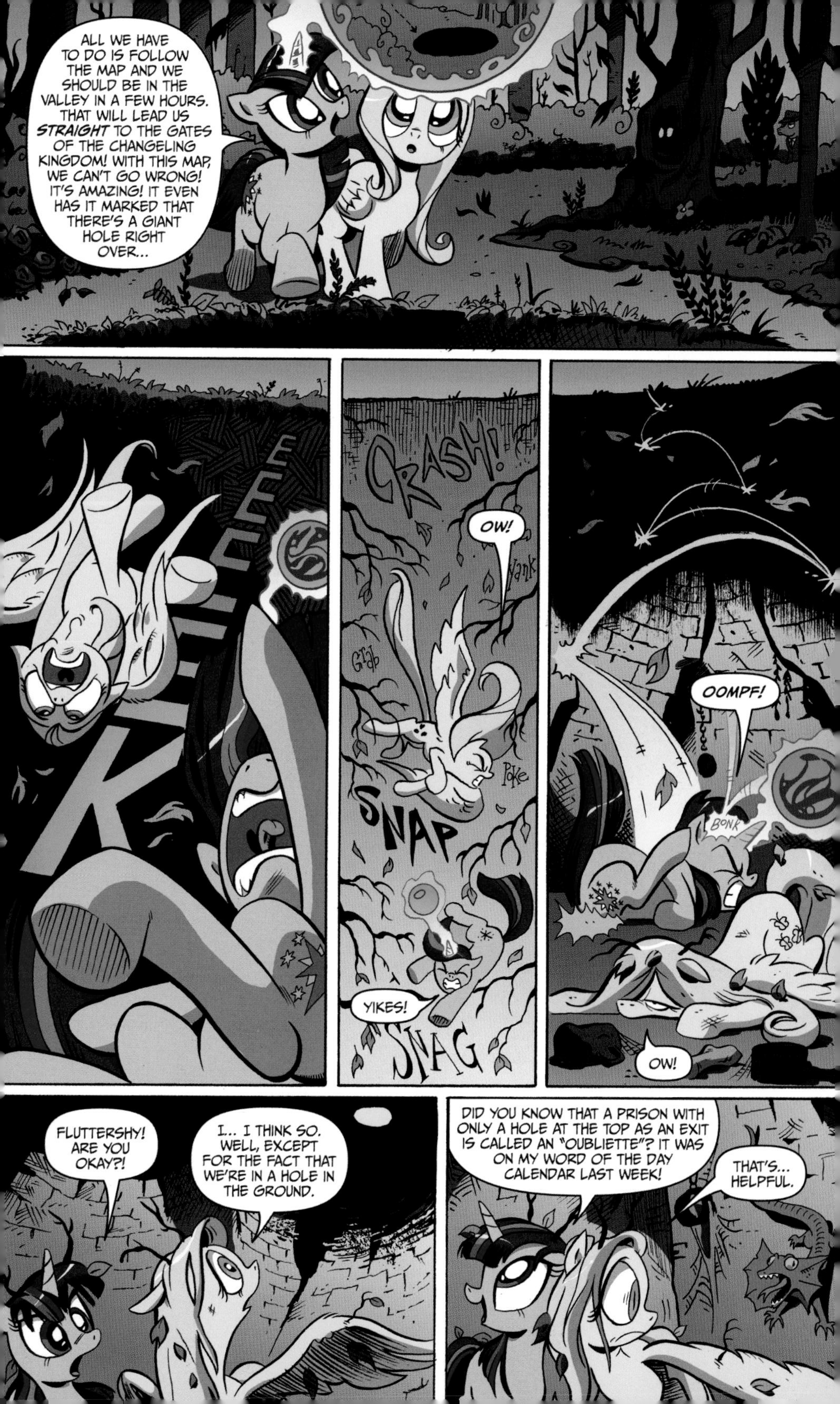
ALL WE HAVE TO DO IS FOLLOW THE MAP AND WE SHOULD BE IN THE VALLEY IN A FEW HOURS. THAT WILL LEAD US *STRAIGHT* TO THE GATES OF THE CHANGELING KINGDOM! WITH THIS MAP, WE CAN'T GO WRONG! IT'S AMAZING! IT EVEN HAS IT MARKED THAT THERE'S A GIANT HOLE RIGHT OVER...
CRASH!
OW!
Yank
Grab
Poke
SNAP
YIKES!
SNAG
OOMPF!
BONK
OW!
FLUTTERSHY! ARE YOU OKAY?!
I... I THINK SO. WELL, EXCEPT FOR THE FACT THAT WE'RE IN A HOLE IN THE GROUND.
DID YOU KNOW THAT A PRISON WITH ONLY A HOLE AT THE TOP AS AN EXIT IS CALLED AN "OUBLIETTE"? IT WAS ON MY WORD OF THE DAY CALENDAR LAST WEEK!
THAT'S... HELPFUL.

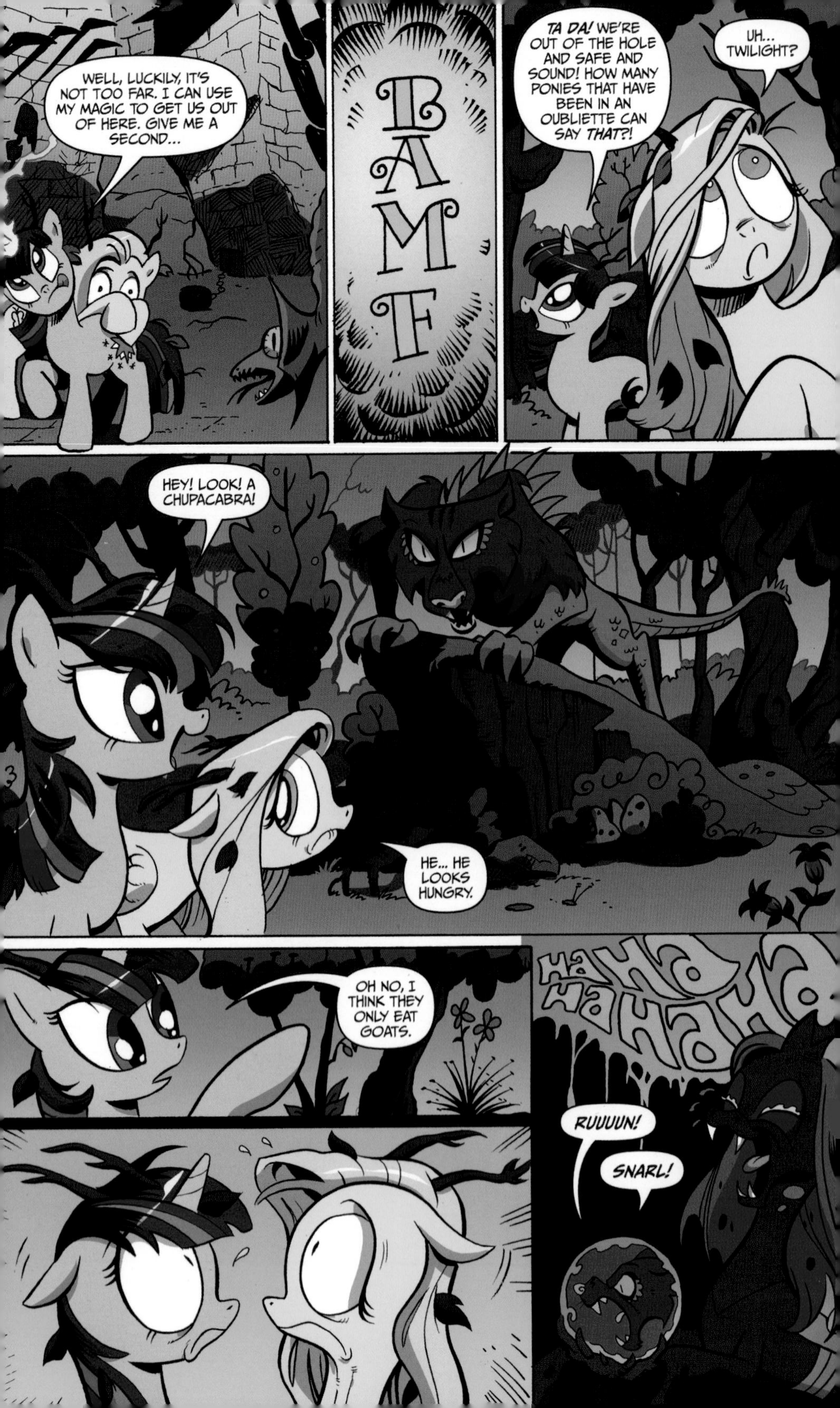
WELL, LUCKILY, IT'S NOT TOO FAR. I CAN USE MY MAGIC TO GET US OUT OF HERE. GIVE ME A SECOND...
BAMF
TA DA! WE'RE OUT OF THE HOLE AND SAFE AND SOUND! HOW MANY PONIES THAT HAVE BEEN IN AN OUBLIETTE CAN SAY THAT?!
UH... TWILIGHT?
HEY! LOOK! A CHUPACABRA!
HE... HE LOOKS HUNGRY.
OH NO, I THINK THEY ONLY EAT GOATS.
HAHAHA HAHAHAHA
RUUUUN!
SNARL!

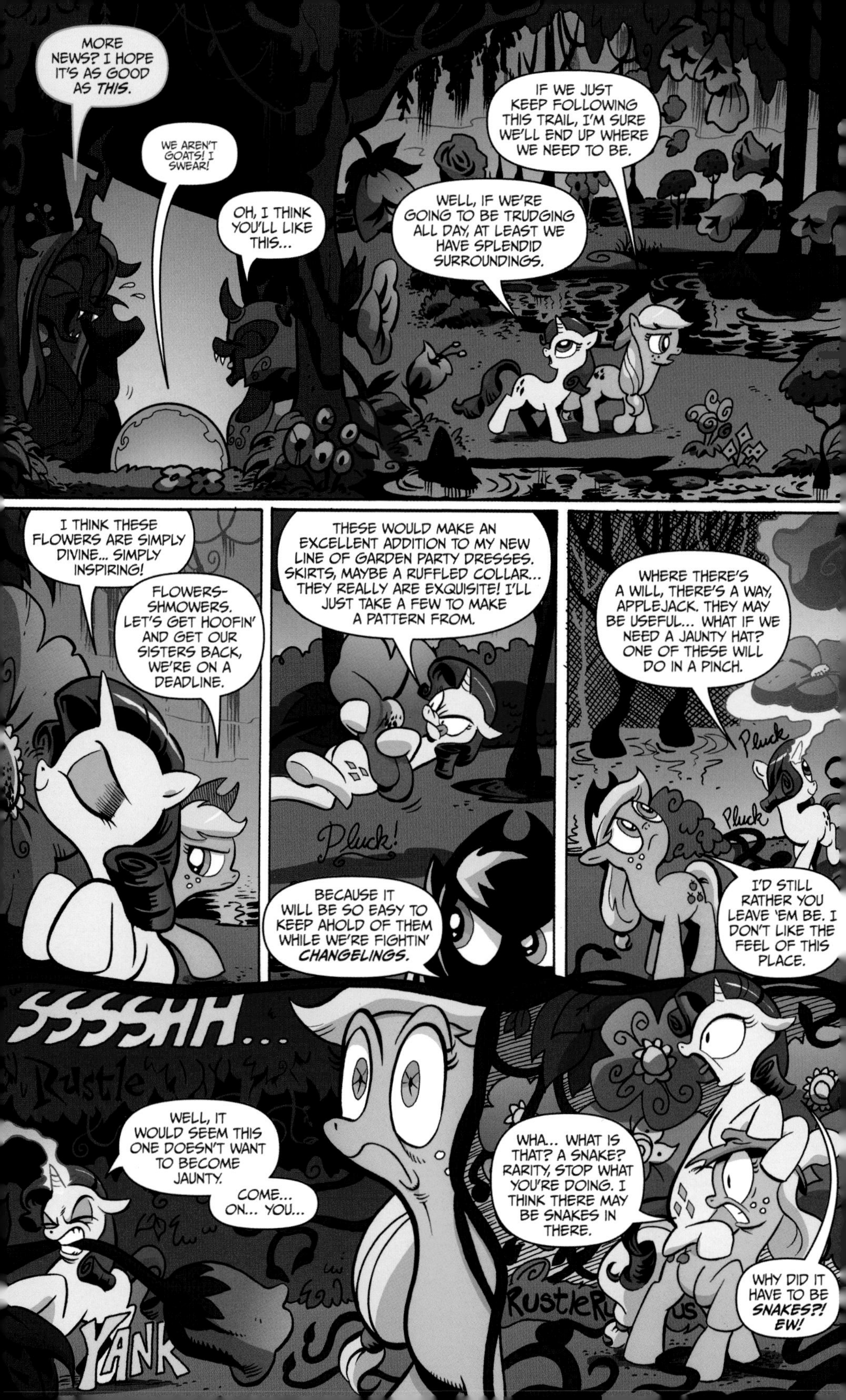
MORE NEWS? I HOPE IT'S AS GOOD AS THIS.
WE AREN'T GOATS! I SWEAR!
OH, I THINK YOU'LL LIKE THIS...
IF WE JUST KEEP FOLLOWING THIS TRAIL, I'M SURE WE'LL END UP WHERE WE NEED TO BE.
WELL, IF WE'RE GOING TO BE TRUDGING ALL DAY, AT LEAST WE HAVE SPLENDID SURROUNDINGS.
I THINK THESE FLOWERS ARE SIMPLY DIVINE... SIMPLY INSPIRING!
FLOWERS-SHMOWERS. LET'S GET HOOFIN' AND GET OUR SISTERS BACK, WE'RE ON A DEADLINE.
THESE WOULD MAKE AN EXCELLENT ADDITION TO MY NEW LINE OF GARDEN PARTY DRESSES. SKIRTS, MAYBE A RUFFLED COLLAR... THEY REALLY ARE EXQUISITE! I'LL JUST TAKE A FEW TO MAKE A PATTERN FROM.
Pluck!
BECAUSE IT WILL BE SO EASY TO KEEP AHOLD OF THEM WHILE WE'RE FIGHTIN' CHANGELINGS.
WHERE THERE'S A WILL, THERE'S A WAY, APPLEJACK. THEY MAY BE USEFUL... WHAT IF WE NEED A JAUNTY HAT? ONE OF THESE WILL DO IN A PINCH.
Pluck
Pluck
I'D STILL RATHER YOU LEAVE 'EM BE. I DON'T LIKE THE FEEL OF THIS PLACE.
SSSSHH...
Rustle
WELL, IT WOULD SEEM THIS ONE DOESN'T WANT TO BECOME JAUNTY.
COME... ON... YOU...
YANK
WHA... WHAT IS THAT? A SNAKE? RARITY, STOP WHAT YOU'RE DOING. I THINK THERE MAY BE SNAKES IN THERE.
Rustle
WHY DID IT HAVE TO BE SNAKES?! EW!

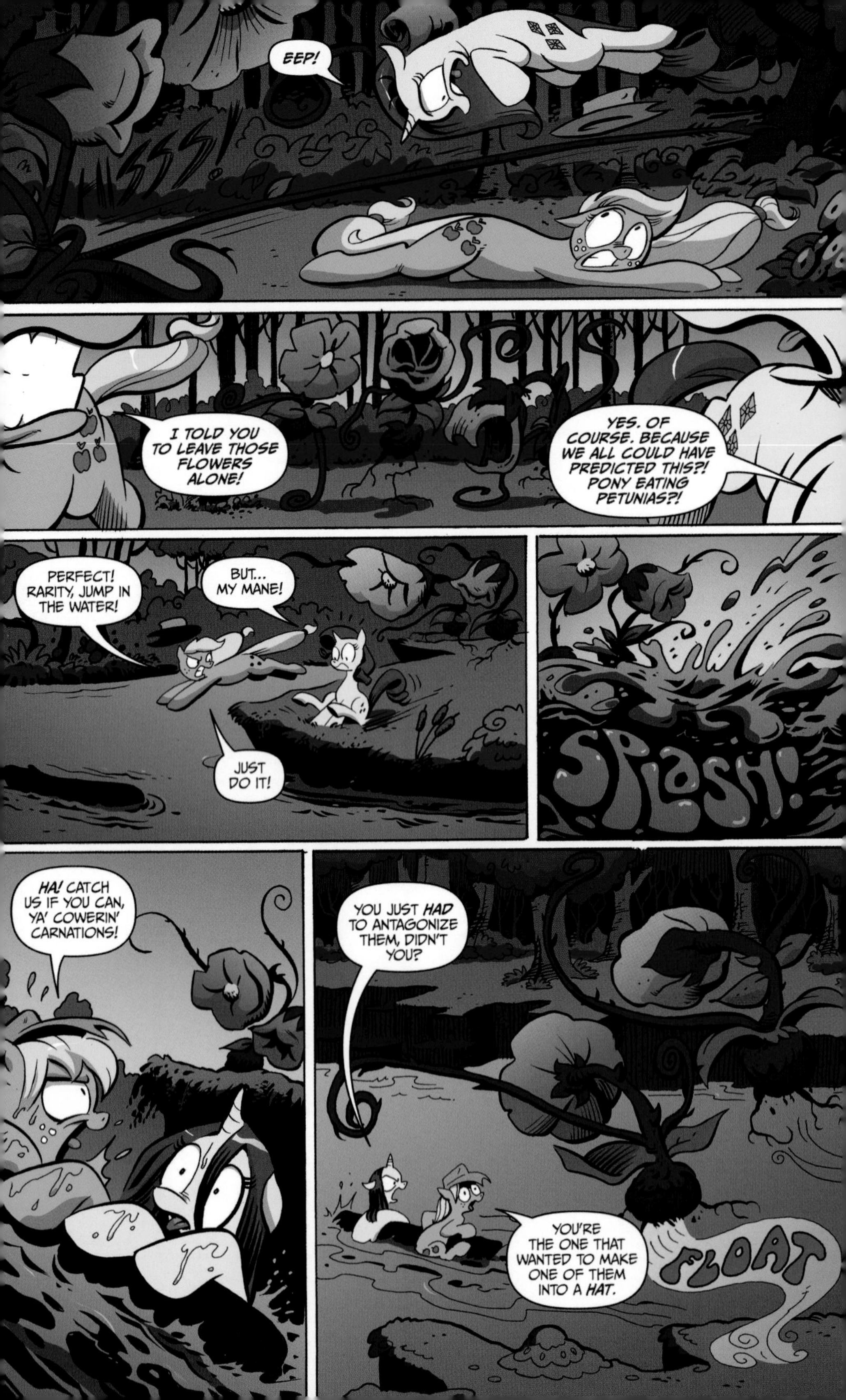
EEP!
HISSS!
I TOLD YOU TO LEAVE THOSE FLOWERS ALONE!
YES. OF COURSE. BECAUSE WE ALL COULD HAVE PREDICTED THIS?! PONY EATING PETUNIAS?!
PERFECT! RARITY, JUMP IN THE WATER!
BUT... MY MANE!
JUST DO IT!
SPLASH!
HA! CATCH US IF YOU CAN, YA' COWERIN' CARNATIONS!
YOU JUST HAD TO ANTAGONIZE THEM, DIDN'T YOU?
YOU'RE THE ONE THAT WANTED TO MAKE ONE OF THEM INTO A HAT.
FLOAT

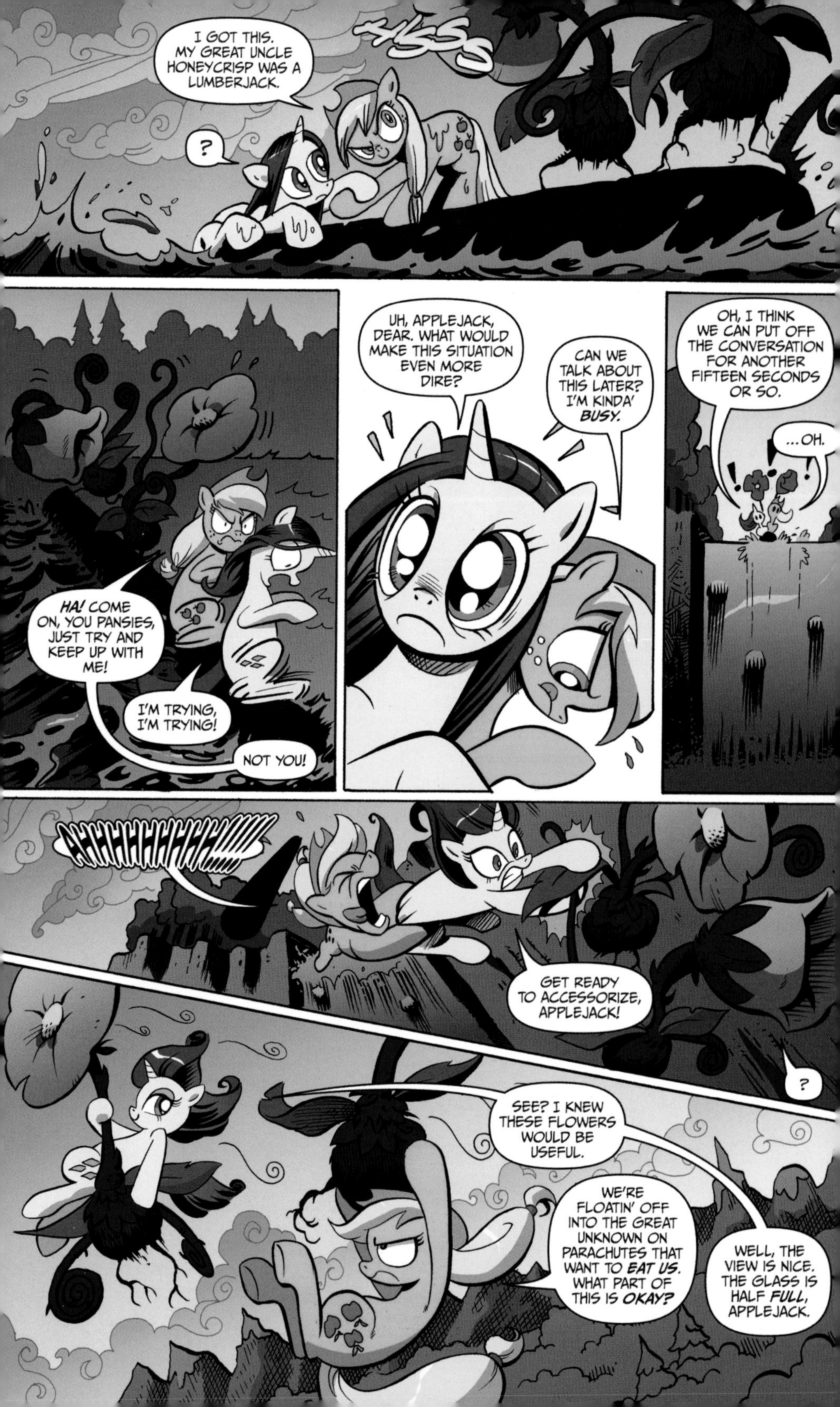
I GOT THIS. MY GREAT UNCLE HONEYCRISP WAS A LUMBERJACK.
HISSS
?
UH, APPLEJACK, DEAR. WHAT WOULD MAKE THIS SITUATION EVEN MORE DIRE?
CAN WE TALK ABOUT THIS LATER? I'M KINDA' BUSY.
OH, I THINK WE CAN PUT OFF THE CONVERSATION FOR ANOTHER FIFTEEN SECONDS OR SO.
...OH.
HA! COME ON, YOU PANSIES, JUST TRY AND KEEP UP WITH ME!
I'M TRYING, I'M TRYING!
NOT YOU!
AHHHHHHHHH!!!!!
GET READY TO ACCESSORIZE, APPLEJACK!
?
SEE? I KNEW THESE FLOWERS WOULD BE USEFUL.
WE'RE FLOATIN' OFF INTO THE GREAT UNKNOWN ON PARACHUTES THAT WANT TO EAT US. WHAT PART OF THIS IS OKAY?
WELL, THE VIEW IS NICE. THE GLASS IS HALF FULL, APPLEJACK.

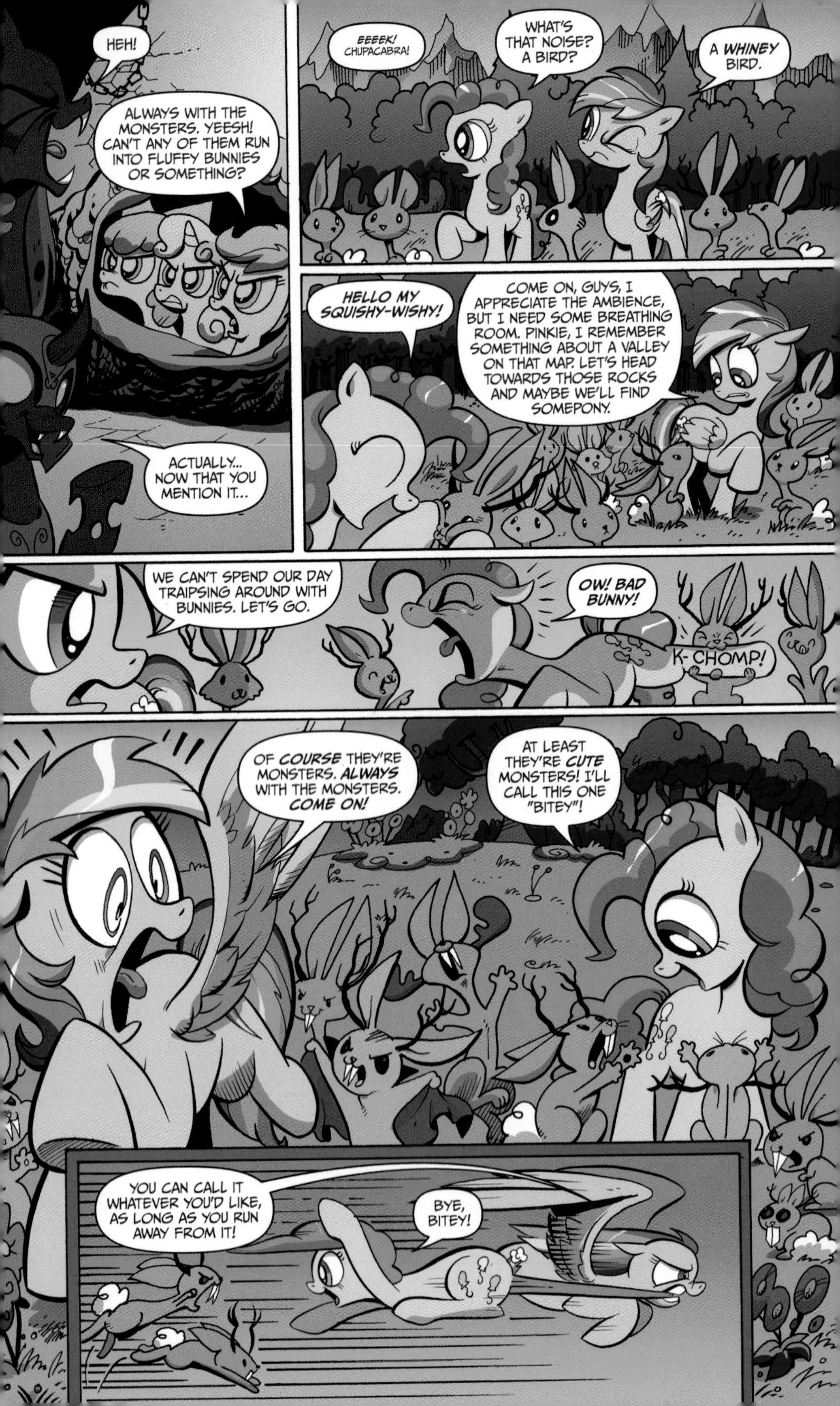
HEH!
ALWAYS WITH THE MONSTERS. YEESH! CAN'T ANY OF THEM RUN INTO FLUFFY BUNNIES OR SOMETHING?
ACTUALLY... NOW THAT YOU MENTION IT...
EEEEK! CHUPACABRA!
WHAT'S THAT NOISE? A BIRD?
A WHINEY BIRD.
HELLO MY SQUISHY-WISHY!
COME ON, GUYS, I APPRECIATE THE AMBIENCE, BUT I NEED SOME BREATHING ROOM. PINKIE, I REMEMBER SOMETHING ABOUT A VALLEY ON THAT MAP. LET'S HEAD TOWARDS THOSE ROCKS AND MAYBE WE'LL FIND SOMEPONY.
WE CAN'T SPEND OUR DAY TRAIPSING AROUND WITH BUNNIES. LET'S GO.
OW! BAD BUNNY!
K-CHOMP!
OF COURSE THEY'RE MONSTERS. ALWAYS WITH THE MONSTERS. COME ON!
AT LEAST THEY'RE CUTE MONSTERS! I'LL CALL THIS ONE "BITEY"!
YOU CAN CALL IT WHATEVER YOU'D LIKE, AS LONG AS YOU RUN AWAY FROM IT!
BYE, BITEY!

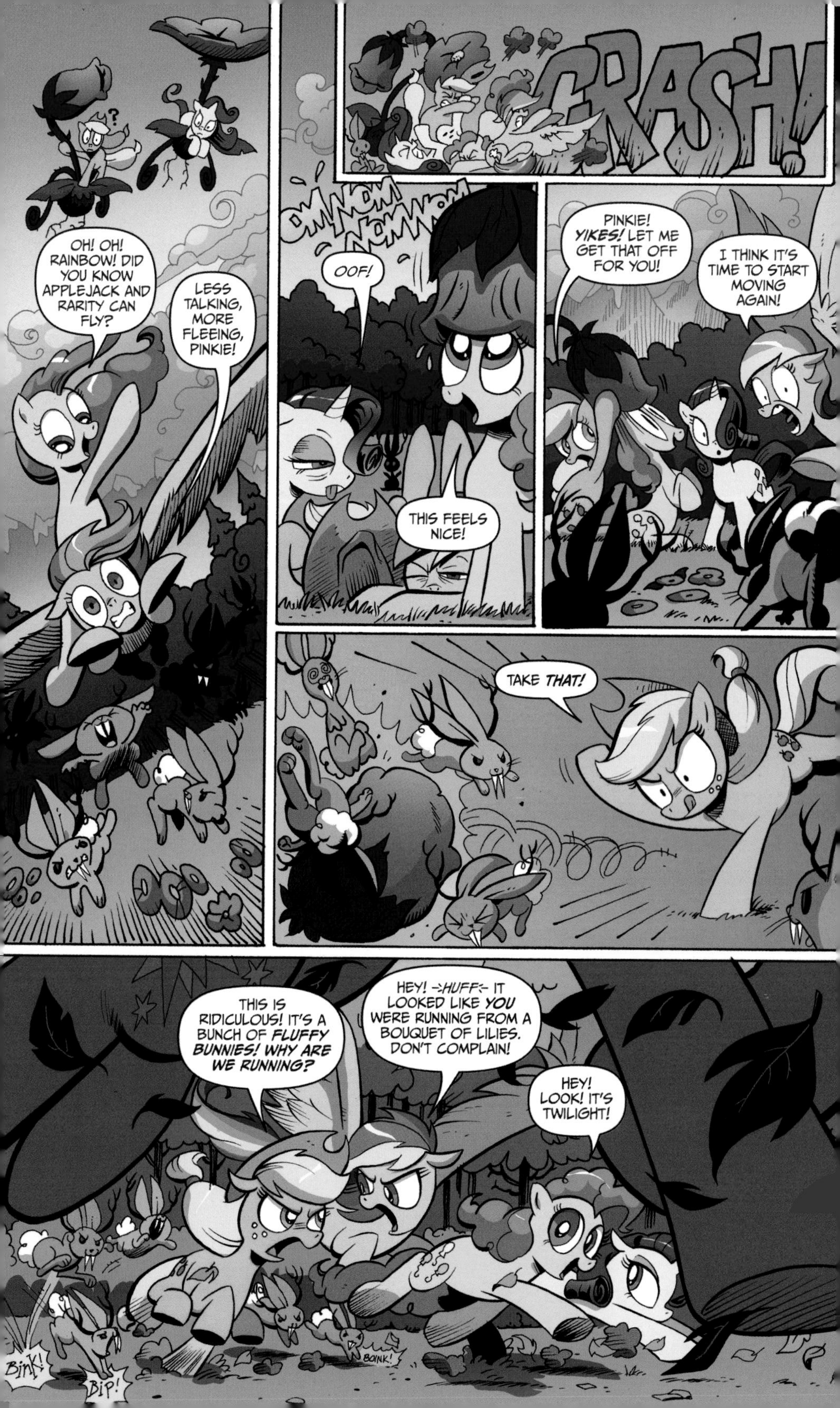
CRASH!
OH! OH! RAINBOW! DID YOU KNOW APPLEJACK AND RARITY CAN FLY?
LESS TALKING, MORE FLEEING, PINKIE!
OM NOM NOM NOM NOM NOM
OOF!
THIS FEELS NICE!
PINKIE! YIKES! LET ME GET THAT OFF FOR YOU!
I THINK IT'S TIME TO START MOVING AGAIN!
TAKE THAT!
THIS IS RIDICULOUS! IT'S A BUNCH OF FLUFFY BUNNIES! WHY ARE WE RUNNING?
HEY! -HUFF- IT LOOKED LIKE YOU WERE RUNNING FROM A BOUQUET OF LILIES. DON'T COMPLAIN!
HEY! LOOK! IT'S TWILIGHT!
BINK!
BIP!
BOINK!

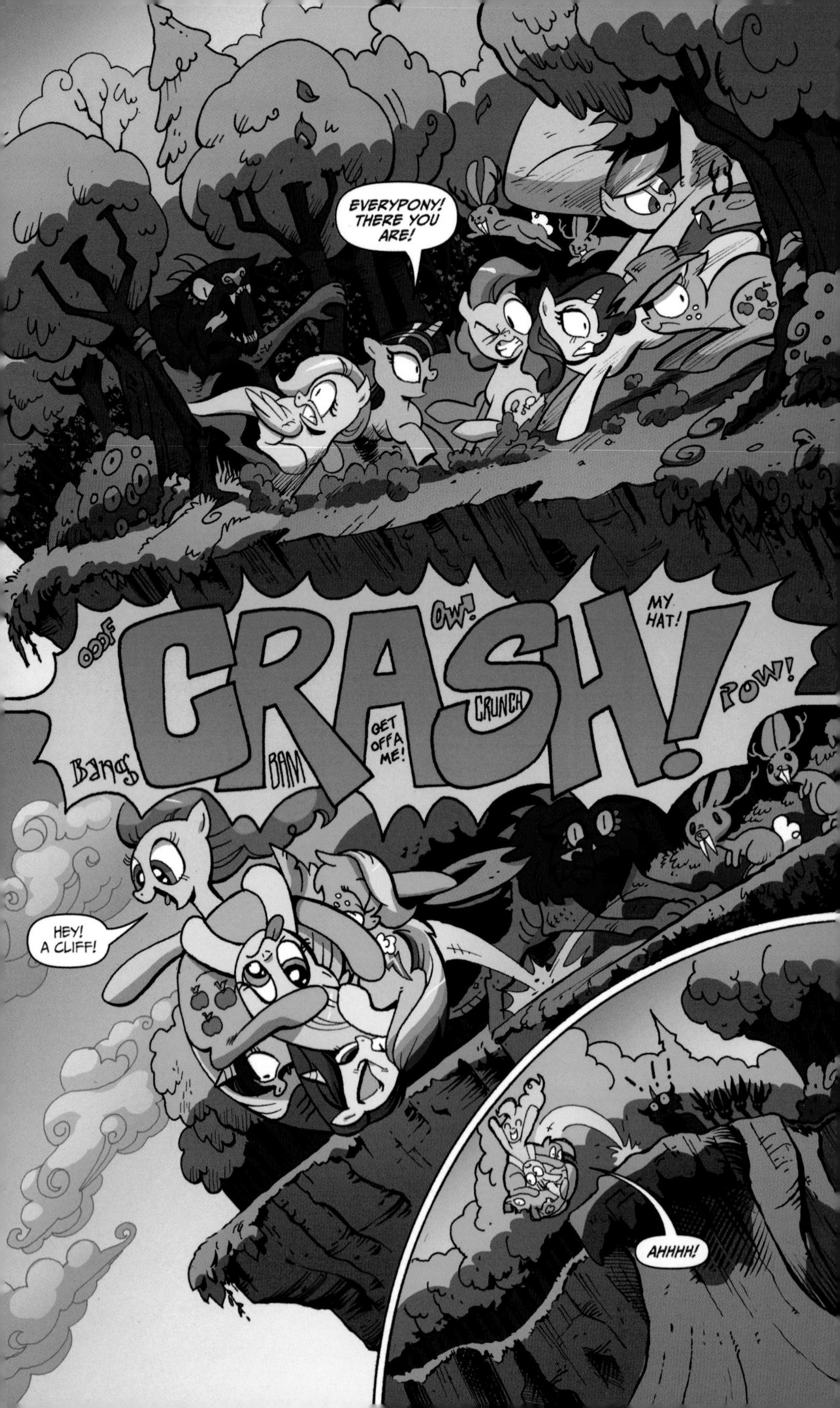
EVERYPONY! THERE YOU ARE!
OOOF
OW!
MY HAT!
CRASH!
CRUNCH
POW!
BANG
BAM
GET OFFA ME!
HEY! A CLIFF!
AHHHH!

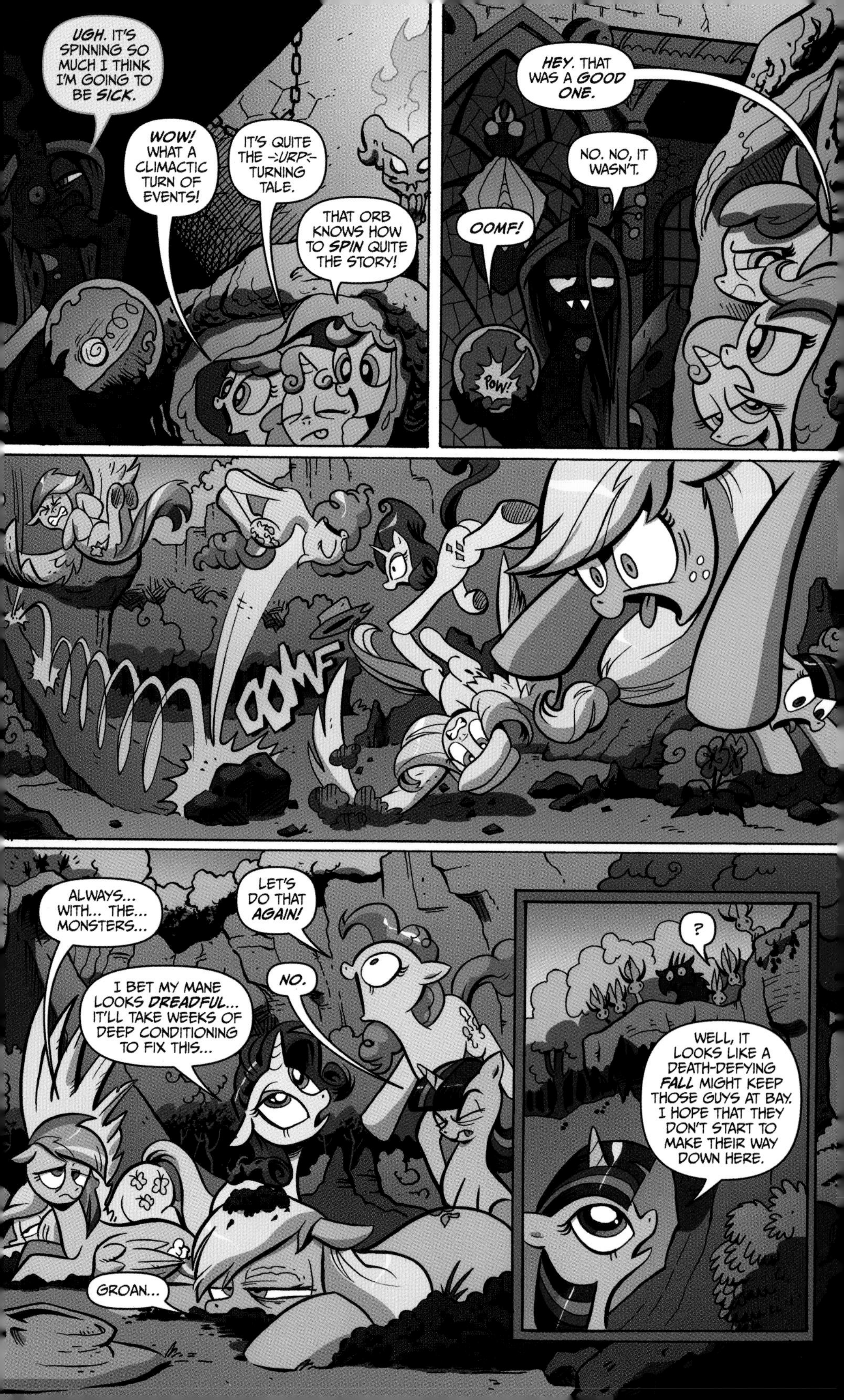

UGH. IT'S SPINNING SO MUCH I THINK I'M GOING TO BE SICK.
WOW! WHAT A CLIMACTIC TURN OF EVENTS!
IT'S QUITE THE -URP- TURNING TALE.
THAT ORB KNOWS HOW TO SPIN QUITE THE STORY!
HEY. THAT WAS A GOOD ONE.
NO. NO, IT WASN'T.
OOMF!
POW!
OOMF
ALWAYS... WITH... THE... MONSTERS...
LET'S DO THAT AGAIN!
I BET MY MANE LOOKS DREADFUL... IT'LL TAKE WEEKS OF DEEP CONDITIONING TO FIX THIS...
NO.
GROAN...
?
WELL, IT LOOKS LIKE A DEATH-DEFYING FALL MIGHT KEEP THOSE GUYS AT BAY. I HOPE THAT THEY DON'T START TO MAKE THEIR WAY DOWN HERE.

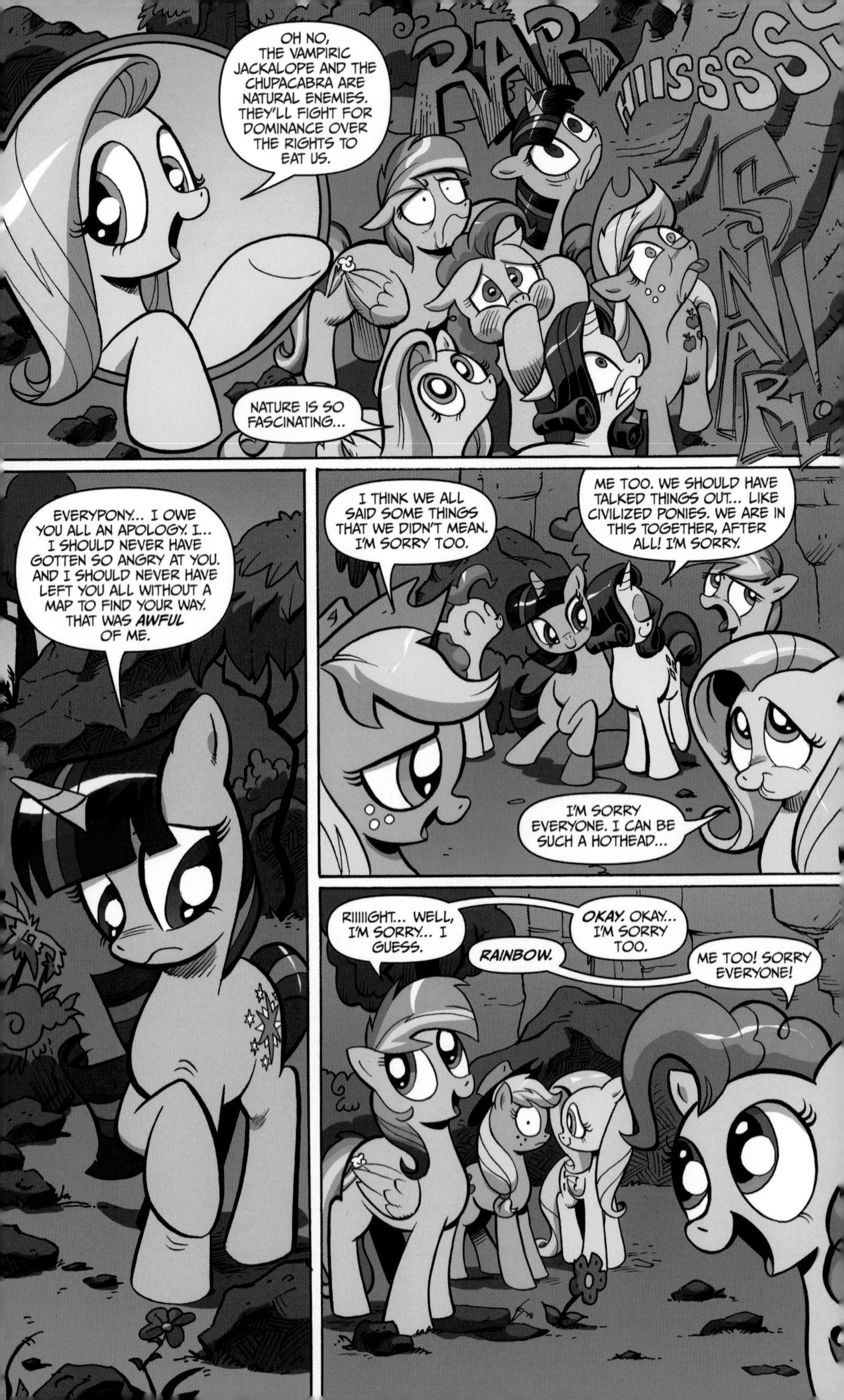
OH NO, THE VAMPIRIC JACKALOPE AND THE CHUPACABRA ARE NATURAL ENEMIES. THEY'LL FIGHT FOR DOMINANCE OVER THE RIGHTS TO EAT US.
RAR
HIISSSSS
NATURE IS SO FASCINATING...
EVERYPONY... I OWE YOU ALL AN APOLOGY. I... I SHOULD NEVER HAVE GOTTEN SO ANGRY AT YOU. AND I SHOULD NEVER HAVE LEFT YOU ALL WITHOUT A MAP TO FIND YOUR WAY. THAT WAS AWFUL OF ME.
I THINK WE ALL SAID SOME THINGS THAT WE DIDN'T MEAN. I'M SORRY TOO.
ME TOO. WE SHOULD HAVE TALKED THINGS OUT... LIKE CIVILIZED PONIES. WE ARE IN THIS TOGETHER, AFTER ALL! I'M SORRY.
I'M SORRY EVERYONE. I CAN BE SUCH A HOTHEAD...
RIIIIIGHT... WELL, I'M SORRY... I GUESS.
RAINBOW.
OKAY. OKAY... I'M SORRY TOO.
ME TOO! SORRY EVERYONE!

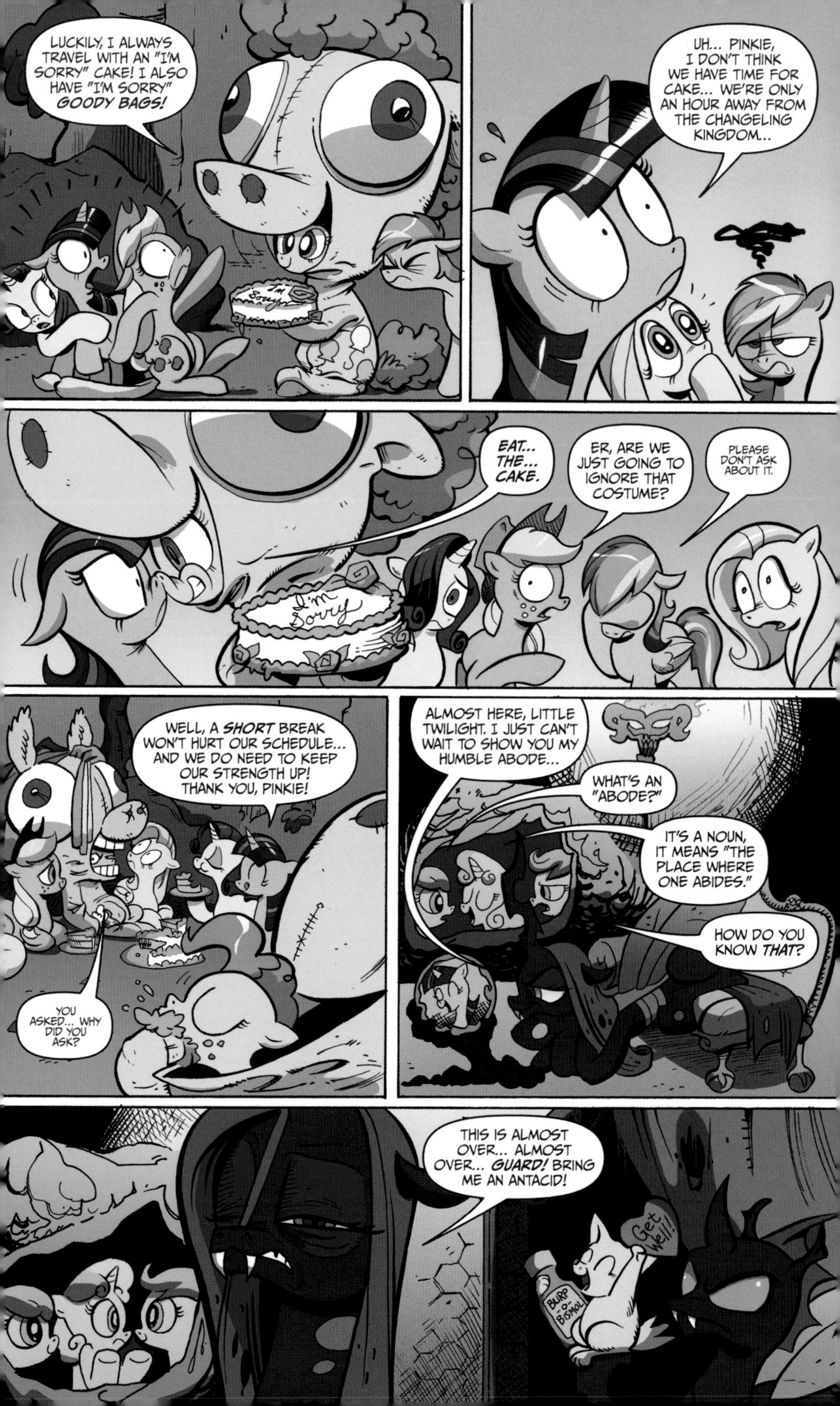
LUCKILY, I ALWAYS TRAVEL WITH AN "I'M SORRY" CAKE! I ALSO HAVE "I'M SORRY" GOODY BAGS!
I'm Sorry
UH... PINKIE, I DON'T THINK WE HAVE TIME FOR CAKE... WE'RE ONLY AN HOUR AWAY FROM THE CHANGELING KINGDOM...
EAT... THE... CAKE.
ER, ARE WE JUST GOING TO IGNORE THAT COSTUME?
PLEASE DON'T ASK ABOUT IT.
I'm Sorry
WELL, A SHORT BREAK WON'T HURT OUR SCHEDULE... AND WE DO NEED TO KEEP OUR STRENGTH UP! THANK YOU, PINKIE!
YOU ASKED... WHY DID YOU ASK?
ALMOST HERE, LITTLE TWILIGHT. I JUST CAN'T WAIT TO SHOW YOU MY HUMBLE ABODE...
WHAT'S AN "ABODE?"
IT'S A NOUN, IT MEANS "THE PLACE WHERE ONE ABIDES."
HOW DO YOU KNOW THAT?
THIS IS ALMOST OVER... ALMOST OVER... GUARD! BRING ME AN ANTACID!
Get Well!
BURP -o- BISMOL

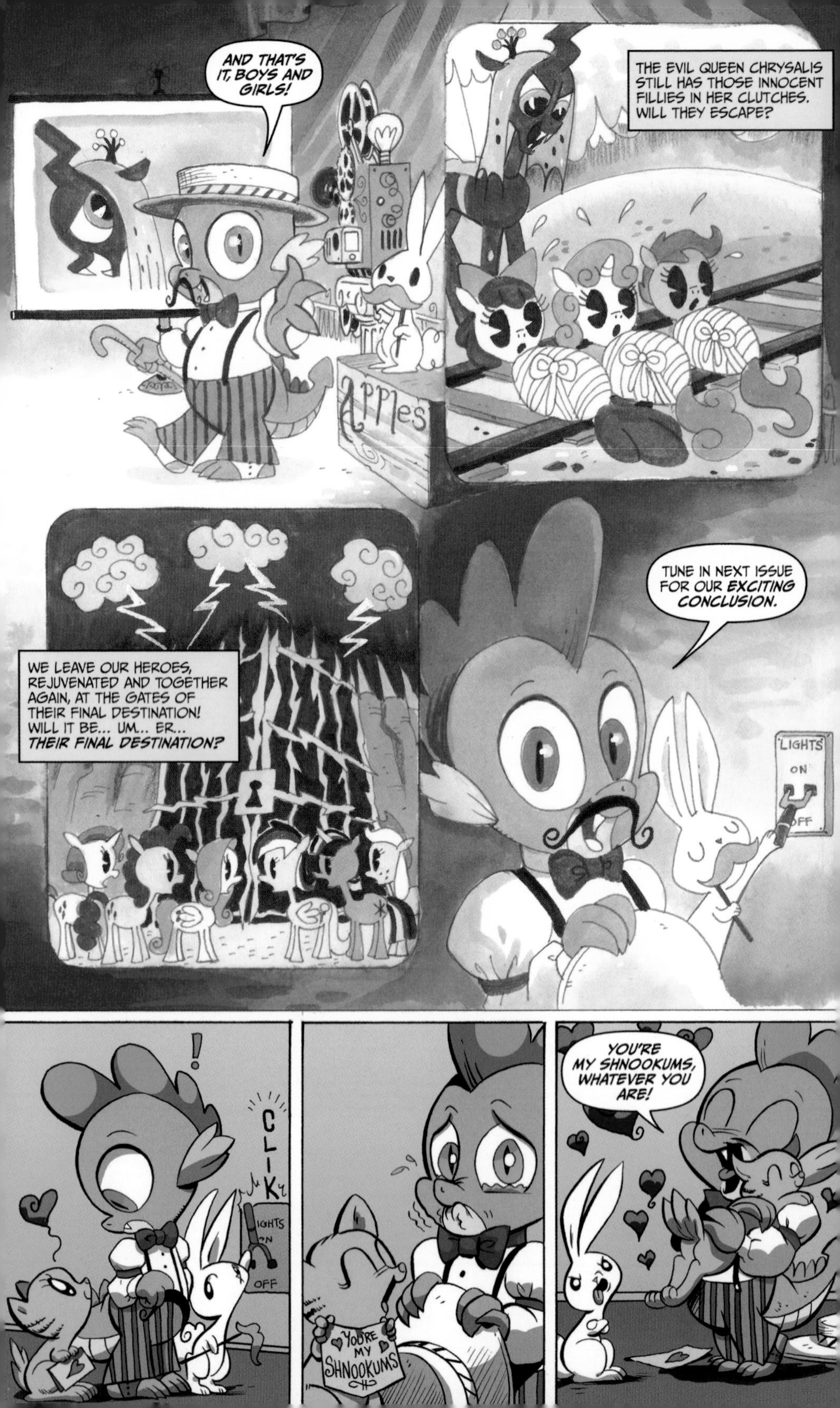

AND THAT'S IT, BOYS AND GIRLS!
THE EVIL QUEEN CHRYSALIS STILL HAS THOSE INNOCENT FILLIES IN HER CLUTCHES. WILL THEY ESCAPE?
APPLES
WE LEAVE OUR HEROES, REJUVENATED AND TOGETHER AGAIN, AT THE GATES OF THEIR FINAL DESTINATION! WILL IT BE... UM... ER... THEIR FINAL DESTINATION?
TUNE IN NEXT ISSUE FOR OUR EXCITING CONCLUSION.
LIGHTS
ON
OFF
!
CLIK
LIGHTS
ON
OFF
YOU'RE MY SHNOOKUMS
YOU'RE MY SHNOOKUMS, WHATEVER YOU ARE!

Art by
Stephanie Buscema

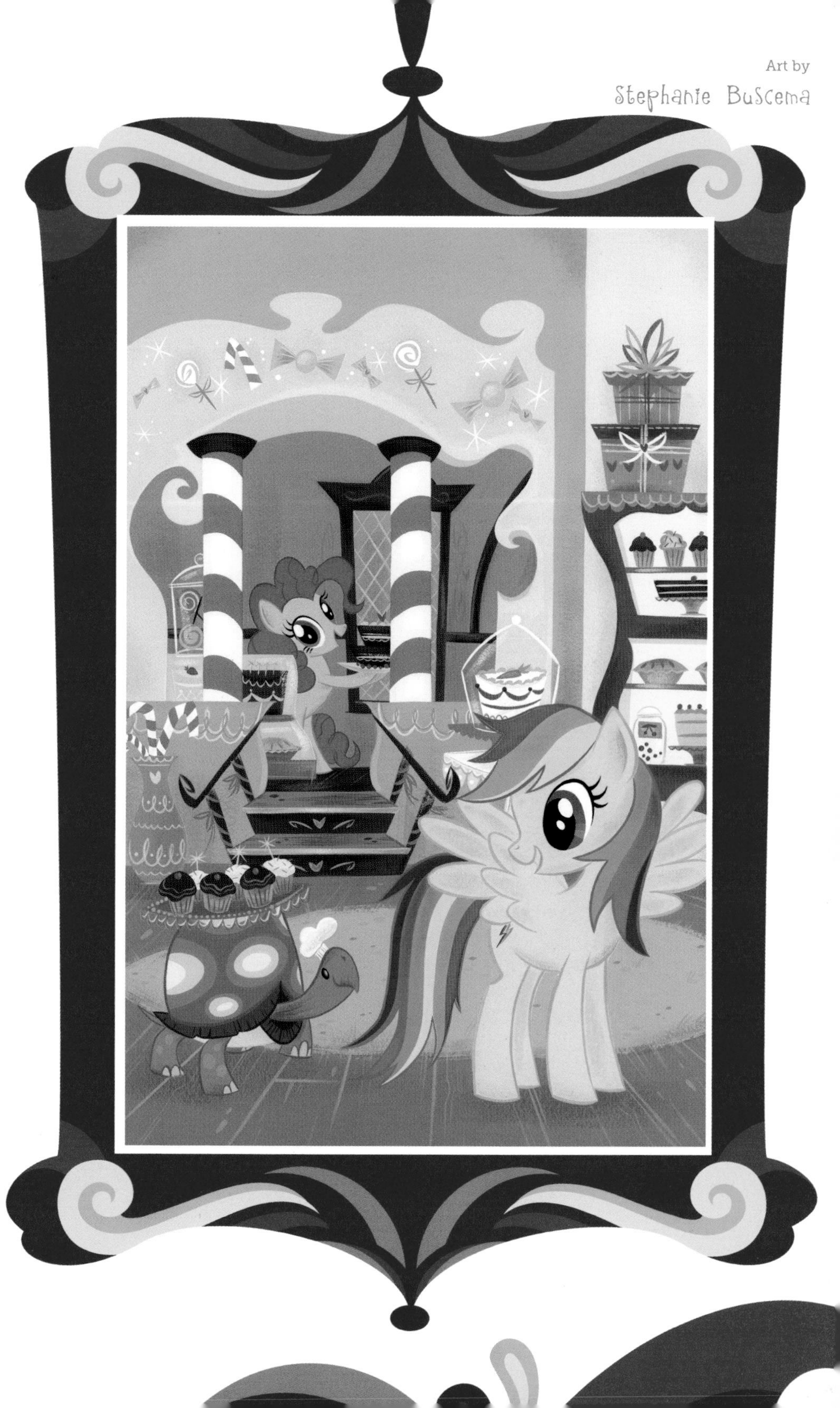

Art by
Amanda Conner

Colors by
Paul Mounts

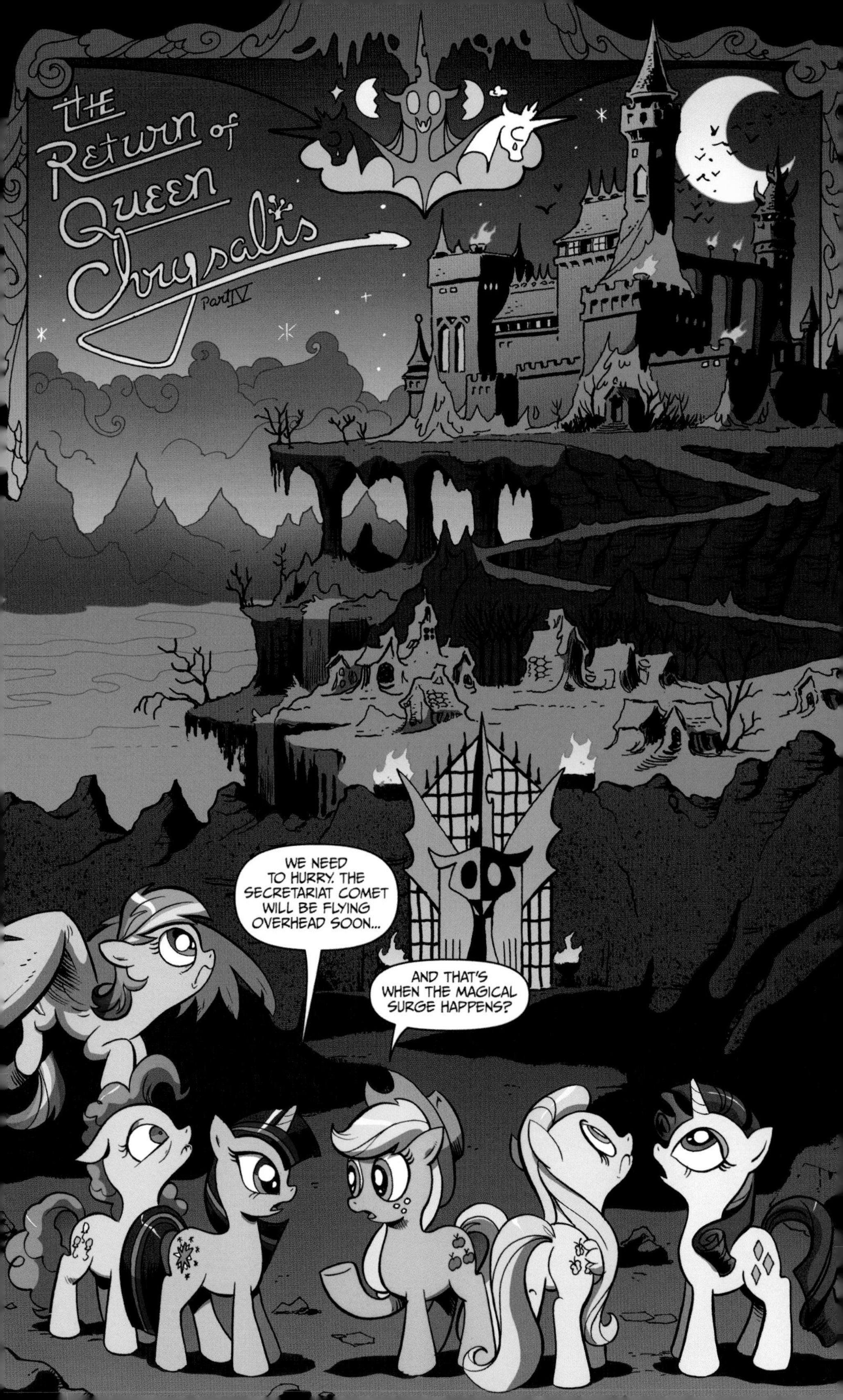
The Return of Queen Chrysalis
Part IV
WE NEED TO HURRY. THE SECRETARIAT COMET WILL BE FLYING OVERHEAD SOON...
AND THAT'S WHEN THE MAGICAL SURGE HAPPENS?

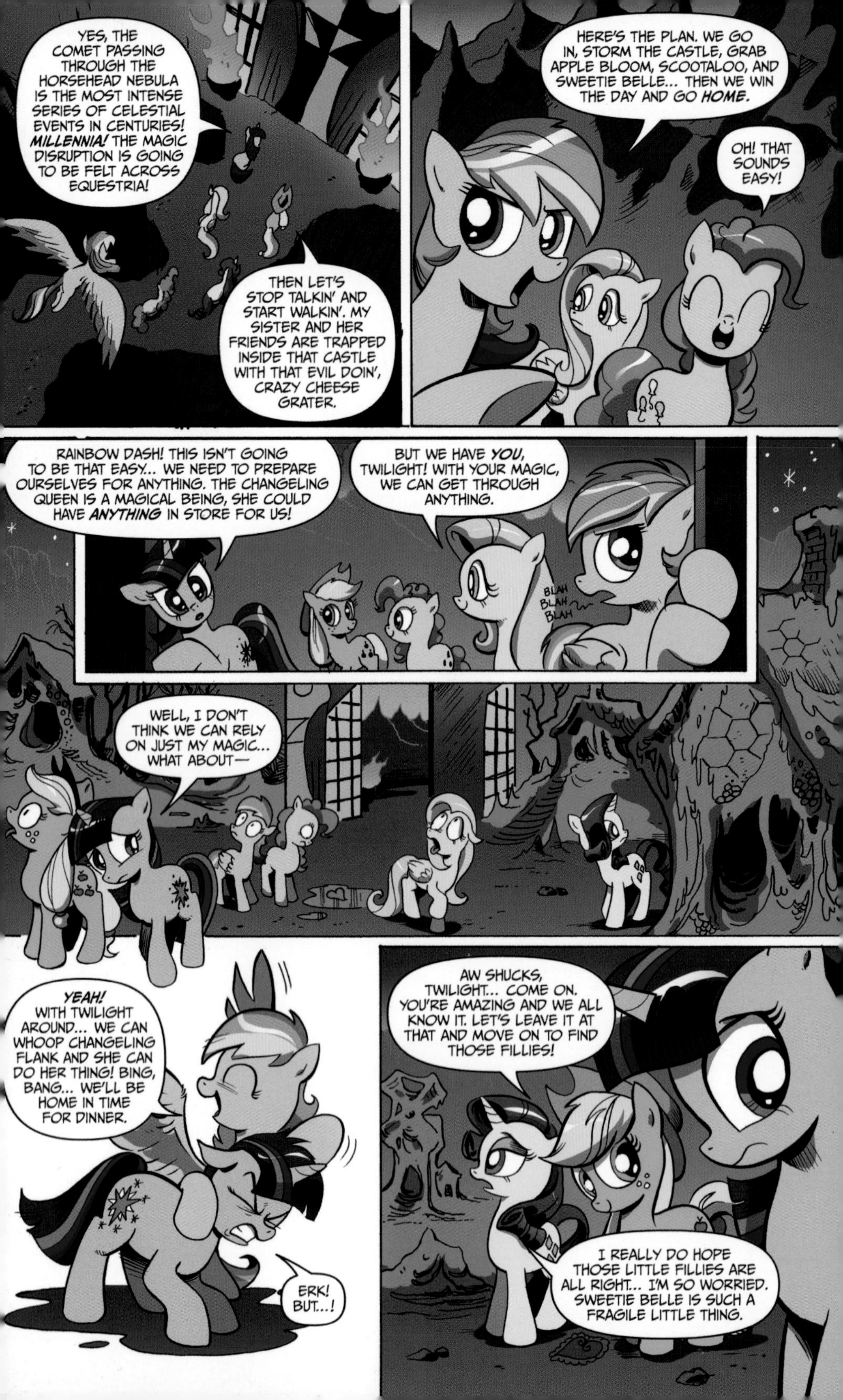

YES, THE COMET PASSING THROUGH THE HORSEHEAD NEBULA IS THE MOST INTENSE SERIES OF CELESTIAL EVENTS IN CENTURIES! *MILLENNIA!* THE MAGIC DISRUPTION IS GOING TO BE FELT ACROSS EQUESTRIA!
THEN LET'S STOP TALKIN' AND START WALKIN'. MY SISTER AND HER FRIENDS ARE TRAPPED INSIDE THAT CASTLE WITH THAT EVIL DOIN', CRAZY CHEESE GRATER.
HERE'S THE PLAN. WE GO IN, STORM THE CASTLE, GRAB APPLE BLOOM, SCOOTALOO, AND SWEETIE BELLE... THEN WE WIN THE DAY AND GO *HOME.*
OH! THAT SOUNDS EASY!
RAINBOW DASH! THIS ISN'T GOING TO BE THAT EASY... WE NEED TO PREPARE OURSELVES FOR ANYTHING. THE CHANGELING QUEEN IS A MAGICAL BEING, SHE COULD HAVE *ANYTHING* IN STORE FOR US!
BUT WE HAVE *YOU*, TWILIGHT! WITH YOUR MAGIC, WE CAN GET THROUGH ANYTHING.
BLAH BLAH BLAH
WELL, I DON'T THINK WE CAN RELY ON JUST MY MAGIC... WHAT ABOUT—
YEAH! WITH TWILIGHT AROUND... WE CAN WHOOP CHANGELING FLANK AND SHE CAN DO HER THING! BING, BANG... WE'LL BE HOME IN TIME FOR DINNER.
ERK! BUT...!
AW SHUCKS, TWILIGHT... COME ON. YOU'RE AMAZING AND WE ALL KNOW IT. LET'S LEAVE IT AT THAT AND MOVE ON TO FIND THOSE FILLIES!
I REALLY DO HOPE THOSE LITTLE FILLIES ARE ALL RIGHT... I'M SO WORRIED. SWEETIE BELLE IS SUCH A FRAGILE LITTLE THING.

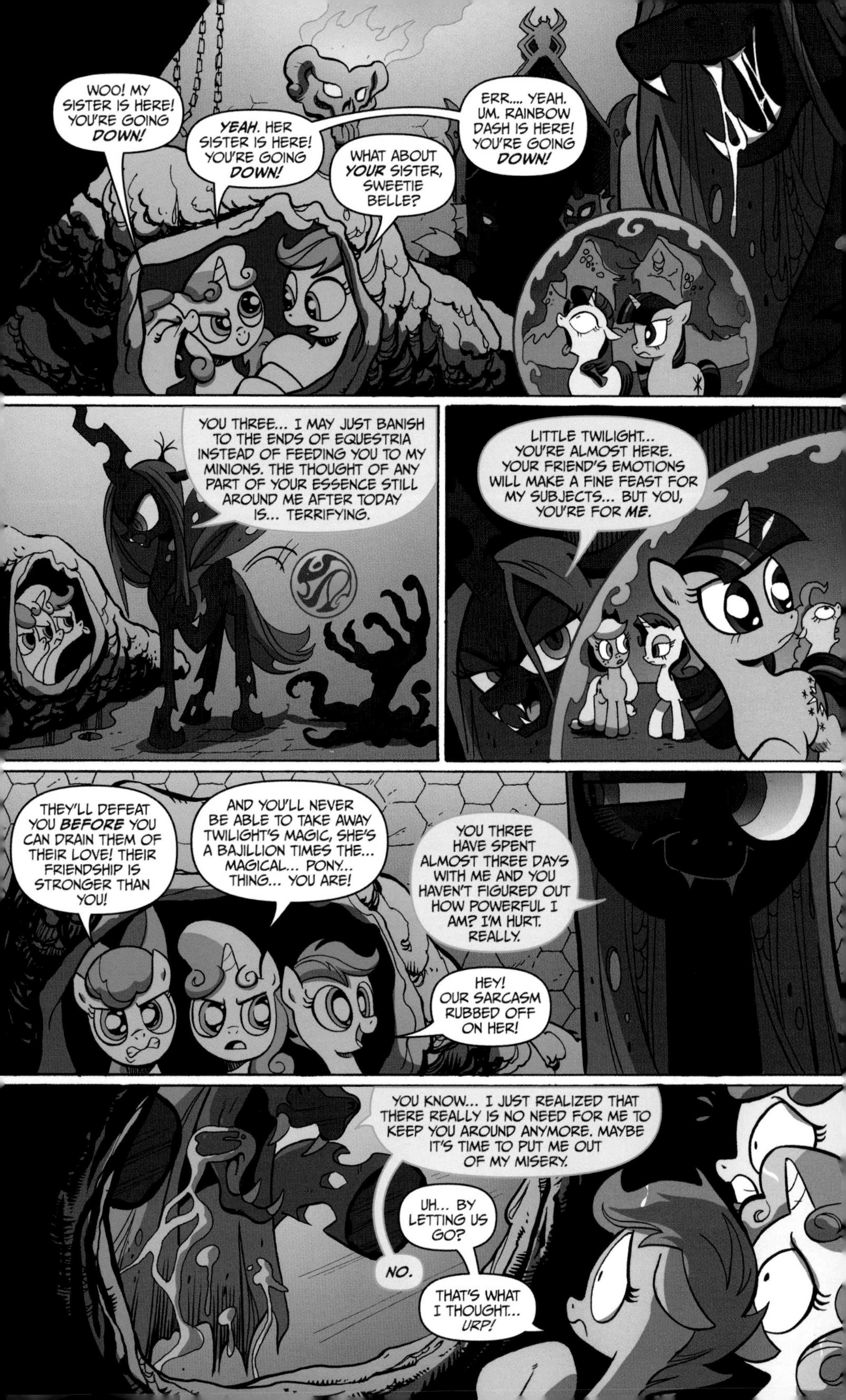
WOO! MY SISTER IS HERE! YOU'RE GOING DOWN!
YEAH. HER SISTER IS HERE! YOU'RE GOING DOWN!
WHAT ABOUT YOUR SISTER, SWEETIE BELLE?
ERR.... YEAH. UM. RAINBOW DASH IS HERE! YOU'RE GOING DOWN!
YOU THREE... I MAY JUST BANISH TO THE ENDS OF EQUESTRIA INSTEAD OF FEEDING YOU TO MY MINIONS. THE THOUGHT OF ANY PART OF YOUR ESSENCE STILL AROUND ME AFTER TODAY IS... TERRIFYING.
LITTLE TWILIGHT... YOU'RE ALMOST HERE. YOUR FRIEND'S EMOTIONS WILL MAKE A FINE FEAST FOR MY SUBJECTS... BUT YOU, YOU'RE FOR ME.
THEY'LL DEFEAT YOU BEFORE YOU CAN DRAIN THEM OF THEIR LOVE! THEIR FRIENDSHIP IS STRONGER THAN YOU!
AND YOU'LL NEVER BE ABLE TO TAKE AWAY TWILIGHT'S MAGIC, SHE'S A BAJILLION TIMES THE... MAGICAL... PONY... THING... YOU ARE!
YOU THREE HAVE SPENT ALMOST THREE DAYS WITH ME AND YOU HAVEN'T FIGURED OUT HOW POWERFUL I AM? I'M HURT. REALLY.
HEY! OUR SARCASM RUBBED OFF ON HER!
YOU KNOW... I JUST REALIZED THAT THERE REALLY IS NO NEED FOR ME TO KEEP YOU AROUND ANYMORE. MAYBE IT'S TIME TO PUT ME OUT OF MY MISERY.
UH... BY LETTING US GO?
NO.
THAT'S WHAT I THOUGHT... URP!

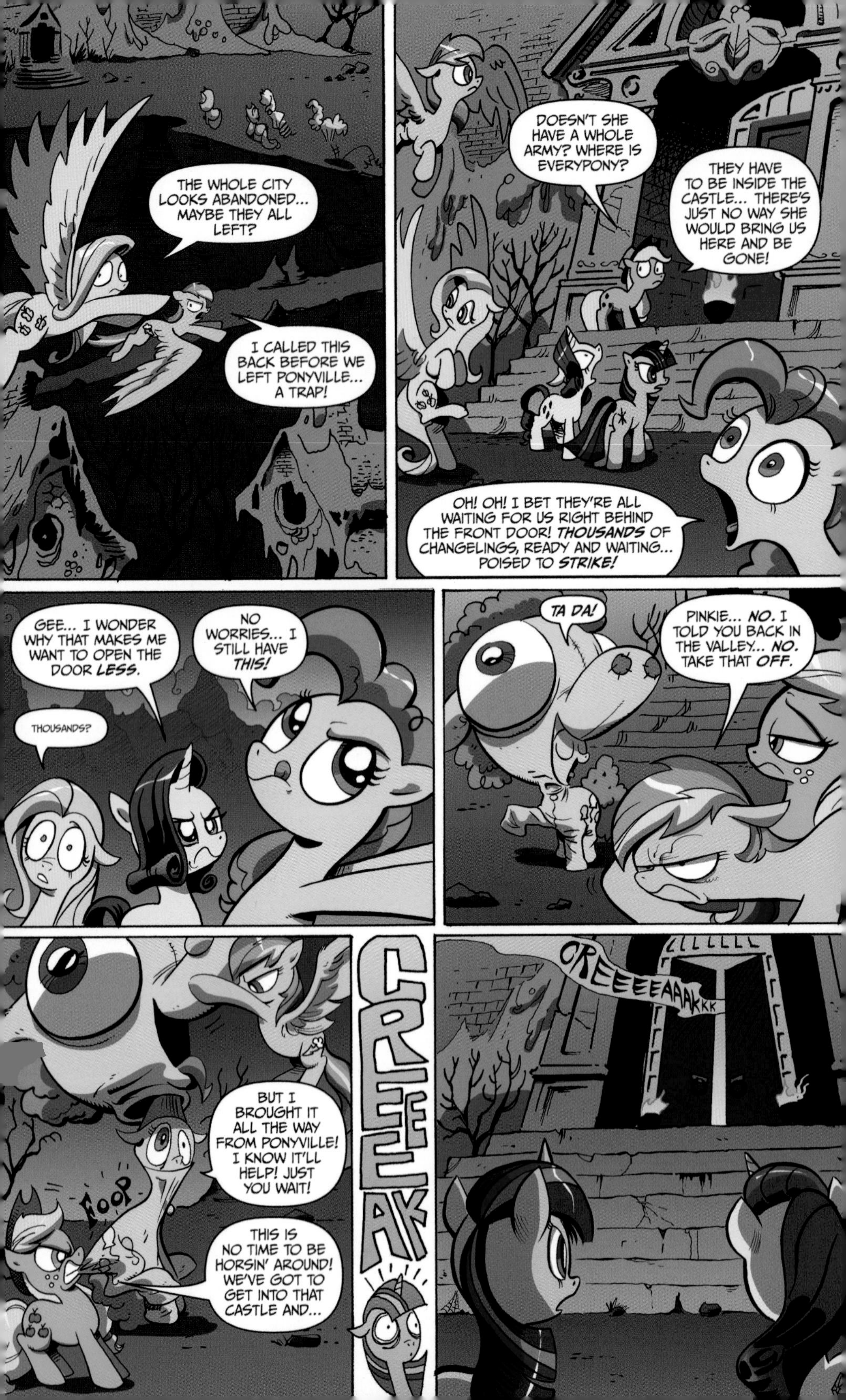
THE WHOLE CITY LOOKS ABANDONED... MAYBE THEY ALL LEFT?
I CALLED THIS BACK BEFORE WE LEFT PONYVILLE... A TRAP!
DOESN'T SHE HAVE A WHOLE ARMY? WHERE IS EVERYPONY?
THEY HAVE TO BE INSIDE THE CASTLE... THERE'S JUST NO WAY SHE WOULD BRING US HERE AND BE GONE!
OH! OH! I BET THEY'RE ALL WAITING FOR US RIGHT BEHIND THE FRONT DOOR! THOUSANDS OF CHANGELINGS, READY AND WAITING... POISED TO STRIKE!
GEE... I WONDER WHY THAT MAKES ME WANT TO OPEN THE DOOR LESS.
NO WORRIES... I STILL HAVE THIS!
THOUSANDS?
TA DA!
PINKIE... NO. I TOLD YOU BACK IN THE VALLEY... NO. TAKE THAT OFF.
BUT I BROUGHT IT ALL THE WAY FROM PONYVILLE! I KNOW IT'LL HELP! JUST YOU WAIT!
FOOP
THIS IS NO TIME TO BE HORSIN' AROUND! WE'VE GOT TO GET INTO THAT CASTLE AND...
CREEEAK
CREEEEEAAAKKK

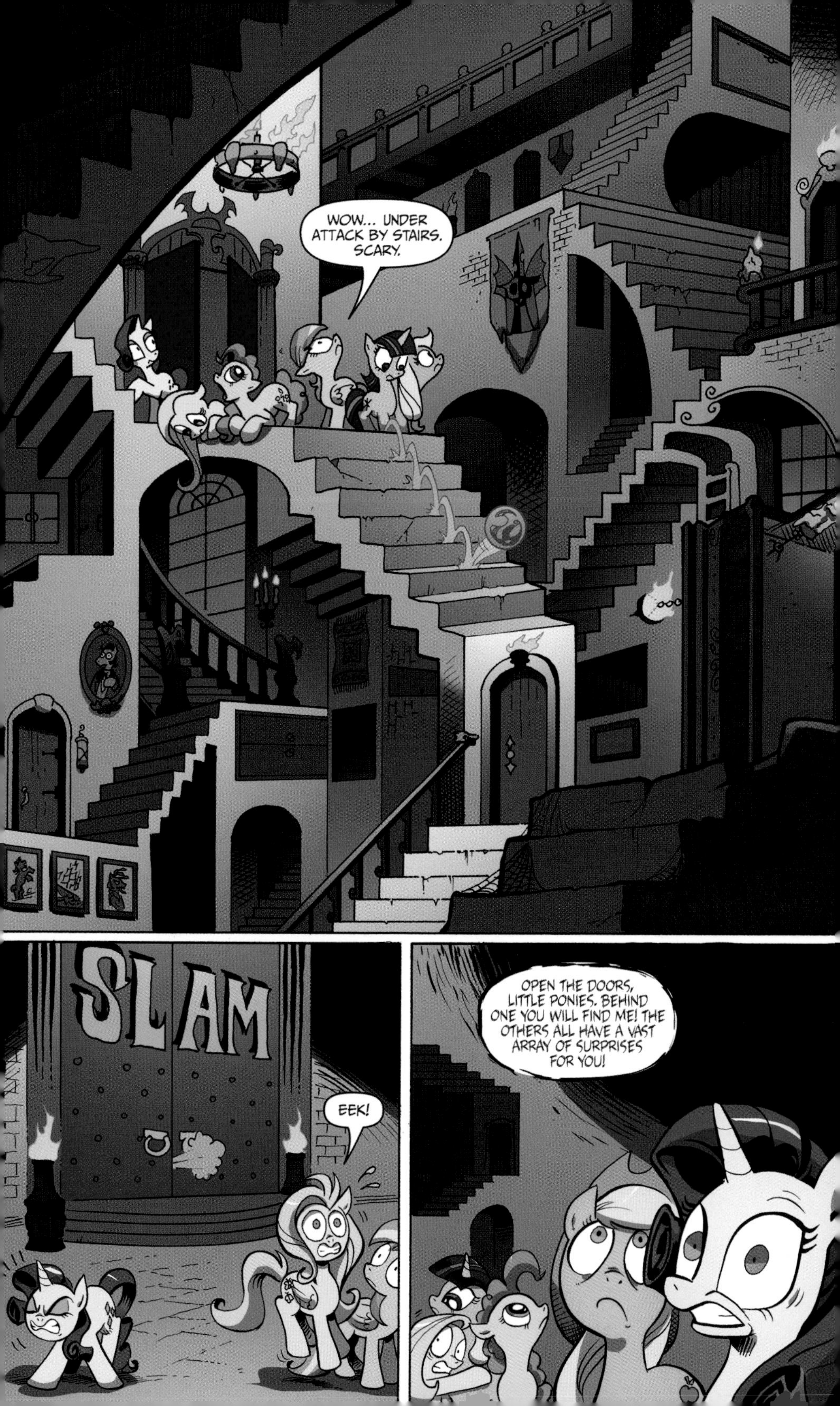
WOW... UNDER ATTACK BY STAIRS. SCARY.
SLAM
EEK!
OPEN THE DOORS, LITTLE PONIES. BEHIND ONE YOU WILL FIND ME! THE OTHERS ALL HAVE A VAST ARRAY OF SURPRISES FOR YOU!

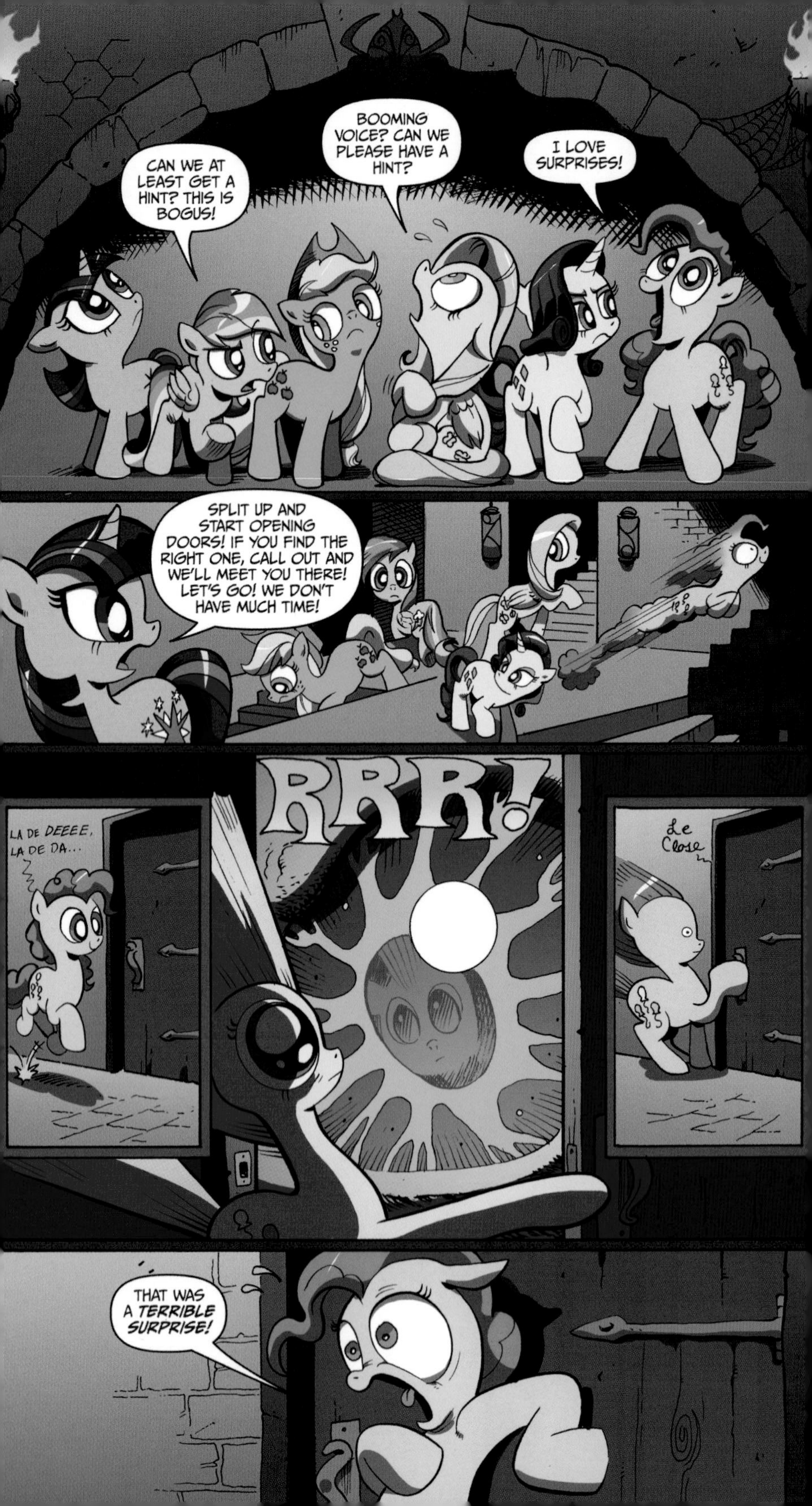
CAN WE AT LEAST GET A HINT? THIS IS BOGUS!
BOOMING VOICE? CAN WE PLEASE HAVE A HINT?
I LOVE SURPRISES!
SPLIT UP AND START OPENING DOORS! IF YOU FIND THE RIGHT ONE, CALL OUT AND WE'LL MEET YOU THERE! LET'S GO! WE DON'T HAVE MUCH TIME!
RRR!
LA DE DEEEE, LA DE DA...
Le Close
THAT WAS A TERRIBLE SURPRISE!

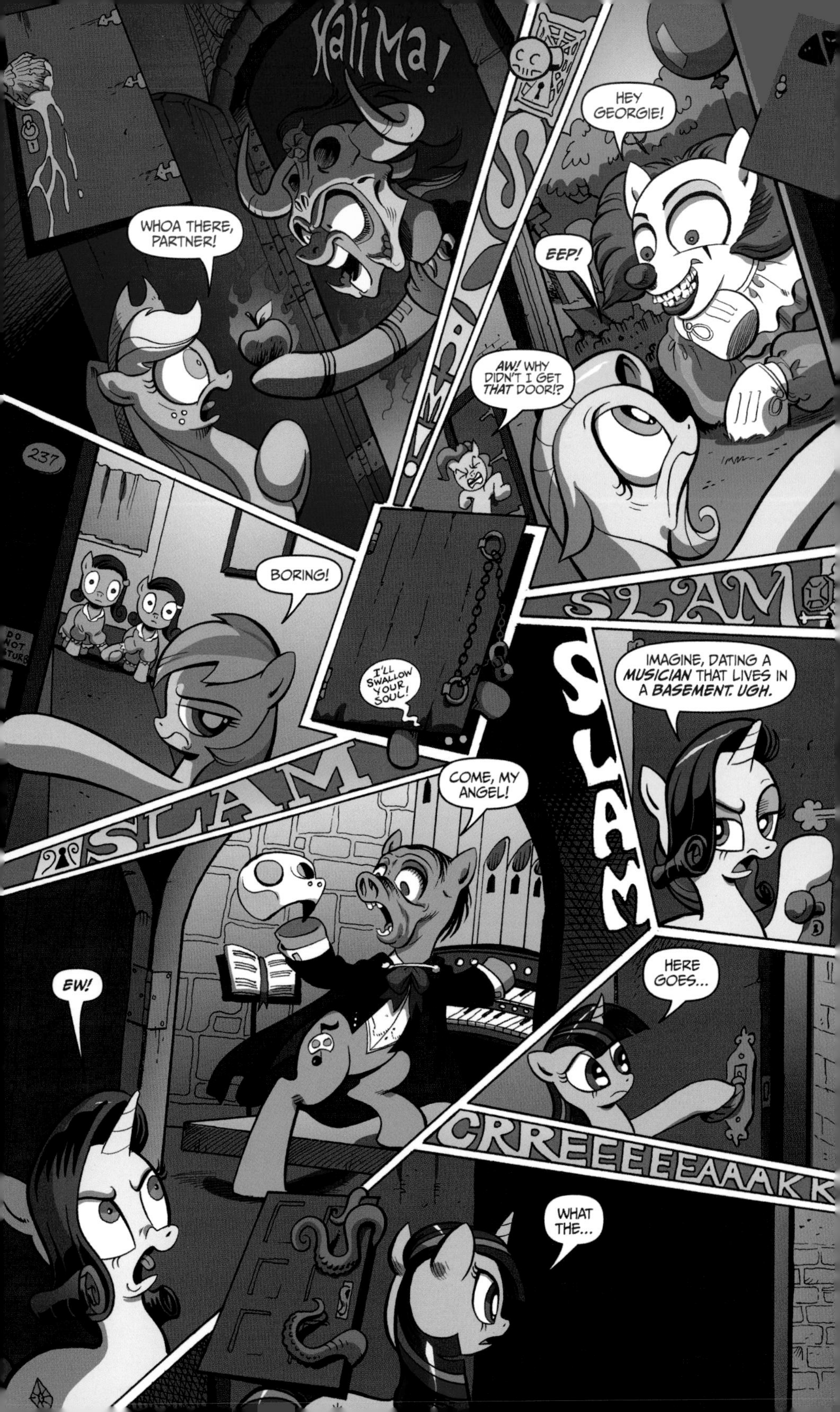
KALI MA!
WHOA THERE, PARTNER!
HEY GEORGIE!
EEP!
AW! WHY DIDN'T I GET THAT DOOR!?
SLAM
237
BORING!
DO NOT
I'LL SWALLOW YOUR SOUL!
SLAM
SLAM
IMAGINE, DATING A MUSICIAN THAT LIVES IN A BASEMENT. UGH.
COME, MY ANGEL!
EW!
HERE GOES...
CRREEEEEEAAAKK
WHAT THE...

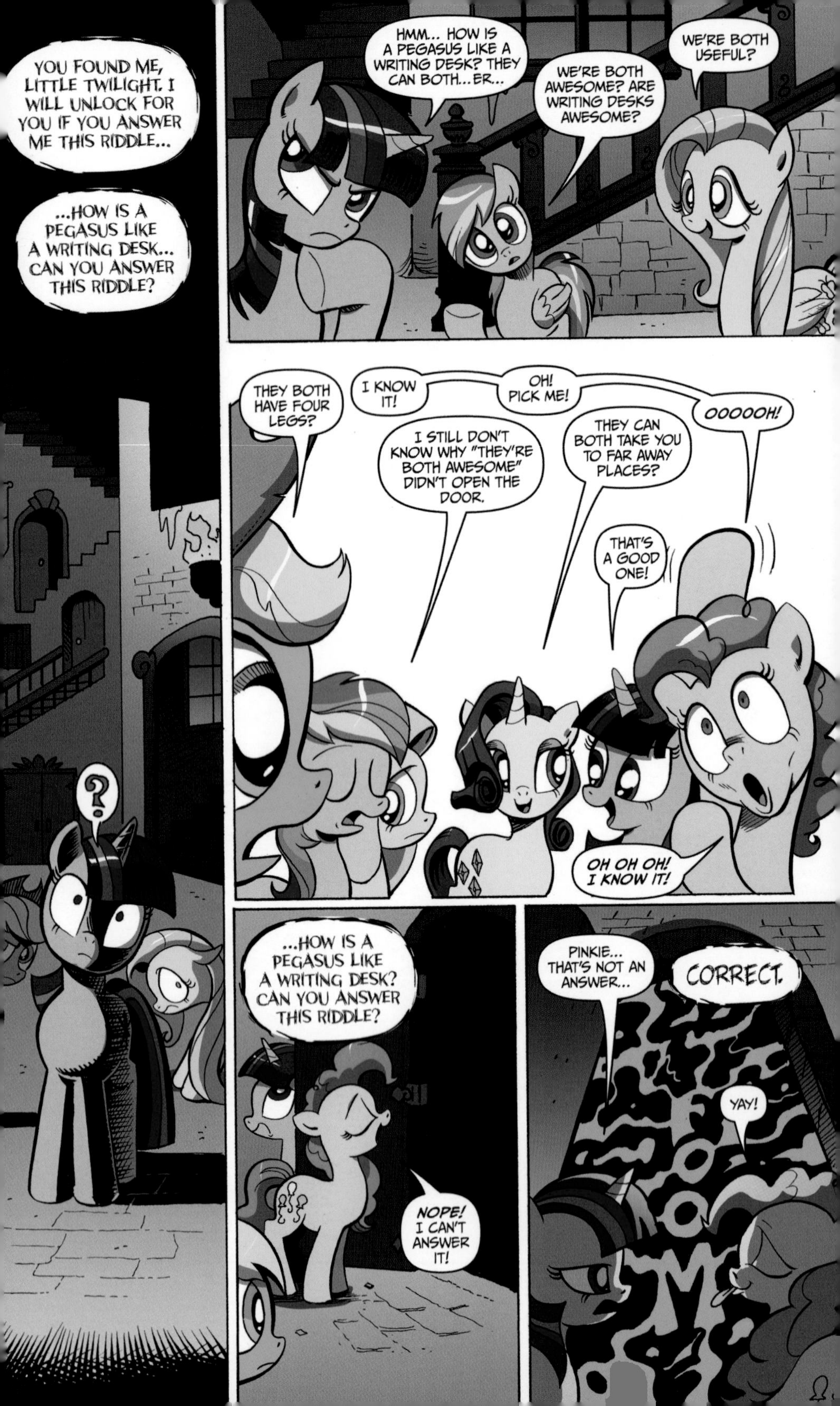

YOU FOUND ME, LITTLE TWILIGHT. I WILL UNLOCK FOR YOU IF YOU ANSWER ME THIS RIDDLE...
...HOW IS A PEGASUS LIKE A WRITING DESK... CAN YOU ANSWER THIS RIDDLE?
?
HMM... HOW IS A PEGASUS LIKE A WRITING DESK? THEY CAN BOTH... ER...
WE'RE BOTH AWESOME? ARE WRITING DESKS AWESOME?
WE'RE BOTH USEFUL?
THEY BOTH HAVE FOUR LEGS?
I KNOW IT!
OH! PICK ME!
OOOOOH!
I STILL DON'T KNOW WHY "THEY'RE BOTH AWESOME" DIDN'T OPEN THE DOOR.
THEY CAN BOTH TAKE YOU TO FAR AWAY PLACES?
THAT'S A GOOD ONE!
OH OH OH! I KNOW IT!
...HOW IS A PEGASUS LIKE A WRITING DESK? CAN YOU ANSWER THIS RIDDLE?
NOPE! I CAN'T ANSWER IT!
PINKIE... THAT'S NOT AN ANSWER...
CORRECT.
YAY!

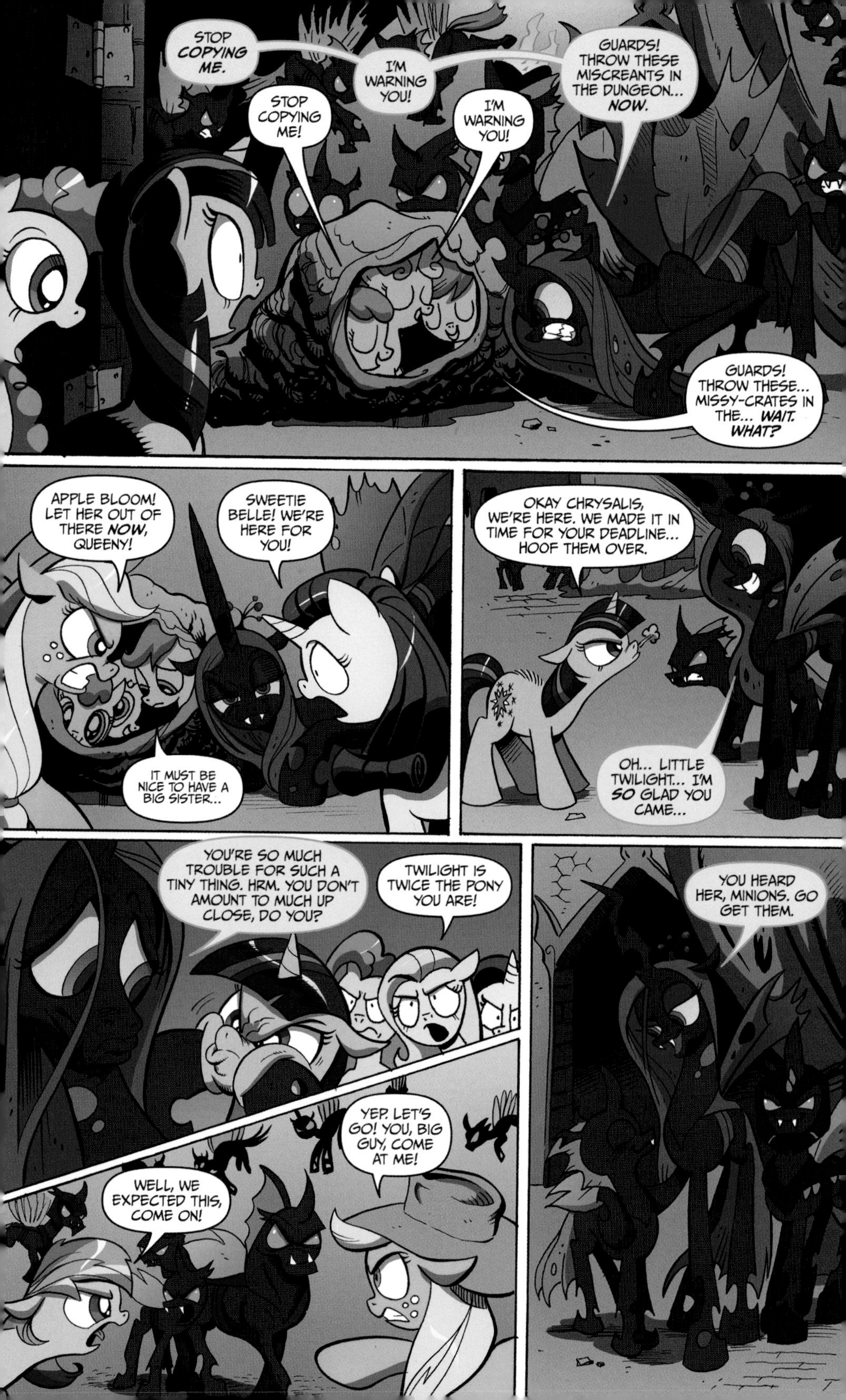
STOP COPYING ME.
STOP COPYING ME!
I'M WARNING YOU!
I'M WARNING YOU!
GUARDS! THROW THESE MISCREANTS IN THE DUNGEON... NOW.
GUARDS! THROW THESE... MISSY-CRATES IN THE... WAIT. WHAT?
APPLE BLOOM! LET HER OUT OF THERE NOW, QUEENY!
SWEETIE BELLE! WE'RE HERE FOR YOU!
IT MUST BE NICE TO HAVE A BIG SISTER...
OKAY CHRYSALIS, WE'RE HERE. WE MADE IT IN TIME FOR YOUR DEADLINE... HOOF THEM OVER.
OH... LITTLE TWILIGHT... I'M SO GLAD YOU CAME...
YOU'RE SO MUCH TROUBLE FOR SUCH A TINY THING. HRM. YOU DON'T AMOUNT TO MUCH UP CLOSE, DO YOU?
TWILIGHT IS TWICE THE PONY YOU ARE!
YOU HEARD HER, MINIONS. GO GET THEM.
WELL, WE EXPECTED THIS, COME ON!
YEP. LET'S GO! YOU, BIG GUY, COME AT ME!

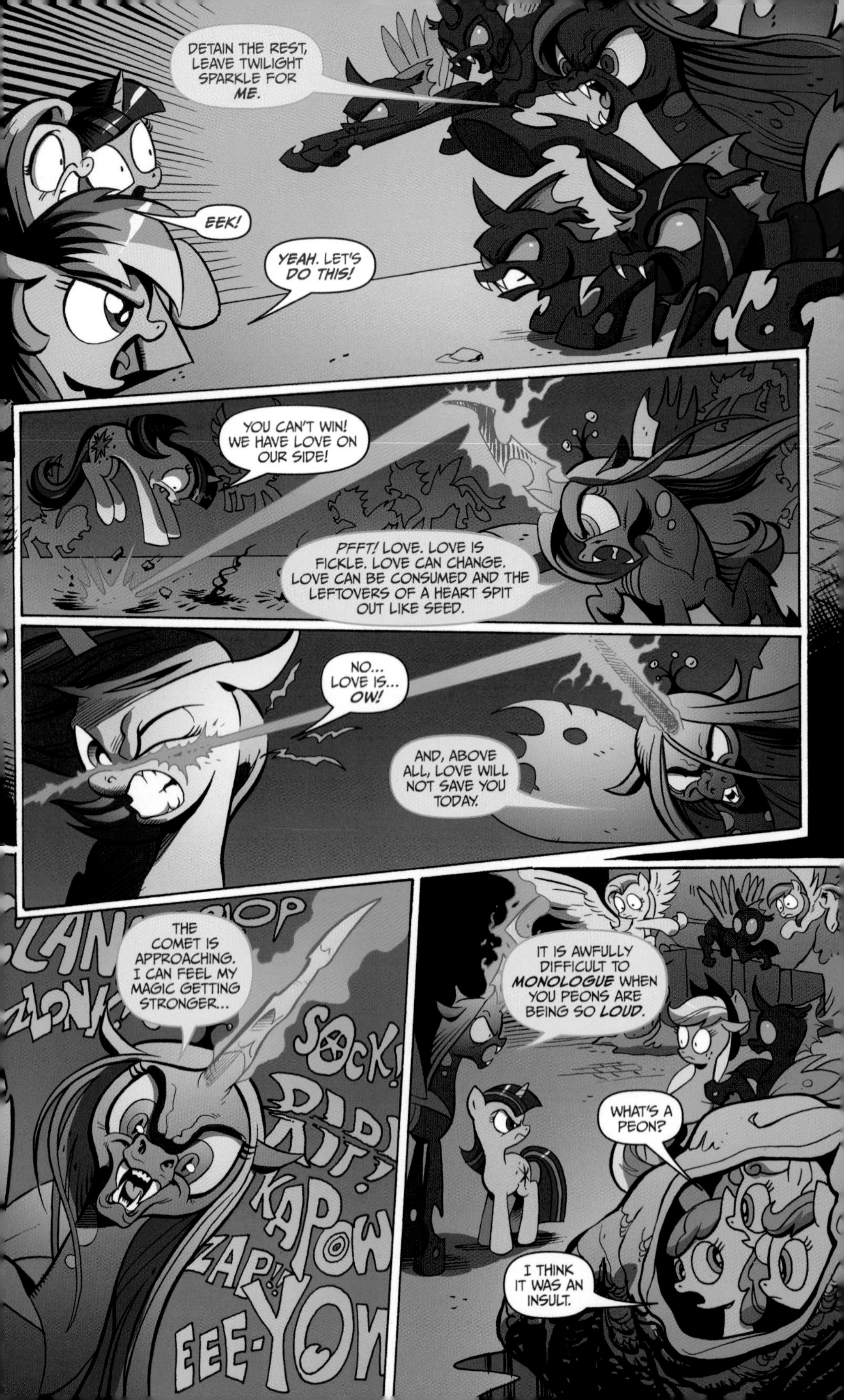
DETAIN THE REST, LEAVE TWILIGHT SPARKLE FOR *ME*.
EEK!
YEAH. LET'S *DO THIS!*
YOU CAN'T WIN! WE HAVE LOVE ON OUR SIDE!
PFFT! LOVE. LOVE IS FICKLE. LOVE CAN CHANGE. LOVE CAN BE CONSUMED AND THE LEFTOVERS OF A HEART SPIT OUT LIKE SEED.
NO... LOVE IS... *OW!*
AND, ABOVE ALL, LOVE WILL NOT SAVE YOU TODAY.
THE COMET IS APPROACHING. I CAN FEEL MY MAGIC GETTING STRONGER...
SOCK!
RIP!
KAPOW
ZAP!
EEE-YOW
IT IS AWFULLY DIFFICULT TO ***MONOLOGUE*** WHEN YOU PEONS ARE BEING SO ***LOUD***.
WHAT'S A PEON?
I THINK IT WAS AN INSULT.

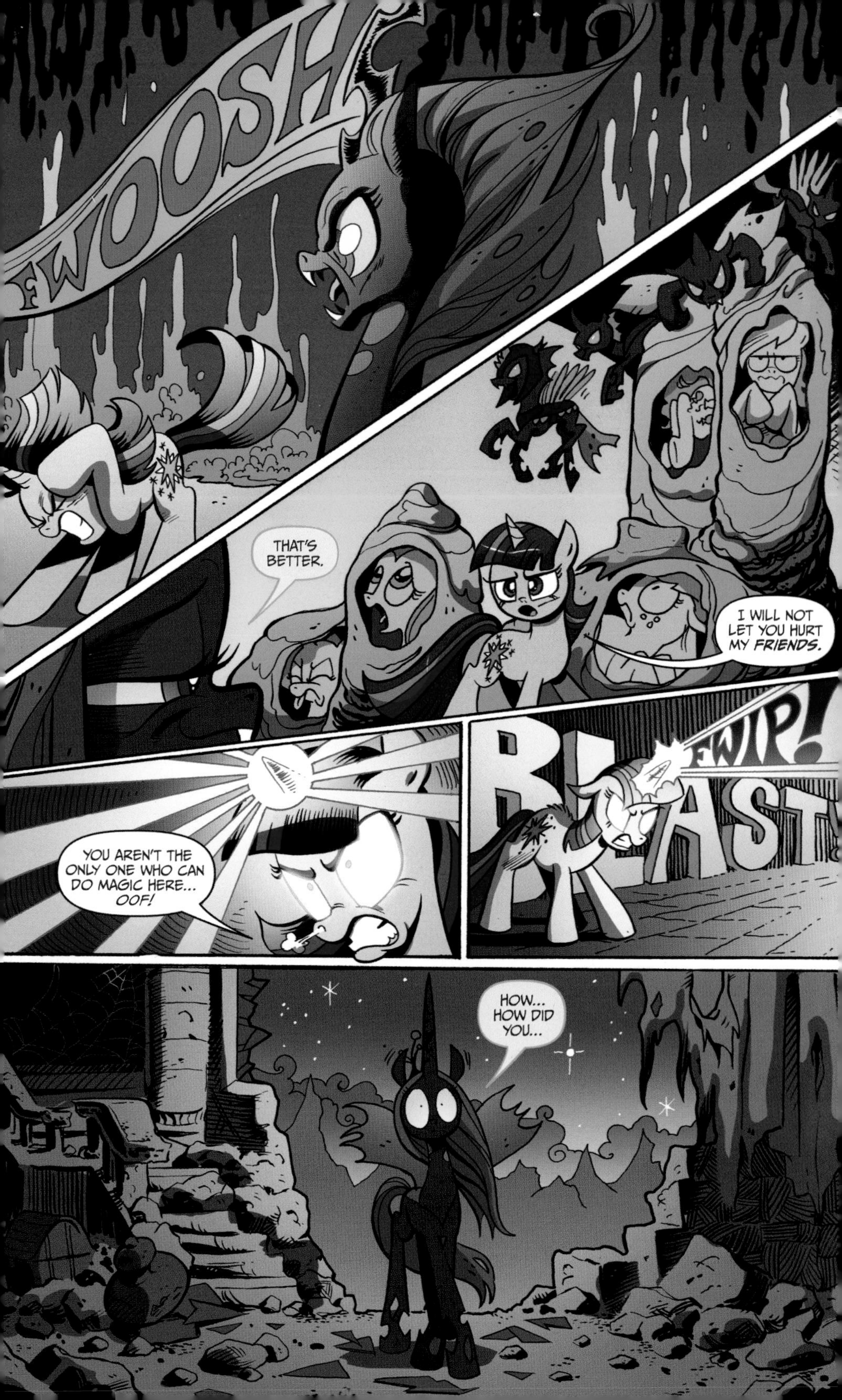
FWOOSH!
THAT'S BETTER.
I WILL NOT LET YOU HURT MY FRIENDS.
YOU AREN'T THE ONLY ONE WHO CAN DO MAGIC HERE... OOF!
BLAST
FWIP!
HOW... HOW DID YOU...

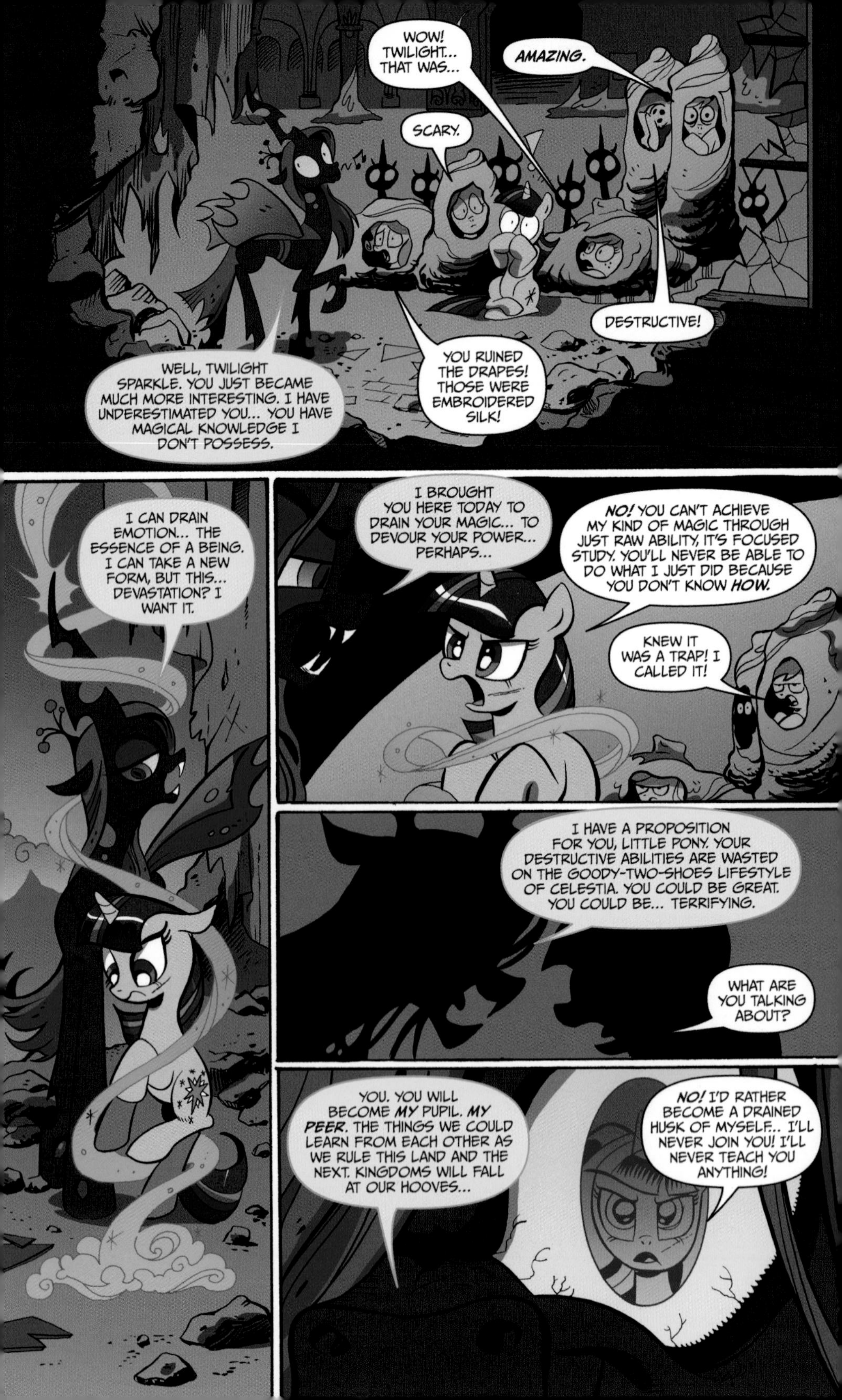
WOW! TWILIGHT... THAT WAS...
AMAZING.
SCARY.
DESTRUCTIVE!
YOU RUINED THE DRAPES! THOSE WERE EMBROIDERED SILK!
WELL, TWILIGHT SPARKLE. YOU JUST BECAME MUCH MORE INTERESTING. I HAVE UNDERESTIMATED YOU... YOU HAVE MAGICAL KNOWLEDGE I DON'T POSSESS.
I CAN DRAIN EMOTION... THE ESSENCE OF A BEING. I CAN TAKE A NEW FORM, BUT THIS... DEVASTATION? I WANT IT.
I BROUGHT YOU HERE TODAY TO DRAIN YOUR MAGIC... TO DEVOUR YOUR POWER... PERHAPS...
NO! YOU CAN'T ACHIEVE MY KIND OF MAGIC THROUGH JUST RAW ABILITY, IT'S FOCUSED STUDY. YOU'LL NEVER BE ABLE TO DO WHAT I JUST DID BECAUSE YOU DON'T KNOW HOW.
KNEW IT WAS A TRAP! I CALLED IT!
I HAVE A PROPOSITION FOR YOU, LITTLE PONY. YOUR DESTRUCTIVE ABILITIES ARE WASTED ON THE GOODY-TWO-SHOES LIFESTYLE OF CELESTIA. YOU COULD BE GREAT. YOU COULD BE... TERRIFYING.
WHAT ARE YOU TALKING ABOUT?
YOU. YOU WILL BECOME MY PUPIL. MY PEER. THE THINGS WE COULD LEARN FROM EACH OTHER AS WE RULE THIS LAND AND THE NEXT. KINGDOMS WILL FALL AT OUR HOOVES...
NO! I'D RATHER BECOME A DRAINED HUSK OF MYSELF... I'LL NEVER JOIN YOU! I'LL NEVER TEACH YOU ANYTHING!

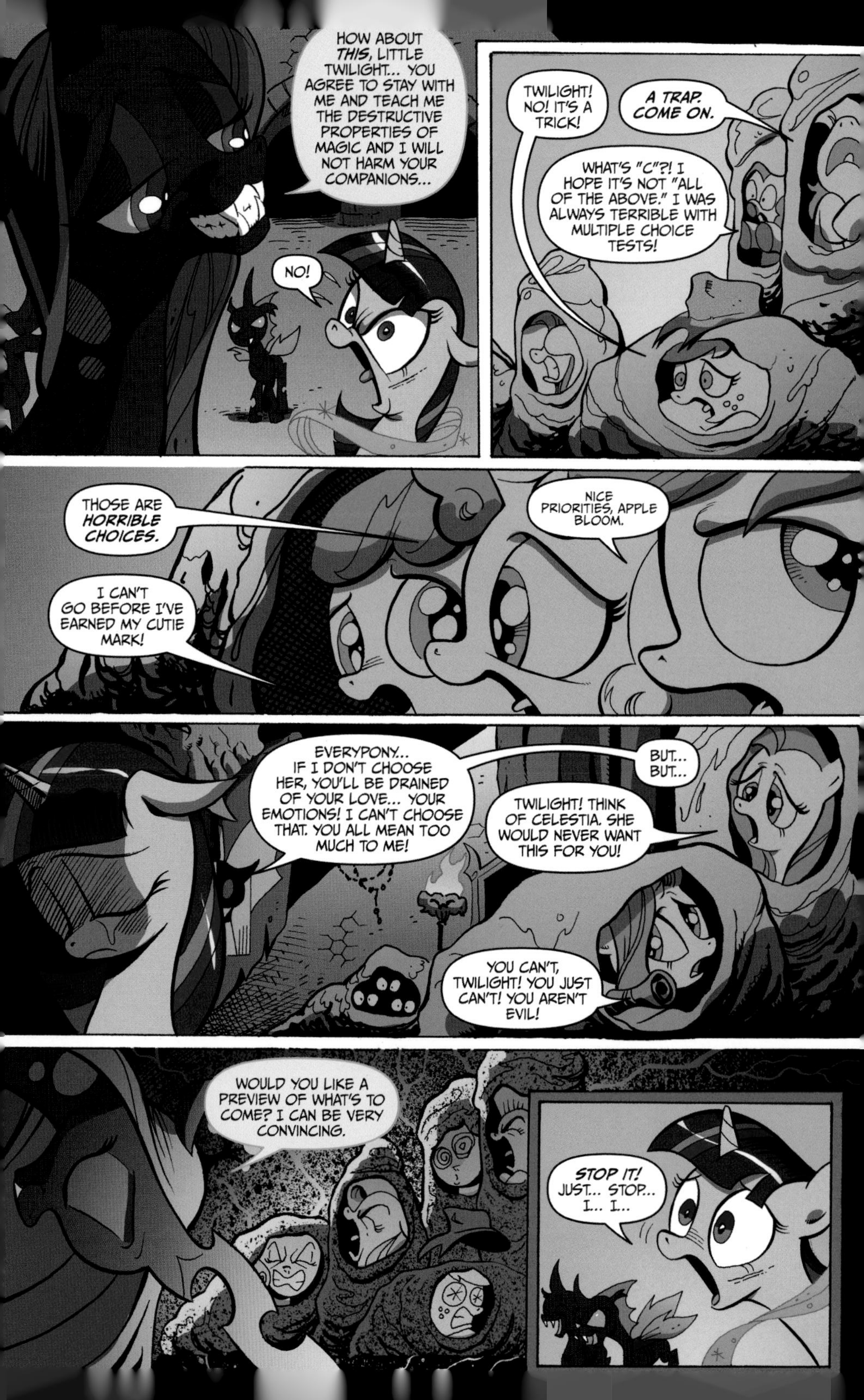
HOW ABOUT *THIS*, LITTLE TWILIGHT... YOU AGREE TO STAY WITH ME AND TEACH ME THE DESTRUCTIVE PROPERTIES OF MAGIC AND I WILL NOT HARM YOUR COMPANIONS...
NO!
TWILIGHT! NO! IT'S A TRICK!
A TRAP. COME ON.
WHAT'S "C"?! I HOPE IT'S NOT "ALL OF THE ABOVE." I WAS ALWAYS TERRIBLE WITH MULTIPLE CHOICE TESTS!
THOSE ARE *HORRIBLE CHOICES.*
NICE PRIORITIES, APPLE BLOOM.
I CAN'T GO BEFORE I'VE EARNED MY CUTIE MARK!
EVERYPONY... IF I DON'T CHOOSE HER, YOU'LL BE DRAINED OF YOUR LOVE... YOUR EMOTIONS! I CAN'T CHOOSE THAT. YOU ALL MEAN TOO MUCH TO ME!
BUT... BUT...
TWILIGHT! THINK OF CELESTIA. SHE WOULD NEVER WANT THIS FOR YOU!
YOU CAN'T, TWILIGHT! YOU JUST CAN'T! YOU AREN'T EVIL!
WOULD YOU LIKE A PREVIEW OF WHAT'S TO COME? I CAN BE VERY CONVINCING.
STOP IT! JUST... STOP... I... I...

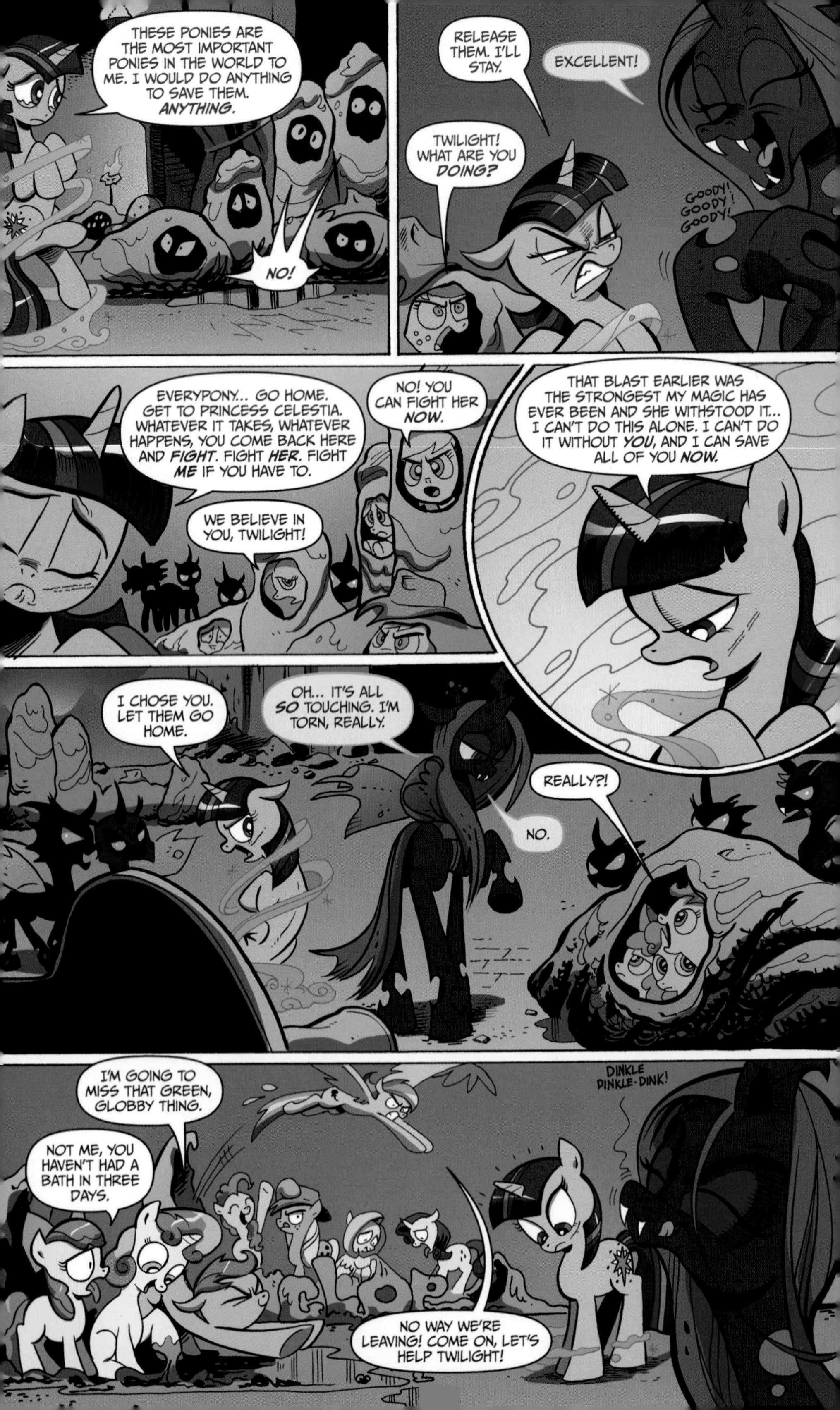
THESE PONIES ARE THE MOST IMPORTANT PONIES IN THE WORLD TO ME. I WOULD DO ANYTHING TO SAVE THEM. ANYTHING.
NO!
RELEASE THEM. I'LL STAY.
EXCELLENT!
TWILIGHT! WHAT ARE YOU DOING?
GOODY! GOODY! GOODY!
EVERYPONY... GO HOME. GET TO PRINCESS CELESTIA. WHATEVER IT TAKES, WHATEVER HAPPENS, YOU COME BACK HERE AND FIGHT. FIGHT HER. FIGHT ME IF YOU HAVE TO.
NO! YOU CAN FIGHT HER NOW.
WE BELIEVE IN YOU, TWILIGHT!
THAT BLAST EARLIER WAS THE STRONGEST MY MAGIC HAS EVER BEEN AND SHE WITHSTOOD IT... I CAN'T DO THIS ALONE. I CAN'T DO IT WITHOUT YOU, AND I CAN SAVE ALL OF YOU NOW.
I CHOSE YOU. LET THEM GO HOME.
OH... IT'S ALL SO TOUCHING. I'M TORN, REALLY.
REALLY?!
NO.
I'M GOING TO MISS THAT GREEN, GLOBBY THING.
NOT ME, YOU HAVEN'T HAD A BATH IN THREE DAYS.
DINKLE DINKLE-DINK!
NO WAY WE'RE LEAVING! COME ON, LET'S HELP TWILIGHT!

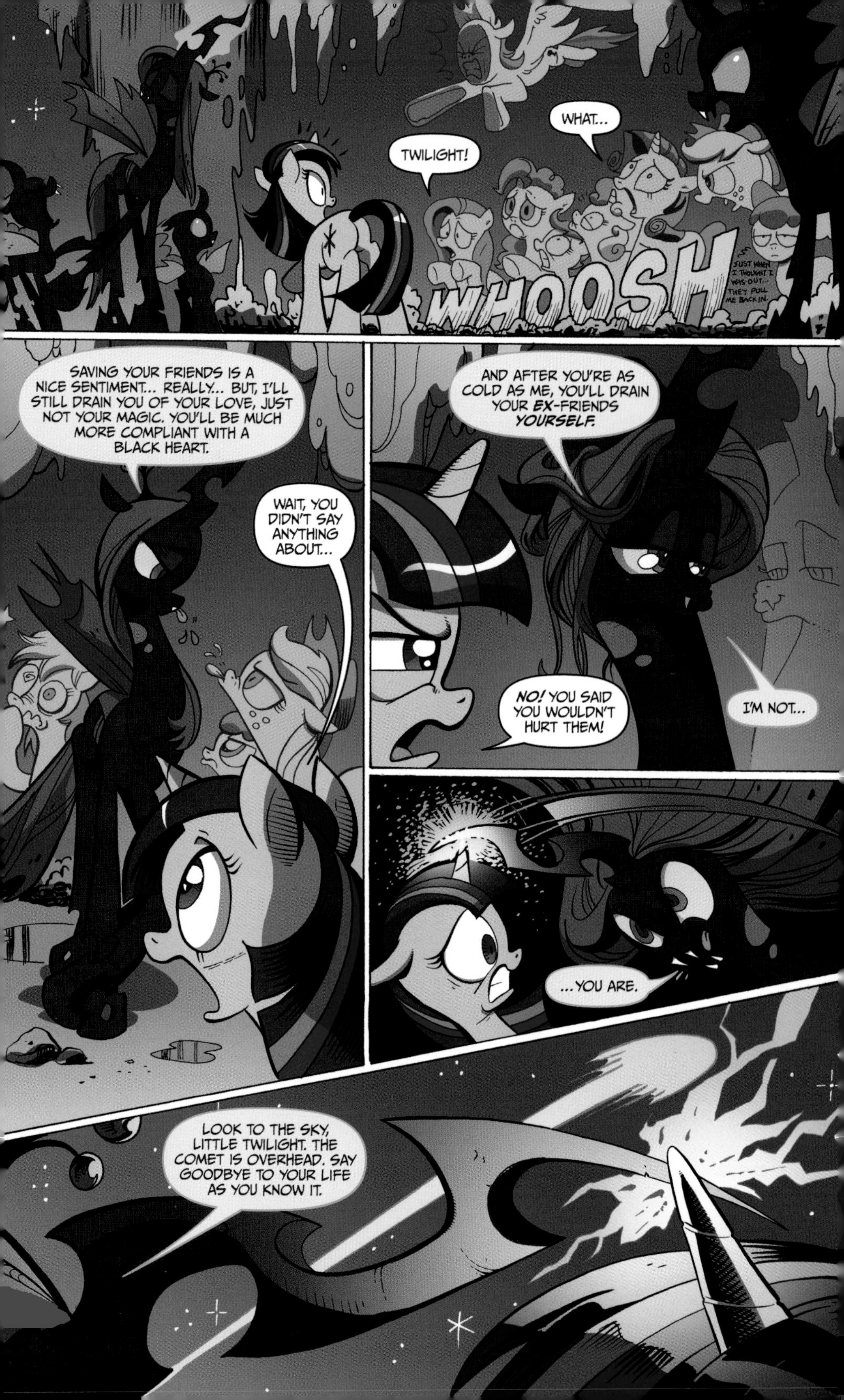
WHAT...
TWILIGHT!
WHOOSH
JUST WHEN I THOUGHT I WAS OUT... THEY PULL ME BACK IN.
SAVING YOUR FRIENDS IS A NICE SENTIMENT... REALLY... BUT, I'LL STILL DRAIN YOU OF YOUR LOVE, JUST NOT YOUR MAGIC. YOU'LL BE MUCH MORE COMPLIANT WITH A BLACK HEART.
WAIT, YOU DIDN'T SAY ANYTHING ABOUT...
AND AFTER YOU'RE AS COLD AS ME, YOU'LL DRAIN YOUR EX-FRIENDS YOURSELF.
NO! YOU SAID YOU WOULDN'T HURT THEM!
I'M NOT...
...YOU ARE.
LOOK TO THE SKY, LITTLE TWILIGHT. THE COMET IS OVERHEAD. SAY GOODBYE TO YOUR LIFE AS YOU KNOW IT.

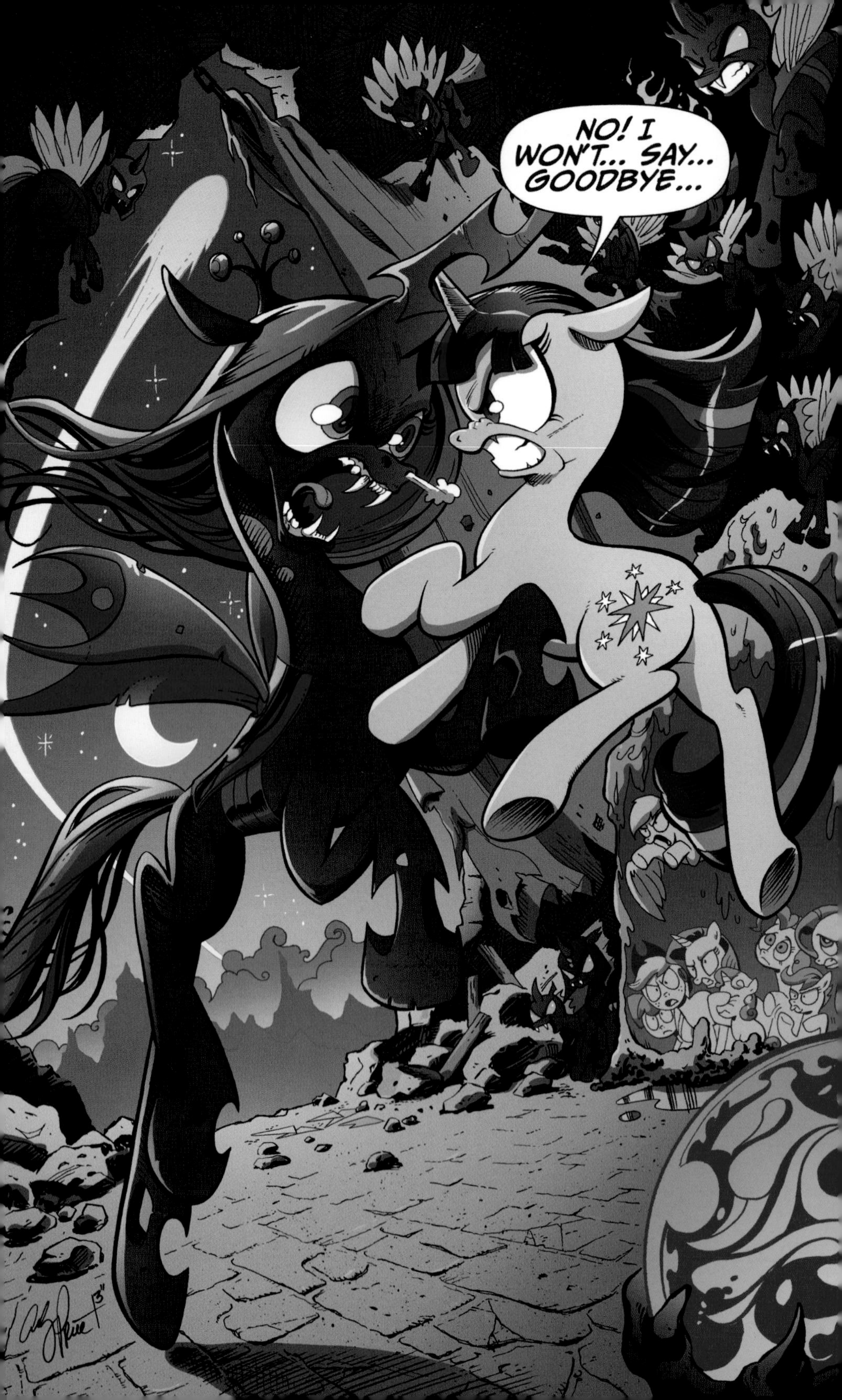
NO! I WON'T... SAY... GOODBYE...

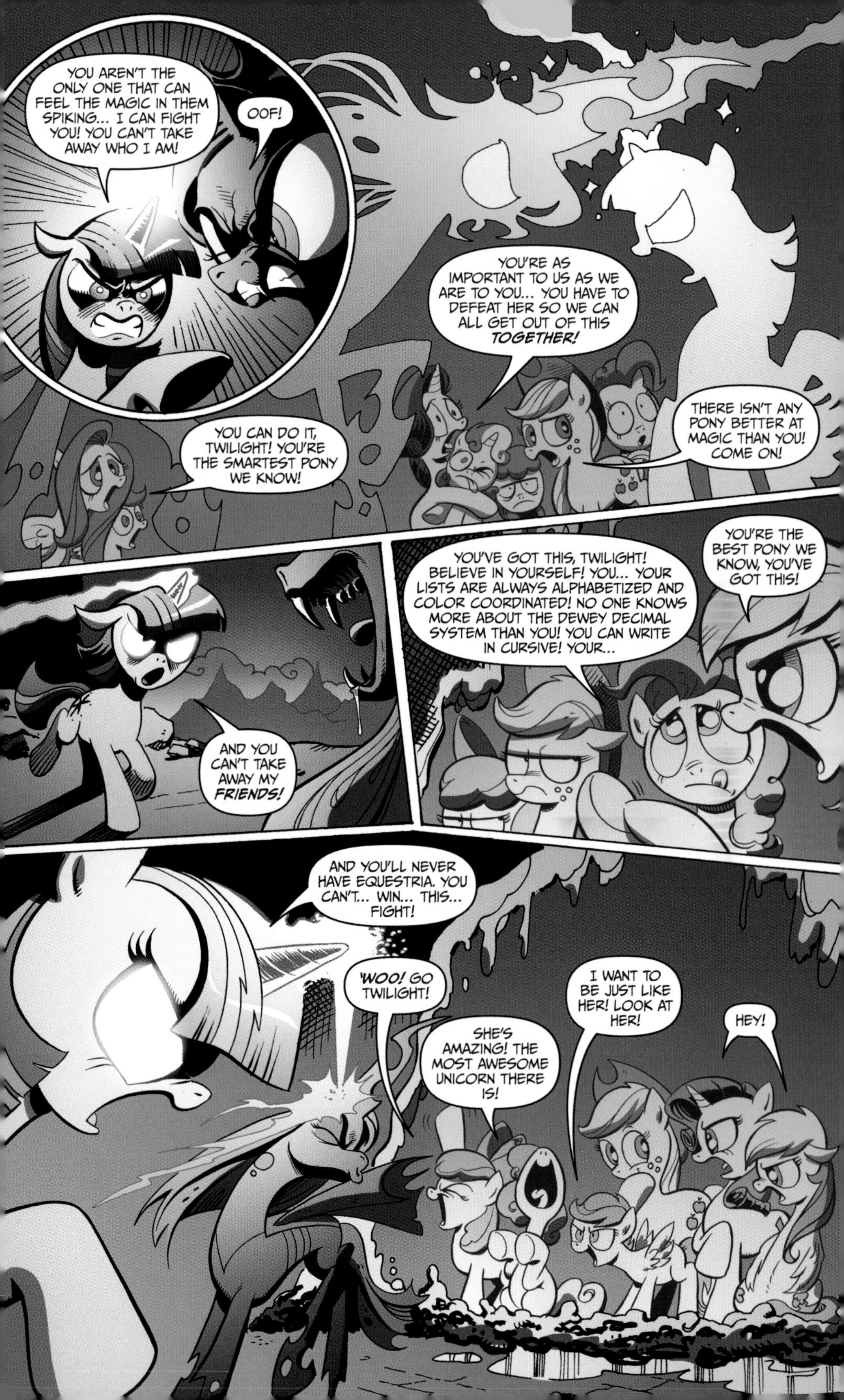
YOU AREN'T THE ONLY ONE THAT CAN FEEL THE MAGIC IN THEM SPIKING... I CAN FIGHT YOU! YOU CAN'T TAKE AWAY WHO I AM!
OOF!
YOU'RE AS IMPORTANT TO US AS WE ARE TO YOU... YOU HAVE TO DEFEAT HER SO WE CAN ALL GET OUT OF THIS *TOGETHER!*
YOU CAN DO IT, TWILIGHT! YOU'RE THE SMARTEST PONY WE KNOW!
THERE ISN'T ANY PONY BETTER AT MAGIC THAN YOU! COME ON!
AND YOU CAN'T TAKE AWAY MY *FRIENDS!*
YOU'VE GOT THIS, TWILIGHT! BELIEVE IN YOURSELF! YOU... YOUR LISTS ARE ALWAYS ALPHABETIZED AND COLOR COORDINATED! NO ONE KNOWS MORE ABOUT THE DEWEY DECIMAL SYSTEM THAN YOU! YOU CAN WRITE IN CURSIVE! YOUR...
YOU'RE THE BEST PONY WE KNOW, YOU'VE GOT THIS!
AND YOU'LL NEVER HAVE EQUESTRIA. YOU CAN'T... WIN... THIS... FIGHT!
'WOO! GO TWILIGHT!
SHE'S AMAZING! THE MOST AWESOME UNICORN THERE IS!
I WANT TO BE JUST LIKE HER! LOOK AT HER!
HEY!

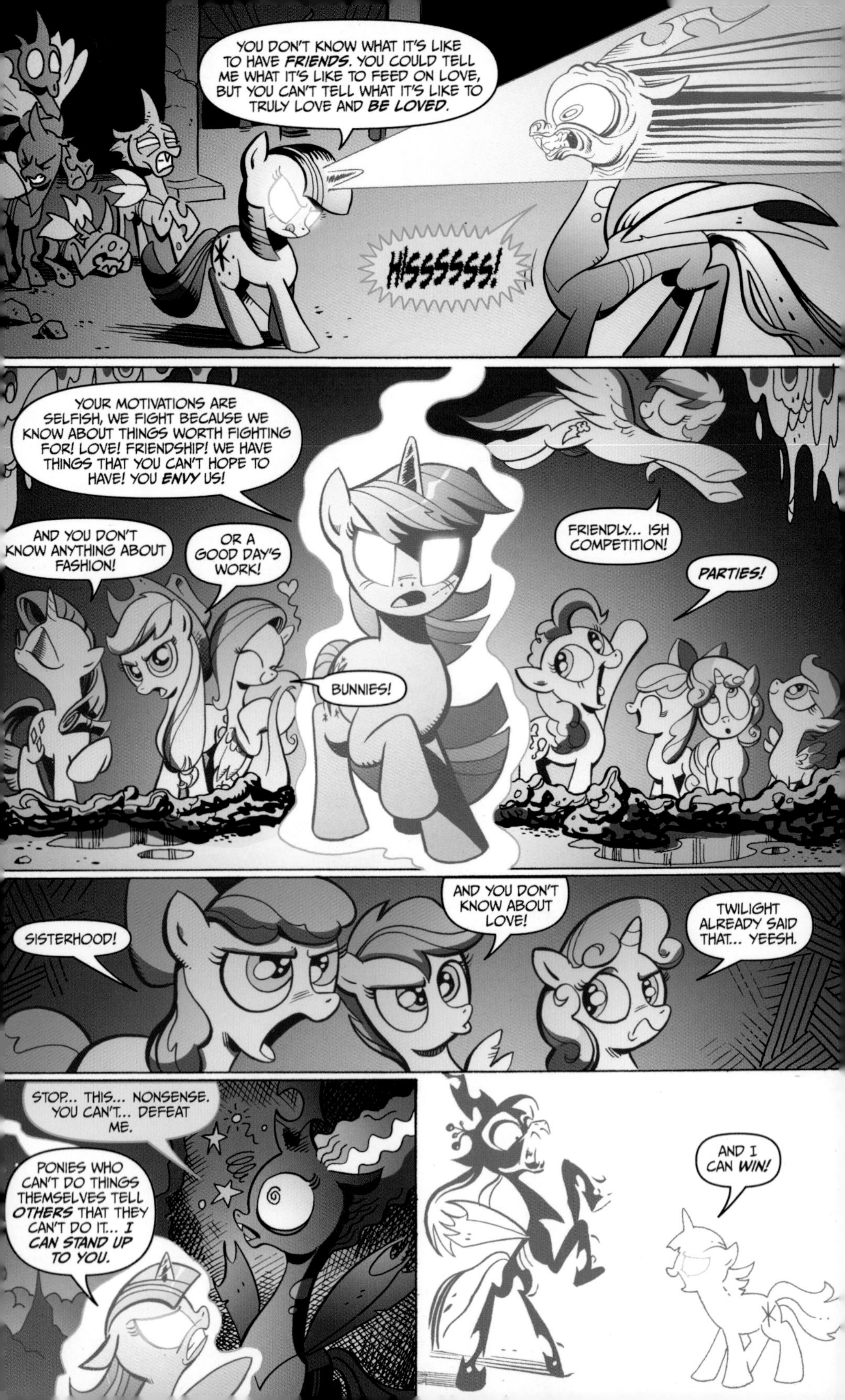
YOU DON'T KNOW WHAT IT'S LIKE TO HAVE FRIENDS. YOU COULD TELL ME WHAT IT'S LIKE TO FEED ON LOVE, BUT YOU CAN'T TELL WHAT IT'S LIKE TO TRULY LOVE AND BE LOVED.
HISSSSSS!
YOUR MOTIVATIONS ARE SELFISH, WE FIGHT BECAUSE WE KNOW ABOUT THINGS WORTH FIGHTING FOR! LOVE! FRIENDSHIP! WE HAVE THINGS THAT YOU CAN'T HOPE TO HAVE! YOU ENVY US!
AND YOU DON'T KNOW ANYTHING ABOUT FASHION!
OR A GOOD DAY'S WORK!
FRIENDLY... ISH COMPETITION!
PARTIES!
BUNNIES!
SISTERHOOD!
AND YOU DON'T KNOW ABOUT LOVE!
TWILIGHT ALREADY SAID THAT... YEESH.
STOP... THIS... NONSENSE. YOU CAN'T... DEFEAT ME.
PONIES WHO CAN'T DO THINGS THEMSELVES TELL OTHERS THAT THEY CAN'T DO IT... I CAN STAND UP TO YOU.
AND I CAN WIN!

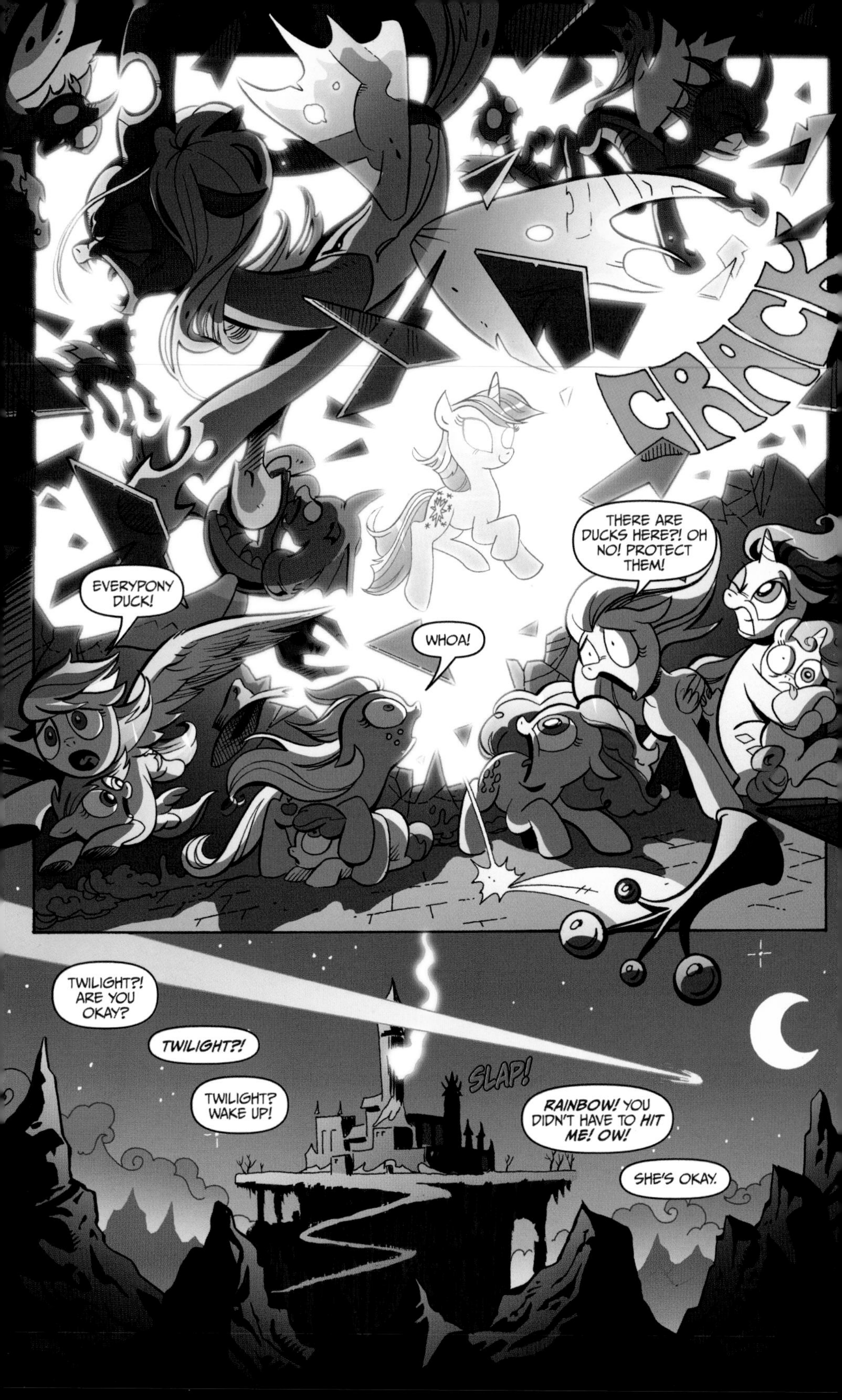
CRACK
EVERYPONY DUCK!
WHOA!
THERE ARE DUCKS HERE?! OH NO! PROTECT THEM!
TWILIGHT?! ARE YOU OKAY?
TWILIGHT?!
TWILIGHT? WAKE UP!
SLAP!
RAINBOW! YOU DIDN'T HAVE TO HIT ME! OW!
SHE'S OKAY.

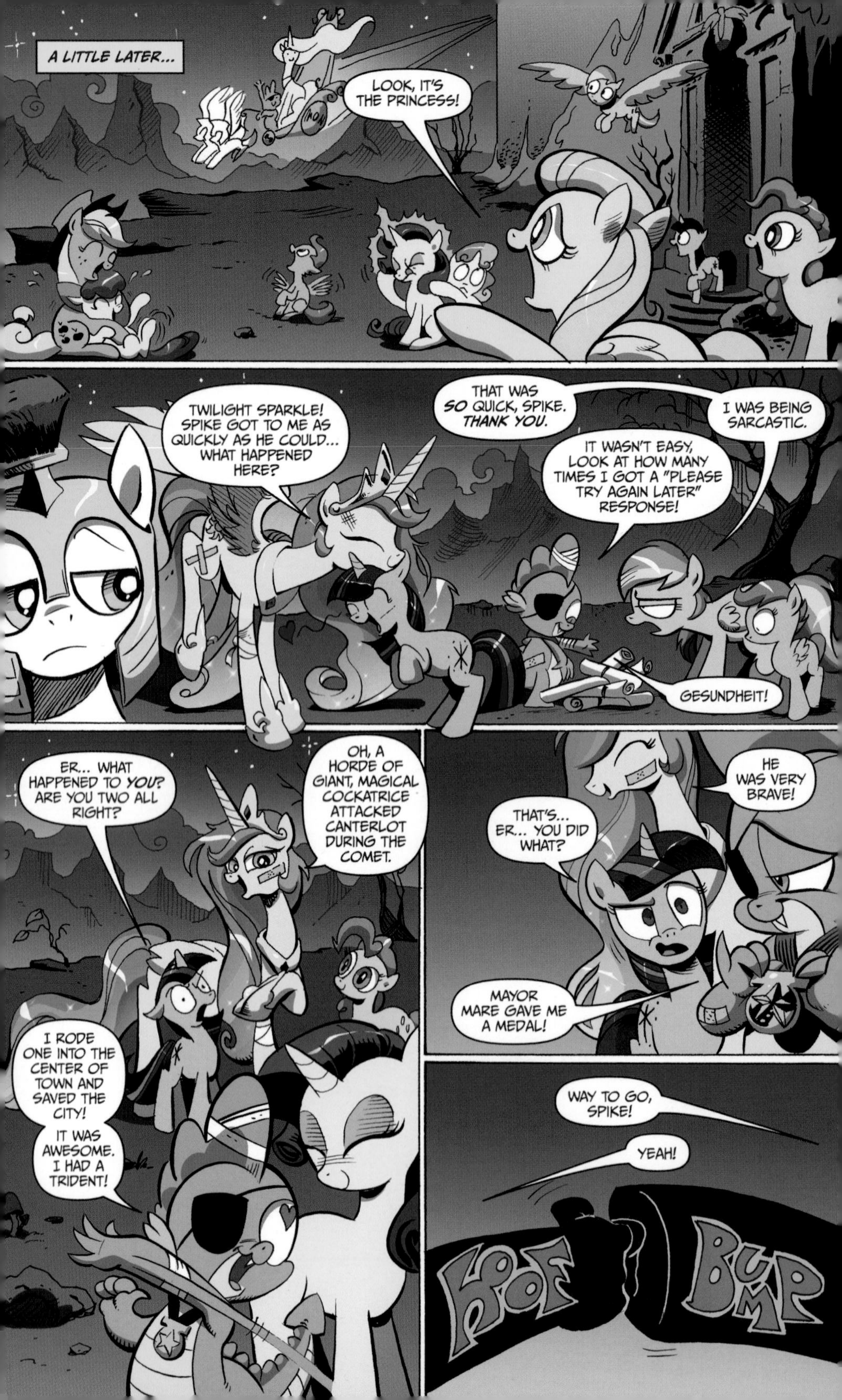
A LITTLE LATER...
LOOK, IT'S THE PRINCESS!
TWILIGHT SPARKLE! SPIKE GOT TO ME AS QUICKLY AS HE COULD... WHAT HAPPENED HERE?
THAT WAS SO QUICK, SPIKE. THANK YOU.
I WAS BEING SARCASTIC.
IT WASN'T EASY, LOOK AT HOW MANY TIMES I GOT A "PLEASE TRY AGAIN LATER" RESPONSE!
GESUNDHEIT!
ER... WHAT HAPPENED TO YOU? ARE YOU TWO ALL RIGHT?
OH, A HORDE OF GIANT, MAGICAL COCKATRICE ATTACKED CANTERLOT DURING THE COMET.
I RODE ONE INTO THE CENTER OF TOWN AND SAVED THE CITY!
IT WAS AWESOME. I HAD A TRIDENT!
HE WAS VERY BRAVE!
THAT'S... ER... YOU DID WHAT?
MAYOR MARE GAVE ME A MEDAL!
WAY TO GO, SPIKE!
YEAH!
WOOF
BUMP

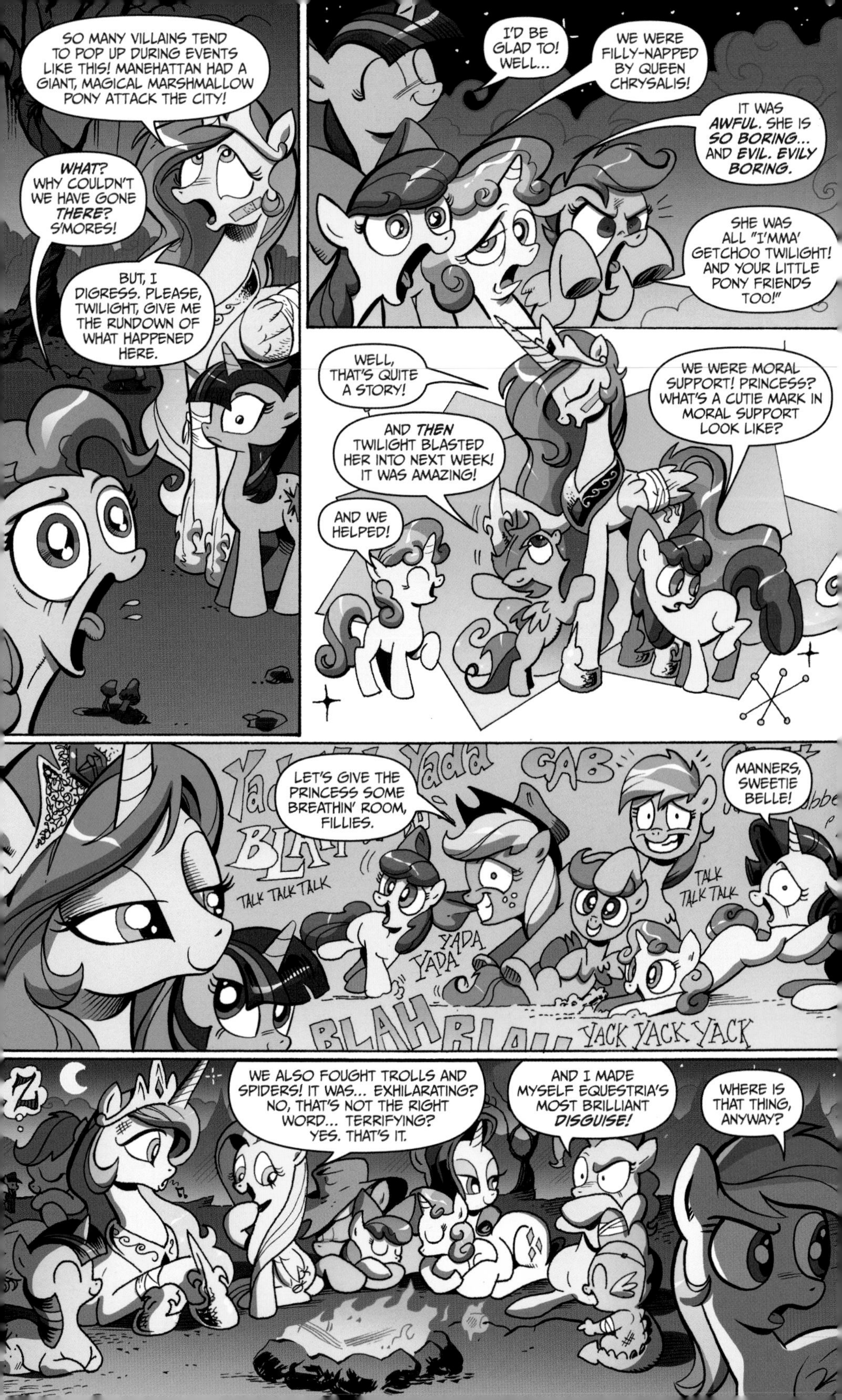

SO MANY VILLAINS TEND TO POP UP DURING EVENTS LIKE THIS! MANEHATTAN HAD A GIANT, MAGICAL MARSHMALLOW PONY ATTACK THE CITY!
WHAT? WHY COULDN'T WE HAVE GONE THERE? S'MORES!
BUT, I DIGRESS. PLEASE, TWILIGHT, GIVE ME THE RUNDOWN OF WHAT HAPPENED HERE.
I'D BE GLAD TO! WELL...
WE WERE FILLY-NAPPED BY QUEEN CHRYSALIS!
IT WAS AWFUL. SHE IS SO BORING... AND EVIL. EVILY BORING.
SHE WAS ALL "I'MMA' GETCHOO TWILIGHT! AND YOUR LITTLE PONY FRIENDS TOO!"
WELL, THAT'S QUITE A STORY!
AND THEN TWILIGHT BLASTED HER INTO NEXT WEEK! IT WAS AMAZING!
AND WE HELPED!
WE WERE MORAL SUPPORT! PRINCESS? WHAT'S A CUTIE MARK IN MORAL SUPPORT LOOK LIKE?
LET'S GIVE THE PRINCESS SOME BREATHIN' ROOM, FILLIES.
MANNERS, SWEETIE BELLE!
GAB
TALK TALK TALK
TALK TALK TALK
YADA YADA
BLAH
YACK YACK YACK
WE ALSO FOUGHT TROLLS AND SPIDERS! IT WAS... EXHILARATING? NO, THAT'S NOT THE RIGHT WORD... TERRIFYING? YES. THAT'S IT.
AND I MADE MYSELF EQUESTRIA'S MOST BRILLIANT DISGUISE!
WHERE IS THAT THING, ANYWAY?

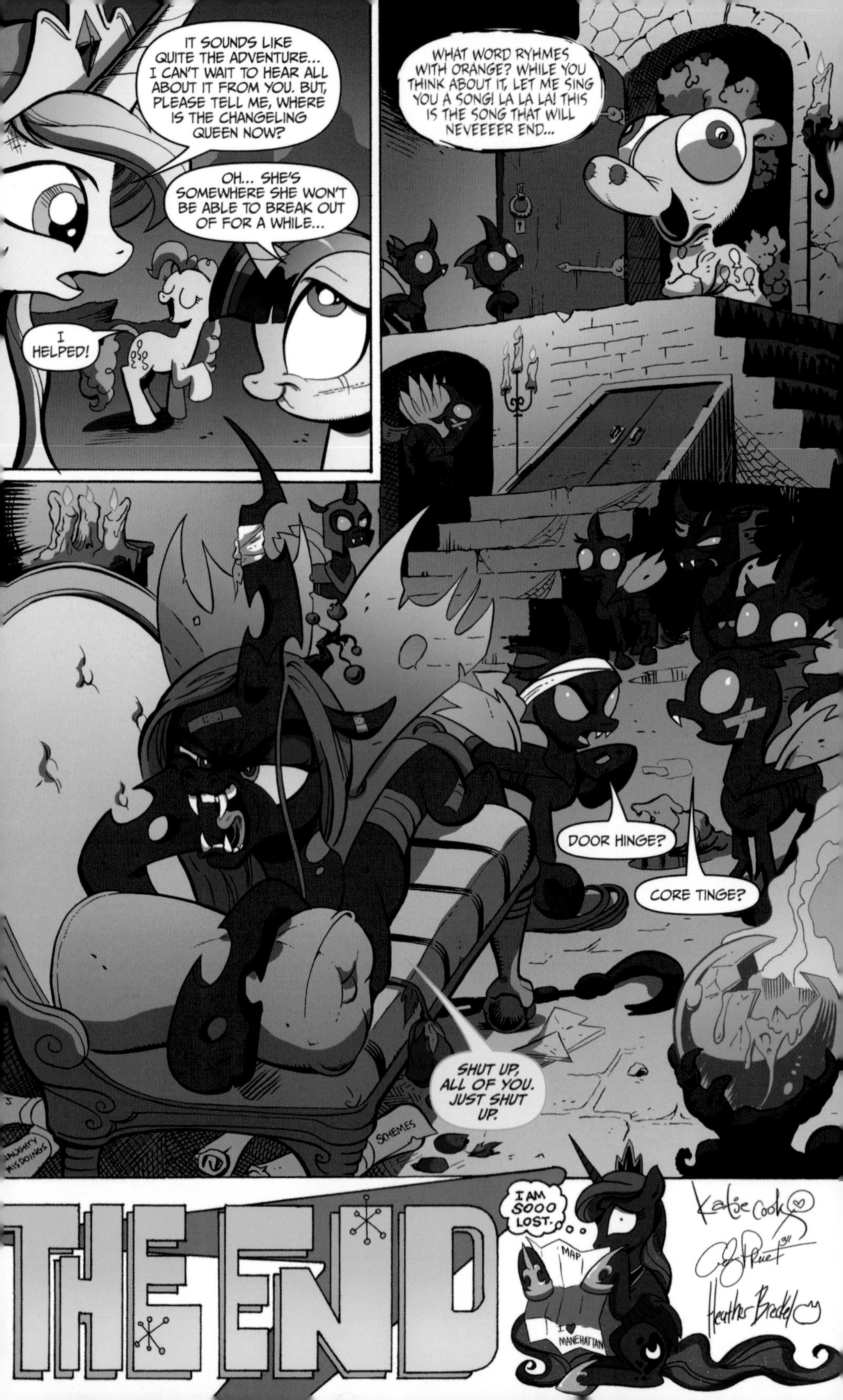
IT SOUNDS LIKE QUITE THE ADVENTURE... I CAN'T WAIT TO HEAR ALL ABOUT IT FROM YOU. BUT, PLEASE TELL ME, WHERE IS THE CHANGELING QUEEN NOW?
OH... SHE'S SOMEWHERE SHE WON'T BE ABLE TO BREAK OUT OF FOR A WHILE...
I HELPED!
WHAT WORD RYHMES WITH ORANGE? WHILE YOU THINK ABOUT IT, LET ME SING YOU A SONG! LA LA LA! THIS IS THE SONG THAT WILL NEVEEEER END...
DOOR HINGE?
CORE TINGE?
SHUT UP, ALL OF YOU. JUST SHUT UP.
NAUGHTY MISDOINGS
SCHEMES
THE END
I AM SOOO LOST.
MAP
I ♥ MANEHATTAN
Katie Cook
Heather Breckel

Art by
Amy Mebberson

Art by
Amy Mebberson

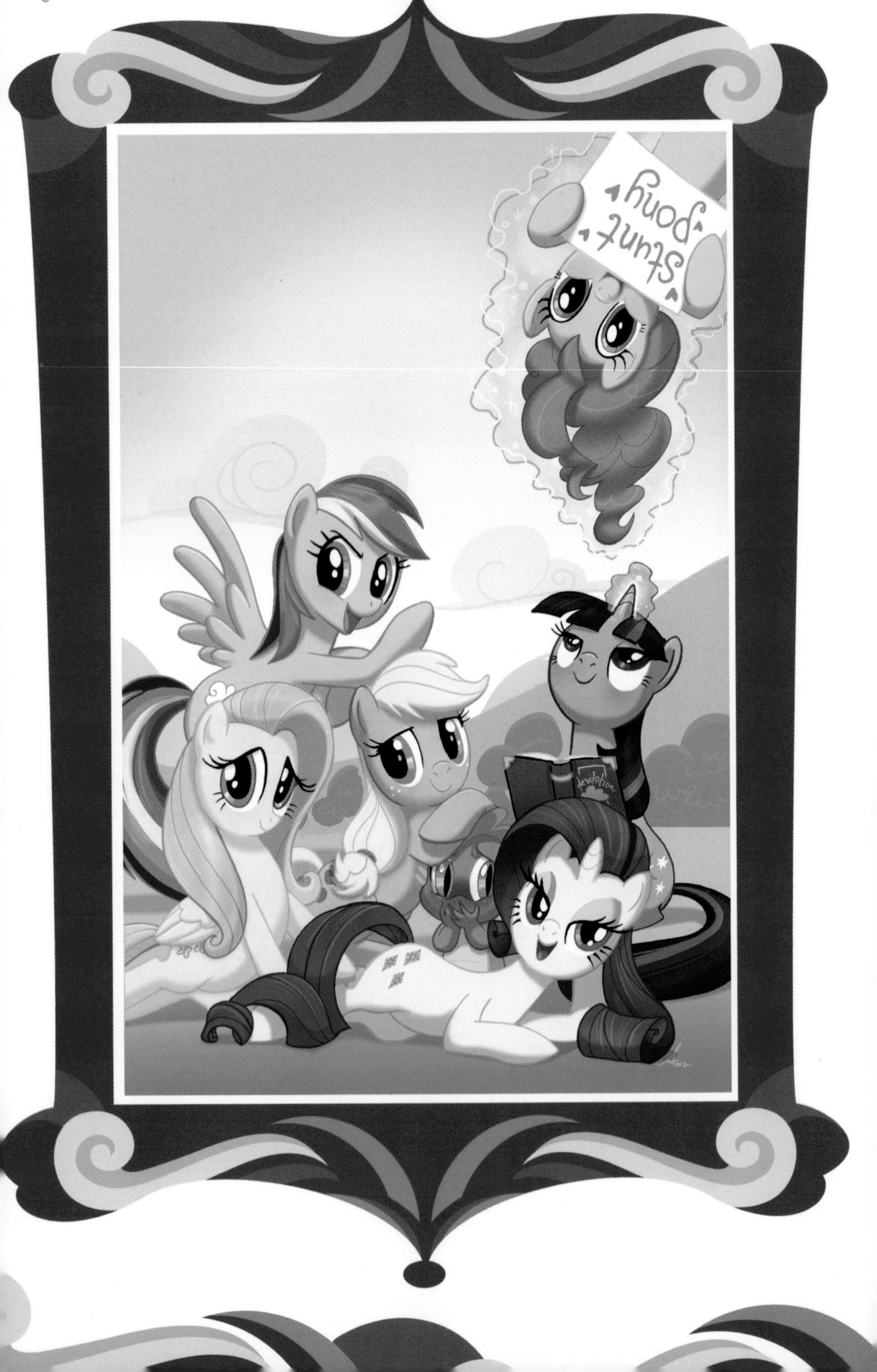
Stunt pony
Levitation

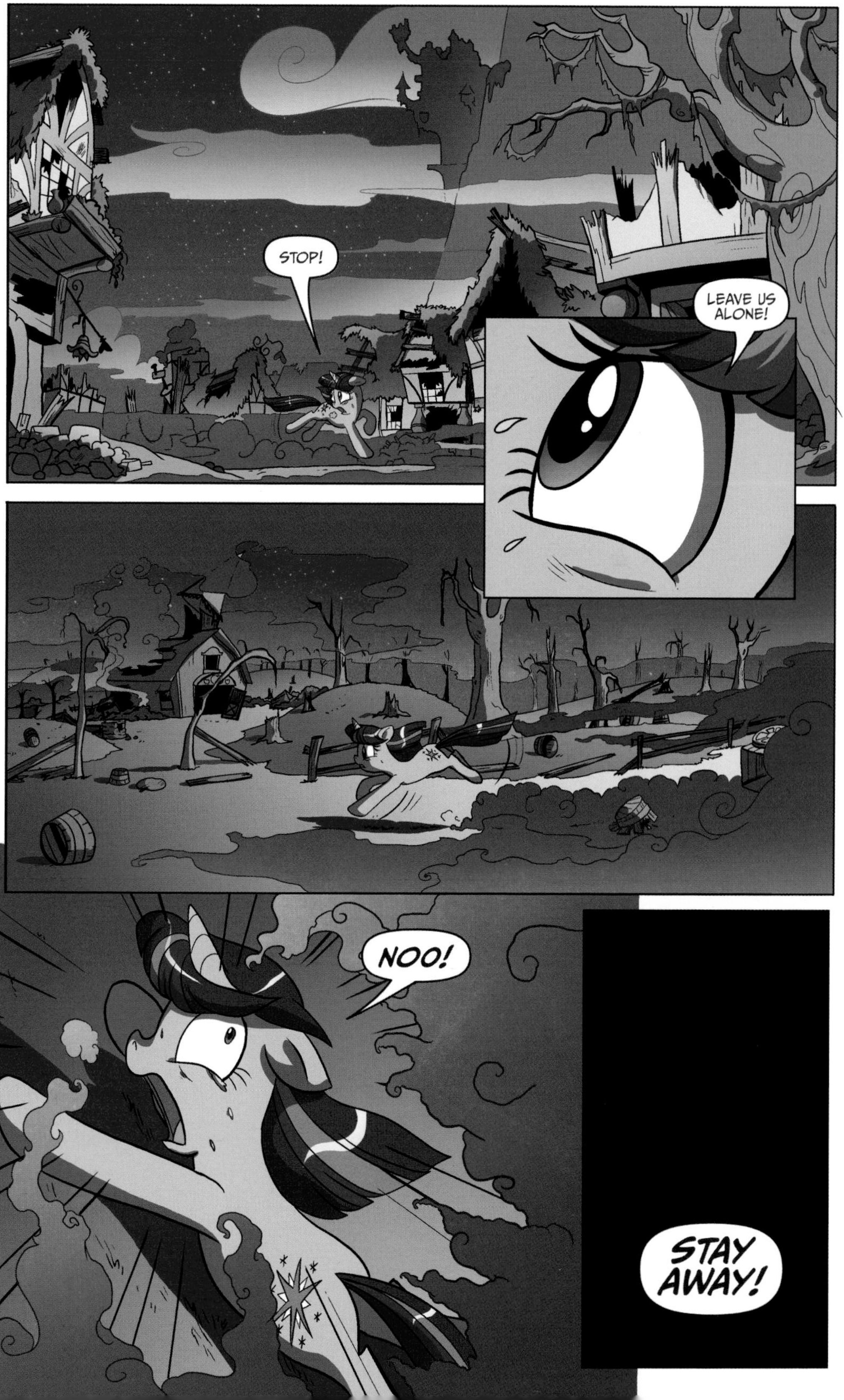
STOP!
LEAVE US ALONE!
NOO!
STAY AWAY!

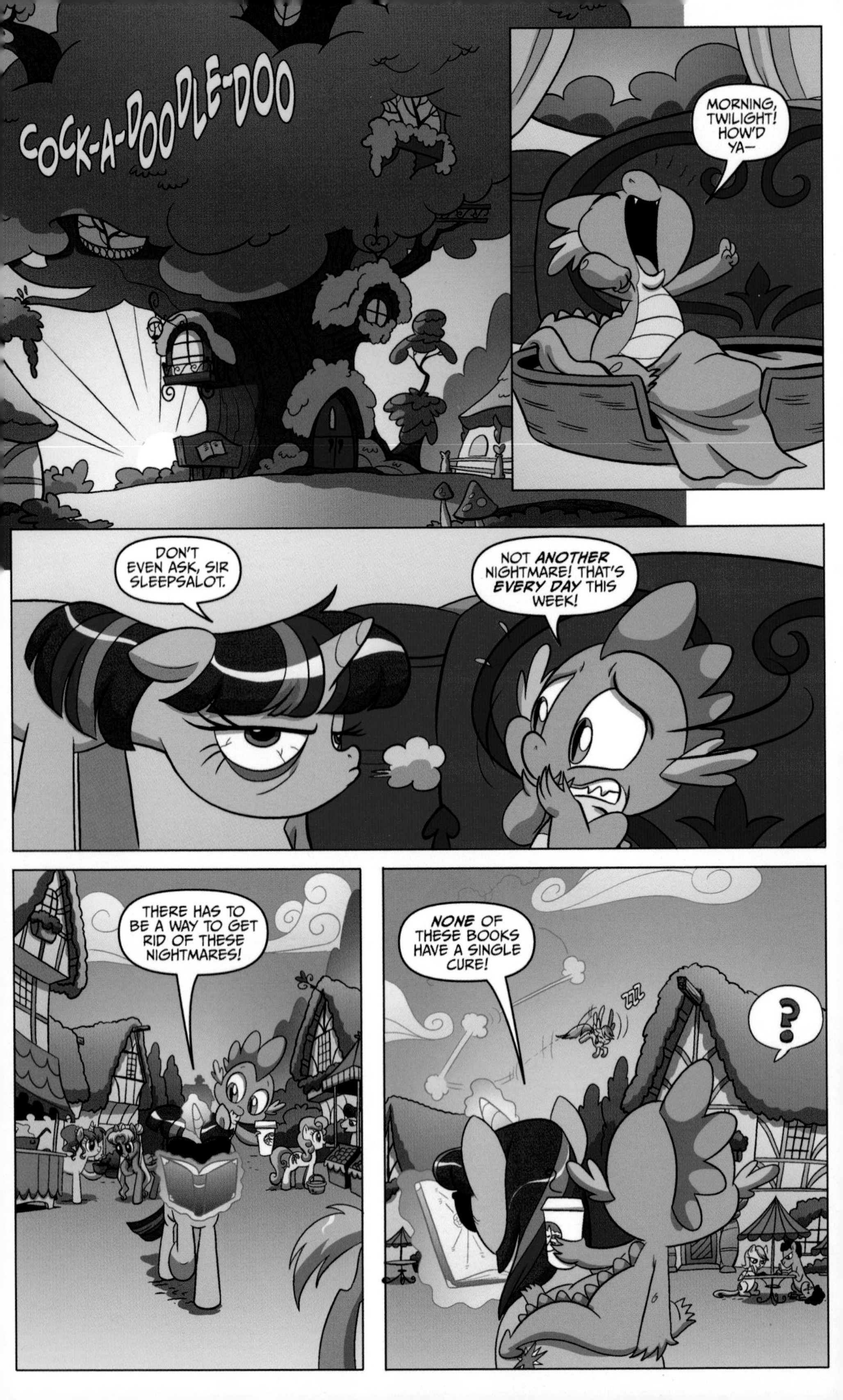

COCK-A-DOODLE-DOO
MORNING, TWILIGHT! HOW'D YA—
DON'T EVEN ASK, SIR SLEEPSALOT.
NOT ANOTHER NIGHTMARE! THAT'S EVERY DAY THIS WEEK!
THERE HAS TO BE A WAY TO GET RID OF THESE NIGHTMARES!
NONE OF THESE BOOKS HAVE A SINGLE CURE!
ZZZ
?

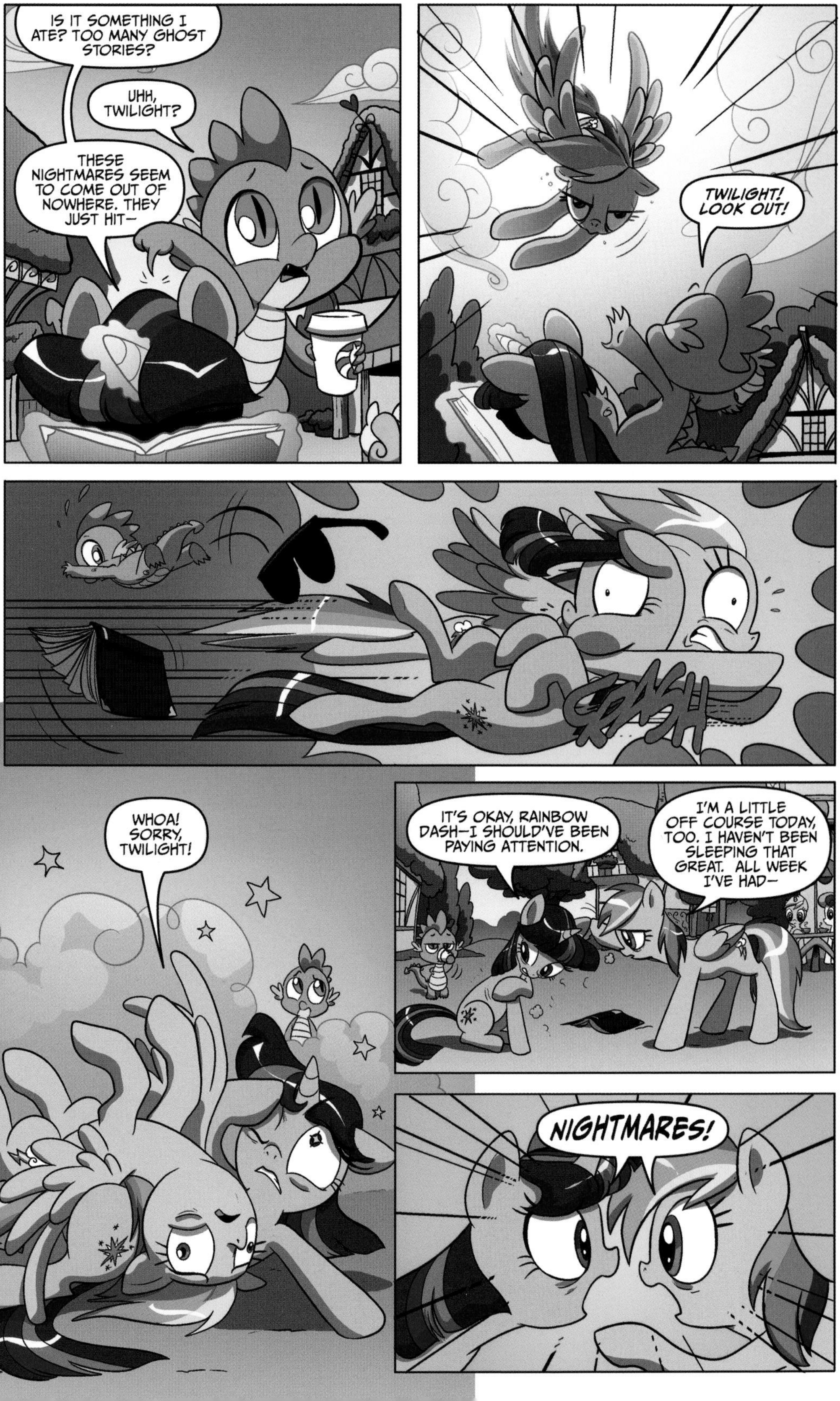
IS IT SOMETHING I ATE? TOO MANY GHOST STORIES?
UHH, TWILIGHT?
THESE NIGHTMARES SEEM TO COME OUT OF NOWHERE. THEY JUST HIT—
TWILIGHT! LOOK OUT!
CRASH
WHOA! SORRY, TWILIGHT!
IT'S OKAY, RAINBOW DASH—I SHOULD'VE BEEN PAYING ATTENTION.
I'M A LITTLE OFF COURSE TODAY, TOO. I HAVEN'T BEEN SLEEPING THAT GREAT. ALL WEEK I'VE HAD—
NIGHTMARES!

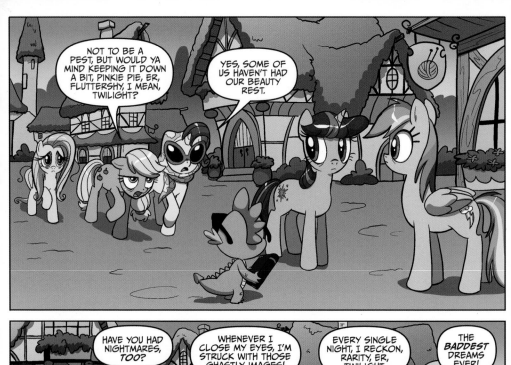

NOT TO BE A PEST, BUT WOULD YA MIND KEEPING IT DOWN A BIT, PINKIE PIE, ER, FLUTTERSHY, I MEAN, TWILIGHT?

YES, SOME OF US HAVEN'T HAD OUR BEAUTY REST.

HAVE YOU HAD NIGHTMARES, TOO?

WHENEVER I CLOSE MY EYES, I'M STRUCK WITH THOSE GHASTLY IMAGES!

EVERY SINGLE NIGHT, I RECKON, RARITY, ER, TWILIGHT.

THE BADDEST DREAMS EVER!

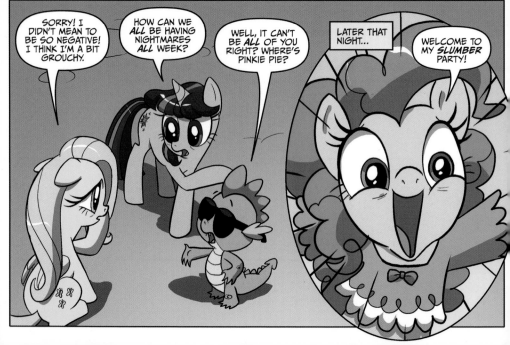

SORRY! I DIDN'T MEAN TO BE SO NEGATIVE! I THINK I'M A BIT GROUCHY.

HOW CAN WE ALL BE HAVING NIGHTMARES ALL WEEK?

WELL, IT CAN'T BE ALL OF YOU RIGHT? WHERE'S PINKIE PIE?

LATER THAT NIGHT...

WELCOME TO MY SLUMBER PARTY!

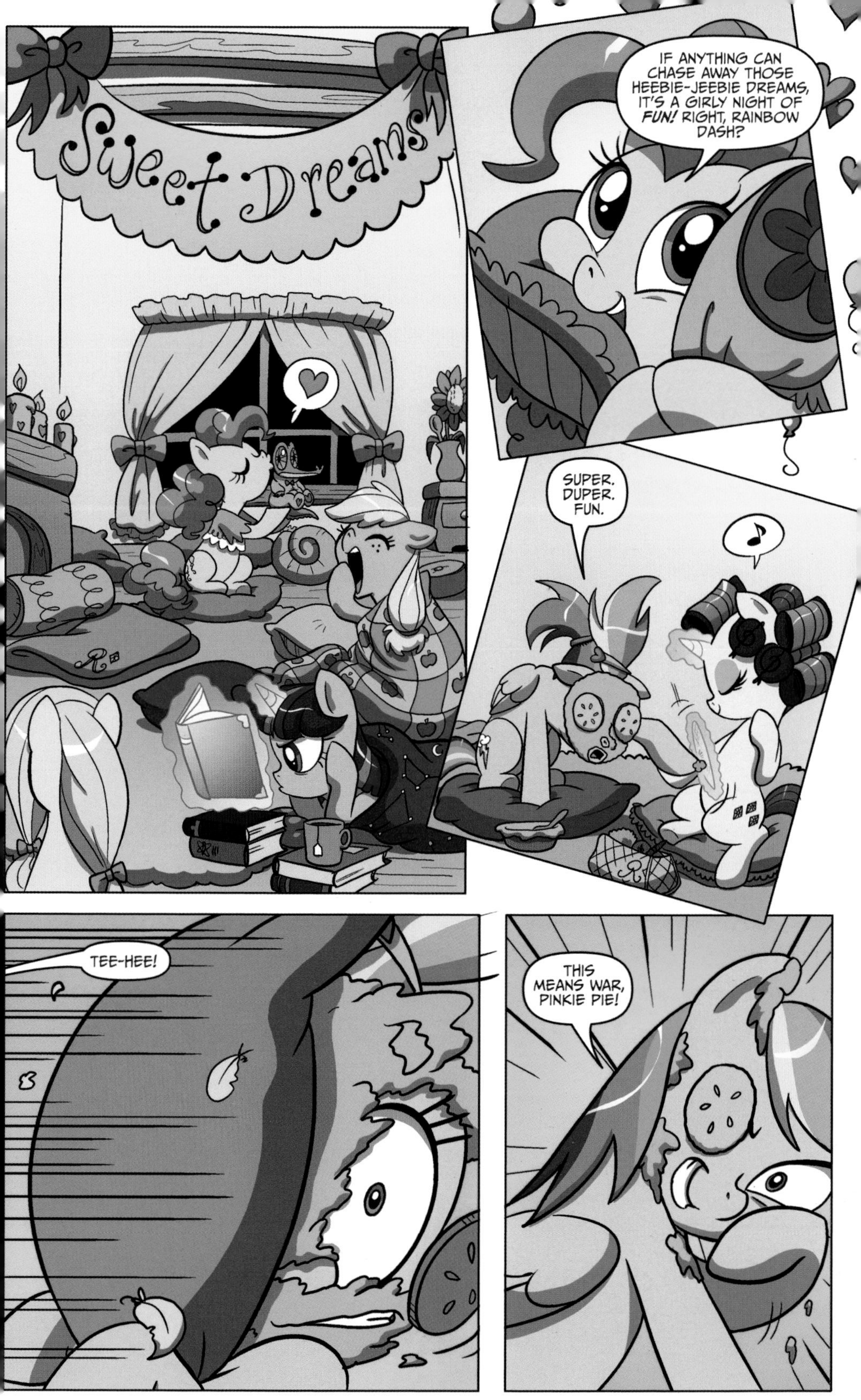
Sweet Dreams
IF ANYTHING CAN CHASE AWAY THOSE HEEBIE-JEEBIE DREAMS, IT'S A GIRLY NIGHT OF *FUN!* RIGHT, RAINBOW DASH?
SUPER. DUPER. FUN.
TEE-HEE!
THIS MEANS WAR, PINKIE PIE!

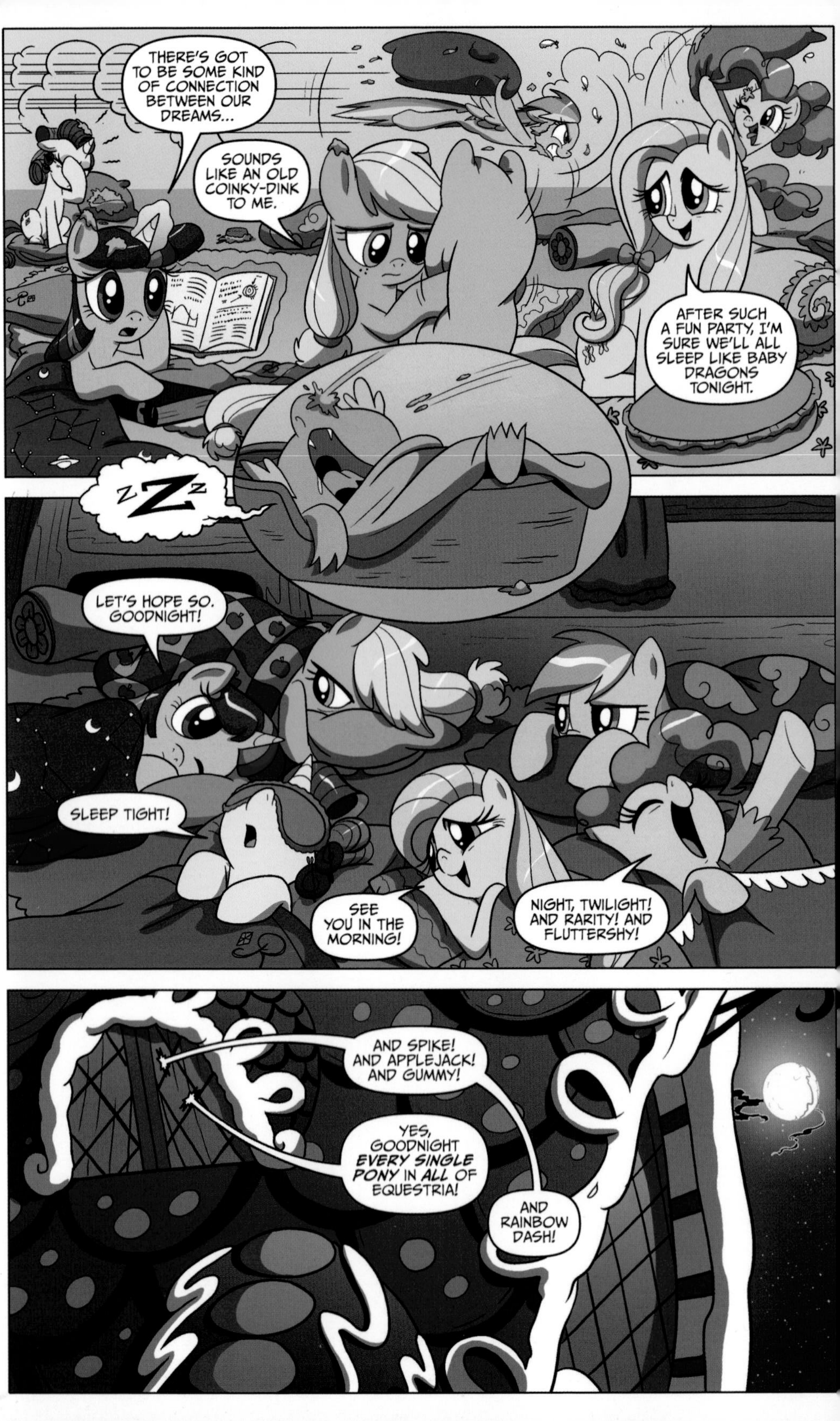
THERE'S GOT TO BE SOME KIND OF CONNECTION BETWEEN OUR DREAMS...
SOUNDS LIKE AN OLD COINKY-DINK TO ME.
AFTER SUCH A FUN PARTY, I'M SURE WE'LL ALL SLEEP LIKE BABY DRAGONS TONIGHT.
ZZZ
LET'S HOPE SO. GOODNIGHT!
SLEEP TIGHT!
SEE YOU IN THE MORNING!
NIGHT, TWILIGHT! AND RARITY! AND FLUTTERSHY!
AND SPIKE! AND APPLEJACK! AND GUMMY!
YES, GOODNIGHT ***EVERY SINGLE PONY*** IN ***ALL*** OF EQUESTRIA!
AND RAINBOW DASH!

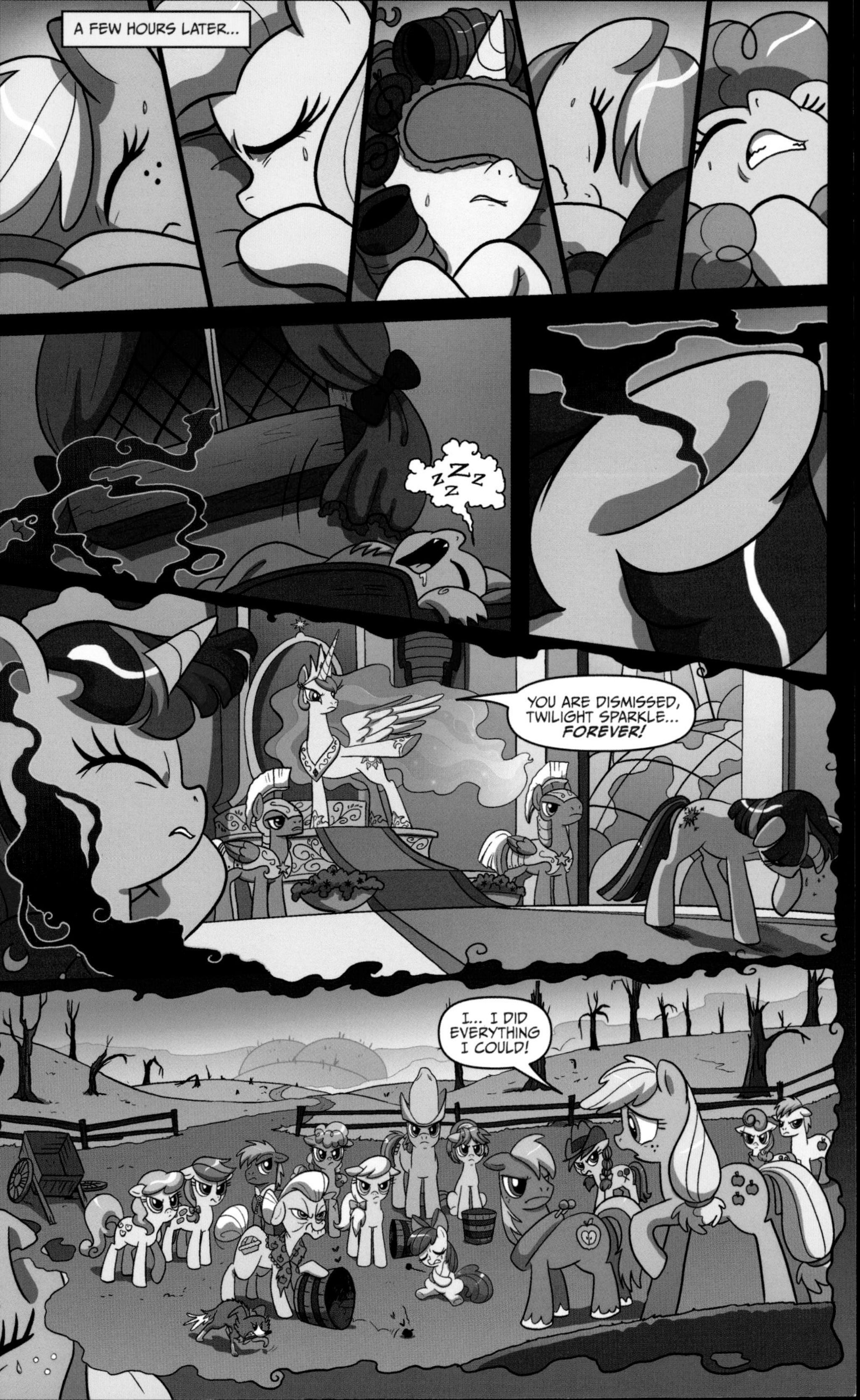
A FEW HOURS LATER...
ZZZZ
YOU ARE DISMISSED, TWILIGHT SPARKLE... *FOREVER!*
I... I DID EVERYTHING I COULD!

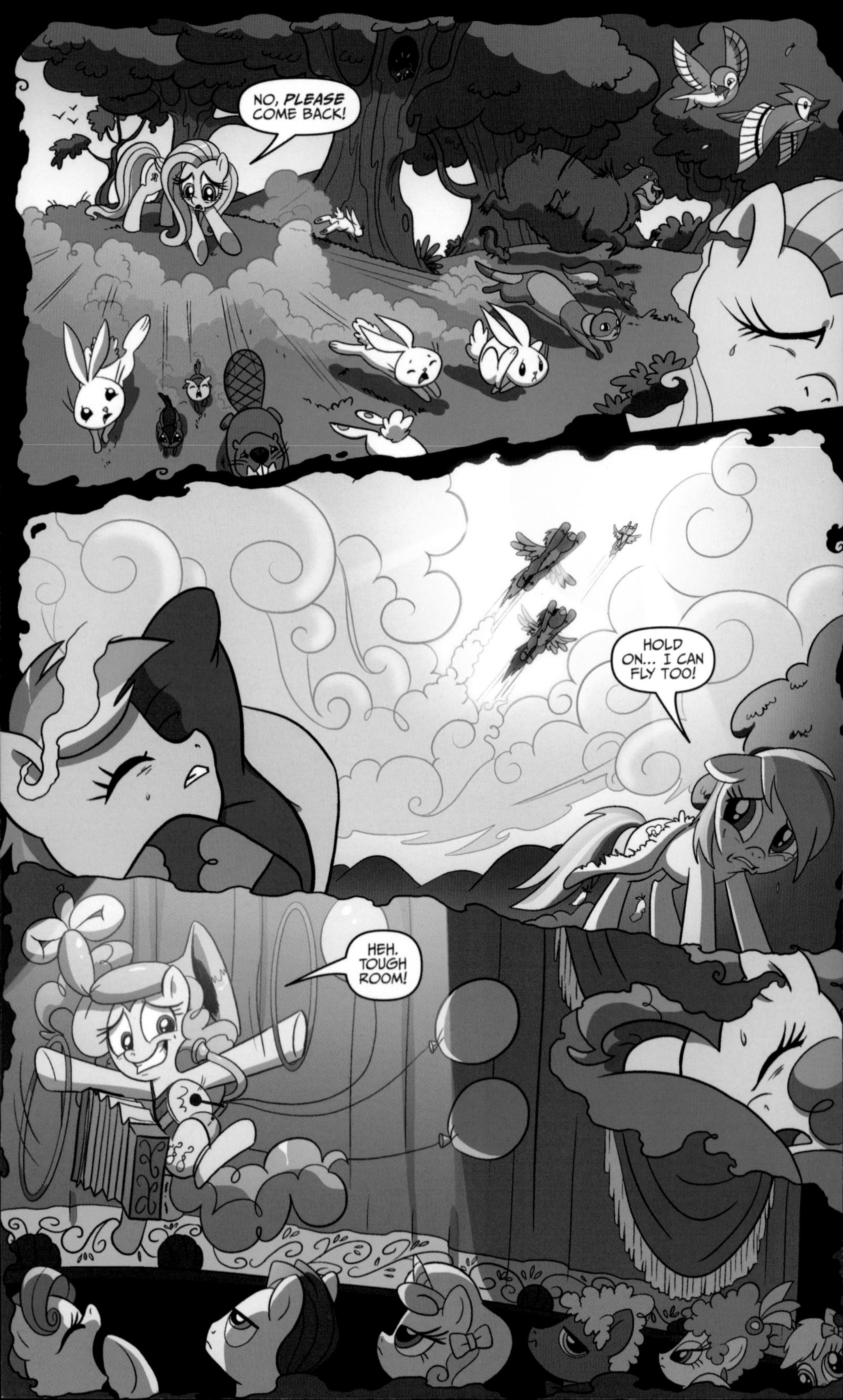

NO, PLEASE COME BACK!
HOLD ON... I CAN FLY TOO!
HEH. TOUGH ROOM!

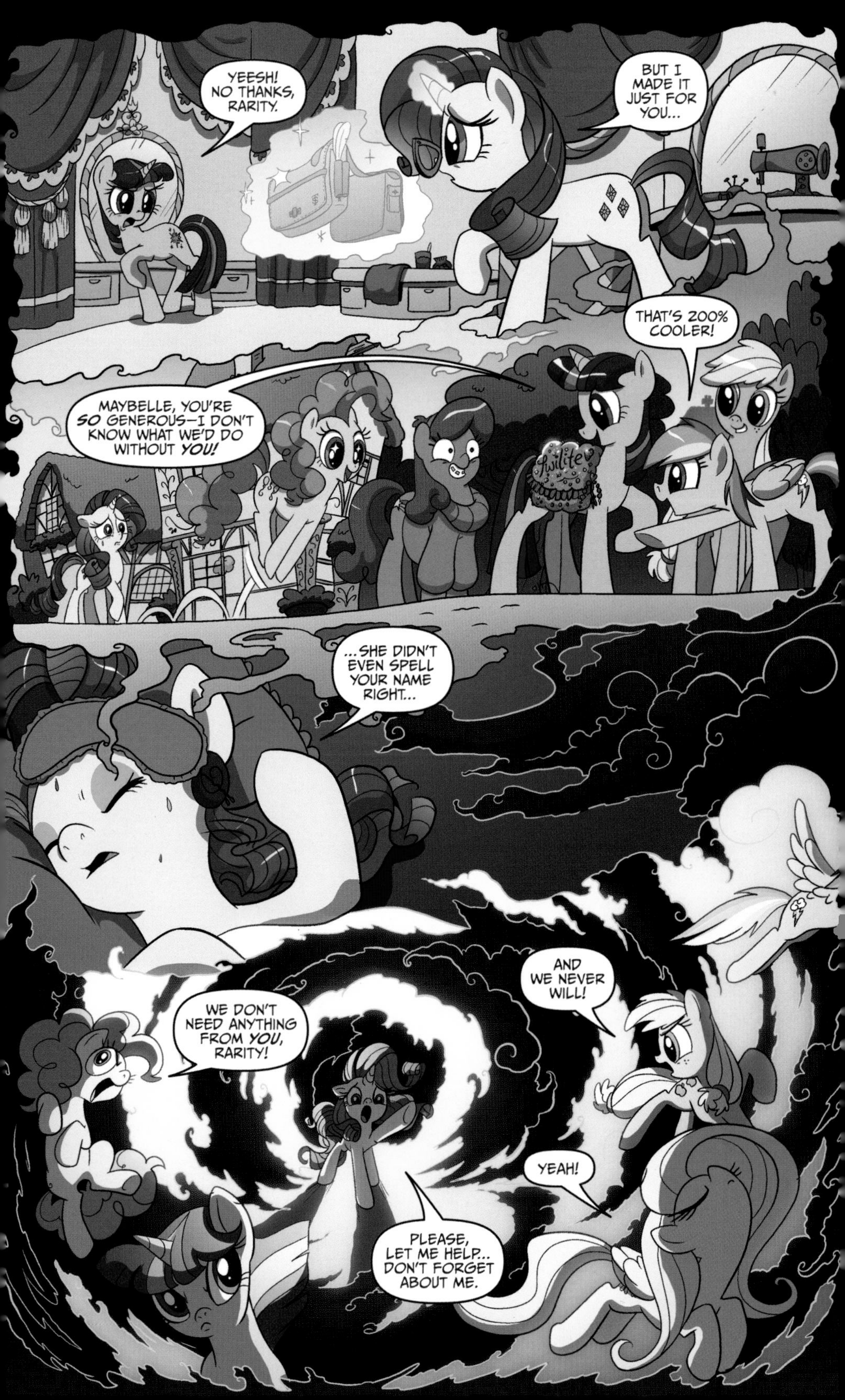
YEESH! NO THANKS, RARITY.
BUT I MADE IT JUST FOR YOU...
THAT'S 200% COOLER!
MAYBELLE, YOU'RE *SO* GENEROUS—I DON'T KNOW WHAT WE'D DO WITHOUT *YOU!*
Twilite
...SHE DIDN'T EVEN SPELL YOUR NAME RIGHT...
WE DON'T NEED ANYTHING FROM *YOU*, RARITY!
AND WE NEVER WILL!
YEAH!
PLEASE, LET ME HELP... DON'T FORGET ABOUT ME.

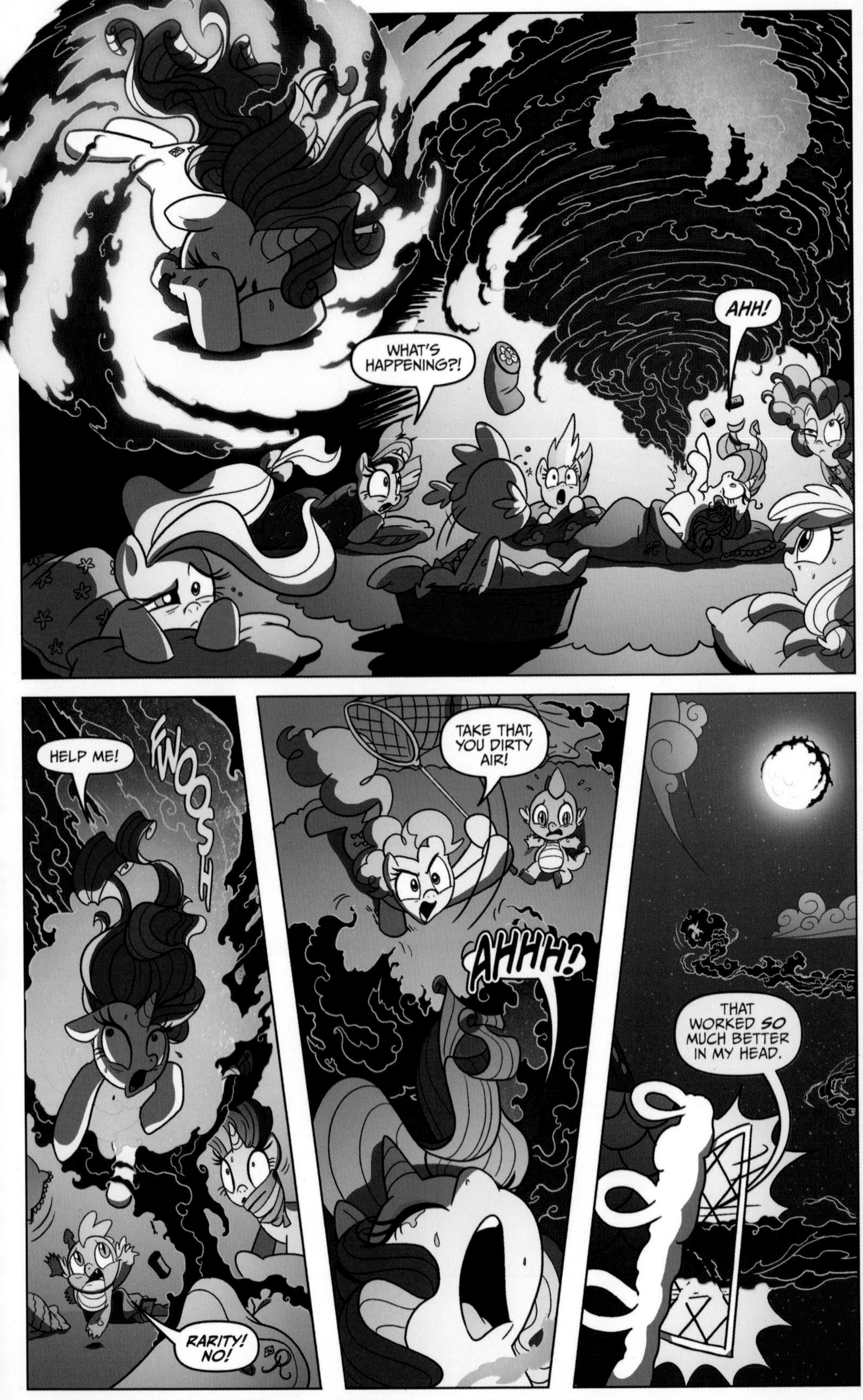
WHAT'S HAPPENING?!
AHH!
HELP ME!
FWOOSH
RARITY! NO!
TAKE THAT, YOU DIRTY AIR!
AHHH!
THAT WORKED SO MUCH BETTER IN MY HEAD.

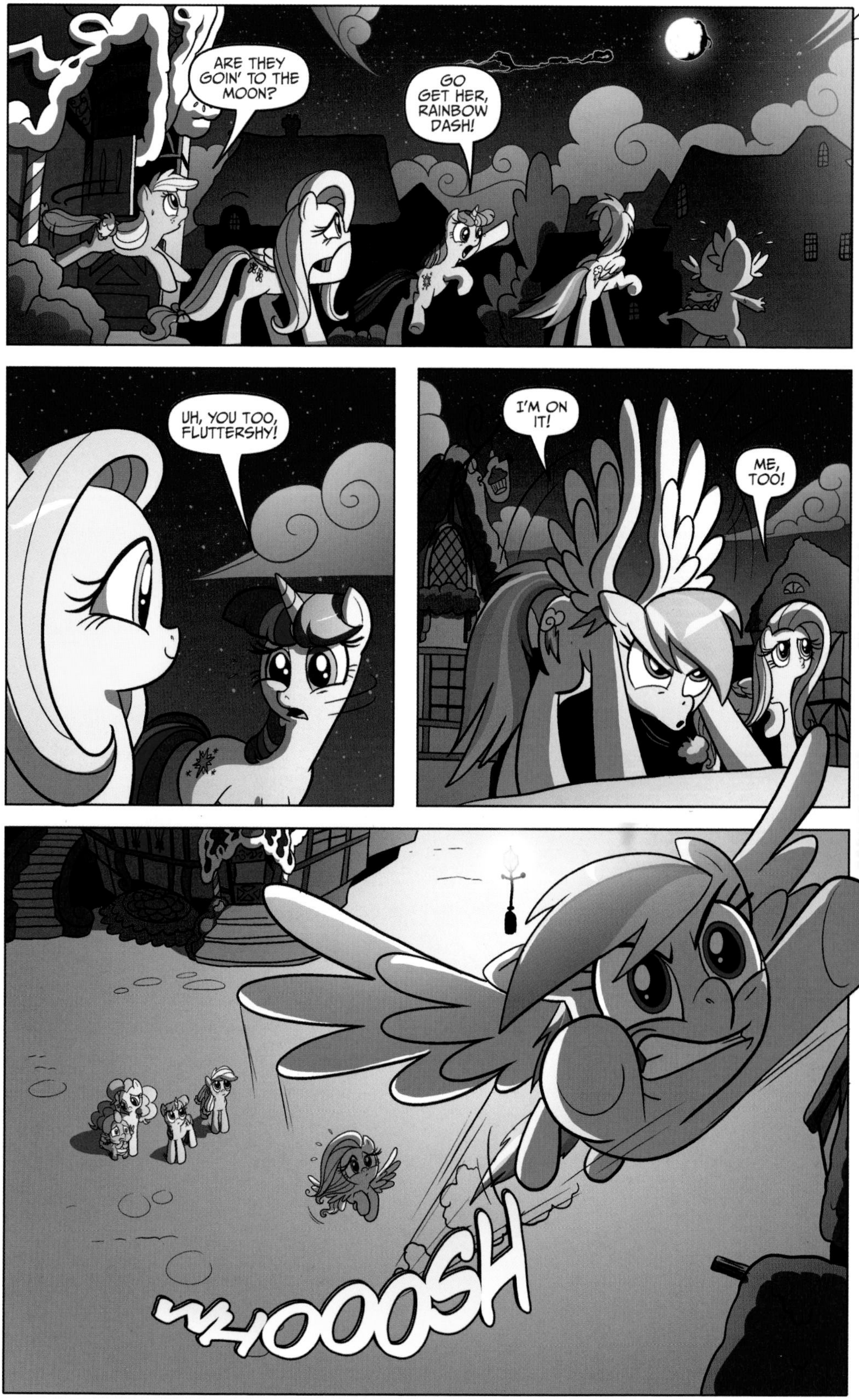
ARE THEY GOIN' TO THE MOON?
GO GET HER, RAINBOW DASH!
UH, YOU TOO, FLUTTERSHY!
I'M ON IT!
ME, TOO!
WHOOOOSH

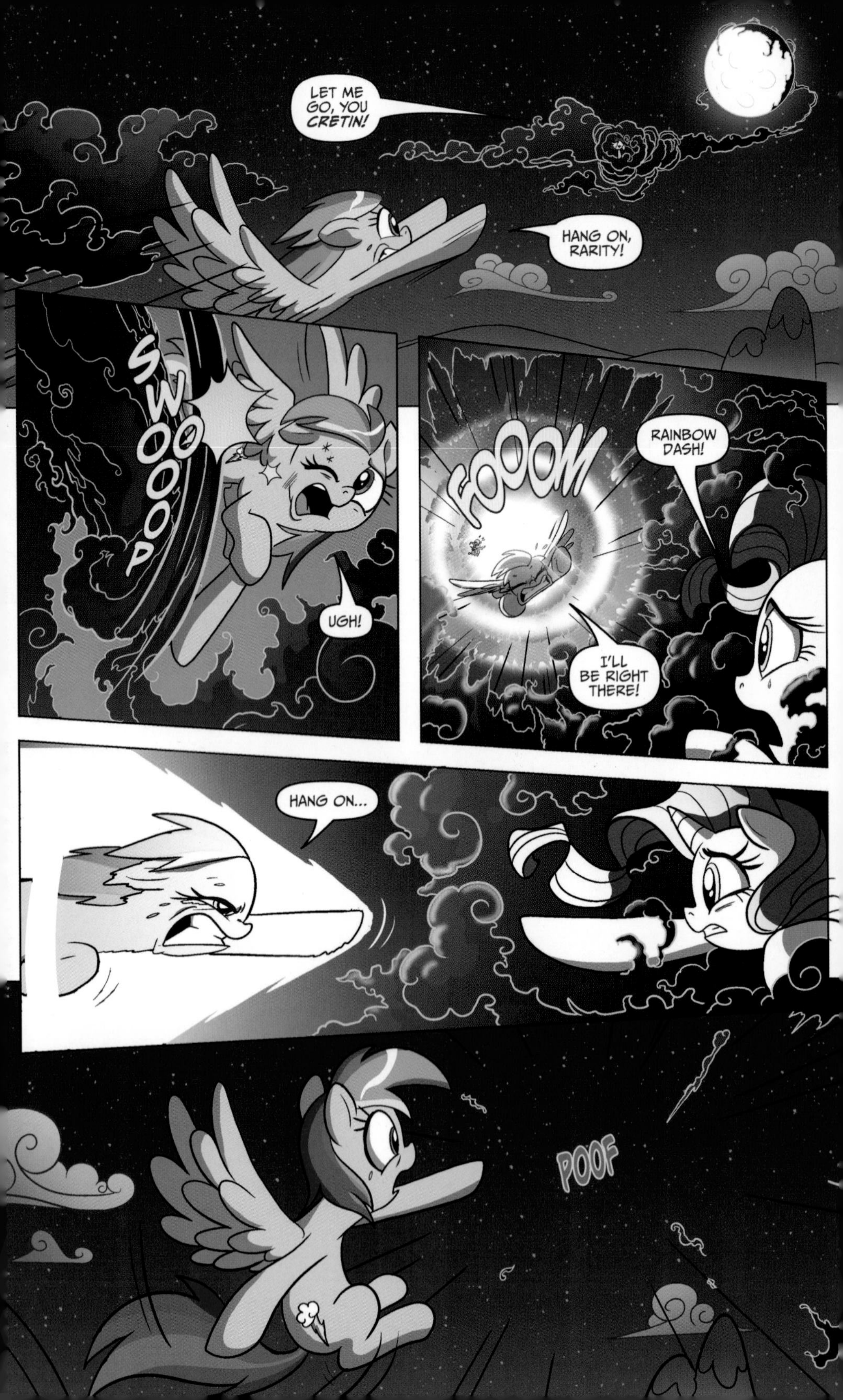
LET ME GO, YOU CRETIN!
HANG ON, RARITY!
SWOOOOP
UGH!
FOOOM
RAINBOW DASH!
I'LL BE RIGHT THERE!
HANG ON...
POOF

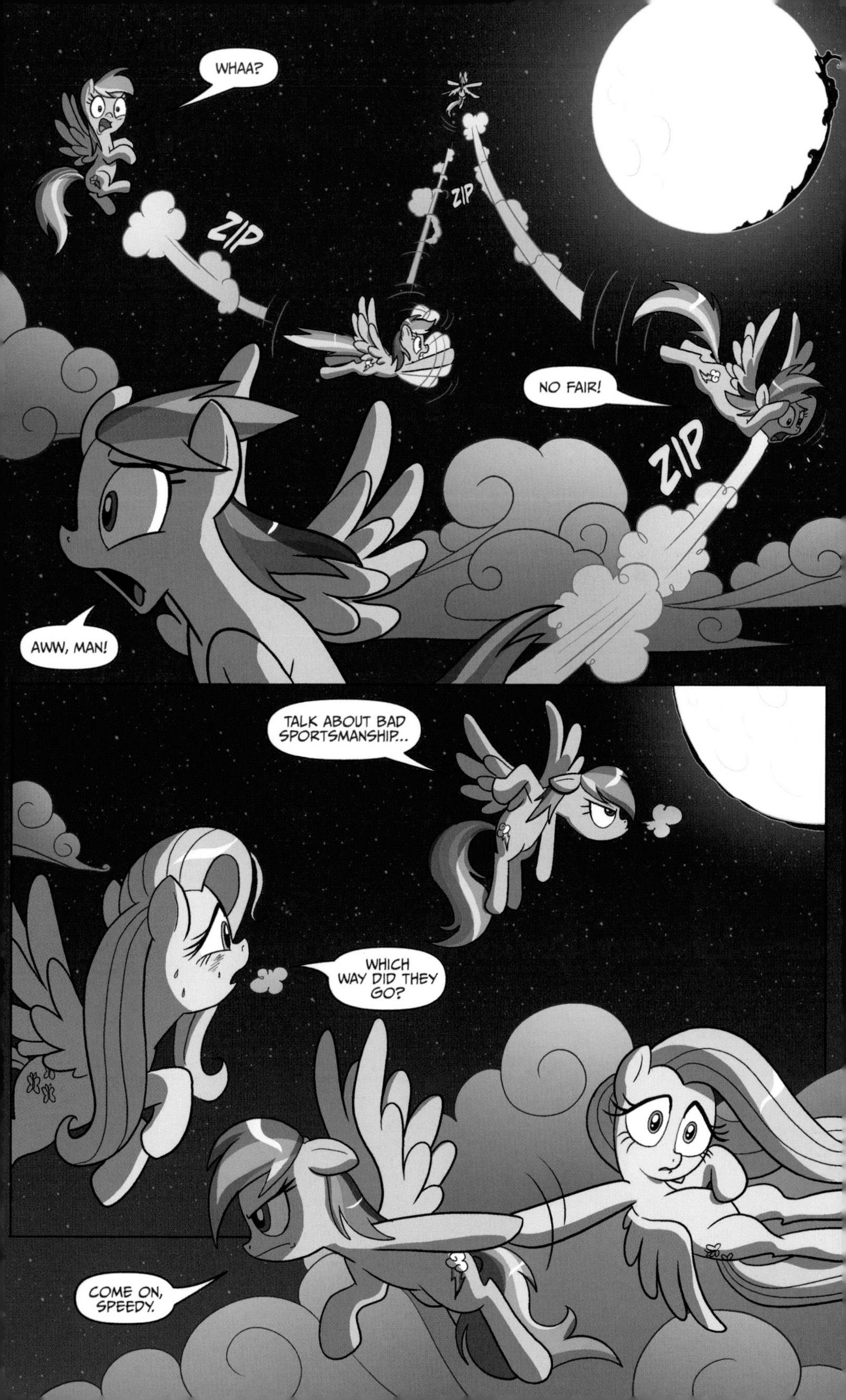
WHAA?
ZIP
ZIP
NO FAIR!
ZIP
AWW, MAN!
TALK ABOUT BAD SPORTSMANSHIP...
WHICH WAY DID THEY GO?
COME ON, SPEEDY.

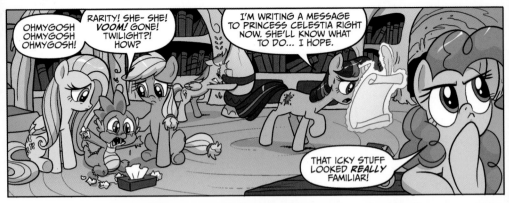

OHMYGOSH OHMYGOSH OHMYGOSH!

RARITY! SHE- SHE! *VOOM!* GONE! TWILIGHT?! HOW?!

I'M WRITING A MESSAGE TO PRINCESS CELESTIA RIGHT NOW. SHE'LL KNOW WHAT TO DO... I HOPE.

THAT ICKY STUFF LOOKED *REALLY* FAMILIAR!

PINKIE'S RIGHT— IT WAS IN MY NIGHTMARE.

I SAW IT IN MINE!

ME, TOO!

SO, THERE HAS TO BE A LINK BETWEEN THIS... STUFF, AND OUR BAD DREAMS. IT MAKES SENSE.

LET ME GET THIS STRAIGHT—YOU'RE TELLING ME THAT THIS GLORIFIED *SMOG* SOMEHOW GOT INTO OUR *BRAINS?*

GASP! BRAINS?! ZOMBIES?!

WHERE DO WE EVEN BEGIN?

PRINCESS LUNA! SHE'S THE PROTECTOR OF DREAMS. *AND* SHE WAS TAKEN OVER BY NIGHTMARE MOON! SHE CAN HELP US INTERPRET OUR NIGHTMARES AND FIND RARITY!

PRINCESS LUNA IS OUR ONLY HOPE!

ANYONE HAVE A SCROLL?

YOU CAN ASK HER IN PONY.

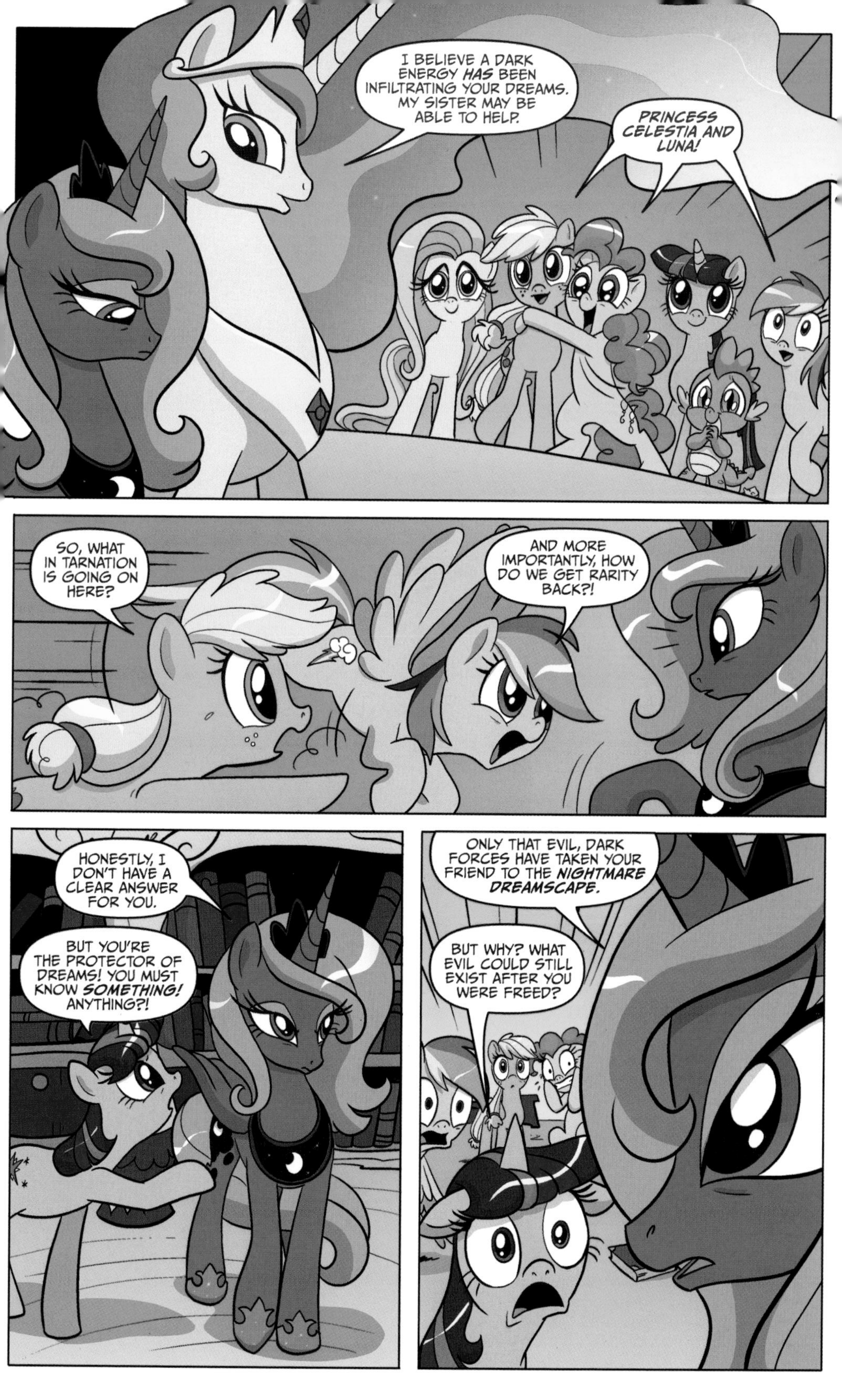

I BELIEVE A DARK ENERGY HAS BEEN INFILTRATING YOUR DREAMS. MY SISTER MAY BE ABLE TO HELP.
PRINCESS CELESTIA AND LUNA!
SO, WHAT IN TARNATION IS GOING ON HERE?
AND MORE IMPORTANTLY, HOW DO WE GET RARITY BACK?!
HONESTLY, I DON'T HAVE A CLEAR ANSWER FOR YOU.
BUT YOU'RE THE PROTECTOR OF DREAMS! YOU MUST KNOW SOMETHING! ANYTHING?!
ONLY THAT EVIL, DARK FORCES HAVE TAKEN YOUR FRIEND TO THE NIGHTMARE DREAMSCAPE.
BUT WHY? WHAT EVIL COULD STILL EXIST AFTER YOU WERE FREED?

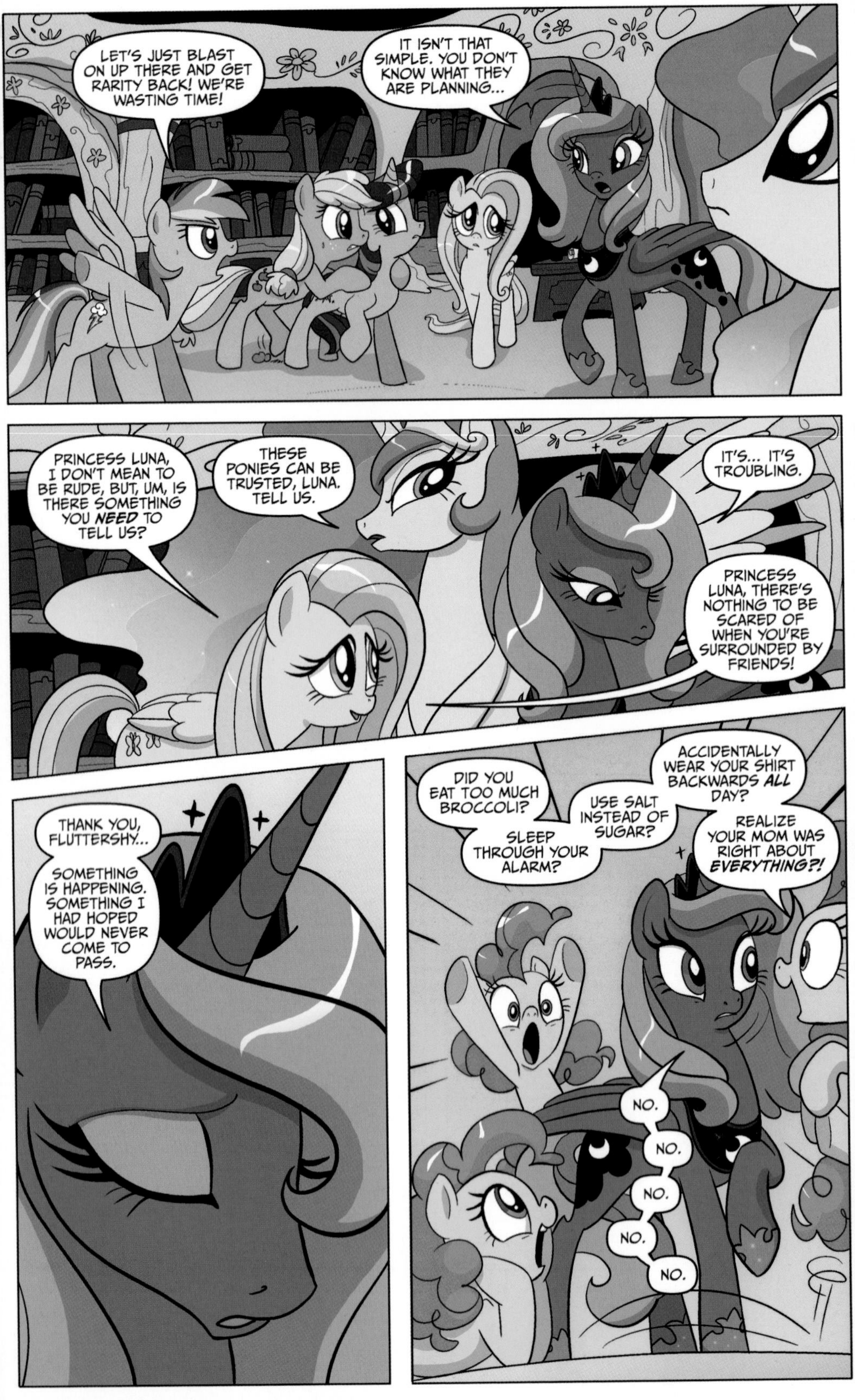
LET'S JUST BLAST ON UP THERE AND GET RARITY BACK! WE'RE WASTING TIME!
IT ISN'T THAT SIMPLE. YOU DON'T KNOW WHAT THEY ARE PLANNING...
PRINCESS LUNA, I DON'T MEAN TO BE RUDE, BUT, UM, IS THERE SOMETHING YOU *NEED* TO TELL US?
THESE PONIES CAN BE TRUSTED, LUNA. TELL US.
IT'S... IT'S TROUBLING.
PRINCESS LUNA, THERE'S NOTHING TO BE SCARED OF WHEN YOU'RE SURROUNDED BY FRIENDS!
THANK YOU, FLUTTERSHY...
SOMETHING IS HAPPENING. SOMETHING I HAD HOPED WOULD NEVER COME TO PASS.
DID YOU EAT TOO MUCH BROCCOLI?
SLEEP THROUGH YOUR ALARM?
USE SALT INSTEAD OF SUGAR?
ACCIDENTALLY WEAR YOUR SHIRT BACKWARDS *ALL* DAY?
REALIZE YOUR MOM WAS RIGHT ABOUT *EVERYTHING?!*
NO.
NO.
NO.
NO.
NO.

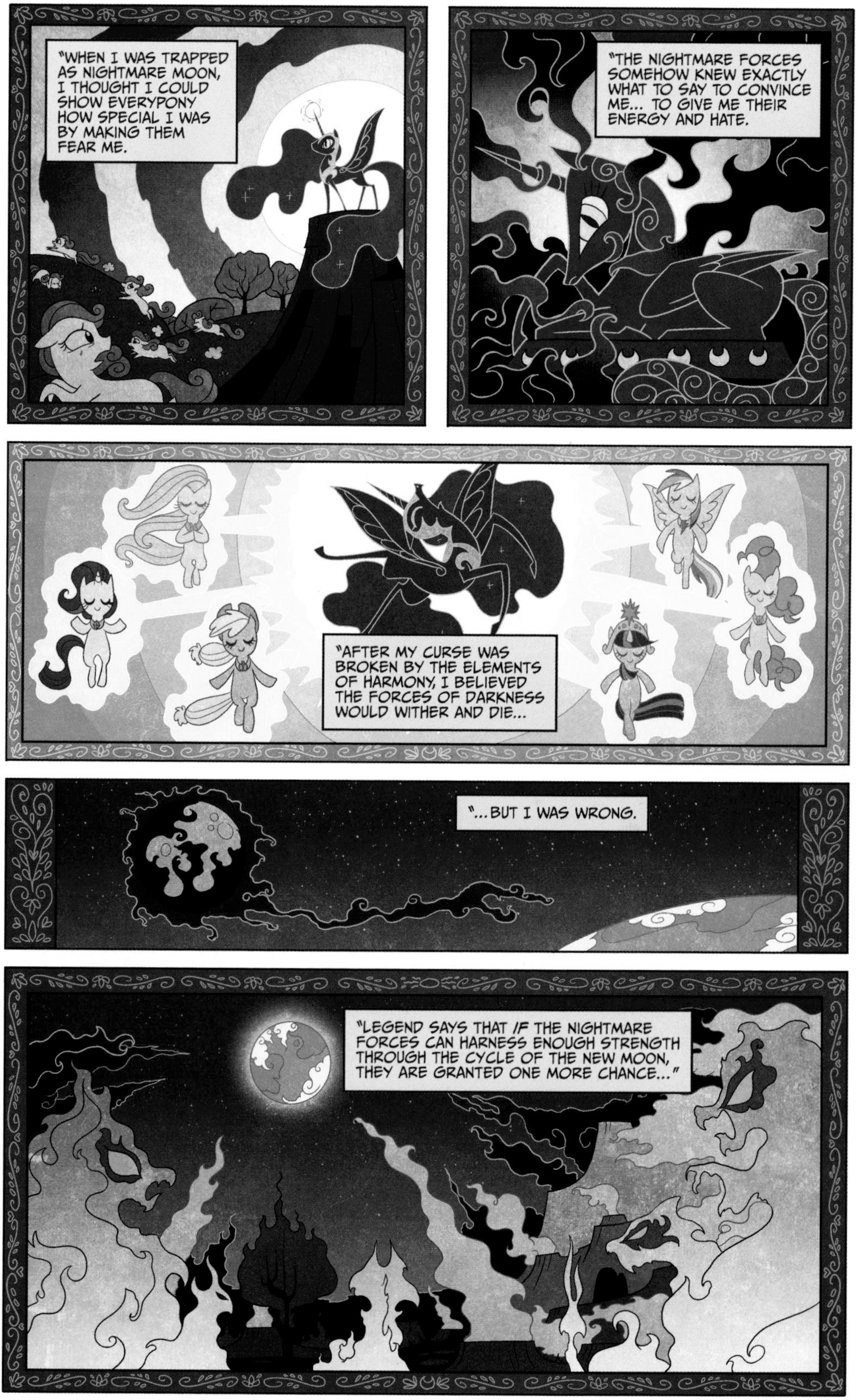
"WHEN I WAS TRAPPED AS NIGHTMARE MOON, I THOUGHT I COULD SHOW EVERYPONY HOW SPECIAL I WAS BY MAKING THEM FEAR ME.
"THE NIGHTMARE FORCES SOMEHOW KNEW EXACTLY WHAT TO SAY TO CONVINCE ME... TO GIVE ME THEIR ENERGY AND HATE.
"AFTER MY CURSE WAS BROKEN BY THE ELEMENTS OF HARMONY, I BELIEVED THE FORCES OF DARKNESS WOULD WITHER AND DIE...
"...BUT I WAS WRONG.
"LEGEND SAYS THAT *IF* THE NIGHTMARE FORCES CAN HARNESS ENOUGH STRENGTH THROUGH THE CYCLE OF THE NEW MOON, THEY ARE GRANTED ONE MORE CHANCE..."

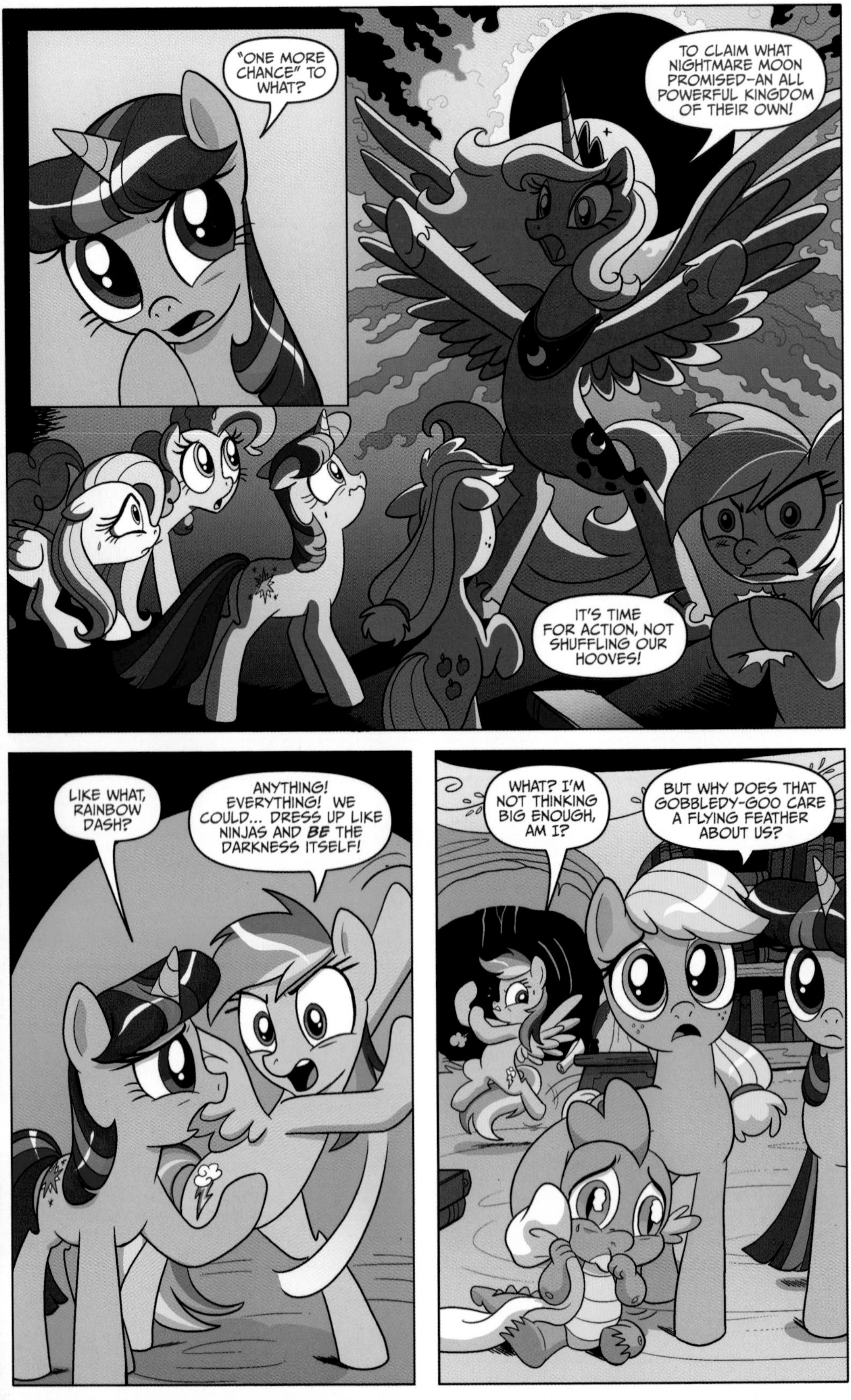
"ONE MORE CHANCE" TO WHAT?
TO CLAIM WHAT NIGHTMARE MOON PROMISED–AN ALL POWERFUL KINGDOM OF THEIR OWN!
IT'S TIME FOR ACTION, NOT SHUFFLING OUR HOOVES!
LIKE WHAT, RAINBOW DASH?
ANYTHING! EVERYTHING! WE COULD... DRESS UP LIKE NINJAS AND *BE* THE DARKNESS ITSELF!
WHAT? I'M NOT THINKING BIG ENOUGH, AM I?
BUT WHY DOES THAT GOBBLEDY-GOO CARE A FLYING FEATHER ABOUT US?

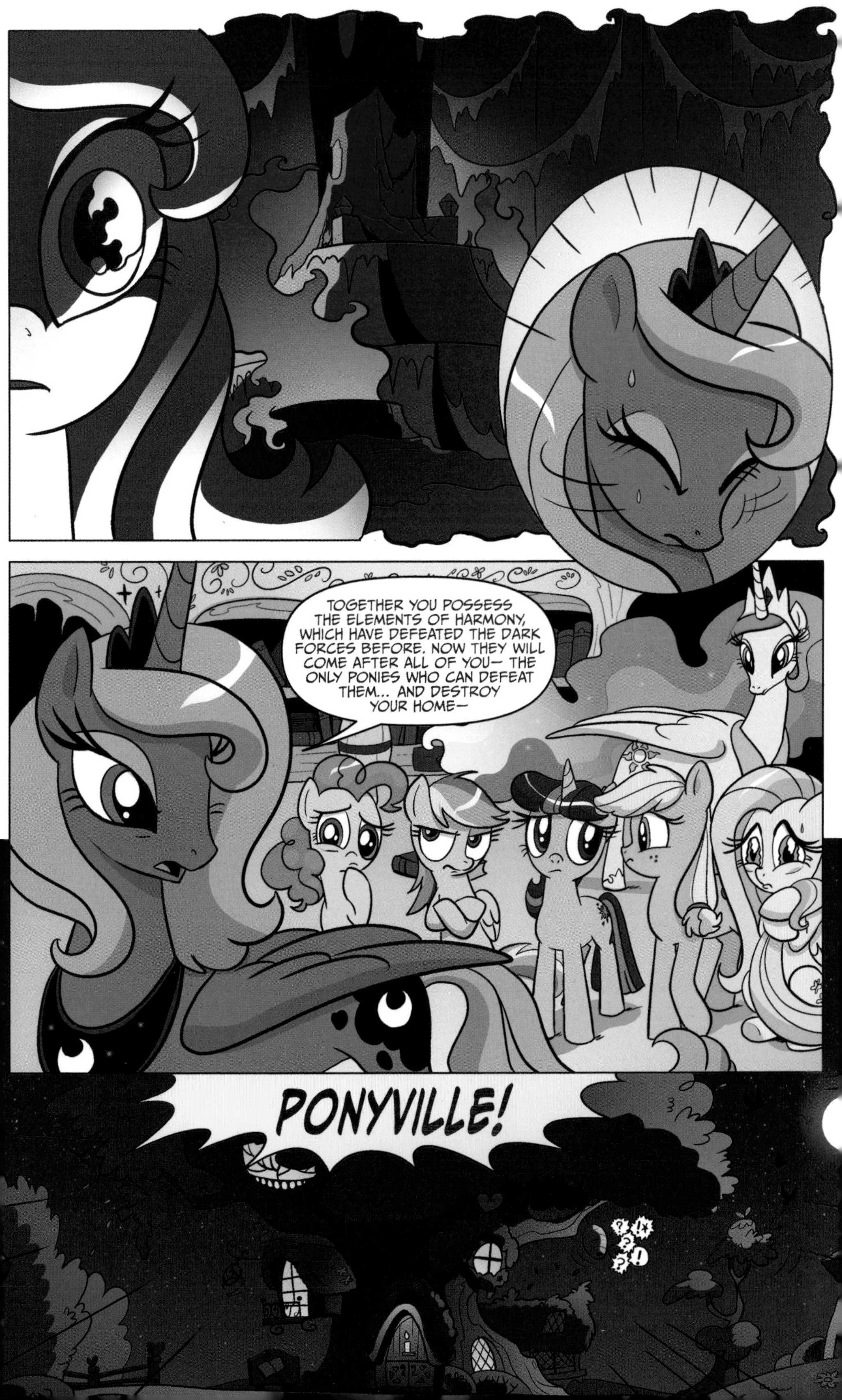
TOGETHER YOU POSSESS THE ELEMENTS OF HARMONY, WHICH HAVE DEFEATED THE DARK FORCES BEFORE. NOW THEY WILL COME AFTER ALL OF YOU— THE ONLY PONIES WHO CAN DEFEAT THEM... AND DESTROY YOUR HOME—
PONYVILLE!
?!
?!

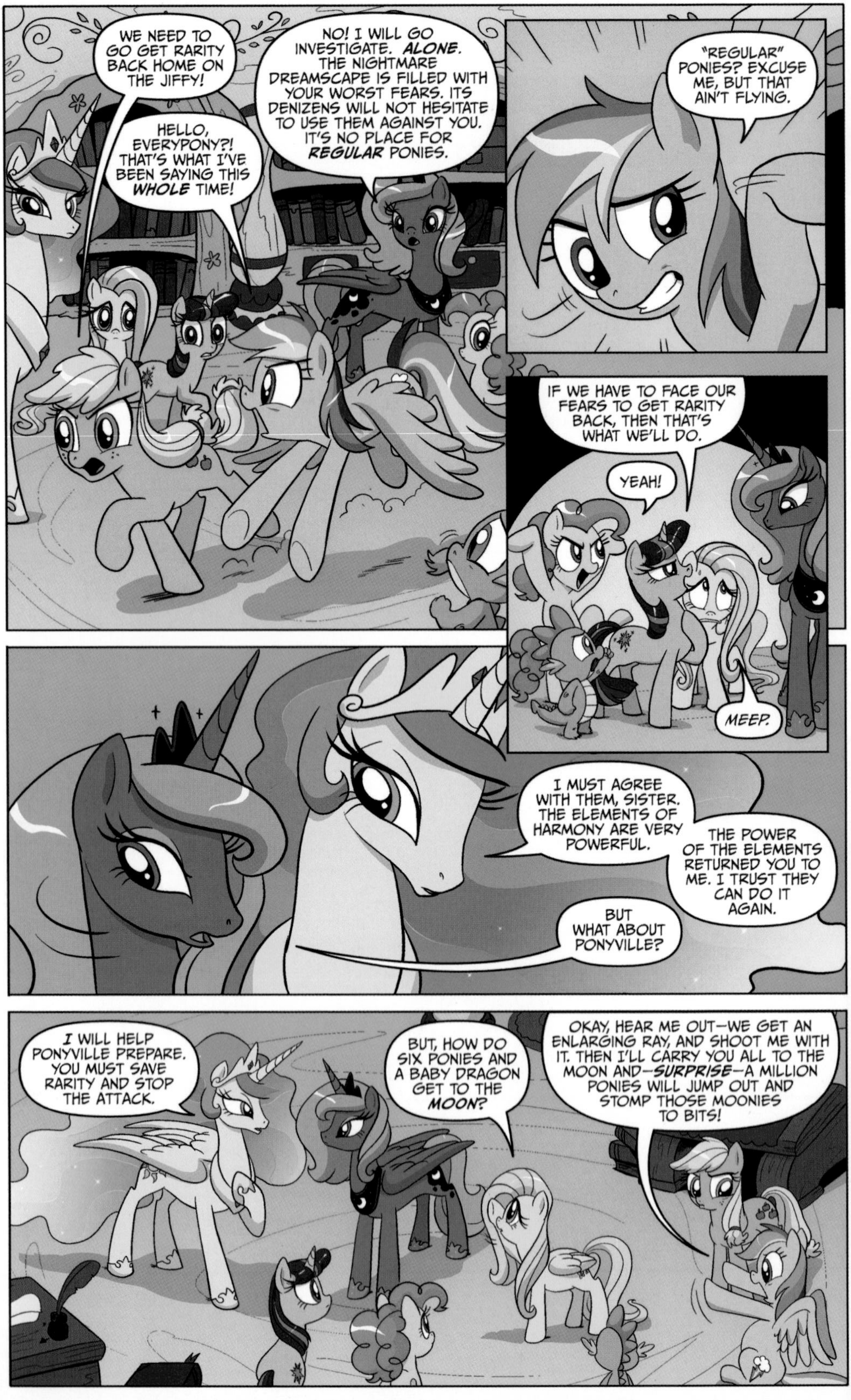
WE NEED TO GO GET RARITY BACK HOME ON THE JIFFY!
HELLO, EVERYPONY?! THAT'S WHAT I'VE BEEN SAYING THIS WHOLE TIME!
NO! I WILL GO INVESTIGATE. ALONE. THE NIGHTMARE DREAMSCAPE IS FILLED WITH YOUR WORST FEARS. ITS DENIZENS WILL NOT HESITATE TO USE THEM AGAINST YOU. IT'S NO PLACE FOR REGULAR PONIES.
"REGULAR" PONIES? EXCUSE ME, BUT THAT AIN'T FLYING.
IF WE HAVE TO FACE OUR FEARS TO GET RARITY BACK, THEN THAT'S WHAT WE'LL DO.
YEAH!
MEEP.
I MUST AGREE WITH THEM, SISTER. THE ELEMENTS OF HARMONY ARE VERY POWERFUL.
THE POWER OF THE ELEMENTS RETURNED YOU TO ME. I TRUST THEY CAN DO IT AGAIN.
BUT WHAT ABOUT PONYVILLE?
I WILL HELP PONYVILLE PREPARE. YOU MUST SAVE RARITY AND STOP THE ATTACK.
BUT, HOW DO SIX PONIES AND A BABY DRAGON GET TO THE MOON?
OKAY, HEAR ME OUT—WE GET AN ENLARGING RAY, AND SHOOT ME WITH IT. THEN I'LL CARRY YOU ALL TO THE MOON AND—SURPRISE—A MILLION PONIES WILL JUMP OUT AND STOMP THOSE MOONIES TO BITS!

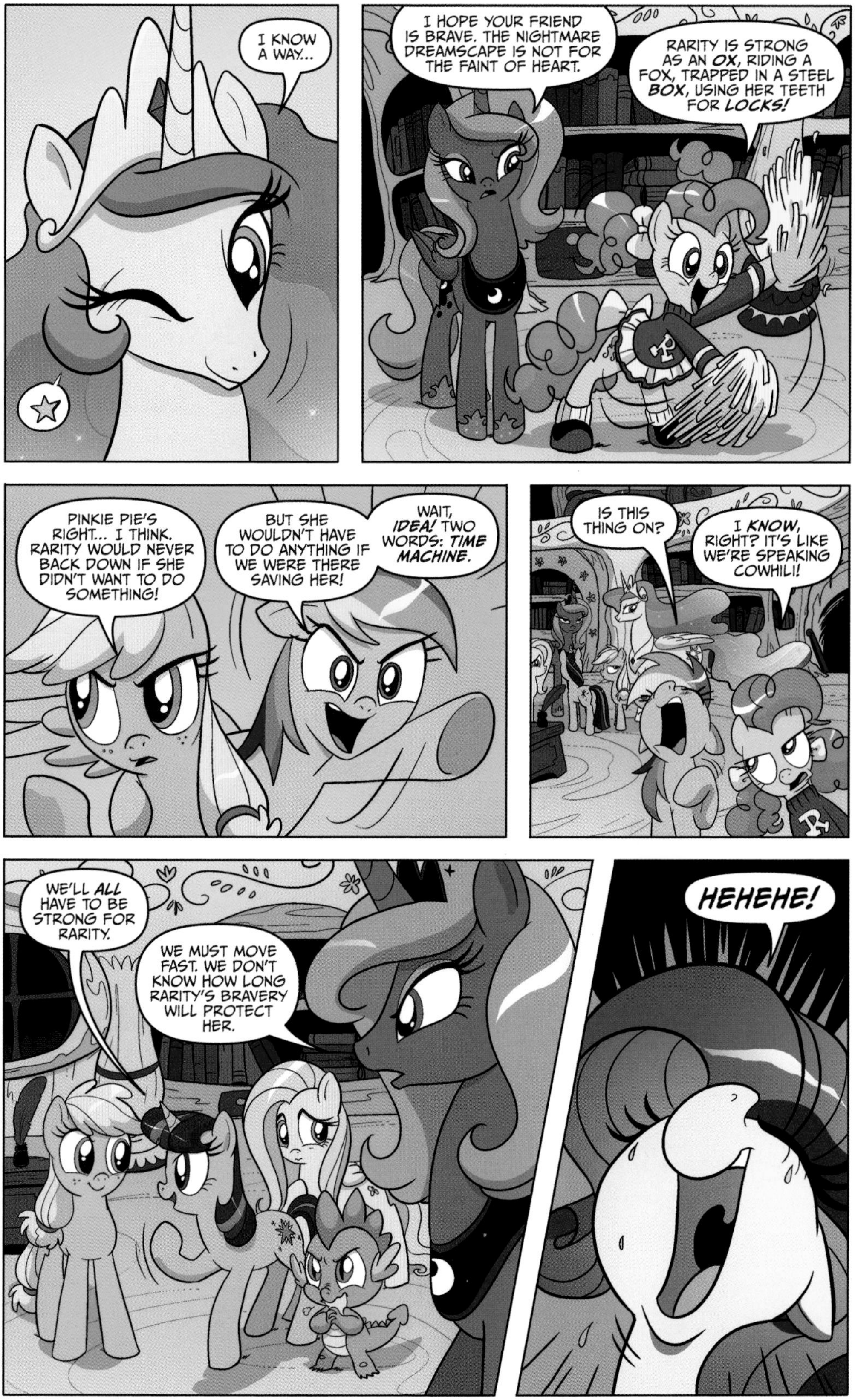

I KNOW A WAY...
I HOPE YOUR FRIEND IS BRAVE. THE NIGHTMARE DREAMSCAPE IS NOT FOR THE FAINT OF HEART.
RARITY IS STRONG AS AN OX, RIDING A FOX, TRAPPED IN A STEEL BOX, USING HER TEETH FOR LOCKS!
PINKIE PIE'S RIGHT... I THINK. RARITY WOULD NEVER BACK DOWN IF SHE DIDN'T WANT TO DO SOMETHING!
BUT SHE WOULDN'T HAVE TO DO ANYTHING IF WE WERE THERE SAVING HER!
WAIT, IDEA! TWO WORDS: TIME MACHINE.
IS THIS THING ON?
I KNOW, RIGHT? IT'S LIKE WE'RE SPEAKING COWHILI!
WE'LL ALL HAVE TO BE STRONG FOR RARITY.
WE MUST MOVE FAST. WE DON'T KNOW HOW LONG RARITY'S BRAVERY WILL PROTECT HER.
HEHEHE!

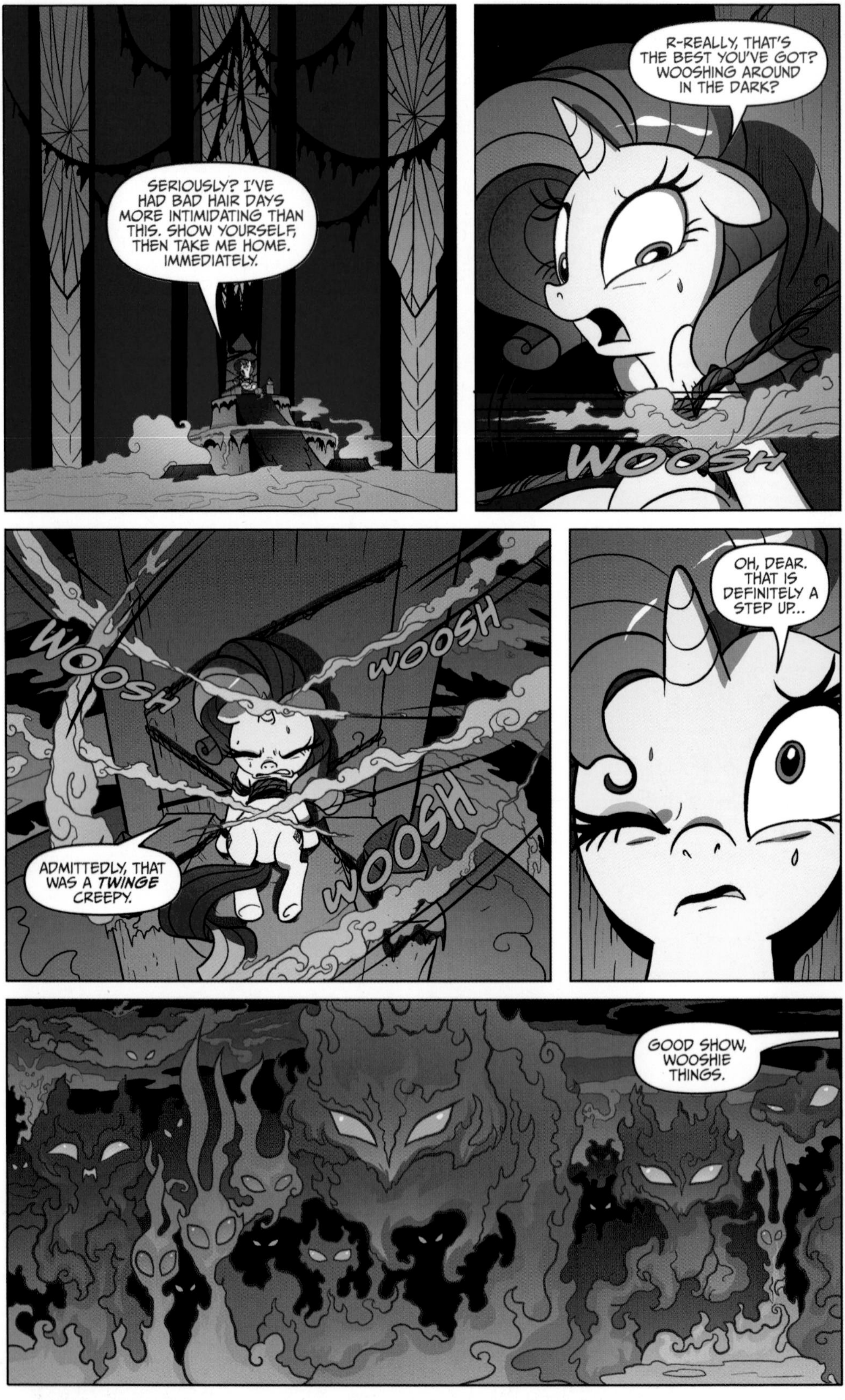

SERIOUSLY? I'VE HAD BAD HAIR DAYS MORE INTIMIDATING THAN THIS. SHOW YOURSELF, THEN TAKE ME HOME. IMMEDIATELY.
R-REALLY, THAT'S THE BEST YOU'VE GOT? WOOSHING AROUND IN THE DARK?
WOOSH
WOOSH
WOOSH
WOOSH
ADMITTEDLY, THAT WAS A *TWINGE* CREEPY.
OH, DEAR. THAT IS DEFINITELY A STEP UP...
GOOD SHOW, WOOSHIE THINGS.

Art by
Andy Price

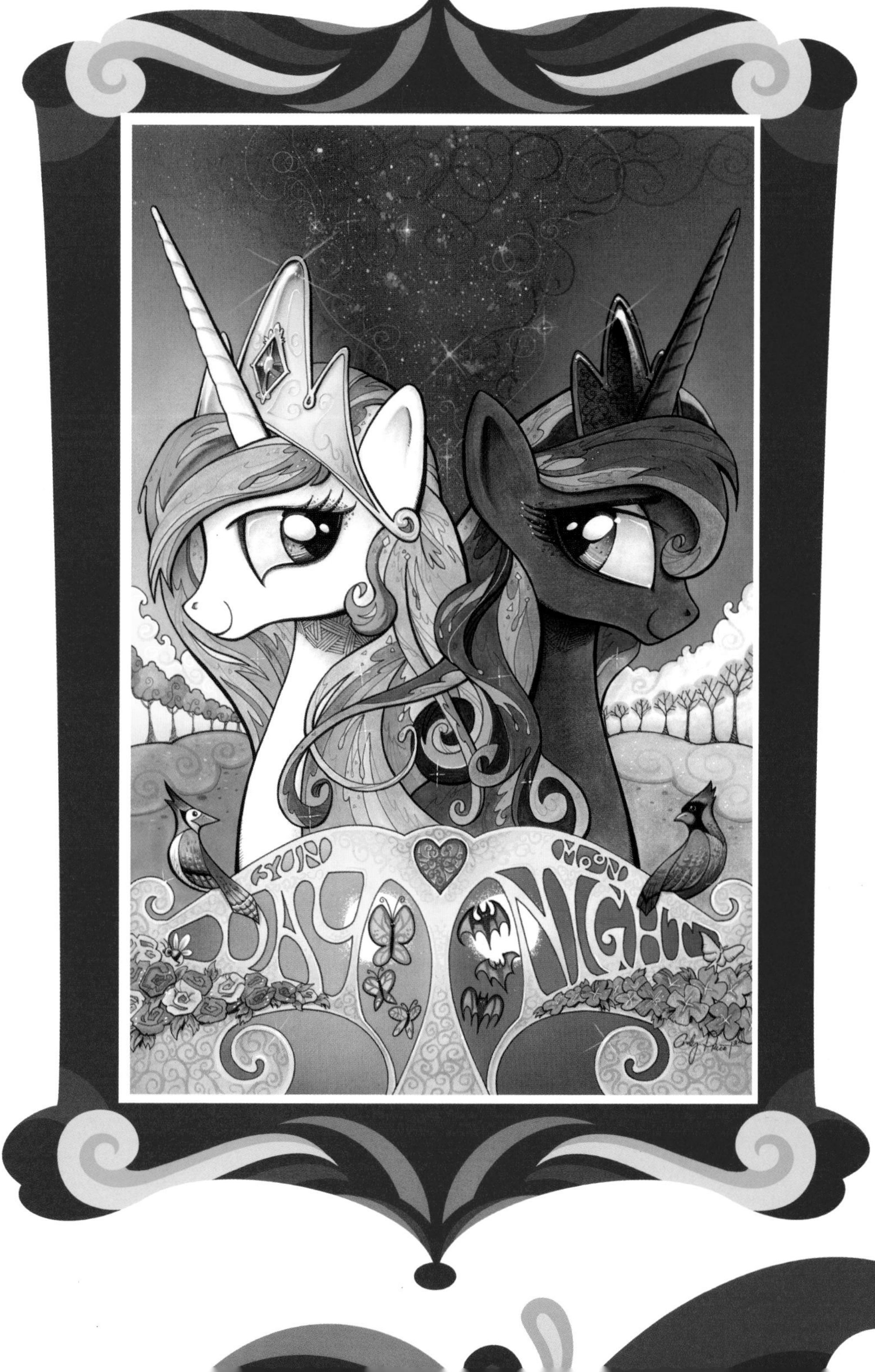

Art by
Amy Mebberson

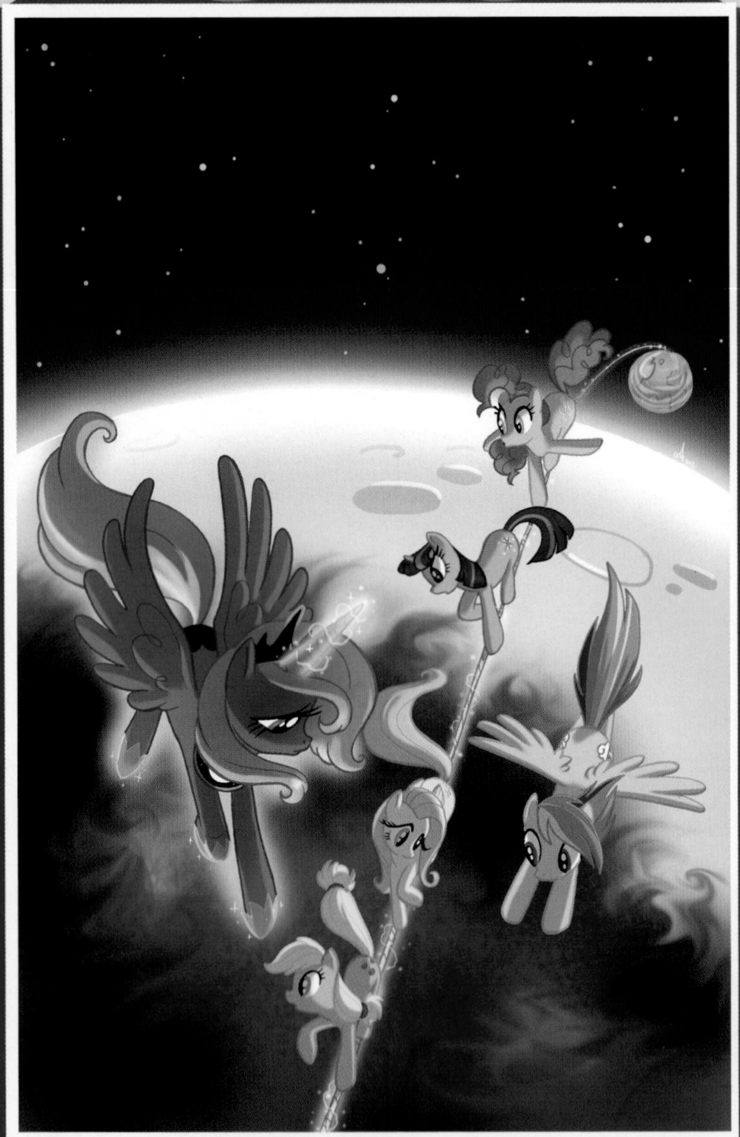

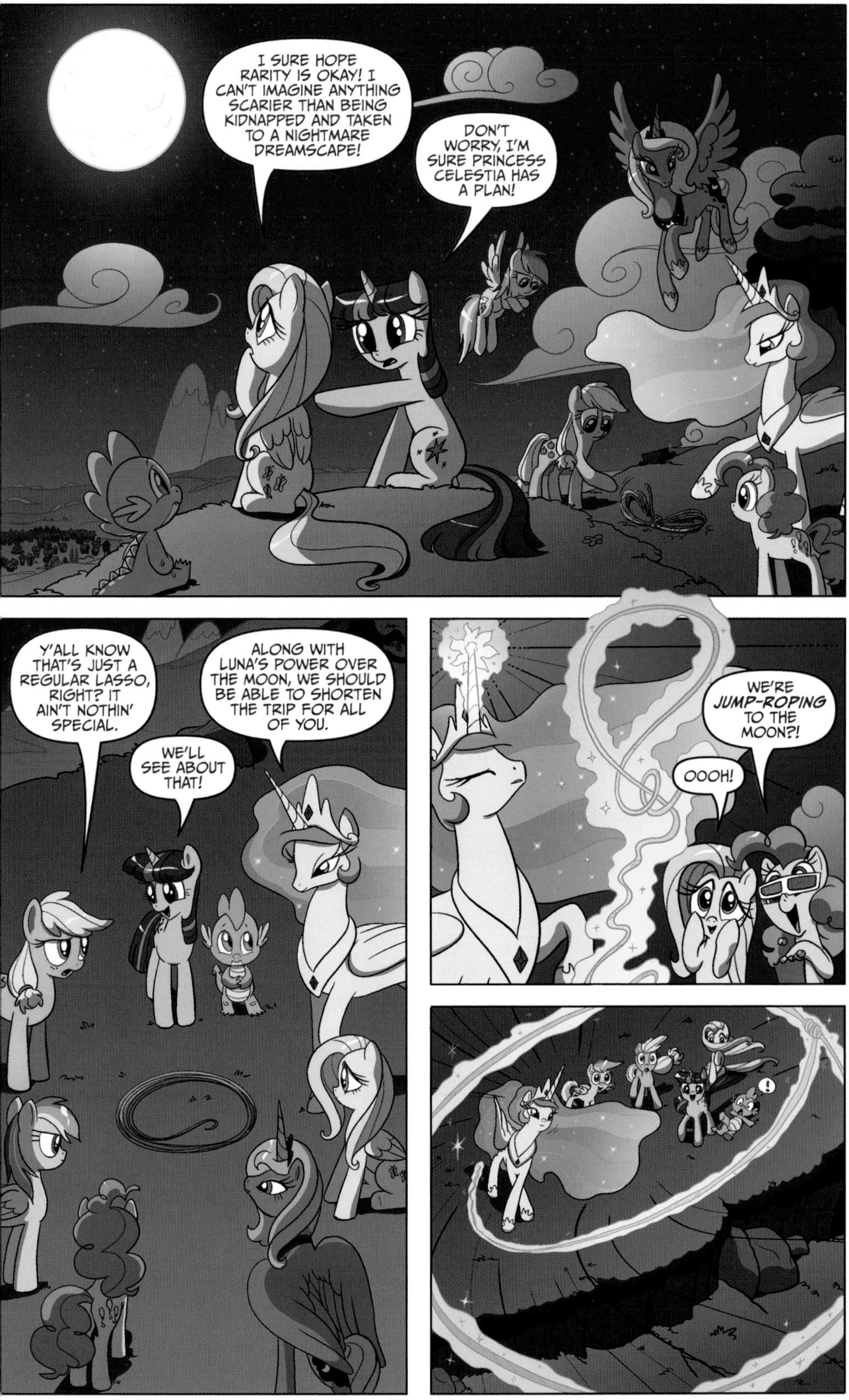

I SURE HOPE RARITY IS OKAY! I CAN'T IMAGINE ANYTHING SCARIER THAN BEING KIDNAPPED AND TAKEN TO A NIGHTMARE DREAMSCAPE!
DON'T WORRY, I'M SURE PRINCESS CELESTIA HAS A PLAN!
Y'ALL KNOW THAT'S JUST A REGULAR LASSO, RIGHT? IT AIN'T NOTHIN' SPECIAL.
ALONG WITH LUNA'S POWER OVER THE MOON, WE SHOULD BE ABLE TO SHORTEN THE TRIP FOR ALL OF YOU.
WE'LL SEE ABOUT THAT!
WE'RE JUMP-ROPING TO THE MOON?!
OOOH!
!

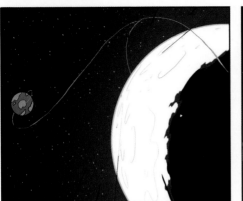

CAREFUL...

...USING MY POWERS TO BRING THE MOON *CLOSER* TO THE EARTH IS HARDER THAN I IMAGINED!

WE'RE RIGHT THERE WITH YA, SISTER!

EVERYONE CONCENTRATE.

I COULD SURE USE A FEW ENCHANTED APPLE CARTS DURING HARVEST SEASON, WHADDYA THINK, PRINCESS CELESTIA?

THEN LET'S PUT OUR CUTIE BOOTIES INTO HIGH GEAR AND *PULL!*

WELL, IF WE DON'T MOVE THIS MOON, WE'LL HAVE HEAVIER PROBLEMS THAN APPLE CARTS!

BONK!

THAT'S IT! WELL DONE, MY PONIES. I WILL BEGIN TO PREPARE PONYVILLE. GOOD LUCK!

THE WINGLESS PONIES WILL HAVE TO USE SURE FOOTING...

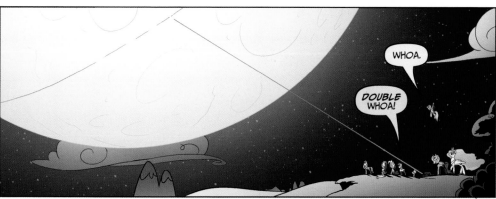

WHOA.

DOUBLE WHOA!

THIS IS YOUR LAST CHANCE TO CHANGE YOUR MINDS. REMEMBER, THE DARK FORCES THAT TOOK RARITY WILL USE ALL OF THEIR POWER TO SCARE YOU. THEY WILL UNRAVEL YOU WITH YOUR GREATEST FEARS.

HOPEFULLY IT'S NOT TOO LATE...

WHEN WE'RE TOGETHER, THE ELEMENTS OF HARMONY CAN OVERCOME ANYTHING.

AS LONG AS WE GET RARITY BACK, IT'LL ALL TURN OUT JUST DANDY.

LET'S DO THIS!

KLOP-SPROIIING

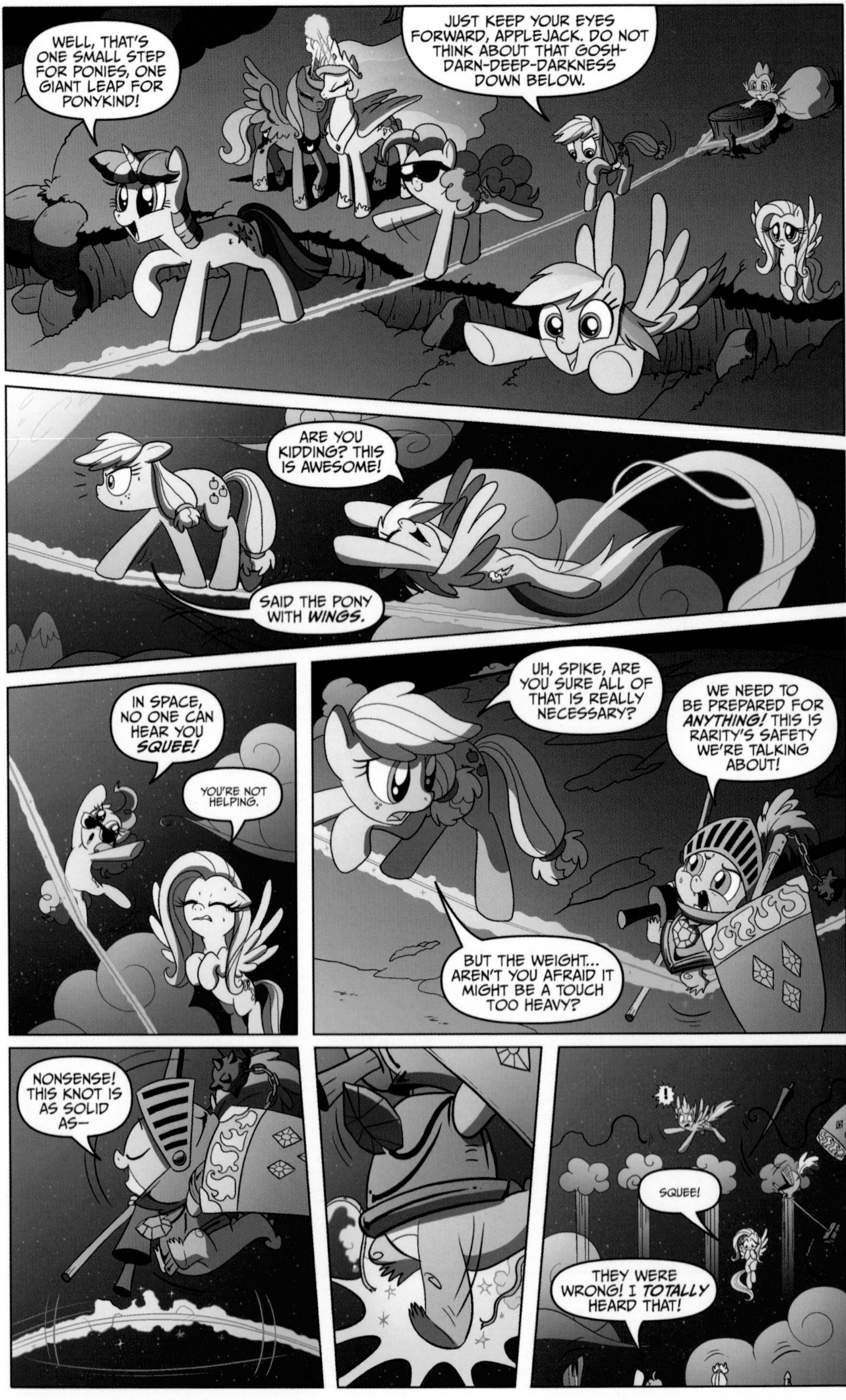
WELL, THAT'S ONE SMALL STEP FOR PONIES, ONE GIANT LEAP FOR PONYKIND!
JUST KEEP YOUR EYES FORWARD, APPLEJACK. DO NOT THINK ABOUT THAT GOSH-DARN-DEEP-DARKNESS DOWN BELOW.
ARE YOU KIDDING? THIS IS AWESOME!
SAID THE PONY WITH WINGS.
IN SPACE, NO ONE CAN HEAR YOU SQUEE!
YOU'RE NOT HELPING.
UH, SPIKE, ARE YOU SURE ALL OF THAT IS REALLY NECESSARY?
WE NEED TO BE PREPARED FOR ANYTHING! THIS IS RARITY'S SAFETY WE'RE TALKING ABOUT!
BUT THE WEIGHT... AREN'T YOU AFRAID IT MIGHT BE A TOUCH TOO HEAVY?
NONSENSE! THIS KNOT IS AS SOLID AS—
!
SQUEE!
THEY WERE WRONG! I TOTALLY HEARD THAT!

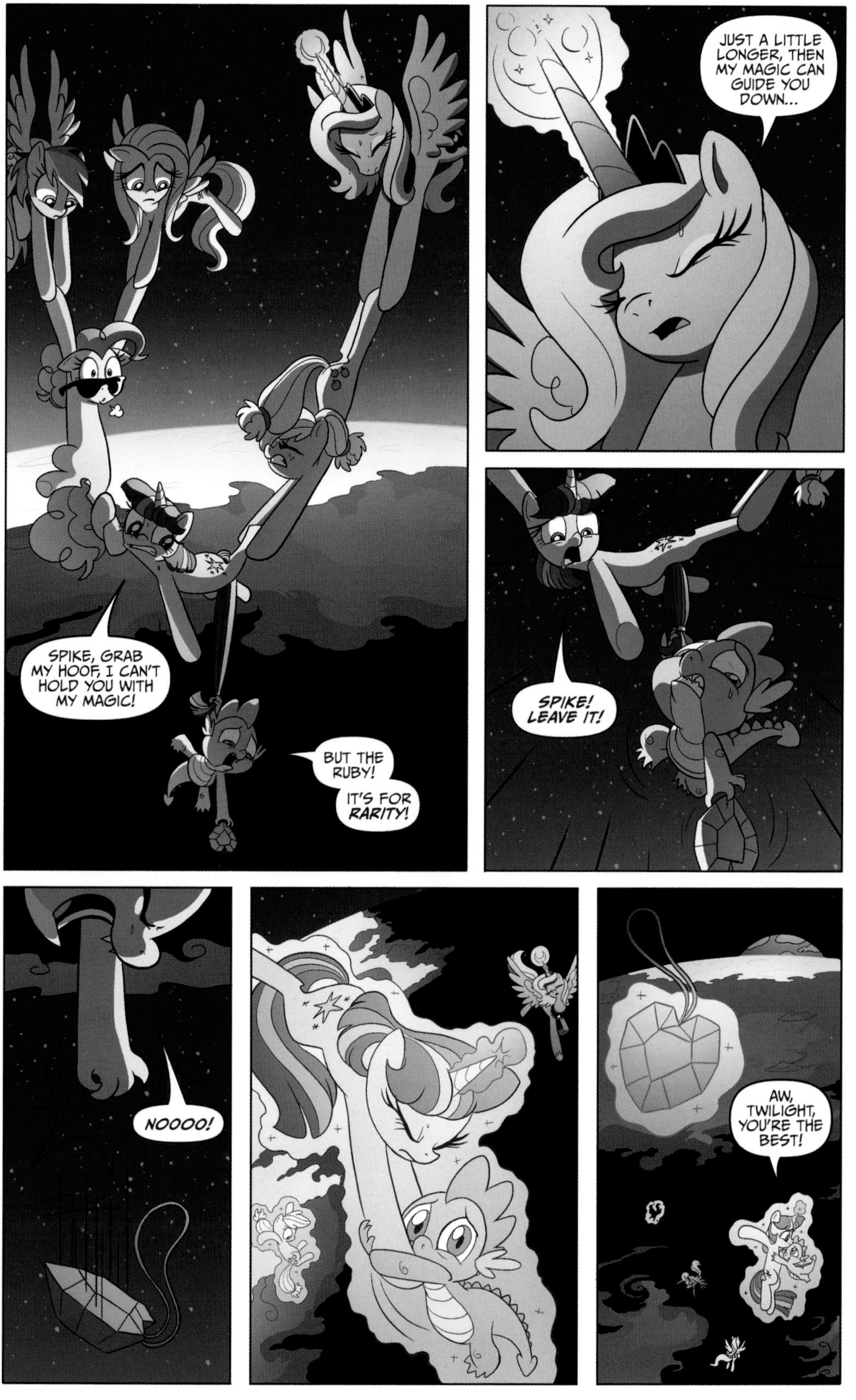
SPIKE, GRAB MY HOOF, I CAN'T HOLD YOU WITH MY MAGIC!
BUT THE RUBY!
IT'S FOR *RARITY*!
JUST A LITTLE LONGER, THEN MY MAGIC CAN GUIDE YOU DOWN...
SPIKE! LEAVE IT!
NOOOO!
AW, TWILIGHT, YOU'RE THE BEST!

FINDING RARITY IN THE PITCH BLACK? NO PROBLEM AT ALL!

WE'LL TAKE CARE OF THAT!

NOW WE MUST HURRY, *THEY'LL* KNOW WE'RE HERE!

AND WHO IS "THEY," EXACTLY?

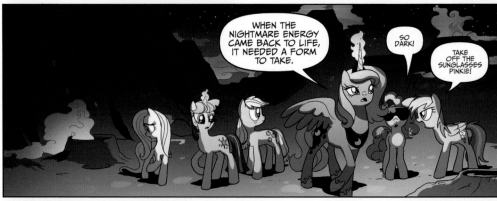

WHEN THE NIGHTMARE ENERGY CAME BACK TO LIFE, IT NEEDED A FORM TO TAKE.

SO DARK!

TAKE OFF THE SUNGLASSES PINKIE!

UNFORTUNATELY, THE PEACEFUL INHABITANTS OF THE MOON BECAME ITS VICTIMS AND ARE NOW TRAPPED UNDER ITS SPELL.

GASP! HOW COULD THEY DO THAT TO SWEET LITTLE ANIMALS?

THEY AREN'T SWEET ANYMORE...

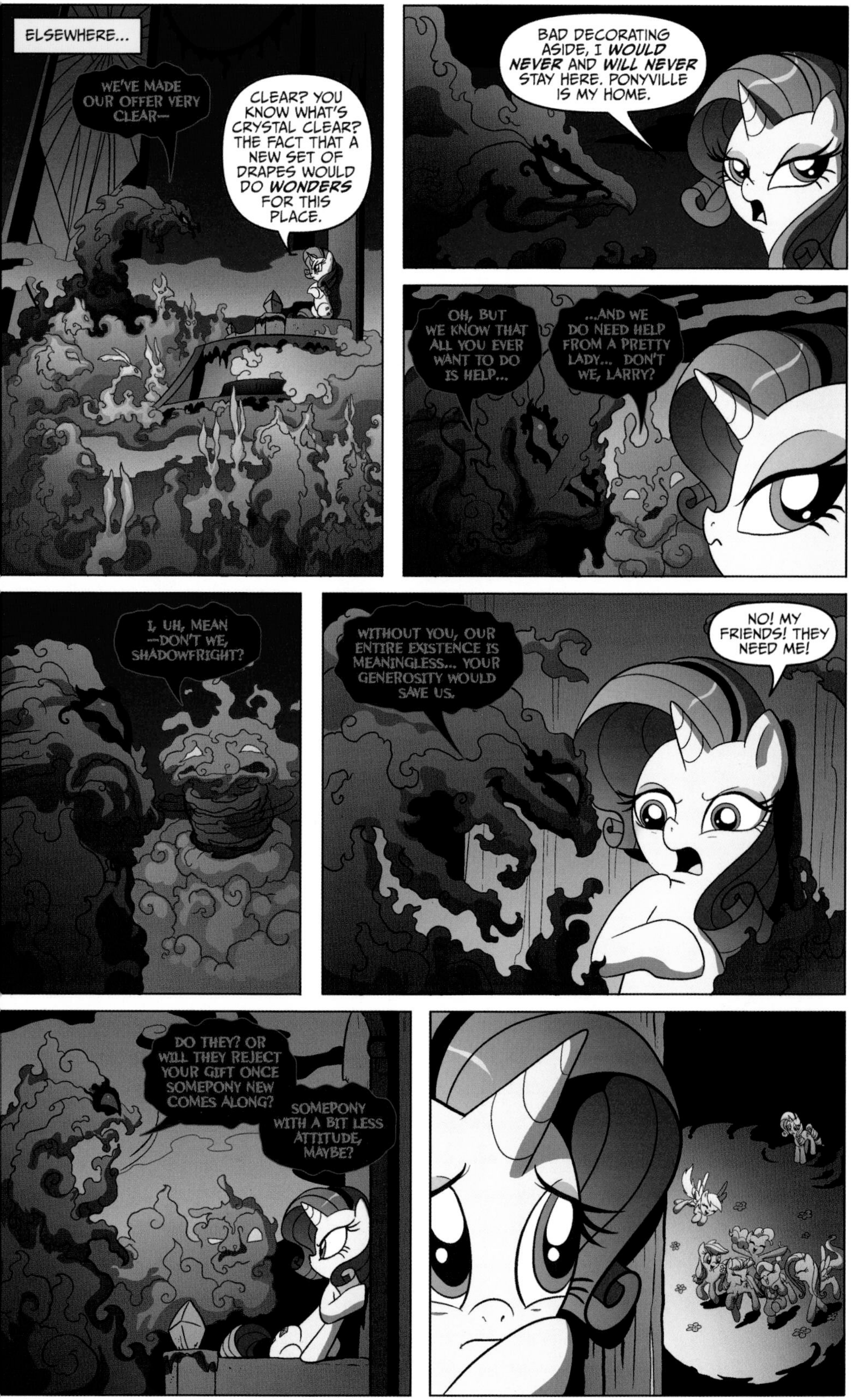
ELSEWHERE...
WE'VE MADE OUR OFFER VERY CLEAR—
CLEAR? YOU KNOW WHAT'S CRYSTAL CLEAR? THE FACT THAT A NEW SET OF DRAPES WOULD DO WONDERS FOR THIS PLACE.
BAD DECORATING ASIDE, I WOULD NEVER AND WILL NEVER STAY HERE. PONYVILLE IS MY HOME.
OH, BUT WE KNOW THAT ALL YOU EVER WANT TO DO IS HELP...
...AND WE DO NEED HELP FROM A PRETTY LADY... DON'T WE, LARRY?
I, UH, MEAN —DON'T WE, SHADOWFRIGHT?
WITHOUT YOU, OUR ENTIRE EXISTENCE IS MEANINGLESS... YOUR GENEROSITY WOULD SAVE US.
NO! MY FRIENDS! THEY NEED ME!
DO THEY? OR WILL THEY REJECT YOUR GIFT ONCE SOMEPONY NEW COMES ALONG?
SOMEPONY WITH A BIT LESS ATTITUDE, MAYBE?

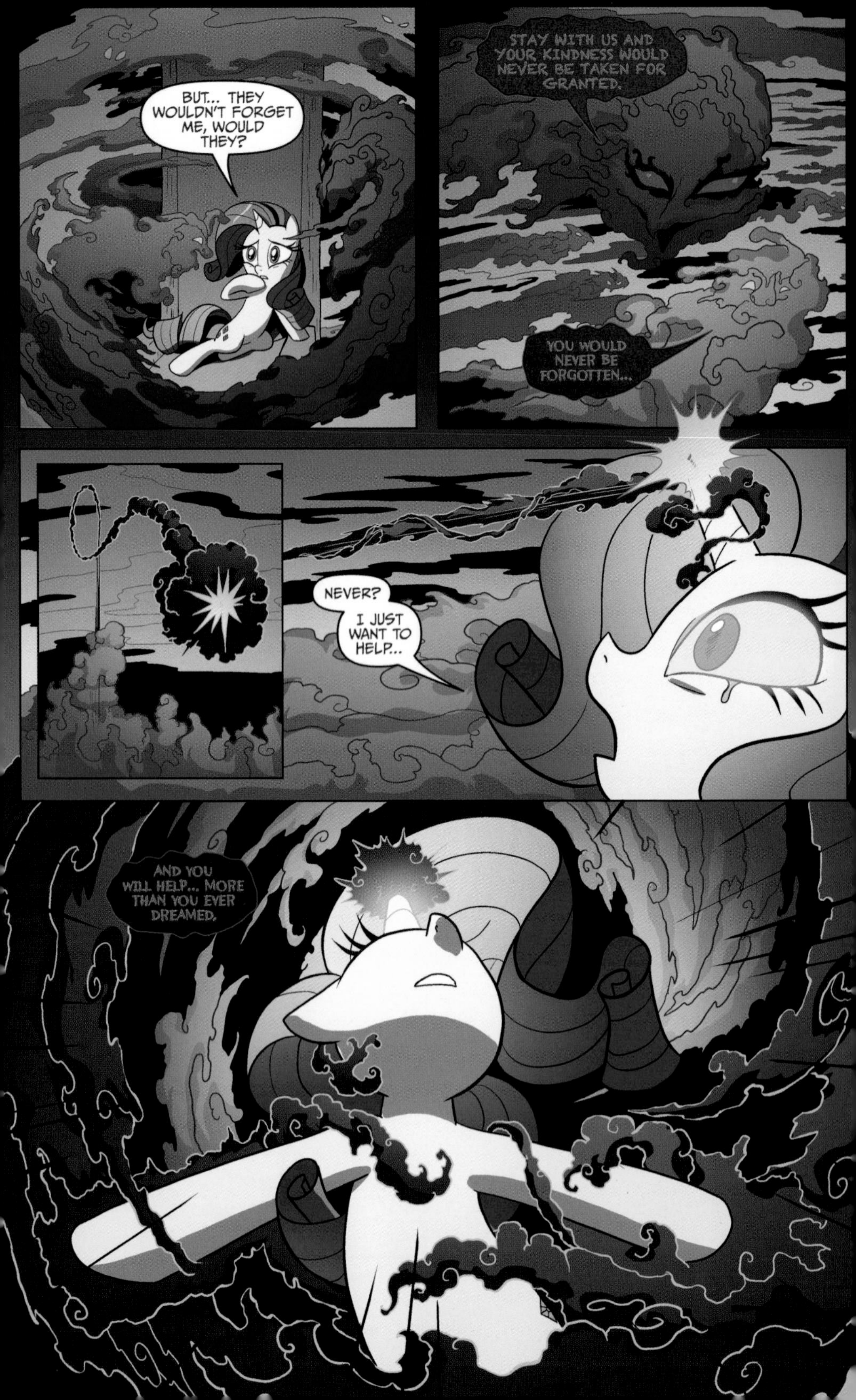
BUT... THEY WOULDN'T FORGET ME, WOULD THEY?
STAY WITH US AND YOUR KINDNESS WOULD NEVER BE TAKEN FOR GRANTED.
YOU WOULD NEVER BE FORGOTTEN...
NEVER? I JUST WANT TO HELP...
AND YOU WILL HELP... MORE THAN YOU EVER DREAMED.

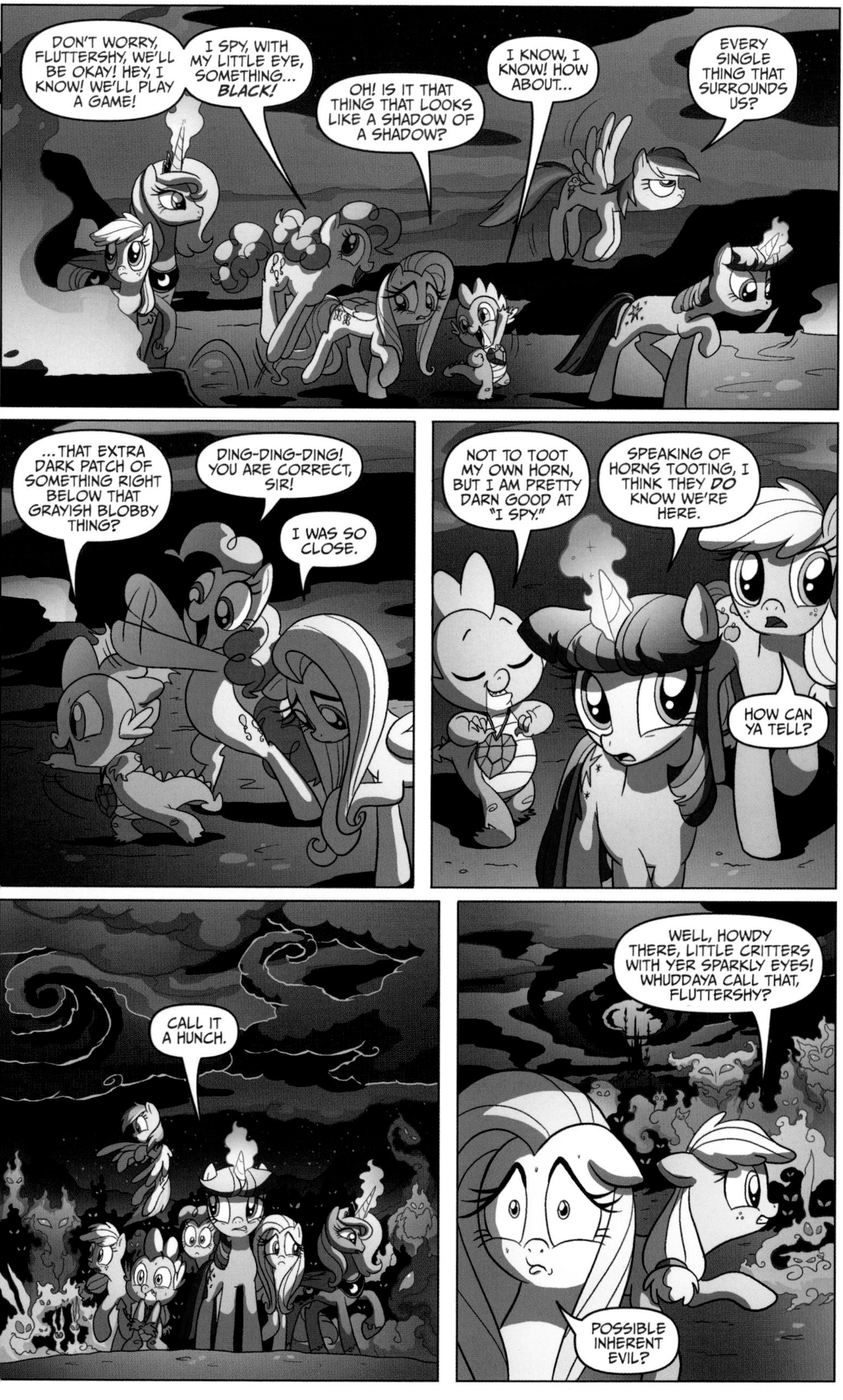
DON'T WORRY, FLUTTERSHY, WE'LL BE OKAY! HEY, I KNOW! WE'LL PLAY A GAME!
I SPY, WITH MY LITTLE EYE, SOMETHING... BLACK!
OH! IS IT THAT THING THAT LOOKS LIKE A SHADOW OF A SHADOW?
I KNOW, I KNOW! HOW ABOUT...
EVERY SINGLE THING THAT SURROUNDS US?
...THAT EXTRA DARK PATCH OF SOMETHING RIGHT BELOW THAT GRAYISH BLOBBY THING?
DING-DING-DING! YOU ARE CORRECT, SIR!
I WAS SO CLOSE.
NOT TO TOOT MY OWN HORN, BUT I AM PRETTY DARN GOOD AT "I SPY."
SPEAKING OF HORNS TOOTING, I THINK THEY DO KNOW WE'RE HERE.
HOW CAN YA TELL?
CALL IT A HUNCH.
WELL, HOWDY THERE, LITTLE CRITTERS WITH YER SPARKLY EYES! WHUDDAYA CALL THAT, FLUTTERSHY?
POSSIBLE INHERENT EVIL?

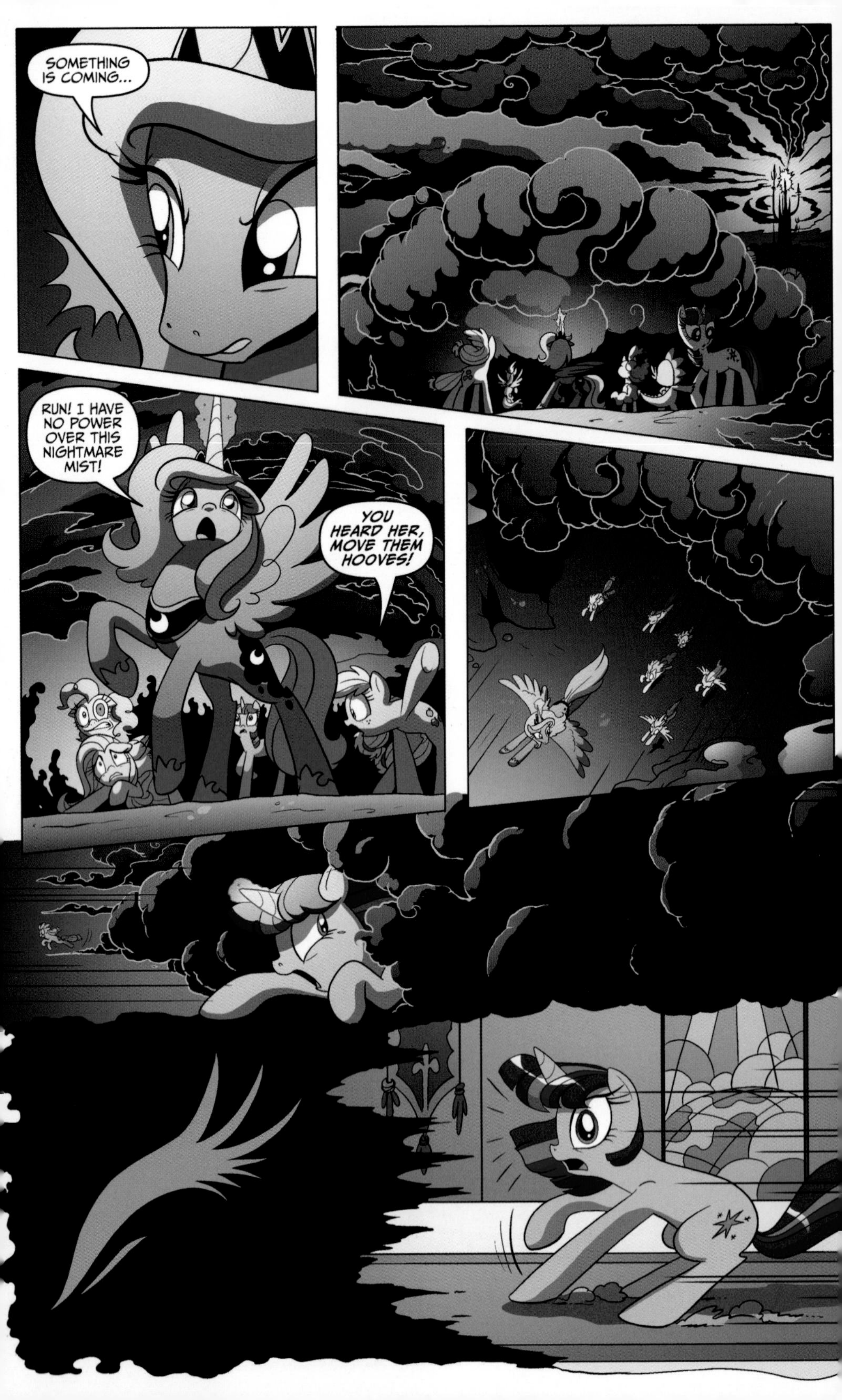
SOMETHING IS COMING...
RUN! I HAVE NO POWER OVER THIS NIGHTMARE MIST!
YOU HEARD HER, MOVE THEM HOOVES!

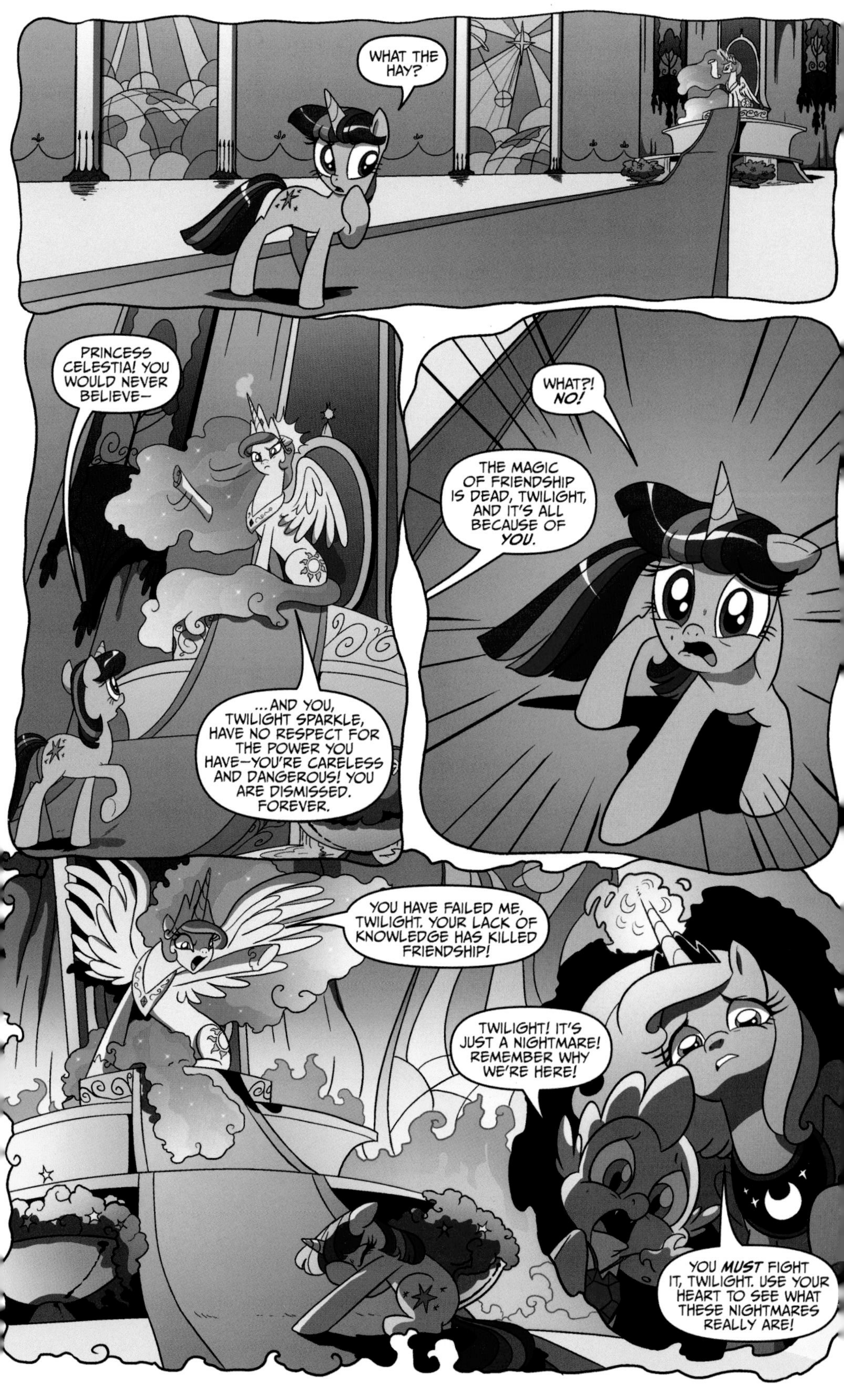
WHAT THE HAY?
PRINCESS CELESTIA! YOU WOULD NEVER BELIEVE—
...AND YOU, TWILIGHT SPARKLE, HAVE NO RESPECT FOR THE POWER YOU HAVE—YOU'RE CARELESS AND DANGEROUS! YOU ARE DISMISSED. FOREVER.
WHAT?! NO!
THE MAGIC OF FRIENDSHIP IS DEAD, TWILIGHT, AND IT'S ALL BECAUSE OF YOU.
YOU HAVE FAILED ME, TWILIGHT. YOUR LACK OF KNOWLEDGE HAS KILLED FRIENDSHIP!
TWILIGHT! IT'S JUST A NIGHTMARE! REMEMBER WHY WE'RE HERE!
YOU MUST FIGHT IT, TWILIGHT. USE YOUR HEART TO SEE WHAT THESE NIGHTMARES REALLY ARE!

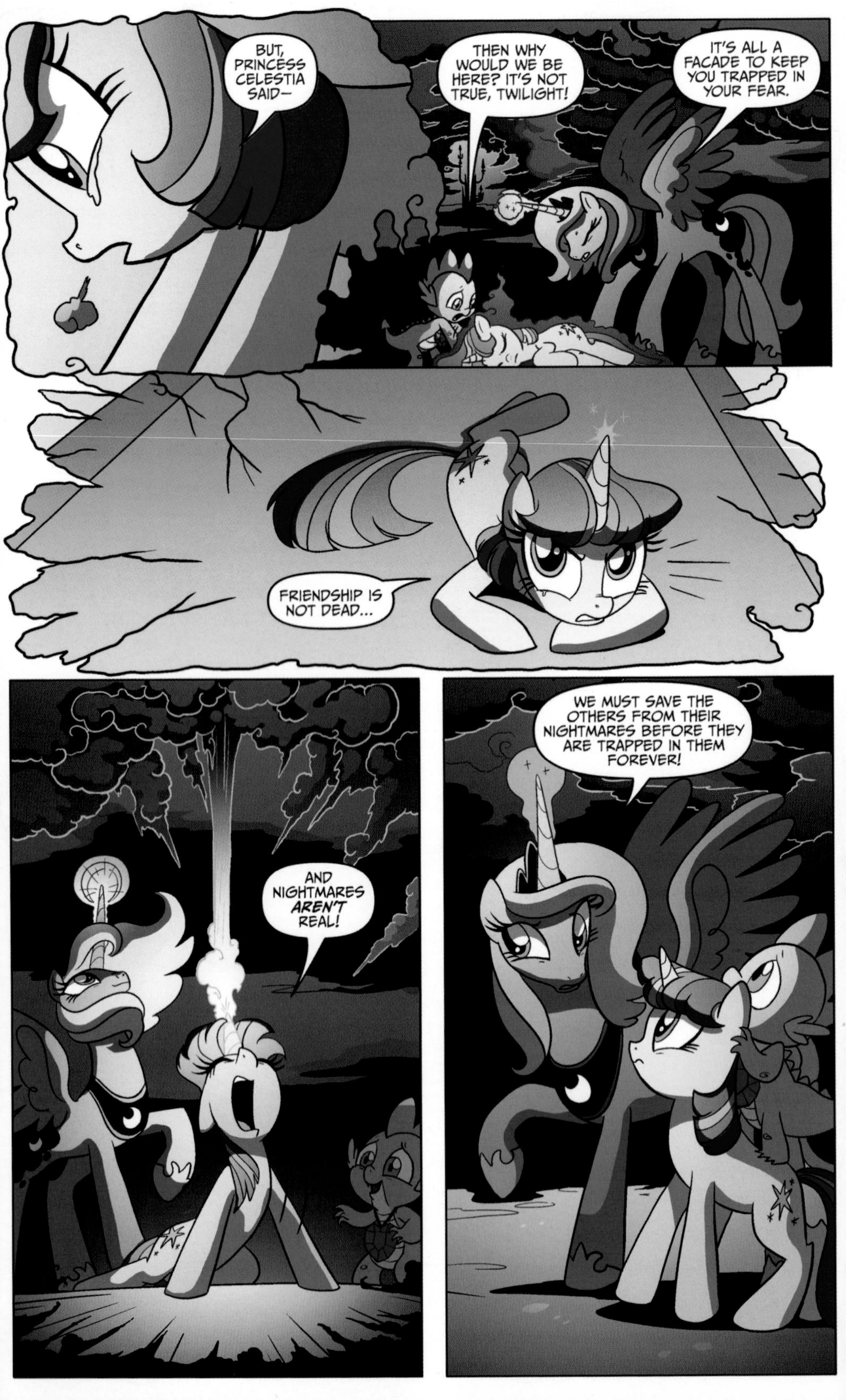
BUT, PRINCESS CELESTIA SAID—
THEN WHY WOULD WE BE HERE? IT'S NOT TRUE, TWILIGHT!
IT'S ALL A FACADE TO KEEP YOU TRAPPED IN YOUR FEAR.
FRIENDSHIP IS NOT DEAD...
AND NIGHTMARES *AREN'T* REAL!
WE MUST SAVE THE OTHERS FROM THEIR NIGHTMARES BEFORE THEY ARE TRAPPED IN THEM FOREVER!

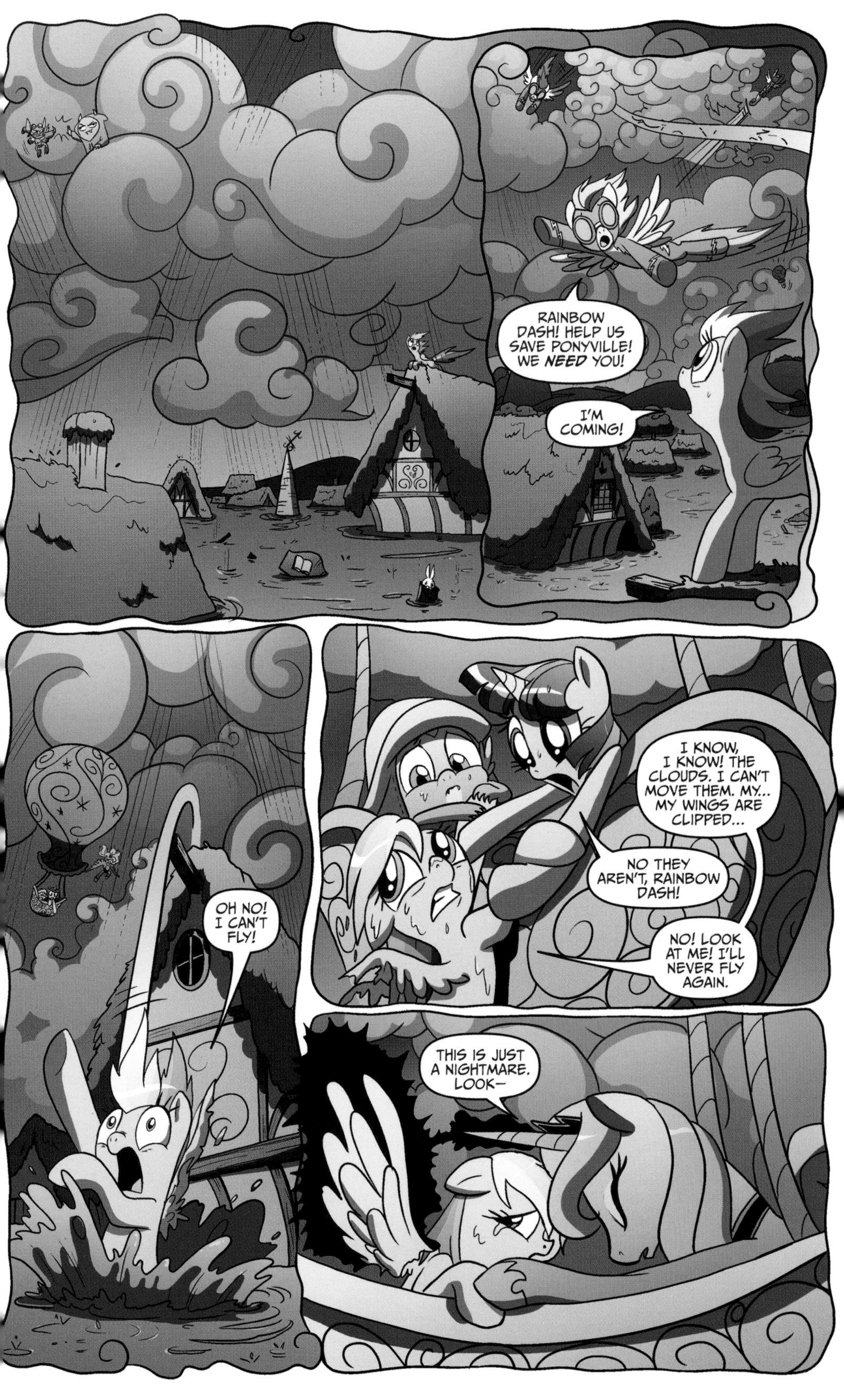
RAINBOW DASH! HELP US SAVE PONYVILLE! WE **NEED** YOU!
I'M COMING!
OH NO! I CAN'T FLY!
I KNOW, I KNOW! THE CLOUDS. I CAN'T MOVE THEM. MY... MY WINGS ARE CLIPPED...
NO THEY AREN'T, RAINBOW DASH!
NO! LOOK AT ME! I'LL NEVER FLY AGAIN.
THIS IS JUST A NIGHTMARE. LOOK—

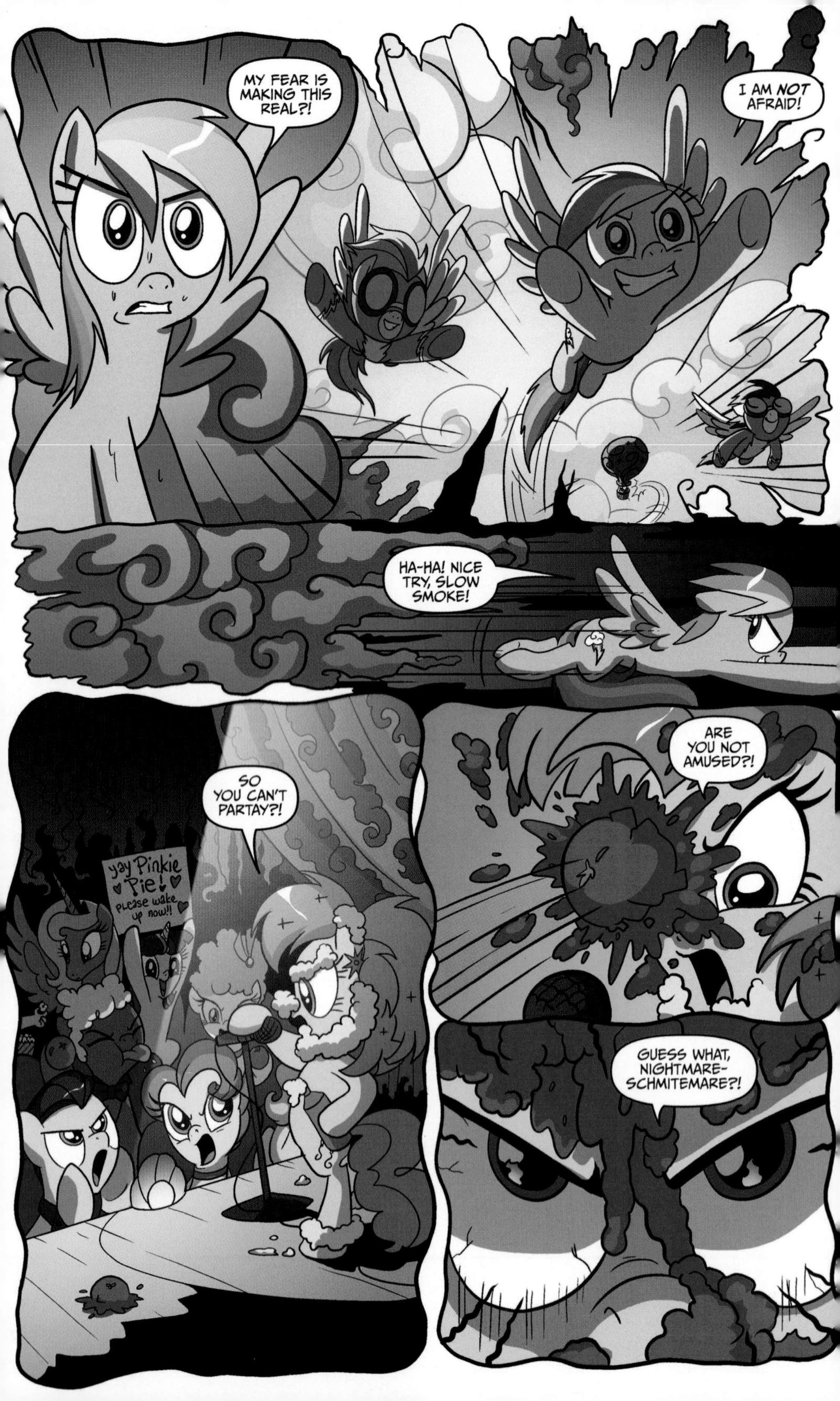
MY FEAR IS MAKING THIS REAL?!
I AM NOT AFRAID!
HA-HA! NICE TRY, SLOW SMOKE!
SO YOU CAN'T PARTAY?!
yay Pinkie Pie! please wake up now!!
ARE YOU NOT AMUSED?!
GUESS WHAT, NIGHTMARE-SCHMITEMARE?!

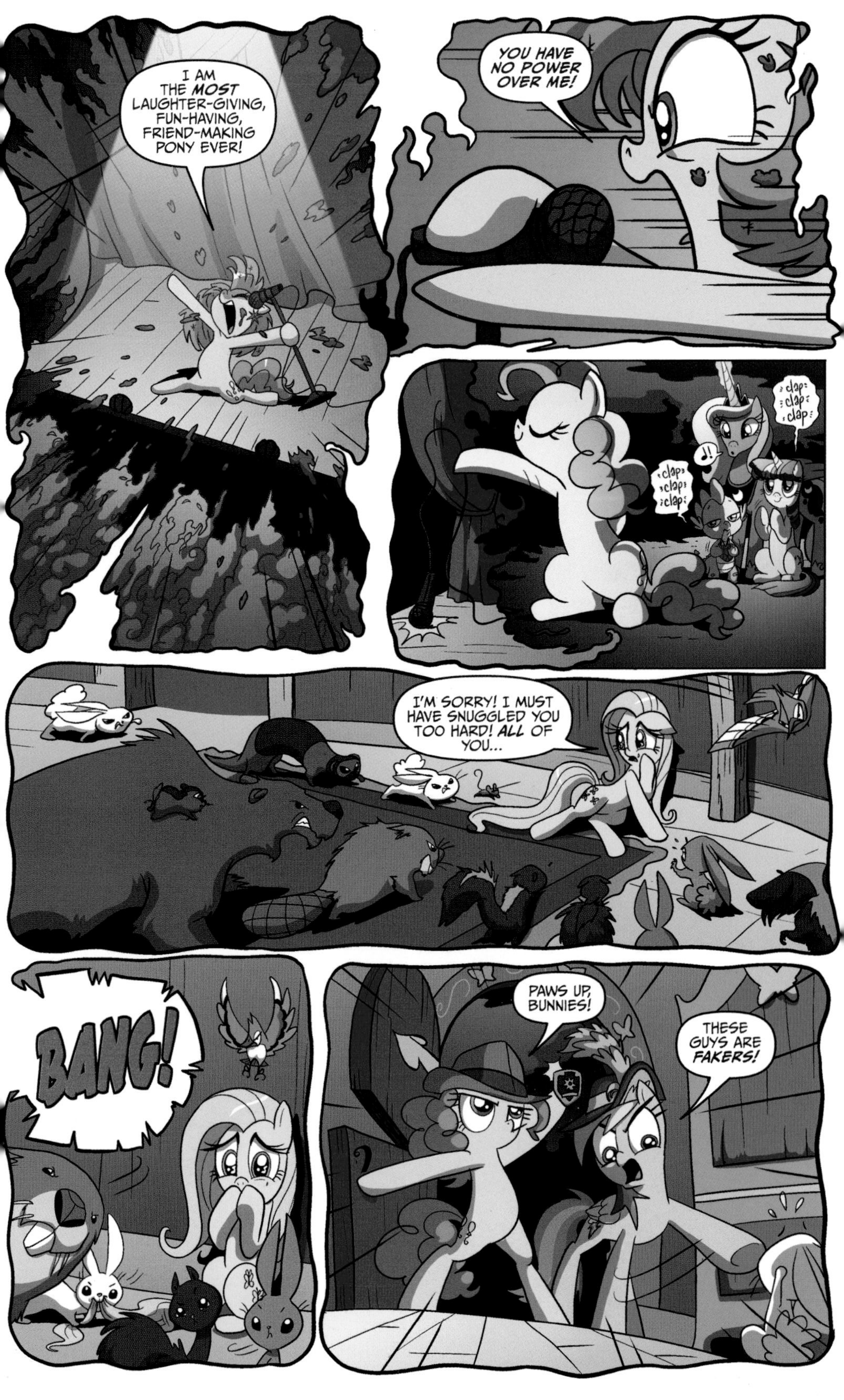
I AM THE MOST LAUGHTER-GIVING, FUN-HAVING, FRIEND-MAKING PONY EVER!
YOU HAVE NO POWER OVER ME!
clap clap clap
clap clap clap
I'M SORRY! I MUST HAVE SNUGGLED YOU TOO HARD! ALL OF YOU...
BANG!
PAWS UP, BUNNIES!
THESE GUYS ARE FAKERS!

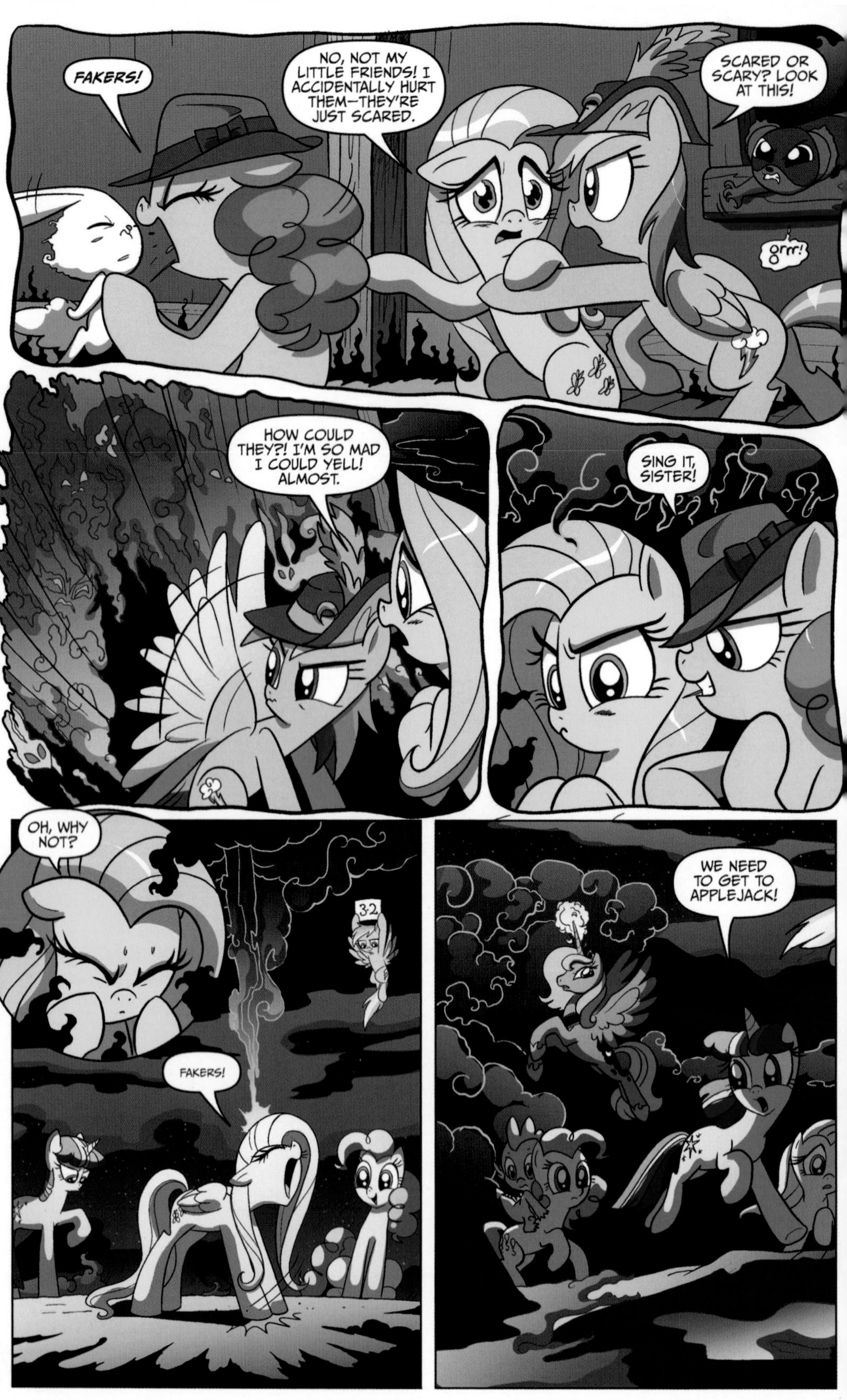
FAKERS!
NO, NOT MY LITTLE FRIENDS! I ACCIDENTALLY HURT THEM—THEY'RE JUST SCARED.
SCARED OR SCARY? LOOK AT THIS!
grrr!
HOW COULD THEY?! I'M SO MAD I COULD YELL! ALMOST.
SING IT, SISTER!
OH, WHY NOT?
3.2
FAKERS!
WE NEED TO GET TO APPLEJACK!

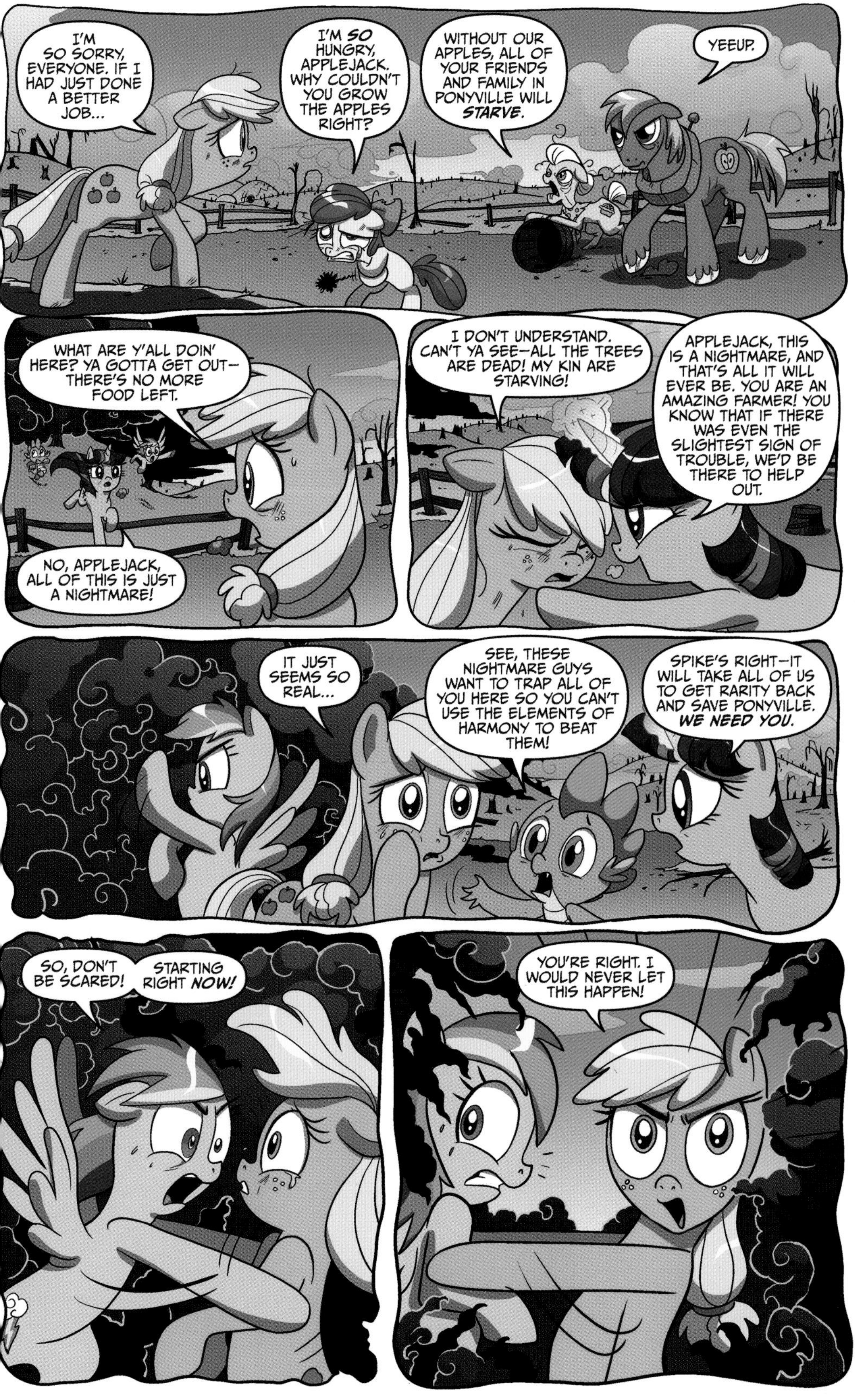

I'M SO SORRY, EVERYONE. IF I HAD JUST DONE A BETTER JOB...
I'M SO HUNGRY, APPLEJACK. WHY COULDN'T YOU GROW THE APPLES RIGHT?
WITHOUT OUR APPLES, ALL OF YOUR FRIENDS AND FAMILY IN PONYVILLE WILL STARVE.
YEEUP.
WHAT ARE Y'ALL DOIN' HERE? YA GOTTA GET OUT— THERE'S NO MORE FOOD LEFT.
NO, APPLEJACK, ALL OF THIS IS JUST A NIGHTMARE!
I DON'T UNDERSTAND. CAN'T YA SEE—ALL THE TREES ARE DEAD! MY KIN ARE STARVING!
APPLEJACK, THIS IS A NIGHTMARE, AND THAT'S ALL IT WILL EVER BE. YOU ARE AN AMAZING FARMER! YOU KNOW THAT IF THERE WAS EVEN THE SLIGHTEST SIGN OF TROUBLE, WE'D BE THERE TO HELP OUT.
IT JUST SEEMS SO REAL...
SEE, THESE NIGHTMARE GUYS WANT TO TRAP ALL OF YOU HERE SO YOU CAN'T USE THE ELEMENTS OF HARMONY TO BEAT THEM!
SPIKE'S RIGHT—IT WILL TAKE ALL OF US TO GET RARITY BACK AND SAVE PONYVILLE. WE NEED YOU.
SO, DON'T BE SCARED!
STARTING RIGHT NOW!
YOU'RE RIGHT. I WOULD NEVER LET THIS HAPPEN!

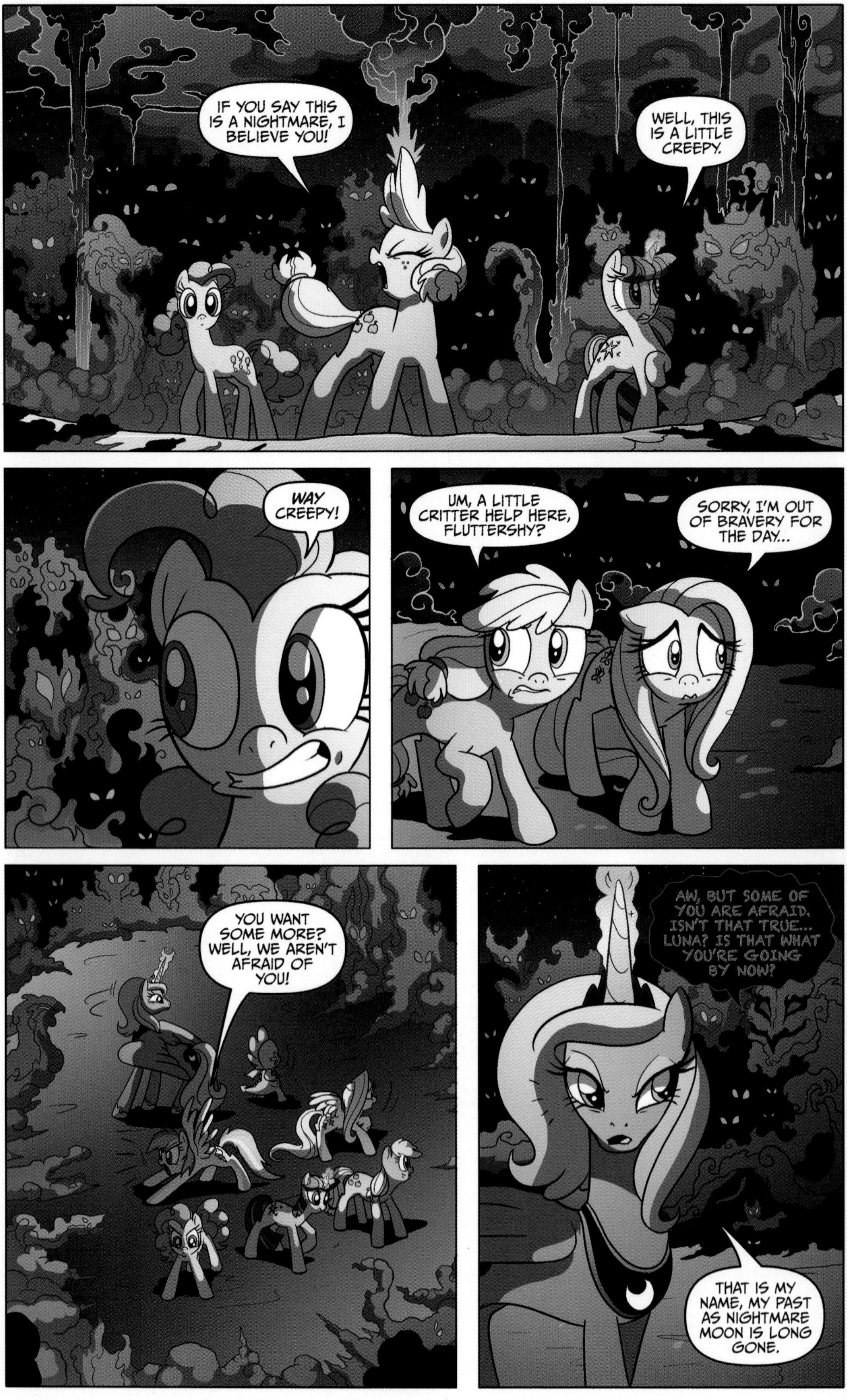

IF YOU SAY THIS IS A NIGHTMARE, I BELIEVE YOU!
WELL, THIS IS A LITTLE CREEPY.
WAY CREEPY!
UM, A LITTLE CRITTER HELP HERE, FLUTTERSHY?
SORRY, I'M OUT OF BRAVERY FOR THE DAY...
YOU WANT SOME MORE? WELL, WE AREN'T AFRAID OF YOU!
AW, BUT SOME OF YOU ARE AFRAID. ISN'T THAT TRUE... LUNA? IS THAT WHAT YOU'RE GOING BY NOW?
THAT IS MY NAME, MY PAST AS NIGHTMARE MOON IS LONG GONE.

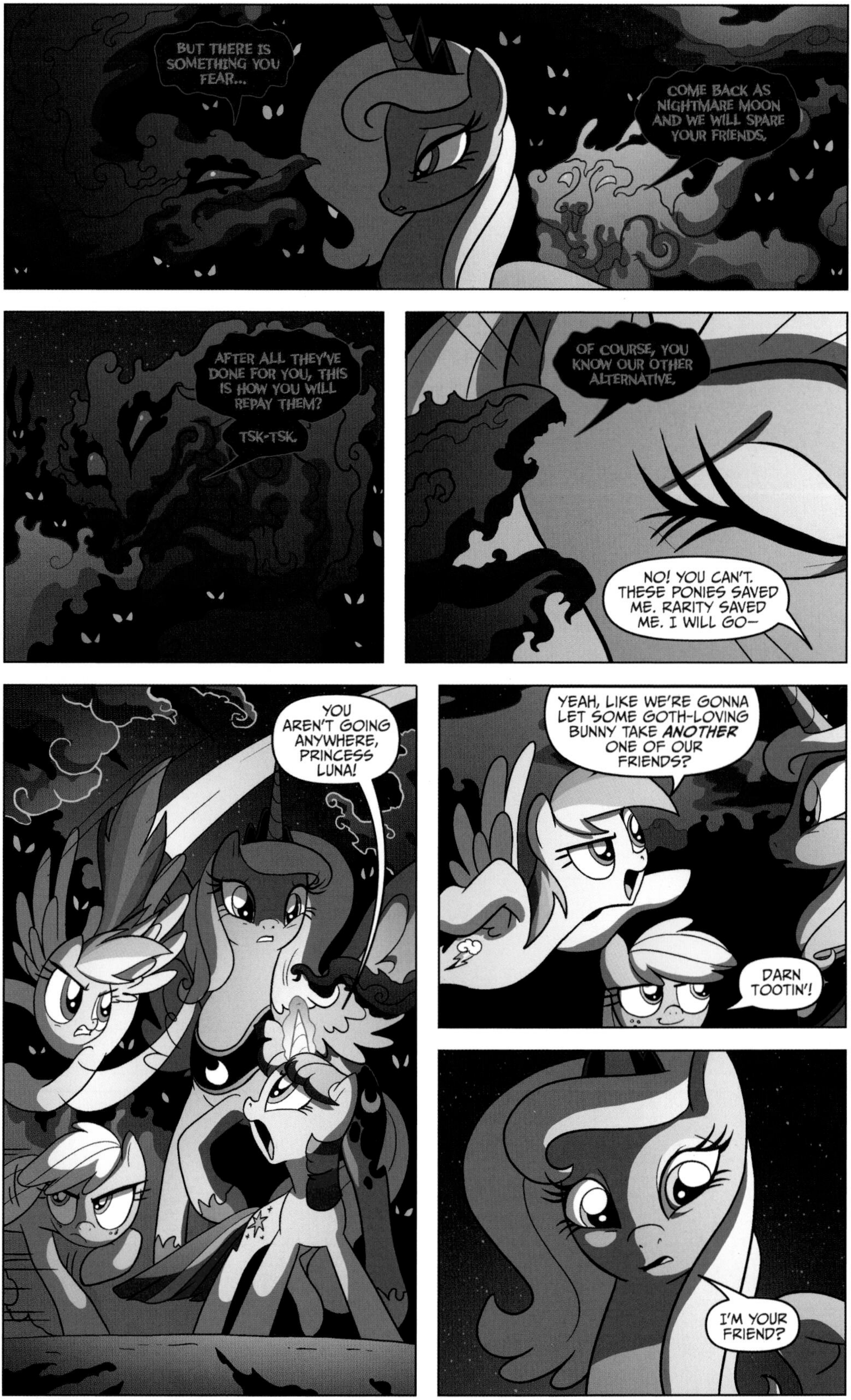
BUT THERE IS SOMETHING YOU FEAR...
COME BACK AS NIGHTMARE MOON AND WE WILL SPARE YOUR FRIENDS.
AFTER ALL THEY'VE DONE FOR YOU, THIS IS HOW YOU WILL REPAY THEM?
TSK-TSK.
OF COURSE, YOU KNOW OUR OTHER ALTERNATIVE.
NO! YOU CAN'T. THESE PONIES SAVED ME. RARITY SAVED ME. I WILL GO—
YOU AREN'T GOING ANYWHERE, PRINCESS LUNA!
YEAH, LIKE WE'RE GONNA LET SOME GOTH-LOVING BUNNY TAKE ANOTHER ONE OF OUR FRIENDS?
DARN TOOTIN'!
I'M YOUR FRIEND?

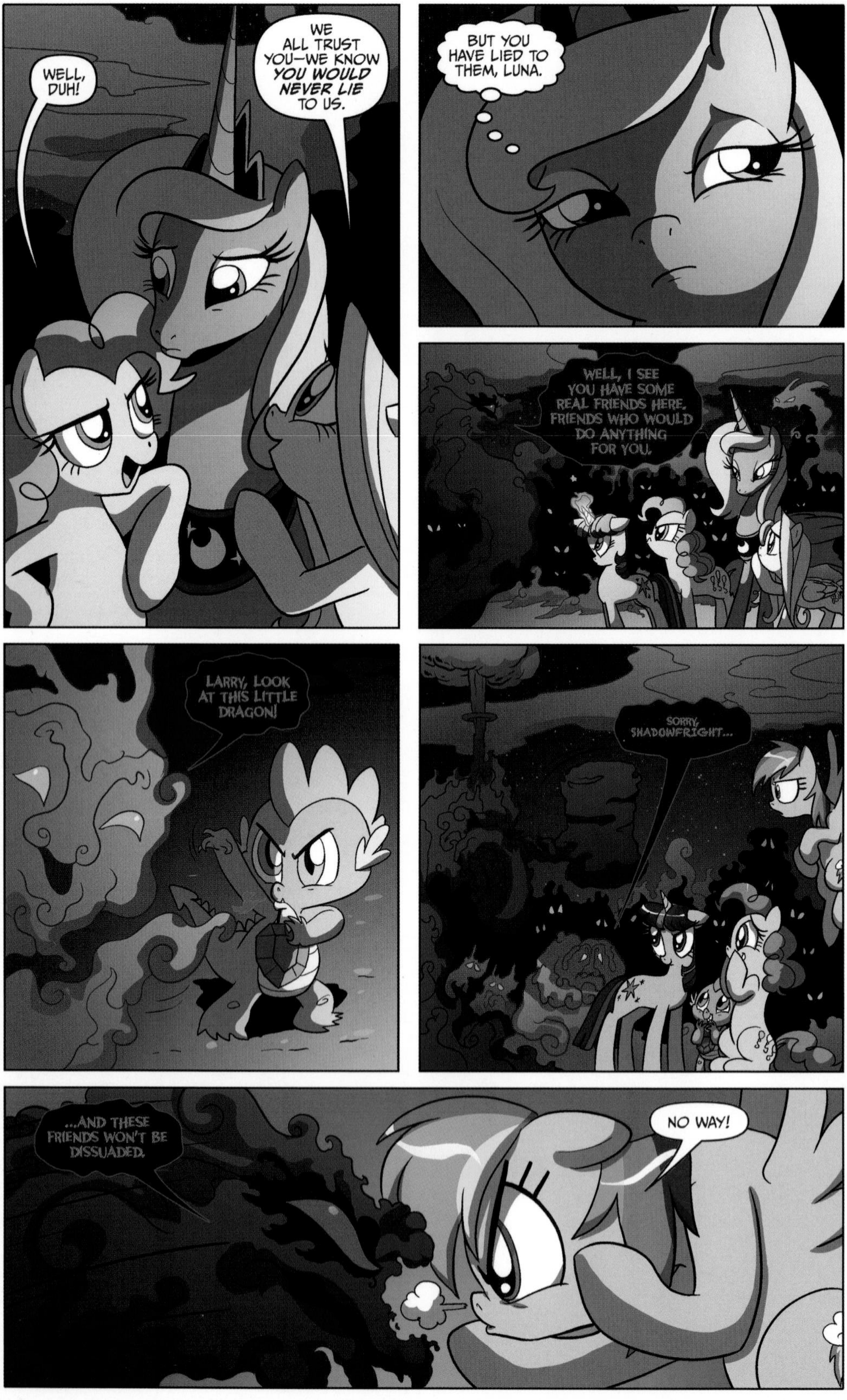
WELL, DUH!
WE ALL TRUST YOU—WE KNOW *YOU WOULD NEVER LIE* TO US.
BUT YOU HAVE LIED TO THEM, LUNA.
WELL, I SEE YOU HAVE SOME REAL FRIENDS HERE, FRIENDS WHO WOULD DO ANYTHING FOR YOU.
LARRY, LOOK AT THIS LITTLE DRAGON!
SORRY, SHADOWFRIGHT...
...AND THESE FRIENDS WON'T BE DISSUADED.
NO WAY!

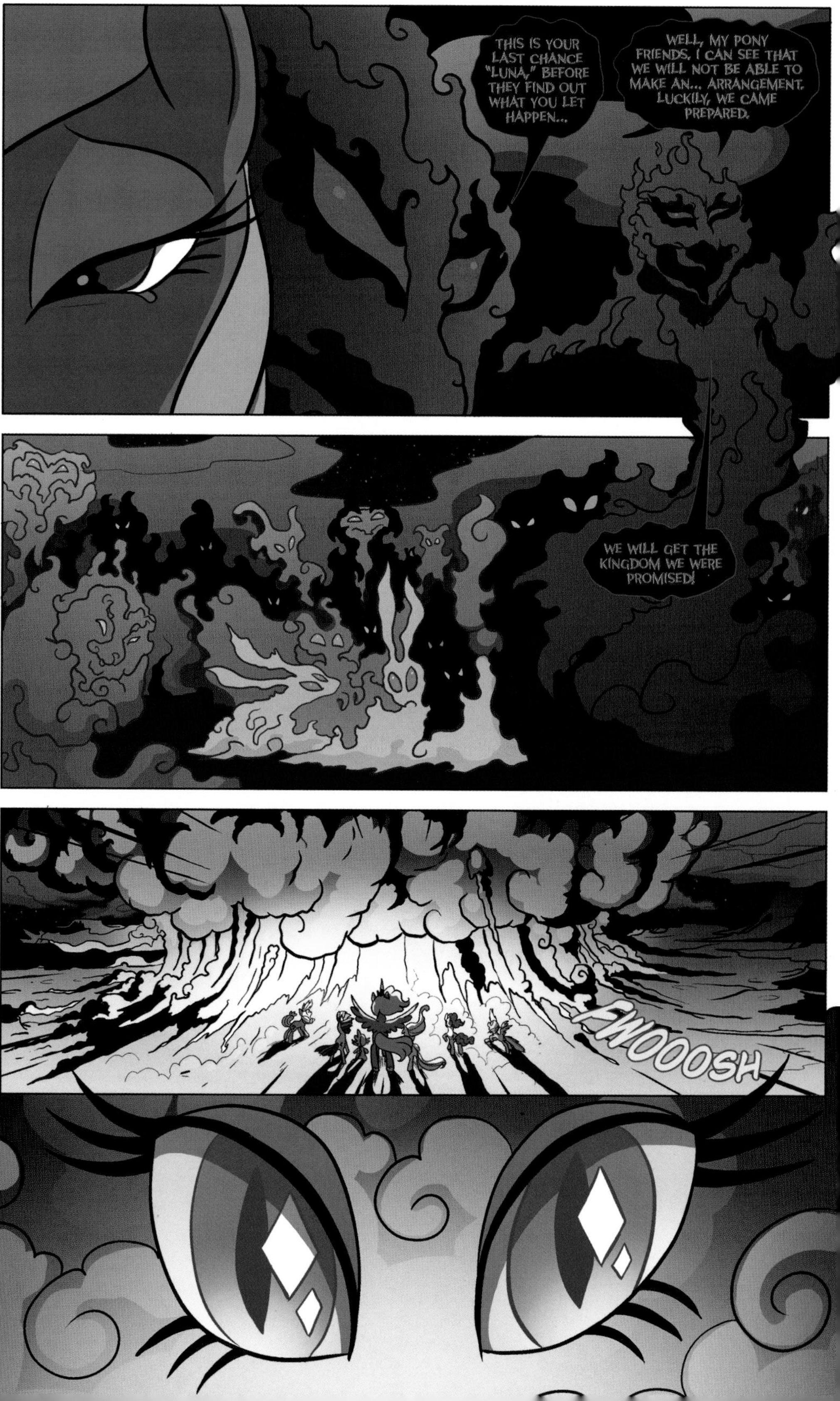
THIS IS YOUR LAST CHANCE "LUNA," BEFORE THEY FIND OUT WHAT YOU LET HAPPEN...
WELL, MY PONY FRIENDS, I CAN SEE THAT WE WILL NOT BE ABLE TO MAKE AN... ARRANGEMENT. LUCKILY, WE CAME PREPARED.
WE WILL GET THE KINGDOM WE WERE PROMISED!
FWOOOSH

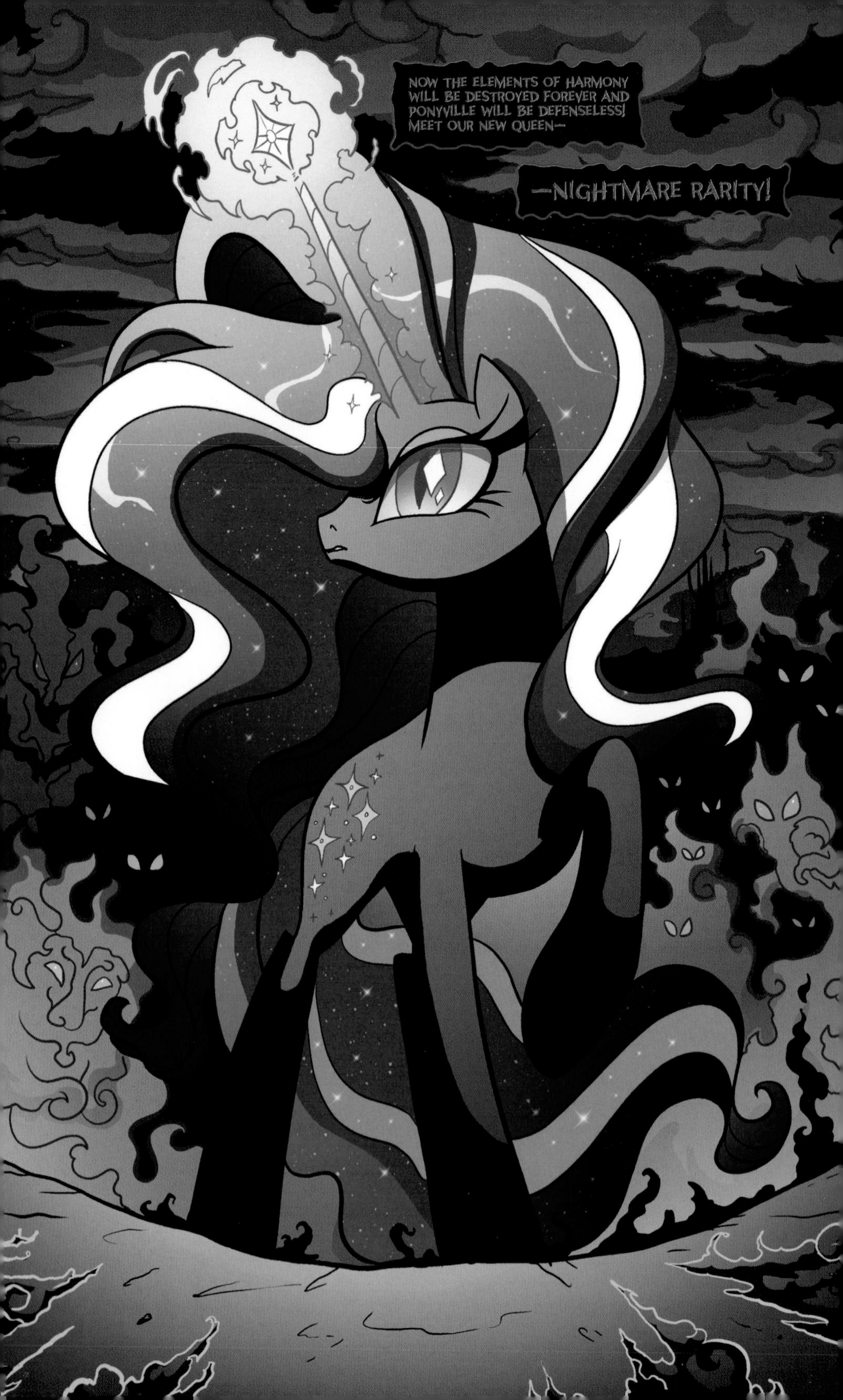
NOW THE ELEMENTS OF HARMONY WILL BE DESTROYED FOREVER AND PONYVILLE WILL BE DEFENSELESS! MEET OUR NEW QUEEN—
—NIGHTMARE RARITY!

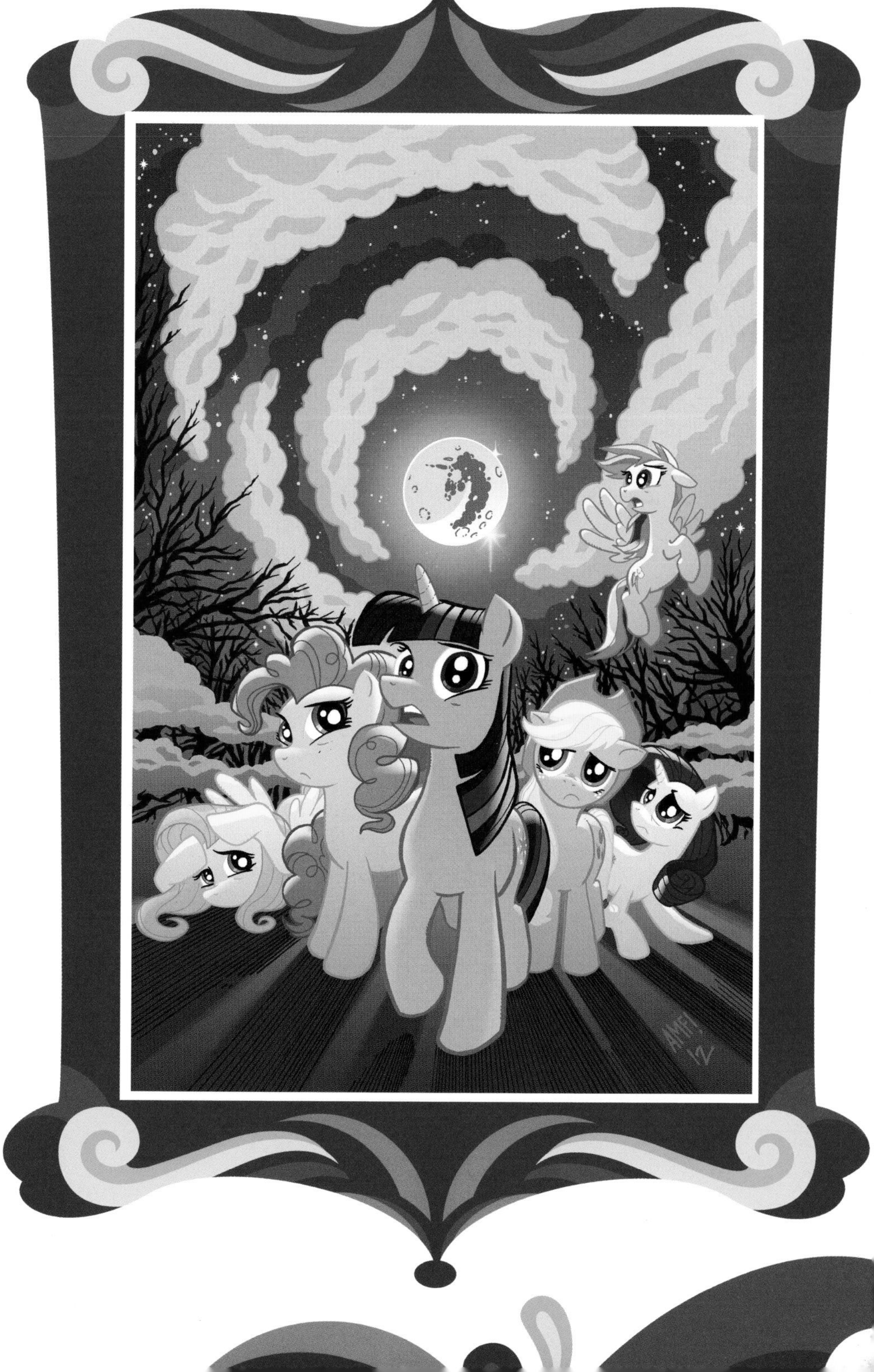

Art by
Tony Fleecs

Art by
Amy Mebberson

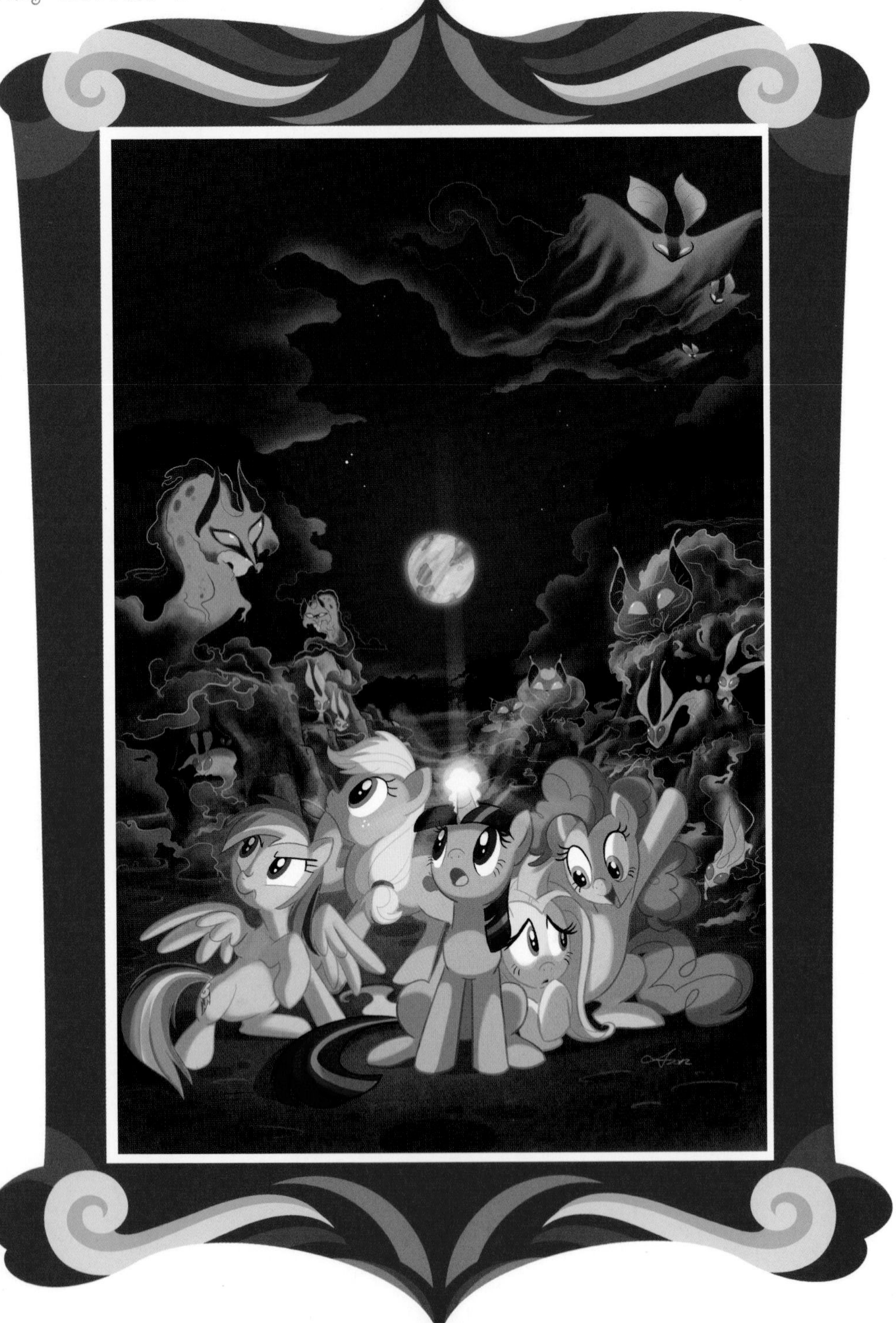

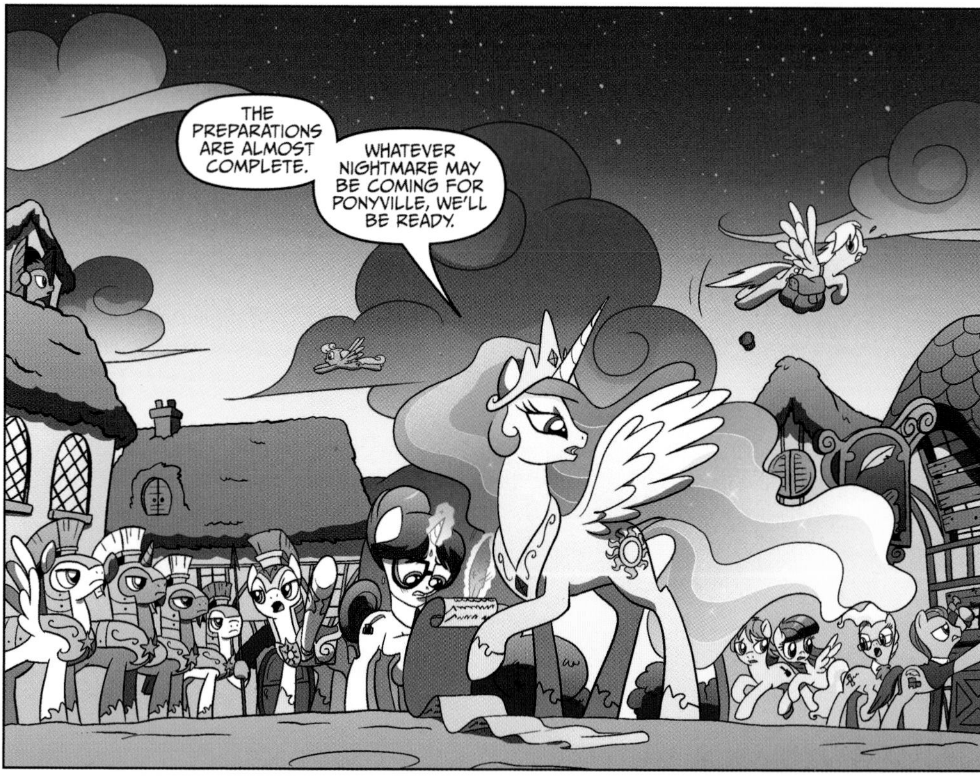
THE PREPARATIONS ARE ALMOST COMPLETE.
WHATEVER NIGHTMARE MAY BE COMING FOR PONYVILLE, WE'LL BE READY.

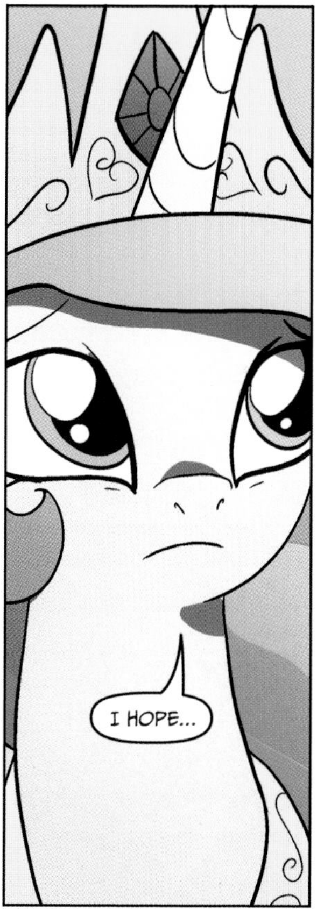
I HOPE...

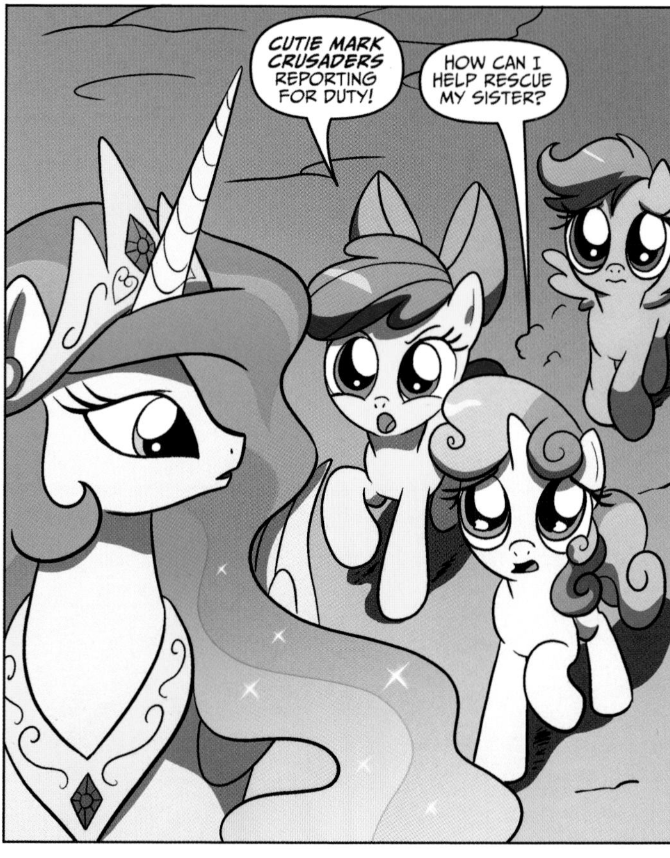
CUTIE MARK CRUSADERS REPORTING FOR DUTY!
HOW CAN I HELP RESCUE MY SISTER?

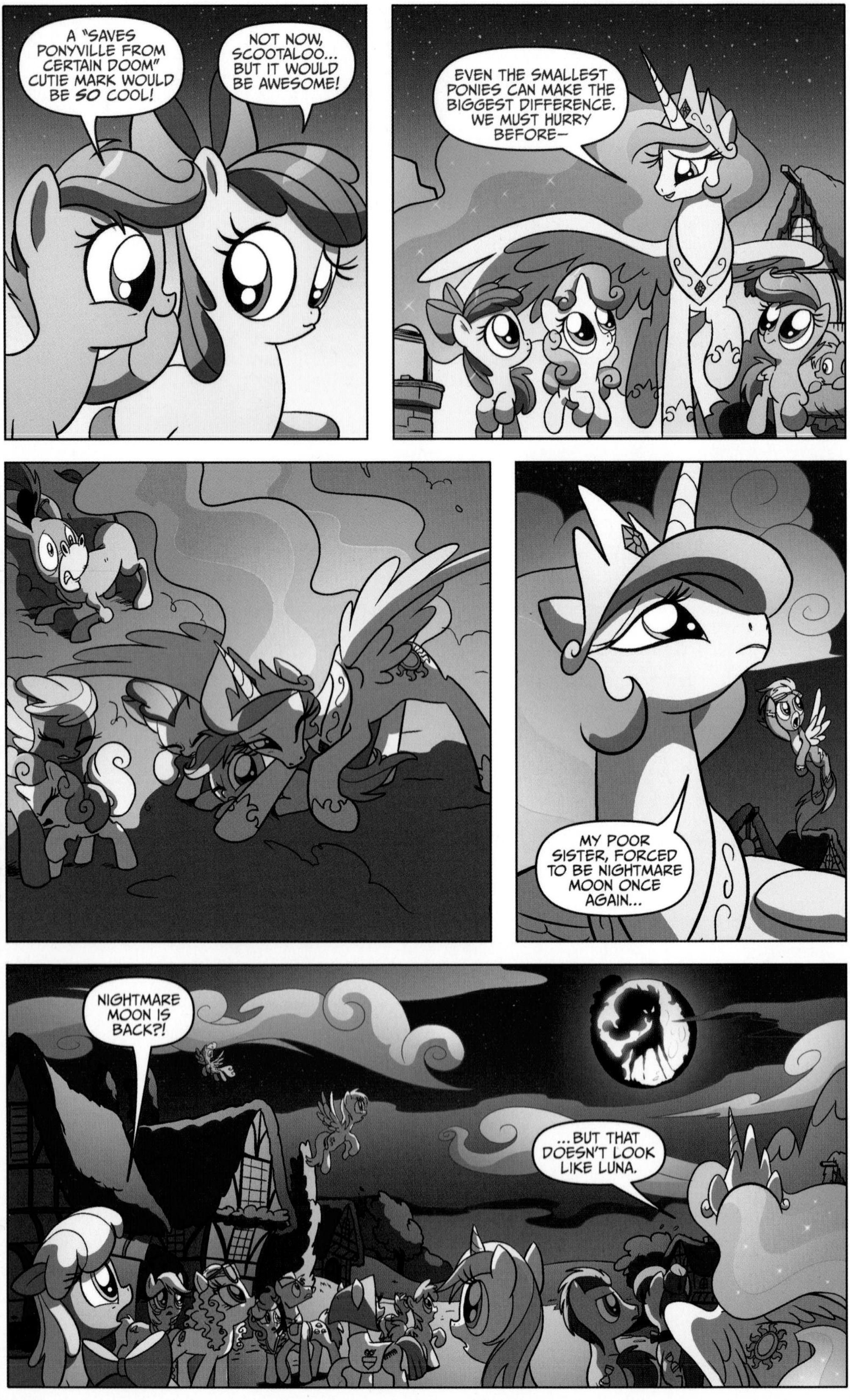
A "SAVES PONYVILLE FROM CERTAIN DOOM" CUTIE MARK WOULD BE SO COOL!
NOT NOW, SCOOTALOO... BUT IT WOULD BE AWESOME!
EVEN THE SMALLEST PONIES CAN MAKE THE BIGGEST DIFFERENCE. WE MUST HURRY BEFORE—
MY POOR SISTER, FORCED TO BE NIGHTMARE MOON ONCE AGAIN...
NIGHTMARE MOON IS BACK?!
...BUT THAT DOESN'T LOOK LIKE LUNA.

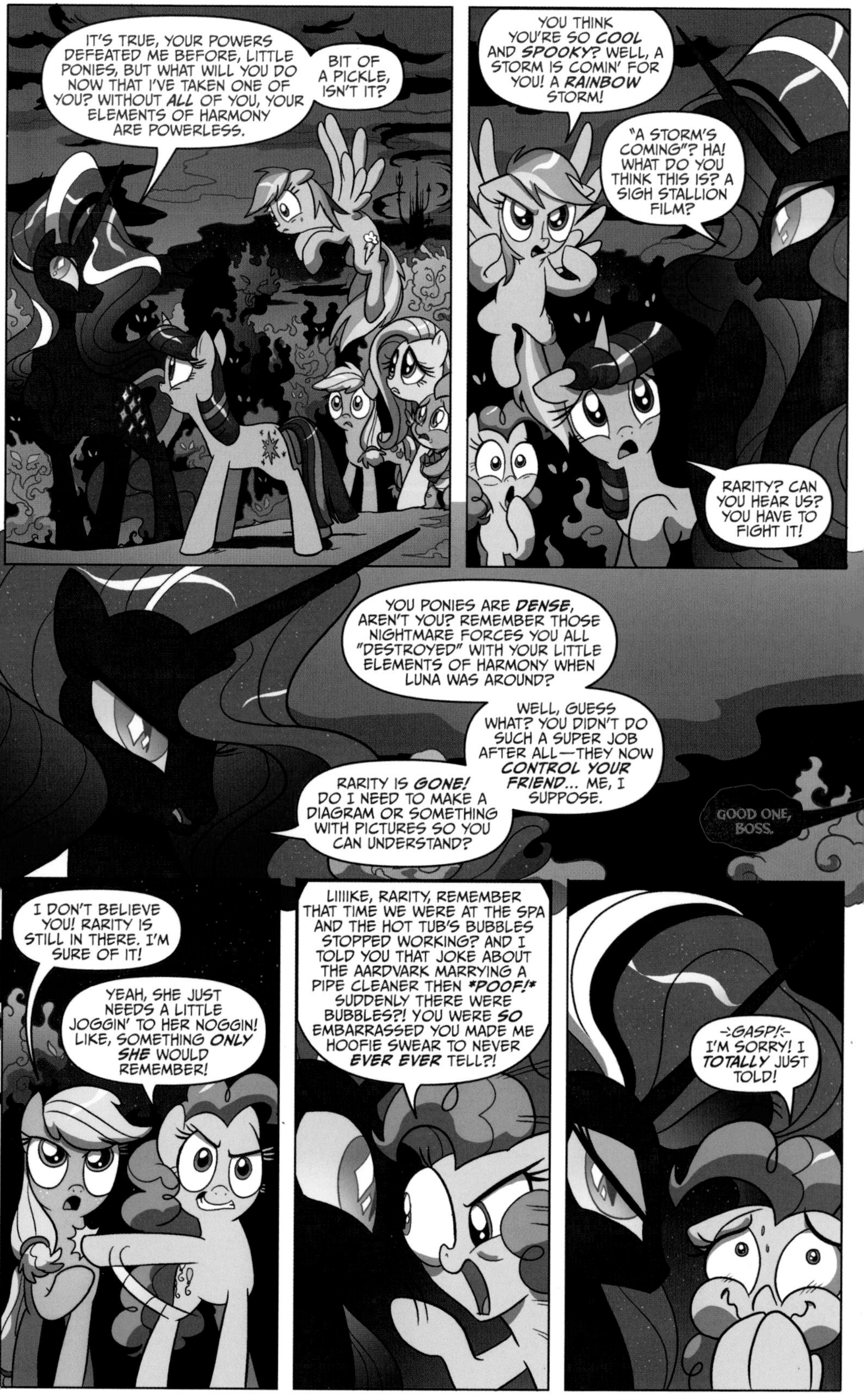

IT'S TRUE, YOUR POWERS DEFEATED ME BEFORE, LITTLE PONIES, BUT WHAT WILL YOU DO NOW THAT I'VE TAKEN ONE OF YOU? WITHOUT *ALL* OF YOU, YOUR ELEMENTS OF HARMONY ARE POWERLESS.
BIT OF A PICKLE, ISN'T IT?
YOU THINK YOU'RE SO *COOL* AND *SPOOKY*? WELL, A STORM IS COMIN' FOR YOU! A *RAINBOW* STORM!
"A STORM'S COMING"? HA! WHAT DO YOU THINK THIS IS? A SIGH STALLION FILM?
RARITY? CAN YOU HEAR US? YOU HAVE TO FIGHT IT!
YOU PONIES ARE *DENSE*, AREN'T YOU? REMEMBER THOSE NIGHTMARE FORCES YOU ALL "DESTROYED" WITH YOUR LITTLE ELEMENTS OF HARMONY WHEN LUNA WAS AROUND?
WELL, GUESS WHAT? YOU DIDN'T DO SUCH A SUPER JOB AFTER ALL—THEY NOW ***CONTROL YOUR FRIEND***... ME, I SUPPOSE.
RARITY IS *GONE!* DO I NEED TO MAKE A DIAGRAM OR SOMETHING WITH PICTURES SO YOU CAN UNDERSTAND?
GOOD ONE, BOSS.
I DON'T BELIEVE YOU! RARITY IS STILL IN THERE. I'M SURE OF IT!
YEAH, SHE JUST NEEDS A LITTLE JOGGIN' TO HER NOGGIN! LIKE, SOMETHING *ONLY SHE* WOULD REMEMBER!
LIIIIKE, RARITY, REMEMBER THAT TIME WE WERE AT THE SPA AND THE HOT TUB'S BUBBLES STOPPED WORKING? AND I TOLD YOU THAT JOKE ABOUT THE AARDVARK MARRYING A PIPE CLEANER THEN **POOF!** SUDDENLY THERE WERE BUBBLES?! YOU WERE *SO* EMBARRASSED YOU MADE ME HOOFIE SWEAR TO NEVER *EVER EVER* TELL?!
-GASP!- I'M SORRY! I *TOTALLY* JUST TOLD!

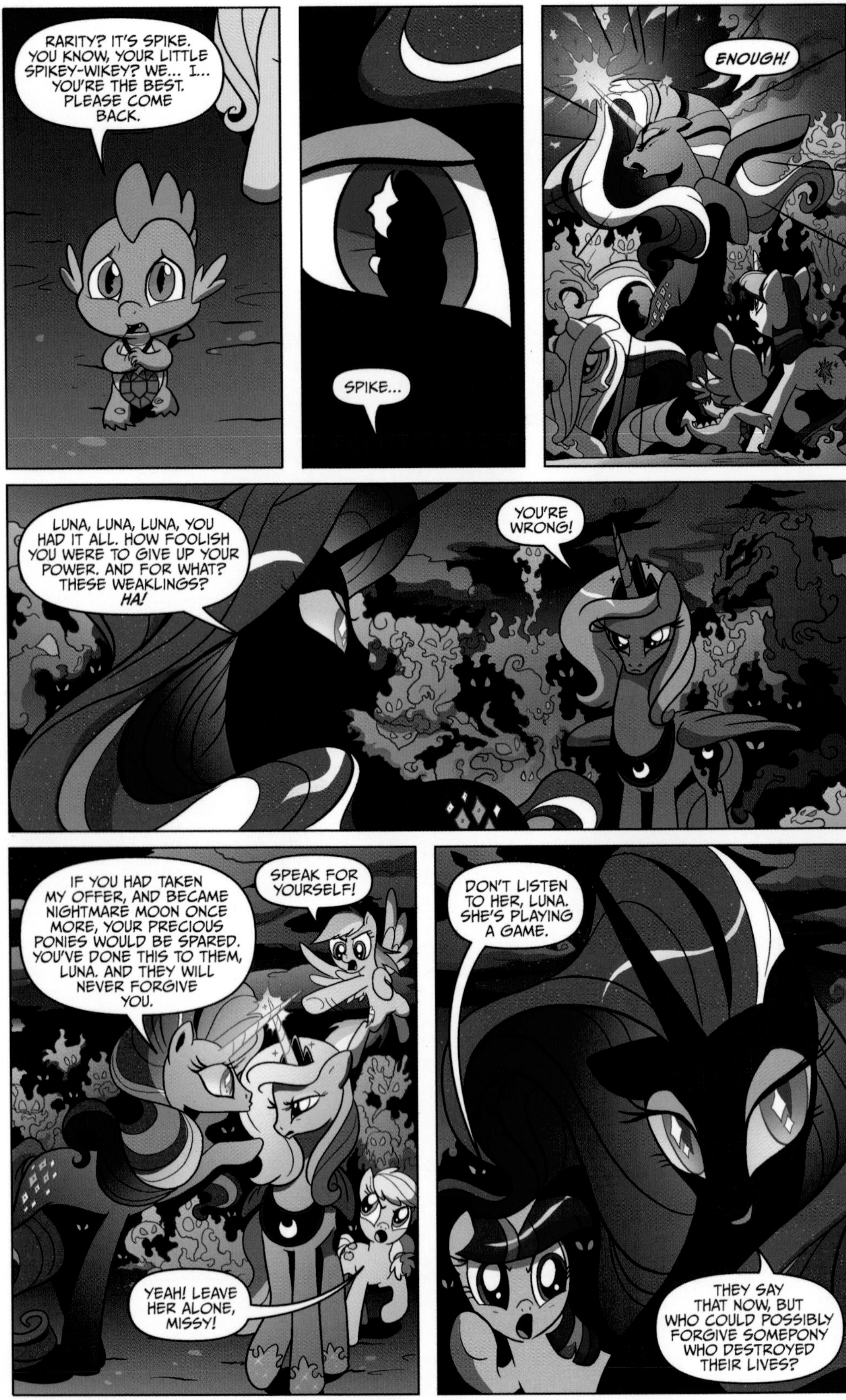
RARITY? IT'S SPIKE. YOU KNOW, YOUR LITTLE SPIKEY-WIKEY? WE... I... YOU'RE THE BEST. PLEASE COME BACK.
SPIKE...
ENOUGH!
LUNA, LUNA, LUNA, YOU HAD IT ALL. HOW FOOLISH YOU WERE TO GIVE UP YOUR POWER. AND FOR WHAT? THESE WEAKLINGS? HA!
YOU'RE WRONG!
IF YOU HAD TAKEN MY OFFER, AND BECAME NIGHTMARE MOON ONCE MORE, YOUR PRECIOUS PONIES WOULD BE SPARED. YOU'VE DONE THIS TO THEM, LUNA. AND THEY WILL NEVER FORGIVE YOU.
SPEAK FOR YOURSELF!
YEAH! LEAVE HER ALONE, MISSY!
DON'T LISTEN TO HER, LUNA. SHE'S PLAYING A GAME.
THEY SAY THAT NOW, BUT WHO COULD POSSIBLY FORGIVE SOMEPONY WHO DESTROYED THEIR LIVES?

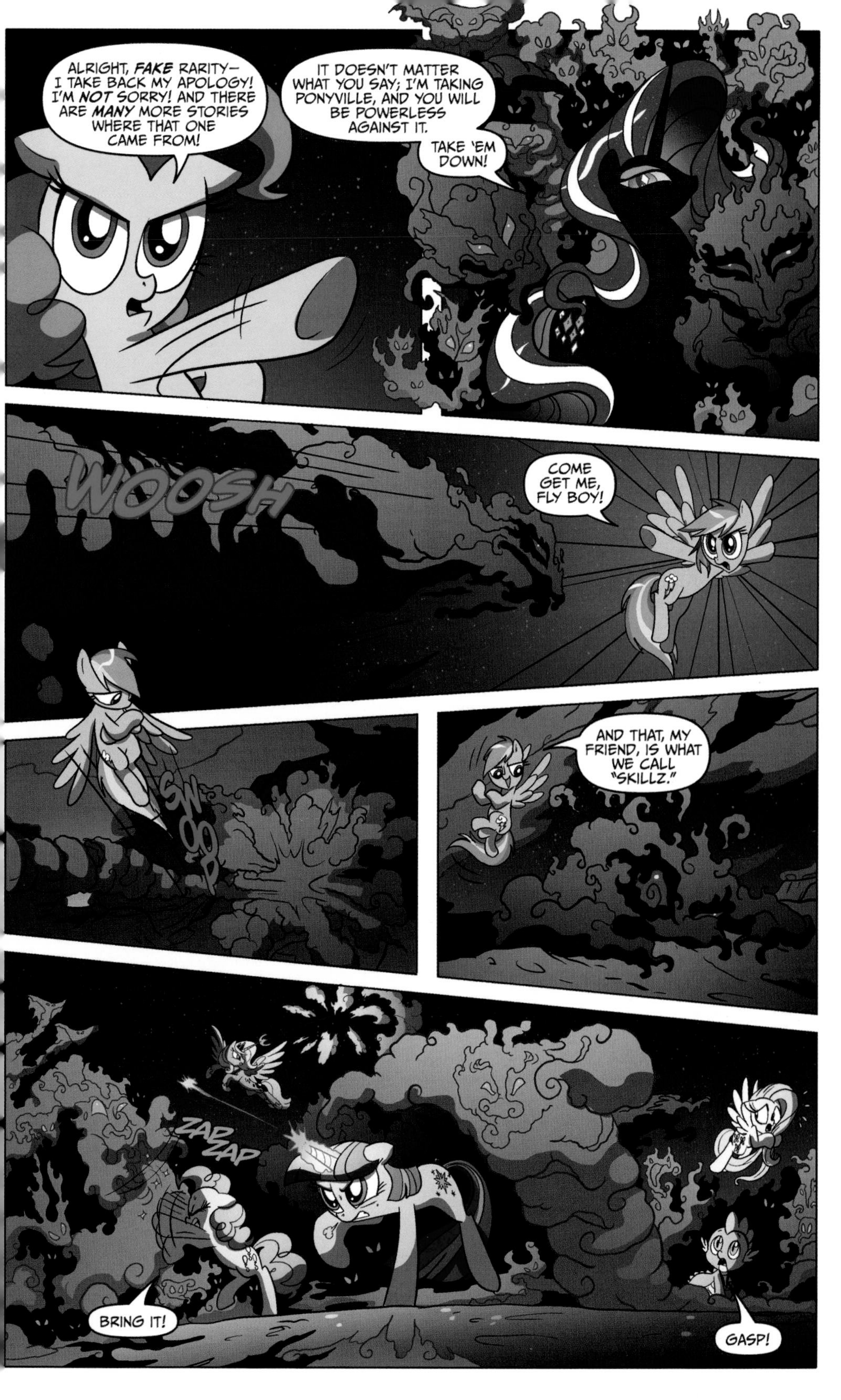
ALRIGHT, FAKE RARITY— I TAKE BACK MY APOLOGY! I'M NOT SORRY! AND THERE ARE MANY MORE STORIES WHERE THAT ONE CAME FROM!
IT DOESN'T MATTER WHAT YOU SAY; I'M TAKING PONYVILLE, AND YOU WILL BE POWERLESS AGAINST IT.
TAKE 'EM DOWN!
WOOSH
COME GET ME, FLY BOY!
SWOOP
AND THAT, MY FRIEND, IS WHAT WE CALL "SKILLZ."
ZAP ZAP
BRING IT!
GASP!

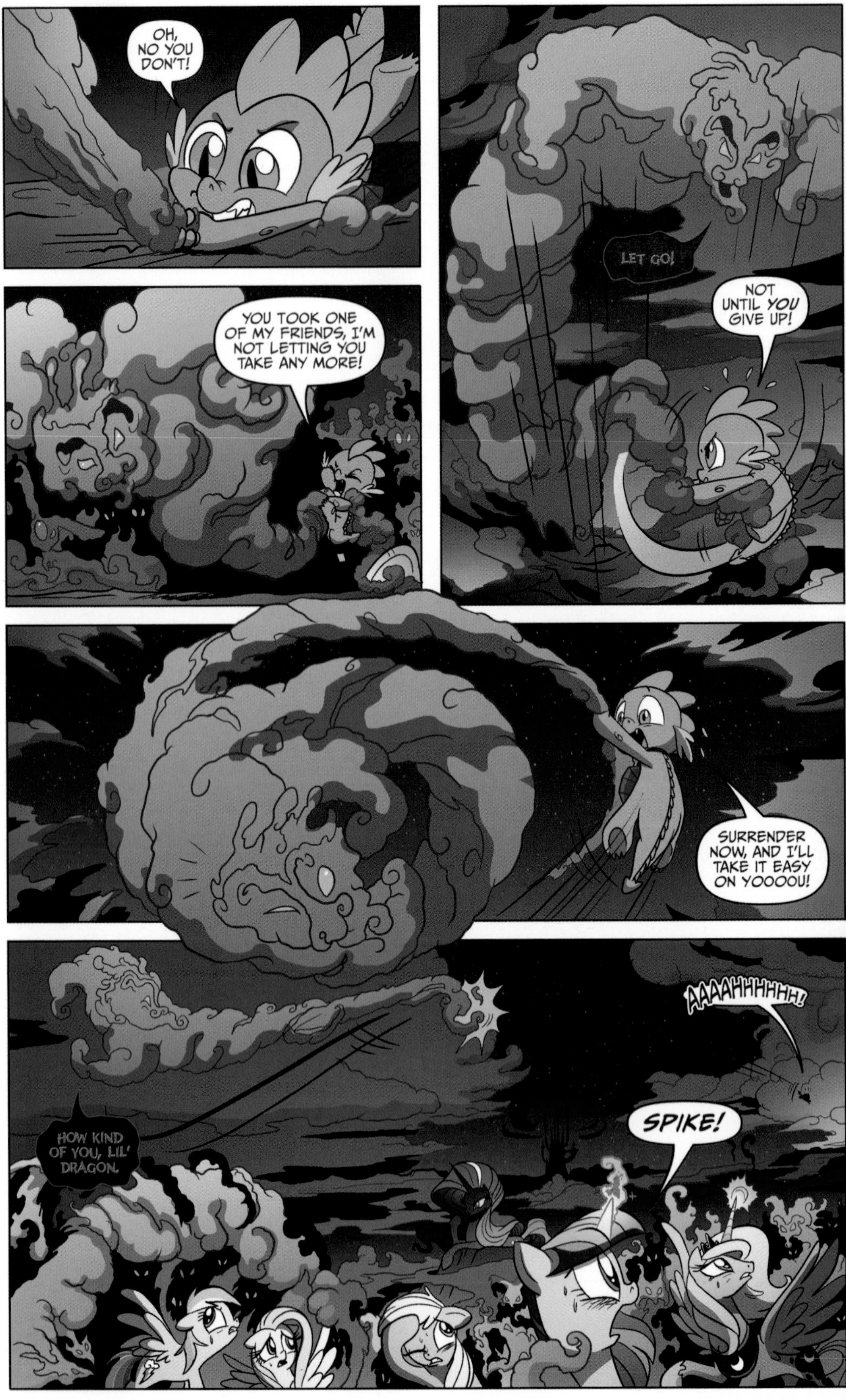
OH, NO YOU DON'T!
YOU TOOK ONE OF MY FRIENDS, I'M NOT LETTING YOU TAKE ANY MORE!
LET GO!
NOT UNTIL YOU GIVE UP!
SURRENDER NOW, AND I'LL TAKE IT EASY ON YOOOOU!
AAAAHHHHHH!
HOW KIND OF YOU, LIL' DRAGON.
SPIKE!

THAT'S IT!

TAKE THAT, YOU MEAN BEAN!

ZAP

OUCH!

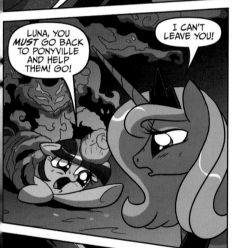

LUNA, YOU *MUST* GO BACK TO PONYVILLE AND HELP THEM! GO!

I CAN'T LEAVE YOU!

RUN, NOW! OR PONYVILLE WON'T STAND A CHANCE!

YER THEIR ONLY HOPE!

BESIDES, WE CAN TAKE CARE OF THESE VARMINTS!

I'LL SAVE YOUR FRIENDS! I SWEAR TO YOU!

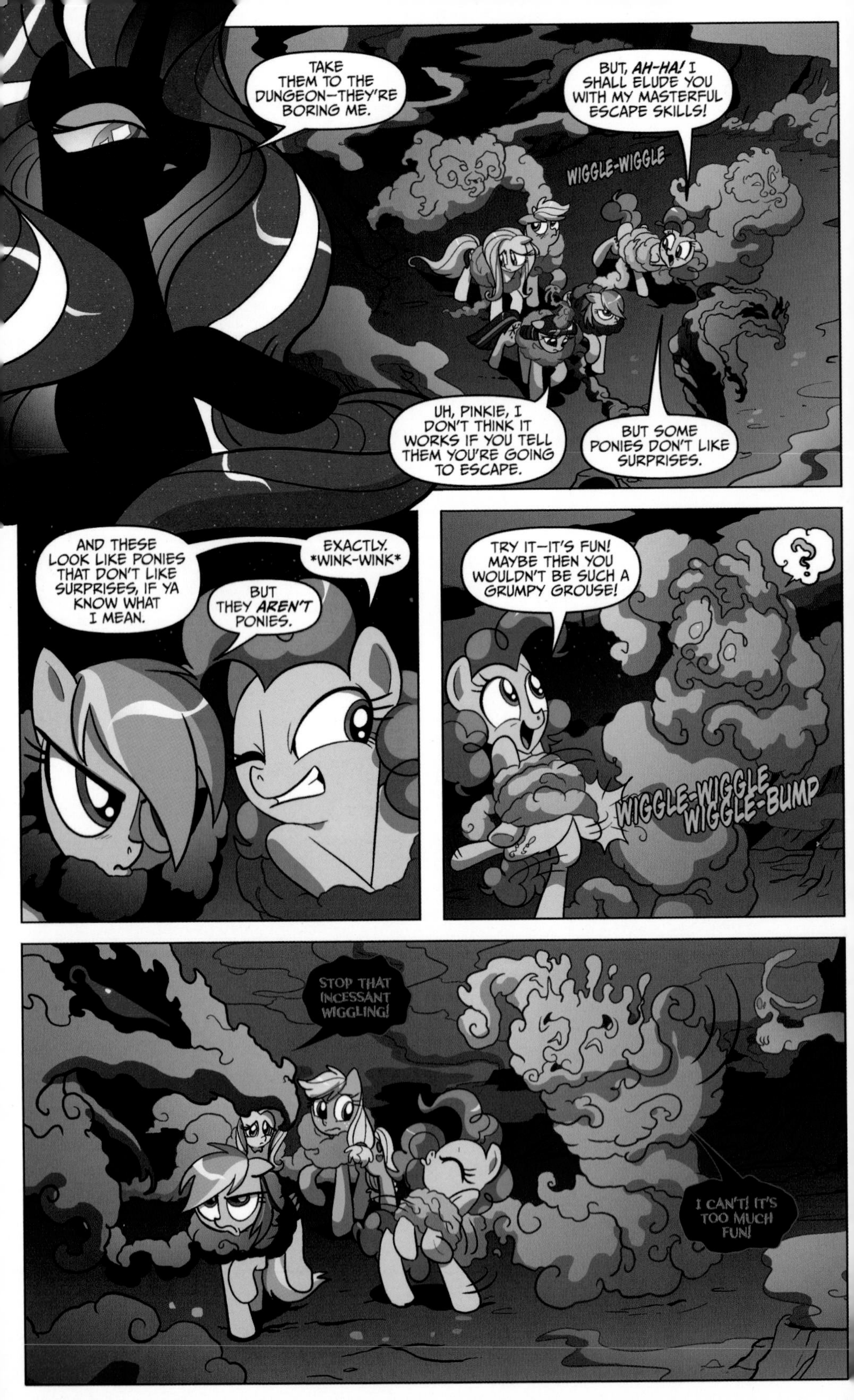
TAKE THEM TO THE DUNGEON—THEY'RE BORING ME.
BUT, AH-HA! I SHALL ELUDE YOU WITH MY MASTERFUL ESCAPE SKILLS!
WIGGLE-WIGGLE
UH, PINKIE, I DON'T THINK IT WORKS IF YOU TELL THEM YOU'RE GOING TO ESCAPE.
BUT SOME PONIES DON'T LIKE SURPRISES.
AND THESE LOOK LIKE PONIES THAT DON'T LIKE SURPRISES, IF YA KNOW WHAT I MEAN.
BUT THEY AREN'T PONIES.
EXACTLY. *WINK-WINK*
TRY IT—IT'S FUN! MAYBE THEN YOU WOULDN'T BE SUCH A GRUMPY GROUSE!
?
WIGGLE-WIGGLE WIGGLE-BUMP
STOP THAT INCESSANT WIGGLING!
I CAN'T! IT'S TOO MUCH FUN!

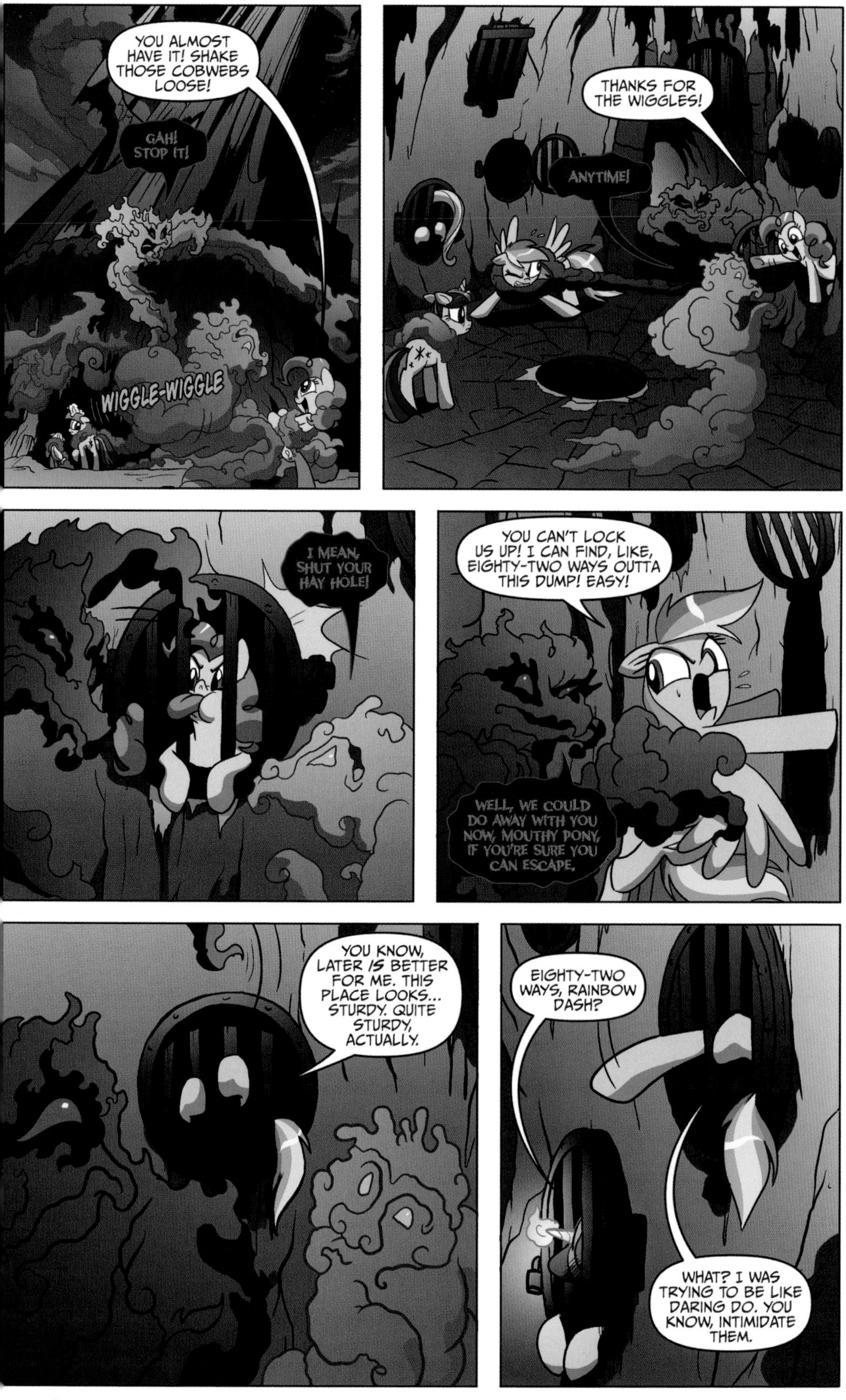
YOU ALMOST HAVE IT! SHAKE THOSE COBWEBS LOOSE!
GAH! STOP IT!
WIGGLE-WIGGLE
THANKS FOR THE WIGGLES!
ANYTIME!
I MEAN, SHUT YOUR HAY HOLE!
YOU CAN'T LOCK US UP! I CAN FIND, LIKE, EIGHTY-TWO WAYS OUTTA THIS DUMP! EASY!
WELL, WE COULD DO AWAY WITH YOU NOW, MOUTHY PONY, IF YOU'RE SURE YOU CAN ESCAPE.
YOU KNOW, LATER IS BETTER FOR ME. THIS PLACE LOOKS... STURDY. QUITE STURDY, ACTUALLY.
EIGHTY-TWO WAYS, RAINBOW DASH?
WHAT? I WAS TRYING TO BE LIKE DARING DO. YOU KNOW, INTIMIDATE THEM.

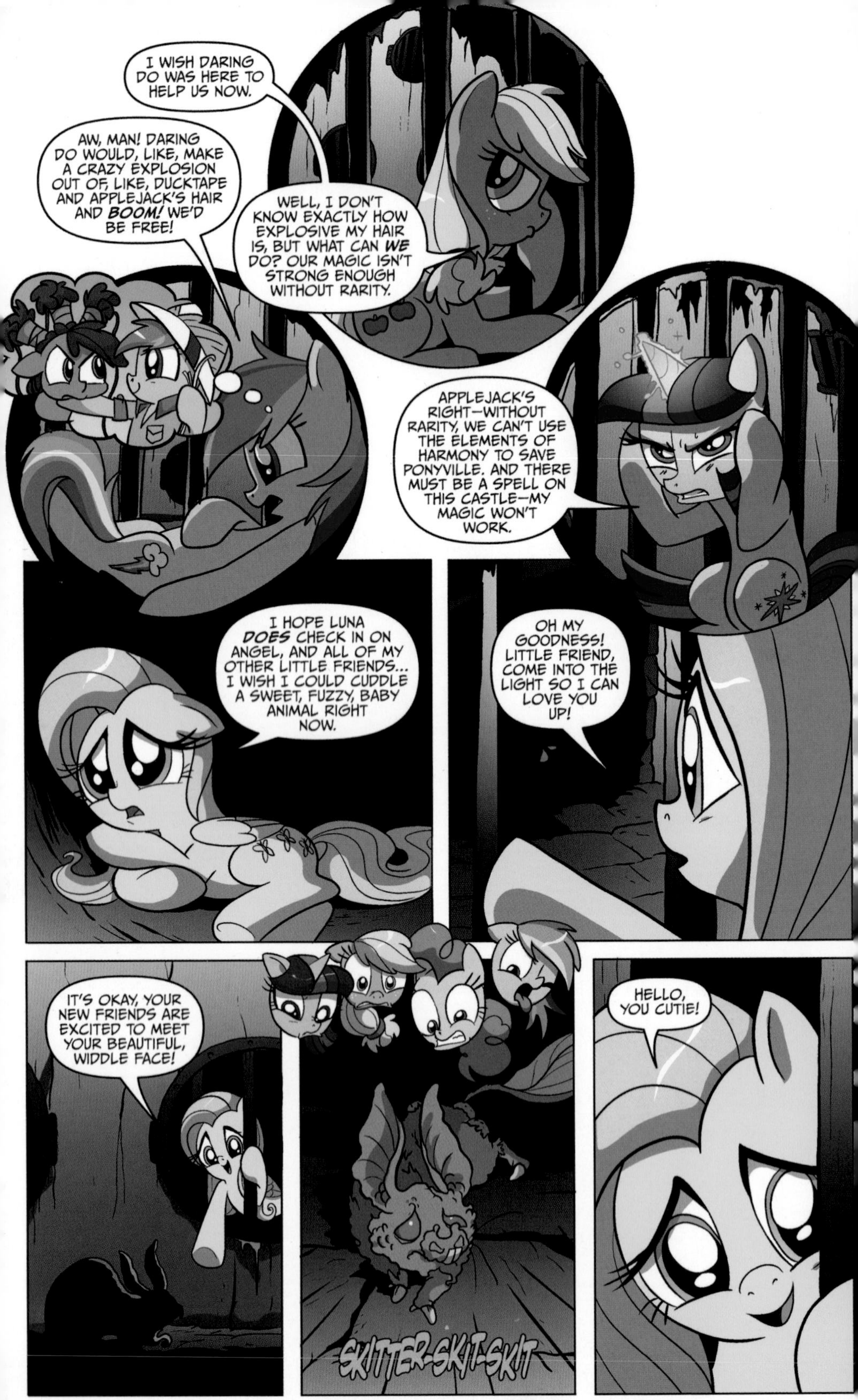
I WISH DARING DO WAS HERE TO HELP US NOW.
AW, MAN! DARING DO WOULD, LIKE, MAKE A CRAZY EXPLOSION OUT OF, LIKE, DUCKTAPE AND APPLEJACK'S HAIR AND BOOM! WE'D BE FREE!
WELL, I DON'T KNOW EXACTLY HOW EXPLOSIVE MY HAIR IS, BUT WHAT CAN WE DO? OUR MAGIC ISN'T STRONG ENOUGH WITHOUT RARITY.
APPLEJACK'S RIGHT—WITHOUT RARITY, WE CAN'T USE THE ELEMENTS OF HARMONY TO SAVE PONYVILLE. AND THERE MUST BE A SPELL ON THIS CASTLE—MY MAGIC WON'T WORK.
I HOPE LUNA DOES CHECK IN ON ANGEL, AND ALL OF MY OTHER LITTLE FRIENDS... I WISH I COULD CUDDLE A SWEET, FUZZY, BABY ANIMAL RIGHT NOW.
OH MY GOODNESS! LITTLE FRIEND, COME INTO THE LIGHT SO I CAN LOVE YOU UP!
IT'S OKAY, YOUR NEW FRIENDS ARE EXCITED TO MEET YOUR BEAUTIFUL, WIDDLE FACE!
SKITTER-SKIT-SKIT
HELLO, YOU CUTIE!

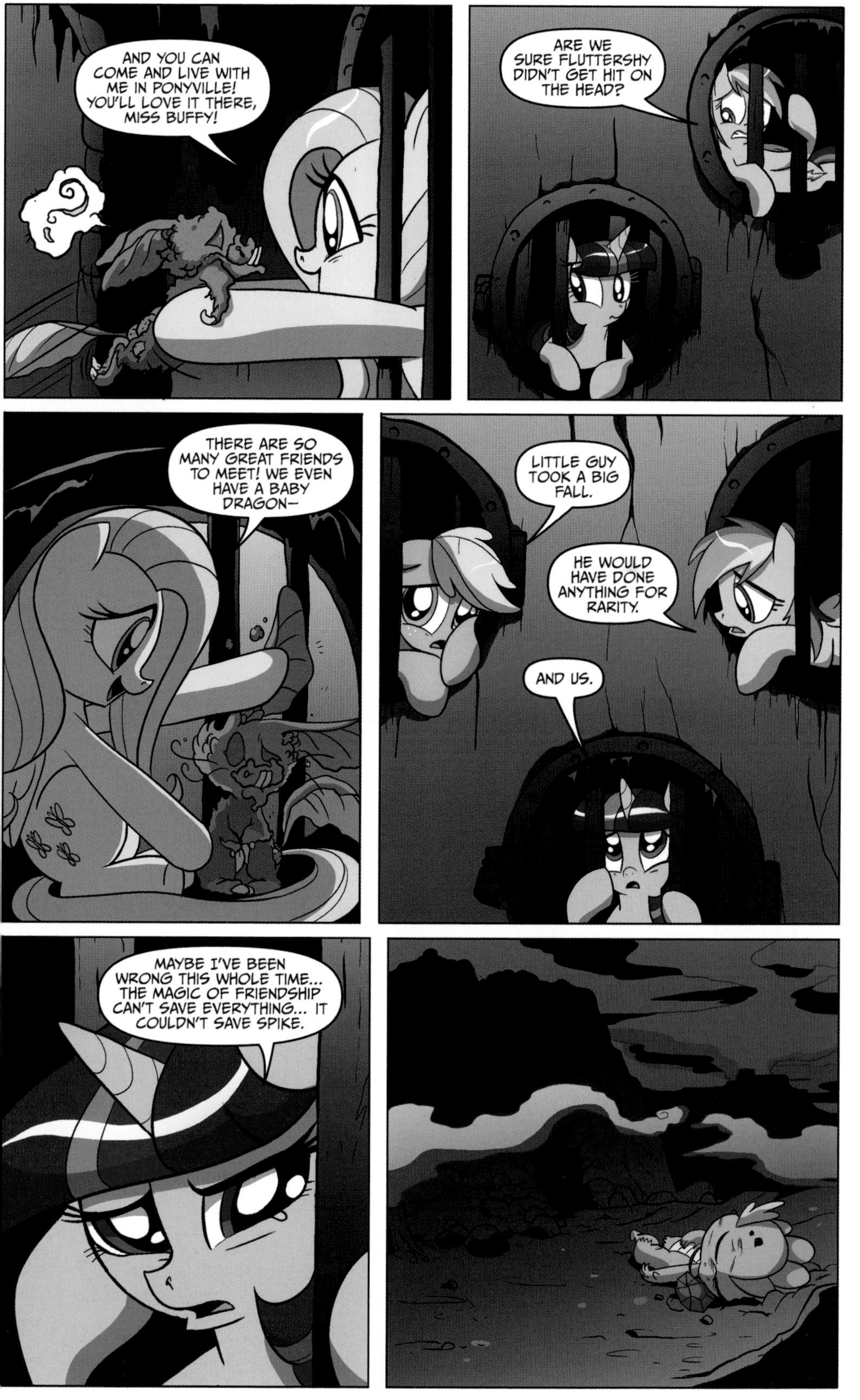
AND YOU CAN COME AND LIVE WITH ME IN PONYVILLE! YOU'LL LOVE IT THERE, MISS BUFFY!
ARE WE SURE FLUTTERSHY DIDN'T GET HIT ON THE HEAD?
THERE ARE SO MANY GREAT FRIENDS TO MEET! WE EVEN HAVE A BABY DRAGON—
LITTLE GUY TOOK A BIG FALL.
HE WOULD HAVE DONE ANYTHING FOR RARITY.
AND US.
MAYBE I'VE BEEN WRONG THIS WHOLE TIME... THE MAGIC OF FRIENDSHIP CAN'T SAVE EVERYTHING... IT COULDN'T SAVE SPIKE.

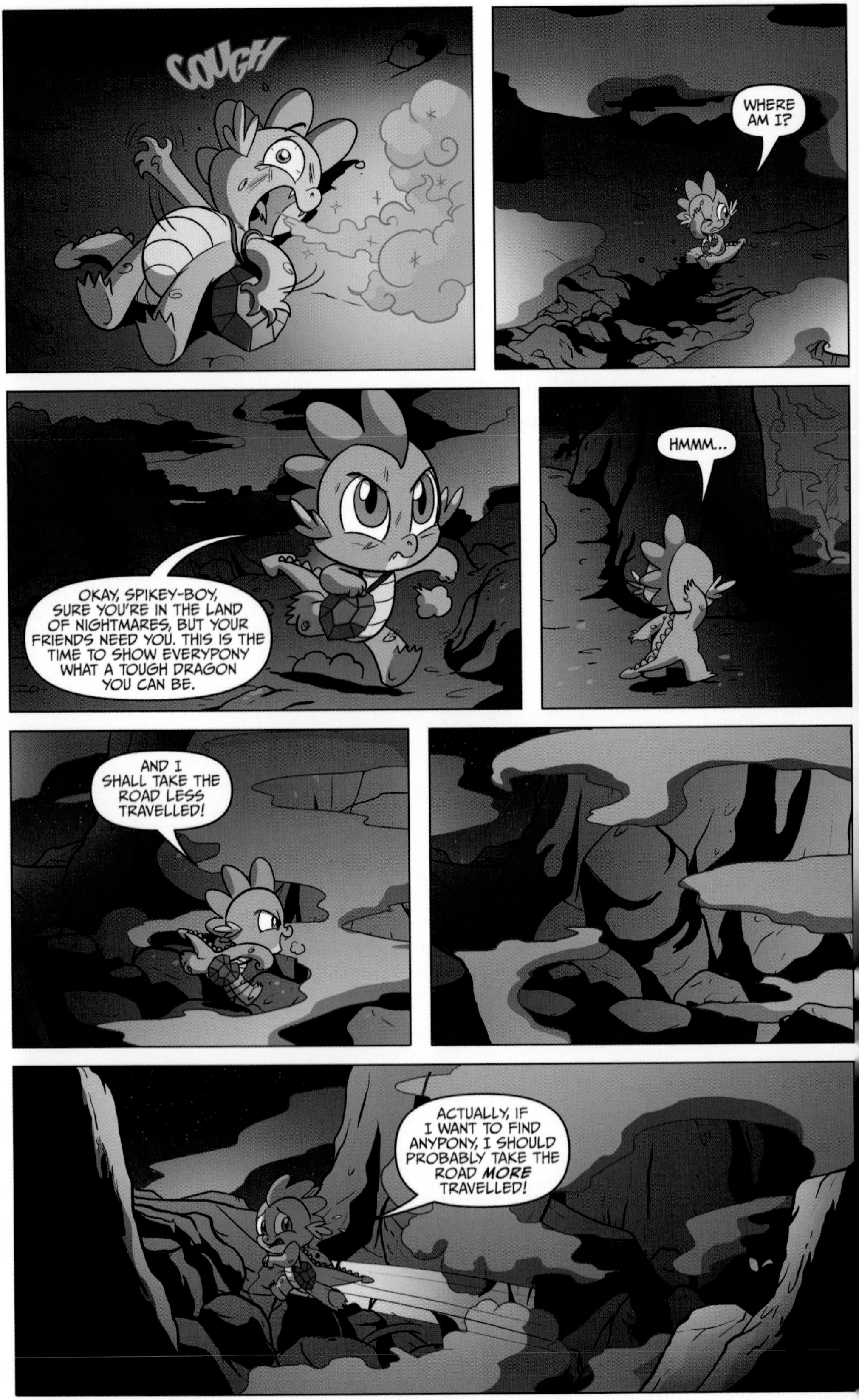
COUGH
WHERE AM I?
OKAY, SPIKEY-BOY, SURE YOU'RE IN THE LAND OF NIGHTMARES, BUT YOUR FRIENDS NEED YOU. THIS IS THE TIME TO SHOW EVERYPONY WHAT A TOUGH DRAGON YOU CAN BE.
HMMM...
AND I SHALL TAKE THE ROAD LESS TRAVELLED!
ACTUALLY, IF I WANT TO FIND ANYPONY, I SHOULD PROBABLY TAKE THE ROAD MORE TRAVELLED!

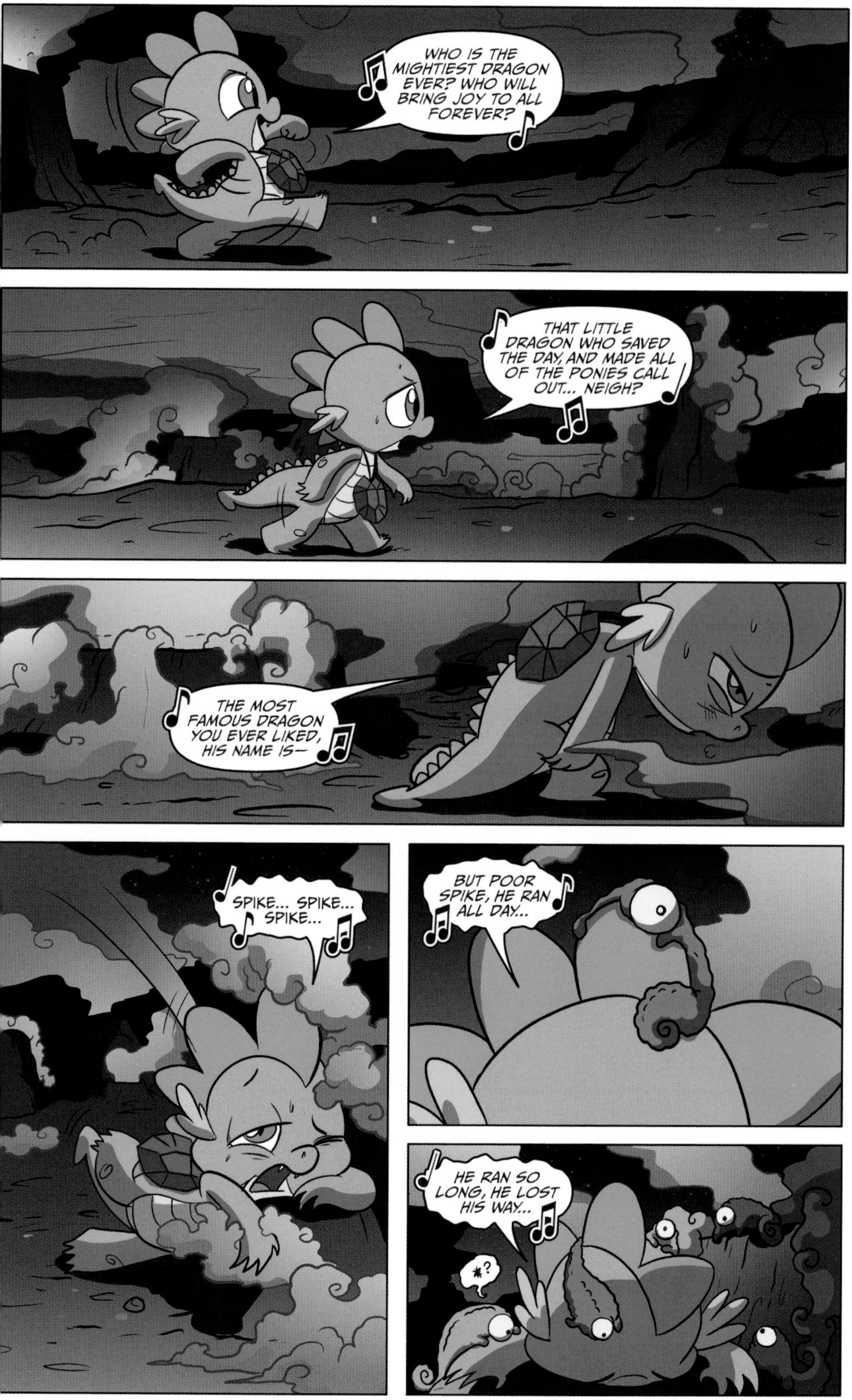
WHO IS THE MIGHTIEST DRAGON EVER? WHO WILL BRING JOY TO ALL FOREVER?
THAT LITTLE DRAGON WHO SAVED THE DAY, AND MADE ALL OF THE PONIES CALL OUT... NEIGH?
THE MOST FAMOUS DRAGON YOU EVER LIKED, HIS NAME IS—
SPIKE... SPIKE... SPIKE...
BUT POOR SPIKE, HE RAN ALL DAY...
HE RAN SO LONG, HE LOST HIS WAY...
*?

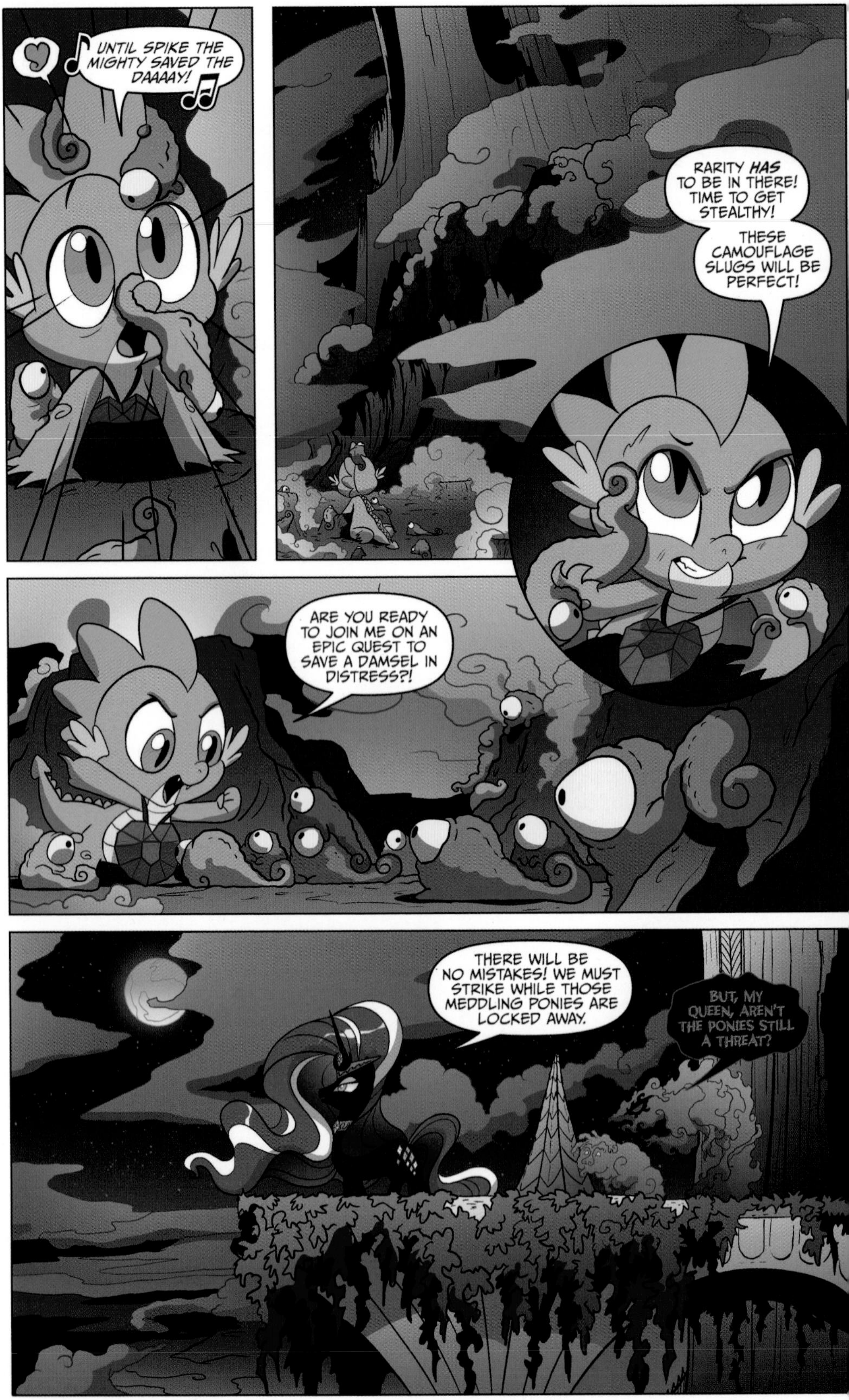
UNTIL SPIKE THE MIGHTY SAVED THE DAAAAY!
RARITY HAS TO BE IN THERE! TIME TO GET STEALTHY!
THESE CAMOUFLAGE SLUGS WILL BE PERFECT!
ARE YOU READY TO JOIN ME ON AN EPIC QUEST TO SAVE A DAMSEL IN DISTRESS?!
THERE WILL BE NO MISTAKES! WE MUST STRIKE WHILE THOSE MEDDLING PONIES ARE LOCKED AWAY.
BUT, MY QUEEN, AREN'T THE PONIES STILL A THREAT?

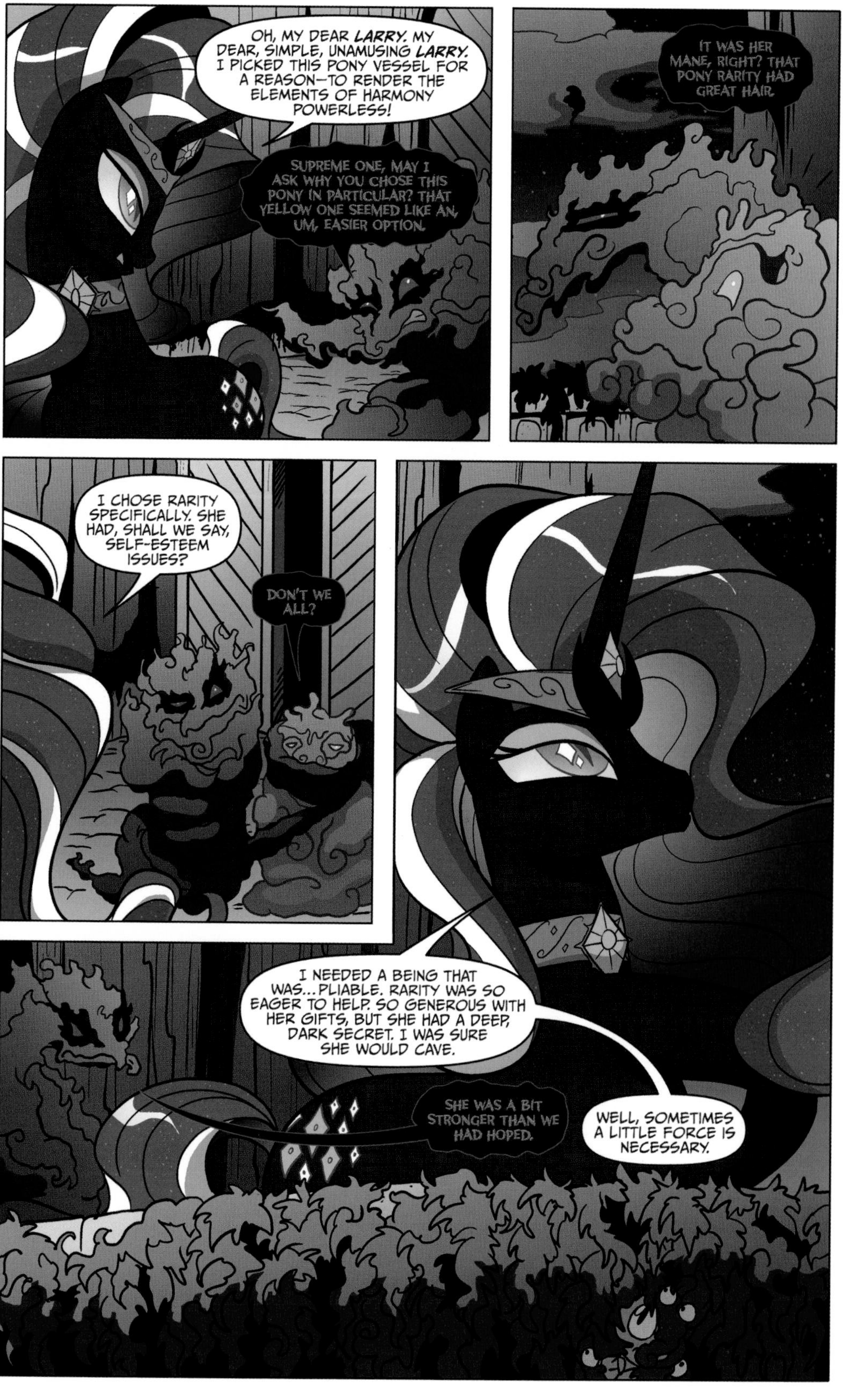

OH, MY DEAR LARRY. MY DEAR, SIMPLE, UNAMUSING LARRY. I PICKED THIS PONY VESSEL FOR A REASON—TO RENDER THE ELEMENTS OF HARMONY POWERLESS!
SUPREME ONE, MAY I ASK WHY YOU CHOSE THIS PONY IN PARTICULAR? THAT YELLOW ONE SEEMED LIKE AN, UM, EASIER OPTION.
IT WAS HER MANE, RIGHT? THAT PONY RARITY HAD GREAT HAIR.
I CHOSE RARITY SPECIFICALLY. SHE HAD, SHALL WE SAY, SELF-ESTEEM ISSUES?
DON'T WE ALL?
I NEEDED A BEING THAT WAS...PLIABLE. RARITY WAS SO EAGER TO HELP. SO GENEROUS WITH HER GIFTS, BUT SHE HAD A DEEP, DARK SECRET. I WAS SURE SHE WOULD CAVE.
SHE WAS A BIT STRONGER THAN WE HAD HOPED.
WELL, SOMETIMES A LITTLE FORCE IS NECESSARY.

AND WHAT WILL WE DO WITH THE PRISONERS ONCE WE'RE VICTORIOUS?

FOR NOW, LEAVE THEM IN THE DUNGEON...

THE DUNGEON?! AT LEAST THEY'RE HERE.

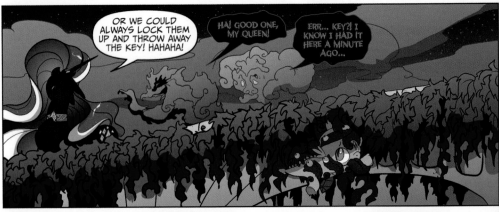

OR WE COULD ALWAYS LOCK THEM UP AND THROW AWAY THE KEY! HAHAHA!

HA! GOOD ONE, MY QUEEN!

ERR... KEY?! I KNOW I HAD IT HERE A MINUTE AGO...

I'LL SAVE THEM FIRST, THEN WE CAN RESCUE RARITY FROM THAT NASTY NO-GOODIE TOGETHER.

DUNGEON HAS TO BE DOWNWARDS, RIGHT?

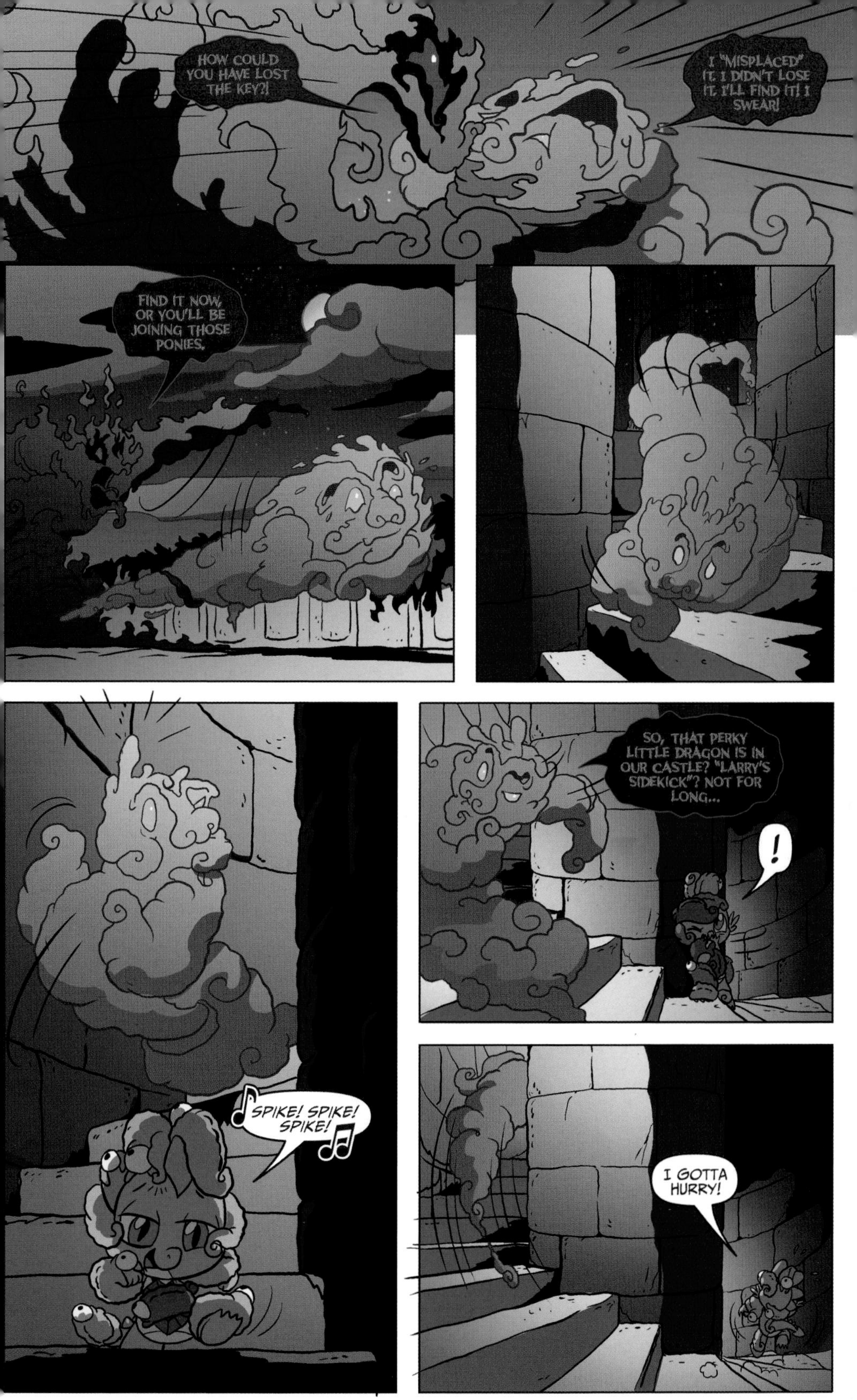

HOW COULD YOU HAVE LOST THE KEY?!
I "MISPLACED" IT. I DIDN'T LOSE IT. I'LL FIND IT! I SWEAR!
FIND IT NOW, OR YOU'LL BE JOINING THOSE PONIES.
SPIKE! SPIKE! SPIKE!
SO, THAT PERKY LITTLE DRAGON IS IN OUR CASTLE? "LARRY'S SIDEKICK"? NOT FOR LONG...
!
I GOTTA HURRY!

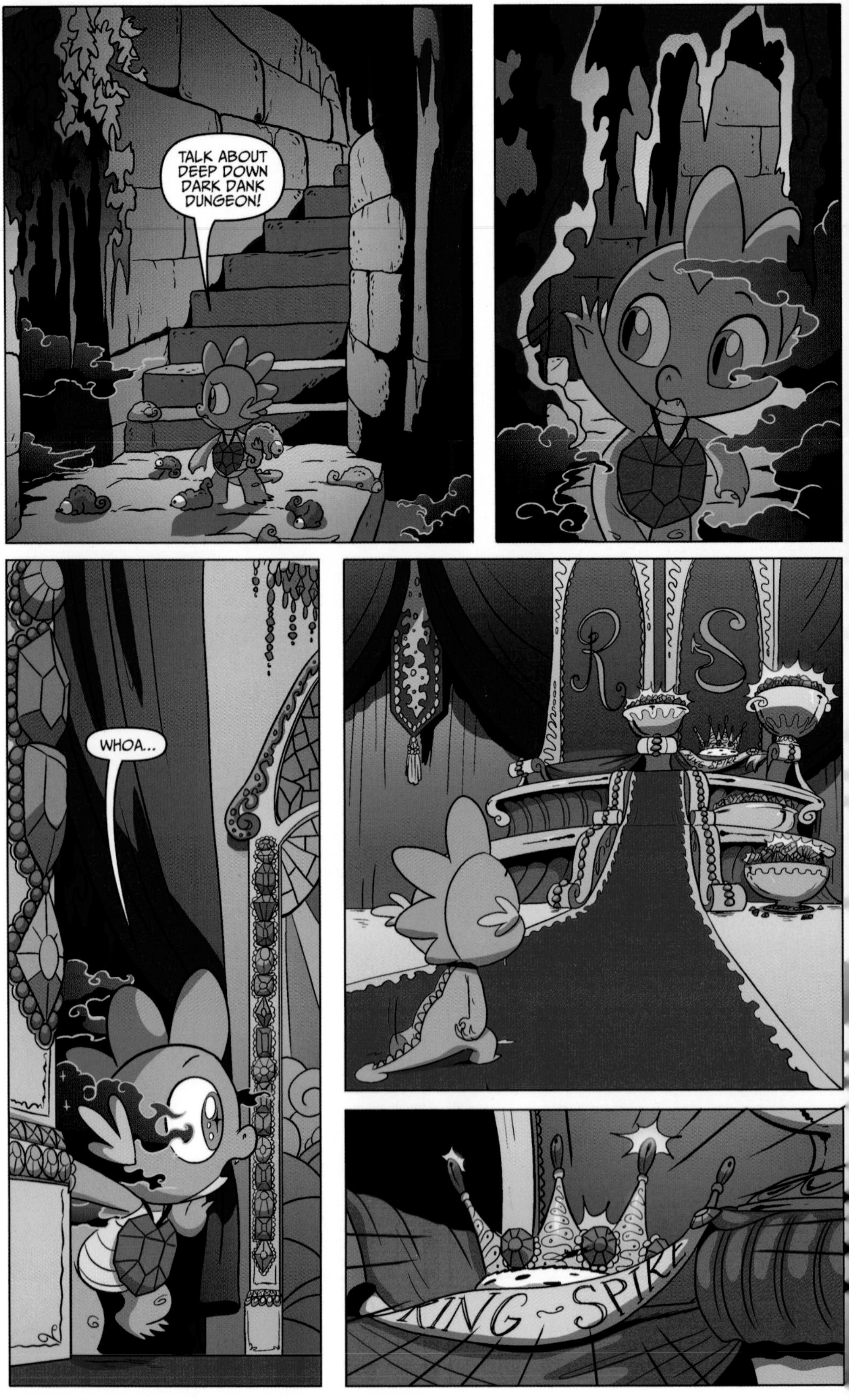
TALK ABOUT DEEP DOWN DARK DANK DUNGEON!
WHOA...
KING ~ SPIKE

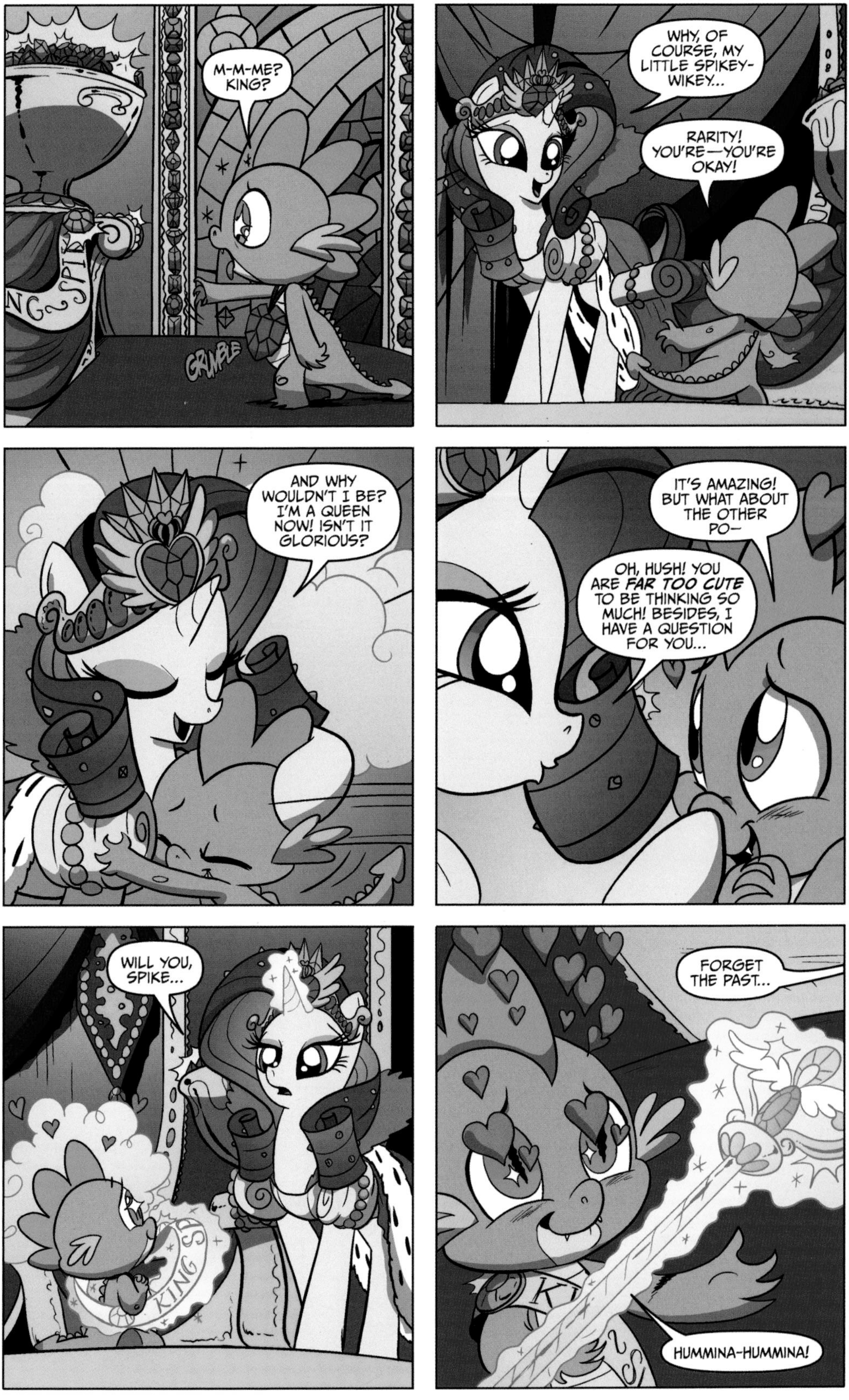
M-M-ME? KING?
KING SPI
GRUMBLE
WHY, OF COURSE, MY LITTLE SPIKEY-WIKEY...
RARITY! YOU'RE—YOU'RE OKAY!
AND WHY WOULDN'T I BE? I'M A QUEEN NOW! ISN'T IT GLORIOUS?
IT'S AMAZING! BUT WHAT ABOUT THE OTHER PO—
OH, HUSH! YOU ARE FAR TOO CUTE TO BE THINKING SO MUCH! BESIDES, I HAVE A QUESTION FOR YOU...
WILL YOU, SPIKE...
KING SP
FORGET THE PAST...
HUMMINA-HUMMINA!

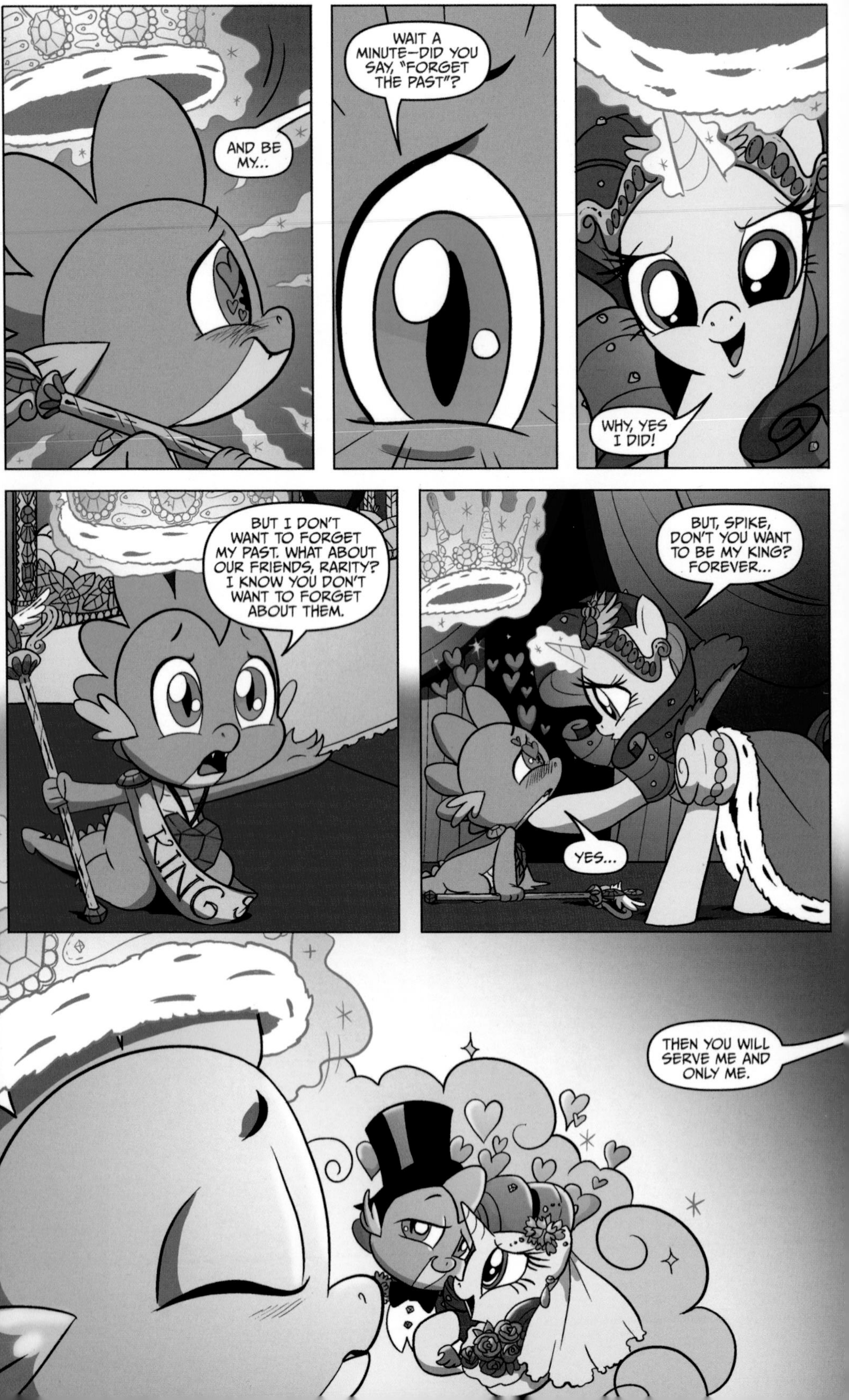
AND BE MY...
WAIT A MINUTE—DID YOU SAY, "FORGET THE PAST"?
WHY, YES I DID!
BUT I DON'T WANT TO FORGET MY PAST. WHAT ABOUT OUR FRIENDS, RARITY? I KNOW YOU DON'T WANT TO FORGET ABOUT THEM.
BUT, SPIKE, DON'T YOU WANT TO BE MY KING? FOREVER...
YES...
KING
THEN YOU WILL SERVE ME AND ONLY ME.

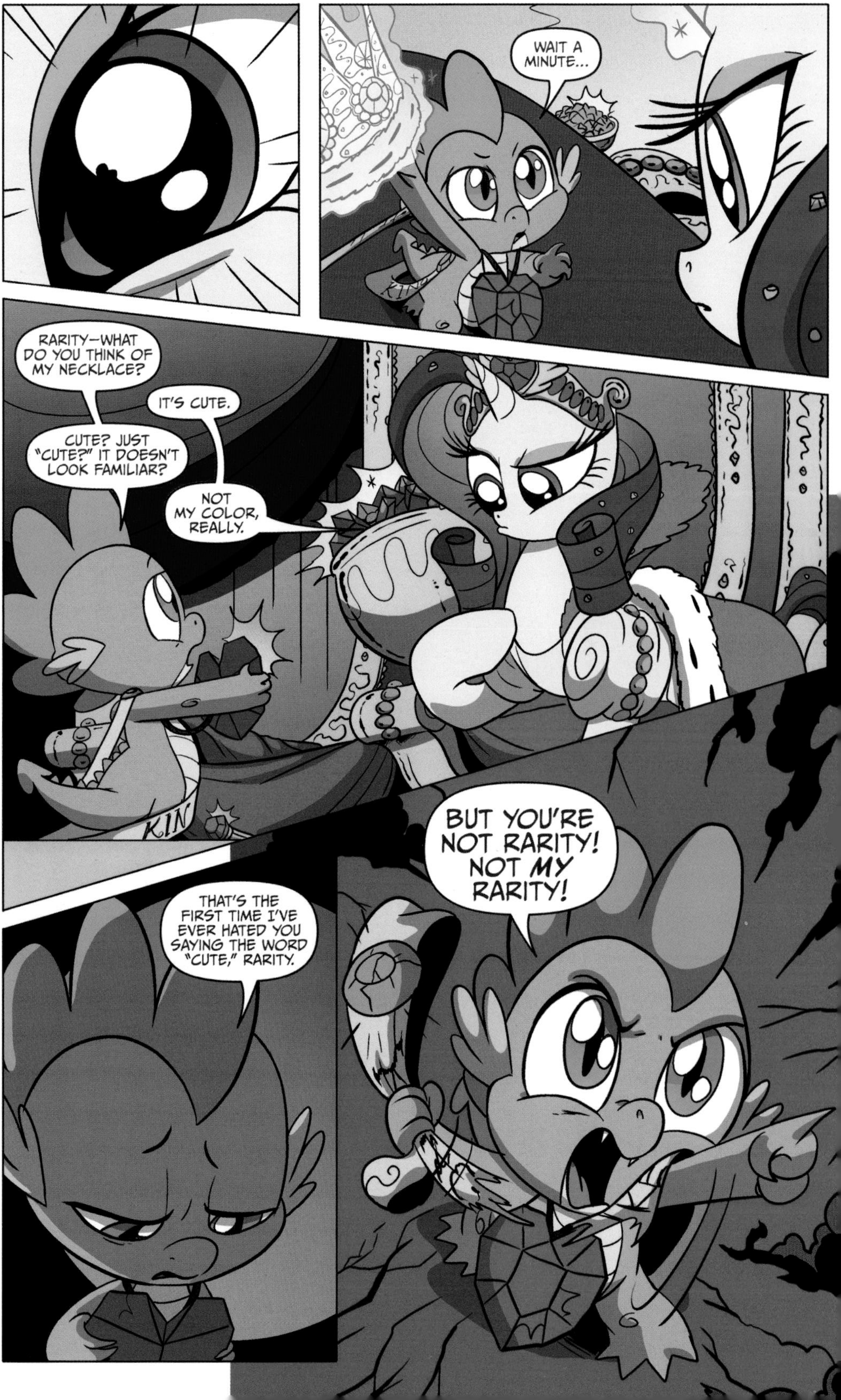
WAIT A MINUTE...
RARITY—WHAT DO YOU THINK OF MY NECKLACE?
IT'S CUTE.
CUTE? JUST "CUTE?" IT DOESN'T LOOK FAMILIAR?
NOT MY COLOR, REALLY.
KIN
BUT YOU'RE NOT RARITY! NOT MY RARITY!
THAT'S THE FIRST TIME I'VE EVER HATED YOU SAYING THE WORD "CUTE," RARITY.

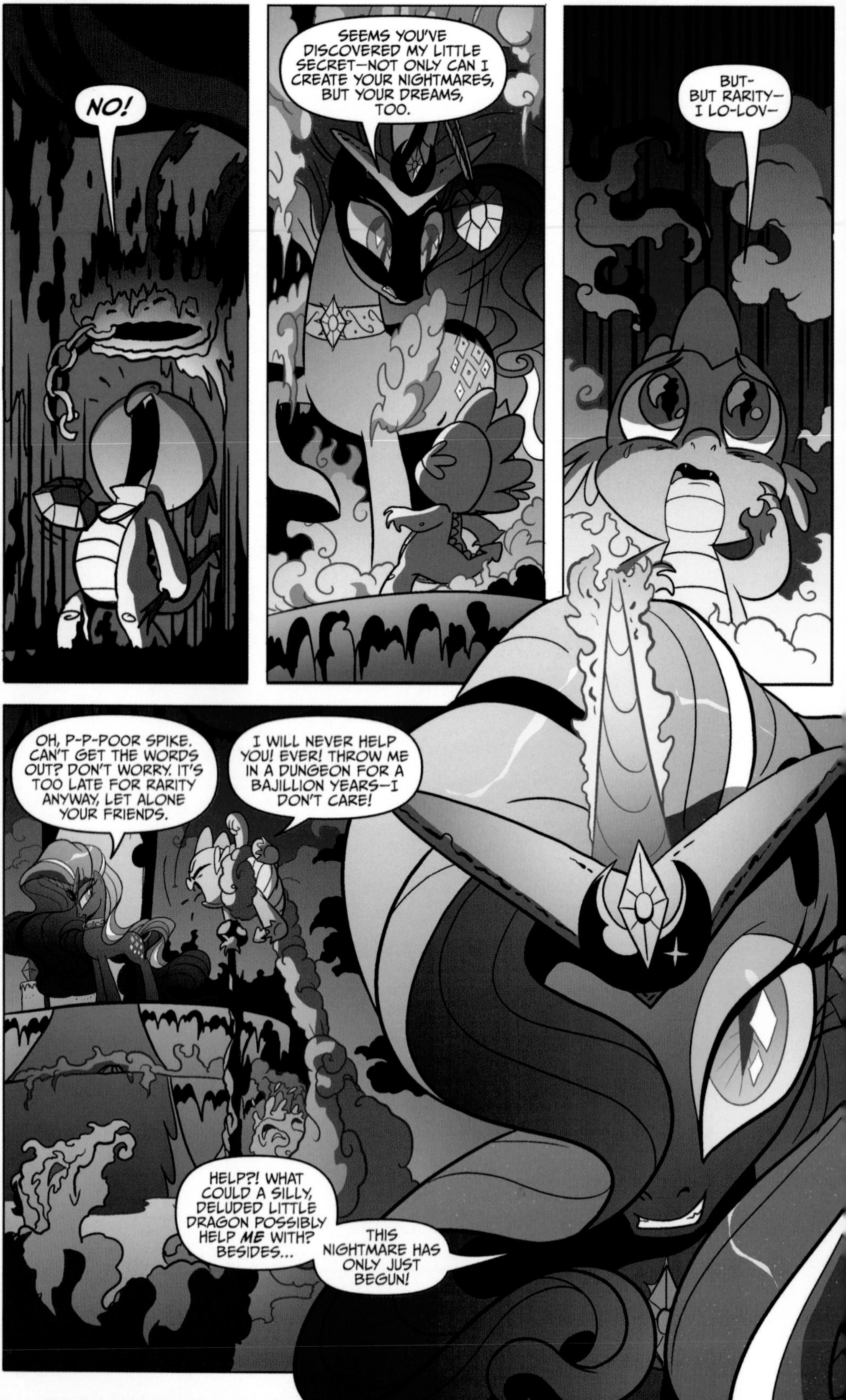

NO!
SEEMS YOU'VE DISCOVERED MY LITTLE SECRET—NOT ONLY CAN I CREATE YOUR NIGHTMARES, BUT YOUR DREAMS, TOO.
BUT- BUT RARITY- I LO-LOV—
OH, P-P-POOR SPIKE. CAN'T GET THE WORDS OUT? DON'T WORRY. IT'S TOO LATE FOR RARITY ANYWAY, LET ALONE YOUR FRIENDS.
I WILL NEVER HELP YOU! EVER! THROW ME IN A DUNGEON FOR A BAJILLION YEARS—I DON'T CARE!
HELP?! WHAT COULD A SILLY, DELUDED LITTLE DRAGON POSSIBLY HELP *ME* WITH? BESIDES...
THIS NIGHTMARE HAS ONLY JUST BEGUN!

Art by
Tony Fleecs

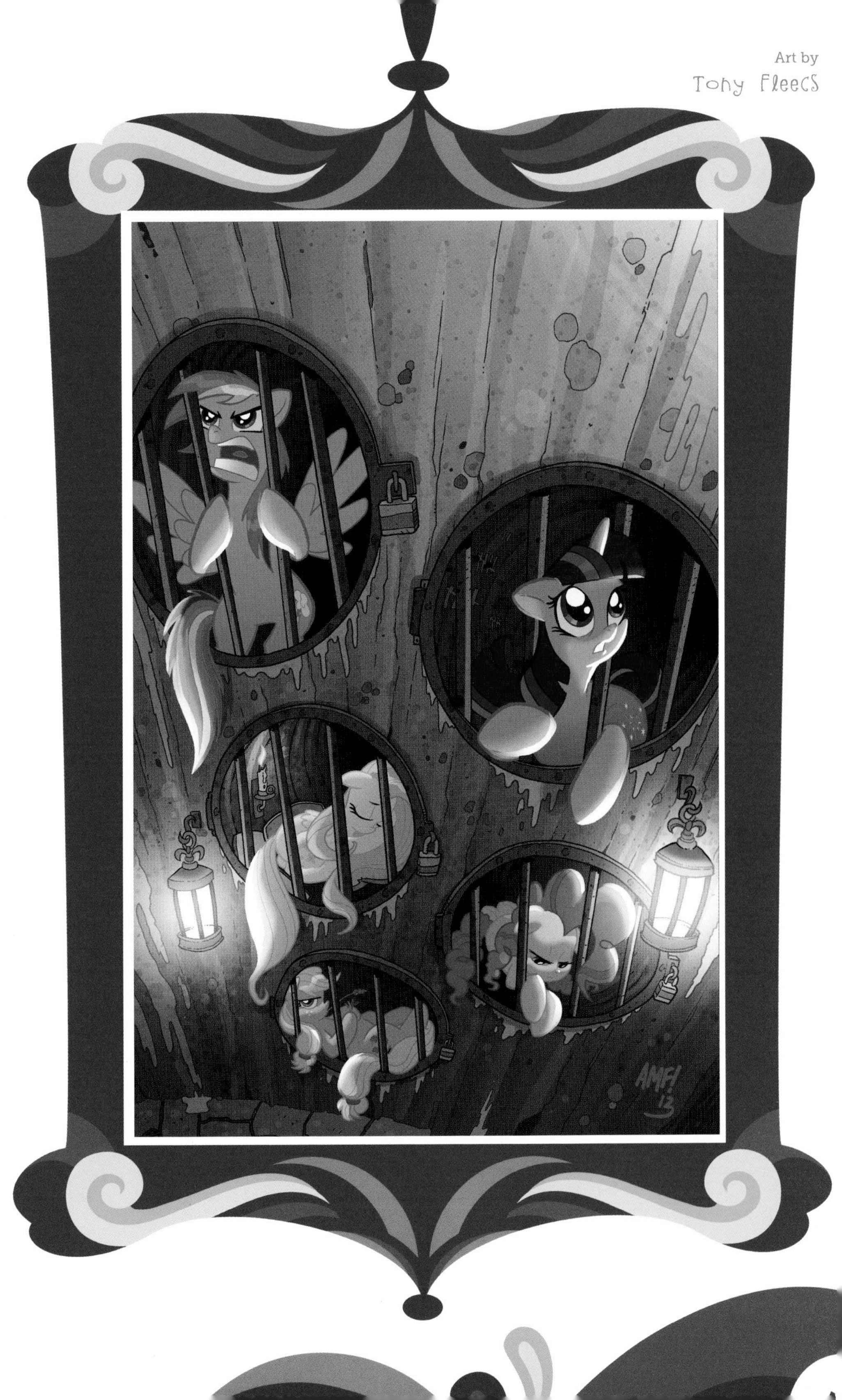

Art by
Amy Mebberson

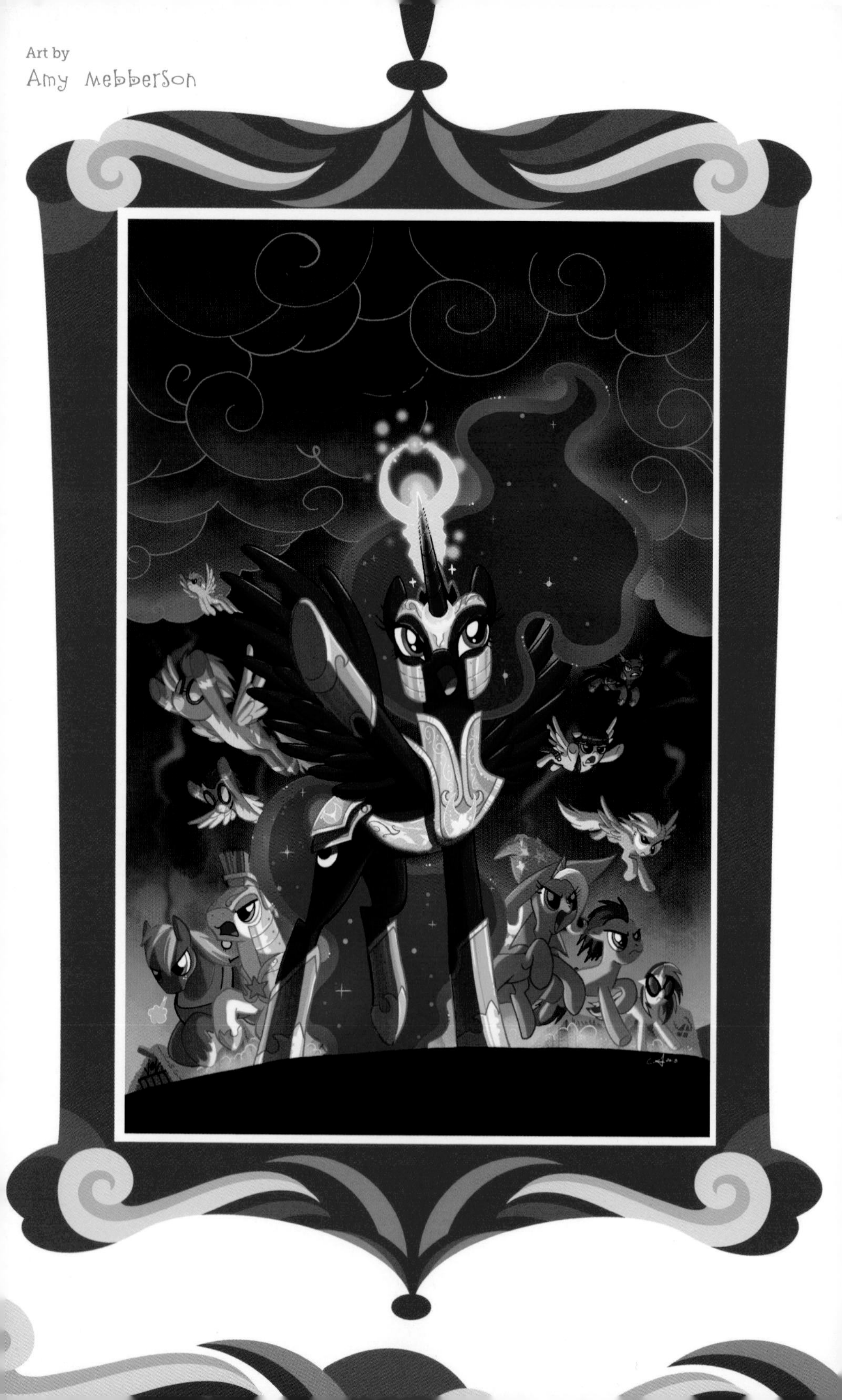

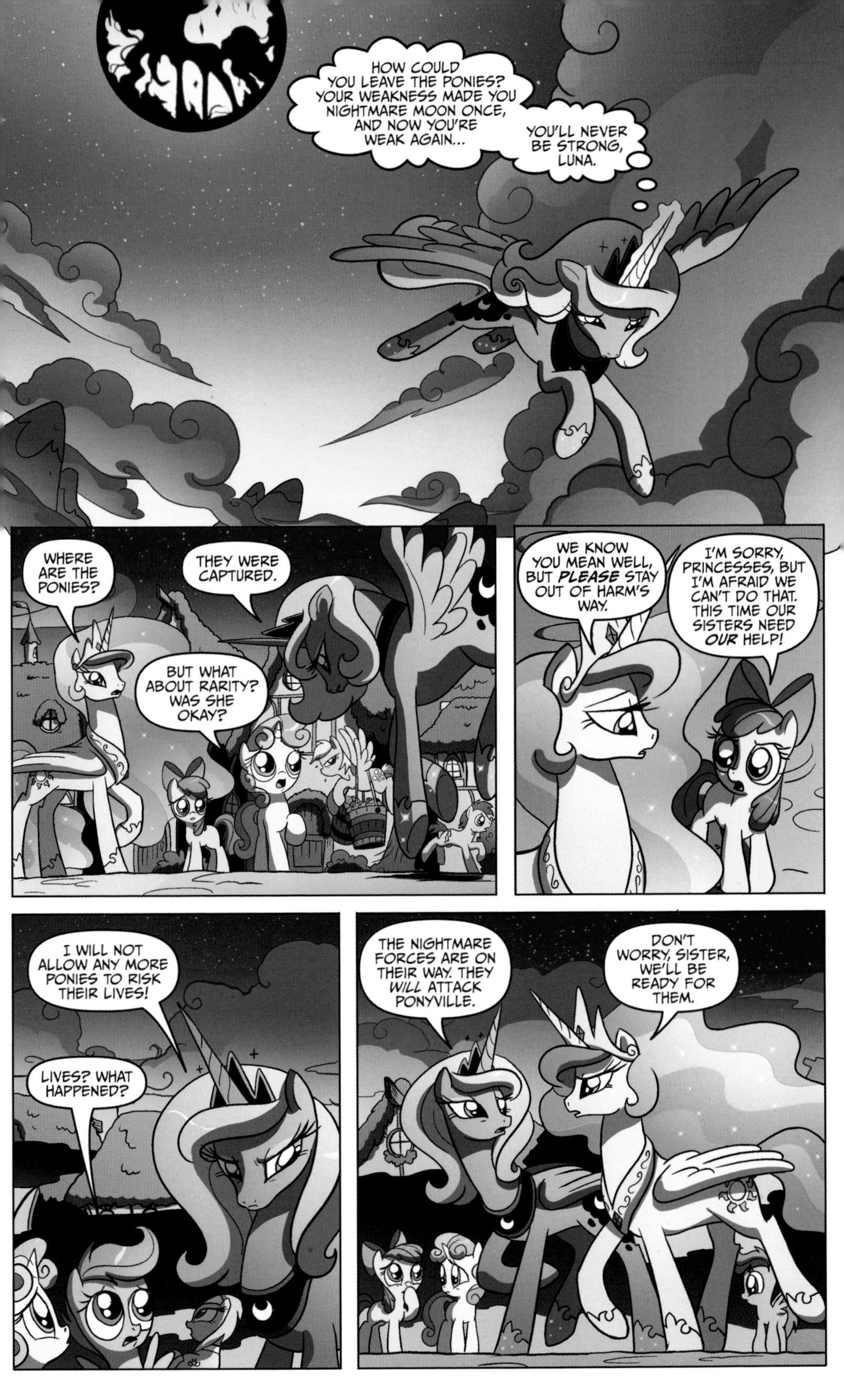
HOW COULD YOU LEAVE THE PONIES? YOUR WEAKNESS MADE YOU NIGHTMARE MOON ONCE, AND NOW YOU'RE WEAK AGAIN...
YOU'LL NEVER BE STRONG, LUNA.
WHERE ARE THE PONIES?
THEY WERE CAPTURED.
BUT WHAT ABOUT RARITY? WAS SHE OKAY?
WE KNOW YOU MEAN WELL, BUT *PLEASE* STAY OUT OF HARM'S WAY.
I'M SORRY, PRINCESSES, BUT I'M AFRAID WE CAN'T DO THAT. THIS TIME OUR SISTERS NEED *OUR* HELP!
I WILL NOT ALLOW ANY MORE PONIES TO RISK THEIR LIVES!
LIVES? WHAT HAPPENED?
THE NIGHTMARE FORCES ARE ON THEIR WAY. THEY *WILL* ATTACK PONYVILLE.
DON'T WORRY, SISTER, WE'LL BE READY FOR THEM.

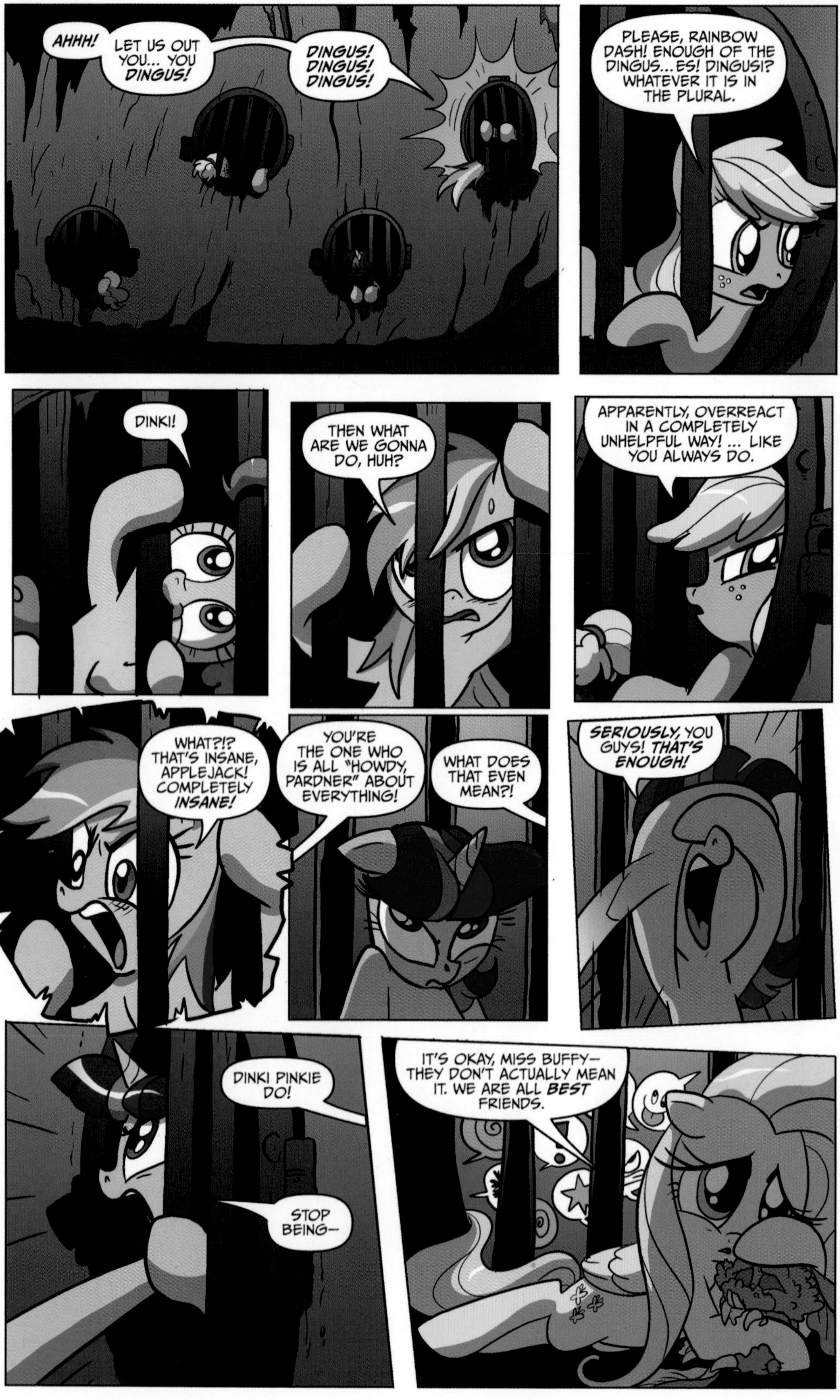
AHHH!
LET US OUT YOU... YOU DINGUS!
DINGUS! DINGUS! DINGUS!
PLEASE, RAINBOW DASH! ENOUGH OF THE DINGUS...ES! DINGUSI? WHATEVER IT IS IN THE PLURAL.
DINKI!
THEN WHAT ARE WE GONNA DO, HUH?
APPARENTLY, OVERREACT IN A COMPLETELY UNHELPFUL WAY! ... LIKE YOU ALWAYS DO.
WHAT?!? THAT'S INSANE, APPLEJACK! COMPLETELY INSANE!
YOU'RE THE ONE WHO IS ALL "HOWDY, PARDNER" ABOUT EVERYTHING!
WHAT DOES THAT EVEN MEAN?!
SERIOUSLY, YOU GUYS! THAT'S ENOUGH!
DINKI PINKIE DO!
STOP BEING—
IT'S OKAY, MISS BUFFY— THEY DON'T ACTUALLY MEAN IT. WE ARE ALL BEST FRIENDS.

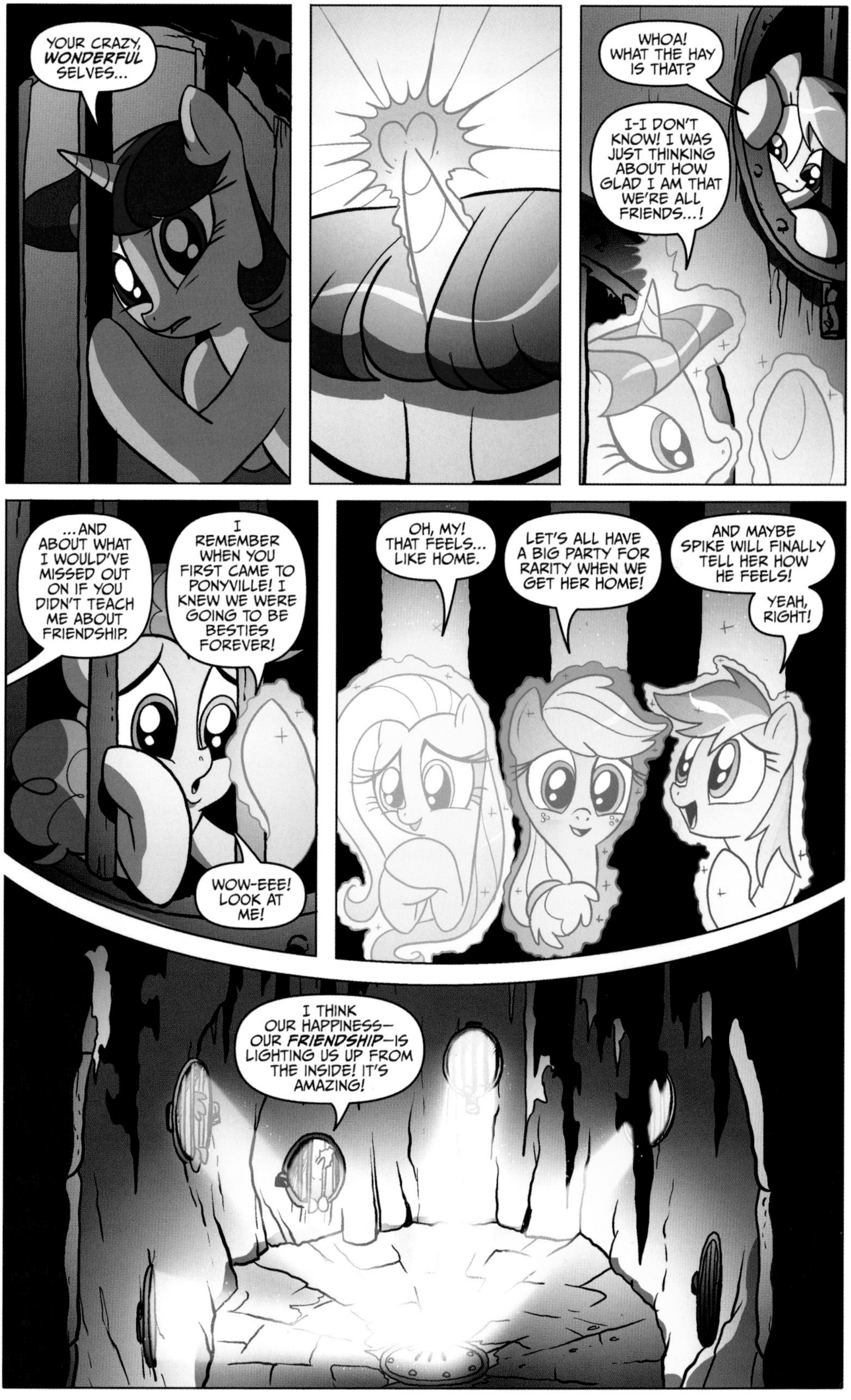
YOUR CRAZY, WONDERFUL SELVES...
WHOA! WHAT THE HAY IS THAT?
I-I DON'T KNOW! I WAS JUST THINKING ABOUT HOW GLAD I AM THAT WE'RE ALL FRIENDS...!
...AND ABOUT WHAT I WOULD'VE MISSED OUT ON IF YOU DIDN'T TEACH ME ABOUT FRIENDSHIP.
I REMEMBER WHEN YOU FIRST CAME TO PONYVILLE! I KNEW WE WERE GOING TO BE BESTIES FOREVER!
WOW-EEE! LOOK AT ME!
OH, MY! THAT FEELS... LIKE HOME.
LET'S ALL HAVE A BIG PARTY FOR RARITY WHEN WE GET HER HOME!
AND MAYBE SPIKE WILL FINALLY TELL HER HOW HE FEELS!
YEAH, RIGHT!
I THINK OUR HAPPINESS— OUR FRIENDSHIP—IS LIGHTING US UP FROM THE INSIDE! IT'S AMAZING!

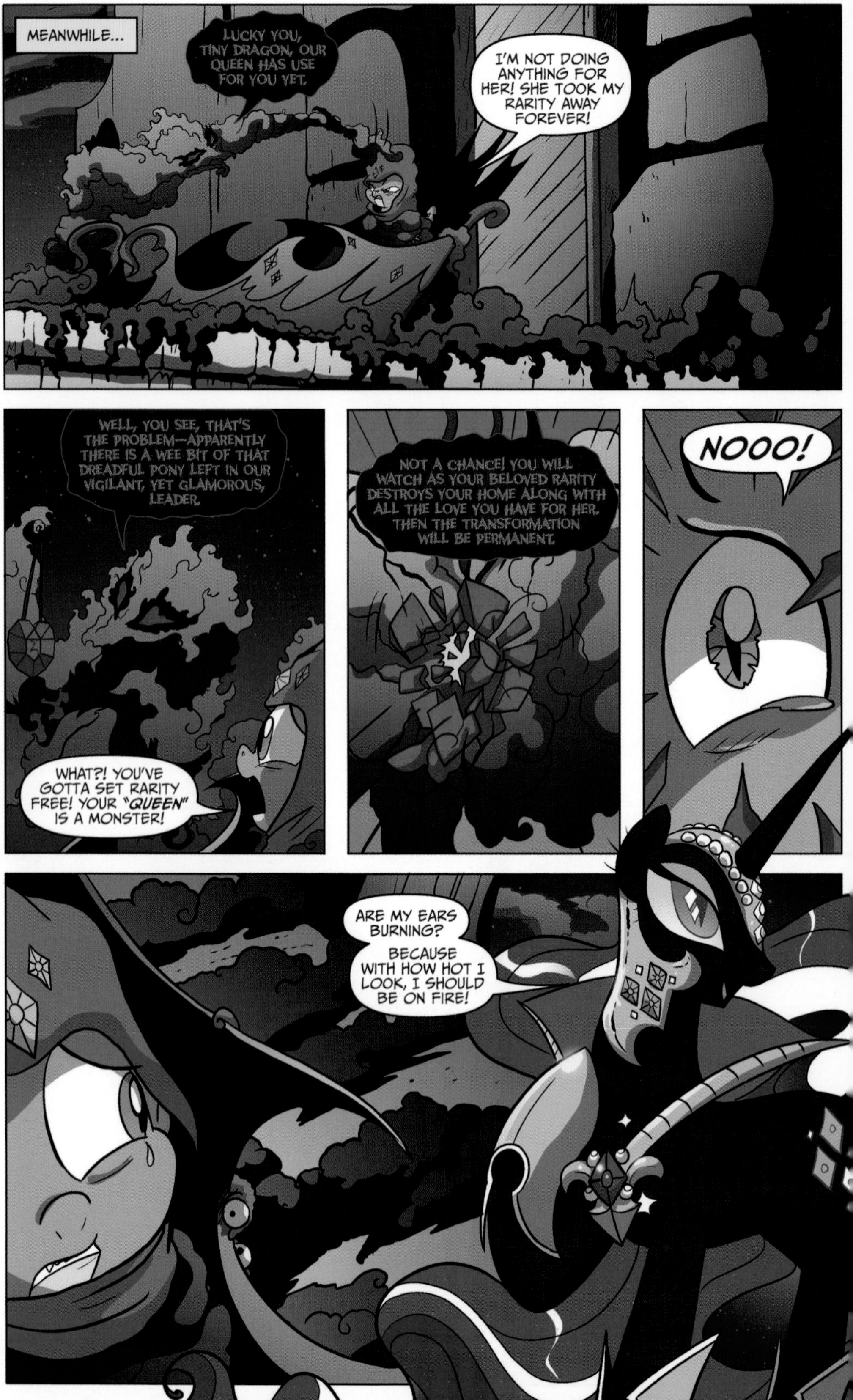
MEANWHILE...
LUCKY YOU, TINY DRAGON, OUR QUEEN HAS USE FOR YOU YET.
I'M NOT DOING ANYTHING FOR HER! SHE TOOK MY RARITY AWAY FOREVER!
WELL, YOU SEE, THAT'S THE PROBLEM—APPARENTLY THERE IS A WEE BIT OF THAT DREADFUL PONY LEFT IN OUR VIGILANT, YET GLAMOROUS, LEADER.
WHAT?! YOU'VE GOTTA SET RARITY FREE! YOUR "*QUEEN*" IS A MONSTER!
NOT A CHANCE! YOU WILL WATCH AS YOUR BELOVED RARITY DESTROYS YOUR HOME ALONG WITH ALL THE LOVE YOU HAVE FOR HER. THEN THE TRANSFORMATION WILL BE PERMANENT.
NOOO!
ARE MY EARS BURNING?
BECAUSE WITH HOW HOT I LOOK, I SHOULD BE ON FIRE!

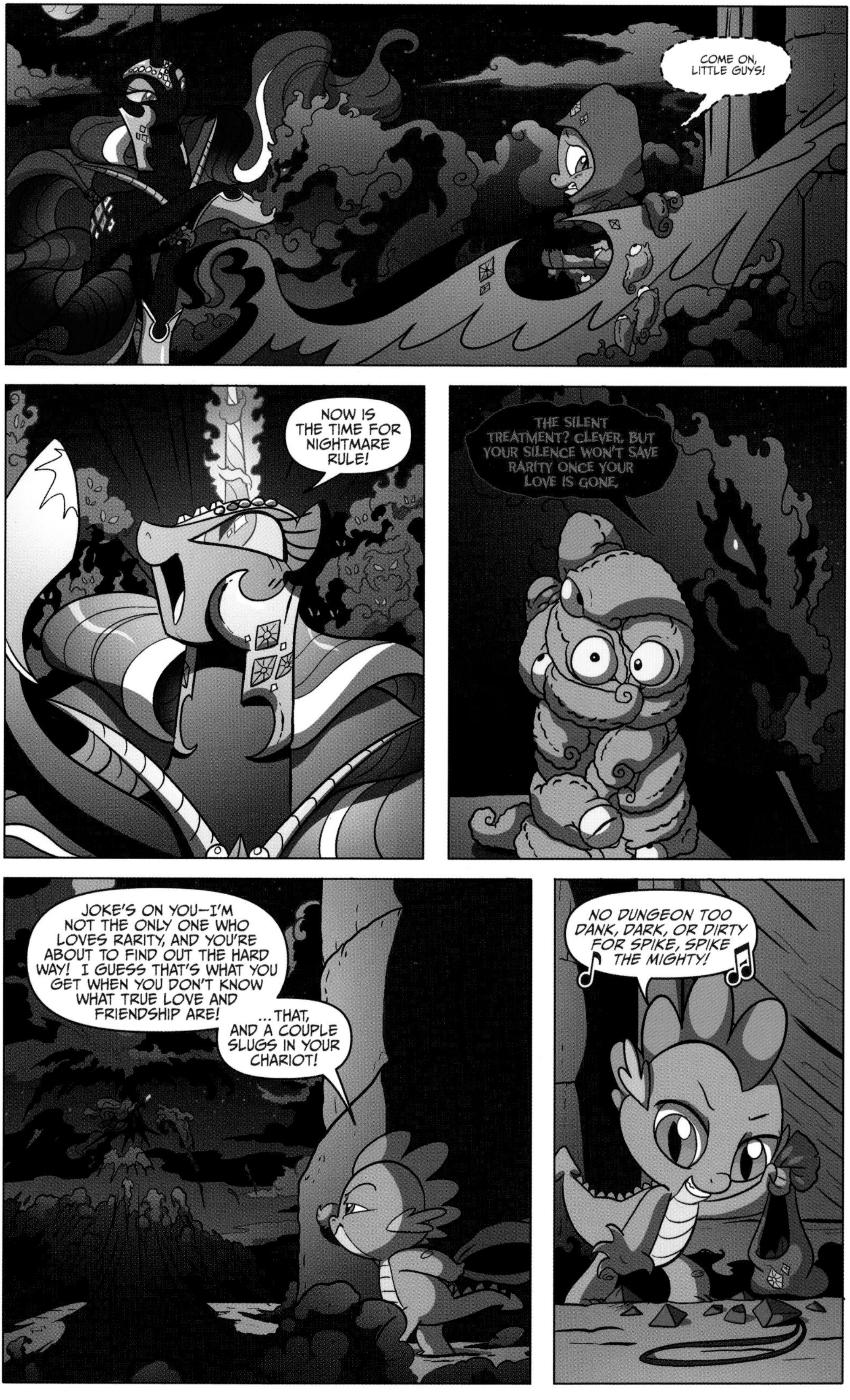
COME ON, LITTLE GUYS!
NOW IS THE TIME FOR NIGHTMARE RULE!
THE SILENT TREATMENT? CLEVER, BUT YOUR SILENCE WON'T SAVE RARITY ONCE YOUR LOVE IS GONE.
JOKE'S ON YOU—I'M NOT THE ONLY ONE WHO LOVES RARITY, AND YOU'RE ABOUT TO FIND OUT THE HARD WAY! I GUESS THAT'S WHAT YOU GET WHEN YOU DON'T KNOW WHAT TRUE LOVE AND FRIENDSHIP ARE!
...THAT, AND A COUPLE SLUGS IN YOUR CHARIOT!
NO DUNGEON TOO DANK, DARK, OR DIRTY FOR SPIKE, SPIKE THE MIGHTY!

THE DUNGEON SHOULDN'T BE *THIS* HARD TO FIND...

IF ANYPONY CAN MAKE BEAUTIFUL LIGHT LIKE THAT, IT'S DEFINITELY *MY* PONIES!

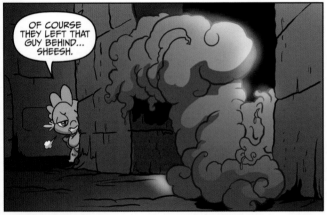

OF COURSE THEY LEFT THAT GUY BEHIND... SHEESH.

SPIKE! YOU'RE OKAY!

YOU ARE ONE TOUGH TINY DUDE!

AW, THANKS! IT WAS NOTHING! JUST A DRAGON DOING HIS MIGHTY DRAGONLY DUTY!

WE GOTTA GET YOU OUT OF HERE FAST! THE BAD GUYS ARE ON THEIR WAY TO PONYVILLE!

UGH! THEY'RE LOCKED!

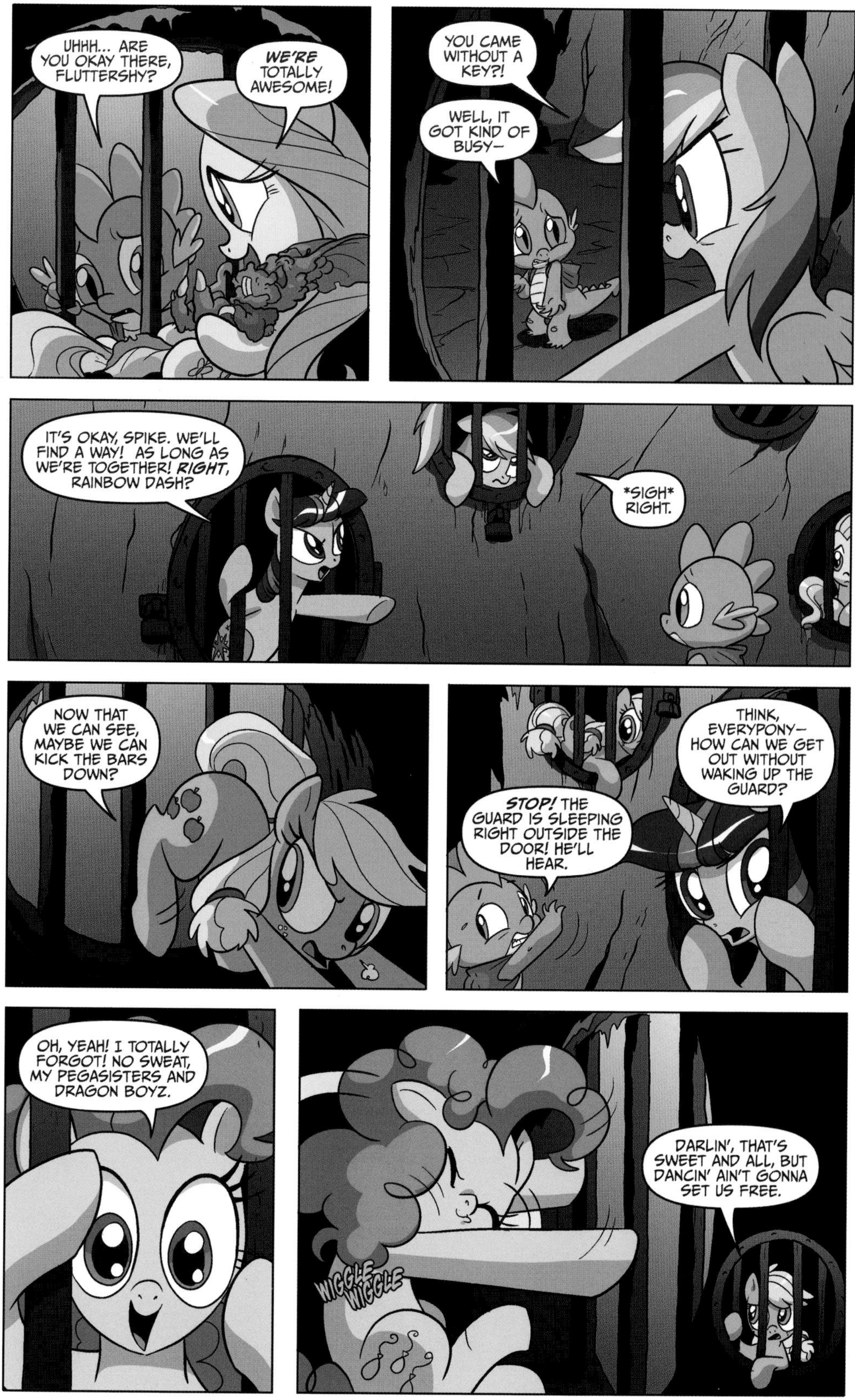
UHHH... ARE YOU OKAY THERE, FLUTTERSHY?
WE'RE TOTALLY AWESOME!
YOU CAME WITHOUT A KEY?!
WELL, IT GOT KIND OF BUSY—
IT'S OKAY, SPIKE. WE'LL FIND A WAY! AS LONG AS WE'RE TOGETHER! RIGHT, RAINBOW DASH?
SIGH RIGHT.
NOW THAT WE CAN SEE, MAYBE WE CAN KICK THE BARS DOWN?
THINK, EVERYPONY— HOW CAN WE GET OUT WITHOUT WAKING UP THE GUARD?
STOP! THE GUARD IS SLEEPING RIGHT OUTSIDE THE DOOR! HE'LL HEAR.
OH, YEAH! I TOTALLY FORGOT! NO SWEAT, MY PEGASISTERS AND DRAGON BOYZ.
WIGGLE WIGGLE
DARLIN', THAT'S SWEET AND ALL, BUT DANCIN' AIN'T GONNA SET US FREE.

WIGGLE WIGGLE WIGGLE

YE OF LITTLE FAITH!

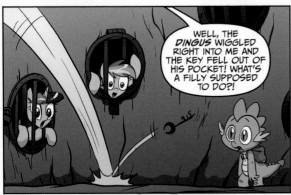

WELL, THE *DINGUS* WIGGLED RIGHT INTO ME AND THE KEY FELL OUT OF HIS POCKET! WHAT'S A FILLY SUPPOSED TO DO?!

NOW, WE HAVE TO GET BACK TO PONYVILLE—THEY SAID THAT SOME OF RARITY WAS STILL ALIVE INSIDE THAT NASTY NOGOODNICK. WE CAN STILL SAVE HER!

NOT SO FAST!

HAVE A NICE NAP THERE? HA-HA!

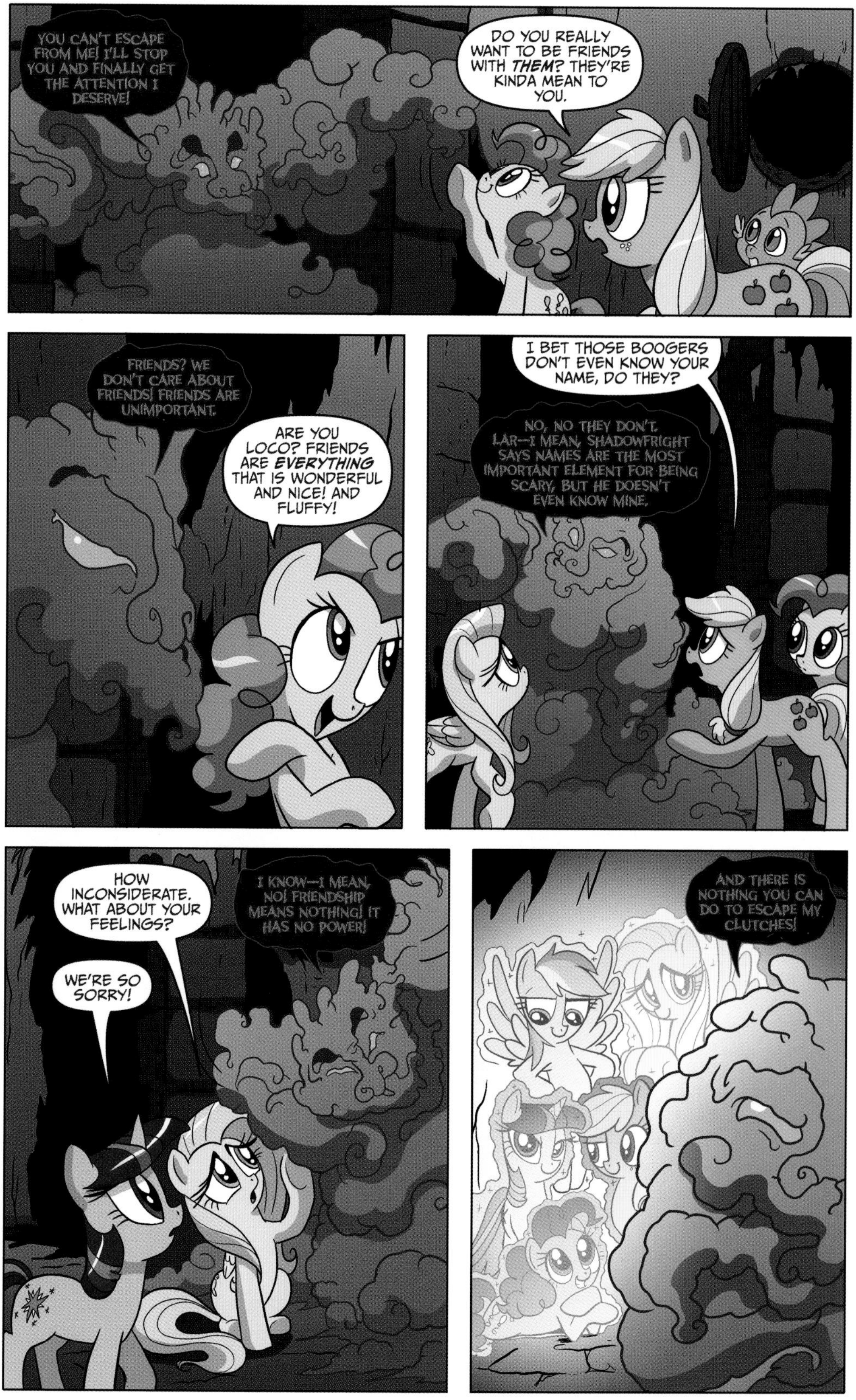

YOU CAN'T ESCAPE FROM ME! I'LL STOP YOU AND FINALLY GET THE ATTENTION I DESERVE!
DO YOU REALLY WANT TO BE FRIENDS WITH *THEM*? THEY'RE KINDA MEAN TO YOU.
FRIENDS? WE DON'T CARE ABOUT FRIENDS! FRIENDS ARE UNIMPORTANT.
ARE YOU LOCO? FRIENDS ARE *EVERYTHING* THAT IS WONDERFUL AND NICE! AND FLUFFY!
I BET THOSE BOOGERS DON'T EVEN KNOW YOUR NAME, DO THEY?
NO, NO THEY DON'T. LAR—I MEAN, SHADOWFRIGHT SAYS NAMES ARE THE MOST IMPORTANT ELEMENT FOR BEING SCARY, BUT HE DOESN'T EVEN KNOW MINE.
HOW INCONSIDERATE. WHAT ABOUT YOUR FEELINGS?
WE'RE SO SORRY!
I KNOW—I MEAN, NO! FRIENDSHIP MEANS NOTHING! IT HAS NO POWER!
AND THERE IS NOTHING YOU CAN DO TO ESCAPE MY CLUTCHES!

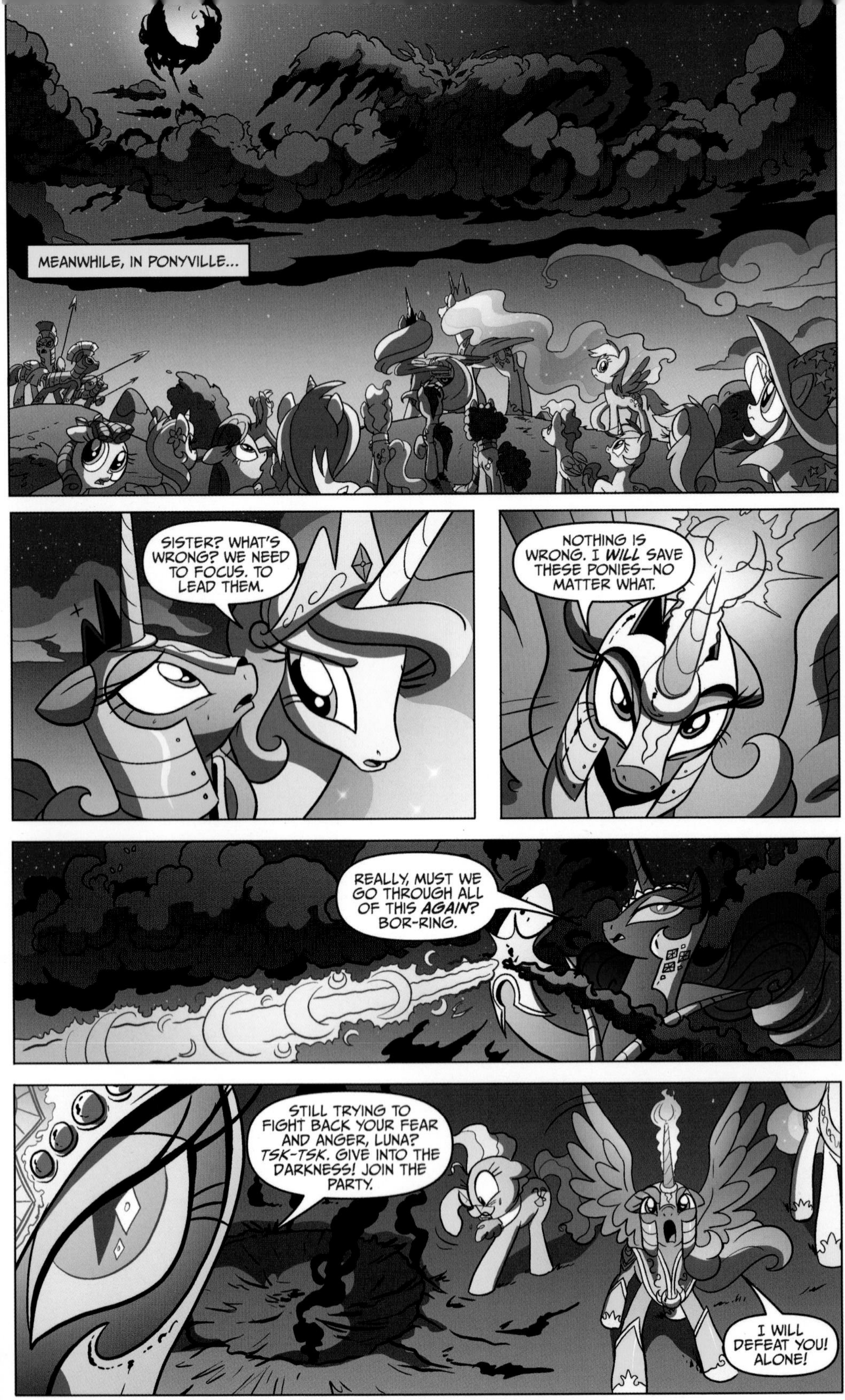
MEANWHILE, IN PONYVILLE...
SISTER? WHAT'S WRONG? WE NEED TO FOCUS. TO LEAD THEM.
NOTHING IS WRONG. I WILL SAVE THESE PONIES—NO MATTER WHAT.
REALLY, MUST WE GO THROUGH ALL OF THIS AGAIN? BOR-RING.
STILL TRYING TO FIGHT BACK YOUR FEAR AND ANGER, LUNA? TSK-TSK. GIVE INTO THE DARKNESS! JOIN THE PARTY.
I WILL DEFEAT YOU! ALONE!

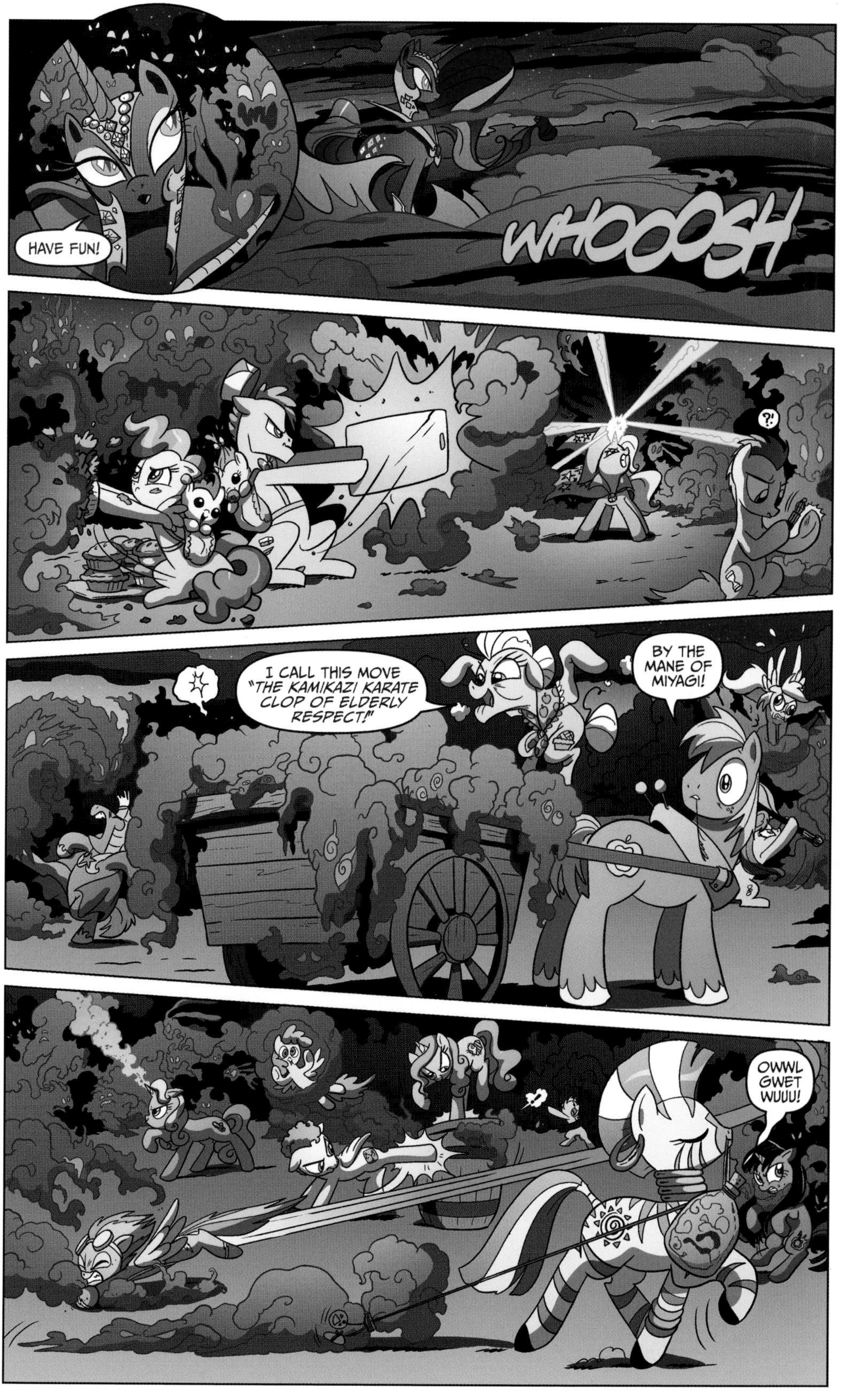
HAVE FUN!
WHOOOSH
?!
I CALL THIS MOVE "THE KAMIKAZI KARATE CLOP OF ELDERLY RESPECT!"
BY THE MANE OF MIYAGI!
OWWL GWET WUUU!

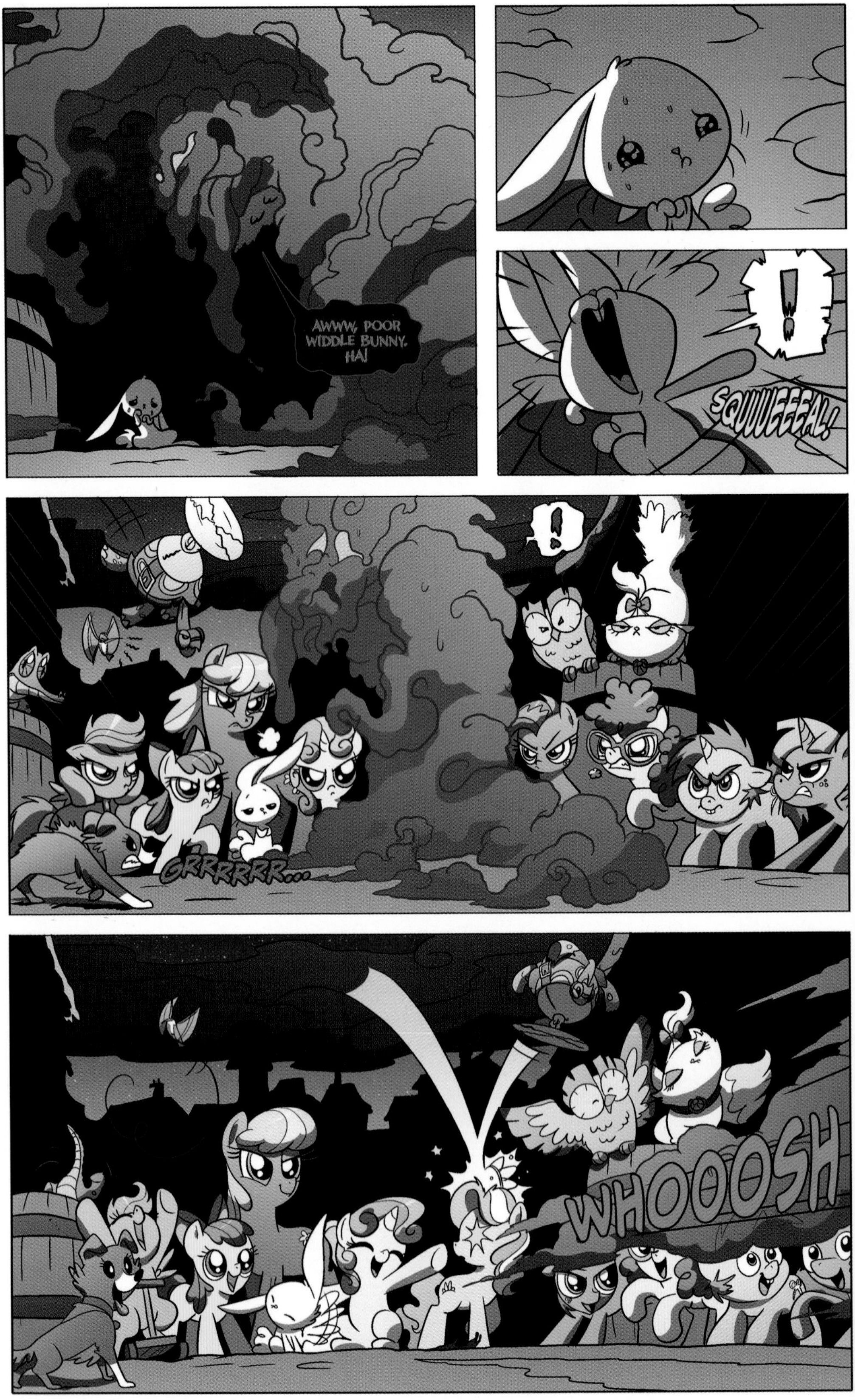

AWWW, POOR WIDDLE BUNNY. HA!
!
SQUUUEEEAL!
!
GRRRRRR...
WHOOOOSH

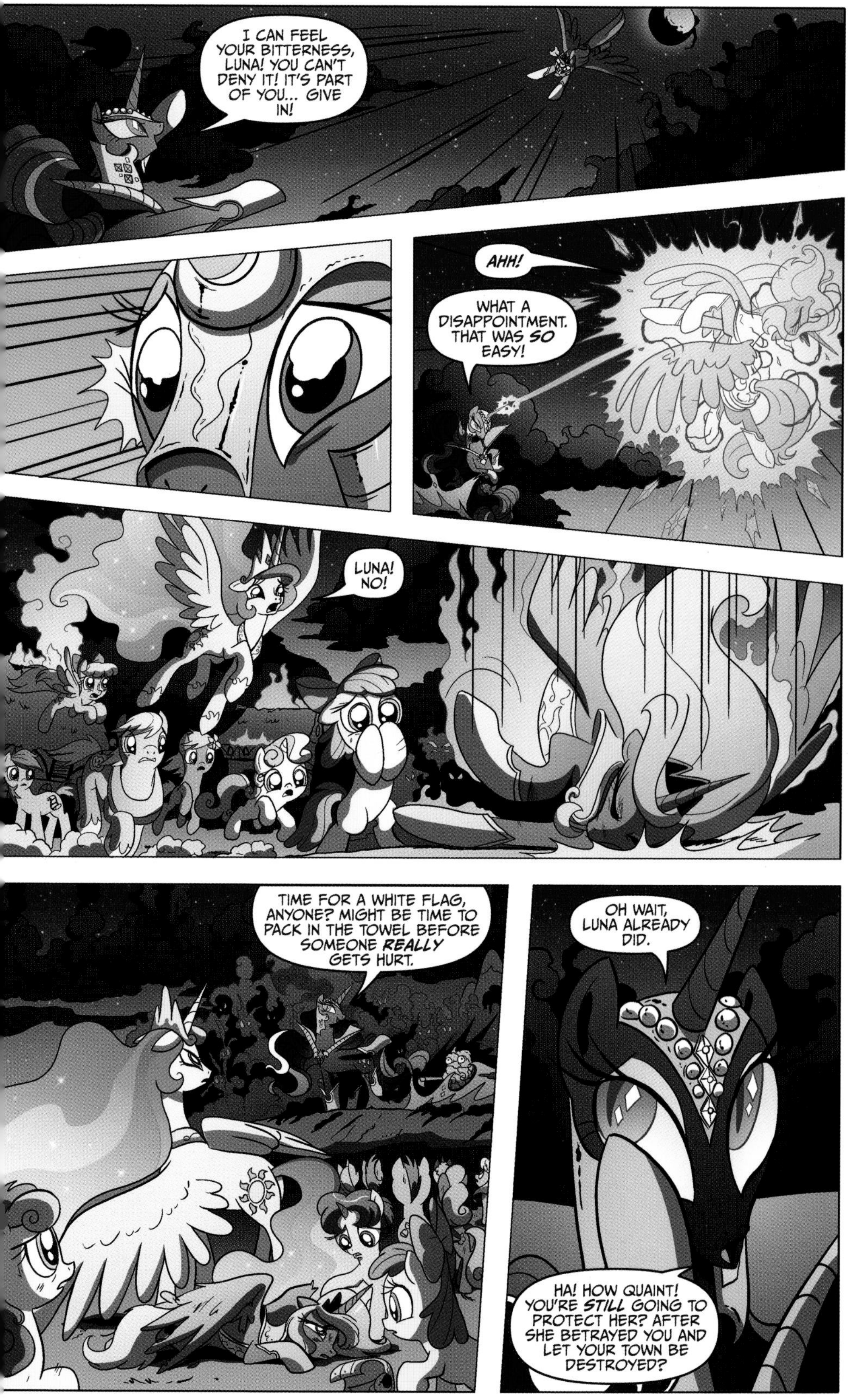
I CAN FEEL YOUR BITTERNESS, LUNA! YOU CAN'T DENY IT! IT'S PART OF YOU... GIVE IN!
AHH!
WHAT A DISAPPOINTMENT. THAT WAS SO EASY!
LUNA! NO!
TIME FOR A WHITE FLAG, ANYONE? MIGHT BE TIME TO PACK IN THE TOWEL BEFORE SOMEONE REALLY GETS HURT.
OH WAIT, LUNA ALREADY DID.
HA! HOW QUAINT! YOU'RE STILL GOING TO PROTECT HER? AFTER SHE BETRAYED YOU AND LET YOUR TOWN BE DESTROYED?

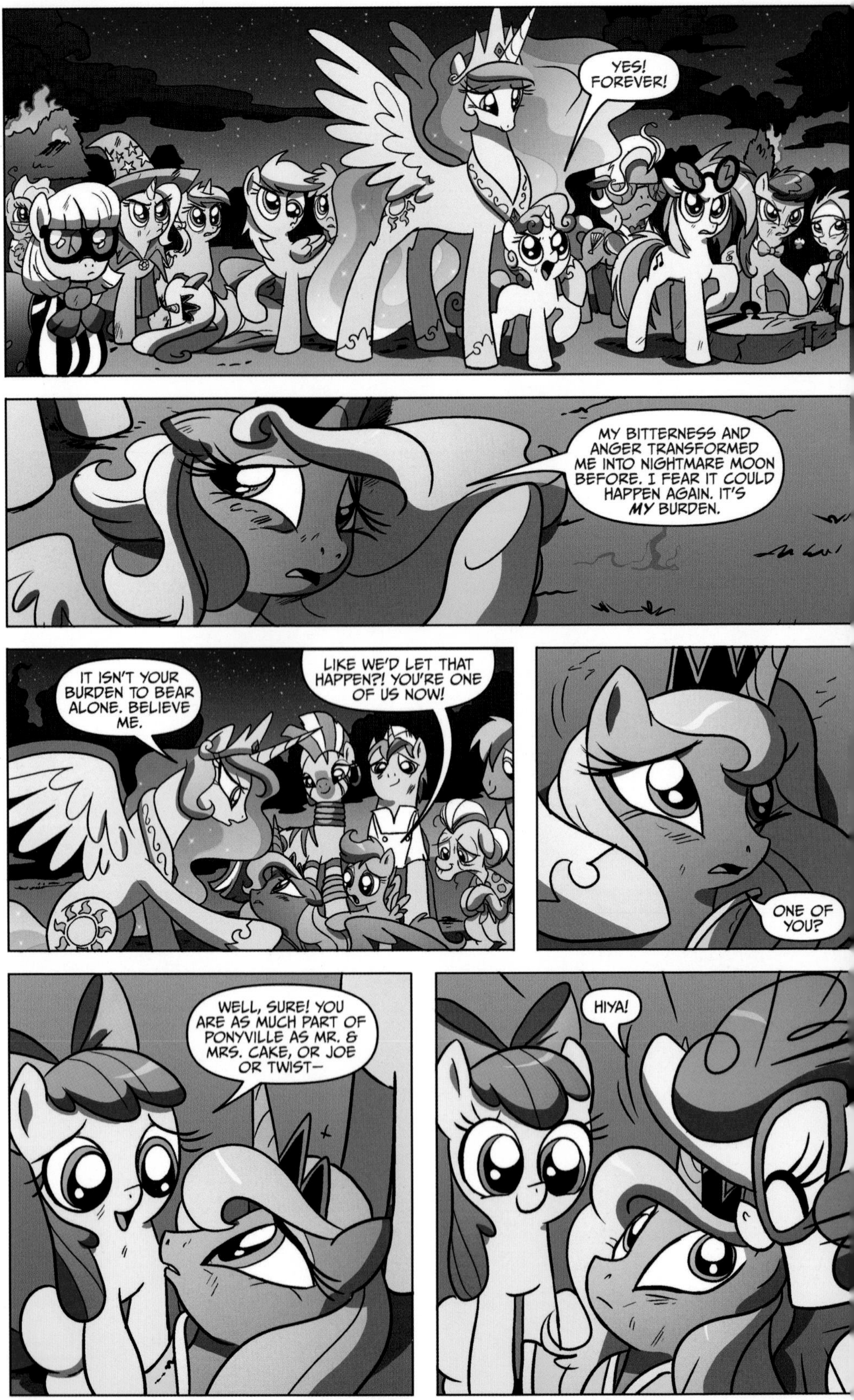
YES! FOREVER!
MY BITTERNESS AND ANGER TRANSFORMED ME INTO NIGHTMARE MOON BEFORE. I FEAR IT COULD HAPPEN AGAIN. IT'S *MY* BURDEN.
IT ISN'T YOUR BURDEN TO BEAR ALONE. BELIEVE ME.
LIKE WE'D LET THAT HAPPEN?! YOU'RE ONE OF US NOW!
ONE OF YOU?
WELL, SURE! YOU ARE AS MUCH PART OF PONYVILLE AS MR. & MRS. CAKE, OR JOE OR TWIST–
HIYA!

WITH ALL OF YOU BESIDE ME, MAYBE I DON'T NEED TO FEAR MY PAST... OR FUTURE.

WHATEVER COMES, WE FACE IT TOGETHER—LIKE A BIG 'OL FAMILY DOES.

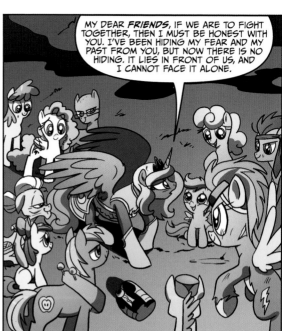

MY DEAR *FRIENDS*, IF WE ARE TO FIGHT TOGETHER, THEN I MUST BE HONEST WITH YOU. I'VE BEEN HIDING MY FEAR AND MY PAST FROM YOU, BUT NOW THERE IS NO HIDING. IT LIES IN FRONT OF US, AND I CANNOT FACE IT ALONE.

IF YOU CAN FORGIVE ME, I SWEAR I WILL NEVER ABANDON YOU AS I ABANDONED THE DENIZENS OF THE MOON. I WILL NEVER LET MY FEAR OF BECOMING NIGHTMARE MOON STOP ME FROM DEFENDING YOU.

EVERYPONY DESERVES A SECOND CHANCE—EVEN A THIRD CHANCE!

TRUST IN YOURSELF, AND IN YOUR FRIENDS. YOU'RE PRINCESS LUNA NOW *AND* FOREVER.

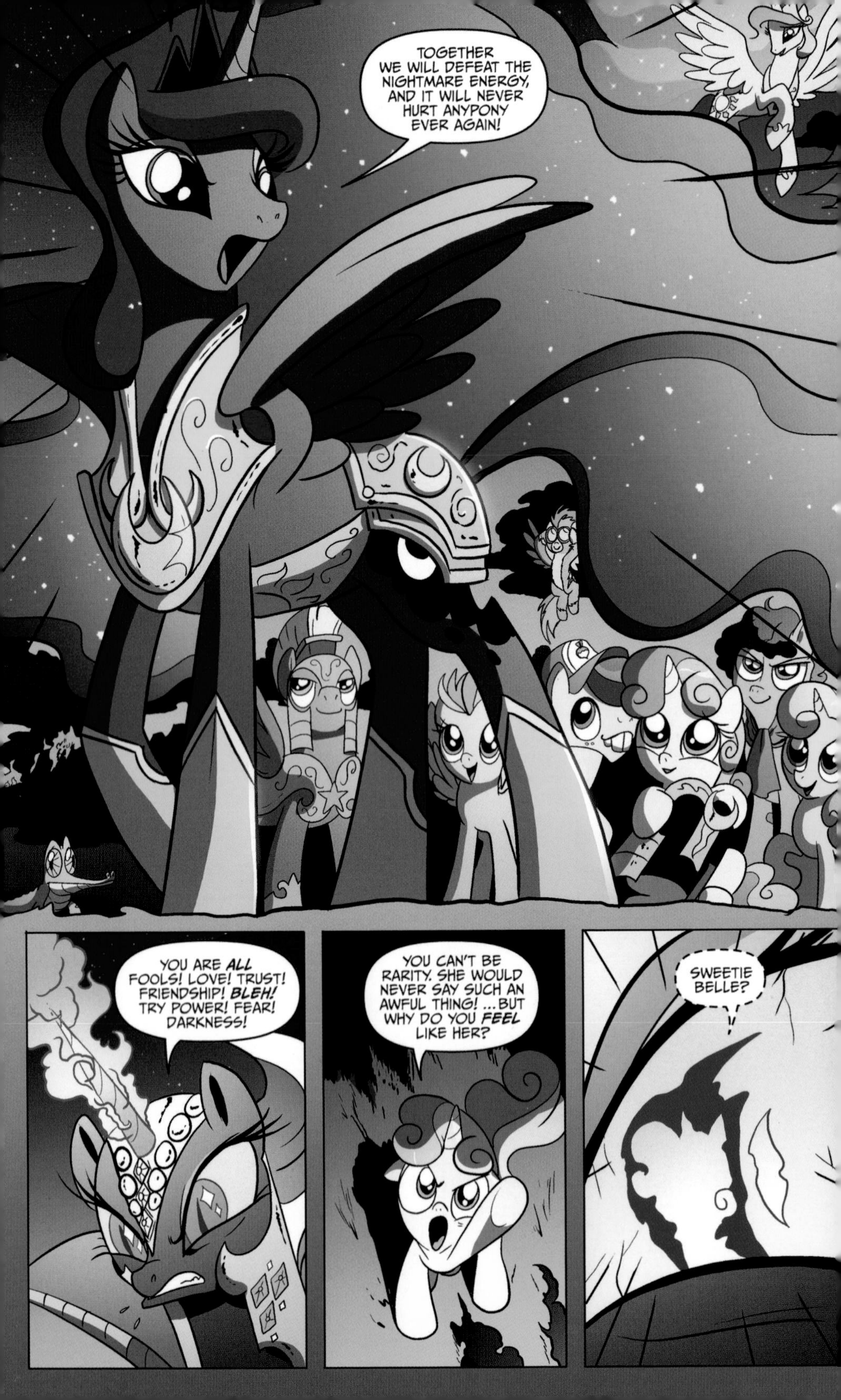
TOGETHER WE WILL DEFEAT THE NIGHTMARE ENERGY, AND IT WILL NEVER HURT ANYPONY EVER AGAIN!
YOU ARE ***ALL*** FOOLS! LOVE! TRUST! FRIENDSHIP! ***BLEH!*** TRY POWER! FEAR! DARKNESS!
YOU CAN'T BE RARITY. SHE WOULD NEVER SAY SUCH AN AWFUL THING! ...BUT WHY DO YOU ***FEEL*** LIKE HER?
SWEETIE BELLE?

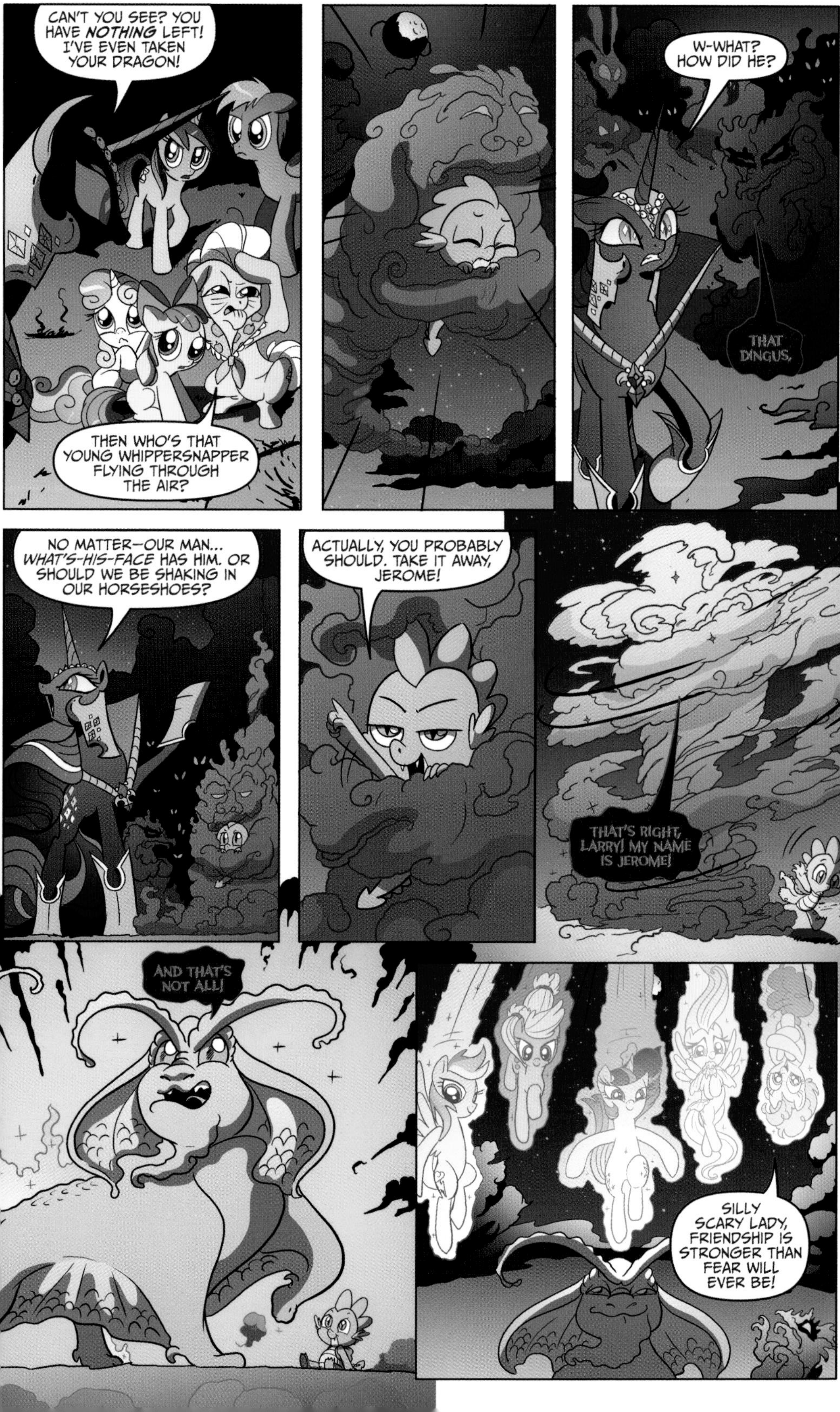
CAN'T YOU SEE? YOU HAVE NOTHING LEFT! I'VE EVEN TAKEN YOUR DRAGON!
THEN WHO'S THAT YOUNG WHIPPERSNAPPER FLYING THROUGH THE AIR?
W-WHAT? HOW DID HE?
THAT DINGUS,
NO MATTER—OUR MAN... WHAT'S-HIS-FACE HAS HIM. OR SHOULD WE BE SHAKING IN OUR HORSESHOES?
ACTUALLY, YOU PROBABLY SHOULD. TAKE IT AWAY, JEROME!
THAT'S RIGHT, LARRY! MY NAME IS JEROME!
AND THAT'S NOT ALL!
SILLY SCARY LADY, FRIENDSHIP IS STRONGER THAN FEAR WILL EVER BE!

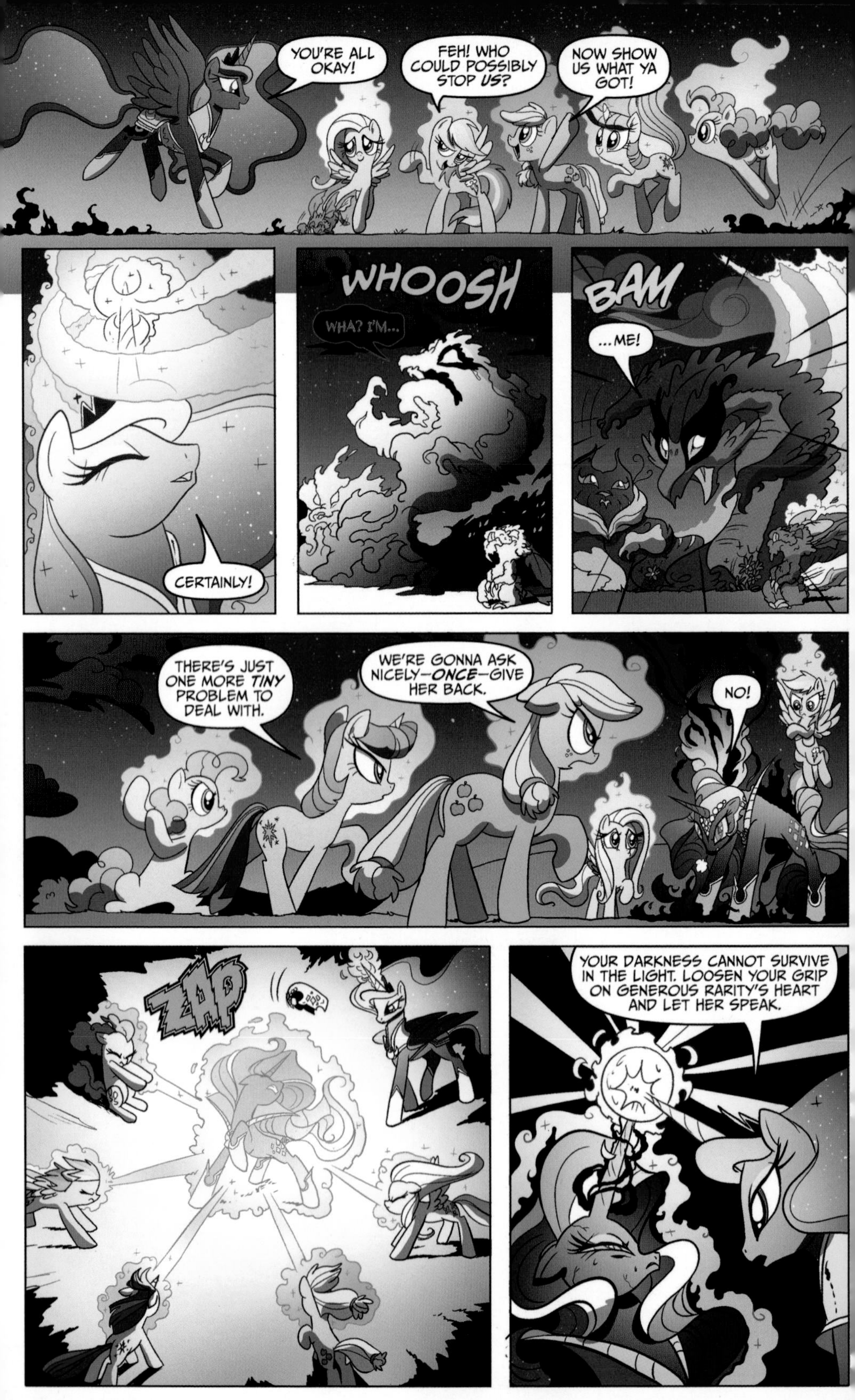
YOU'RE ALL OKAY!
FEH! WHO COULD POSSIBLY STOP US?
NOW SHOW US WHAT YA GOT!
CERTAINLY!
WHOOSH
WHA? I'M...
BAM
...ME!
THERE'S JUST ONE MORE TINY PROBLEM TO DEAL WITH.
WE'RE GONNA ASK NICELY—ONCE—GIVE HER BACK.
NO!
ZAP
YOUR DARKNESS CANNOT SURVIVE IN THE LIGHT. LOOSEN YOUR GRIP ON GENEROUS RARITY'S HEART AND LET HER SPEAK.

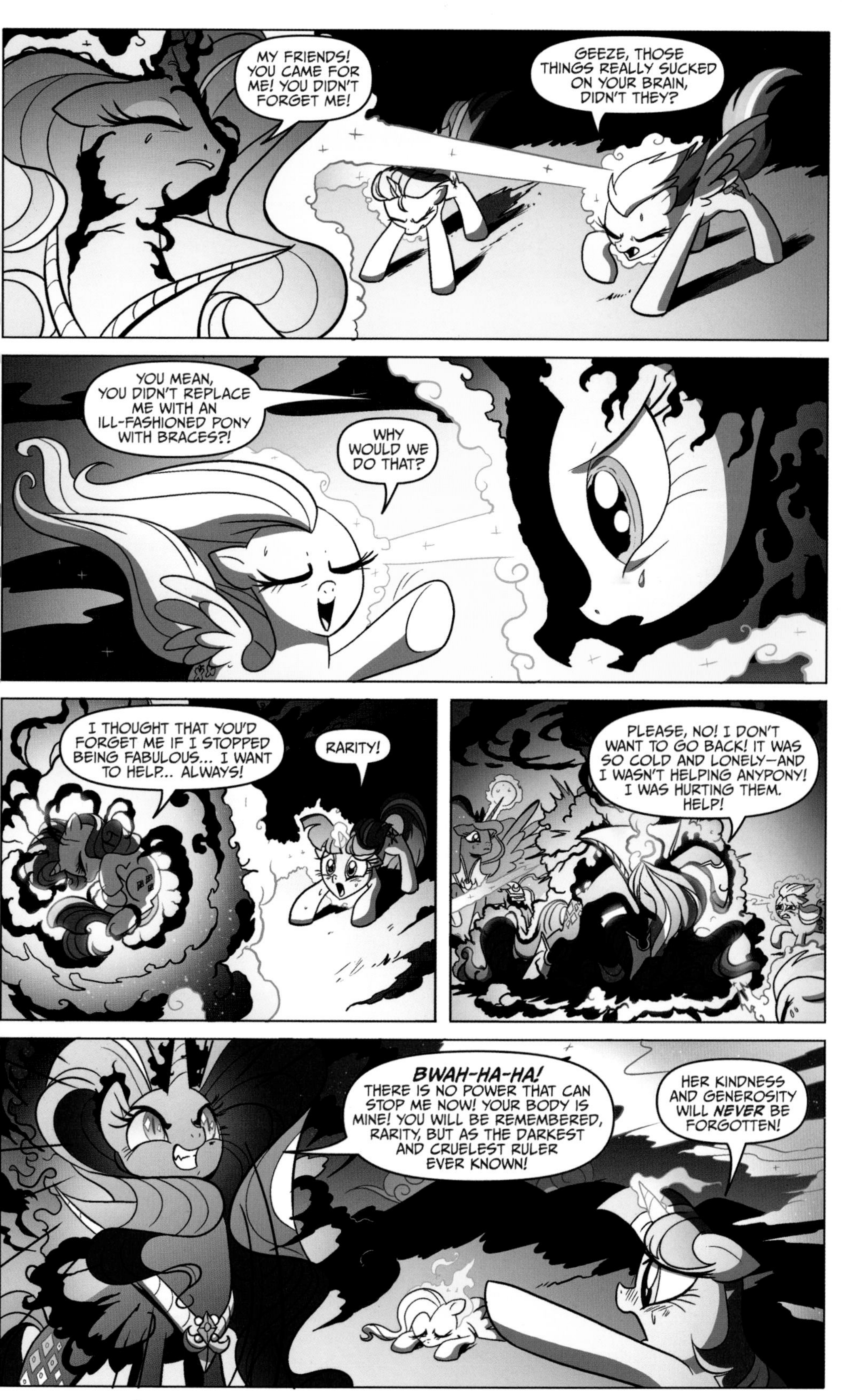
MY FRIENDS! YOU CAME FOR ME! YOU DIDN'T FORGET ME!
GEEZE, THOSE THINGS REALLY SUCKED ON YOUR BRAIN, DIDN'T THEY?
YOU MEAN, YOU DIDN'T REPLACE ME WITH AN ILL-FASHIONED PONY WITH BRACES?!
WHY WOULD WE DO THAT?
I THOUGHT THAT YOU'D FORGET ME IF I STOPPED BEING FABULOUS... I WANT TO HELP... ALWAYS!
RARITY!
PLEASE, NO! I DON'T WANT TO GO BACK! IT WAS SO COLD AND LONELY—AND I WASN'T HELPING ANYPONY! I WAS HURTING THEM. HELP!
BWAH-HA-HA! THERE IS NO POWER THAT CAN STOP ME NOW! YOUR BODY IS MINE! YOU WILL BE REMEMBERED, RARITY, BUT AS THE DARKEST AND CRUELEST RULER EVER KNOWN!
HER KINDNESS AND GENEROSITY WILL NEVER BE FORGOTTEN!

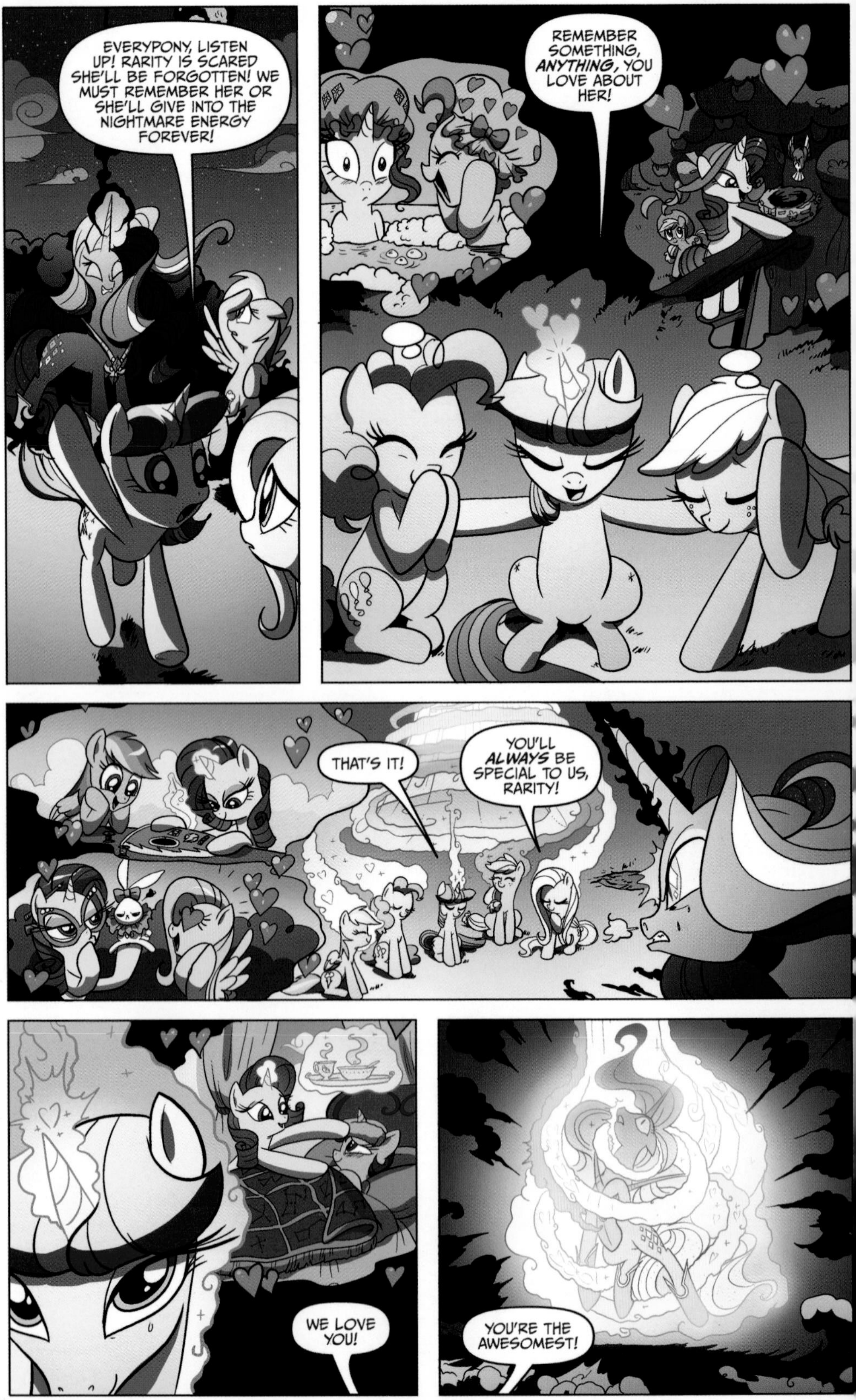
EVERYPONY, LISTEN UP! RARITY IS SCARED SHE'LL BE FORGOTTEN! WE MUST REMEMBER HER OR SHE'LL GIVE INTO THE NIGHTMARE ENERGY FOREVER!
REMEMBER SOMETHING, ANYTHING, YOU LOVE ABOUT HER!
THAT'S IT!
YOU'LL ALWAYS BE SPECIAL TO US, RARITY!
WE LOVE YOU!
YOU'RE THE AWESOMEST!

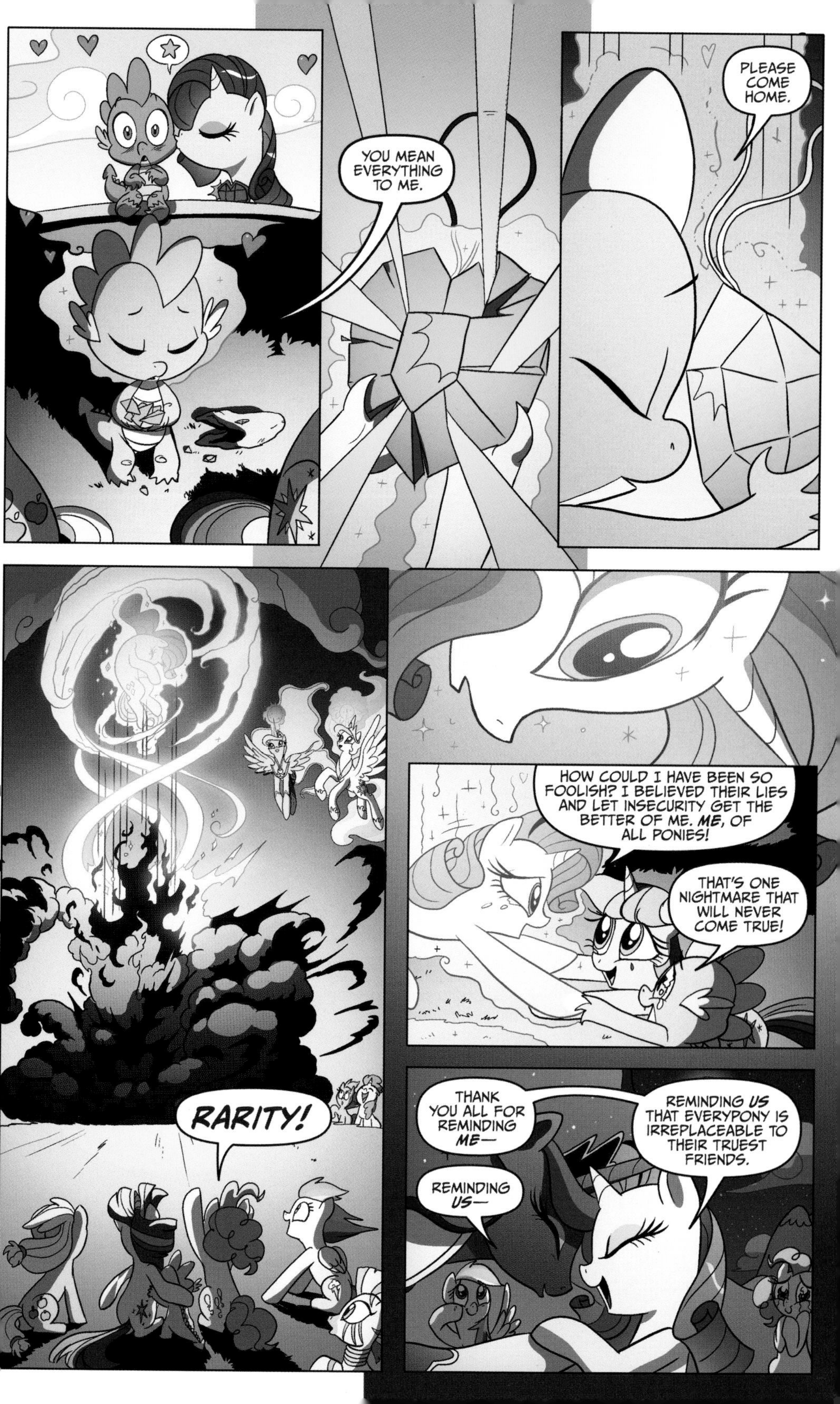
YOU MEAN EVERYTHING TO ME.
PLEASE COME HOME.
HOW COULD I HAVE BEEN SO FOOLISH? I BELIEVED THEIR LIES AND LET INSECURITY GET THE BETTER OF ME. *ME*, OF ALL PONIES!
THAT'S ONE NIGHTMARE THAT WILL NEVER COME TRUE!
RARITY!
THANK YOU ALL FOR REMINDING *ME*—
REMINDING *US*—
REMINDING *US* THAT EVERYPONY IS IRREPLACEABLE TO THEIR TRUEST FRIENDS.

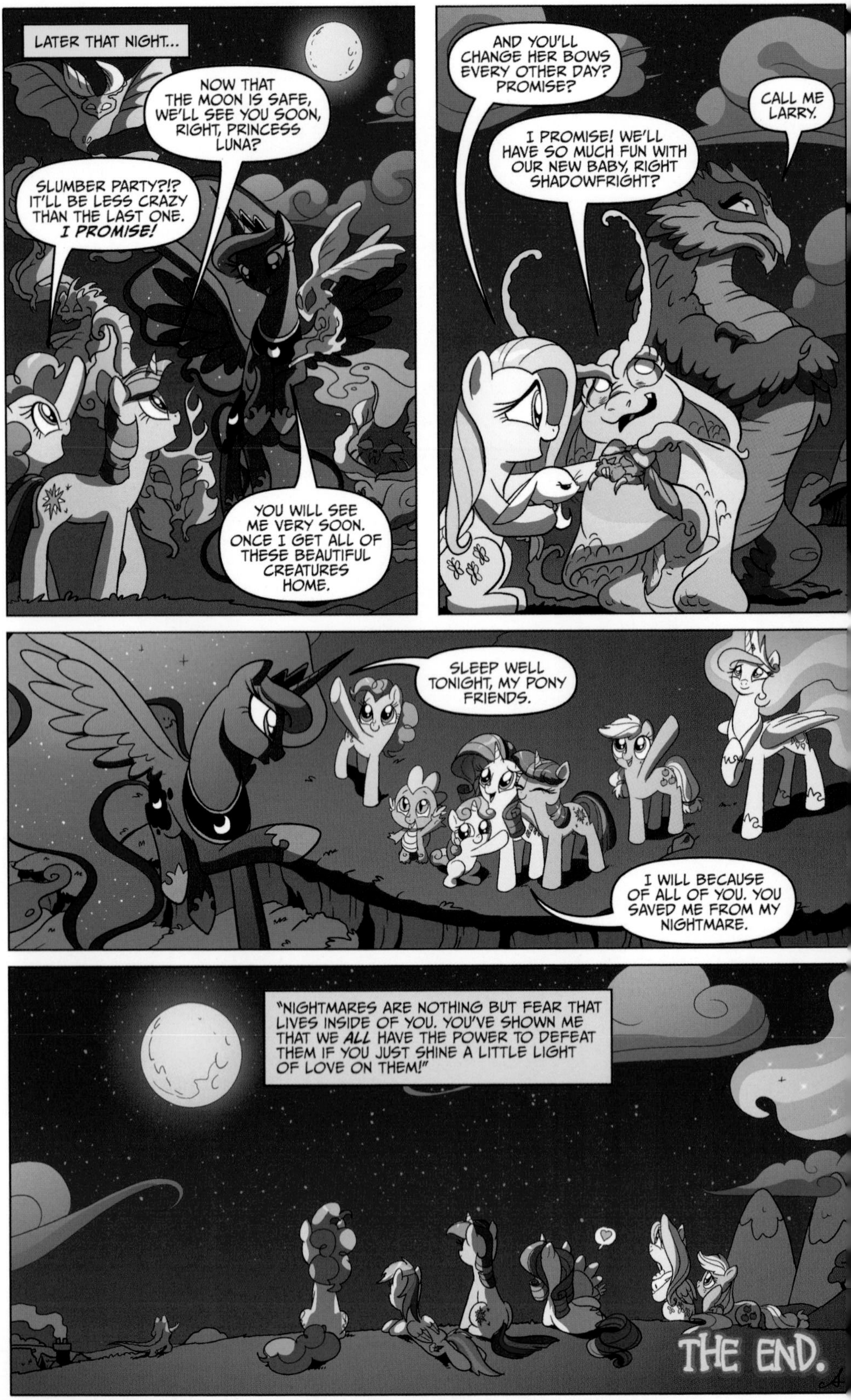
LATER THAT NIGHT...
NOW THAT THE MOON IS SAFE, WE'LL SEE YOU SOON, RIGHT, PRINCESS LUNA?
SLUMBER PARTY?!? IT'LL BE LESS CRAZY THAN THE LAST ONE. *I PROMISE!*
YOU WILL SEE ME VERY SOON. ONCE I GET ALL OF THESE BEAUTIFUL CREATURES HOME.
AND YOU'LL CHANGE HER BOWS EVERY OTHER DAY? PROMISE?
I PROMISE! WE'LL HAVE SO MUCH FUN WITH OUR NEW BABY, RIGHT SHADOWFRIGHT?
CALL ME LARRY.
SLEEP WELL TONIGHT, MY PONY FRIENDS.
I WILL BECAUSE OF ALL OF YOU. YOU SAVED ME FROM MY NIGHTMARE.
"NIGHTMARES ARE NOTHING BUT FEAR THAT LIVES INSIDE OF YOU. YOU'VE SHOWN ME THAT WE *ALL* HAVE THE POWER TO DEFEAT THEM IF YOU JUST SHINE A LITTLE LIGHT OF LOVE ON THEM!"
THE END.

Art by
Andy Price

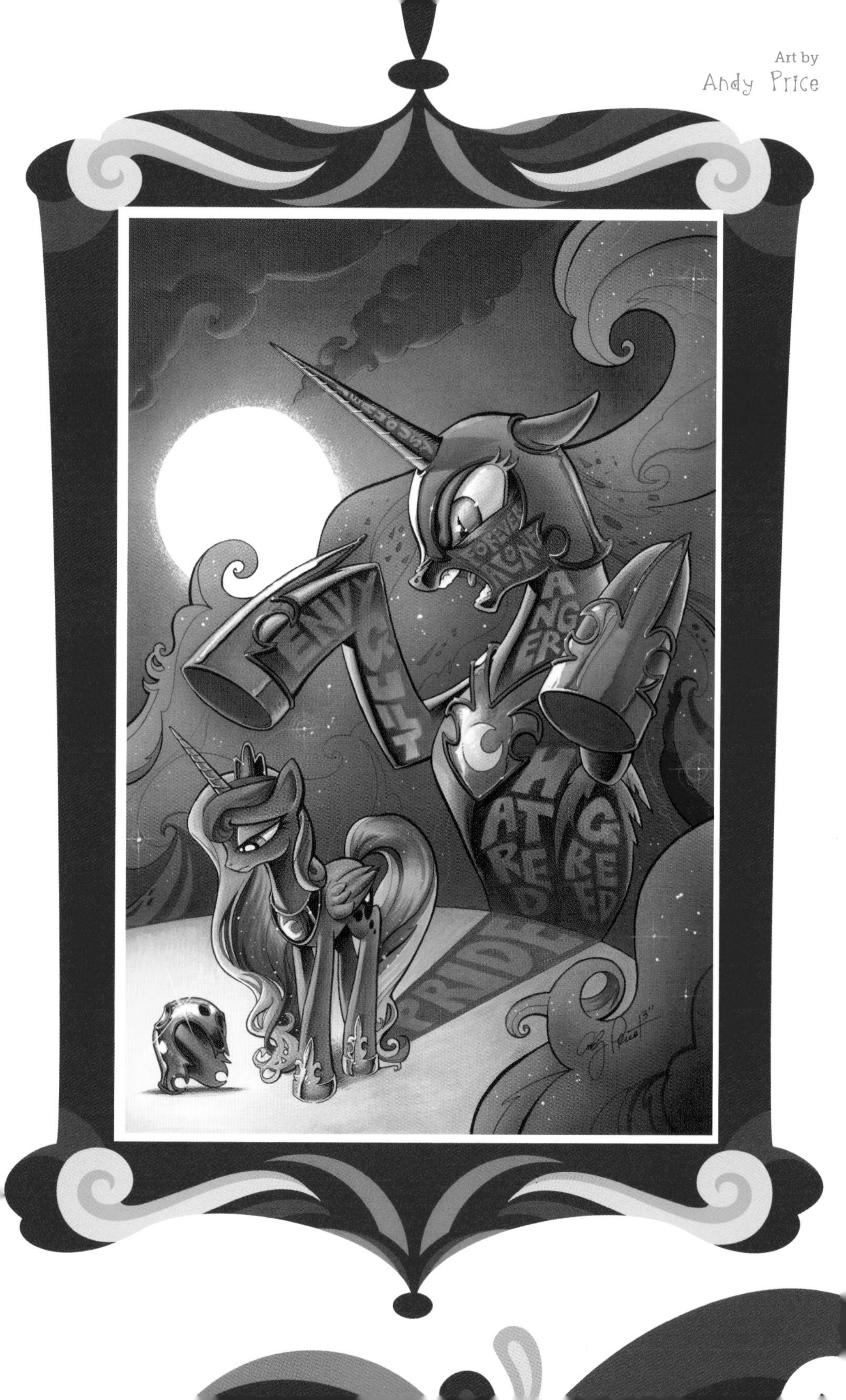

Art by
Andy Price

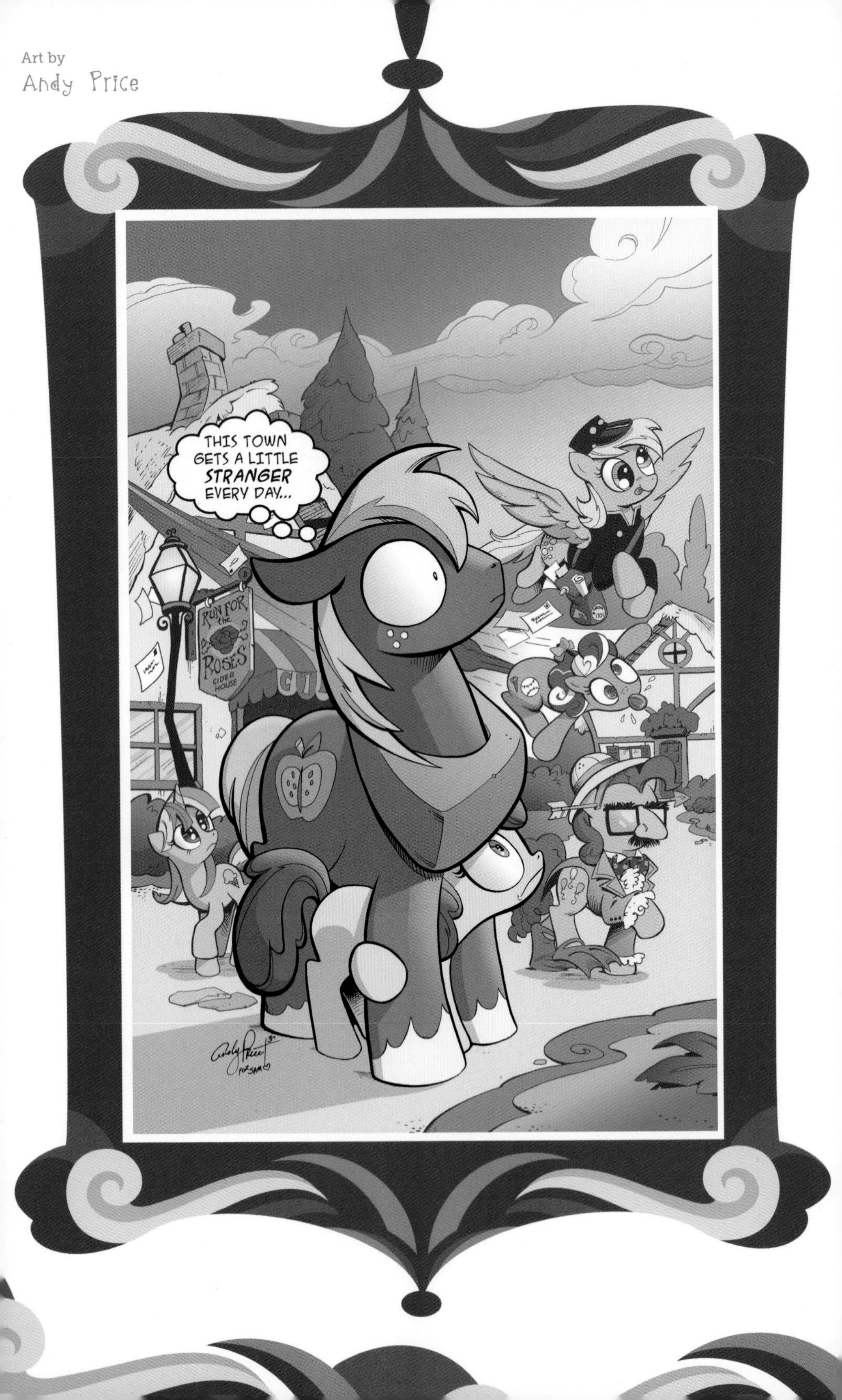
THIS TOWN GETS A LITTLE STRANGER EVERY DAY...
RUN FOR the ROSES CIDER HOUSE

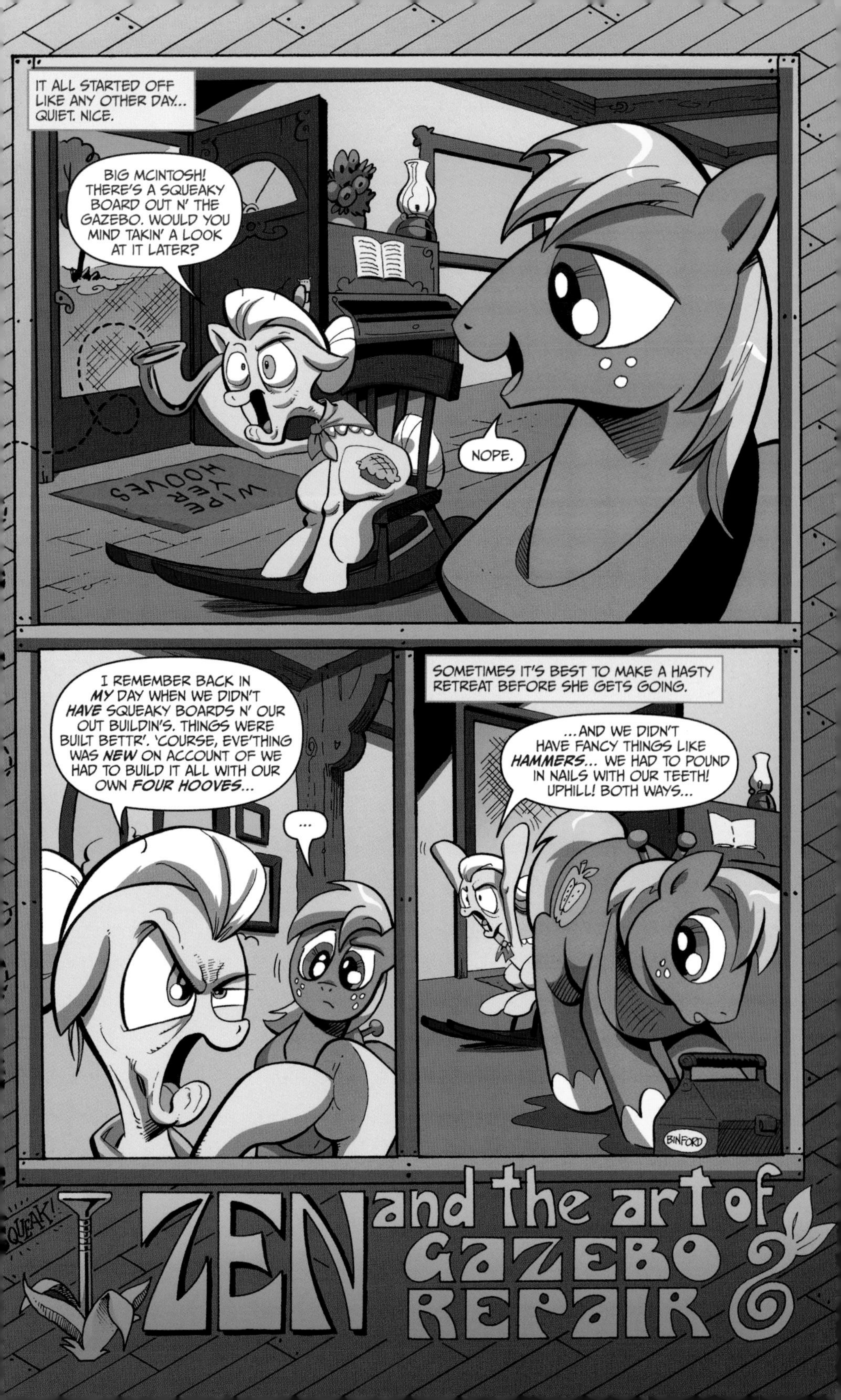
IT ALL STARTED OFF LIKE ANY OTHER DAY... QUIET. NICE.
BIG MCINTOSH! THERE'S A SQUEAKY BOARD OUT N' THE GAZEBO. WOULD YOU MIND TAKIN' A LOOK AT IT LATER?
NOPE.
WIPE YER HOOVES
I REMEMBER BACK IN MY DAY WHEN WE DIDN'T HAVE SQUEAKY BOARDS N' OUR OUT BUILDIN'S. THINGS WERE BUILT BETTR'. 'COURSE, EVE'THING WAS NEW ON ACCOUNT OF WE HAD TO BUILD IT ALL WITH OUR OWN FOUR HOOVES...
...
SOMETIMES IT'S BEST TO MAKE A HASTY RETREAT BEFORE SHE GETS GOING.
...AND WE DIDN'T HAVE FANCY THINGS LIKE HAMMERS... WE HAD TO POUND IN NAILS WITH OUR TEETH! UPHILL! BOTH WAYS...
BINFORD
QUEAK!
ZEN and the art of GAZEBO REPAIR

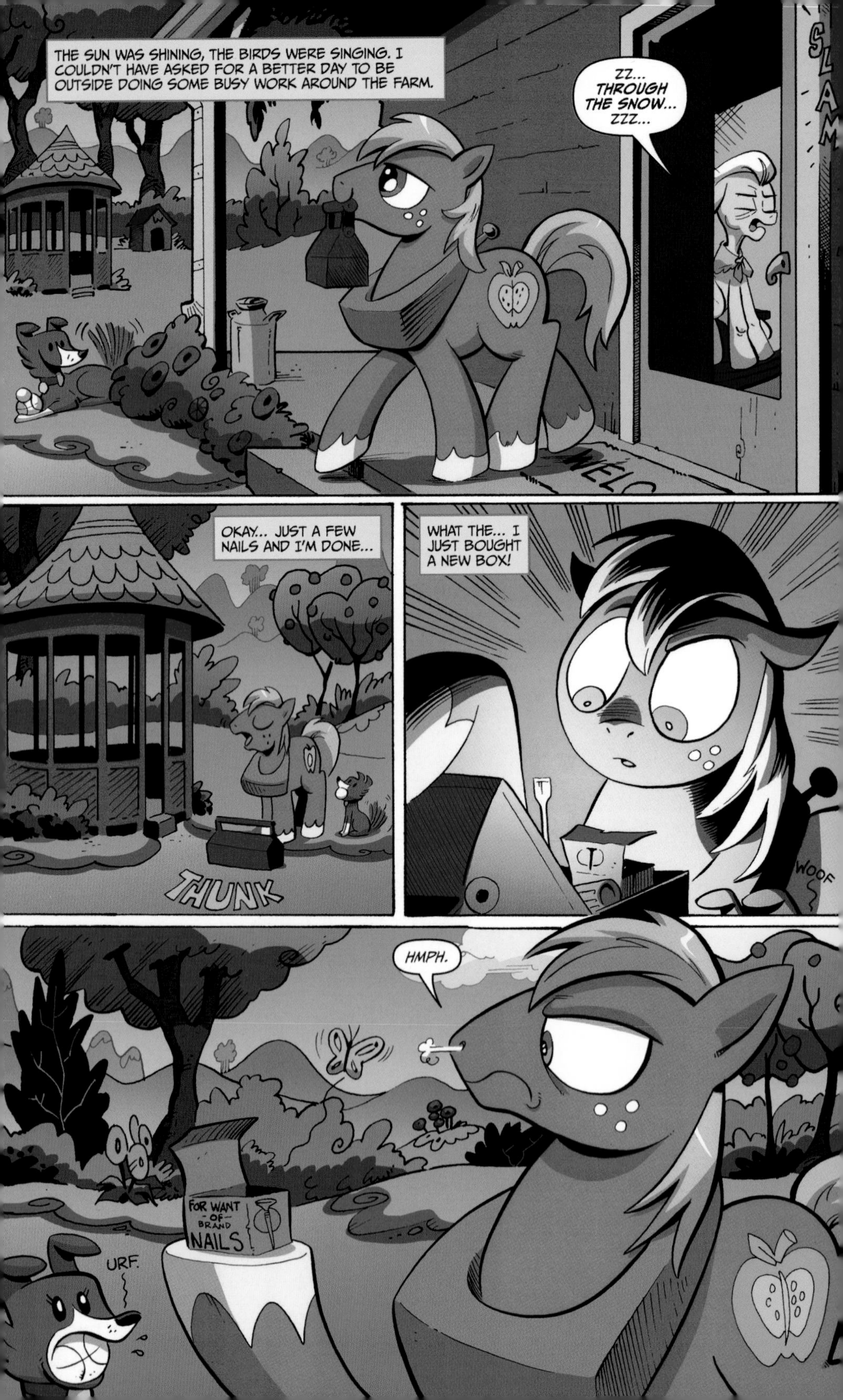
THE SUN WAS SHINING, THE BIRDS WERE SINGING. I COULDN'T HAVE ASKED FOR A BETTER DAY TO BE OUTSIDE DOING SOME BUSY WORK AROUND THE FARM.
ZZ... THROUGH THE SNOW... ZZZ...
SLAM
OKAY... JUST A FEW NAILS AND I'M DONE...
THUNK
WHAT THE... I JUST BOUGHT A NEW BOX!
WOOF
HMPH.
FOR WANT -OF- BRAND NAILS
URF.

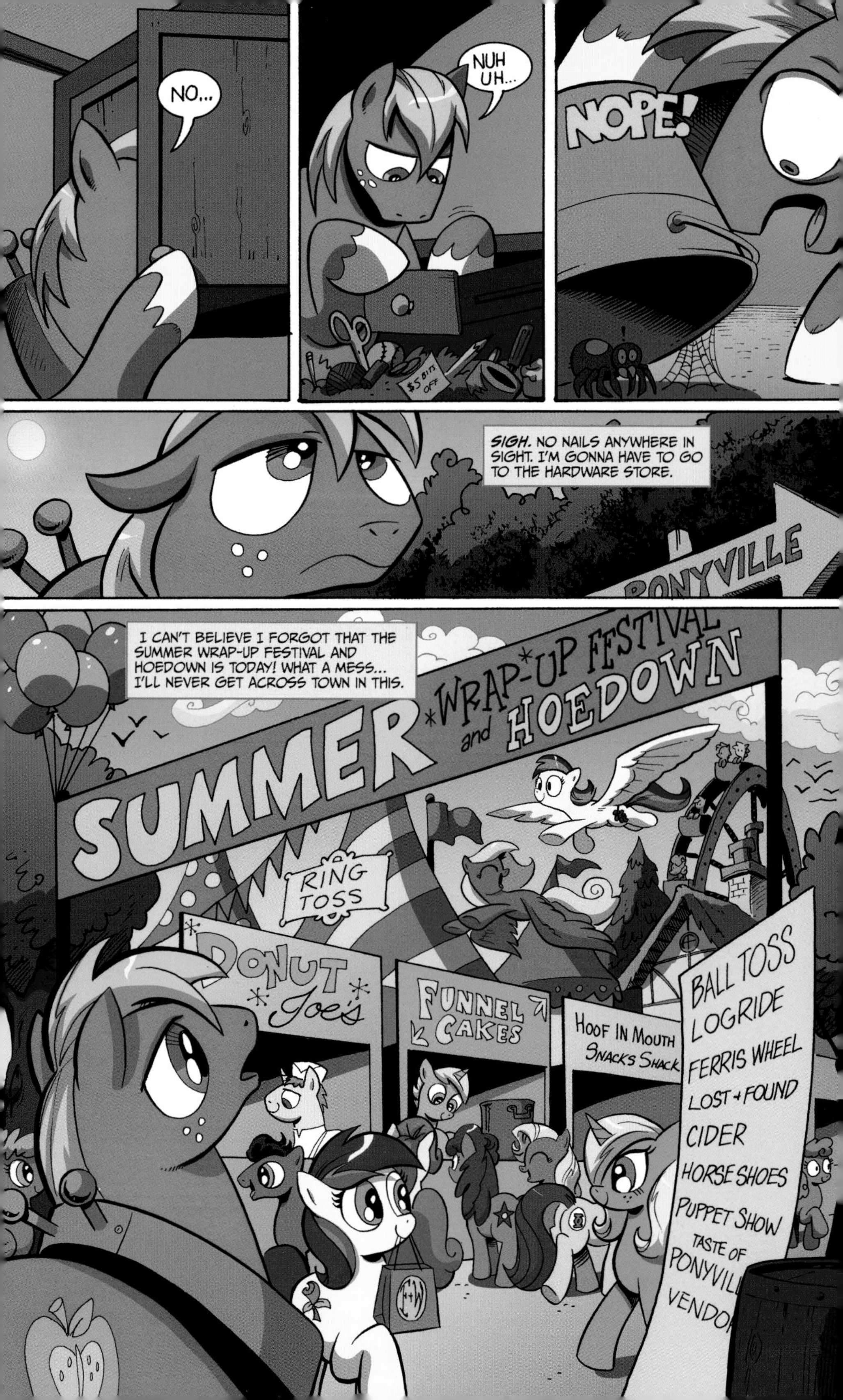
NO...
NUH UH...
NOPE!
$5 BITS OFF
SIGH. NO NAILS ANYWHERE IN SIGHT. I'M GONNA HAVE TO GO TO THE HARDWARE STORE.
PONYVILLE
I CAN'T BELIEVE I FORGOT THAT THE SUMMER WRAP-UP FESTIVAL AND HOEDOWN IS TODAY! WHAT A MESS... I'LL NEVER GET ACROSS TOWN IN THIS.
SUMMER WRAP-UP FESTIVAL and HOEDOWN
RING TOSS
DONUT Joe's
FUNNEL CAKES
HOOF IN MOUTH SNACKS SHACK
BALL TOSS
LOGRIDE
FERRIS WHEEL
LOST + FOUND
CIDER
HORSE SHOES
PUPPET SHOW
TASTE OF PONYVILL
VENDO

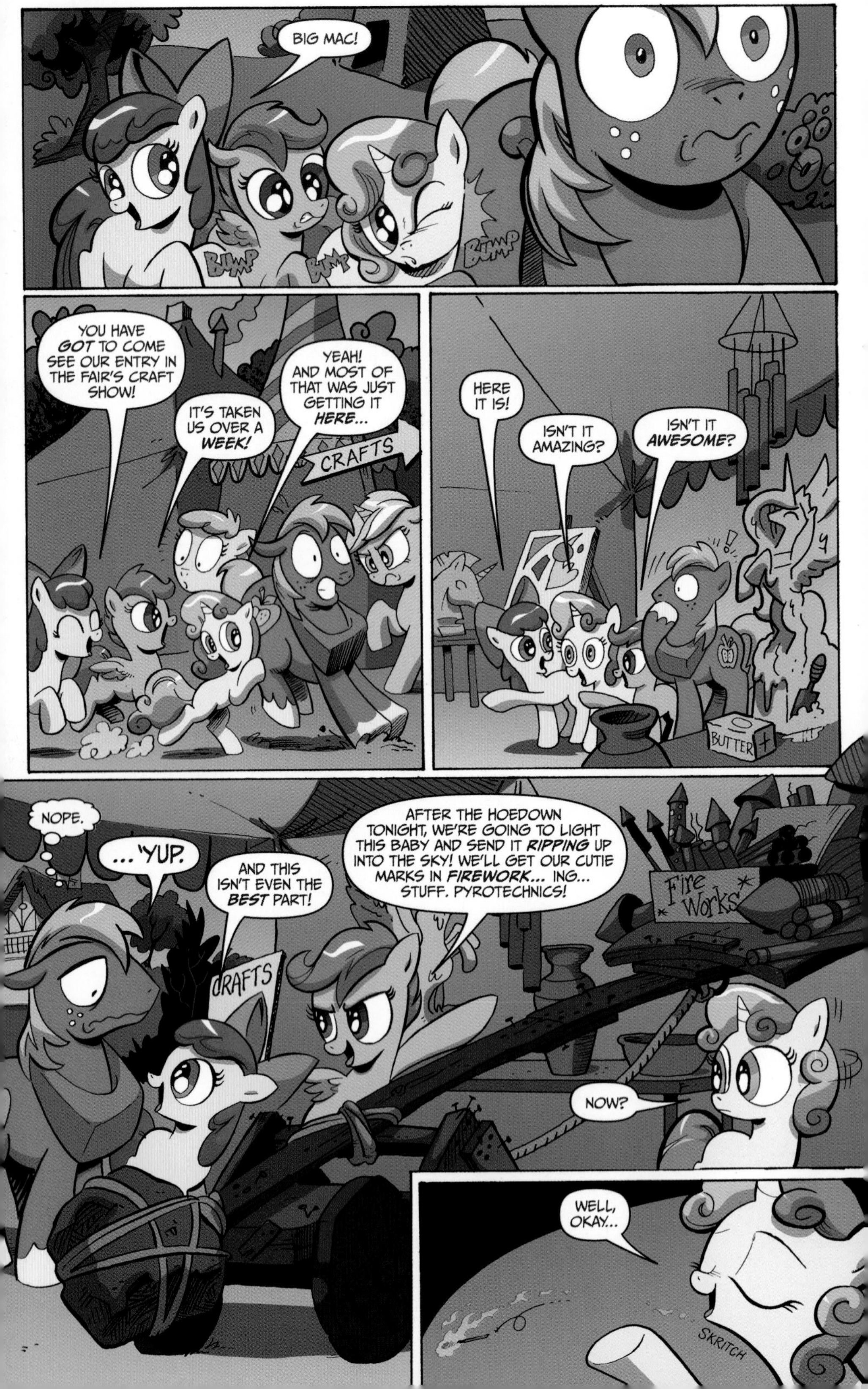

BIG MAC!
BUMP
BUMP
BUMP
YOU HAVE GOT TO COME SEE OUR ENTRY IN THE FAIR'S CRAFT SHOW!
IT'S TAKEN US OVER A WEEK!
YEAH! AND MOST OF THAT WAS JUST GETTING IT HERE...
CRAFTS
HERE IT IS!
ISN'T IT AMAZING?
ISN'T IT AWESOME?
!
BUTTER
NOPE.
...'YUP.
AND THIS ISN'T EVEN THE BEST PART!
AFTER THE HOEDOWN TONIGHT, WE'RE GOING TO LIGHT THIS BABY AND SEND IT RIPPING UP INTO THE SKY! WE'LL GET OUR CUTIE MARKS IN FIREWORK... ING... STUFF. PYROTECHNICS!
Fire Works
CRAFTS
NOW?
WELL, OKAY...
SKRITCH

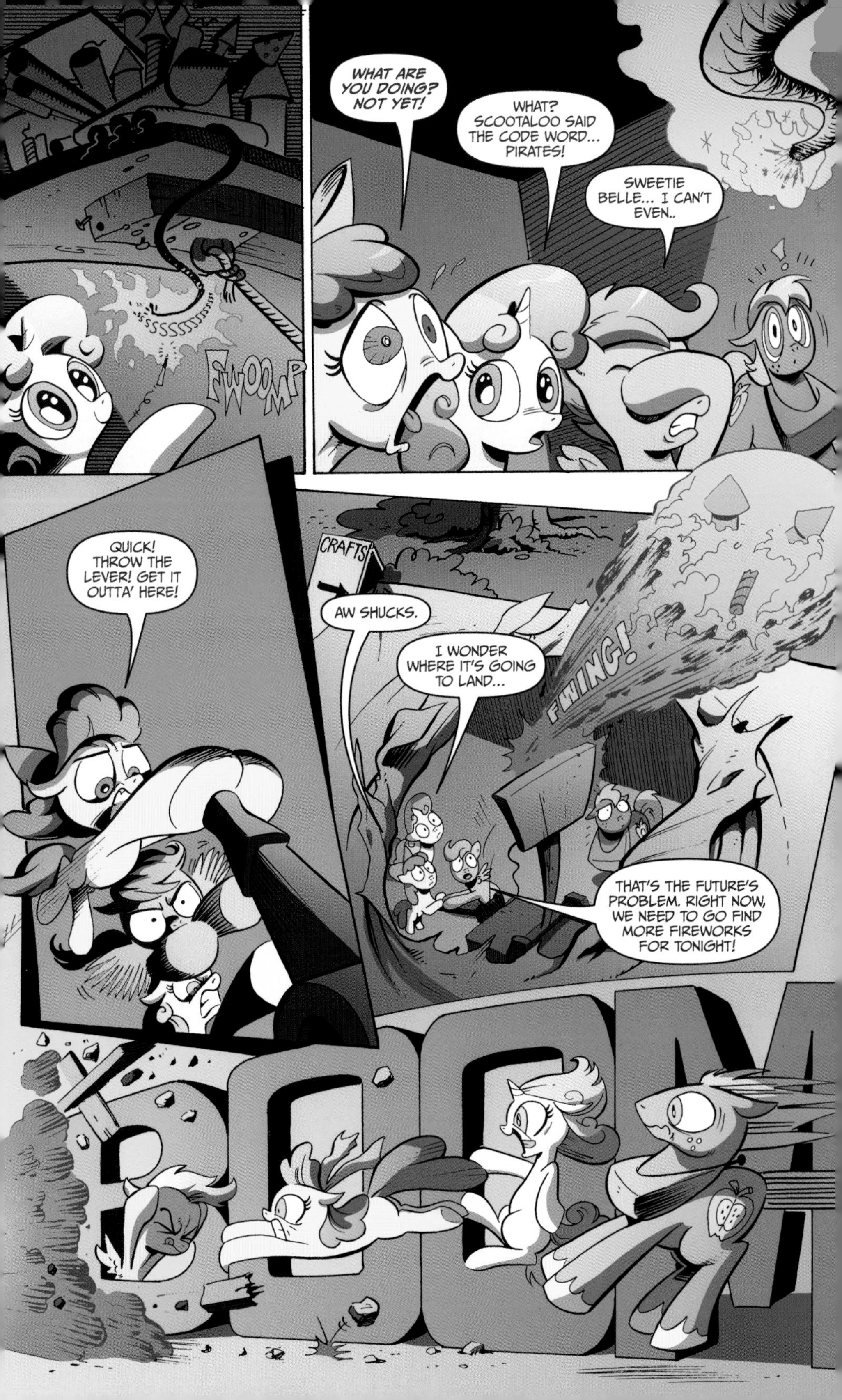
SSSSSSSSSSS
FWOOMP
WHAT ARE YOU DOING? NOT YET!
WHAT? SCOOTALOO SAID THE CODE WORD... PIRATES!
SWEETIE BELLE... I CAN'T EVEN..
QUICK! THROW THE LEVER! GET IT OUTTA' HERE!
CRAFTS
AW SHUCKS.
I WONDER WHERE IT'S GOING TO LAND...
FWING!
THAT'S THE FUTURE'S PROBLEM. RIGHT NOW, WE NEED TO GO FIND MORE FIREWORKS FOR TONIGHT!
BOOM

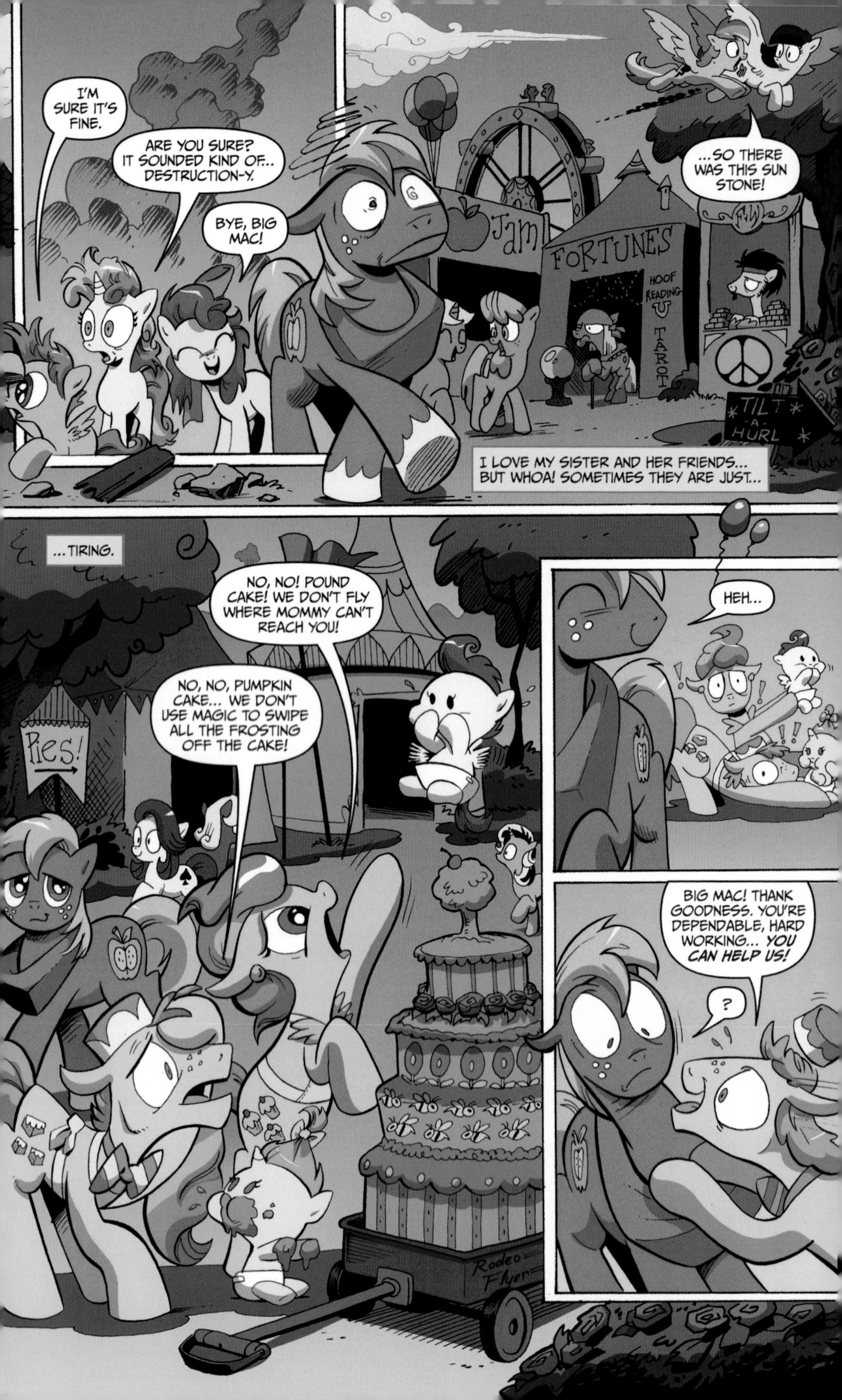
I'M SURE IT'S FINE.
ARE YOU SURE? IT SOUNDED KIND OF... DESTRUCTION-Y.
BYE, BIG MAC!
...SO THERE WAS THIS SUN STONE!
Jam
FORTUNES
HOOF READING
TAROT
TILT -A- HURL
I LOVE MY SISTER AND HER FRIENDS... BUT WHOA! SOMETIMES THEY ARE JUST...
...TIRING.
NO, NO! POUND CAKE! WE DON'T FLY WHERE MOMMY CAN'T REACH YOU!
NO, NO, PUMPKIN CAKE... WE DON'T USE MAGIC TO SWIPE ALL THE FROSTING OFF THE CAKE!
Pies!
Rodeo Flyer
HEH...
BIG MAC! THANK GOODNESS. YOU'RE DEPENDABLE, HARD WORKING... *YOU CAN HELP US!*
?

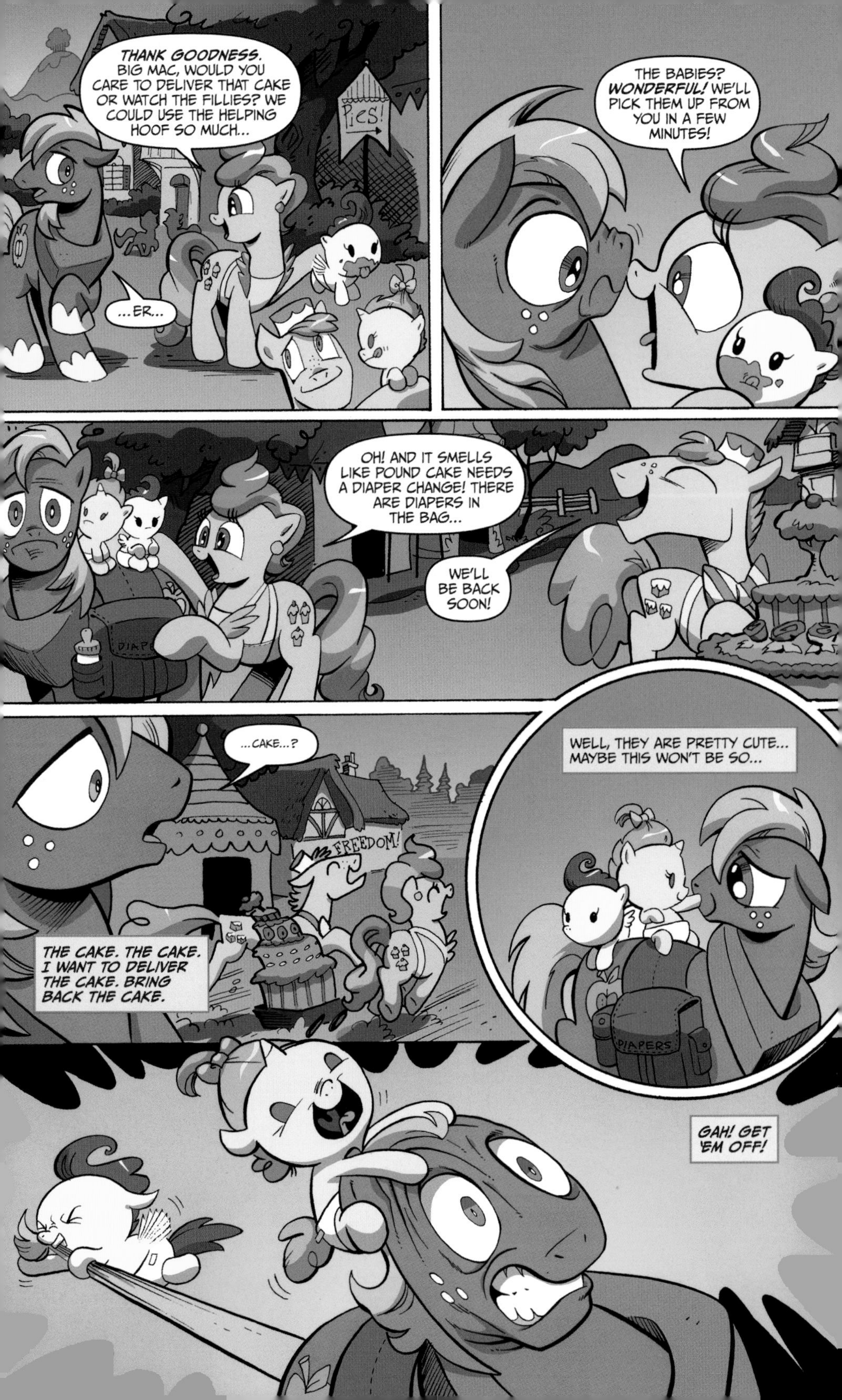

THANK GOODNESS. BIG MAC, WOULD YOU CARE TO DELIVER THAT CAKE OR WATCH THE FILLIES? WE COULD USE THE HELPING HOOF SO MUCH...
PIES!
...ER...
THE BABIES? WONDERFUL! WE'LL PICK THEM UP FROM YOU IN A FEW MINUTES!
OH! AND IT SMELLS LIKE POUND CAKE NEEDS A DIAPER CHANGE! THERE ARE DIAPERS IN THE BAG...
WE'LL BE BACK SOON!
...CAKE...?
FREEDOM!
THE CAKE. THE CAKE. I WANT TO DELIVER THE CAKE. BRING BACK THE CAKE.
WELL, THEY ARE PRETTY CUTE... MAYBE THIS WON'T BE SO...
DIAPERS
GAH! GET 'EM OFF!

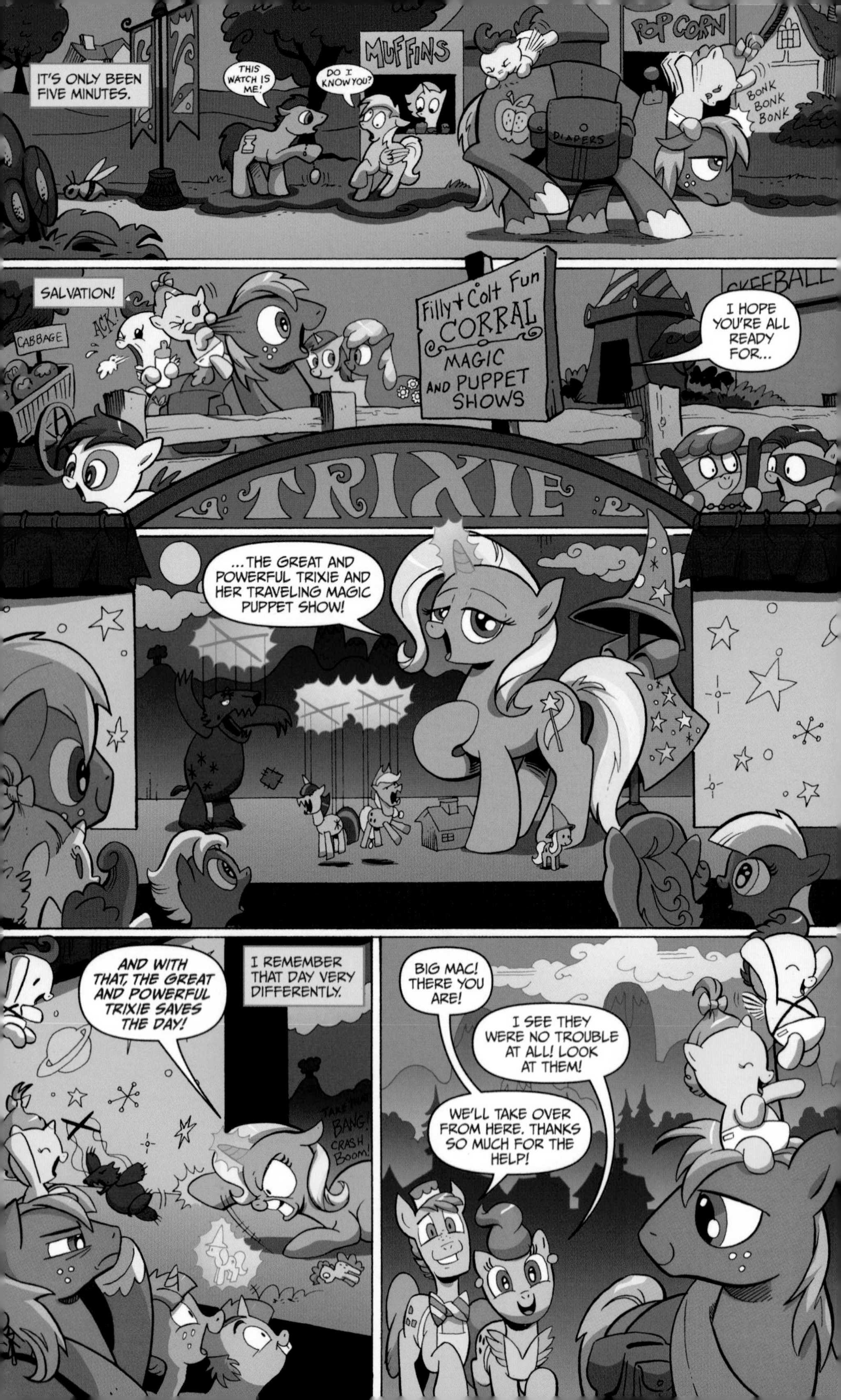

IT'S ONLY BEEN FIVE MINUTES.
MUFFINS
THIS WATCH IS ME!
DO I KNOW YOU?
POP CORN
DIAPERS
BONK BONK BONK
SALVATION!
CABBAGE
ACK!
Filly + Colt Fun CORRAL MAGIC AND PUPPET SHOWS
I HOPE YOU'RE ALL READY FOR...
TRIXIE
...THE GREAT AND POWERFUL TRIXIE AND HER TRAVELING MAGIC PUPPET SHOW!
AND WITH THAT, THE GREAT AND POWERFUL TRIXIE SAVES THE DAY!
I REMEMBER THAT DAY VERY DIFFERENTLY.
TAKE THAT! BANG! CRASH BOOM!
BIG MAC! THERE YOU ARE!
I SEE THEY WERE NO TROUBLE AT ALL! LOOK AT THEM!
WE'LL TAKE OVER FROM HERE. THANKS SO MUCH FOR THE HELP!

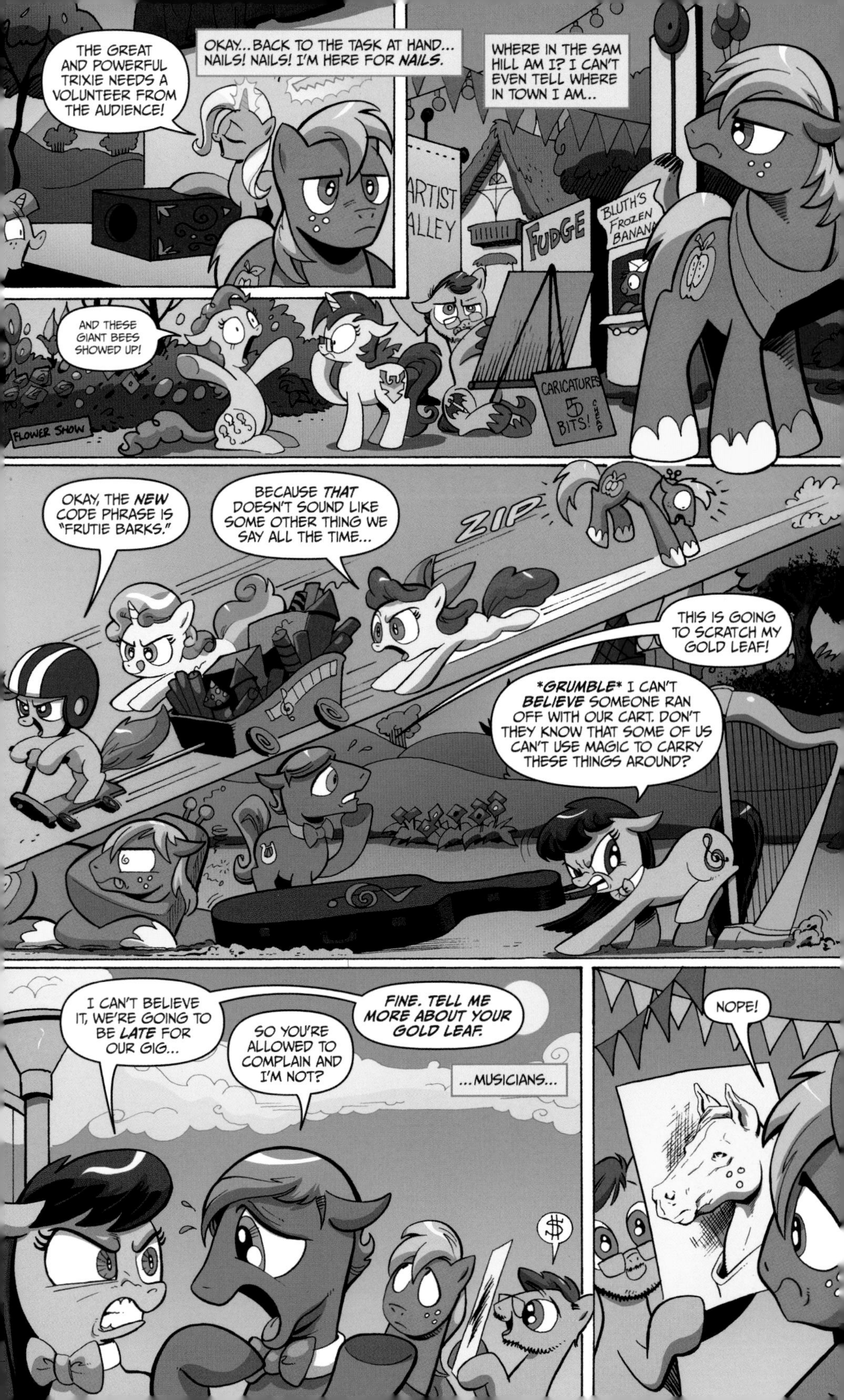
THE GREAT AND POWERFUL TRIXIE NEEDS A VOLUNTEER FROM THE AUDIENCE!
OKAY... BACK TO THE TASK AT HAND... NAILS! NAILS! I'M HERE FOR NAILS.
WHERE IN THE SAM HILL AM I? I CAN'T EVEN TELL WHERE IN TOWN I AM...
ARTIST ALLEY
FUDGE
BLUTH'S Frozen BANANA
AND THESE GIANT BEES SHOWED UP!
FLOWER SHOW
CARICATURES 5 BITS! CHEAP
OKAY, THE NEW CODE PHRASE IS "FRUTIE BARKS."
BECAUSE THAT DOESN'T SOUND LIKE SOME OTHER THING WE SAY ALL THE TIME...
ZIP
THIS IS GOING TO SCRATCH MY GOLD LEAF!
GRUMBLE I CAN'T BELIEVE SOMEONE RAN OFF WITH OUR CART. DON'T THEY KNOW THAT SOME OF US CAN'T USE MAGIC TO CARRY THESE THINGS AROUND?
I CAN'T BELIEVE IT, WE'RE GOING TO BE LATE FOR OUR GIG...
SO YOU'RE ALLOWED TO COMPLAIN AND I'M NOT?
FINE. TELL ME MORE ABOUT YOUR GOLD LEAF.
...MUSICIANS...
$
NOPE!

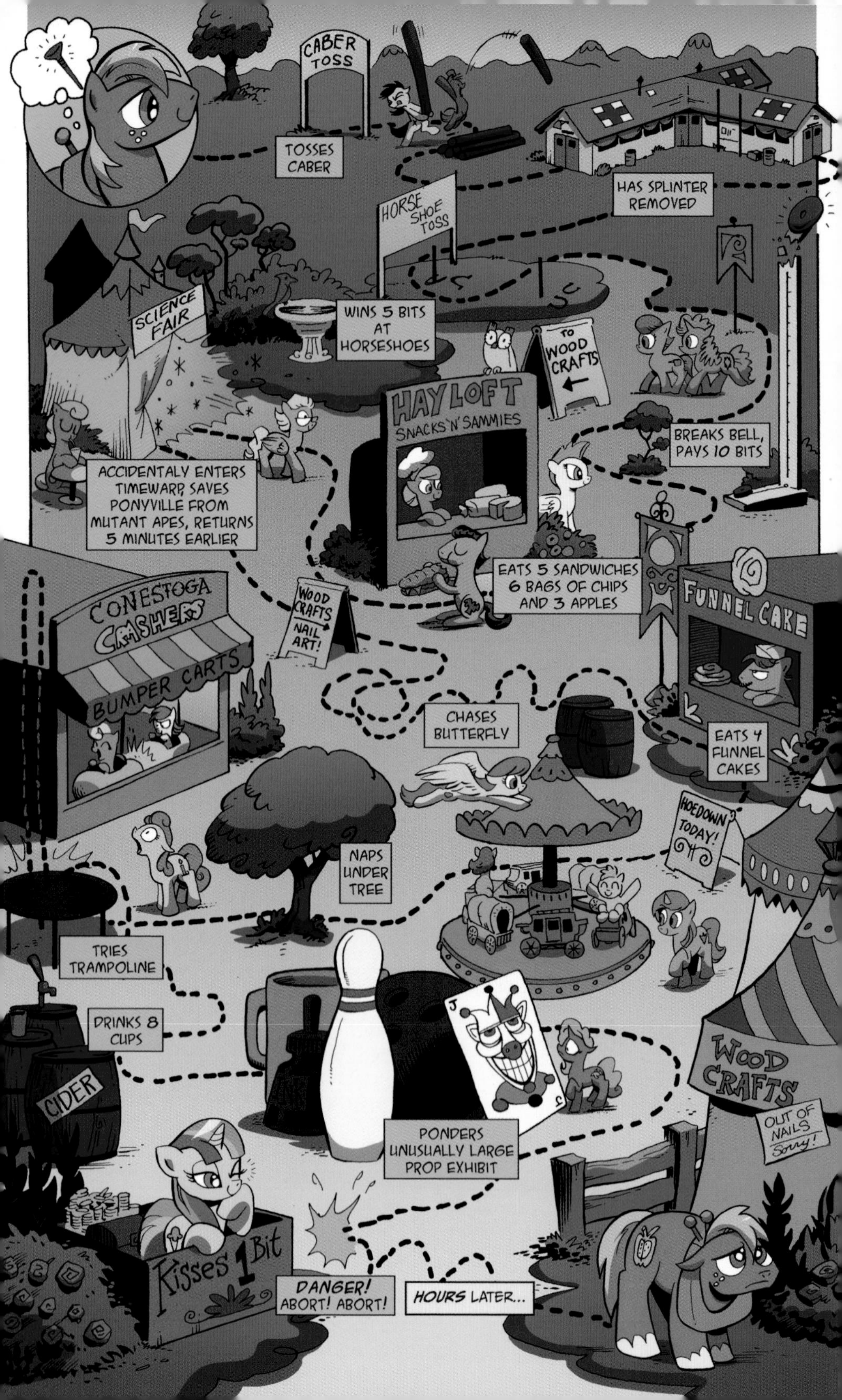
CABER TOSS
TOSSES CABER
HAS SPLINTER REMOVED
HORSE SHOE TOSS
SCIENCE FAIR
WINS 5 BITS AT HORSESHOES
TO WOOD CRAFTS
HAYLOFT SNACKS 'N' SAMMIES
BREAKS BELL, PAYS 10 BITS
ACCIDENTALY ENTERS TIMEWARP, SAVES PONYVILLE FROM MUTANT APES, RETURNS 5 MINUTES EARLIER
CONESTOGA CRASHERS
BUMPER CARTS
WOOD CRAFTS NAIL ART!
EATS 5 SANDWICHES 6 BAGS OF CHIPS AND 3 APPLES
FUNNEL CAKE
CHASES BUTTERFLY
EATS 4 FUNNEL CAKES
HOEDOWN TODAY!
NAPS UNDER TREE
TRIES TRAMPOLINE
DRINKS 8 CUPS
CIDER
WOOD CRAFTS
OUT OF NAILS Sorry!
PONDERS UNUSUALLY LARGE PROP EXHIBIT
Kisses 1 Bit
DANGER! ABORT! ABORT!
HOURS LATER...

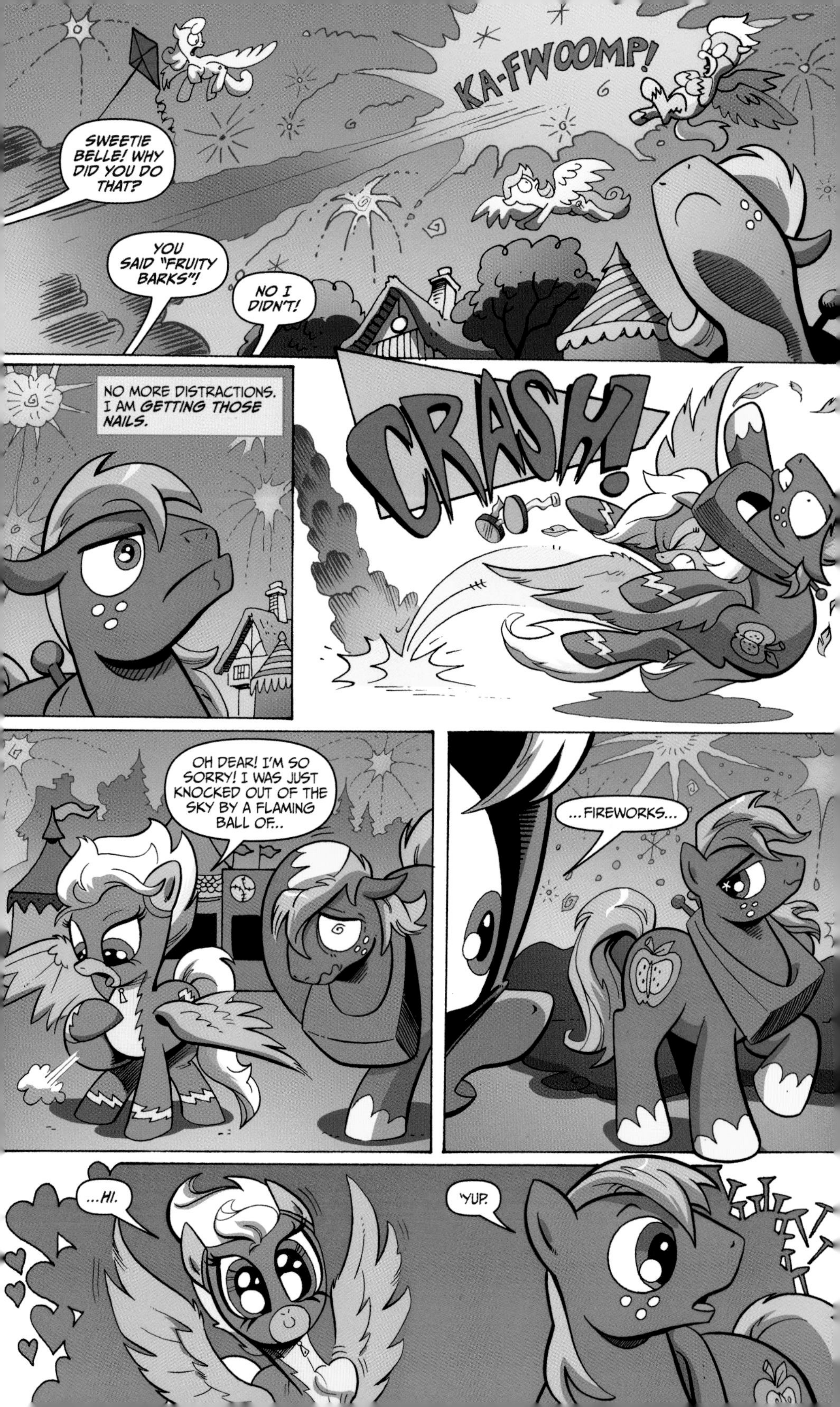
KA-FWOOMP!
SWEETIE BELLE! WHY DID YOU DO THAT?
YOU SAID "FRUITY BARKS"!
NO I DIDN'T!
NO MORE DISTRACTIONS. I AM GETTING THOSE NAILS.
CRASH!
OH DEAR! I'M SO SORRY! I WAS JUST KNOCKED OUT OF THE SKY BY A FLAMING BALL OF...
...FIREWORKS...
...HI.
'YUP.

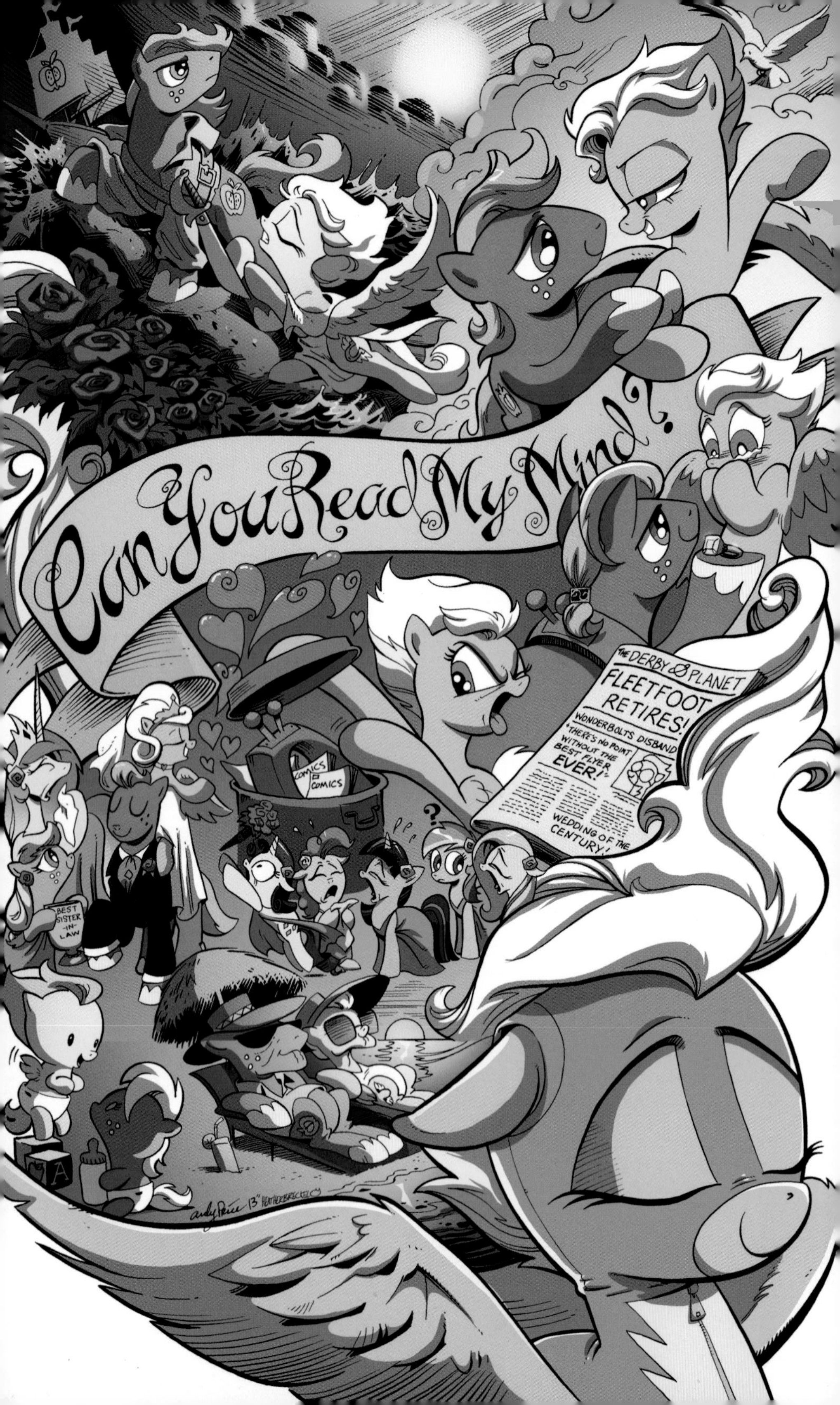

Can You Read My Mind?
THE DERBY PLANET
FLEETFOOT RETIRES!
WONDERBOLTS DISBAND
"THERE'S NO POINT WITHOUT THE BEST FLYER EVER!"
WEDDING OF THE CENTURY!
COMICS
COMICS
BEST SISTER-IN-LAW

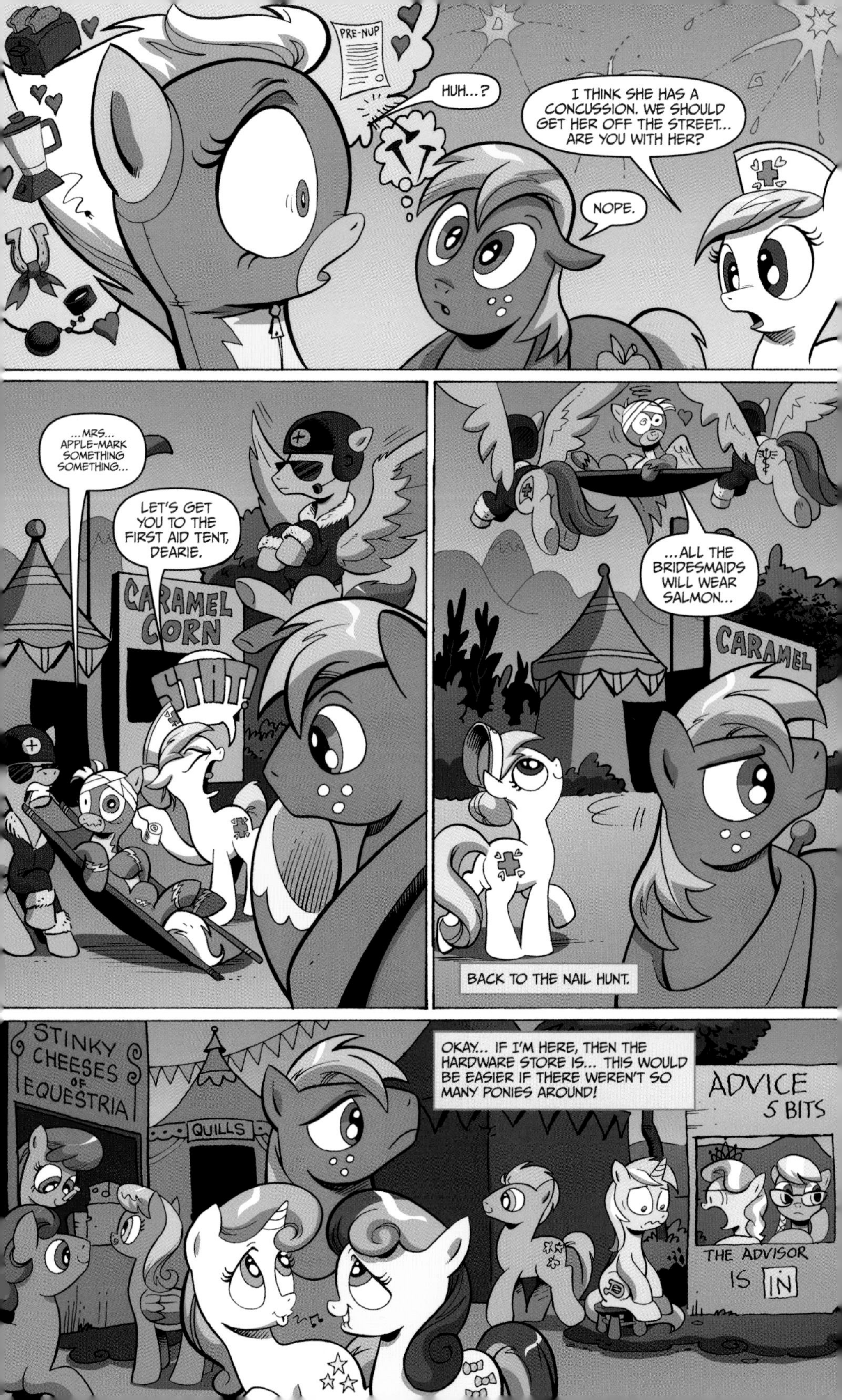
PRE-NUP
HUH...?
I THINK SHE HAS A CONCUSSION. WE SHOULD GET HER OFF THE STREET... ARE YOU WITH HER?
NOPE.
...MRS... APPLE-MARK SOMETHING SOMETHING...
LET'S GET YOU TO THE FIRST AID TENT, DEARIE.
CARAMEL CORN
STAT!
...ALL THE BRIDESMAIDS WILL WEAR SALMON...
CARAMEL
BACK TO THE NAIL HUNT.
STINKY CHEESES OF EQUESTRIA
QUILLS
OKAY... IF I'M HERE, THEN THE HARDWARE STORE IS... THIS WOULD BE EASIER IF THERE WEREN'T SO MANY PONIES AROUND!
ADVICE 5 BITS
THE ADVISOR IS IN

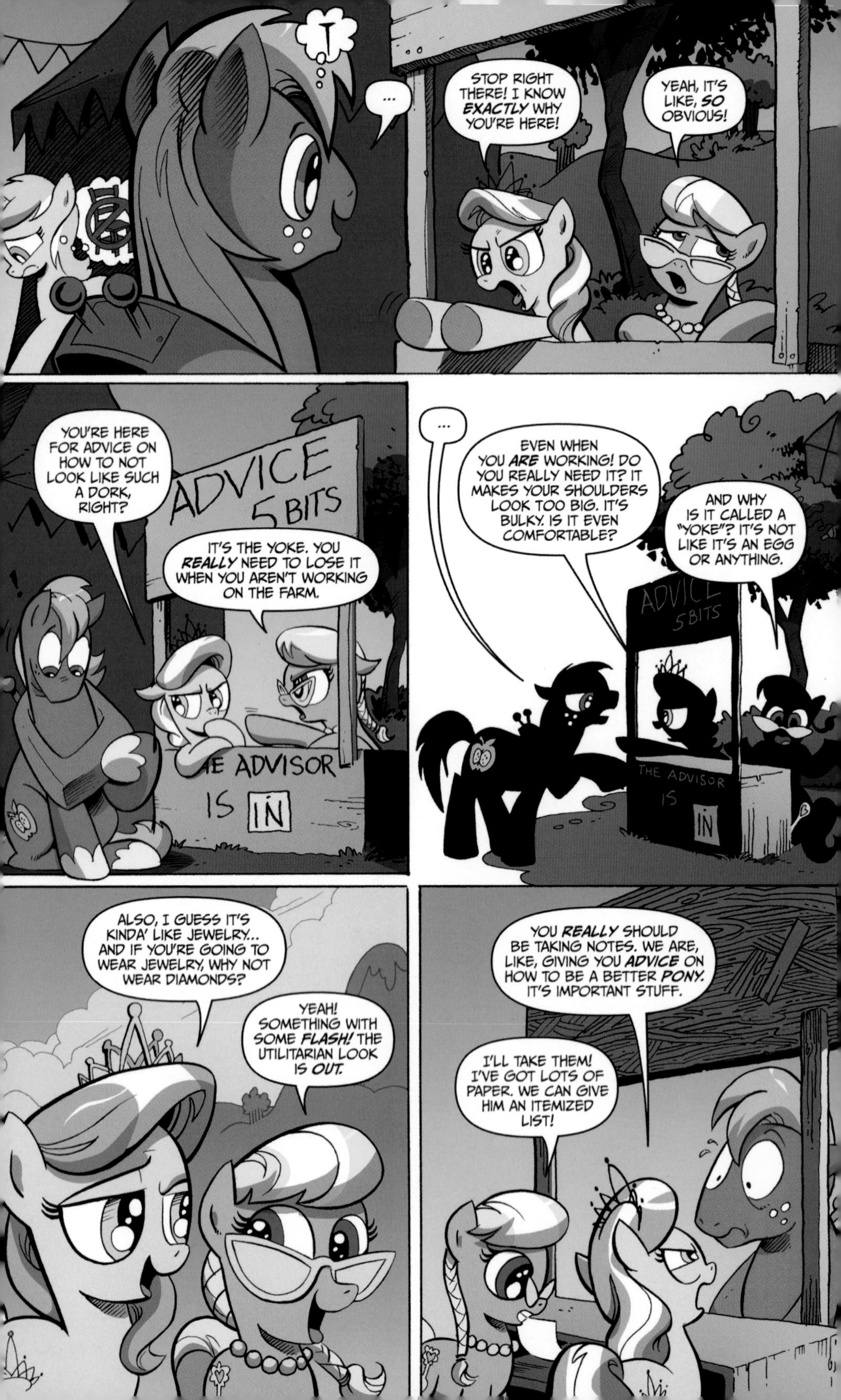
T
...
STOP RIGHT THERE! I KNOW EXACTLY WHY YOU'RE HERE!
YEAH, IT'S LIKE, SO OBVIOUS!
YOU'RE HERE FOR ADVICE ON HOW TO NOT LOOK LIKE SUCH A DORK, RIGHT?
ADVICE 5 BITS
IT'S THE YOKE. YOU REALLY NEED TO LOSE IT WHEN YOU AREN'T WORKING ON THE FARM.
!
HE ADVISOR IS IN
...
EVEN WHEN YOU ARE WORKING! DO YOU REALLY NEED IT? IT MAKES YOUR SHOULDERS LOOK TOO BIG. IT'S BULKY. IS IT EVEN COMFORTABLE?
AND WHY IS IT CALLED A "YOKE"? IT'S NOT LIKE IT'S AN EGG OR ANYTHING.
ADVICE 5 BITS
THE ADVISOR IS IN
ALSO, I GUESS IT'S KINDA' LIKE JEWELRY... AND IF YOU'RE GOING TO WEAR JEWELRY, WHY NOT WEAR DIAMONDS?
YEAH! SOMETHING WITH SOME FLASH! THE UTILITARIAN LOOK IS OUT.
YOU REALLY SHOULD BE TAKING NOTES. WE ARE, LIKE, GIVING YOU ADVICE ON HOW TO BE A BETTER PONY. IT'S IMPORTANT STUFF.
I'LL TAKE THEM! I'VE GOT LOTS OF PAPER. WE CAN GIVE HIM AN ITEMIZED LIST!

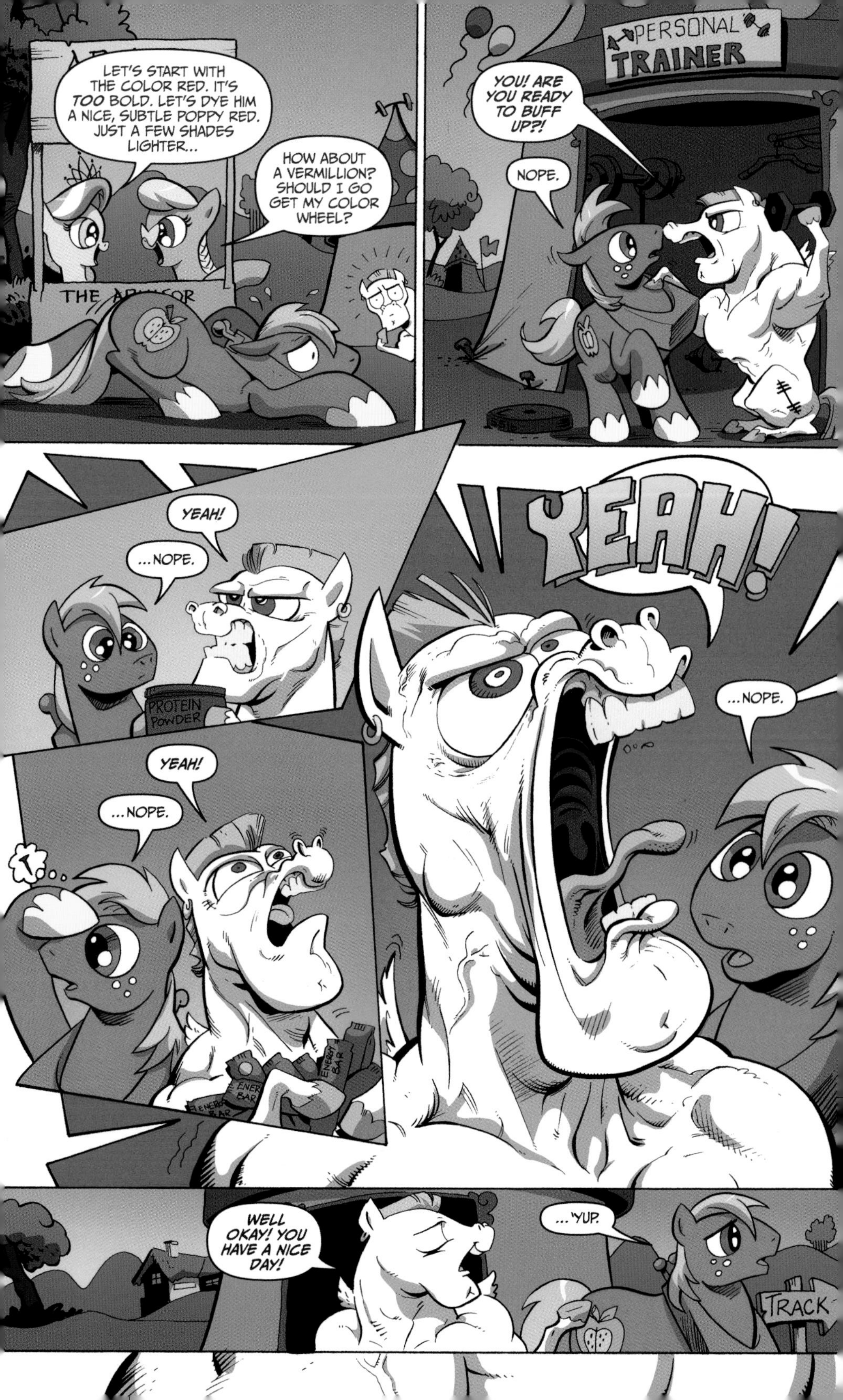
LET'S START WITH THE COLOR RED. IT'S *TOO* BOLD. LET'S DYE HIM A NICE, SUBTLE POPPY RED. JUST A FEW SHADES LIGHTER...
HOW ABOUT A VERMILLION? SHOULD I GO GET MY COLOR WHEEL?
THE A
PERSONAL TRAINER
YOU! ARE YOU READY TO BUFF UP?!
NOPE.
YEAH!
...NOPE.
PROTEIN POWDER
YEAH!
...NOPE.
ENERGY BAR
YEAH!
...NOPE.
WELL OKAY! YOU HAVE A NICE DAY!
...YUP.
TRACK

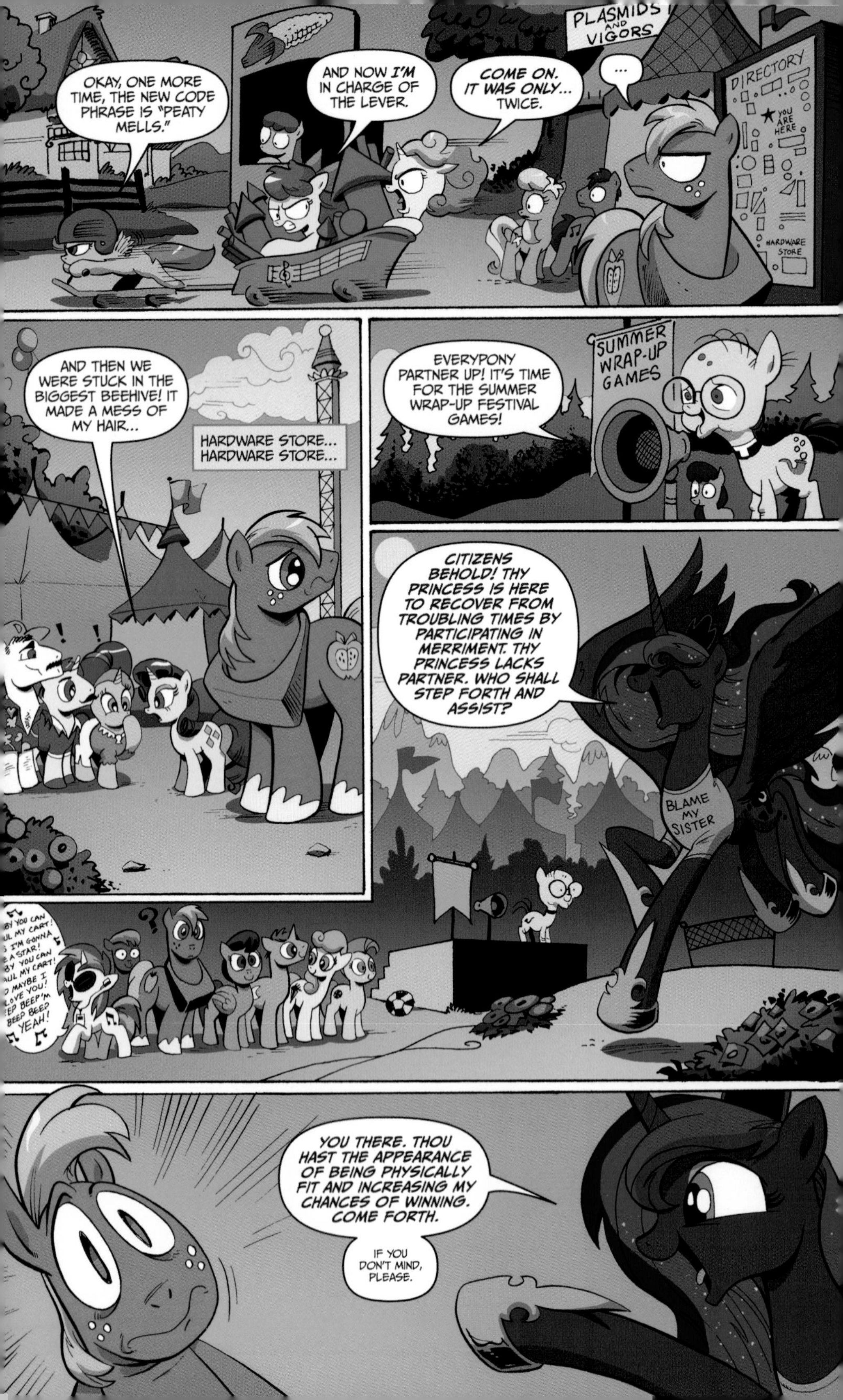
PLASMIDS AND VIGORS
OKAY, ONE MORE TIME, THE NEW CODE PHRASE IS "PEATY MELLS."
AND NOW I'M IN CHARGE OF THE LEVER.
COME ON. IT WAS ONLY... TWICE.
...
DIRECTORY
YOU ARE HERE
HARDWARE STORE
AND THEN WE WERE STUCK IN THE BIGGEST BEEHIVE! IT MADE A MESS OF MY HAIR...
HARDWARE STORE... HARDWARE STORE...
SUMMER WRAP-UP GAMES
EVERYPONY PARTNER UP! IT'S TIME FOR THE SUMMER WRAP-UP FESTIVAL GAMES!
CITIZENS BEHOLD! THY PRINCESS IS HERE TO RECOVER FROM TROUBLING TIMES BY PARTICIPATING IN MERRIMENT. THY PRINCESS LACKS PARTNER. WHO SHALL STEP FORTH AND ASSIST?
BLAME MY SISTER
YOU THERE. THOU HAST THE APPEARANCE OF BEING PHYSICALLY FIT AND INCREASING MY CHANCES OF WINNING. COME FORTH.
IF YOU DON'T MIND, PLEASE.

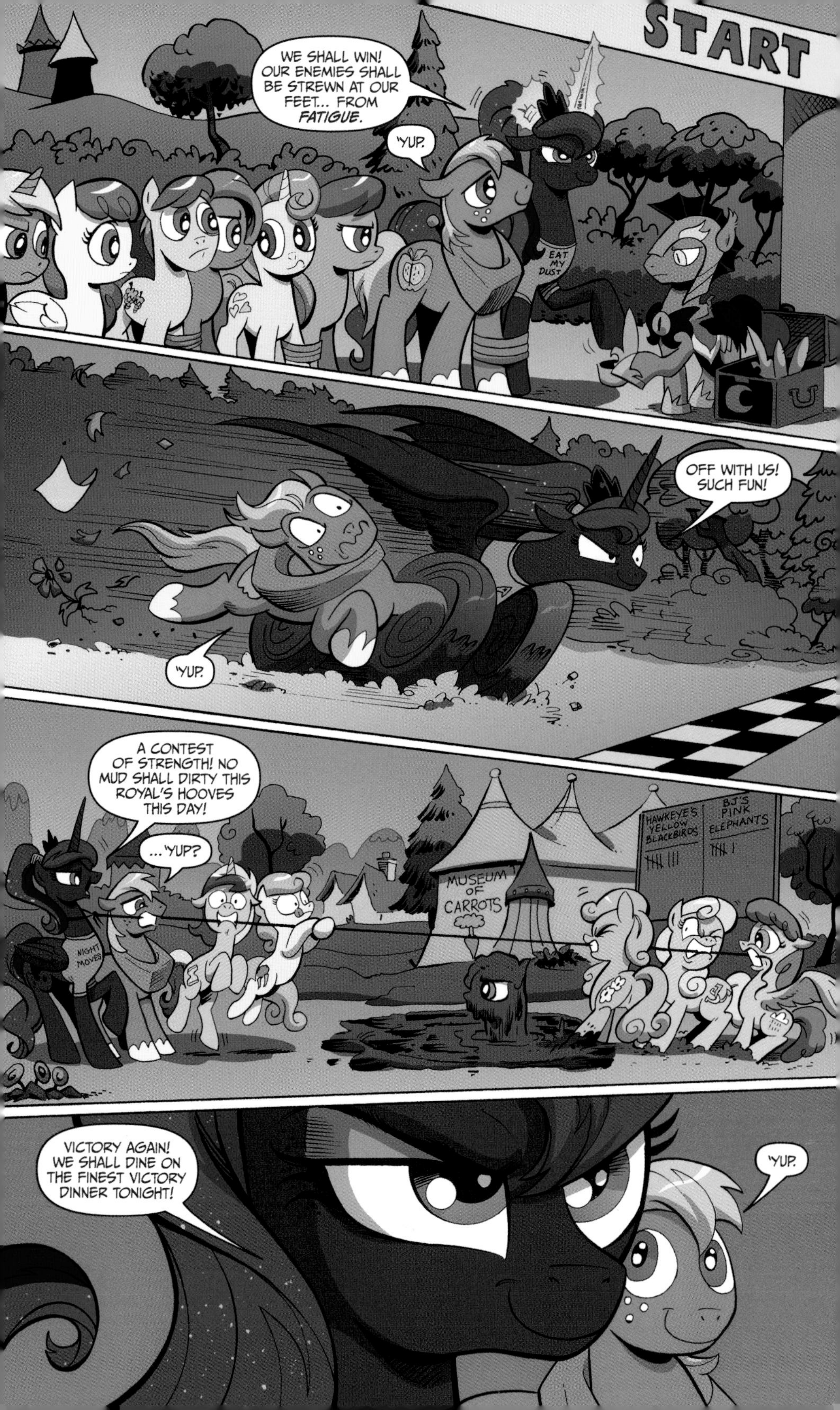
START
WE SHALL WIN! OUR ENEMIES SHALL BE STREWN AT OUR FEET... FROM FATIGUE.
'YUP.
EAT MY DUST
OFF WITH US! SUCH FUN!
'YUP.
A CONTEST OF STRENGTH! NO MUD SHALL DIRTY THIS ROYAL'S HOOVES THIS DAY!
...'YUP?
HAWKEYE'S YELLOW BLACKBIRDS
BJ'S PINK ELEPHANTS
MUSEUM OF CARROTS
NIGHT MOVES
VICTORY AGAIN! WE SHALL DINE ON THE FINEST VICTORY DINNER TONIGHT!
'YUP.

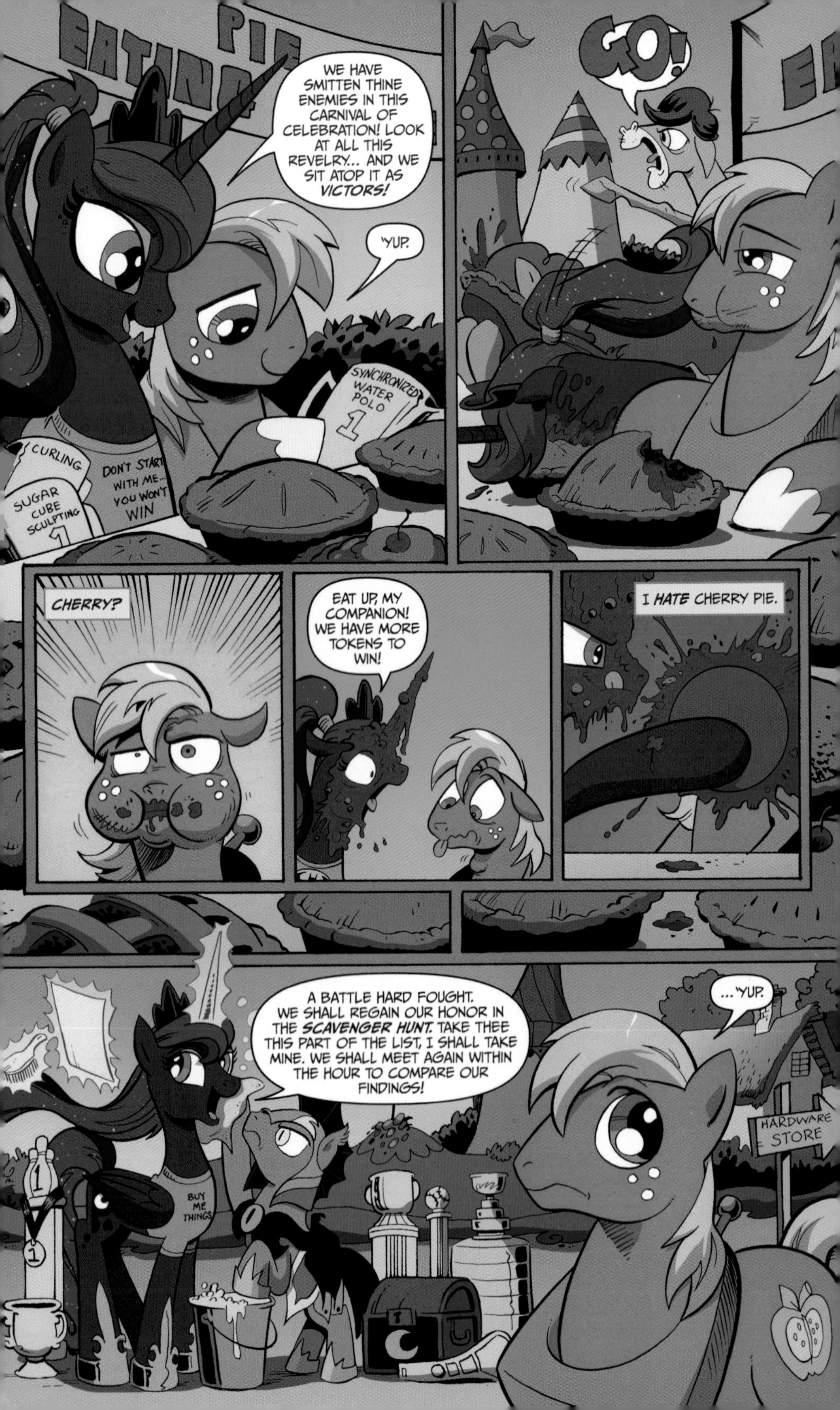
PIE EATING
WE HAVE SMITTEN THINE ENEMIES IN THIS CARNIVAL OF CELEBRATION! LOOK AT ALL THIS REVELRY... AND WE SIT ATOP IT AS VICTORS!
'YUP.
SYNCHRONIZED WATER POLO 1
CURLING
SUGAR CUBE SCULPTING 1
DON'T START WITH ME... YOU WON'T WIN
GO!
CHERRY?
EAT UP, MY COMPANION! WE HAVE MORE TOKENS TO WIN!
I HATE CHERRY PIE.
A BATTLE HARD FOUGHT. WE SHALL REGAIN OUR HONOR IN THE SCAVENGER HUNT. TAKE THEE THIS PART OF THE LIST, I SHALL TAKE MINE. WE SHALL MEET AGAIN WITHIN THE HOUR TO COMPARE OUR FINDINGS!
...'YUP.
HARDWARE STORE
BUY ME THINGS

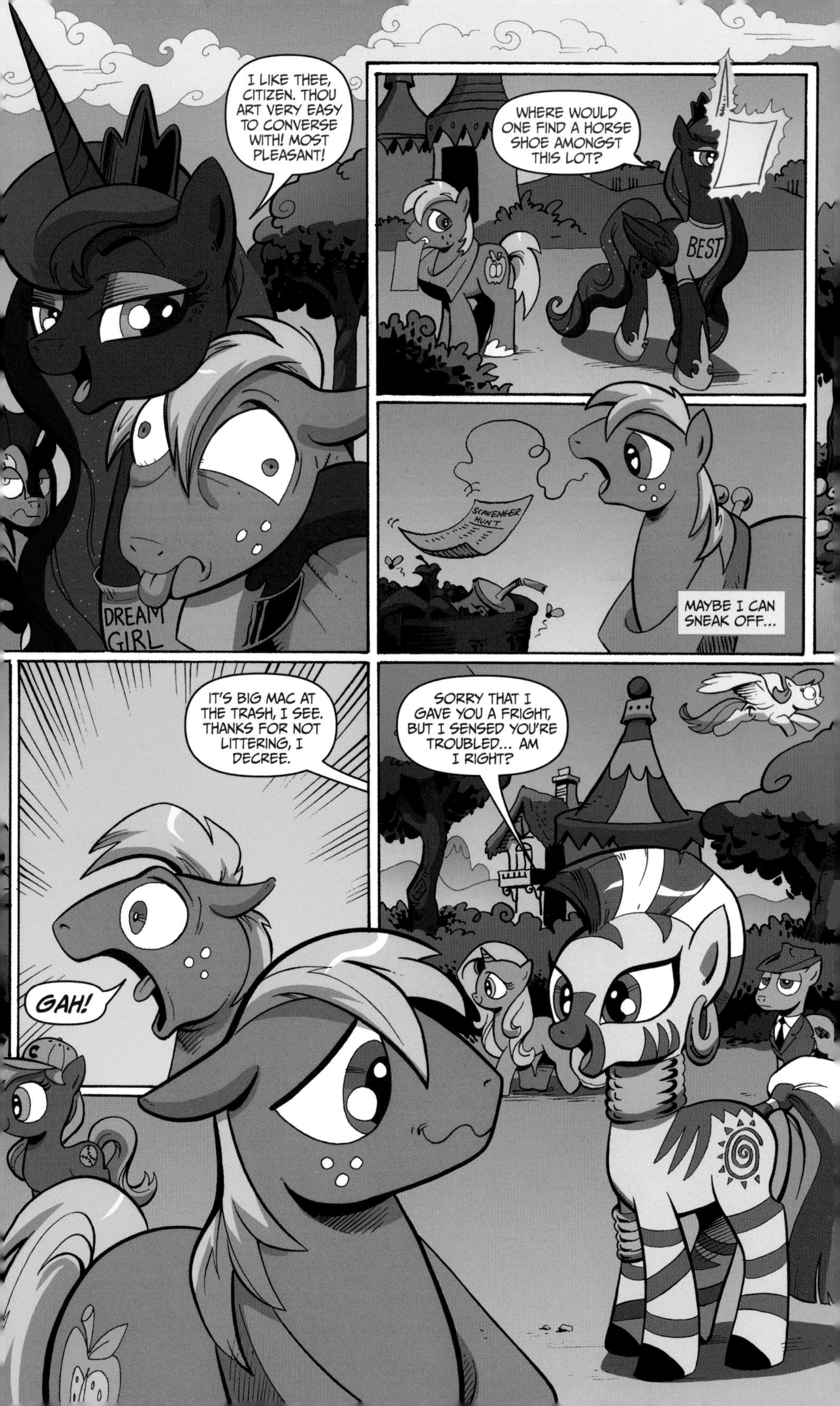
I LIKE THEE, CITIZEN. THOU ART VERY EASY TO CONVERSE WITH! MOST PLEASANT!
DREAM GIRL
WHERE WOULD ONE FIND A HORSE SHOE AMONGST THIS LOT?
BEST
SCAVENGER HUNT
MAYBE I CAN SNEAK OFF...
IT'S BIG MAC AT THE TRASH, I SEE. THANKS FOR NOT LITTERING, I DECREE.
GAH!
SORRY THAT I GAVE YOU A FRIGHT, BUT I SENSED YOU'RE TROUBLED... AM I RIGHT?

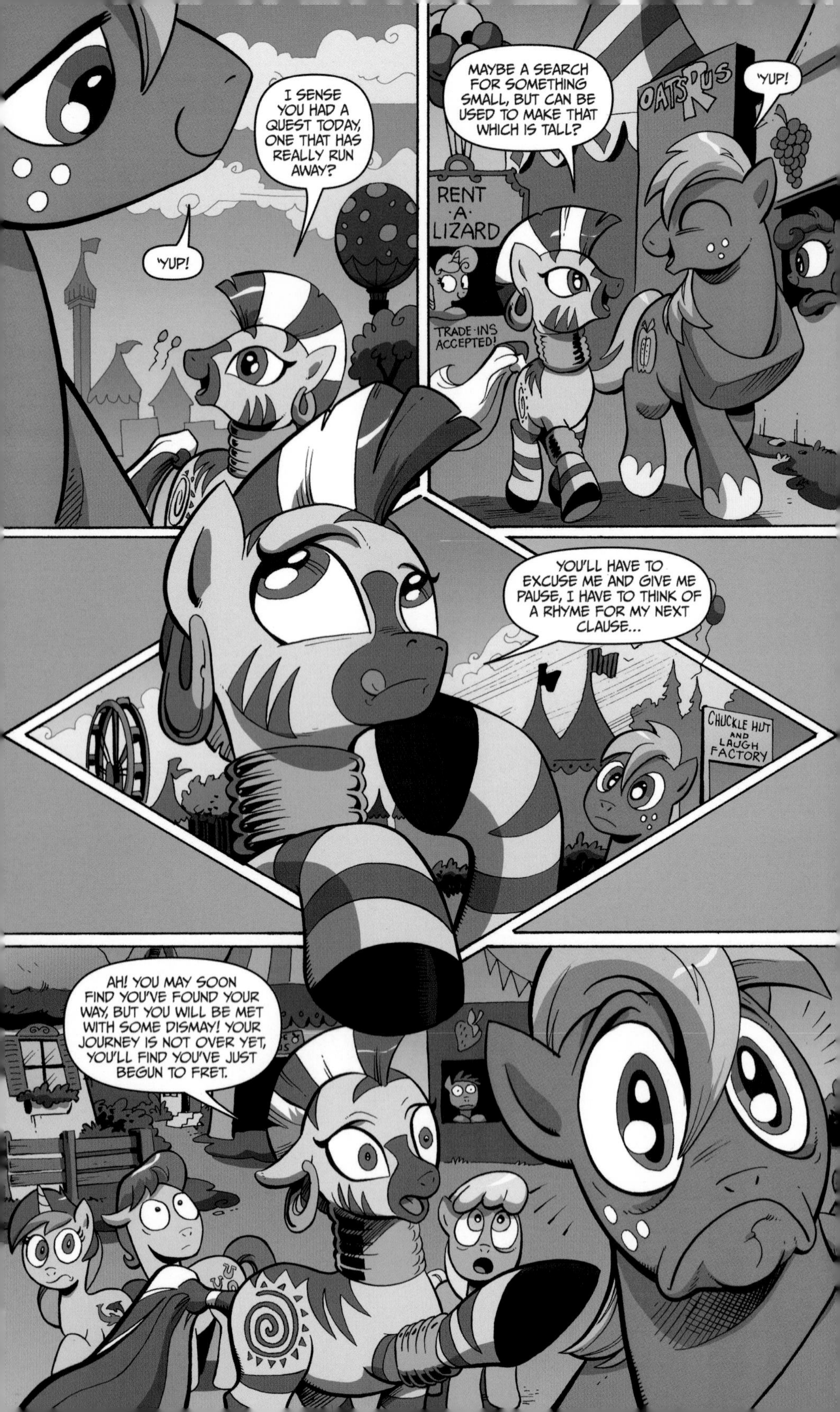
I SENSE YOU HAD A QUEST TODAY, ONE THAT HAS REALLY RUN AWAY?
'YUP!
MAYBE A SEARCH FOR SOMETHING SMALL, BUT CAN BE USED TO MAKE THAT WHICH IS TALL?
'YUP!
OATS R US
RENT A LIZARD
TRADE-INS ACCEPTED!
YOU'LL HAVE TO EXCUSE ME AND GIVE ME PAUSE, I HAVE TO THINK OF A RHYME FOR MY NEXT CLAUSE...
CHUCKLE HUT AND LAUGH FACTORY
AH! YOU MAY SOON FIND YOU'VE FOUND YOUR WAY, BUT YOU WILL BE MET WITH SOME DISMAY! YOUR JOURNEY IS NOT OVER YET, YOU'LL FIND YOU'VE JUST BEGUN TO FRET.

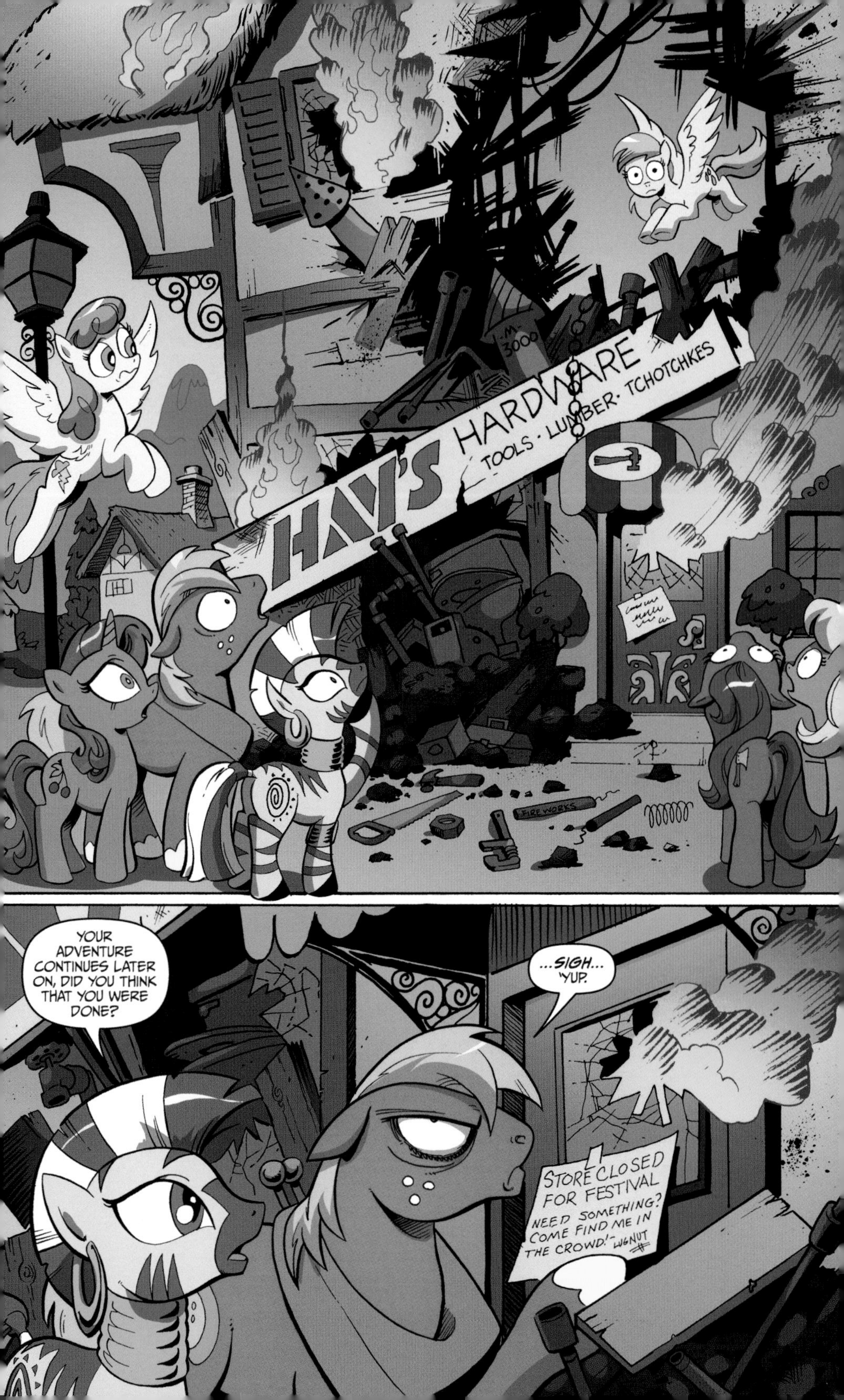

HAY'S HARDWARE
TOOLS · LUMBER · TCHOTCHKES
FIREWORKS
YOUR ADVENTURE CONTINUES LATER ON, DID YOU THINK THAT YOU WERE DONE?
...SIGH... 'YUP.
STORE CLOSED FOR FESTIVAL
NEED SOMETHING? COME FIND ME IN THE CROWD! - LUGNUT

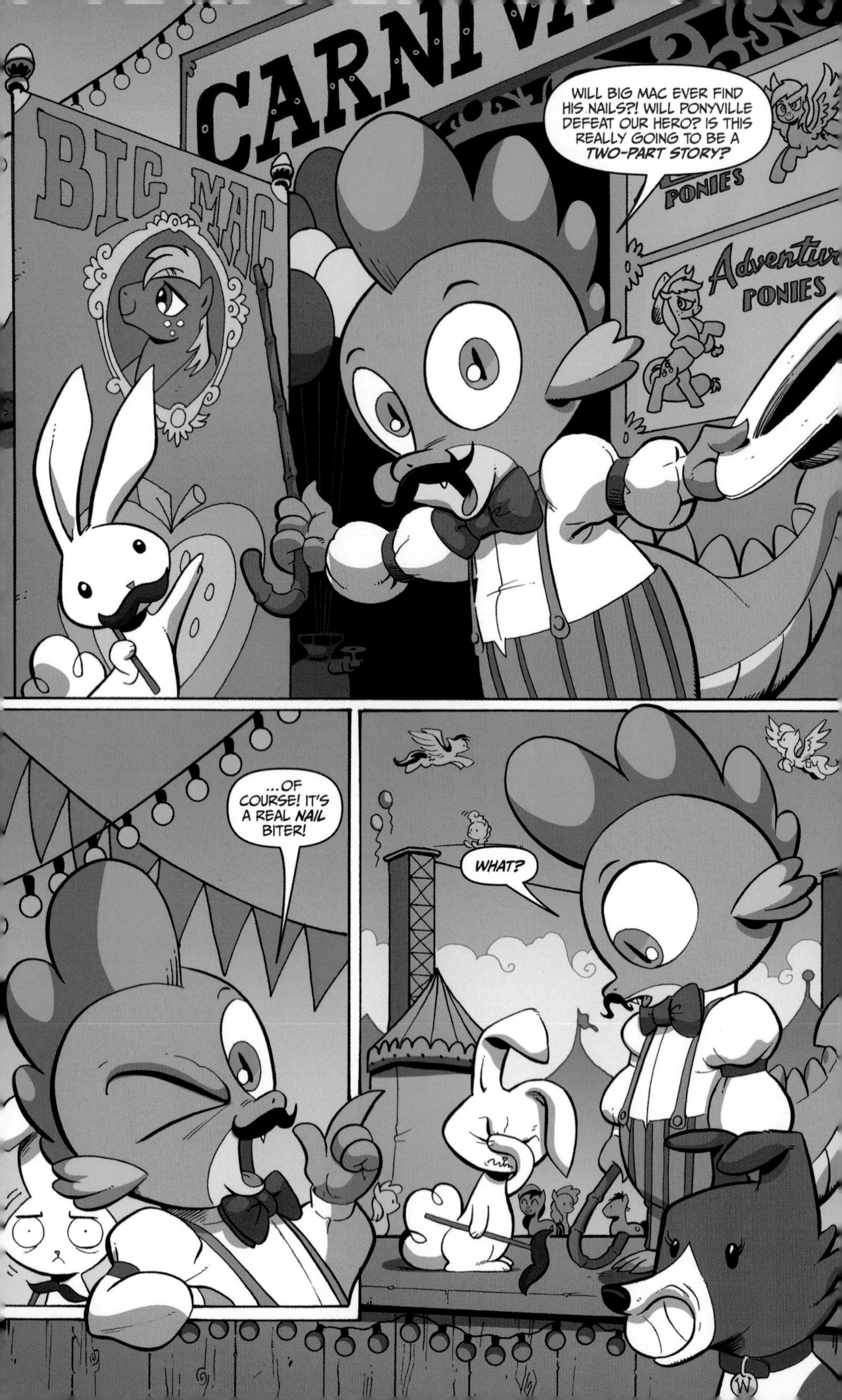
CARNIVAL
BIG MAC
WILL BIG MAC EVER FIND HIS NAILS?! WILL PONYVILLE DEFEAT OUR HERO? IS THIS REALLY GOING TO BE A *TWO-PART STORY?*
PONIES
Adventure PONIES
...OF COURSE! IT'S A REAL *NAIL* BITER!
WHAT?

Art by
Amy Mebberson

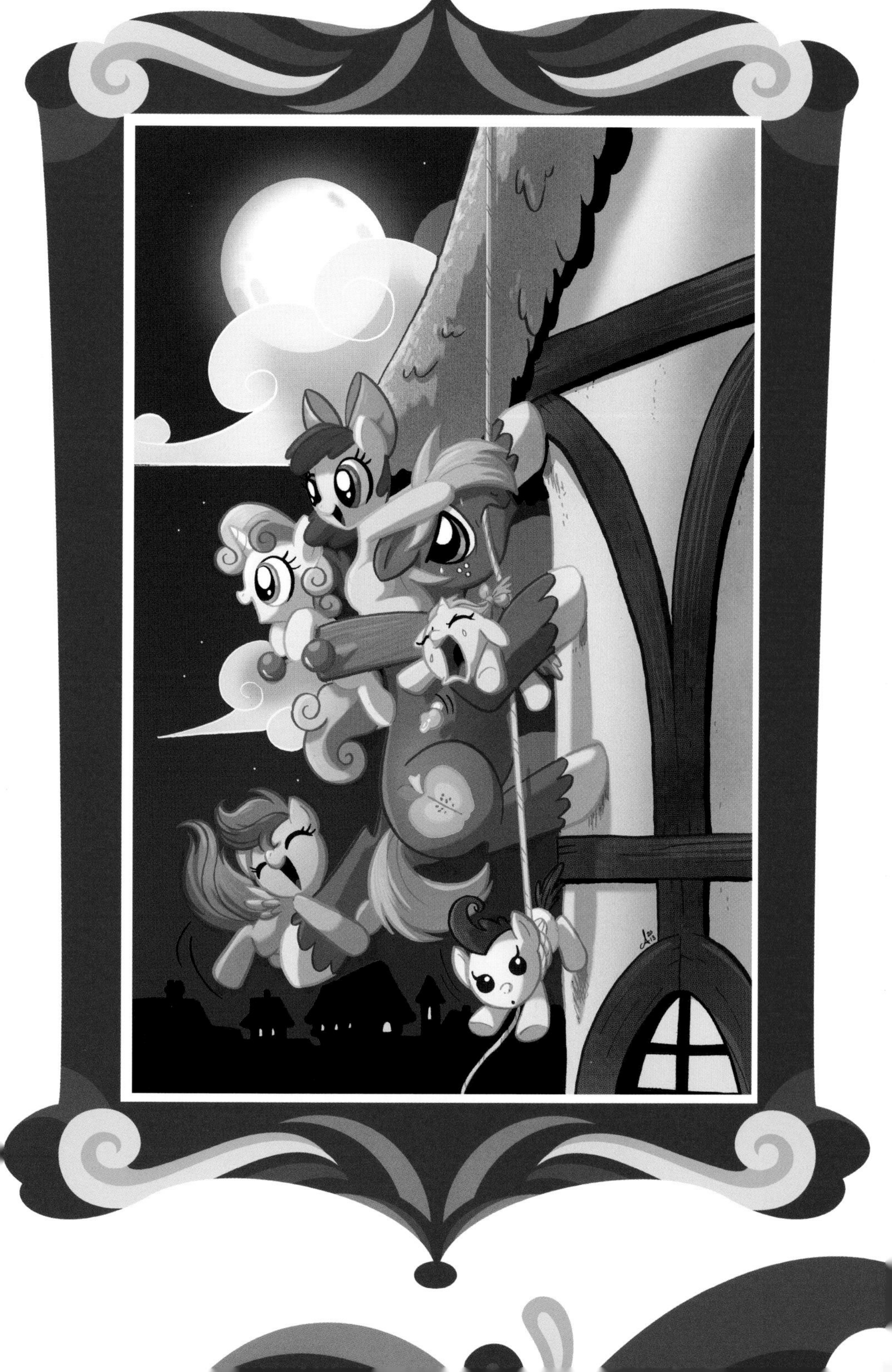

Art by
Andy Price

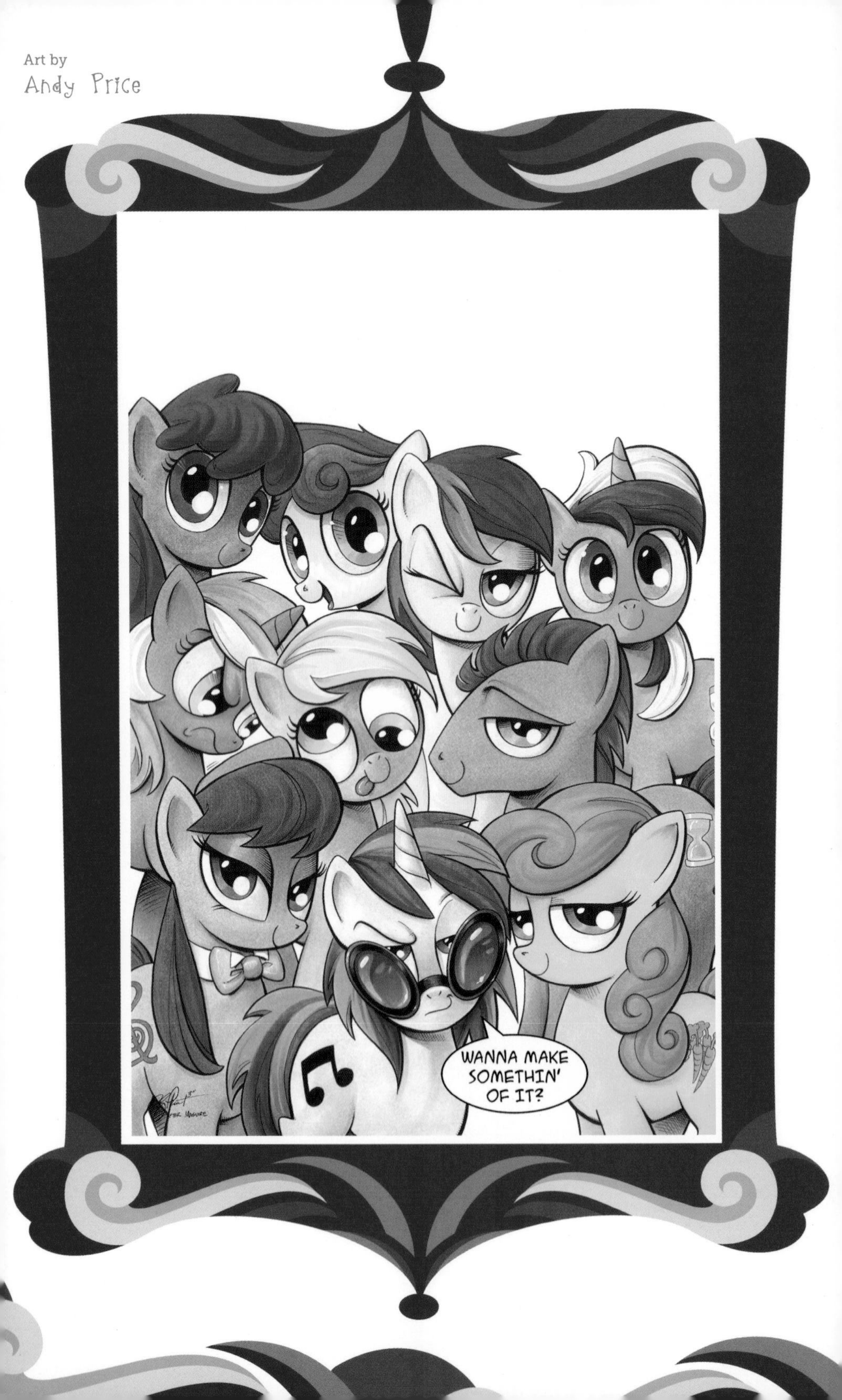
WANNA MAKE SOMETHIN' OF IT?

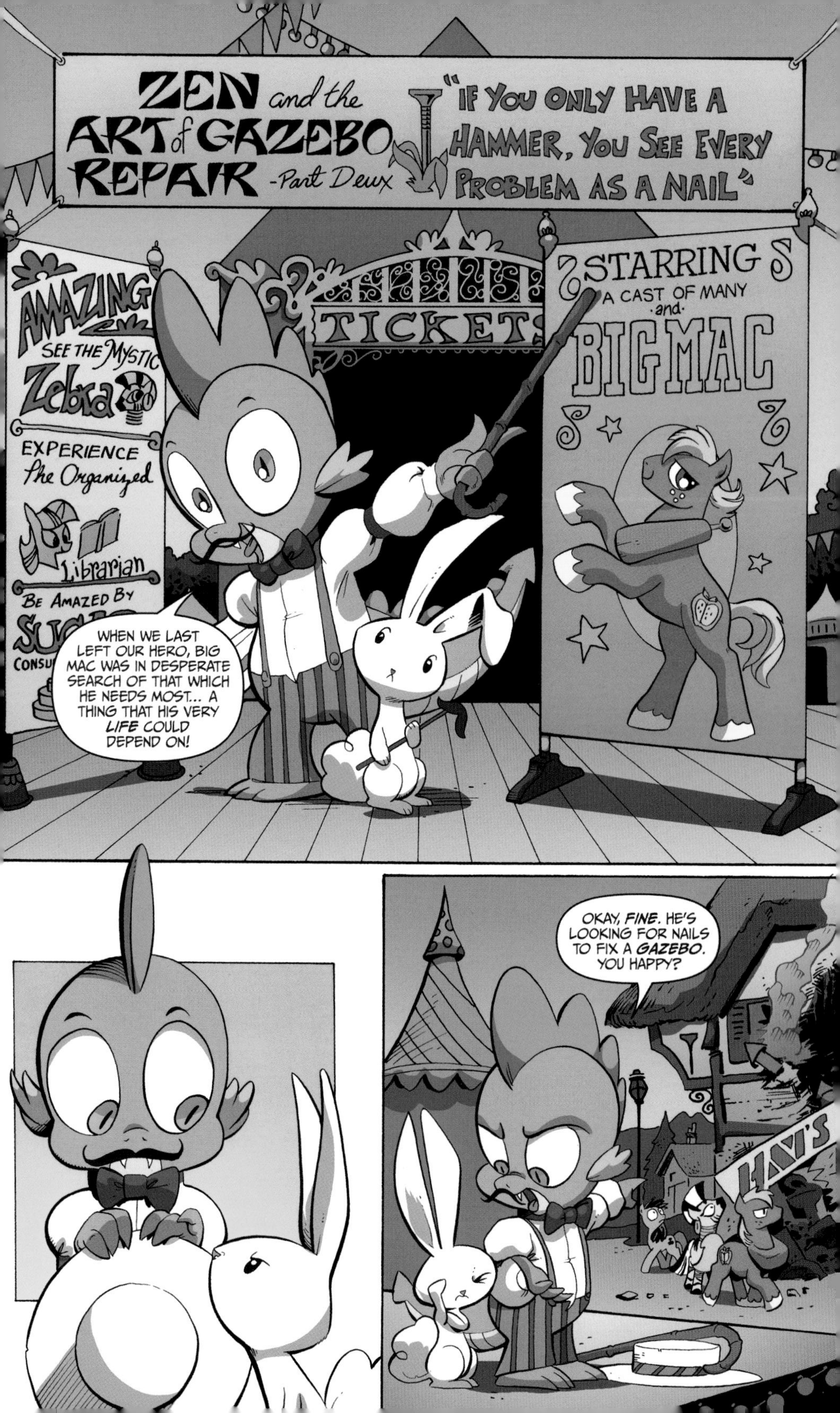
ZEN and the ART of GAZEBO REPAIR -Part Deux
"IF YOU ONLY HAVE A HAMMER, YOU SEE EVERY PROBLEM AS A NAIL"
AMAZING
SEE THE MYSTIC Zebra
EXPERIENCE The Organized Librarian
BE AMAZED BY
TICKETS
STARRING A CAST OF MANY and BIG MAC
WHEN WE LAST LEFT OUR HERO, BIG MAC WAS IN DESPERATE SEARCH OF THAT WHICH HE NEEDS MOST... A THING THAT HIS VERY *LIFE* COULD DEPEND ON!
OKAY, *FINE*. HE'S LOOKING FOR NAILS TO FIX A *GAZEBO*. YOU HAPPY?

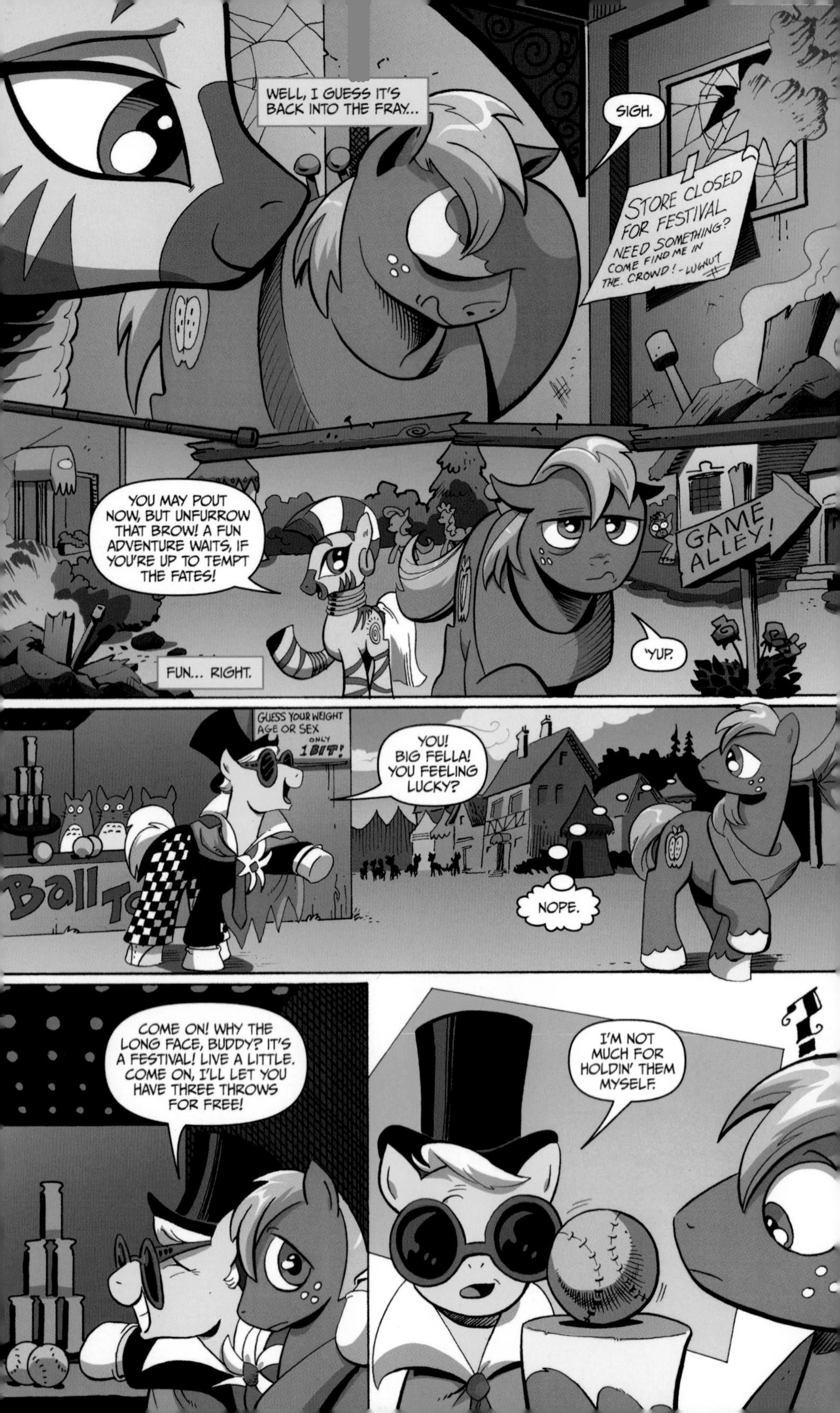
WELL, I GUESS IT'S BACK INTO THE FRAY...
SIGH.
STORE CLOSED FOR FESTIVAL
NEED SOMETHING? COME FIND ME IN THE CROWD! - LUGNUT
YOU MAY POUT NOW, BUT UNFURROW THAT BROW! A FUN ADVENTURE WAITS, IF YOU'RE UP TO TEMPT THE FATES!
GAME ALLEY!
'YUP.
FUN... RIGHT.
GUESS YOUR WEIGHT AGE OR SEX ONLY 1 BIT!
YOU! BIG FELLA! YOU FEELING LUCKY?
NOPE.
COME ON! WHY THE LONG FACE, BUDDY? IT'S A FESTIVAL! LIVE A LITTLE. COME ON, I'LL LET YOU HAVE THREE THROWS FOR FREE!
I'M NOT MUCH FOR HOLDIN' THEM MYSELF.

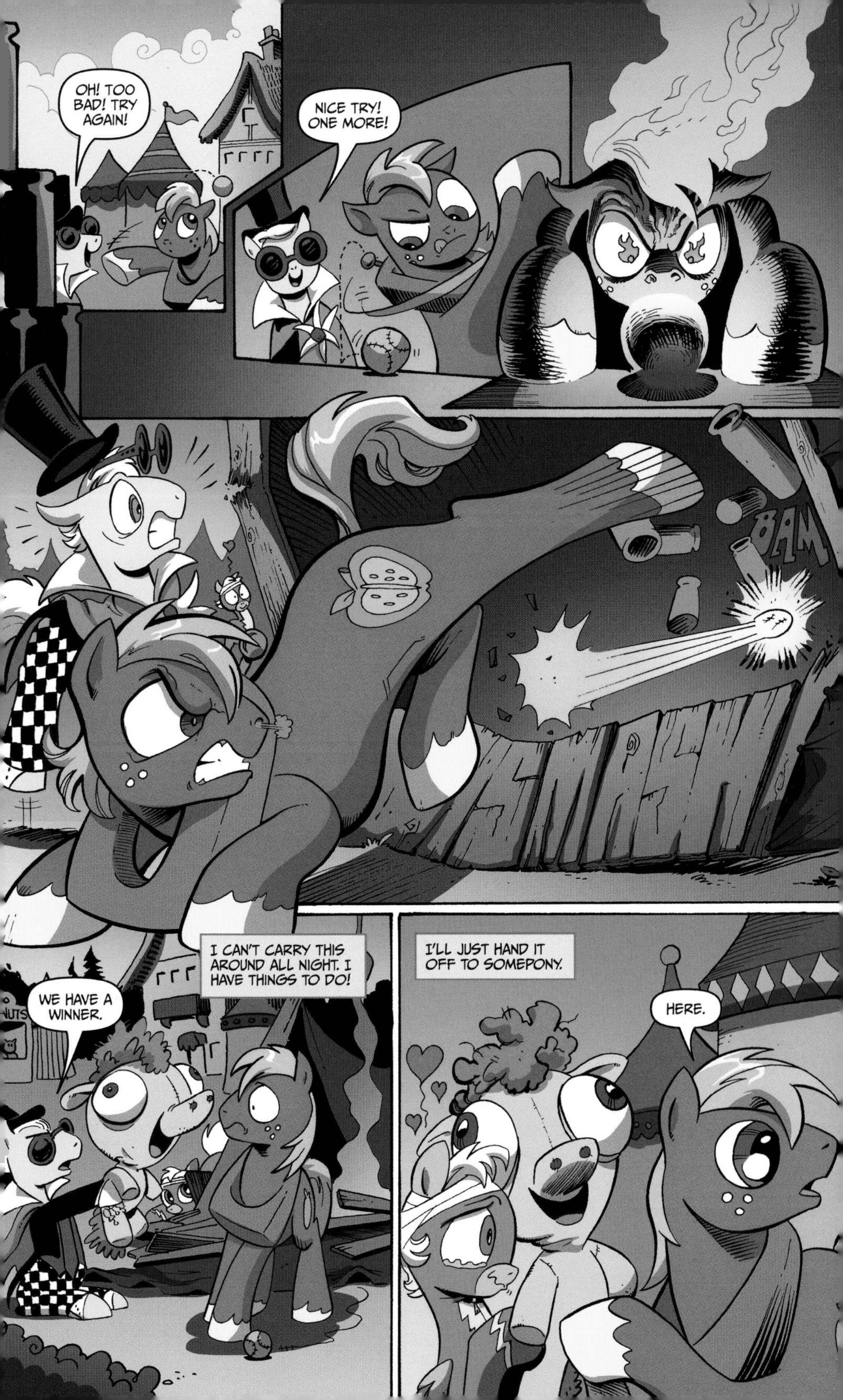
OH! TOO BAD! TRY AGAIN!
NICE TRY! ONE MORE!
BAM
SMASH
I CAN'T CARRY THIS AROUND ALL NIGHT. I HAVE THINGS TO DO!
WE HAVE A WINNER.
I'LL JUST HAND IT OFF TO SOMEPONY.
HERE.

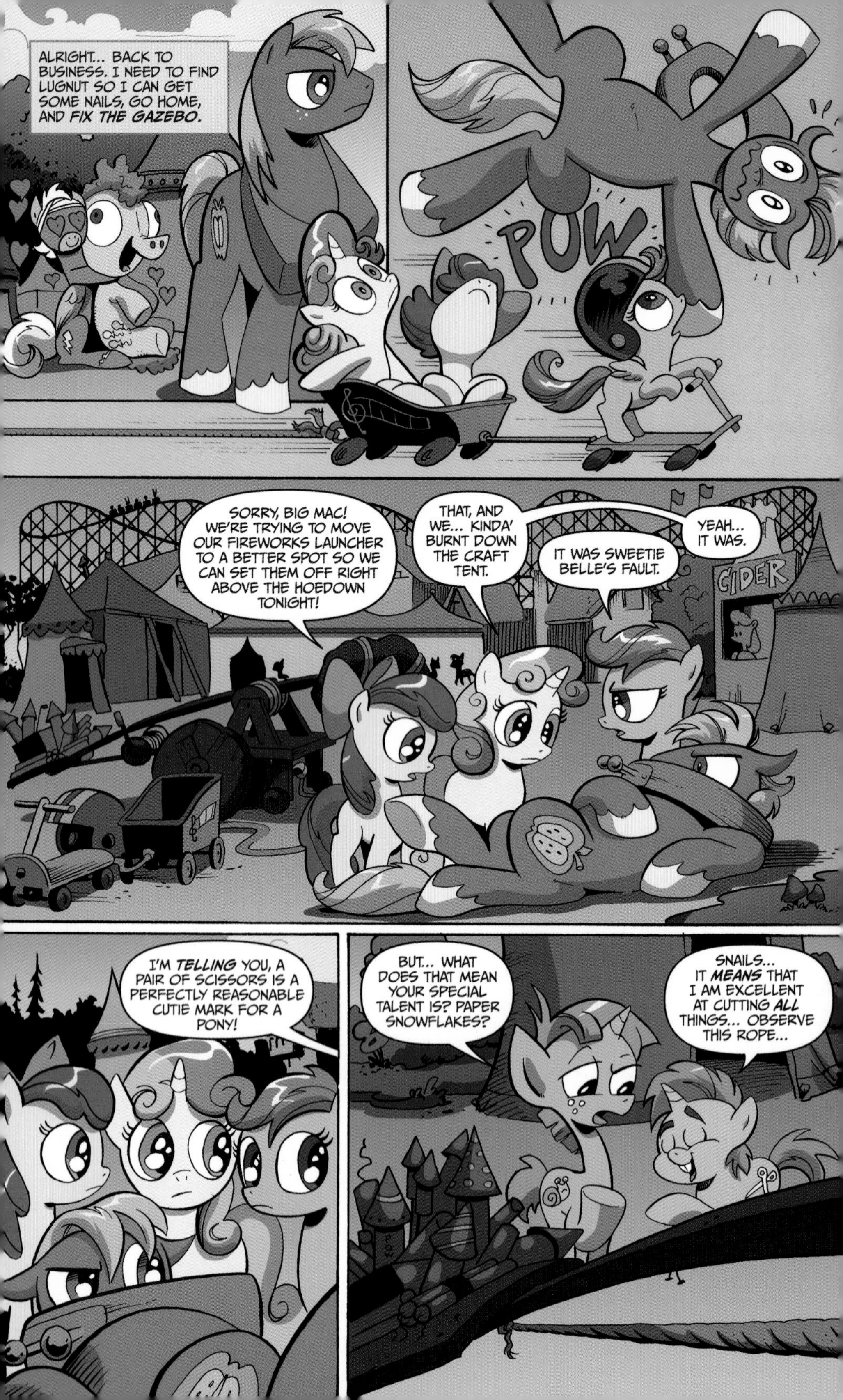
ALRIGHT... BACK TO BUSINESS. I NEED TO FIND LUGNUT SO I CAN GET SOME NAILS, GO HOME, AND *FIX THE GAZEBO*.
POW
SORRY, BIG MAC! WE'RE TRYING TO MOVE OUR FIREWORKS LAUNCHER TO A BETTER SPOT SO WE CAN SET THEM OFF RIGHT ABOVE THE HOEDOWN TONIGHT!
THAT, AND WE... KINDA' BURNT DOWN THE CRAFT TENT.
IT WAS SWEETIE BELLE'S FAULT.
YEAH... IT WAS.
CIDER
I'M *TELLING* YOU, A PAIR OF SCISSORS IS A PERFECTLY REASONABLE CUTIE MARK FOR A PONY!
BUT... WHAT DOES THAT MEAN YOUR SPECIAL TALENT IS? PAPER SNOWFLAKES?
SNAILS... IT *MEANS* THAT I AM EXCELLENT AT CUTTING *ALL* THINGS... OBSERVE THIS ROPE...

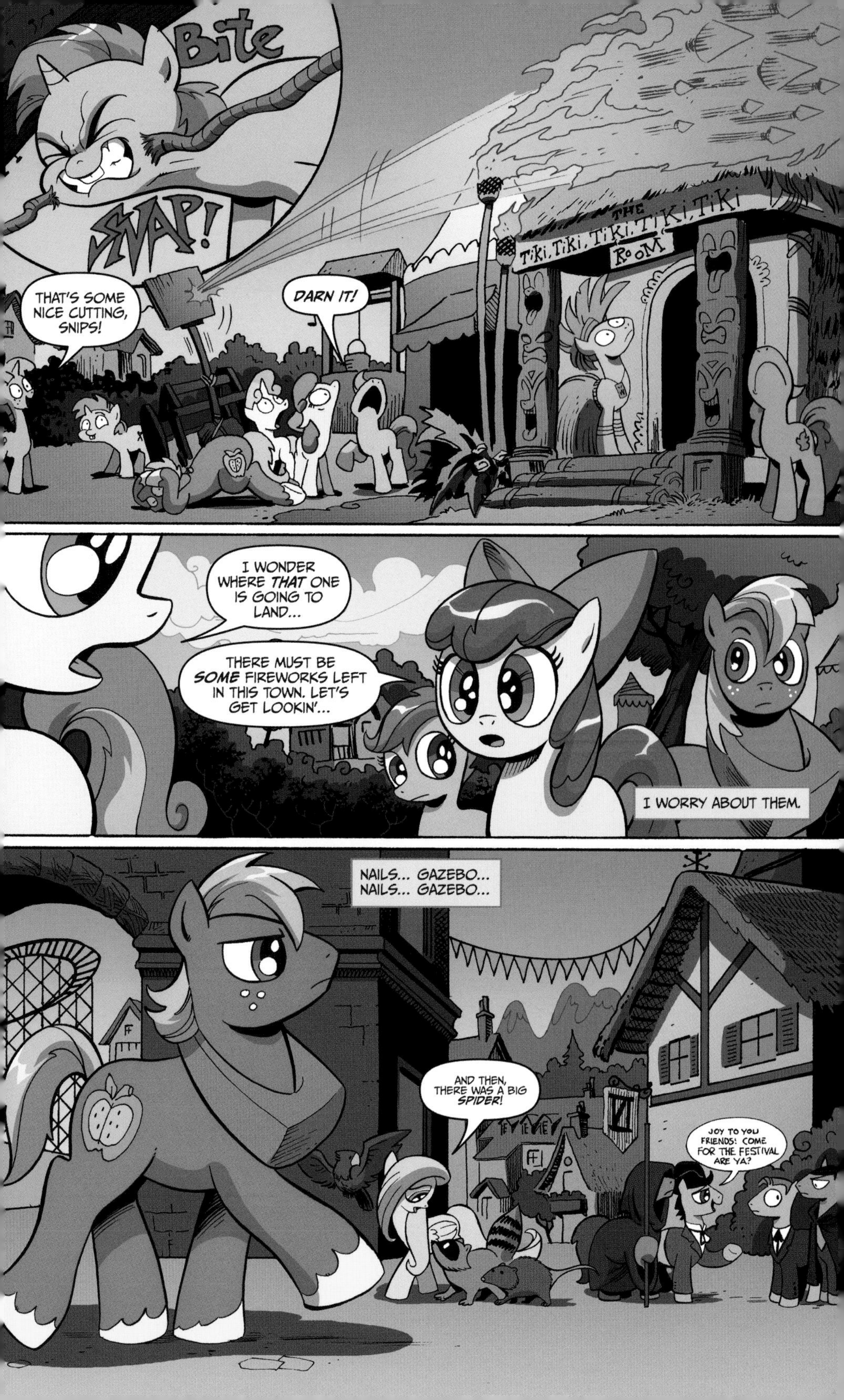
Bite
SNAP!
THE TIKI, TIKI, TIKI, TIKI, TIKI ROOM
THAT'S SOME NICE CUTTING, SNIPS!
DARN IT!
I WONDER WHERE THAT ONE IS GOING TO LAND...
THERE MUST BE SOME FIREWORKS LEFT IN THIS TOWN. LET'S GET LOOKIN'...
I WORRY ABOUT THEM.
NAILS... GAZEBO... NAILS... GAZEBO...
AND THEN, THERE WAS A BIG SPIDER!
JOY TO YOU FRIENDS! COME FOR THE FESTIVAL ARE YA?

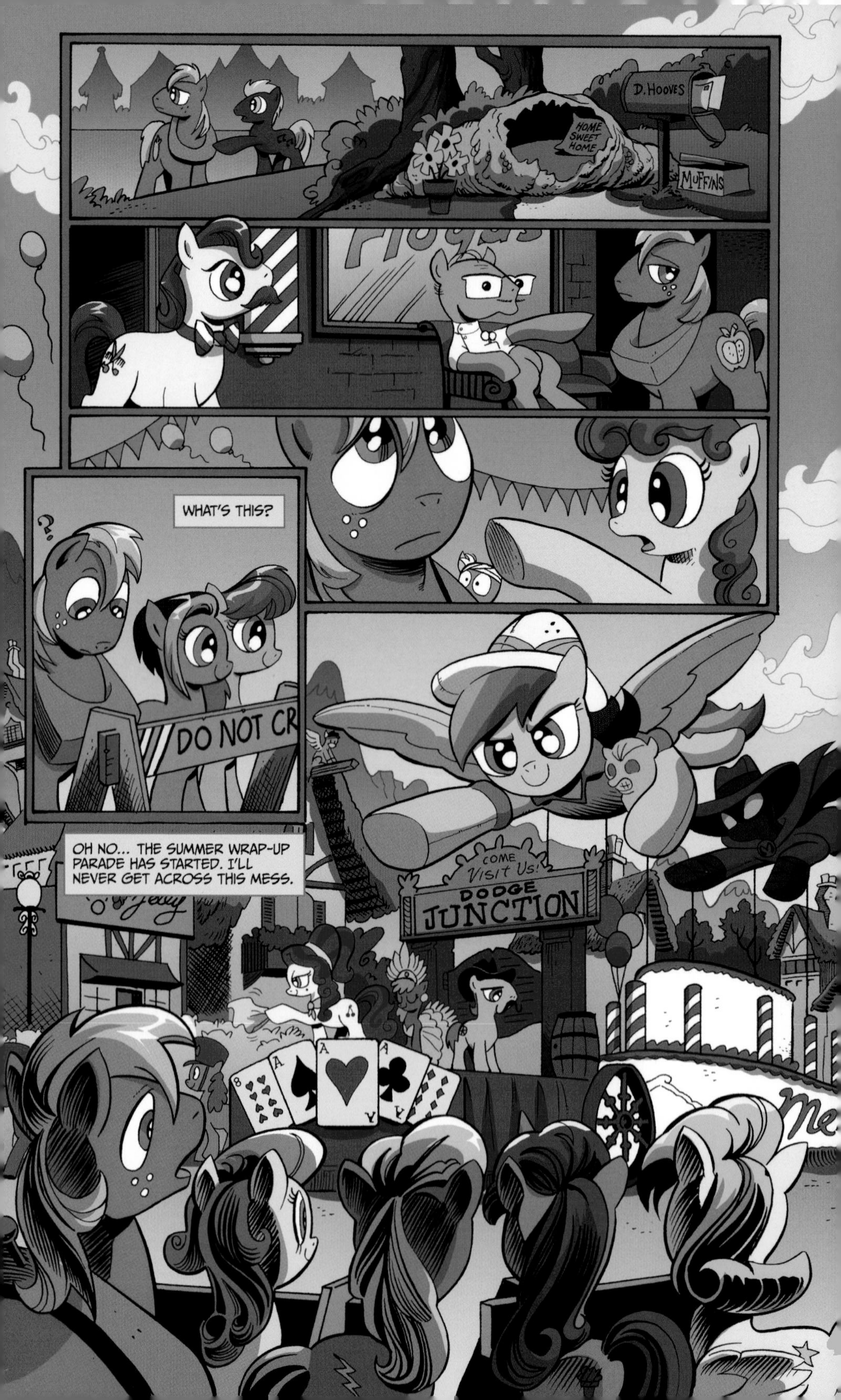
D. HOOVES
HOME SWEET HOME
MUFFINS
WHAT'S THIS?
?
DO NOT CR
OH NO... THE SUMMER WRAP-UP PARADE HAS STARTED. I'LL NEVER GET ACROSS THIS MESS.
COME Visit Us!
DODGE JUNCTION

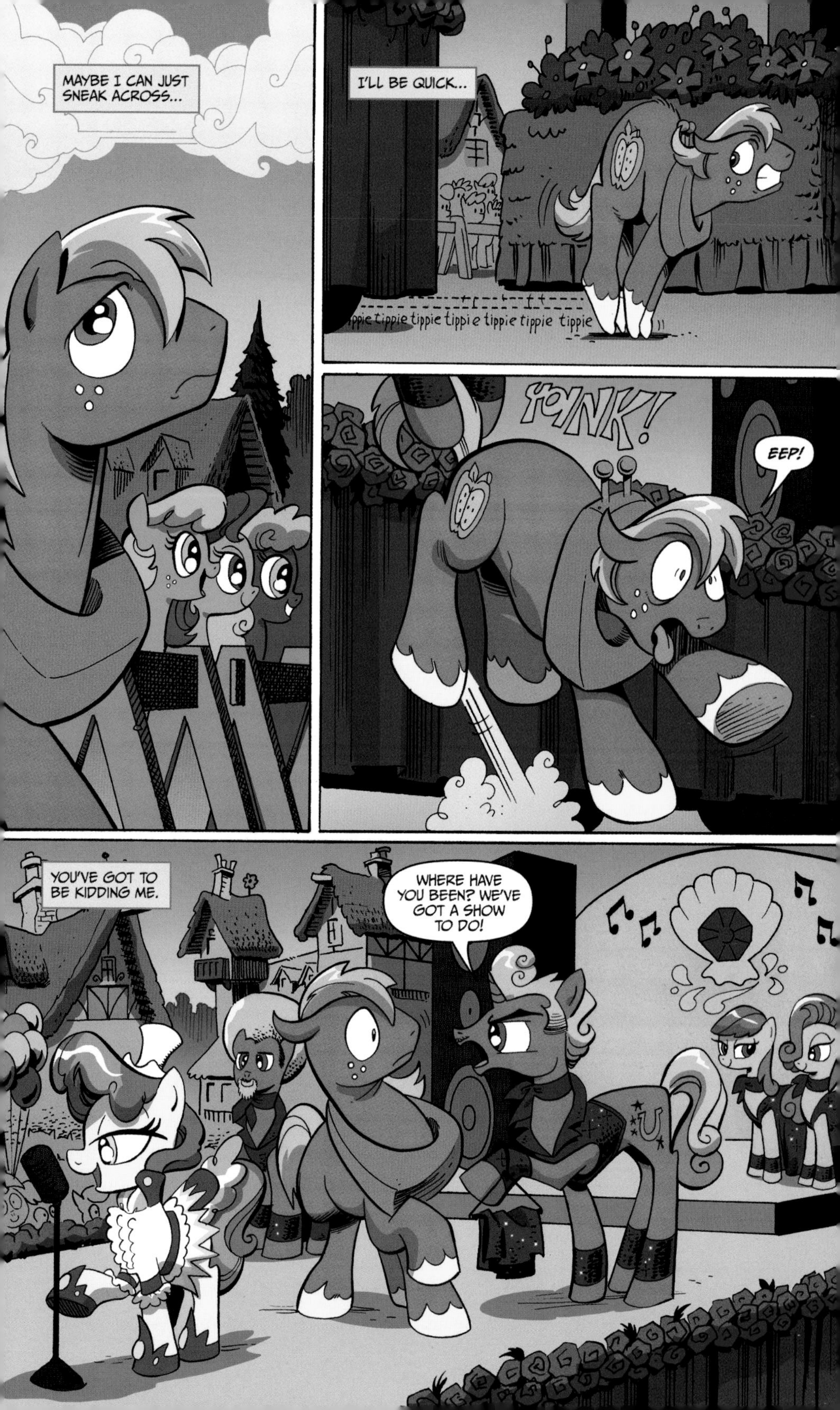
MAYBE I CAN JUST SNEAK ACROSS...
I'LL BE QUICK...
tippie tippie tippie tippie tippie tippie tippie
YOINK!
EEP!
YOU'VE GOT TO BE KIDDING ME.
WHERE HAVE YOU BEEN? WE'VE GOT A SHOW TO DO!

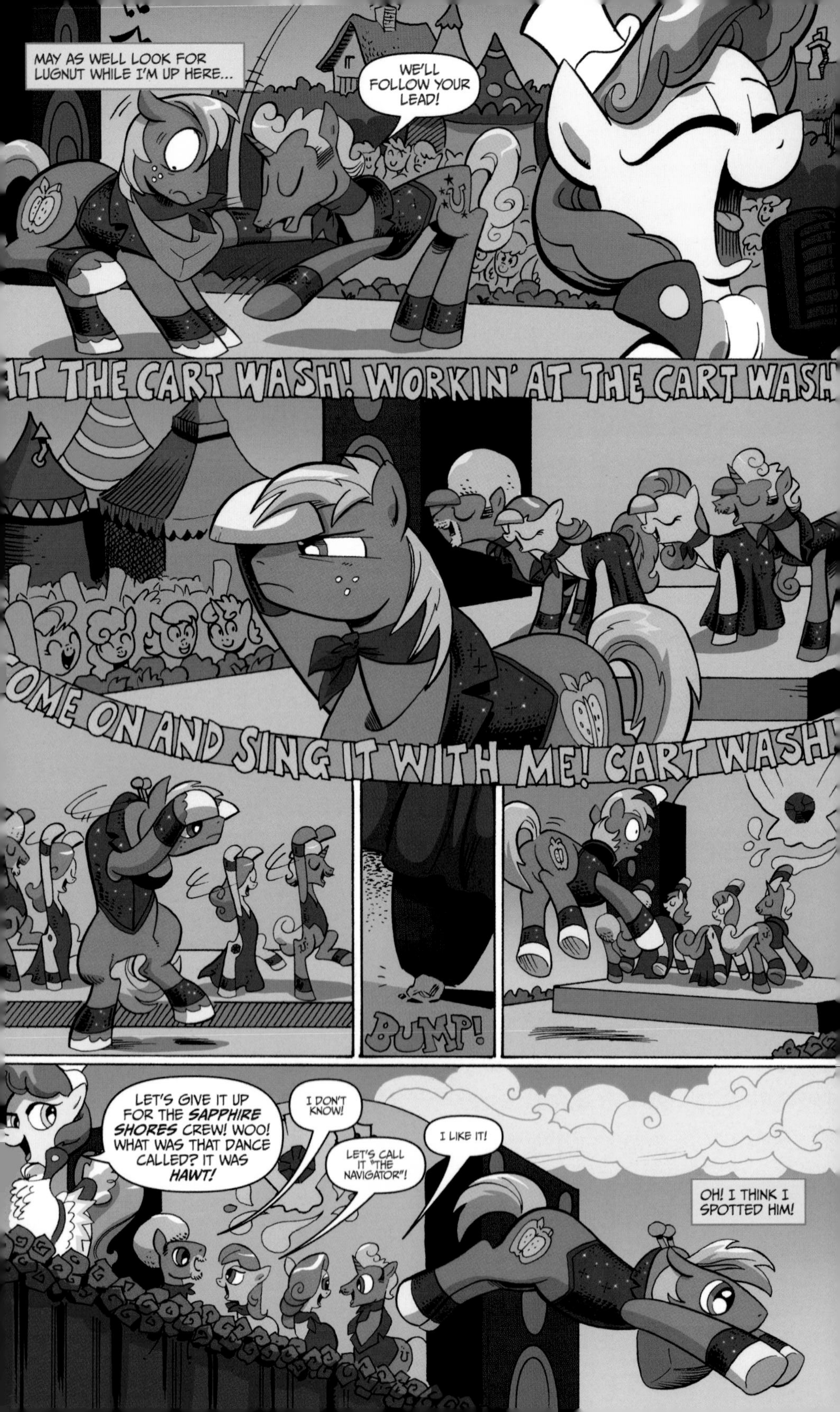
MAY AS WELL LOOK FOR LUGNUT WHILE I'M UP HERE...
WE'LL FOLLOW YOUR LEAD!
IT THE CART WASH! WORKIN' AT THE CART WASH
OME ON AND SING IT WITH ME! CART WASH
BUMP!
LET'S GIVE IT UP FOR THE SAPPHIRE SHORES CREW! WOO! WHAT WAS THAT DANCE CALLED? IT WAS HAWT!
I DON'T KNOW!
LET'S CALL IT "THE NAVIGATOR"!
I LIKE IT!
OH! I THINK I SPOTTED HIM!

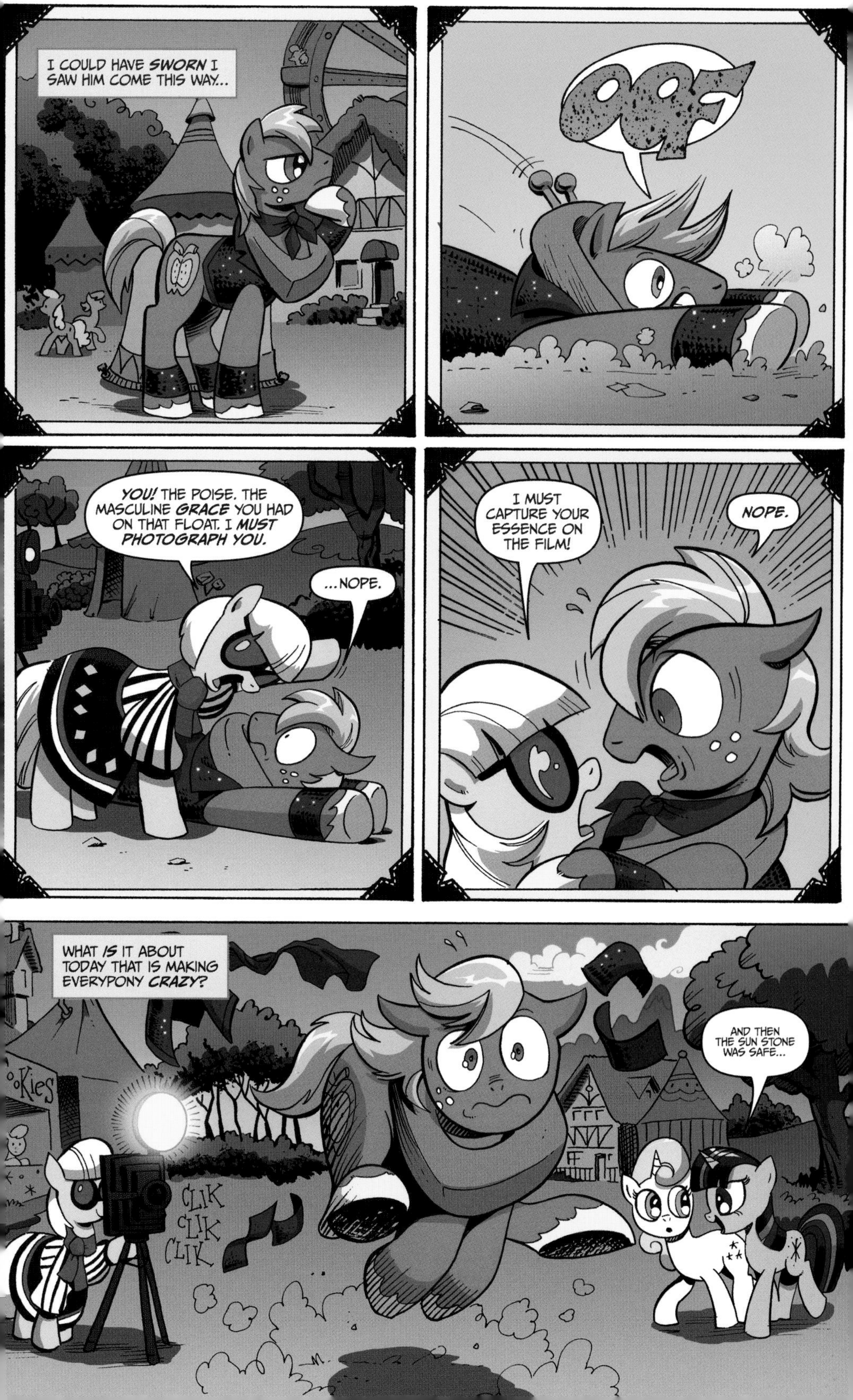
I COULD HAVE SWORN I SAW HIM COME THIS WAY...
OOF
YOU! THE POISE. THE MASCULINE GRACE YOU HAD ON THAT FLOAT. I MUST PHOTOGRAPH YOU.
...NOPE.
I MUST CAPTURE YOUR ESSENCE ON THE FILM!
NOPE.
WHAT IS IT ABOUT TODAY THAT IS MAKING EVERYPONY CRAZY?
OOKIES
CLIK CLIK CLIK
AND THEN THE SUN STONE WAS SAFE...

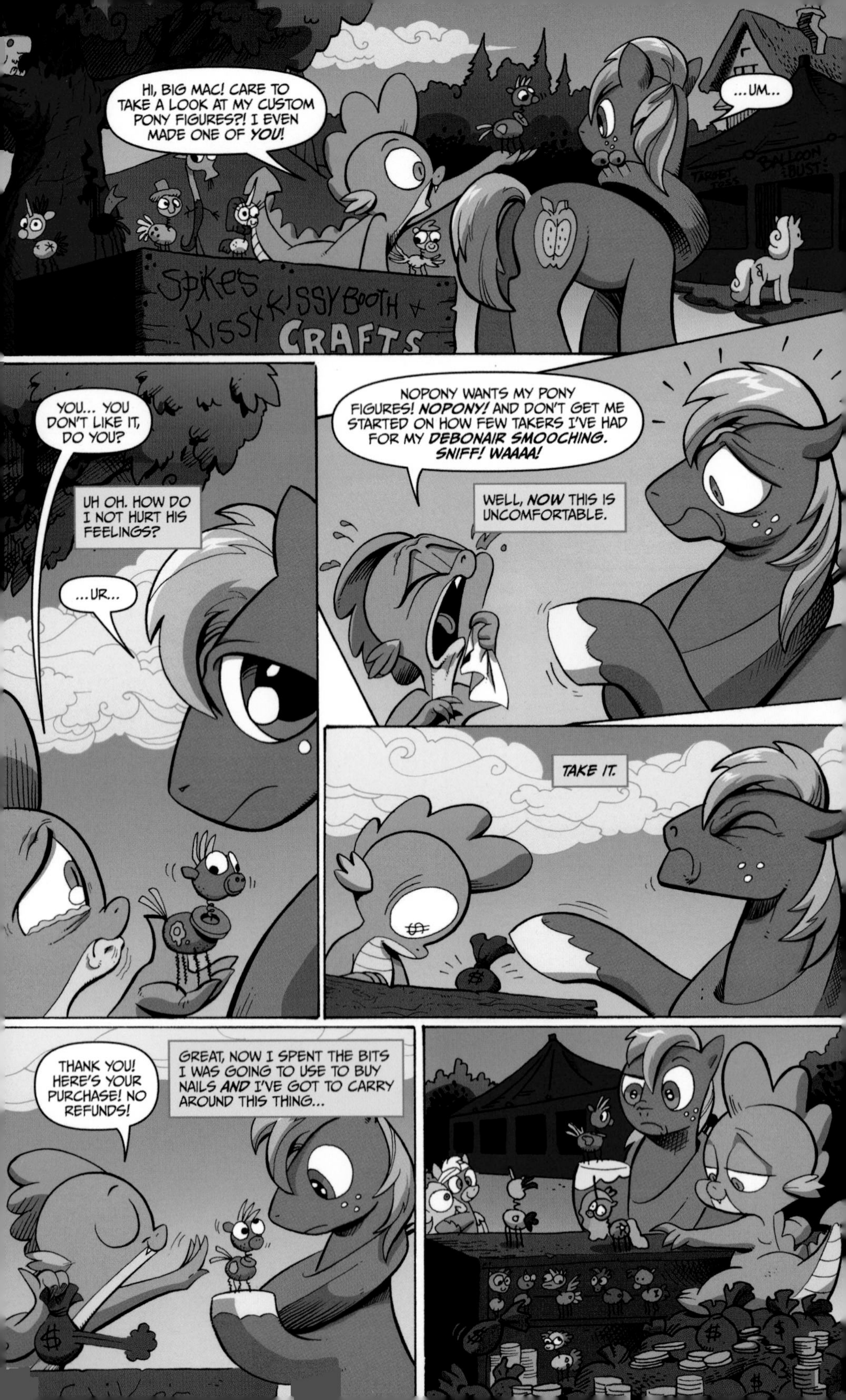
HI, BIG MAC! CARE TO TAKE A LOOK AT MY CUSTOM PONY FIGURES?! I EVEN MADE ONE OF *YOU*!
...UM...
TARGET TOSS
BALLOON BUST
SPIKE'S KISSY KISSY BOOTH + CRAFTS
YOU... YOU DON'T LIKE IT, DO YOU?
UH OH. HOW DO I NOT HURT HIS FEELINGS?
...UR...
NOPONY WANTS MY PONY FIGURES! *NOPONY!* AND DON'T GET ME STARTED ON HOW FEW TAKERS I'VE HAD FOR MY *DEBONAIR SMOOCHING. SNIFF! WAAAA!*
WELL, *NOW* THIS IS UNCOMFORTABLE.
TAKE IT.
THANK YOU! HERE'S YOUR PURCHASE! NO REFUNDS!
GREAT, NOW I SPENT THE BITS I WAS GOING TO USE TO BUY NAILS *AND* I'VE GOT TO CARRY AROUND THIS THING...

HERE.

WELL, *THAT* GOT RID OF *THAT.*

SPRING... WEDDING...

I CAN'T BELIEVE I HAVEN'T FOUND LUGNUT YET. IT'S LIKE LOOKING FOR NEEDLE AT THE HAYSTACK.

AND BY THAT, I MEAN IT'S HARD TO FIND GREAT UNCLE NEEDLE AT THE HAYSTACK APPLE FESTIVAL. THAT PLACE IS A MADHOUSE.

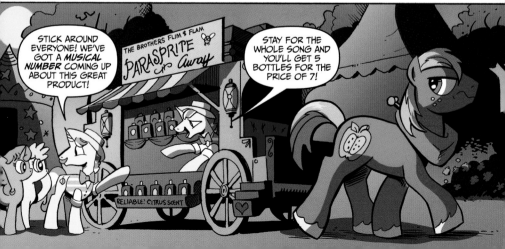

STICK AROUND EVERYONE! WE'VE GOT A *MUSICAL NUMBER* COMING UP ABOUT THIS GREAT PRODUCT!

THE BROTHERS FLIM & FLAM

PARASPRITE Away

STAY FOR THE WHOLE SONG AND YOU'LL GET 5 BOTTLES FOR THE PRICE OF 7!

RELIABLE! CITRUS SCENT

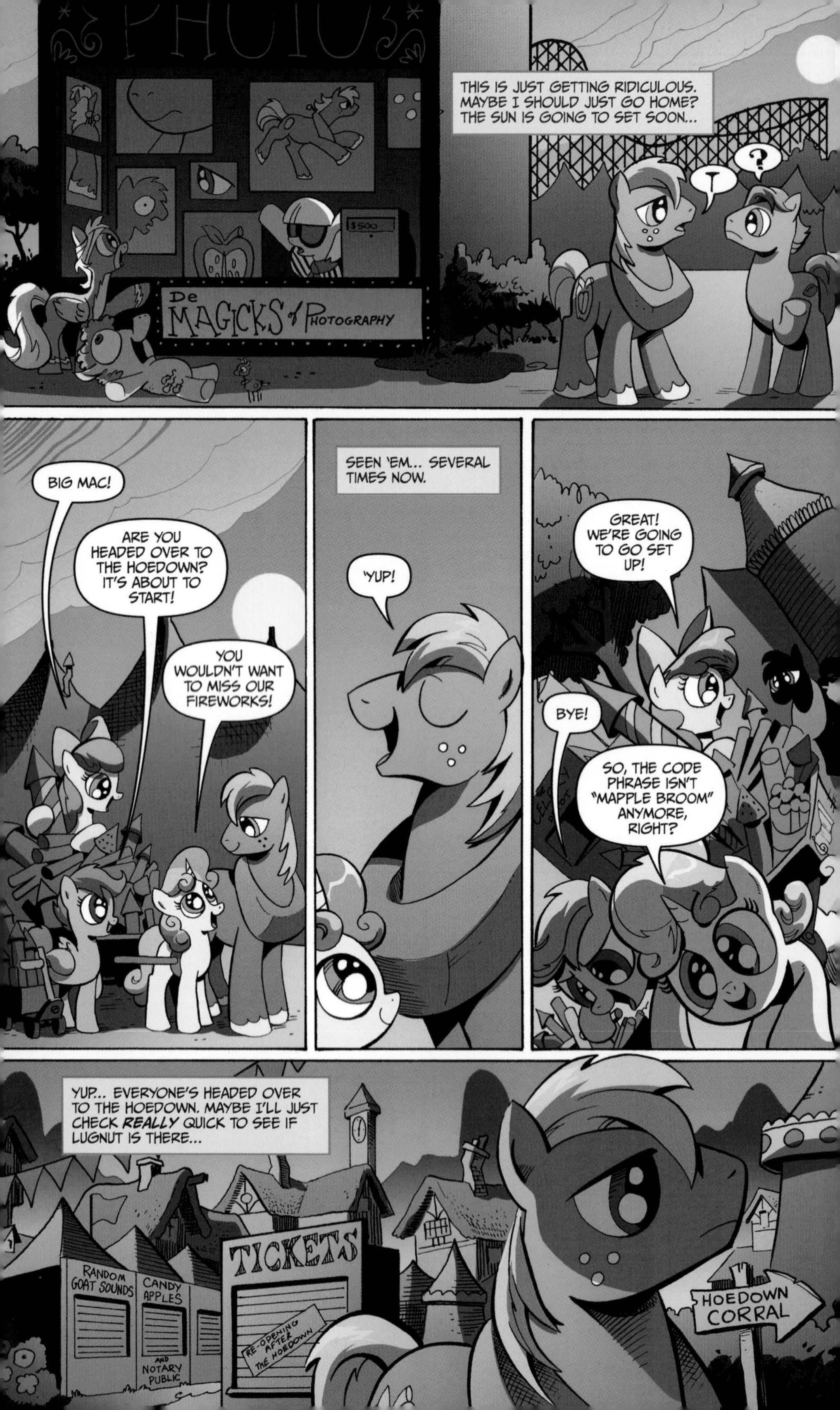
PHOTO
$500
De MAGICKS of PHOTOGRAPHY
THIS IS JUST GETTING RIDICULOUS. MAYBE I SHOULD JUST GO HOME? THE SUN IS GOING TO SET SOON...
?
BIG MAC!
ARE YOU HEADED OVER TO THE HOEDOWN? IT'S ABOUT TO START!
YOU WOULDN'T WANT TO MISS OUR FIREWORKS!
SEEN 'EM... SEVERAL TIMES NOW.
'YUP!
GREAT! WE'RE GOING TO GO SET UP!
BYE!
SO, THE CODE PHRASE ISN'T "MAPPLE BROOM" ANYMORE, RIGHT?
YUP... EVERYONE'S HEADED OVER TO THE HOEDOWN. MAYBE I'LL JUST CHECK ***REALLY*** QUICK TO SEE IF LUGNUT IS THERE...
RANDOM GOAT SOUNDS
CANDY APPLES
AND NOTARY PUBLIC
TICKETS
RE-OPENING AFTER THE HOEDOWN
HOEDOWN CORRAL

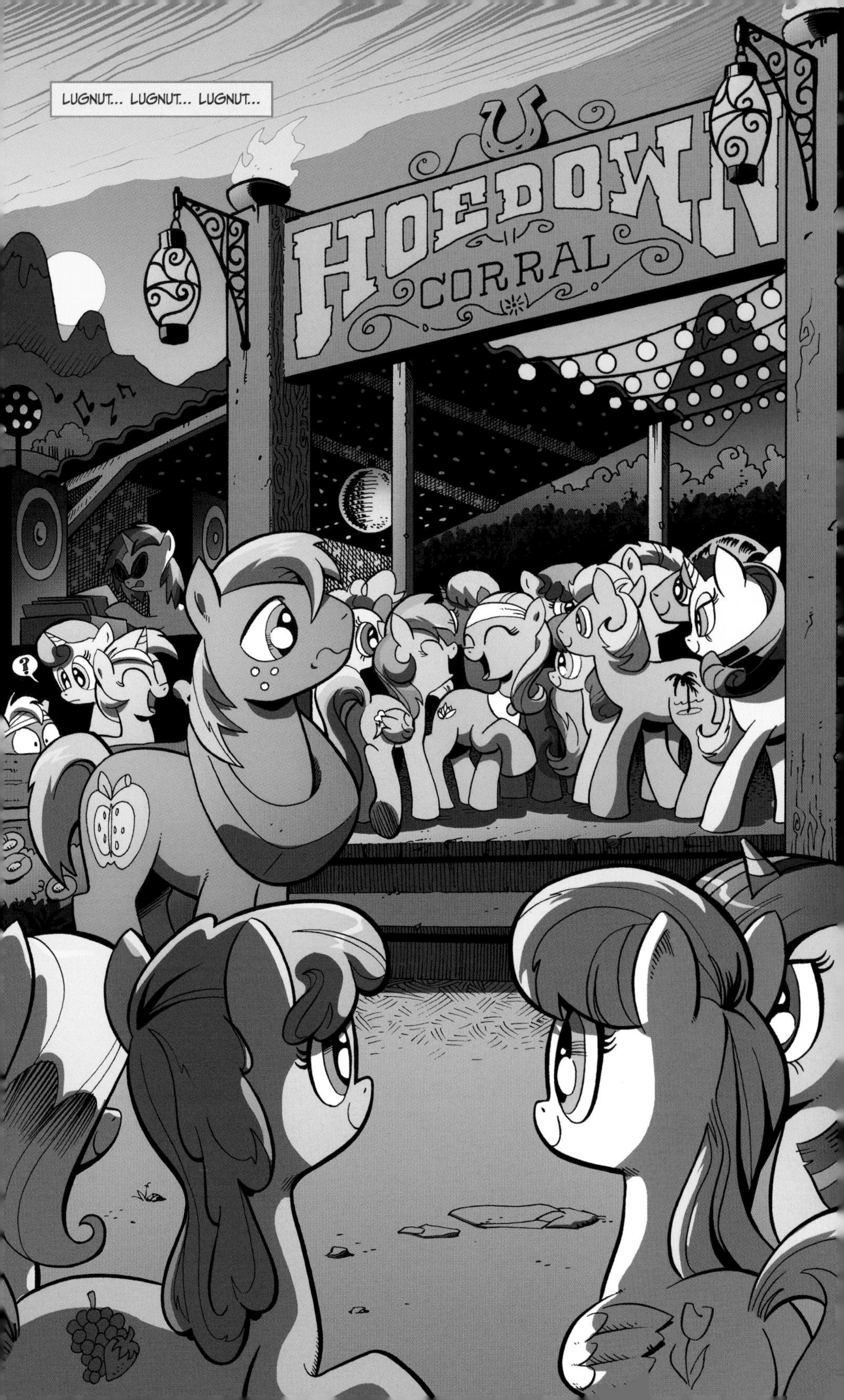
LUGNUT... LUGNUT... LUGNUT...
HOEDOWN
CORRAL
?

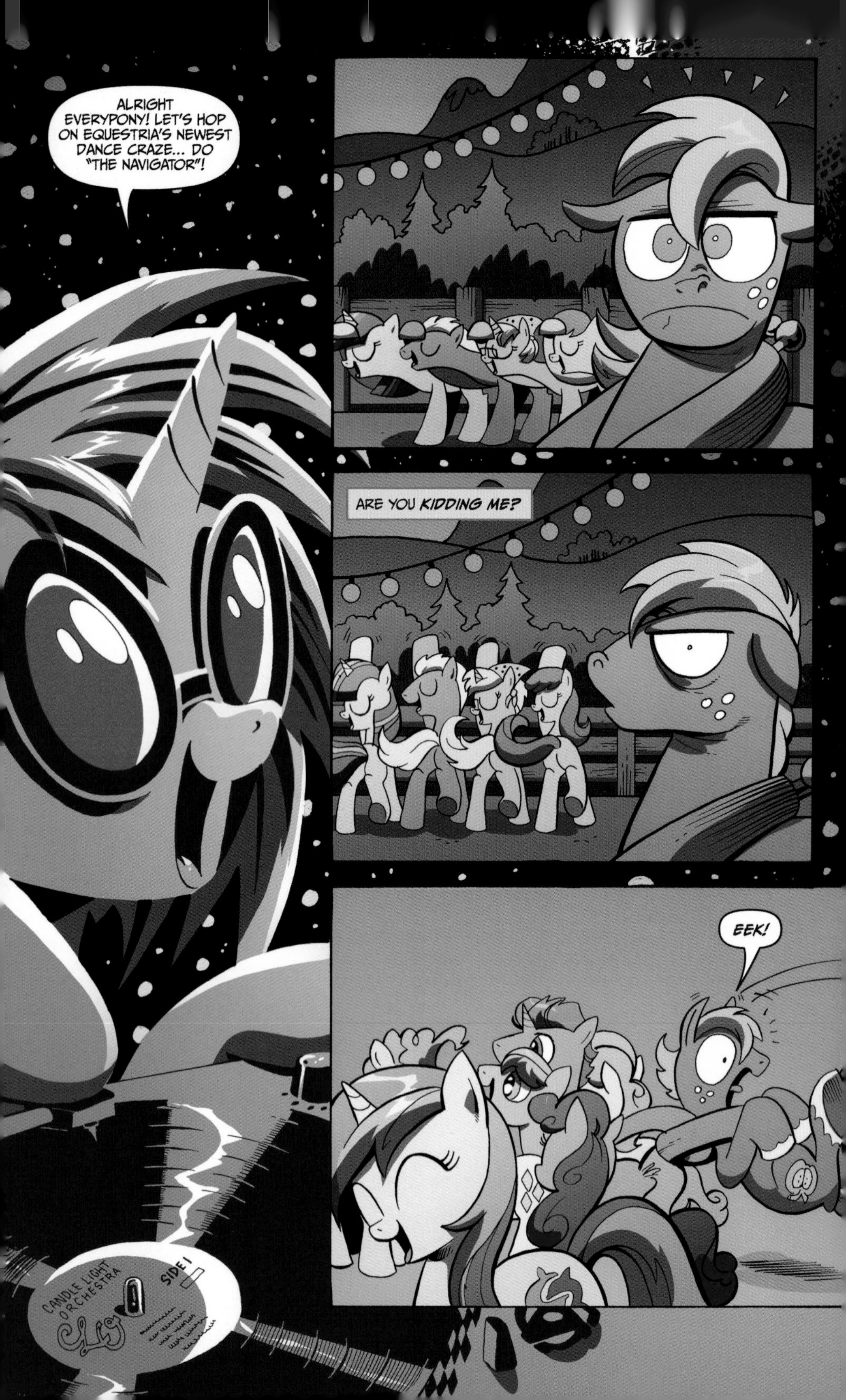
ALRIGHT EVERYPONY! LET'S HOP ON EQUESTRIA'S NEWEST DANCE CRAZE... DO "THE NAVIGATOR"!
ARE YOU KIDDING ME?
EEK!
CANDLE LIGHT ORCHESTRA
SIDE I

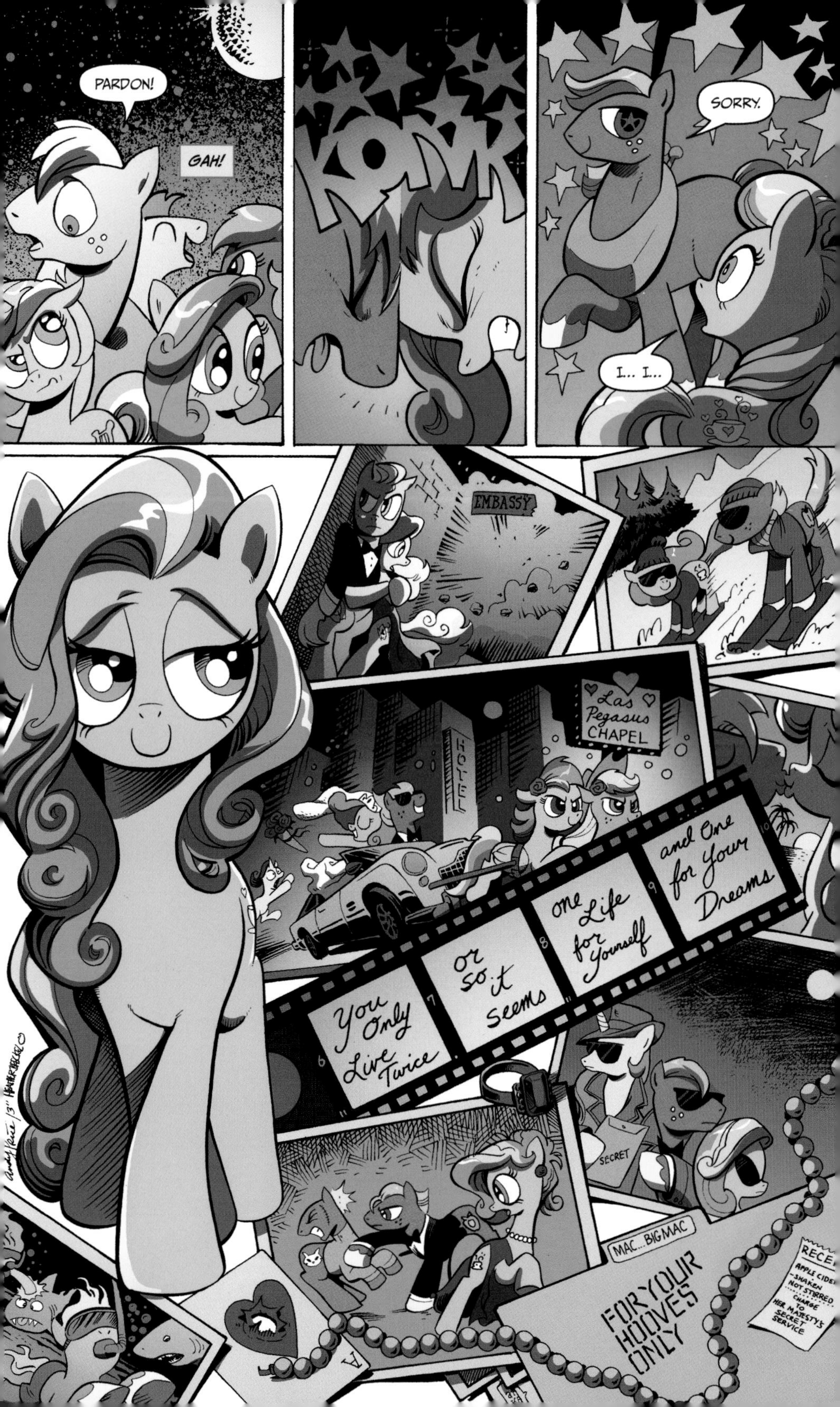
PARDON!
GAH!
KONK
SORRY.
I... I...
EMBASSY
Las Pegasus CHAPEL
HOTEL
You Only Live Twice
or so it seems
one Life for yourself
and One for Your Dreams
SECRET
MAC...BIGMAC
FOR YOUR HOOVES ONLY
RECE
APPLE CIDE
-SHAKEN NOT STIRRED
CHARGE TO HER MAJESTY'S SECRET SERVICE

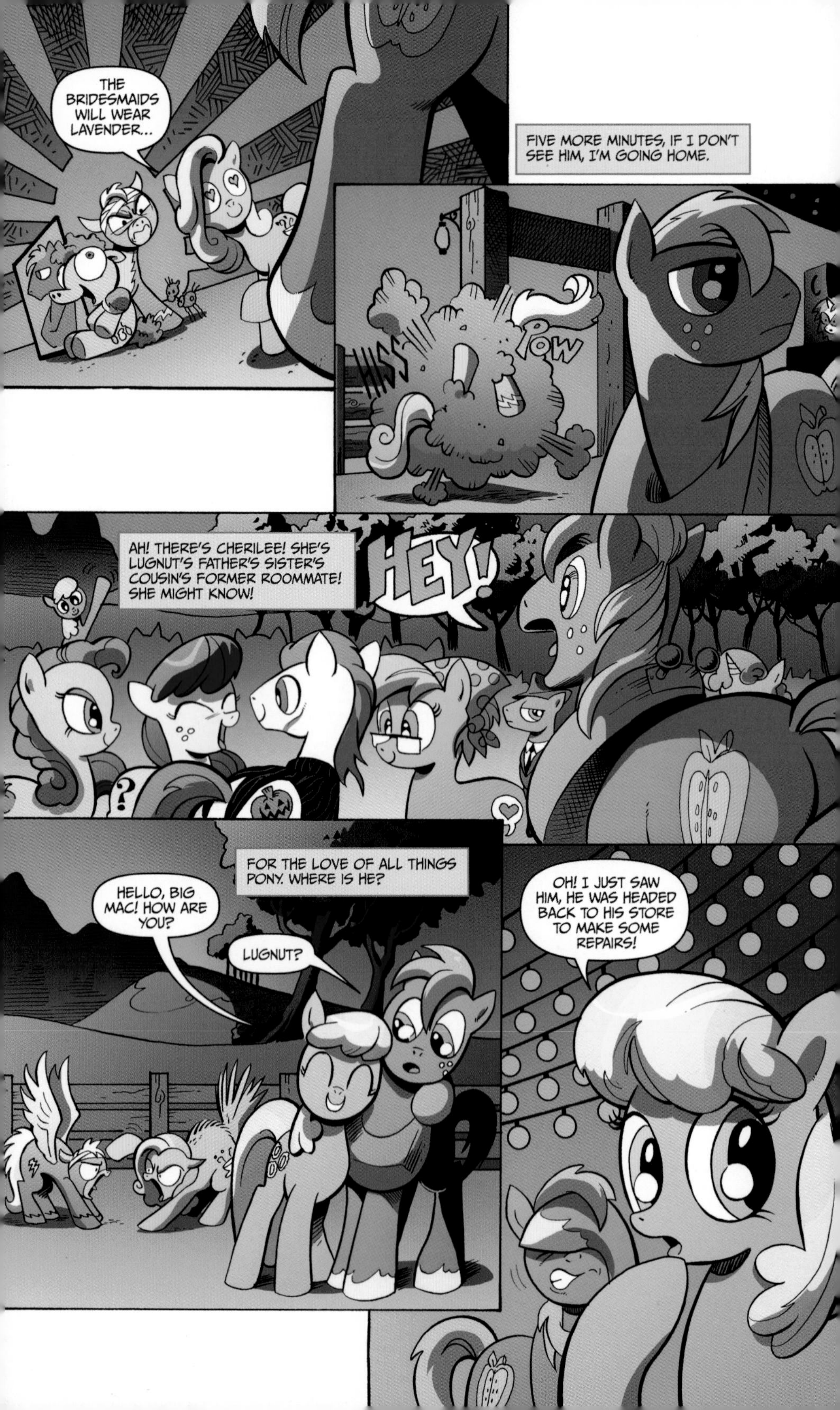
THE BRIDESMAIDS WILL WEAR LAVENDER...
FIVE MORE MINUTES, IF I DON'T SEE HIM, I'M GOING HOME.
HISS
POW
AH! THERE'S CHERILEE! SHE'S LUGNUT'S FATHER'S SISTER'S COUSIN'S FORMER ROOMMATE! SHE MIGHT KNOW!
HEY!
FOR THE LOVE OF ALL THINGS PONY. WHERE IS HE?
HELLO, BIG MAC! HOW ARE YOU?
LUGNUT?
OH! I JUST SAW HIM, HE WAS HEADED BACK TO HIS STORE TO MAKE SOME REPAIRS!

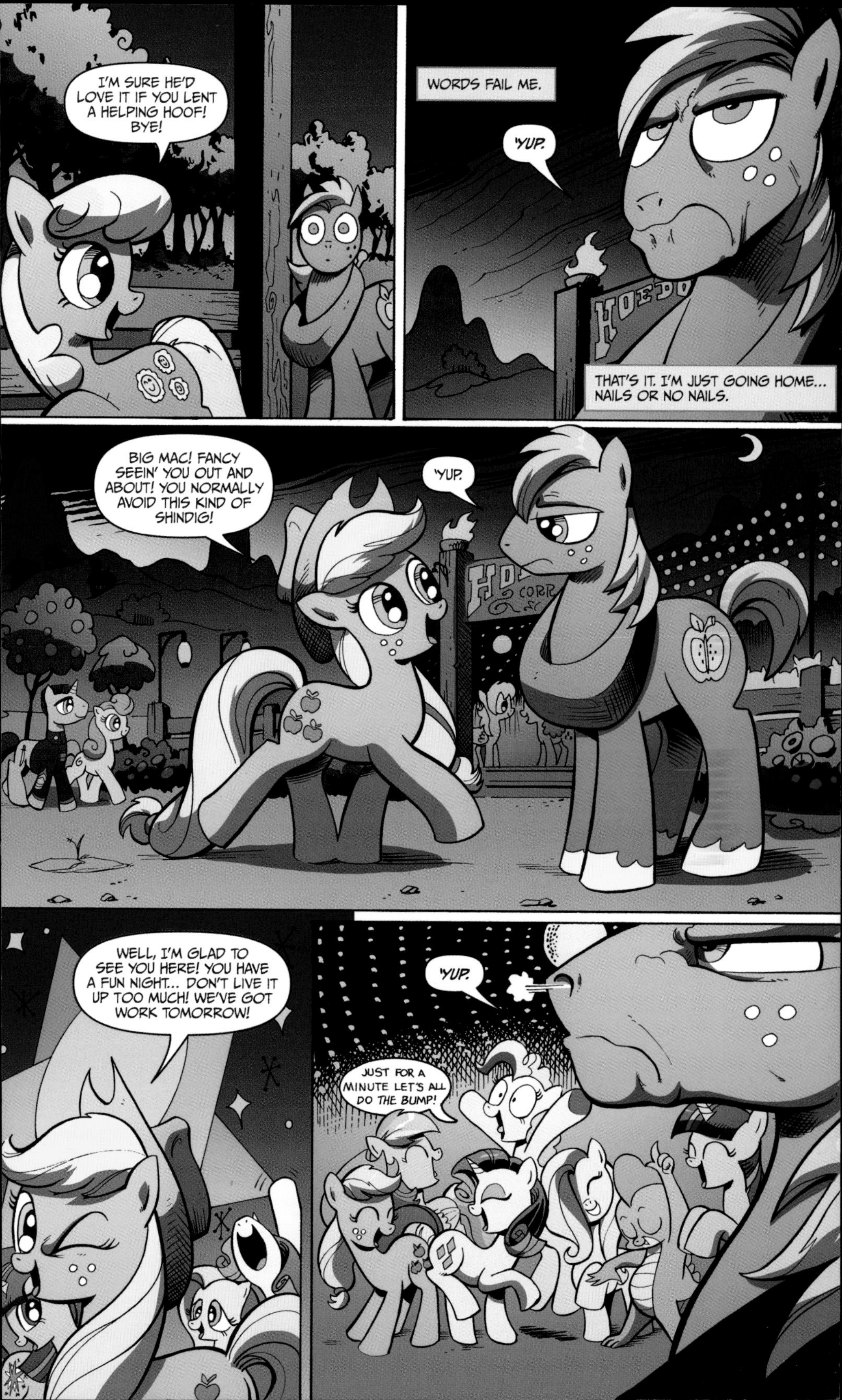
I'M SURE HE'D LOVE IT IF YOU LENT A HELPING HOOF! BYE!
WORDS FAIL ME.
'YUP.
THAT'S IT. I'M JUST GOING HOME... NAILS OR NO NAILS.
BIG MAC! FANCY SEEIN' YOU OUT AND ABOUT! YOU NORMALLY AVOID THIS KIND OF SHINDIG!
'YUP.
WELL, I'M GLAD TO SEE YOU HERE! YOU HAVE A FUN NIGHT... DON'T LIVE IT UP TOO MUCH! WE'VE GOT WORK TOMORROW!
'YUP.
JUST FOR A MINUTE LET'S ALL DO THE BUMP!

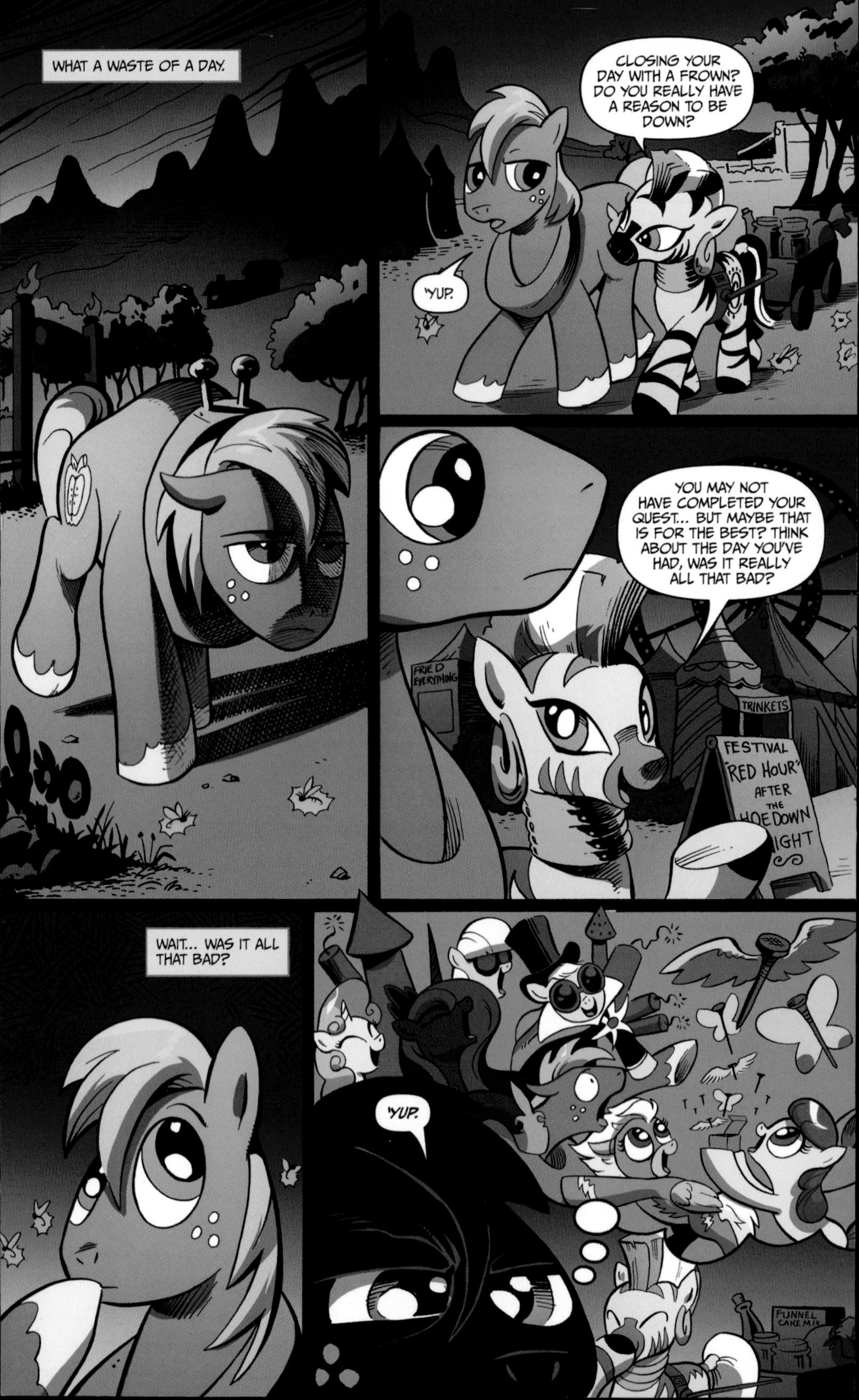
WHAT A WASTE OF A DAY.
CLOSING YOUR DAY WITH A FROWN? DO YOU REALLY HAVE A REASON TO BE DOWN?
'YUP.
YOU MAY NOT HAVE COMPLETED YOUR QUEST... BUT MAYBE THAT IS FOR THE BEST? THINK ABOUT THE DAY YOU'VE HAD, WAS IT REALLY ALL THAT BAD?
FRIED EVERYTHING
TRINKETS
FESTIVAL "RED HOUR" AFTER THE HOEDOWN
WAIT... WAS IT ALL THAT BAD?
'YUP.
FUNNEL CAKE MIX

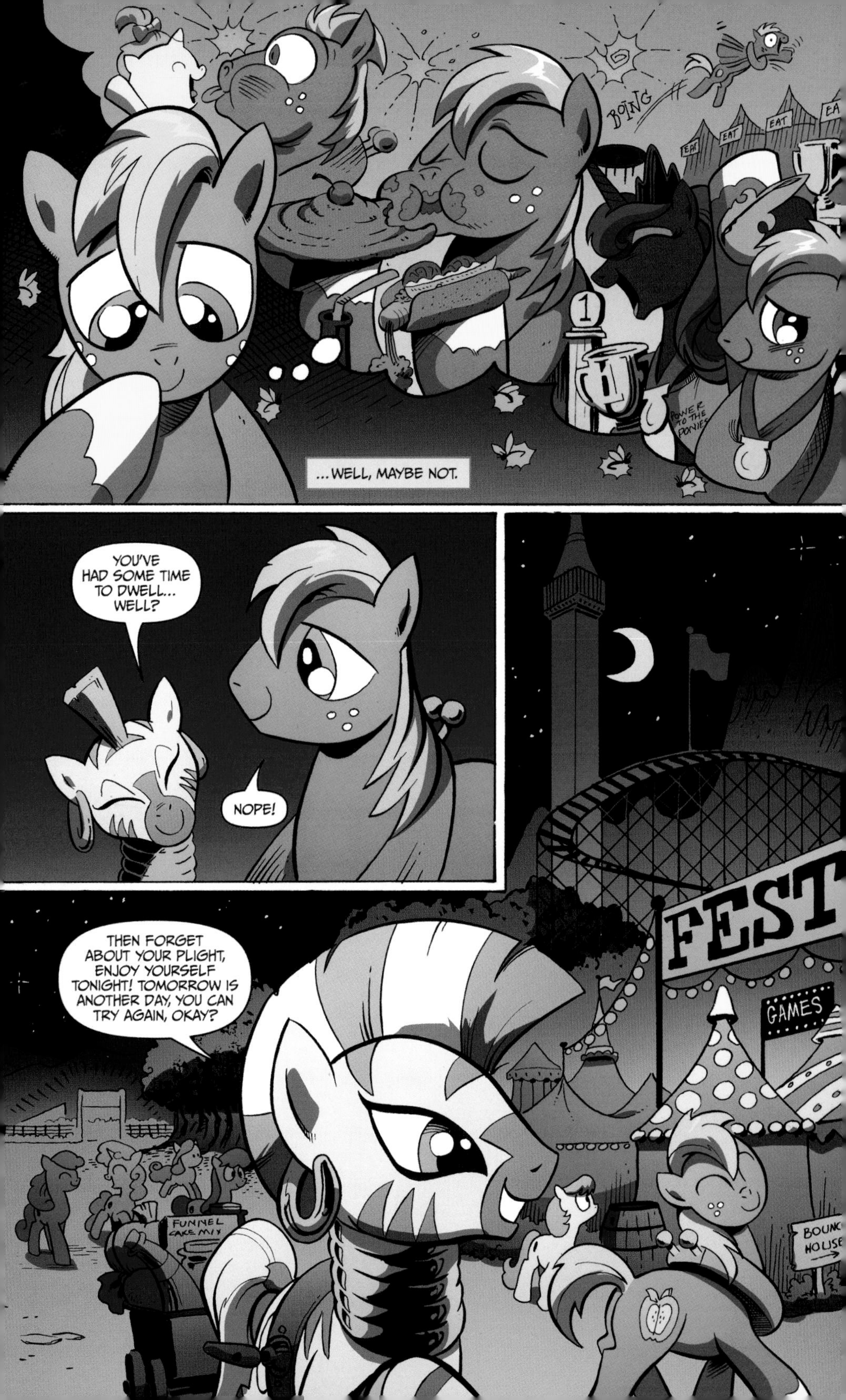
BOING
EAT
EAT
EAT
EAT
1
POWER TO THE PONIES
...WELL, MAYBE NOT.
YOU'VE HAD SOME TIME TO DWELL... WELL?
NOPE!
THEN FORGET ABOUT YOUR PLIGHT, ENJOY YOURSELF TONIGHT! TOMORROW IS ANOTHER DAY, YOU CAN TRY AGAIN, OKAY?
FEST
GAMES
FUNNEL CAKE MIX
BOUNC HOUSE

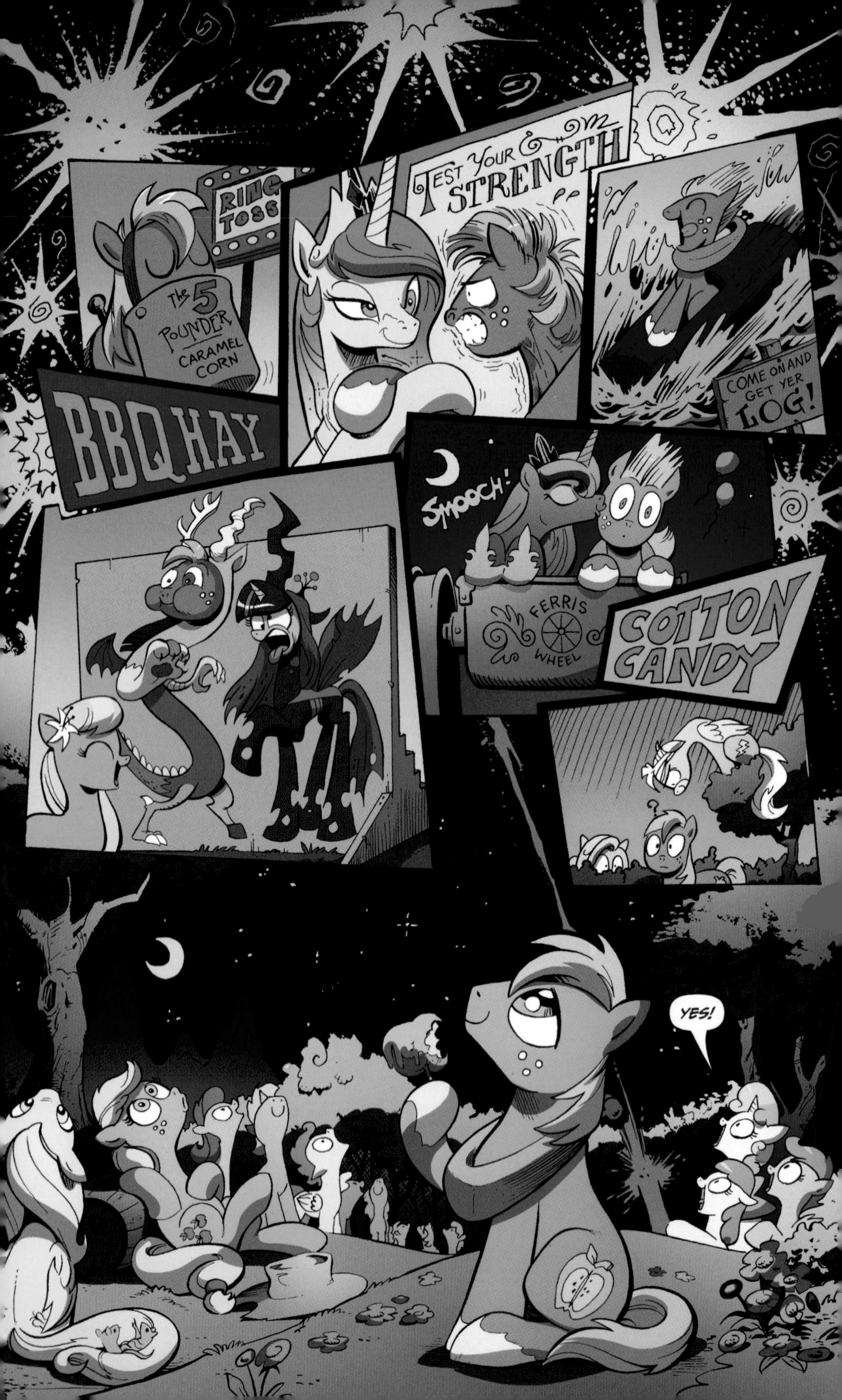

RING TOSS
The 5 POUNDER CARAMEL CORN
BBQ HAY
TEST YOUR STRENGTH
COME ON AND GET YER LOG!
SMOOCH!
FERRIS WHEEL
COTTON CANDY
YES!

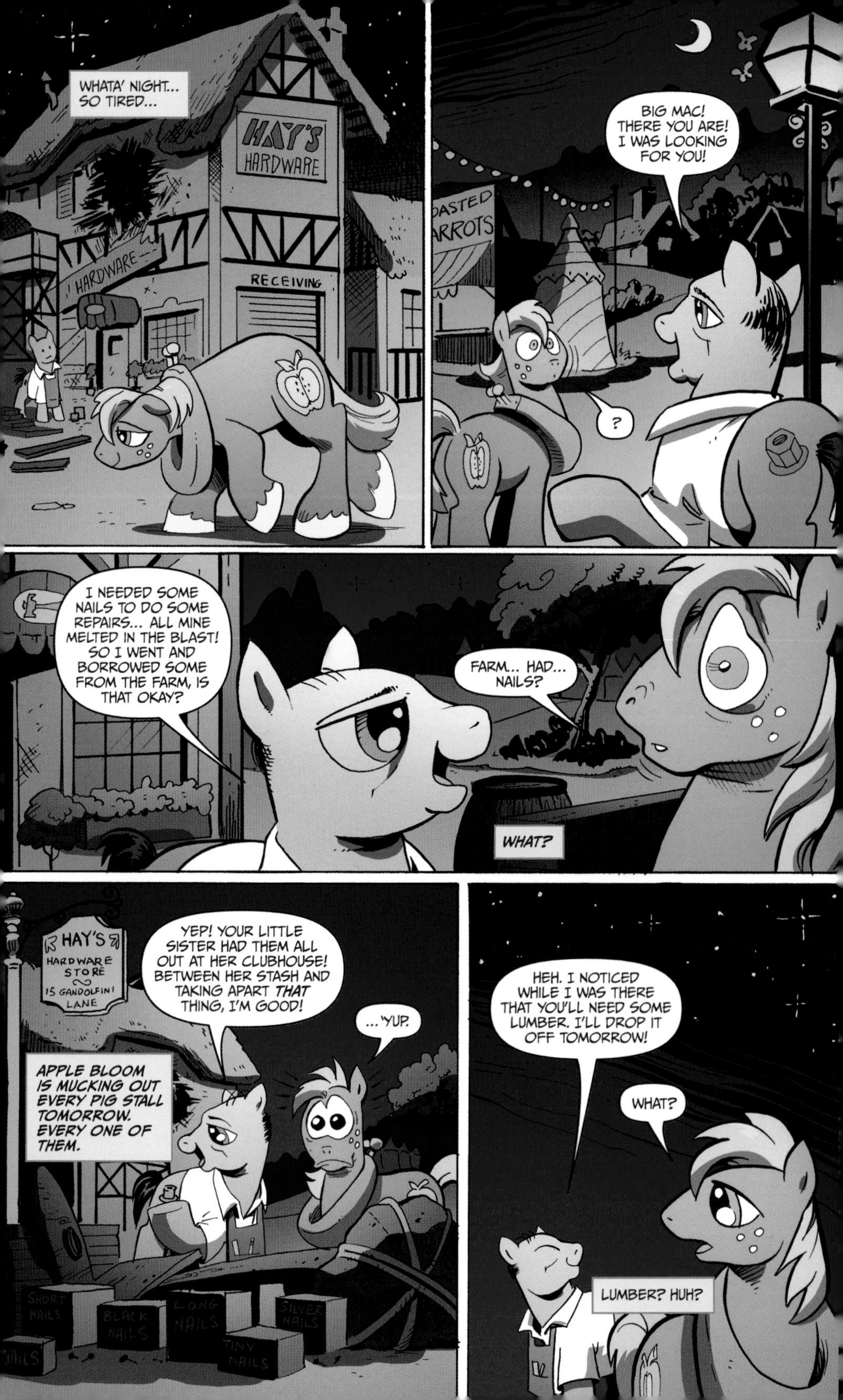
WHATA' NIGHT... SO TIRED...
HAY'S HARDWARE
HARDWARE
RECEIVING
BIG MAC! THERE YOU ARE! I WAS LOOKING FOR YOU!
?
I NEEDED SOME NAILS TO DO SOME REPAIRS... ALL MINE MELTED IN THE BLAST! SO I WENT AND BORROWED SOME FROM THE FARM, IS THAT OKAY?
FARM... HAD... NAILS?
WHAT?
HAY'S HARDWARE STORE 15 GANDOLFINI LANE
YEP! YOUR LITTLE SISTER HAD THEM ALL OUT AT HER CLUBHOUSE! BETWEEN HER STASH AND TAKING APART *THAT* THING, I'M GOOD!
...'YUP.
APPLE BLOOM IS MUCKING OUT EVERY PIG STALL TOMORROW. EVERY ONE OF THEM.
SHORT NAILS
BLACK NAILS
LONG NAILS
SILVER NAILS
TINY NAILS
HEH. I NOTICED WHILE I WAS THERE THAT YOU'LL NEED SOME LUMBER. I'LL DROP IT OFF TOMORROW!
WHAT?
LUMBER? HUH?

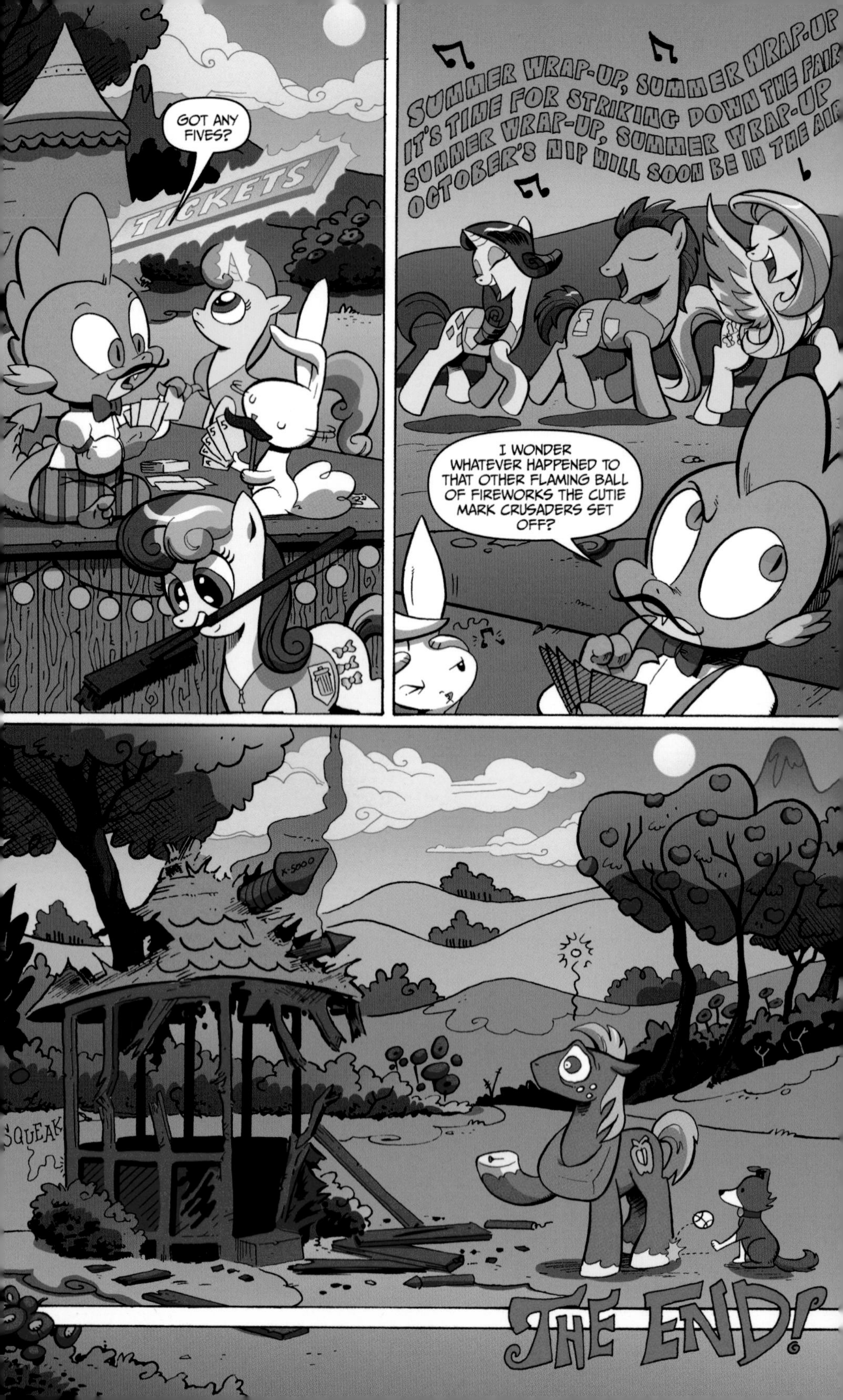
GOT ANY FIVES?
TICKETS
SUMMER WRAP-UP, SUMMER WRAP-UP
IT'S TIME FOR STRIKING DOWN THE FAIR
SUMMER WRAP-UP, SUMMER WRAP-UP
OCTOBER'S NIP WILL SOON BE IN THE AIR
I WONDER WHATEVER HAPPENED TO THAT OTHER FLAMING BALL OF FIREWORKS THE CUTIE MARK CRUSADERS SET OFF?
X-5000
SQUEAK
THE END!

Art by
Katie Cook

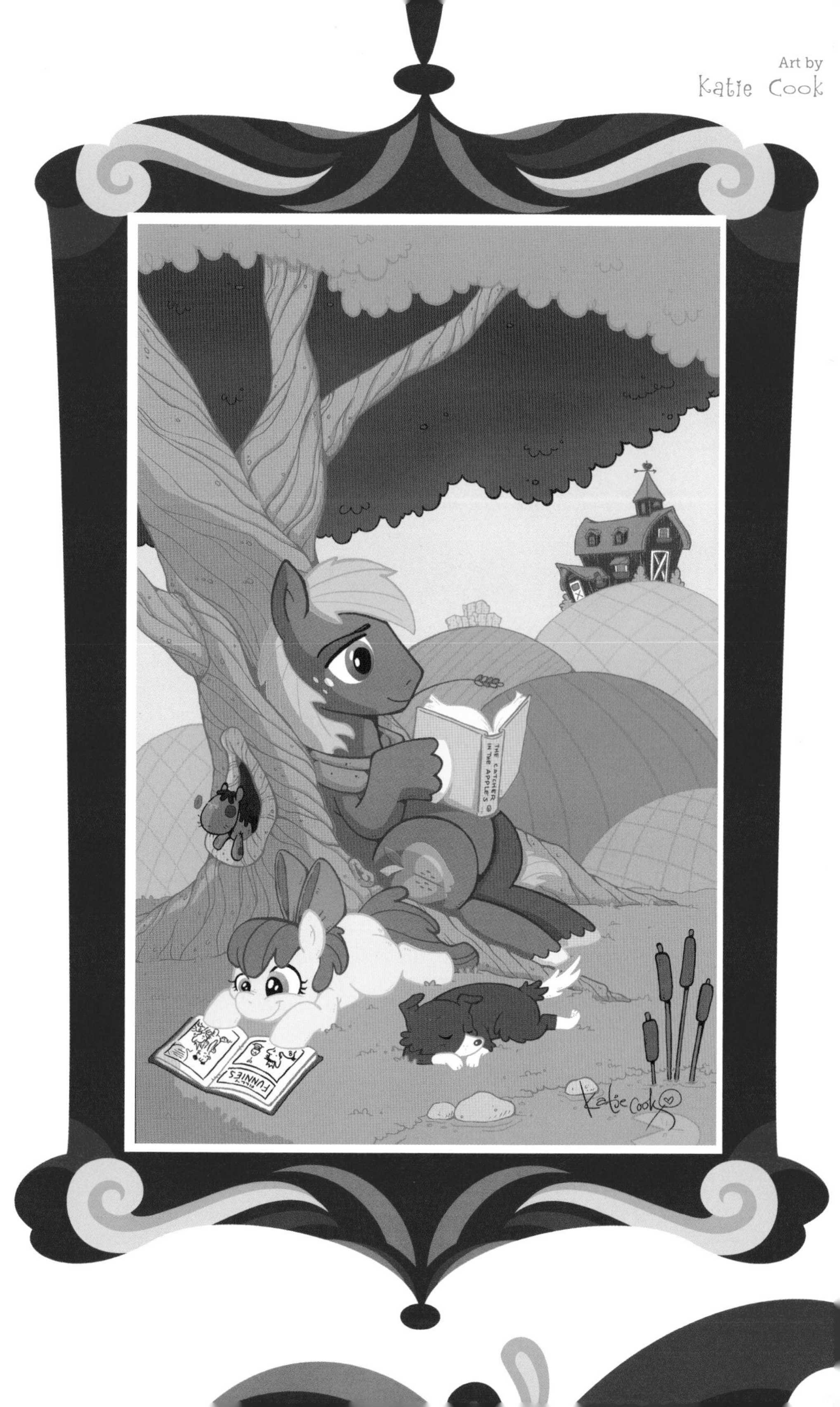
THE CATCHER IN THE APPLES
FUNNIES
Katie Cook

Art by
Andy Price

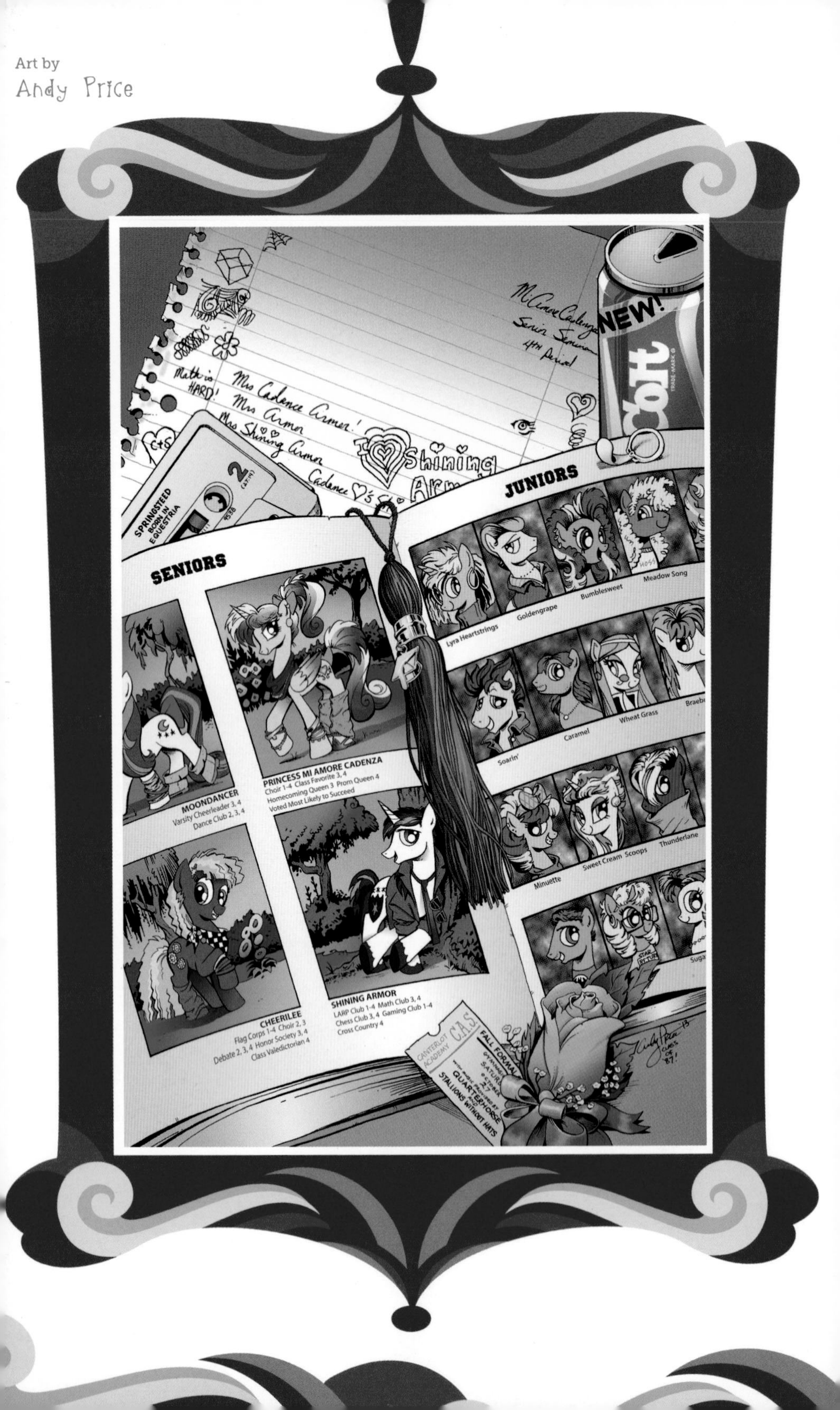
Mi Amore Cadenza
Senior Seminar
4th Period
NEW!
Math is HARD!
Mrs Cadence Armor!
Mrs Armor
Mrs Shining Armor
I ♡ Shining Armor
SPRINGSTEED
BORN IN EQUESTRIA
JUNIORS
Lyra Heartstrings
Goldengrape
Bumblesweet
Meadow Song
Soarin'
Caramel
Wheat Grass
Minuette
Sweet Cream Scoops
Thunderlane
SENIORS
MOONDANCER
Varsity Cheerleader 3, 4
Dance Club 2, 3, 4
PRINCESS MI AMORE CADENZA
Choir 1-4 Class Favorite 3, 4
Homecoming Queen 3 Prom Queen 4
Voted Most Likely to Succeed
CHEERILEE
Flag Corps 1-4 Choir 2, 3
Debate 2, 3, 4 Honor Society 3, 4
Class Valedictorian 4
SHINING ARMOR
LARP Club 1-4 Math Club 3, 4
Chess Club 3, 4 Gaming Club 1-4
Cross Country 4
CANTERLOT ACADEMY
C.A.S.
FALL FORMAL
QUARTERHORSE
STALLIONS WITHOUT HATS

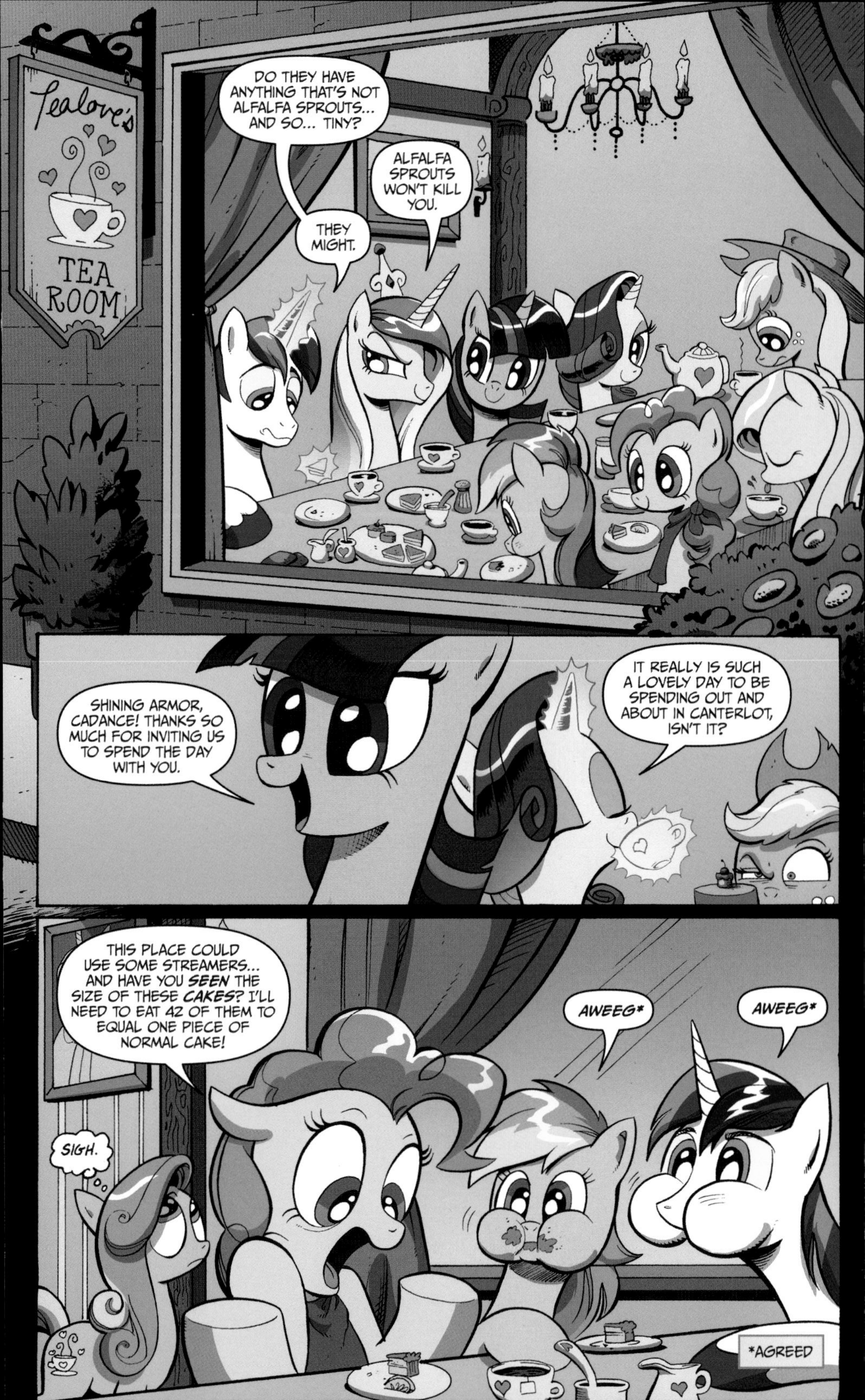
Tealove's
TEA ROOM
DO THEY HAVE ANYTHING THAT'S NOT ALFALFA SPROUTS... AND SO... TINY?
ALFALFA SPROUTS WON'T KILL YOU.
THEY MIGHT.
SHINING ARMOR, CADANCE! THANKS SO MUCH FOR INVITING US TO SPEND THE DAY WITH YOU.
IT REALLY IS SUCH A LOVELY DAY TO BE SPENDING OUT AND ABOUT IN CANTERLOT, ISN'T IT?
THIS PLACE COULD USE SOME STREAMERS... AND HAVE YOU SEEN THE SIZE OF THESE CAKES? I'LL NEED TO EAT 42 OF THEM TO EQUAL ONE PIECE OF NORMAL CAKE!
AWEEG*
AWEEG*
SIGH.
*AGREED

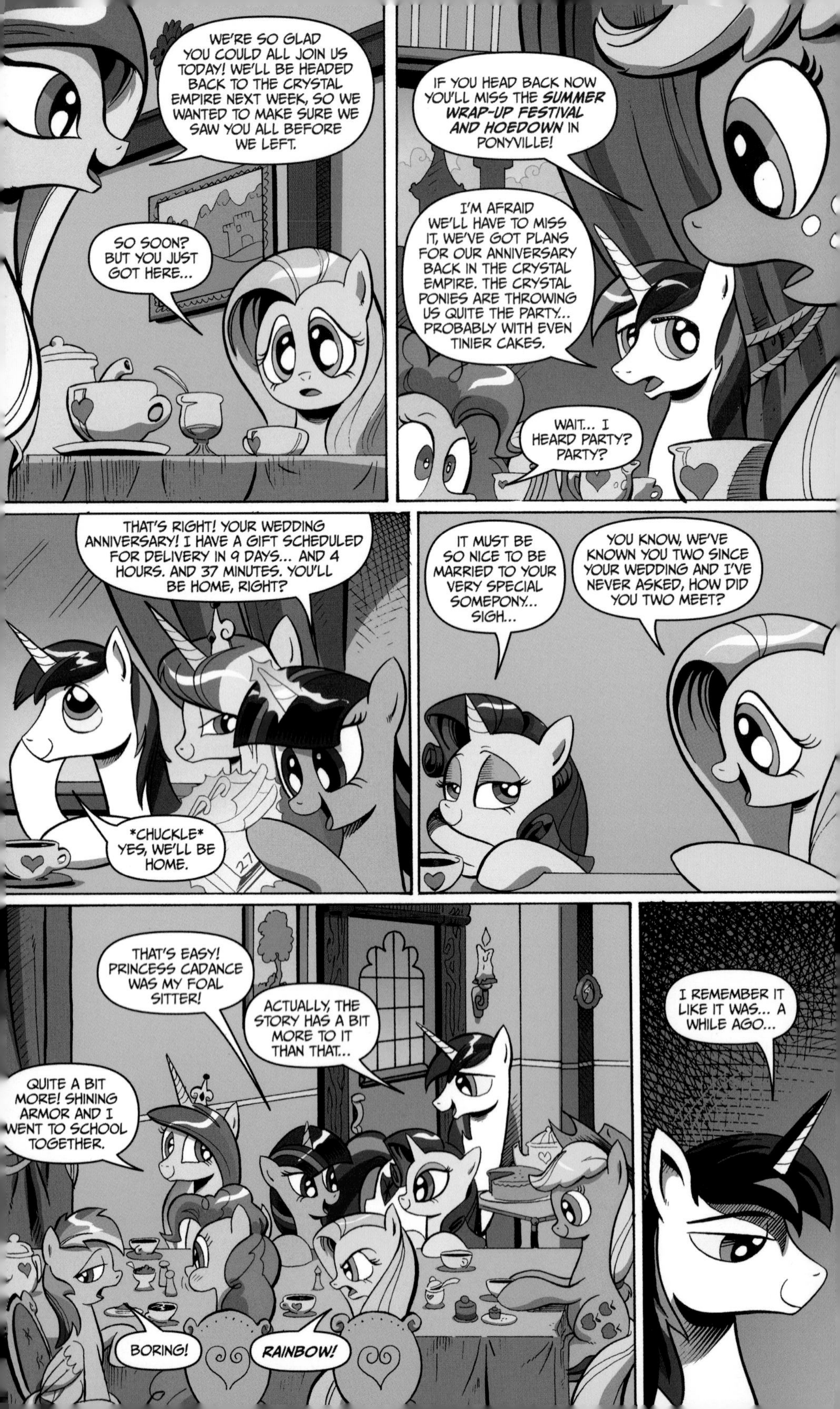

WE'RE SO GLAD YOU COULD ALL JOIN US TODAY! WE'LL BE HEADED BACK TO THE CRYSTAL EMPIRE NEXT WEEK, SO WE WANTED TO MAKE SURE WE SAW YOU ALL BEFORE WE LEFT.
SO SOON? BUT YOU JUST GOT HERE...
IF YOU HEAD BACK NOW YOU'LL MISS THE *SUMMER WRAP-UP FESTIVAL AND HOEDOWN* IN PONYVILLE!
I'M AFRAID WE'LL HAVE TO MISS IT, WE'VE GOT PLANS FOR OUR ANNIVERSARY BACK IN THE CRYSTAL EMPIRE. THE CRYSTAL PONIES ARE THROWING US QUITE THE PARTY... PROBABLY WITH EVEN TINIER CAKES.
WAIT... I HEARD PARTY? PARTY?
THAT'S RIGHT! YOUR WEDDING ANNIVERSARY! I HAVE A GIFT SCHEDULED FOR DELIVERY IN 9 DAYS... AND 4 HOURS. AND 37 MINUTES. YOU'LL BE HOME, RIGHT?
CHUCKLE YES, WE'LL BE HOME.
27
IT MUST BE SO NICE TO BE MARRIED TO YOUR VERY SPECIAL SOMEPONY... SIGH...
YOU KNOW, WE'VE KNOWN YOU TWO SINCE YOUR WEDDING AND I'VE NEVER ASKED, HOW DID YOU TWO MEET?
THAT'S EASY! PRINCESS CADANCE WAS MY FOAL SITTER!
ACTUALLY, THE STORY HAS A BIT MORE TO IT THAN THAT...
QUITE A BIT MORE! SHINING ARMOR AND I WENT TO SCHOOL TOGETHER.
BORING!
RAINBOW!
I REMEMBER IT LIKE IT WAS... A WHILE AGO...

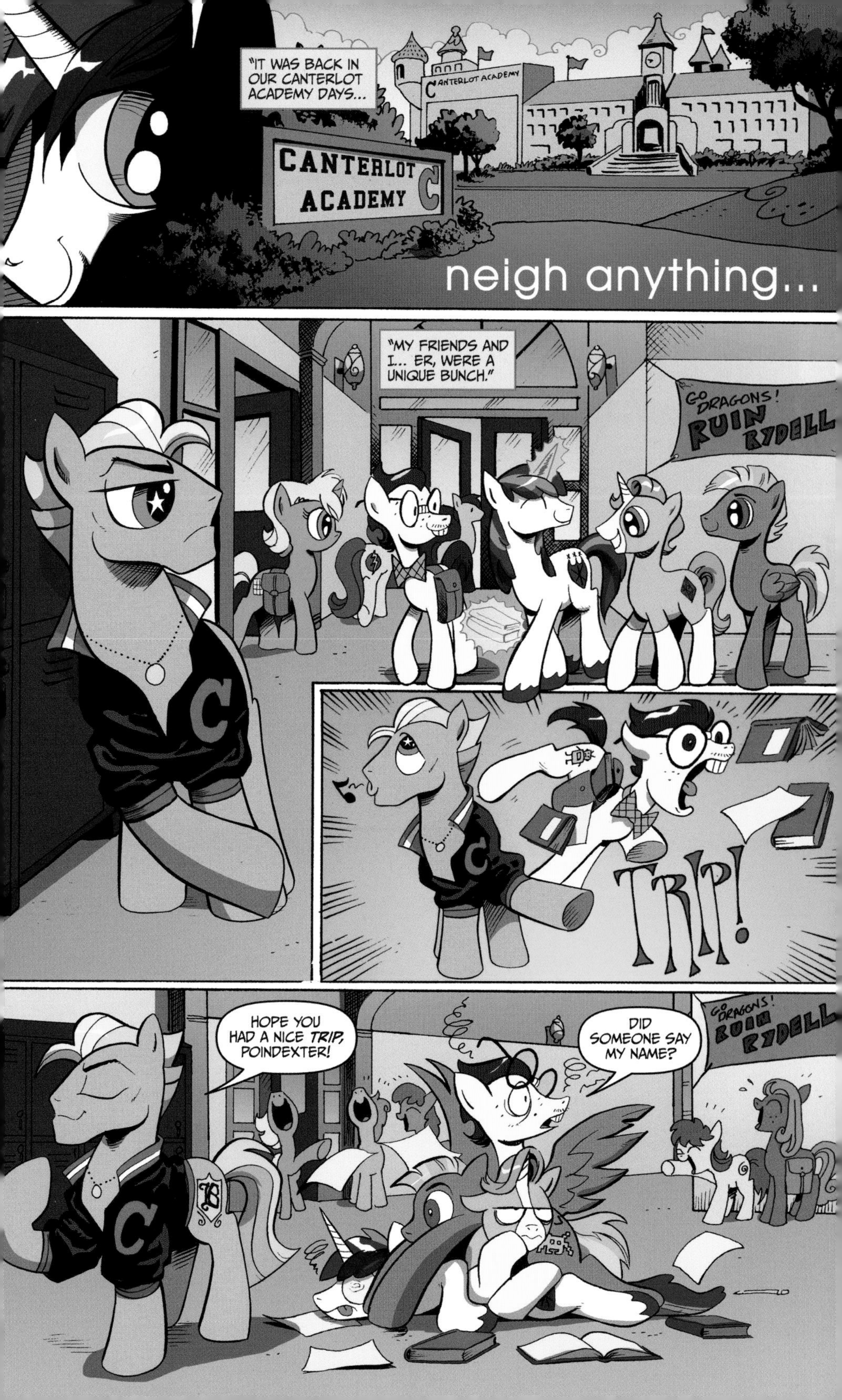
"IT WAS BACK IN OUR CANTERLOT ACADEMY DAYS...
CANTERLOT ACADEMY
CANTERLOT ACADEMY C
neigh anything...
"MY FRIENDS AND I... ER, WERE A UNIQUE BUNCH."
GO DRAGONS! RUIN RYDELL
TRIP!
HOPE YOU HAD A NICE TRIP, POINDEXTER!
DID SOMEONE SAY MY NAME?
GO DRAGONS! RUIN RYDELL

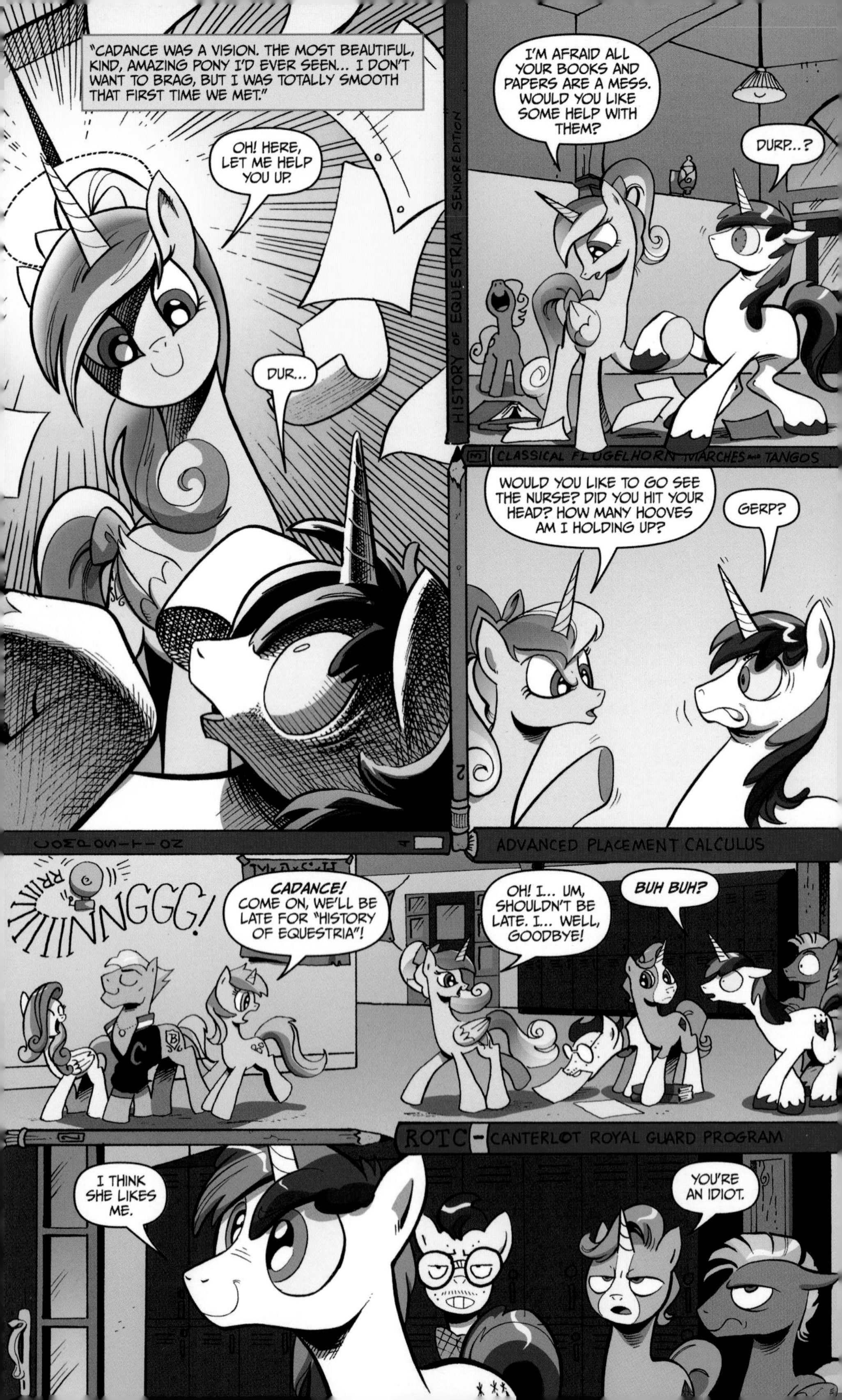
"CADANCE WAS A VISION. THE MOST BEAUTIFUL, KIND, AMAZING PONY I'D EVER SEEN... I DON'T WANT TO BRAG, BUT I WAS TOTALLY SMOOTH THAT FIRST TIME WE MET."
OH! HERE, LET ME HELP YOU UP.
DUR...
HISTORY of EQUESTRIA SENIOR EDITION
I'M AFRAID ALL YOUR BOOKS AND PAPERS ARE A MESS. WOULD YOU LIKE SOME HELP WITH THEM?
DURP...?
CLASSICAL FLUGELHORN MARCHES and TANGOS
WOULD YOU LIKE TO GO SEE THE NURSE? DID YOU HIT YOUR HEAD? HOW MANY HOOVES AM I HOLDING UP?
GERP?
ADVANCED PLACEMENT CALCULUS
RRIIIINNGGG!
CADANCE! COME ON, WE'LL BE LATE FOR "HISTORY OF EQUESTRIA"!
OH! I... UM, SHOULDN'T BE LATE. I... WELL, GOODBYE!
BUH BUH?
ROTC - CANTERLOT ROYAL GUARD PROGRAM
I THINK SHE LIKES ME.
YOU'RE AN IDIOT.

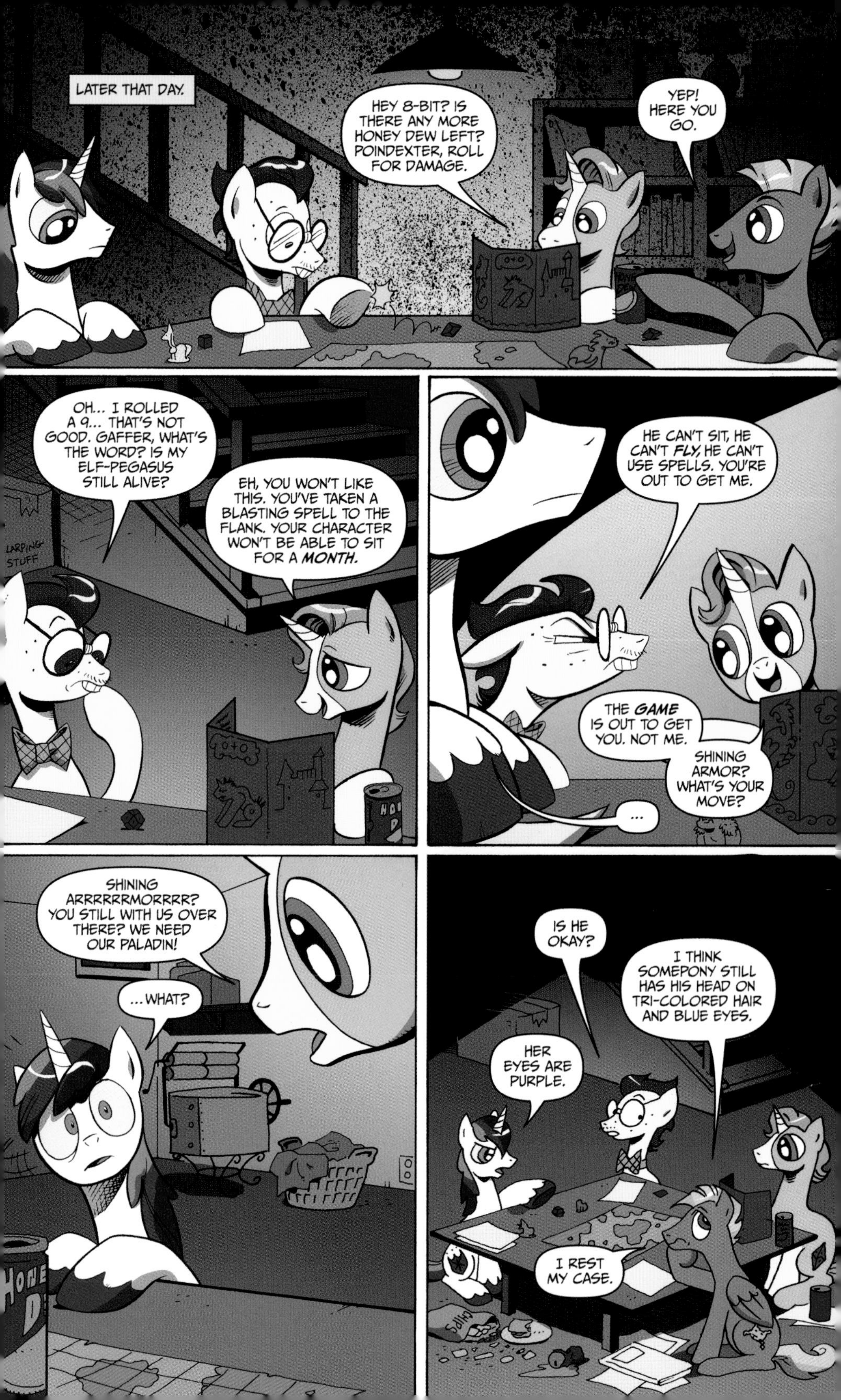
LATER THAT DAY.
HEY 8-BIT? IS THERE ANY MORE HONEY DEW LEFT? POINDEXTER, ROLL FOR DAMAGE.
YEP! HERE YOU GO.
OH... I ROLLED A 9... THAT'S NOT GOOD. GAFFER, WHAT'S THE WORD? IS MY ELF-PEGASUS STILL ALIVE?
EH, YOU WON'T LIKE THIS. YOU'VE TAKEN A BLASTING SPELL TO THE FLANK. YOUR CHARACTER WON'T BE ABLE TO SIT FOR A MONTH.
LARPING STUFF
HE CAN'T SIT, HE CAN'T FLY, HE CAN'T USE SPELLS. YOU'RE OUT TO GET ME.
THE GAME IS OUT TO GET YOU. NOT ME.
SHINING ARMOR? WHAT'S YOUR MOVE?
...
SHINING ARRRRRRMORRRR? YOU STILL WITH US OVER THERE? WE NEED OUR PALADIN!
...WHAT?
IS HE OKAY?
I THINK SOMEPONY STILL HAS HIS HEAD ON TRI-COLORED HAIR AND BLUE EYES.
HER EYES ARE PURPLE.
I REST MY CASE.

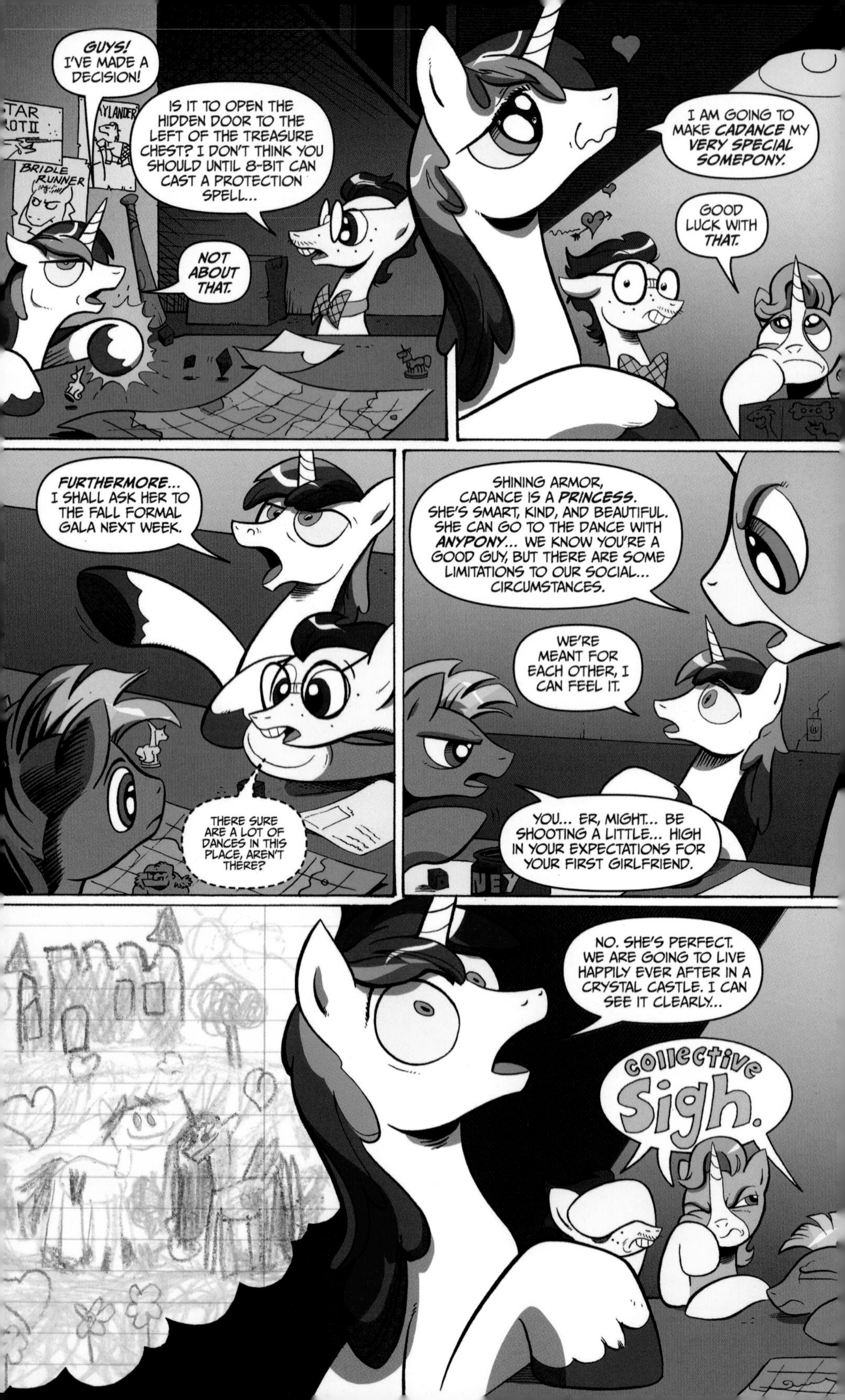
GUYS! I'VE MADE A DECISION!
IS IT TO OPEN THE HIDDEN DOOR TO THE LEFT OF THE TREASURE CHEST? I DON'T THINK YOU SHOULD UNTIL 8-BIT CAN CAST A PROTECTION SPELL...
BRIDLE RUNNER
NOT ABOUT THAT.
I AM GOING TO MAKE CADANCE MY VERY SPECIAL SOMEPONY.
GOOD LUCK WITH THAT.
FURTHERMORE... I SHALL ASK HER TO THE FALL FORMAL GALA NEXT WEEK.
THERE SURE ARE A LOT OF DANCES IN THIS PLACE, AREN'T THERE?
SHINING ARMOR, CADANCE IS A PRINCESS. SHE'S SMART, KIND, AND BEAUTIFUL. SHE CAN GO TO THE DANCE WITH ANYPONY... WE KNOW YOU'RE A GOOD GUY, BUT THERE ARE SOME LIMITATIONS TO OUR SOCIAL... CIRCUMSTANCES.
WE'RE MEANT FOR EACH OTHER, I CAN FEEL IT.
YOU... ER, MIGHT... BE SHOOTING A LITTLE... HIGH IN YOUR EXPECTATIONS FOR YOUR FIRST GIRLFRIEND.
NO. SHE'S PERFECT. WE ARE GOING TO LIVE HAPPILY EVER AFTER IN A CRYSTAL CASTLE. I CAN SEE IT CLEARLY...
Collective Sigh.

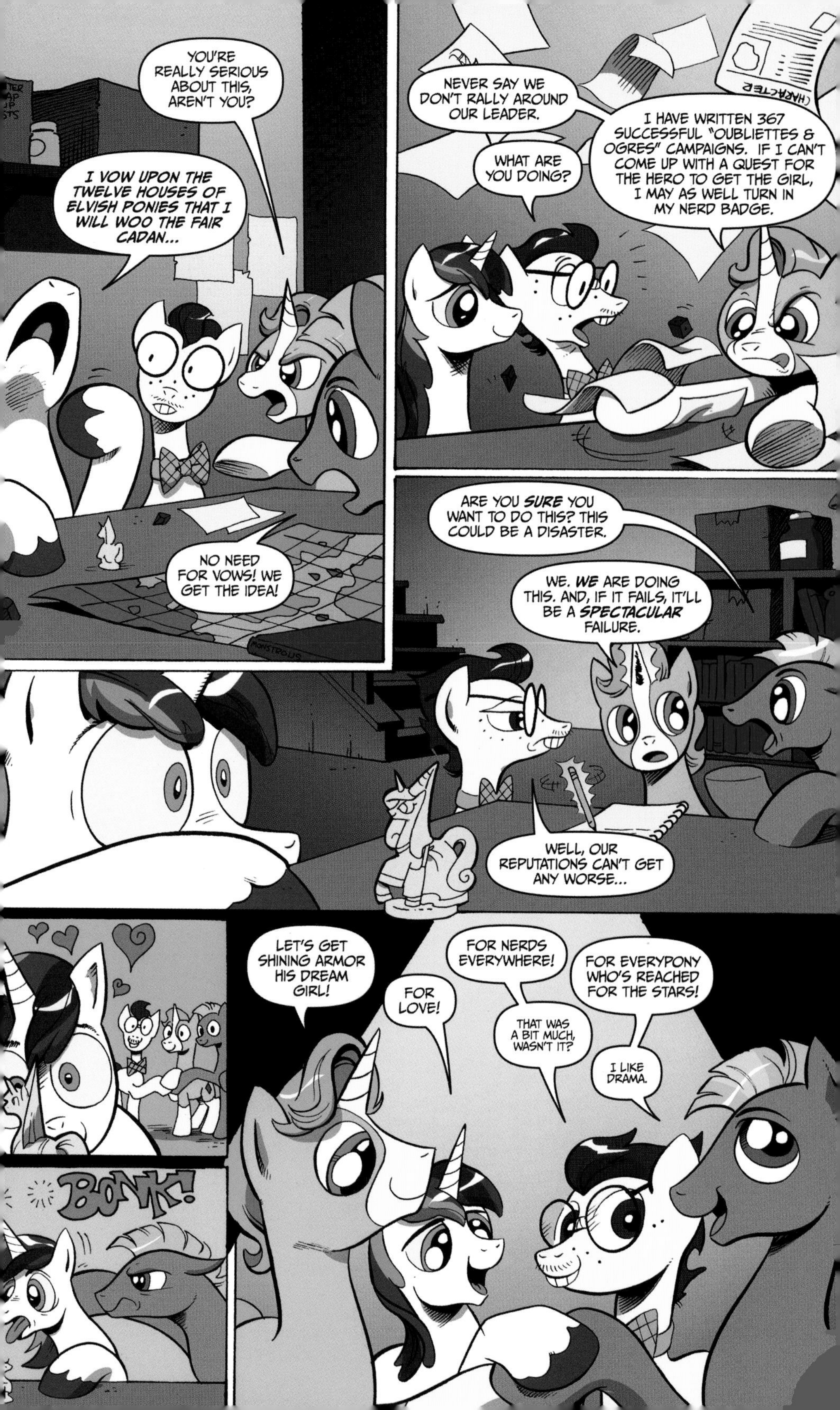
YOU'RE REALLY SERIOUS ABOUT THIS, AREN'T YOU?
I VOW UPON THE TWELVE HOUSES OF ELVISH PONIES THAT I WILL WOO THE FAIR CADAN...
NO NEED FOR VOWS! WE GET THE IDEA!
MONSTROUS
NEVER SAY WE DON'T RALLY AROUND OUR LEADER.
WHAT ARE YOU DOING?
I HAVE WRITTEN 367 SUCCESSFUL "OUBLIETTES & OGRES" CAMPAIGNS. IF I CAN'T COME UP WITH A QUEST FOR THE HERO TO GET THE GIRL, I MAY AS WELL TURN IN MY NERD BADGE.
ARE YOU SURE YOU WANT TO DO THIS? THIS COULD BE A DISASTER.
WE. WE ARE DOING THIS. AND, IF IT FAILS, IT'LL BE A SPECTACULAR FAILURE.
WELL, OUR REPUTATIONS CAN'T GET ANY WORSE...
BONK!
LET'S GET SHINING ARMOR HIS DREAM GIRL!
FOR LOVE!
FOR NERDS EVERYWHERE!
THAT WAS A BIT MUCH, WASN'T IT?
FOR EVERYPONY WHO'S REACHED FOR THE STARS!
I LIKE DRAMA.

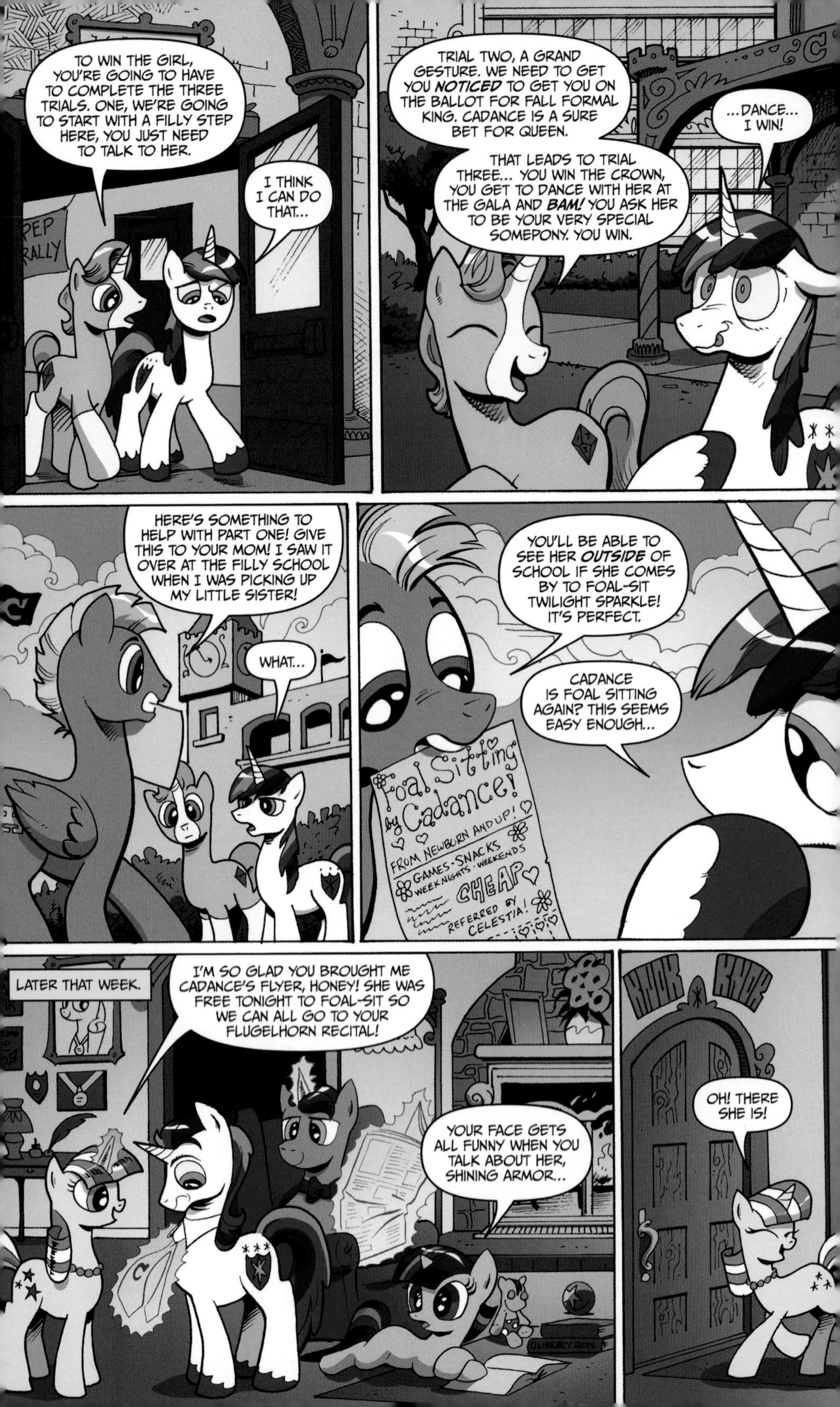
TO WIN THE GIRL, YOU'RE GOING TO HAVE TO COMPLETE THE THREE TRIALS. ONE, WE'RE GOING TO START WITH A FILLY STEP HERE, YOU JUST NEED TO TALK TO HER.
PEP RALLY
I THINK I CAN DO THAT...
TRIAL TWO, A GRAND GESTURE. WE NEED TO GET YOU NOTICED TO GET YOU ON THE BALLOT FOR FALL FORMAL KING. CADANCE IS A SURE BET FOR QUEEN.
THAT LEADS TO TRIAL THREE... YOU WIN THE CROWN, YOU GET TO DANCE WITH HER AT THE GALA AND BAM! YOU ASK HER TO BE YOUR VERY SPECIAL SOMEPONY. YOU WIN.
...DANCE... I WIN!
HERE'S SOMETHING TO HELP WITH PART ONE! GIVE THIS TO YOUR MOM! I SAW IT OVER AT THE FILLY SCHOOL WHEN I WAS PICKING UP MY LITTLE SISTER!
WHAT...
YOU'LL BE ABLE TO SEE HER OUTSIDE OF SCHOOL IF SHE COMES BY TO FOAL-SIT TWILIGHT SPARKLE! IT'S PERFECT.
CADANCE IS FOAL SITTING AGAIN? THIS SEEMS EASY ENOUGH...
Foal Sitting by Cadance!
FROM NEWBORN AND UP!
GAMES · SNACKS
WEEKNIGHTS · WEEKENDS
CHEAP
REFERRED BY CELESTIA!
LATER THAT WEEK.
I'M SO GLAD YOU BROUGHT ME CADANCE'S FLYER, HONEY! SHE WAS FREE TONIGHT TO FOAL-SIT SO WE CAN ALL GO TO YOUR FLUGELHORN RECITAL!
YOUR FACE GETS ALL FUNNY WHEN YOU TALK ABOUT HER, SHINING ARMOR...
KNOK KNOK
OH! THERE SHE IS!

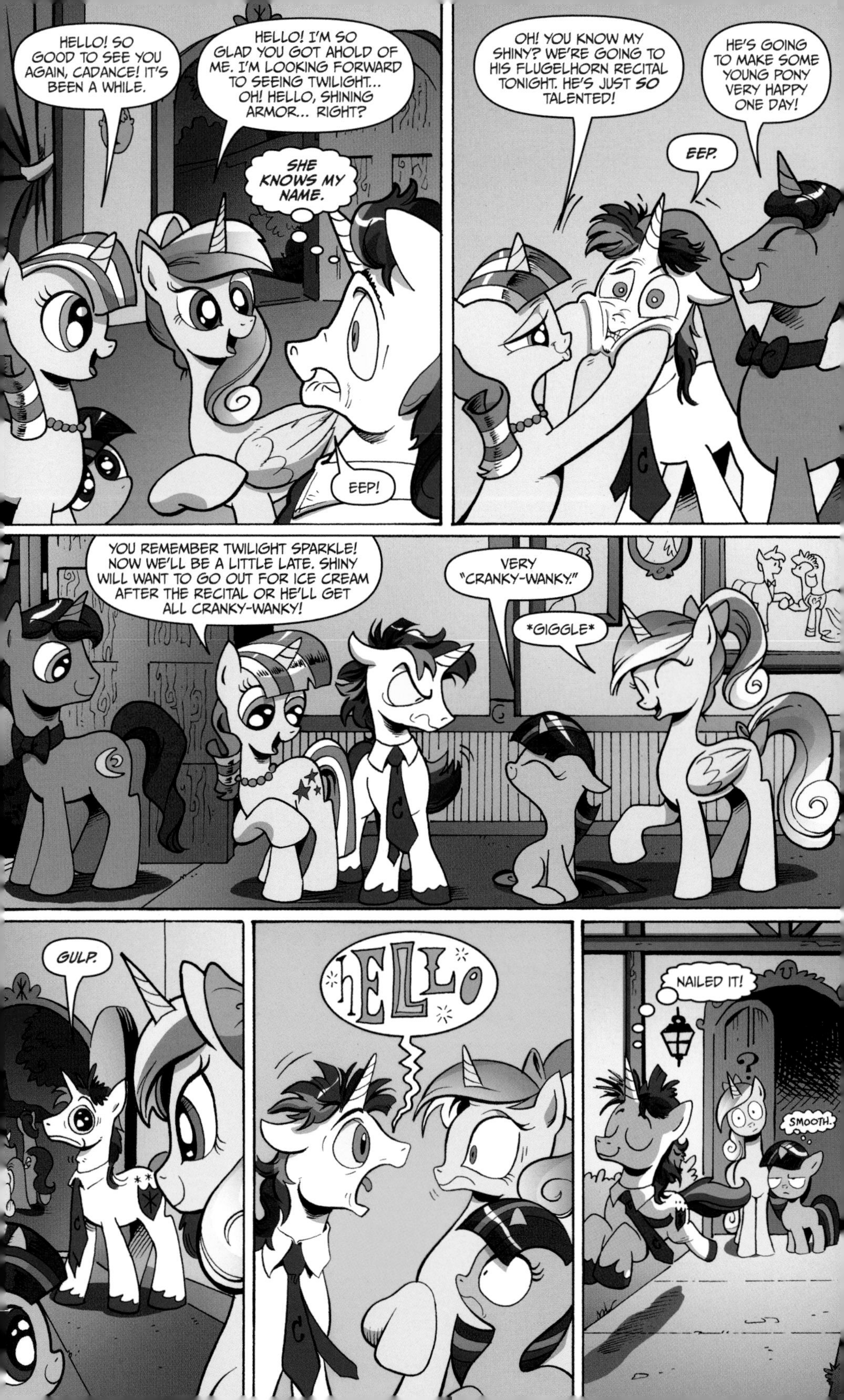
HELLO! SO GOOD TO SEE YOU AGAIN, CADANCE! IT'S BEEN A WHILE.
HELLO! I'M SO GLAD YOU GOT AHOLD OF ME. I'M LOOKING FORWARD TO SEEING TWILIGHT... OH! HELLO, SHINING ARMOR... RIGHT?
SHE KNOWS MY NAME.
EEP!
OH! YOU KNOW MY SHINY? WE'RE GOING TO HIS FLUGELHORN RECITAL TONIGHT. HE'S JUST SO TALENTED!
HE'S GOING TO MAKE SOME YOUNG PONY VERY HAPPY ONE DAY!
EEP.
YOU REMEMBER TWILIGHT SPARKLE! NOW WE'LL BE A LITTLE LATE. SHINY WILL WANT TO GO OUT FOR ICE CREAM AFTER THE RECITAL OR HE'LL GET ALL CRANKY-WANKY!
VERY "CRANKY-WANKY."
GIGGLE
GULP.
hELLo
NAILED IT!
?
SMOOTH.

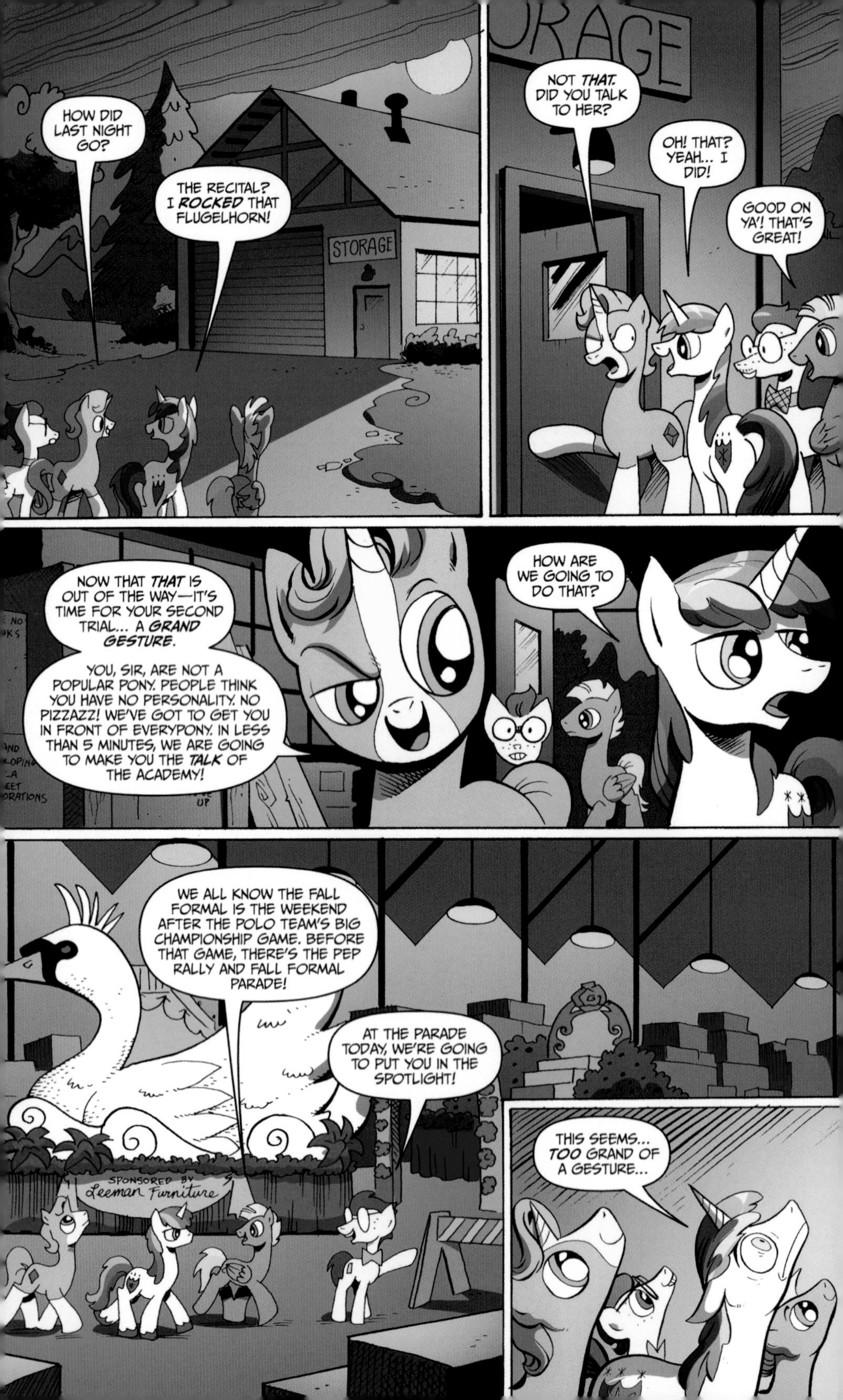
HOW DID LAST NIGHT GO?
THE RECITAL? I *ROCKED* THAT FLUGELHORN!
STORAGE
NOT *THAT.* DID YOU TALK TO HER?
OH! THAT? YEAH... I DID!
GOOD ON YA'! THAT'S GREAT!
NOW THAT *THAT* IS OUT OF THE WAY—IT'S TIME FOR YOUR SECOND TRIAL... A *GRAND GESTURE*.
YOU, SIR, ARE NOT A POPULAR PONY. PEOPLE THINK YOU HAVE NO PERSONALITY. NO PIZZAZZ! WE'VE GOT TO GET YOU IN FRONT OF EVERYPONY. IN LESS THAN 5 MINUTES, WE ARE GOING TO MAKE YOU THE *TALK* OF THE ACADEMY!
HOW ARE WE GOING TO DO THAT?
WE ALL KNOW THE FALL FORMAL IS THE WEEKEND AFTER THE POLO TEAM'S BIG CHAMPIONSHIP GAME. BEFORE THAT GAME, THERE'S THE PEP RALLY AND FALL FORMAL PARADE!
AT THE PARADE TODAY, WE'RE GOING TO PUT YOU IN THE SPOTLIGHT!
SPONSORED BY Leeman Furniture
THIS SEEMS... *TOO* GRAND OF A GESTURE...

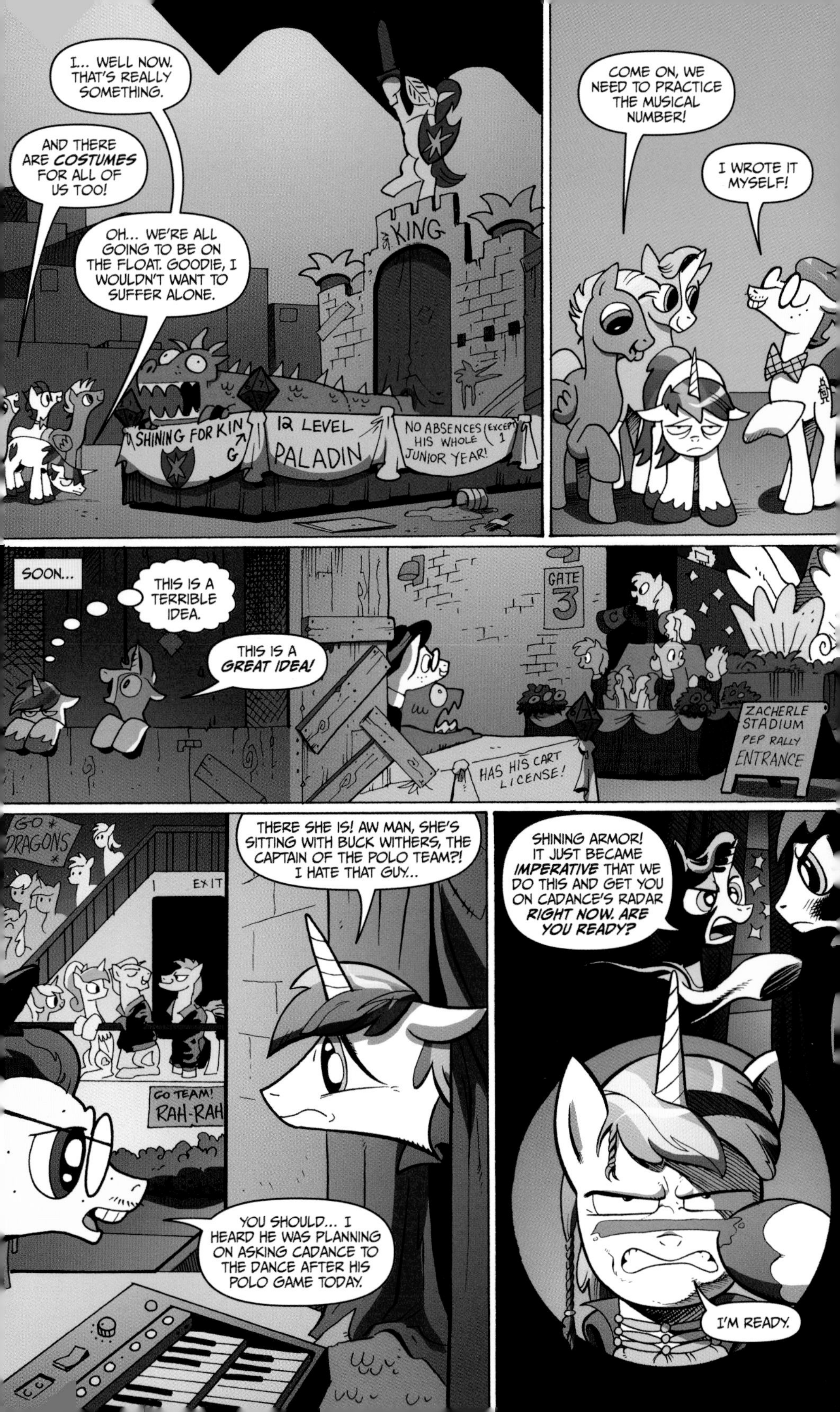

I... WELL NOW. THAT'S REALLY SOMETHING.
AND THERE ARE COSTUMES FOR ALL OF US TOO!
OH... WE'RE ALL GOING TO BE ON THE FLOAT. GOODIE, I WOULDN'T WANT TO SUFFER ALONE.
KING
SHINING FOR KING
12 LEVEL PALADIN
NO ABSENCES (EXCEPT 1) HIS WHOLE JUNIOR YEAR!
COME ON, WE NEED TO PRACTICE THE MUSICAL NUMBER!
I WROTE IT MYSELF!
SOON...
THIS IS A TERRIBLE IDEA.
THIS IS A GREAT IDEA!
GATE 3
HAS HIS CART LICENSE!
ZACHERLE STADIUM PEP RALLY ENTRANCE
GO DRAGONS
EXIT
GO TEAM! RAH-RAH
THERE SHE IS! AW MAN, SHE'S SITTING WITH BUCK WITHERS, THE CAPTAIN OF THE POLO TEAM?! I HATE THAT GUY...
YOU SHOULD... I HEARD HE WAS PLANNING ON ASKING CADANCE TO THE DANCE AFTER HIS POLO GAME TODAY.
SHINING ARMOR! IT JUST BECAME IMPERATIVE THAT WE DO THIS AND GET YOU ON CADANCE'S RADAR RIGHT NOW. ARE YOU READY?
I'M READY.

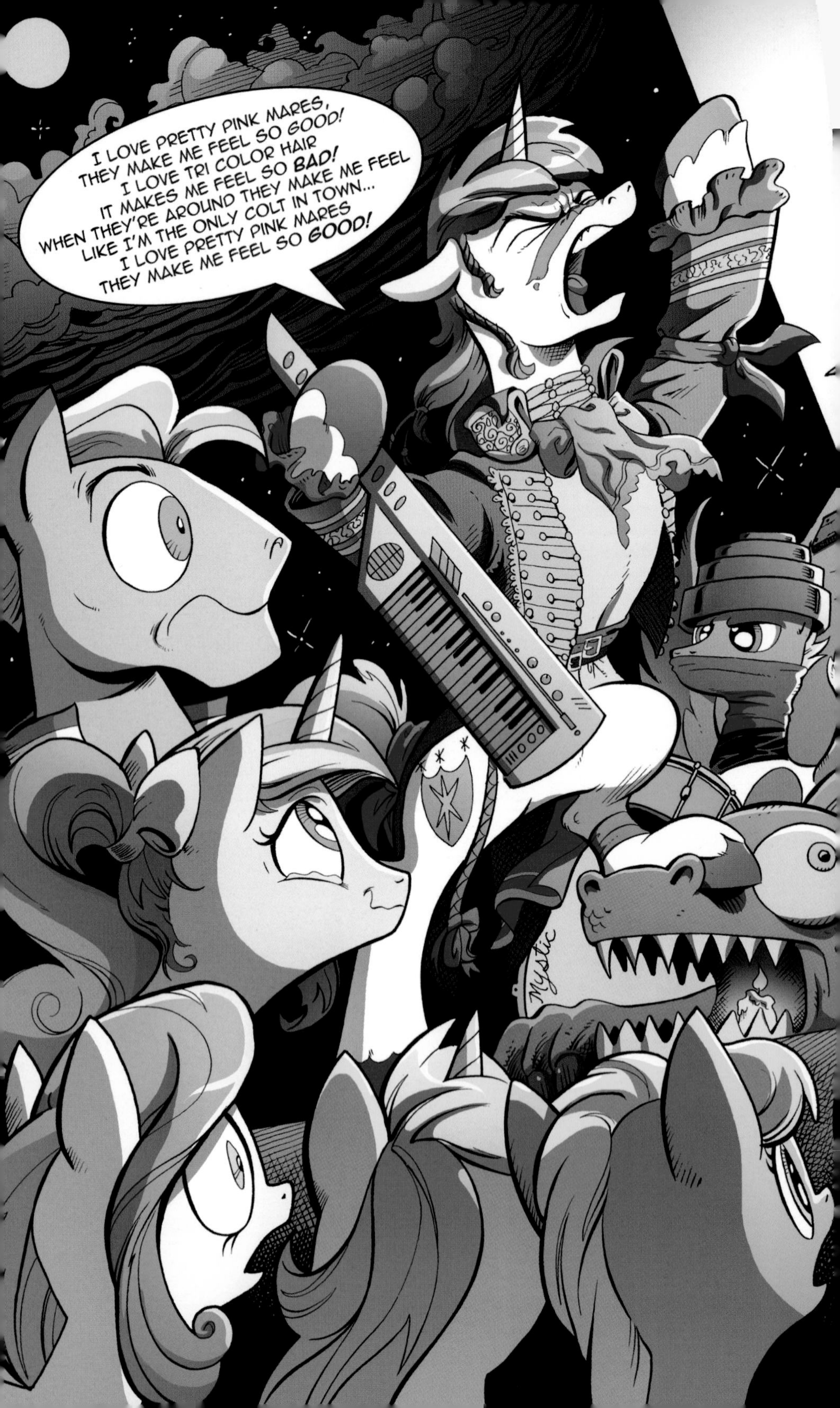
I LOVE PRETTY PINK MARES, THEY MAKE ME FEEL SO GOOD! I LOVE TRI COLOR HAIR IT MAKES ME FEEL SO BAD! WHEN THEY'RE AROUND THEY MAKE ME FEEL LIKE I'M THE ONLY COLT IN TOWN... I LOVE PRETTY PINK MARES THEY MAKE ME FEEL SO GOOD!
Mystic

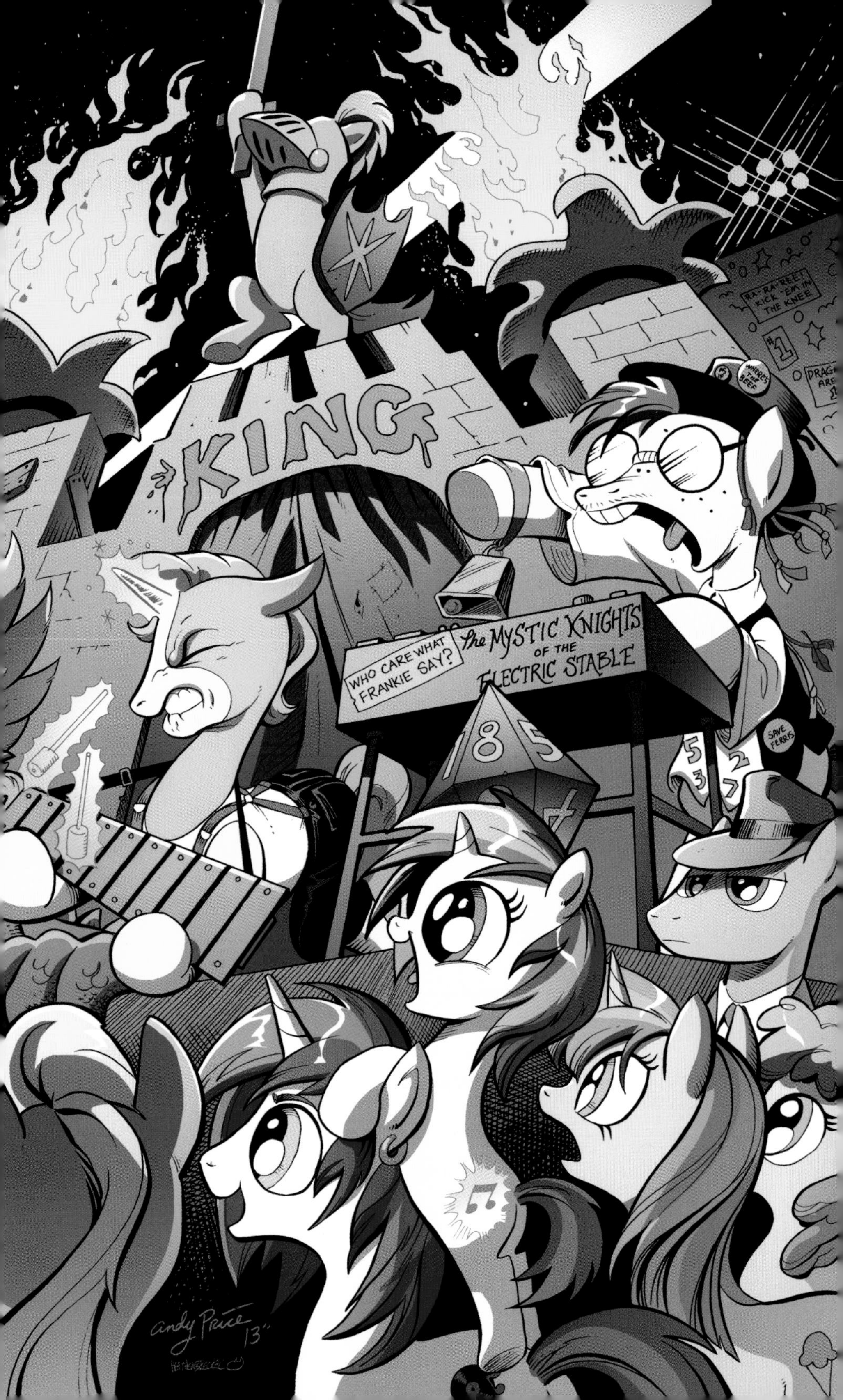
RA-RA-REE! KICK 'EM IN THE KNEE
#1
WHERE'S THE BEEF
KING
WHO CARE WHAT FRANKIE SAY?
The MYSTIC KNIGHTS OF THE ELECTRIC STABLE
SAVE FERRIS
andy Price 13"

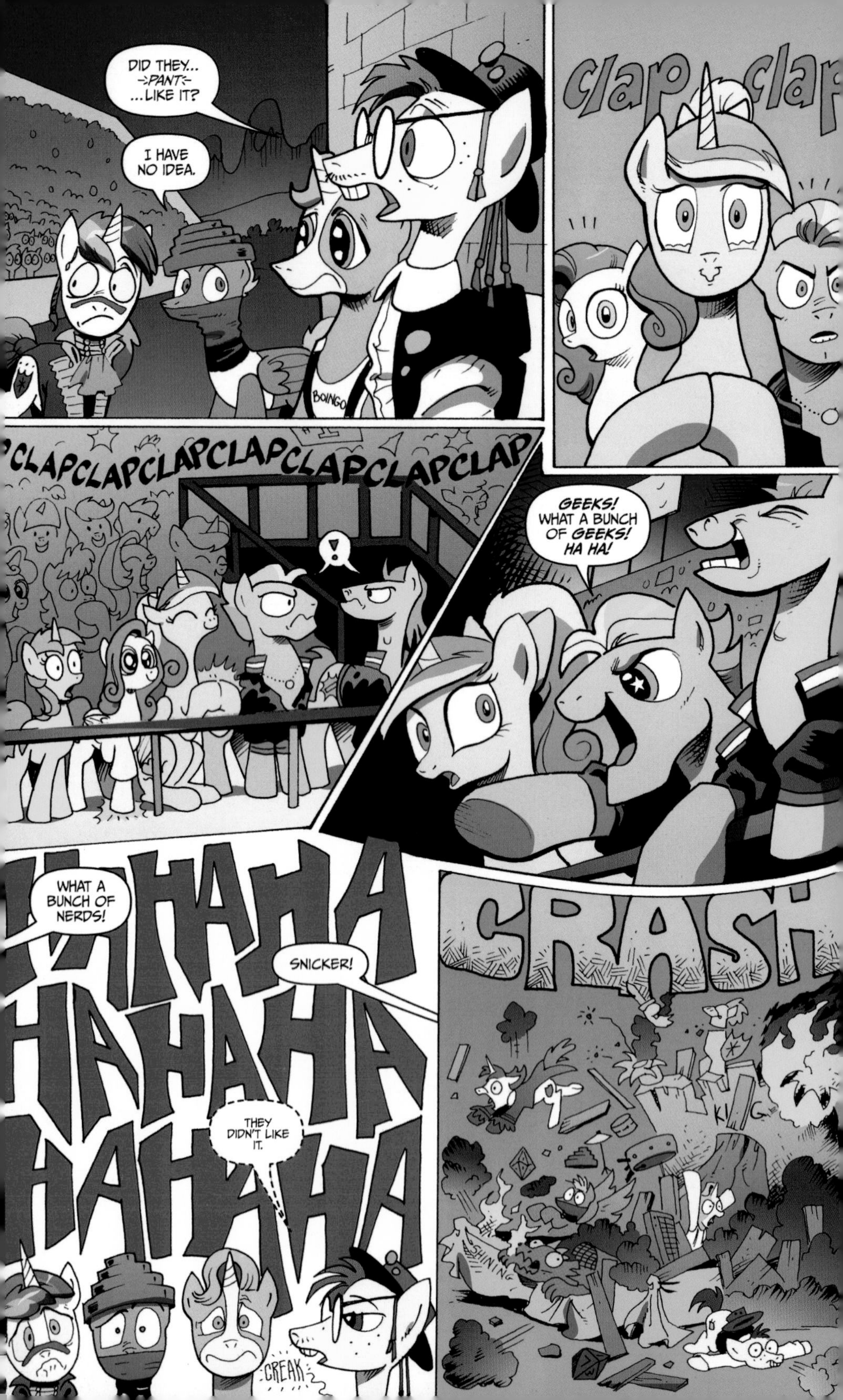

DID THEY... -PANT- ...LIKE IT?
I HAVE NO IDEA.
BOINGO
CLAP CLAP
CLAPCLAPCLAPCLAPCLAPCLAPCLAP
!
GEEKS! WHAT A BUNCH OF GEEKS! HA HA!
HAHAHA HAHAHA HAHAHA
WHAT A BUNCH OF NERDS!
SNICKER!
THEY DIDN'T LIKE IT.
CREAK
CRASH
SHINING

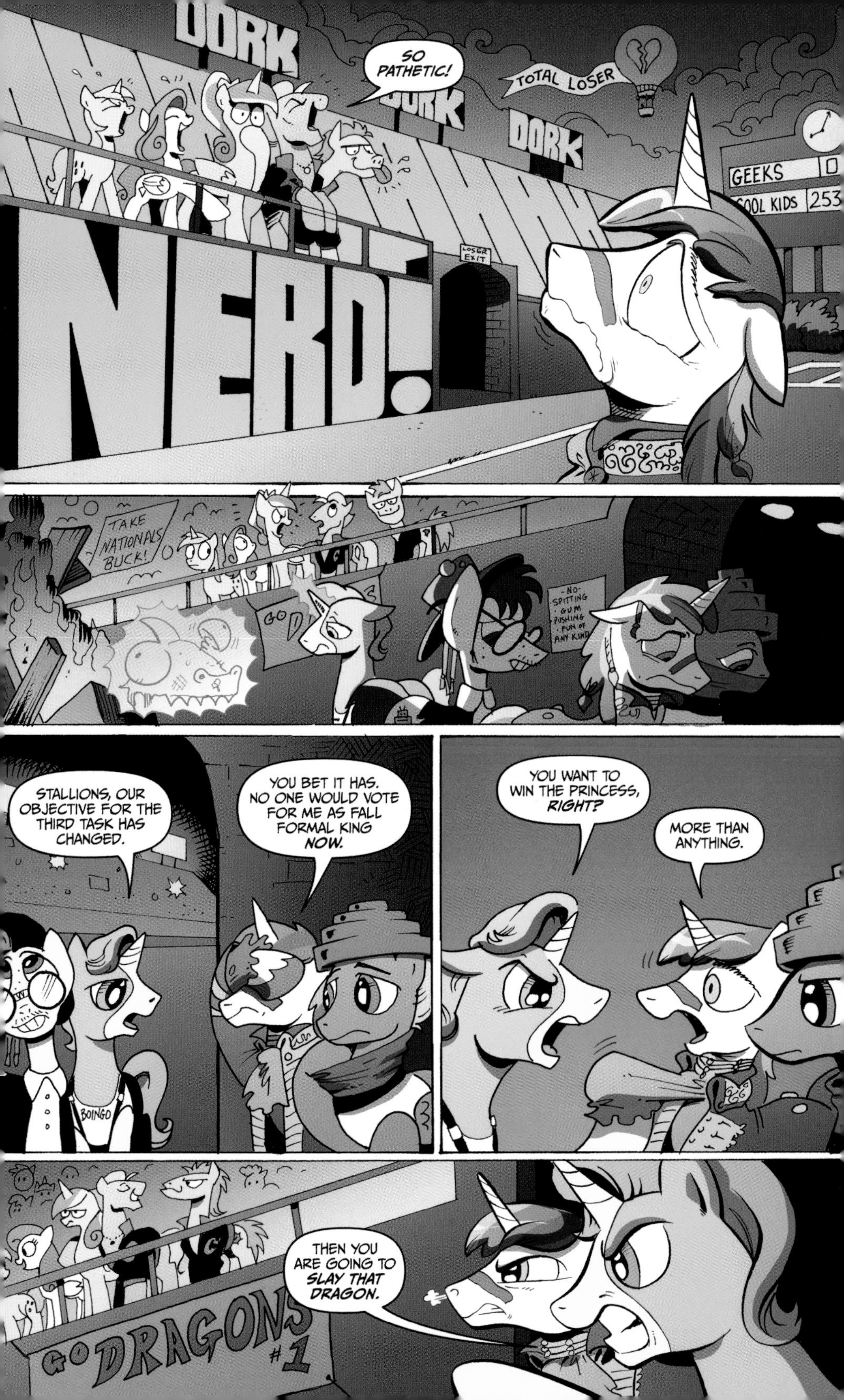
DORK
SO PATHETIC!
DORK
TOTAL LOSER
DORK
GEEKS 0
COOL KIDS 253
LOSER EXIT
NERD!
TAKE NATIONALS BUCK!
-NO- SPITTING · GUM PUSHING · FUN OF ANY KIND
STALLIONS, OUR OBJECTIVE FOR THE THIRD TASK HAS CHANGED.
YOU BET IT HAS. NO ONE WOULD VOTE FOR ME AS FALL FORMAL KING *NOW.*
BOINGO
YOU WANT TO WIN THE PRINCESS, *RIGHT?*
MORE THAN ANYTHING.
THEN YOU ARE GOING TO *SLAY THAT DRAGON.*
GO DRAGONS #1

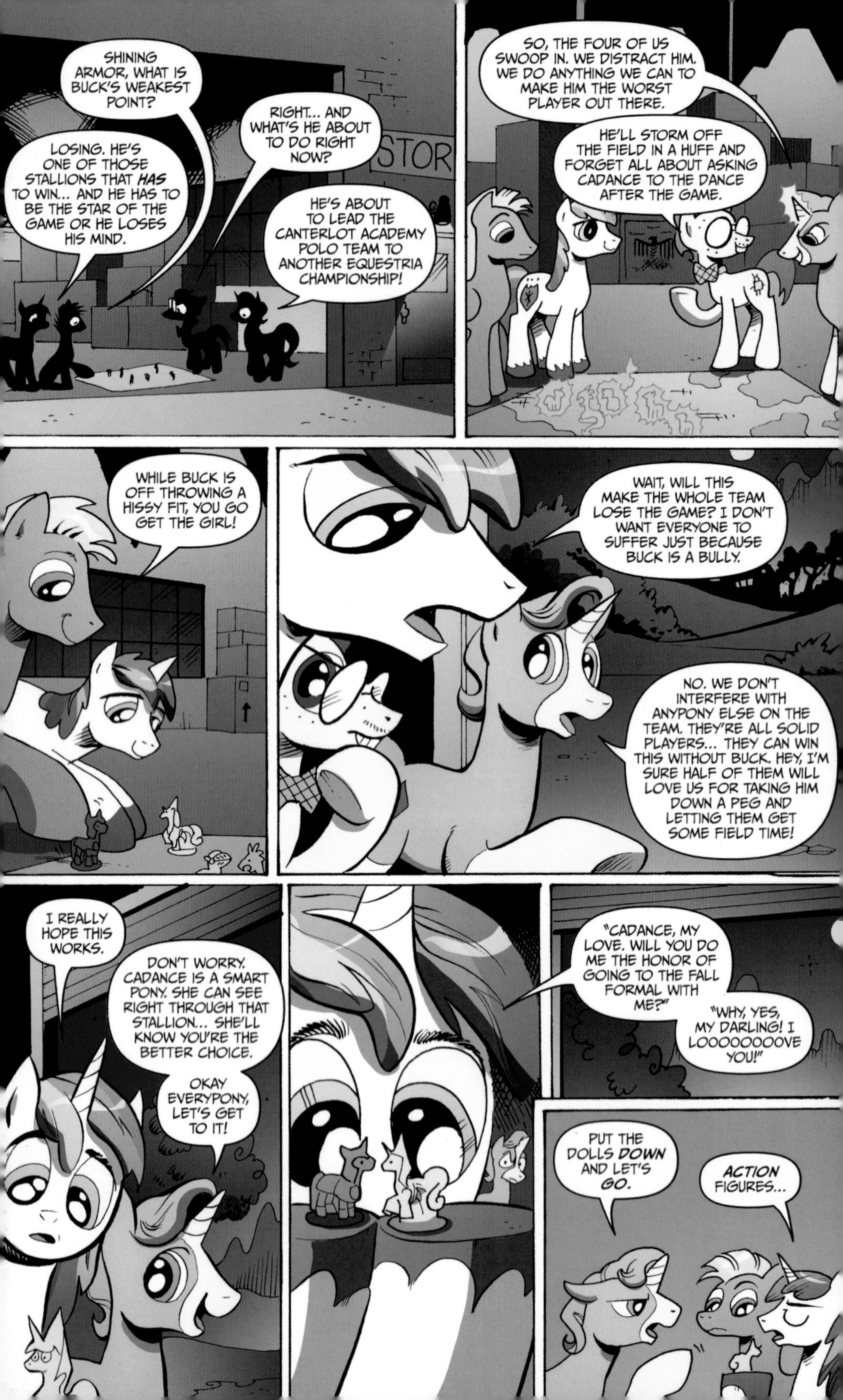

SHINING ARMOR, WHAT IS BUCK'S WEAKEST POINT?
LOSING. HE'S ONE OF THOSE STALLIONS THAT *HAS* TO WIN... AND HE HAS TO BE THE STAR OF THE GAME OR HE LOSES HIS MIND.
RIGHT... AND WHAT'S HE ABOUT TO DO RIGHT NOW?
STOR
HE'S ABOUT TO LEAD THE CANTERLOT ACADEMY POLO TEAM TO ANOTHER EQUESTRIA CHAMPIONSHIP!
SO, THE FOUR OF US SWOOP IN. WE DISTRACT HIM. WE DO ANYTHING WE CAN TO MAKE HIM THE WORST PLAYER OUT THERE.
HE'LL STORM OFF THE FIELD IN A HUFF AND FORGET ALL ABOUT ASKING CADANCE TO THE DANCE AFTER THE GAME.
WHILE BUCK IS OFF THROWING A HISSY FIT, YOU GO GET THE GIRL!
WAIT, WILL THIS MAKE THE WHOLE TEAM LOSE THE GAME? I DON'T WANT EVERYONE TO SUFFER JUST BECAUSE BUCK IS A BULLY.
NO. WE DON'T INTERFERE WITH ANYPONY ELSE ON THE TEAM. THEY'RE ALL SOLID PLAYERS... THEY CAN WIN THIS WITHOUT BUCK. HEY, I'M SURE HALF OF THEM WILL LOVE US FOR TAKING HIM DOWN A PEG AND LETTING THEM GET SOME FIELD TIME!
I REALLY HOPE THIS WORKS.
DON'T WORRY. CADANCE IS A SMART PONY. SHE CAN SEE RIGHT THROUGH THAT STALLION... SHE'LL KNOW YOU'RE THE BETTER CHOICE.
OKAY EVERYPONY, LET'S GET TO IT!
"CADANCE, MY LOVE. WILL YOU DO ME THE HONOR OF GOING TO THE FALL FORMAL WITH ME?"
"WHY, YES, MY DARLING! I LOOOOOOOOVE YOU!"
PUT THE DOLLS *DOWN* AND LET'S *GO*.
ACTION FIGURES...

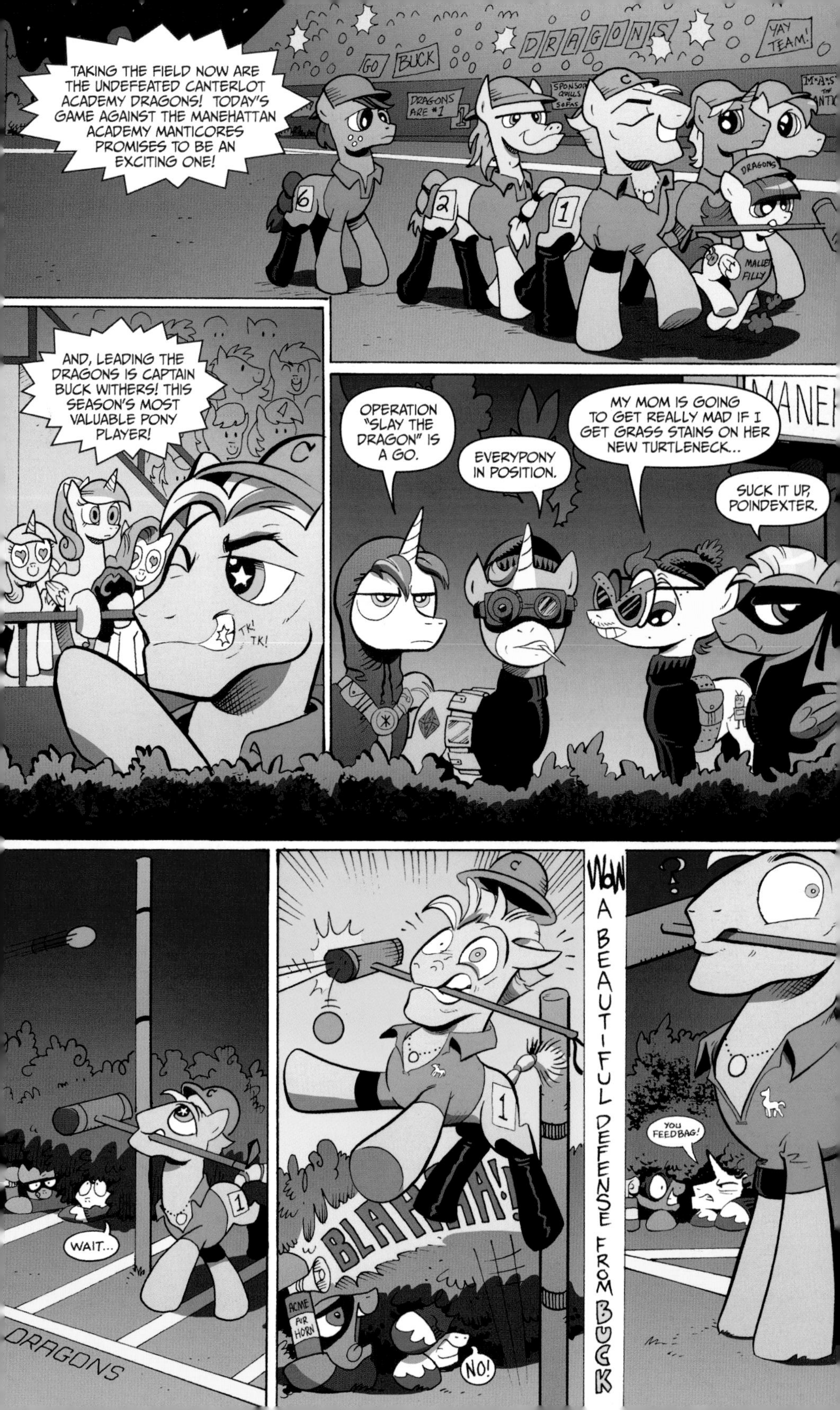

GO
BUCK
DRAGONS
YAY TEAM!
TAKING THE FIELD NOW ARE THE UNDEFEATED CANTERLOT ACADEMY DRAGONS! TODAY'S GAME AGAINST THE MANEHATTAN ACADEMY MANTICORES PROMISES TO BE AN EXCITING ONE!
DRAGONS ARE #1
SPONSOR QUILLS & SOFAS
6
2
1
DRAGONS
MALLET FILLY
AND, LEADING THE DRAGONS IS CAPTAIN BUCK WITHERS! THIS SEASON'S MOST VALUABLE PONY PLAYER!
TK! TK!
OPERATION "SLAY THE DRAGON" IS A GO.
EVERYPONY IN POSITION.
MY MOM IS GOING TO GET REALLY MAD IF I GET GRASS STAINS ON HER NEW TURTLENECK...
SUCK IT UP, POINDEXTER.
MANE
WAIT...
DRAGONS
WOW A BEAUTIFUL DEFENSE FROM BUCK
BLAAAAA!
ACME AIR HORN
NO!
?
YOU FEEDBAG!

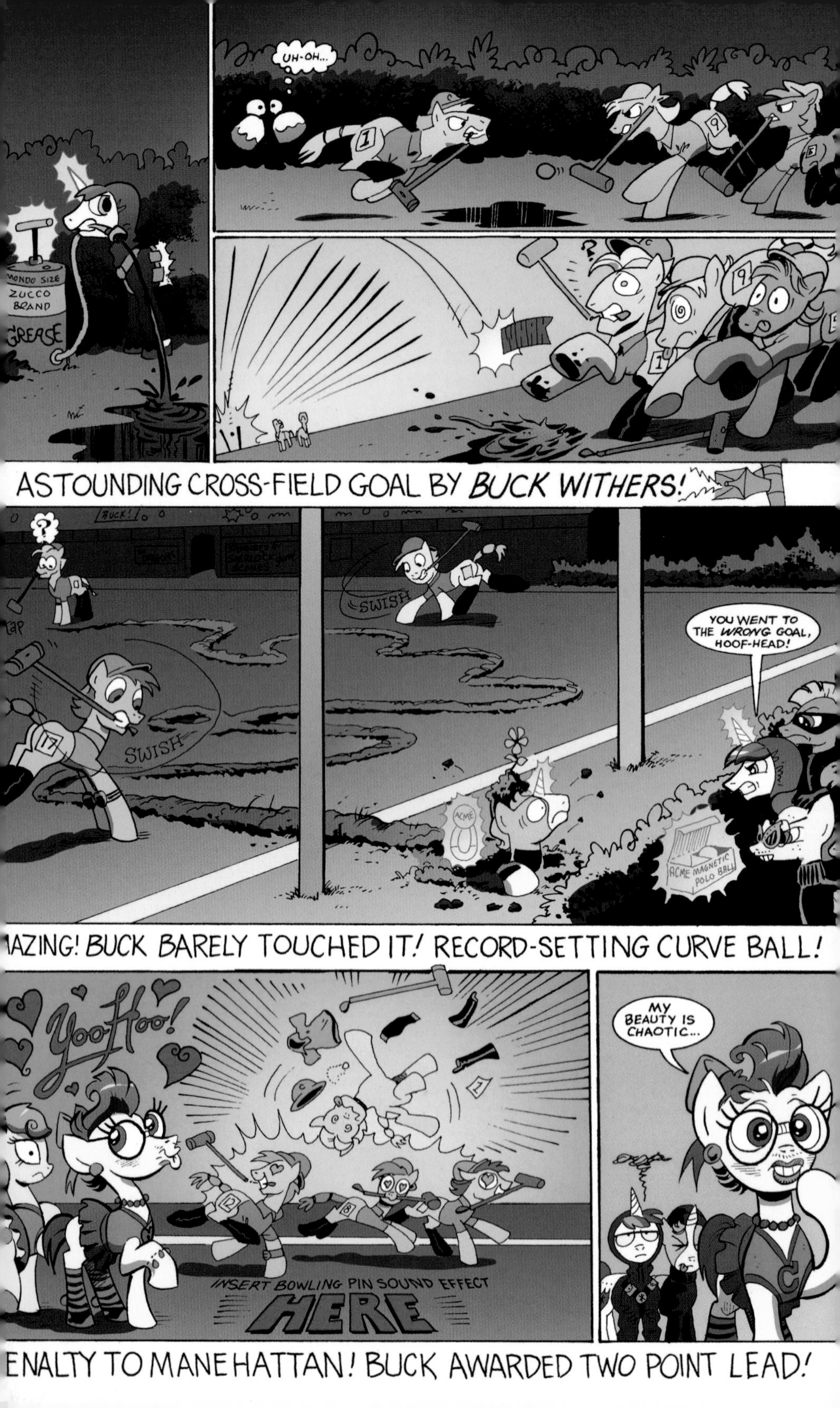

MONDO SIZE
ZUCCO
BRAND
GREASE
UH-OH...
WHAK
ASTOUNDING CROSS-FIELD GOAL BY BUCK WITHERS!
BUCK!
SWISH
TAP
SWISH
YOU WENT TO THE WRONG GOAL, HOOF-HEAD!
ACME
ACME MAGNETIC POLO BALL
AZING! BUCK BARELY TOUCHED IT! RECORD-SETTING CURVE BALL!
Yoo-Hoo!
INSERT BOWLING PIN SOUND EFFECT
HERE
MY BEAUTY IS CHAOTIC...
ENALTY TO MANEHATTAN! BUCK AWARDED TWO POINT LEAD!

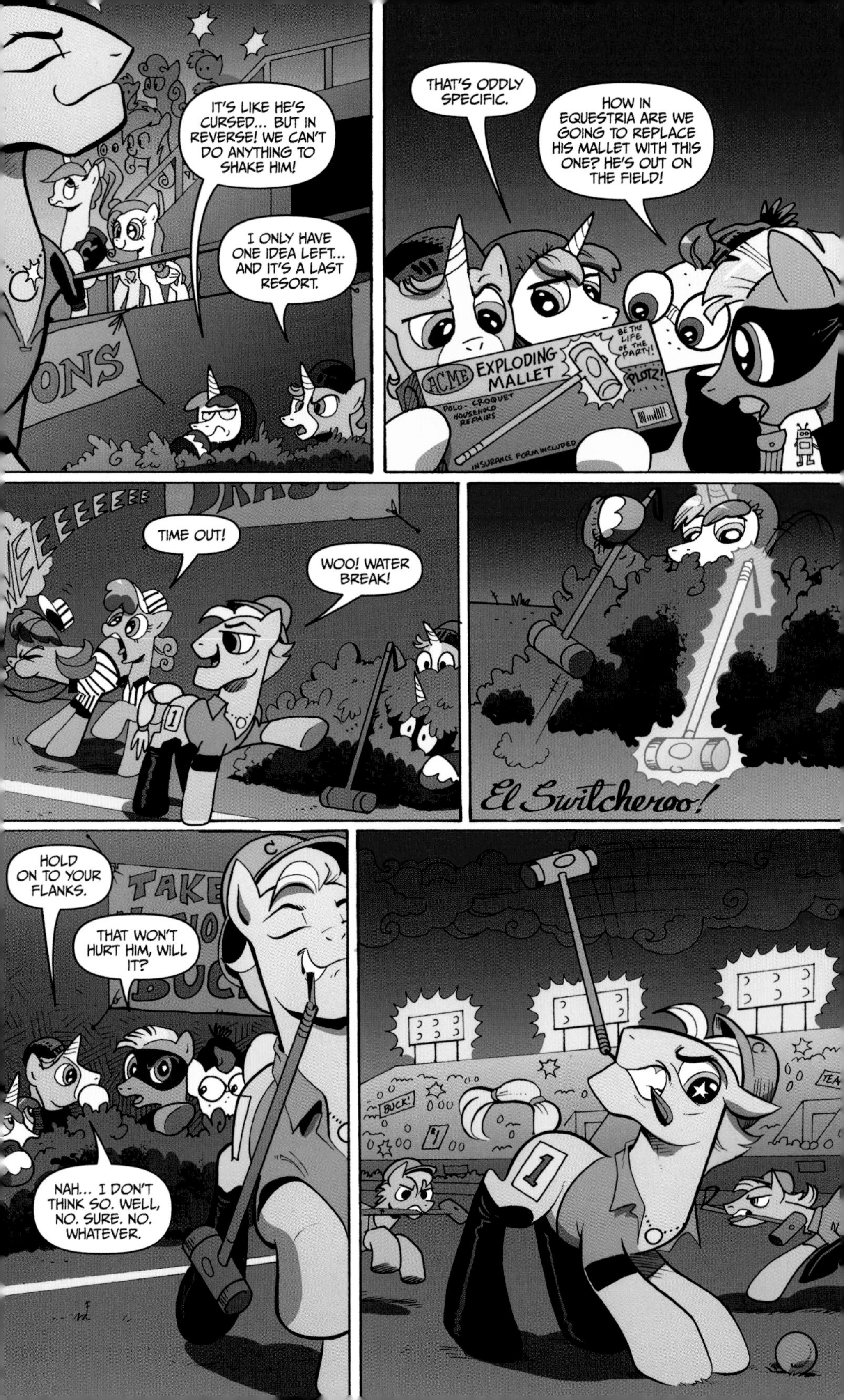
IT'S LIKE HE'S CURSED... BUT IN REVERSE! WE CAN'T DO ANYTHING TO SHAKE HIM!
I ONLY HAVE ONE IDEA LEFT... AND IT'S A LAST RESORT.
ONS
THAT'S ODDLY SPECIFIC.
HOW IN EQUESTRIA ARE WE GOING TO REPLACE HIS MALLET WITH THIS ONE? HE'S OUT ON THE FIELD!
ACME EXPLODING MALLET
BE THE LIFE OF THE PARTY!
PLOTZ!
POLO - CROQUET HOUSEHOLD REPAIRS
INSURANCE FORM INCLUDED
WEEEEEEEEE
TIME OUT!
WOO! WATER BREAK!
El Switcheroo!
HOLD ON TO YOUR FLANKS.
THAT WON'T HURT HIM, WILL IT?
NAH... I DON'T THINK SO. WELL, NO. SURE. NO. WHATEVER.
BUCK!

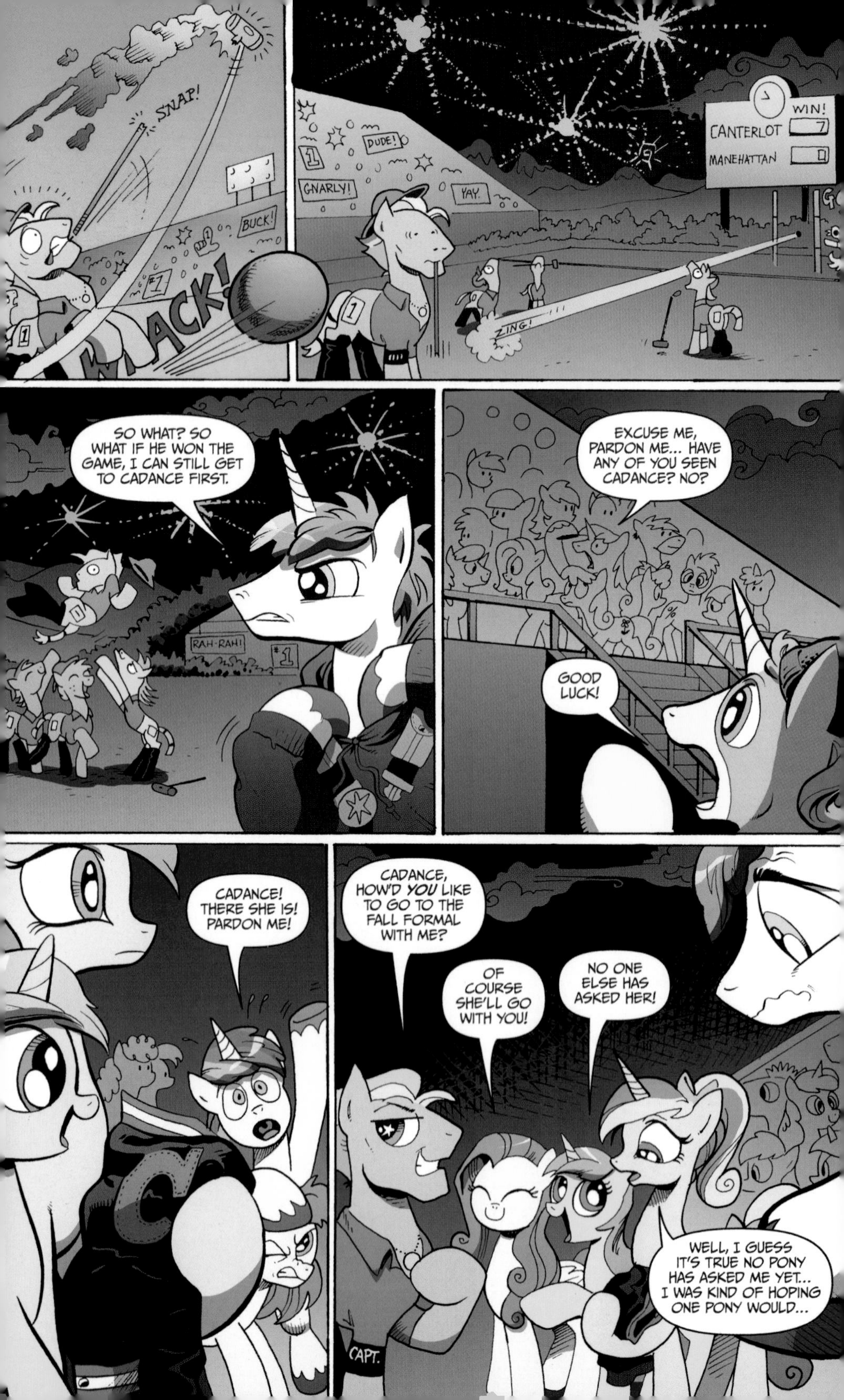
SNAP!
BUCK!
#1
WHACK!
DUDE!
GNARLY!
YAY.
WIN!
CANTERLOT 7
MANEHATTAN 0
ZING!
SO WHAT? SO WHAT IF HE WON THE GAME, I CAN STILL GET TO CADANCE FIRST.
RAH-RAH!
#1
EXCUSE ME, PARDON ME... HAVE ANY OF YOU SEEN CADANCE? NO?
GOOD LUCK!
CADANCE! THERE SHE IS! PARDON ME!
CADANCE, HOW'D *YOU* LIKE TO GO TO THE FALL FORMAL WITH ME?
OF COURSE SHE'LL GO WITH YOU!
NO ONE ELSE HAS ASKED HER!
WELL, I GUESS IT'S TRUE NO PONY HAS ASKED ME YET... I WAS KIND OF HOPING ONE PONY WOULD...
CAPT.

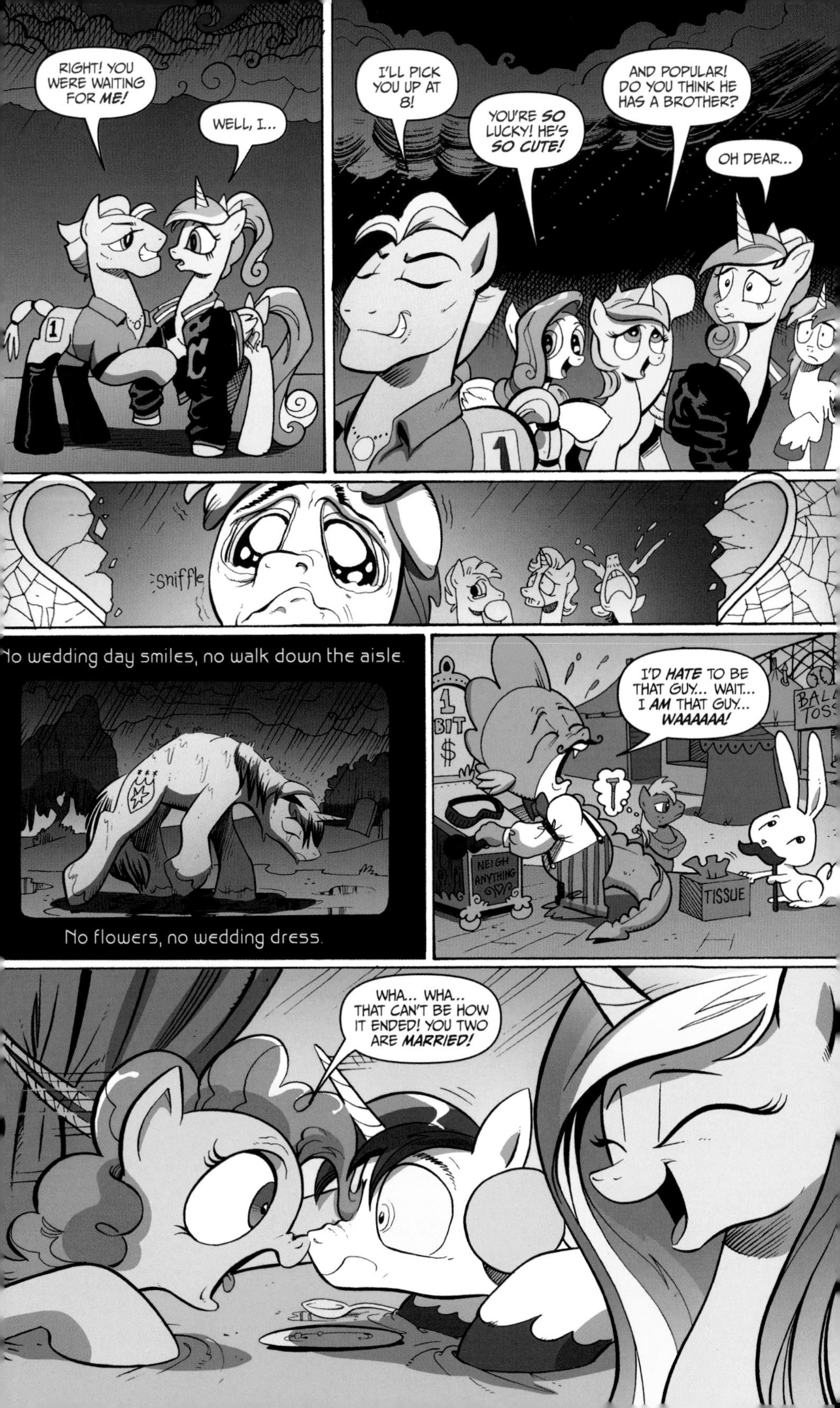
RIGHT! YOU WERE WAITING FOR ME!
WELL, I...
I'LL PICK YOU UP AT 8!
YOU'RE SO LUCKY! HE'S SO CUTE!
AND POPULAR! DO YOU THINK HE HAS A BROTHER?
OH DEAR...
sniffle
No wedding day smiles, no walk down the aisle.
No flowers, no wedding dress.
1 BIT $
NEIGH ANYTHING
BALL TOSS
TISSUE
I'D HATE TO BE THAT GUY... WAIT... I AM THAT GUY... WAAAAAA!
WHA... WHA... THAT CAN'T BE HOW IT ENDED! YOU TWO ARE MARRIED!

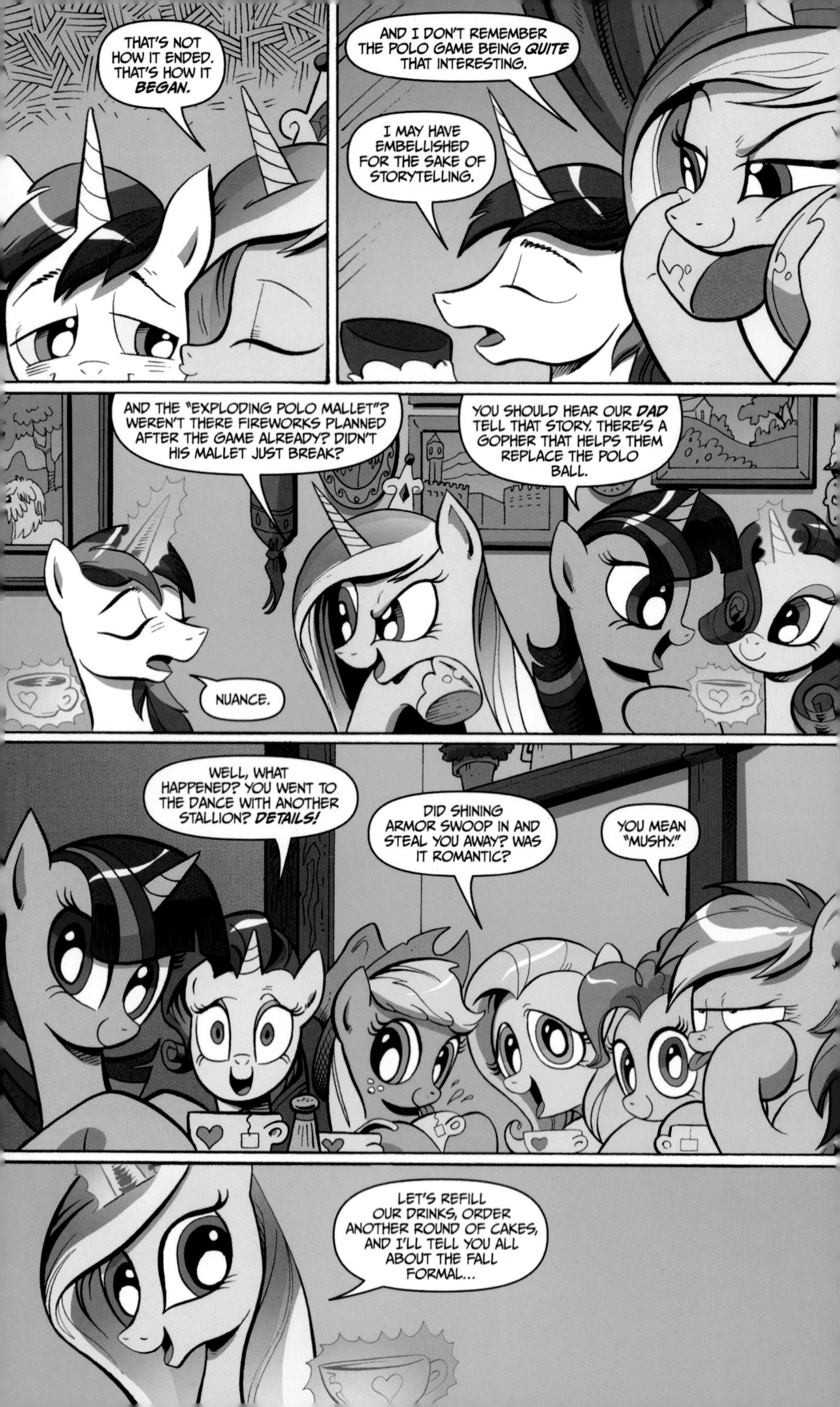
THAT'S NOT HOW IT ENDED. THAT'S HOW IT *BEGAN.*
AND I DON'T REMEMBER THE POLO GAME BEING *QUITE* THAT INTERESTING.
I MAY HAVE EMBELLISHED FOR THE SAKE OF STORYTELLING.
AND THE "EXPLODING POLO MALLET"? WEREN'T THERE FIREWORKS PLANNED AFTER THE GAME ALREADY? DIDN'T HIS MALLET JUST BREAK?
NUANCE.
YOU SHOULD HEAR OUR *DAD* TELL THAT STORY. THERE'S A GOPHER THAT HELPS THEM REPLACE THE POLO BALL.
WELL, WHAT HAPPENED? YOU WENT TO THE DANCE WITH ANOTHER STALLION? *DETAILS!*
DID SHINING ARMOR SWOOP IN AND STEAL YOU AWAY? WAS IT ROMANTIC?
YOU MEAN "MUSHY."
LET'S REFILL OUR DRINKS, ORDER ANOTHER ROUND OF CAKES, AND I'LL TELL YOU ALL ABOUT THE FALL FORMAL...

Art by
Sara Richard

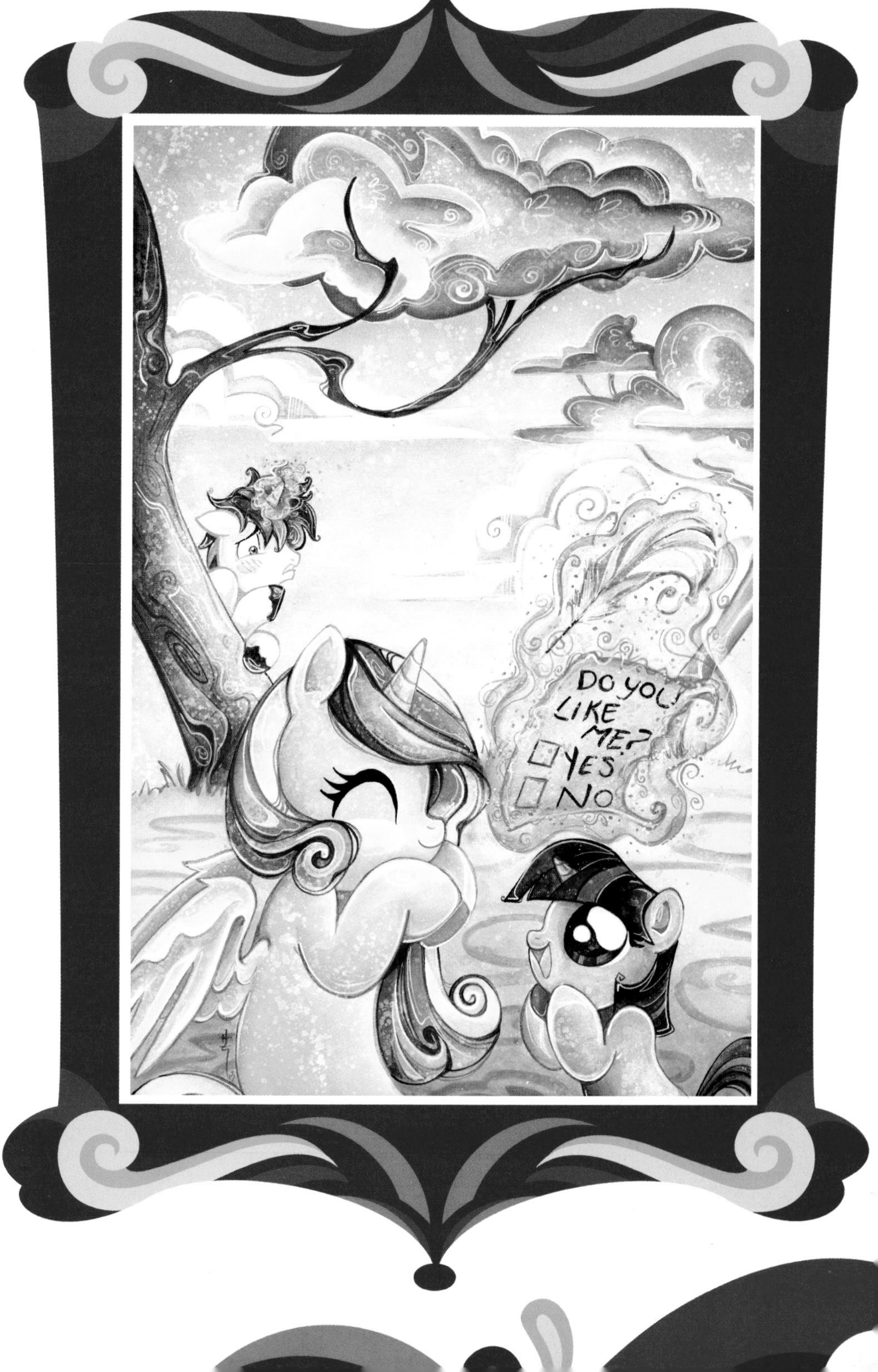
DO YOU LIKE ME?
YES
NO

Art by
Andy Price

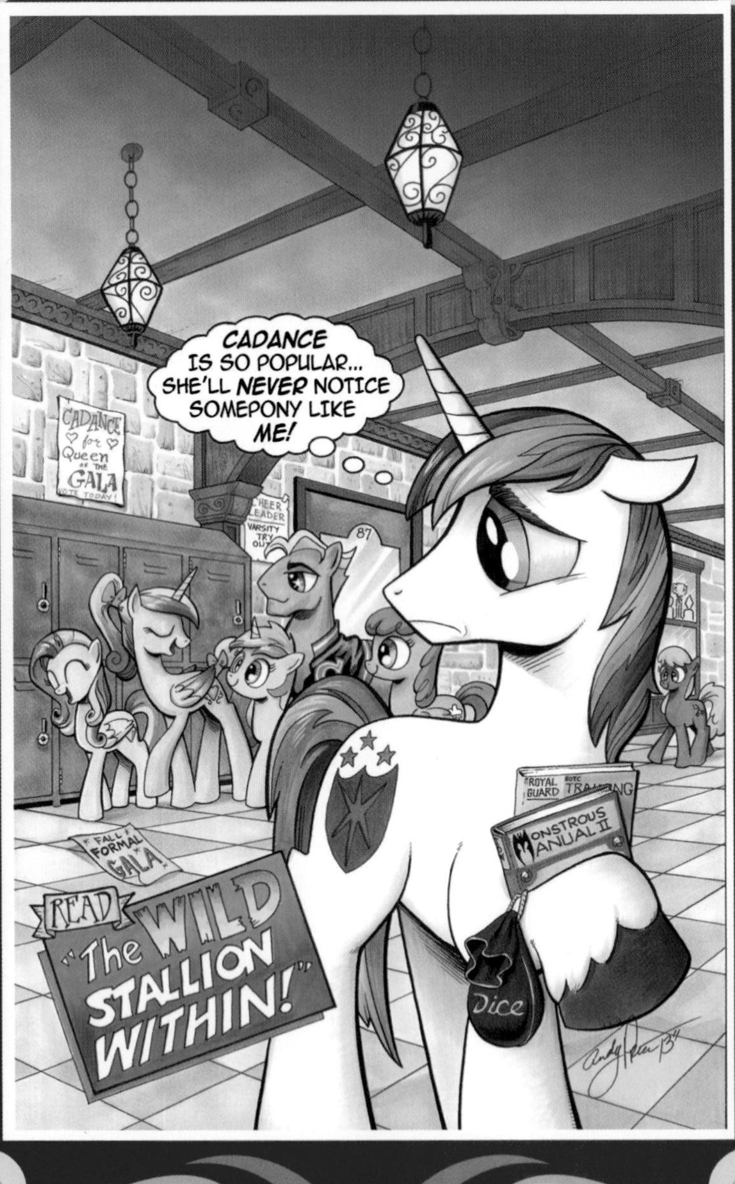

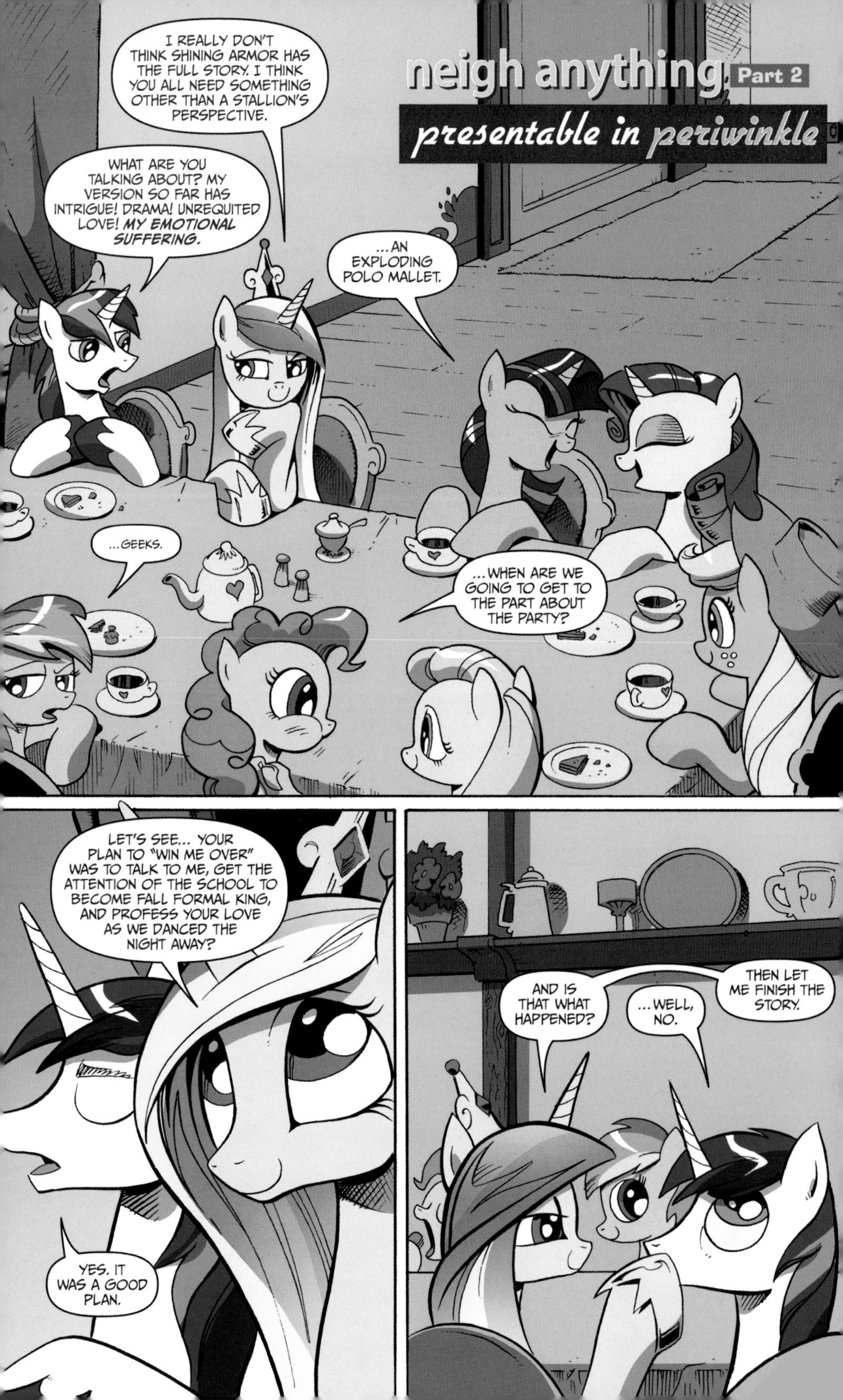
neigh anything Part 2
presentable in periwinkle
I REALLY DON'T THINK SHINING ARMOR HAS THE FULL STORY. I THINK YOU ALL NEED SOMETHING OTHER THAN A STALLION'S PERSPECTIVE.
WHAT ARE YOU TALKING ABOUT? MY VERSION SO FAR HAS INTRIGUE! DRAMA! UNREQUITED LOVE! *MY EMOTIONAL SUFFERING.*
...AN EXPLODING POLO MALLET.
...GEEKS.
...WHEN ARE WE GOING TO GET TO THE PART ABOUT THE PARTY?
LET'S SEE... YOUR PLAN TO "WIN ME OVER" WAS TO TALK TO ME, GET THE ATTENTION OF THE SCHOOL TO BECOME FALL FORMAL KING, AND PROFESS YOUR LOVE AS WE DANCED THE NIGHT AWAY?
YES. IT WAS A GOOD PLAN.
AND IS THAT WHAT HAPPENED?
...WELL, NO.
THEN LET ME FINISH THE STORY.

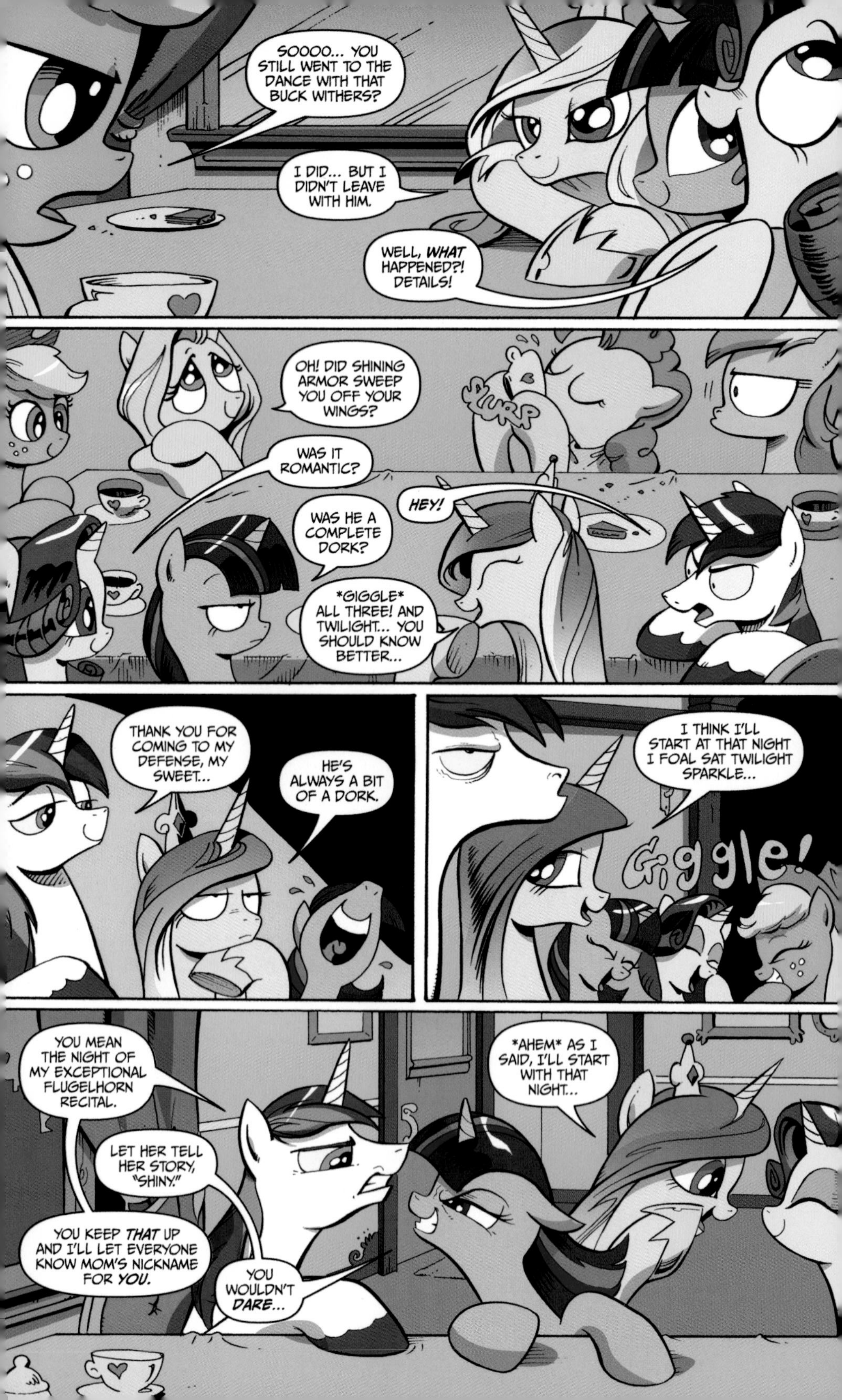
SOOOO... YOU STILL WENT TO THE DANCE WITH THAT BUCK WITHERS?
I DID... BUT I DIDN'T LEAVE WITH HIM.
WELL, WHAT HAPPENED?! DETAILS!
OH! DID SHINING ARMOR SWEEP YOU OFF YOUR WINGS?
SLURP
WAS IT ROMANTIC?
WAS HE A COMPLETE DORK?
HEY!
GIGGLE ALL THREE! AND TWILIGHT... YOU SHOULD KNOW BETTER...
THANK YOU FOR COMING TO MY DEFENSE, MY SWEET...
HE'S ALWAYS A BIT OF A DORK.
I THINK I'LL START AT THAT NIGHT I FOAL SAT TWILIGHT SPARKLE...
GIGGLE!
YOU MEAN THE NIGHT OF MY EXCEPTIONAL FLUGELHORN RECITAL.
AHEM AS I SAID, I'LL START WITH THAT NIGHT...
LET HER TELL HER STORY, "SHINY."
YOU KEEP THAT UP AND I'LL LET EVERYONE KNOW MOM'S NICKNAME FOR YOU.
YOU WOULDN'T DARE...

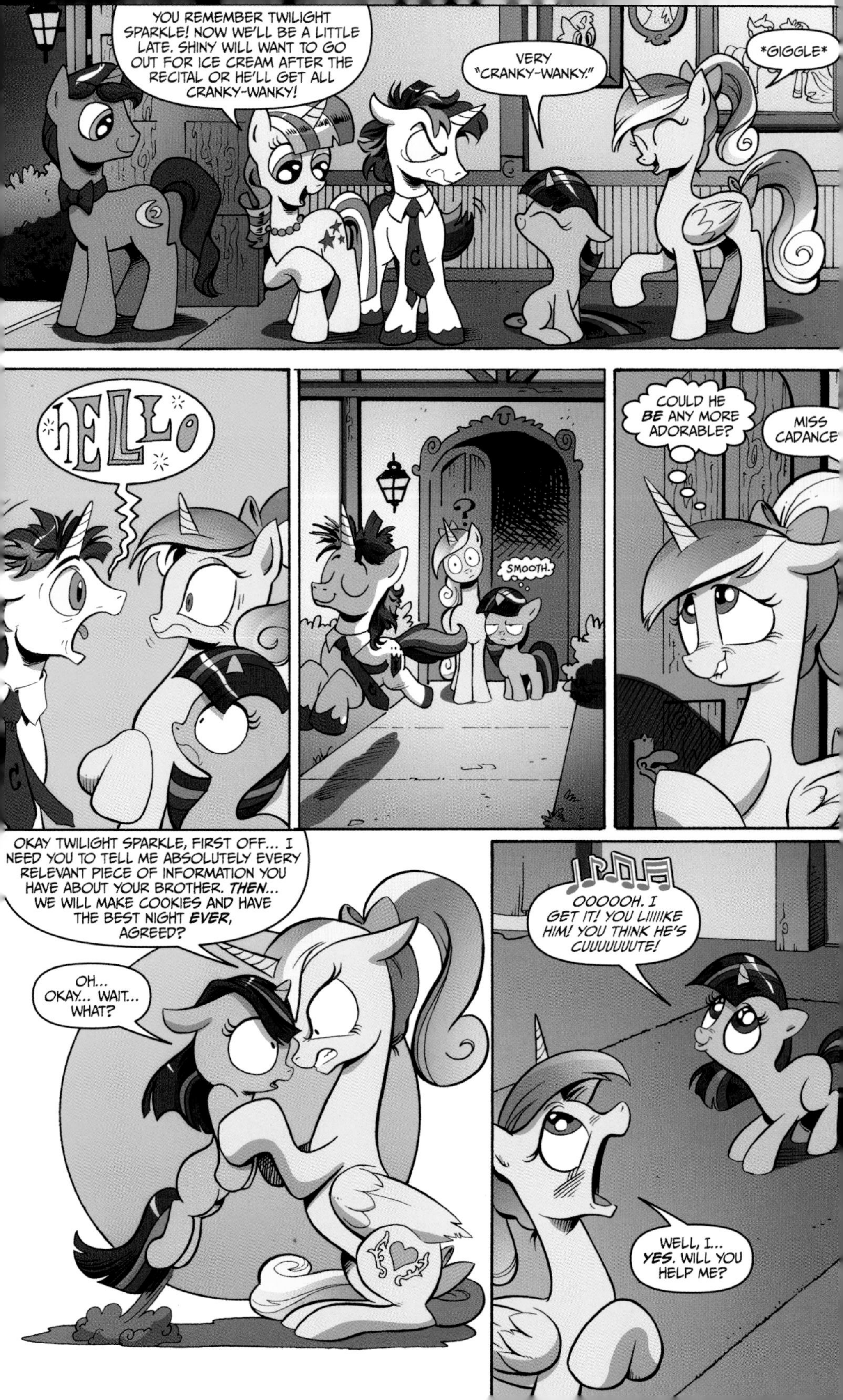
YOU REMEMBER TWILIGHT SPARKLE! NOW WE'LL BE A LITTLE LATE. SHINY WILL WANT TO GO OUT FOR ICE CREAM AFTER THE RECITAL OR HE'LL GET ALL CRANKY-WANKY!
VERY "CRANKY-WANKY."
GIGGLE
HELLO
?
SMOOTH.
COULD HE BE ANY MORE ADORABLE?
MISS CADANCE
OKAY TWILIGHT SPARKLE, FIRST OFF... I NEED YOU TO TELL ME ABSOLUTELY EVERY RELEVANT PIECE OF INFORMATION YOU HAVE ABOUT YOUR BROTHER. THEN... WE WILL MAKE COOKIES AND HAVE THE BEST NIGHT EVER, AGREED?
OH... OKAY... WAIT... WHAT?
OOOOOH. I GET IT! YOU LIIIIIKE HIM! YOU THINK HE'S CUUUUUUUTE!
WELL, I... YES. WILL YOU HELP ME?

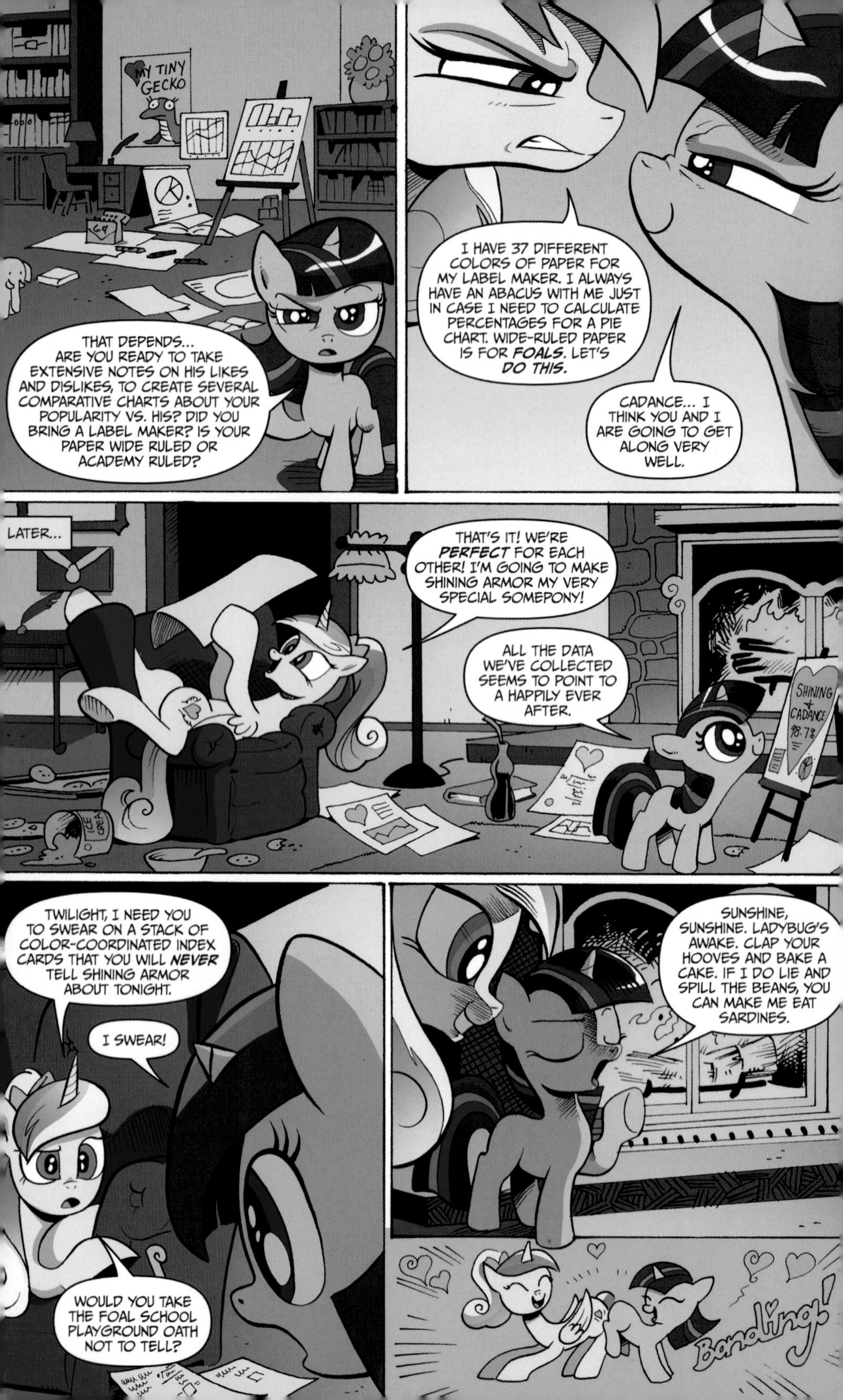
MY TINY GECKO
THAT DEPENDS... ARE YOU READY TO TAKE EXTENSIVE NOTES ON HIS LIKES AND DISLIKES, TO CREATE SEVERAL COMPARATIVE CHARTS ABOUT YOUR POPULARITY VS. HIS? DID YOU BRING A LABEL MAKER? IS YOUR PAPER WIDE RULED OR ACADEMY RULED?
I HAVE 37 DIFFERENT COLORS OF PAPER FOR MY LABEL MAKER. I ALWAYS HAVE AN ABACUS WITH ME JUST IN CASE I NEED TO CALCULATE PERCENTAGES FOR A PIE CHART. WIDE-RULED PAPER IS FOR ***FOALS***. LET'S ***DO THIS.***
CADANCE... I THINK YOU AND I ARE GOING TO GET ALONG VERY WELL.
LATER...
THAT'S IT! WE'RE ***PERFECT*** FOR EACH OTHER! I'M GOING TO MAKE SHINING ARMOR MY VERY SPECIAL SOMEPONY!
ALL THE DATA WE'VE COLLECTED SEEMS TO POINT TO A HAPPILY EVER AFTER.
SHINING + CADANCE 98.7%
ICE CREA
TWILIGHT, I NEED YOU TO SWEAR ON A STACK OF COLOR-COORDINATED INDEX CARDS THAT YOU WILL ***NEVER*** TELL SHINING ARMOR ABOUT TONIGHT.
I SWEAR!
WOULD YOU TAKE THE FOAL SCHOOL PLAYGROUND OATH NOT TO TELL?
SUNSHINE, SUNSHINE. LADYBUG'S AWAKE. CLAP YOUR HOOVES AND BAKE A CAKE. IF I DO LIE AND SPILL THE BEANS, YOU CAN MAKE ME EAT SARDINES.
Bonding!

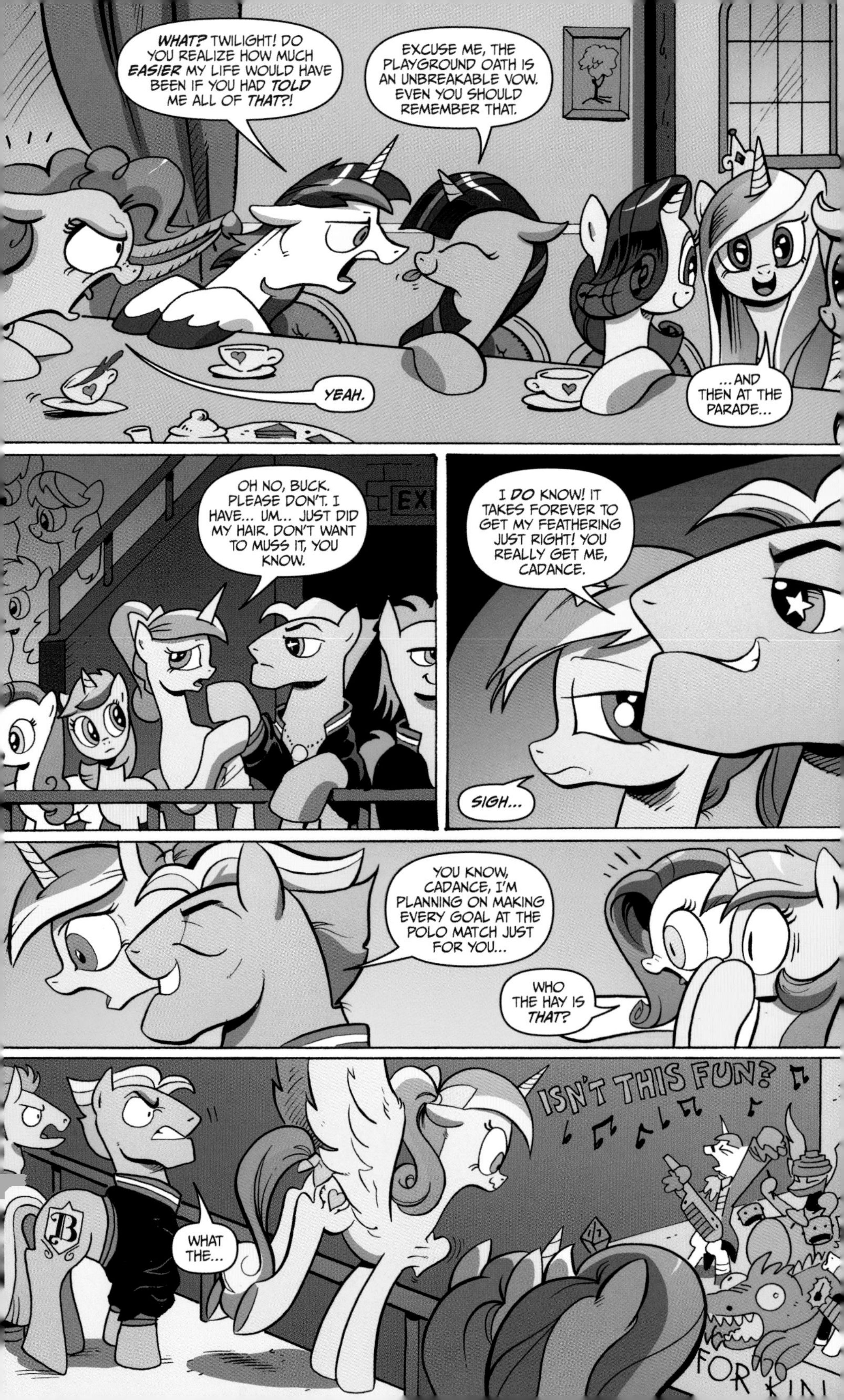
WHAT? TWILIGHT! DO YOU REALIZE HOW MUCH EASIER MY LIFE WOULD HAVE BEEN IF YOU HAD TOLD ME ALL OF THAT?!
EXCUSE ME, THE PLAYGROUND OATH IS AN UNBREAKABLE VOW. EVEN YOU SHOULD REMEMBER THAT.
YEAH.
...AND THEN AT THE PARADE...
OH NO, BUCK. PLEASE DON'T. I HAVE... UM... JUST DID MY HAIR. DON'T WANT TO MUSS IT, YOU KNOW.
I DO KNOW! IT TAKES FOREVER TO GET MY FEATHERING JUST RIGHT! YOU REALLY GET ME, CADANCE.
SIGH...
YOU KNOW, CADANCE, I'M PLANNING ON MAKING EVERY GOAL AT THE POLO MATCH JUST FOR YOU...
WHO THE HAY IS THAT?
ISN'T THIS FUN?
WHAT THE...

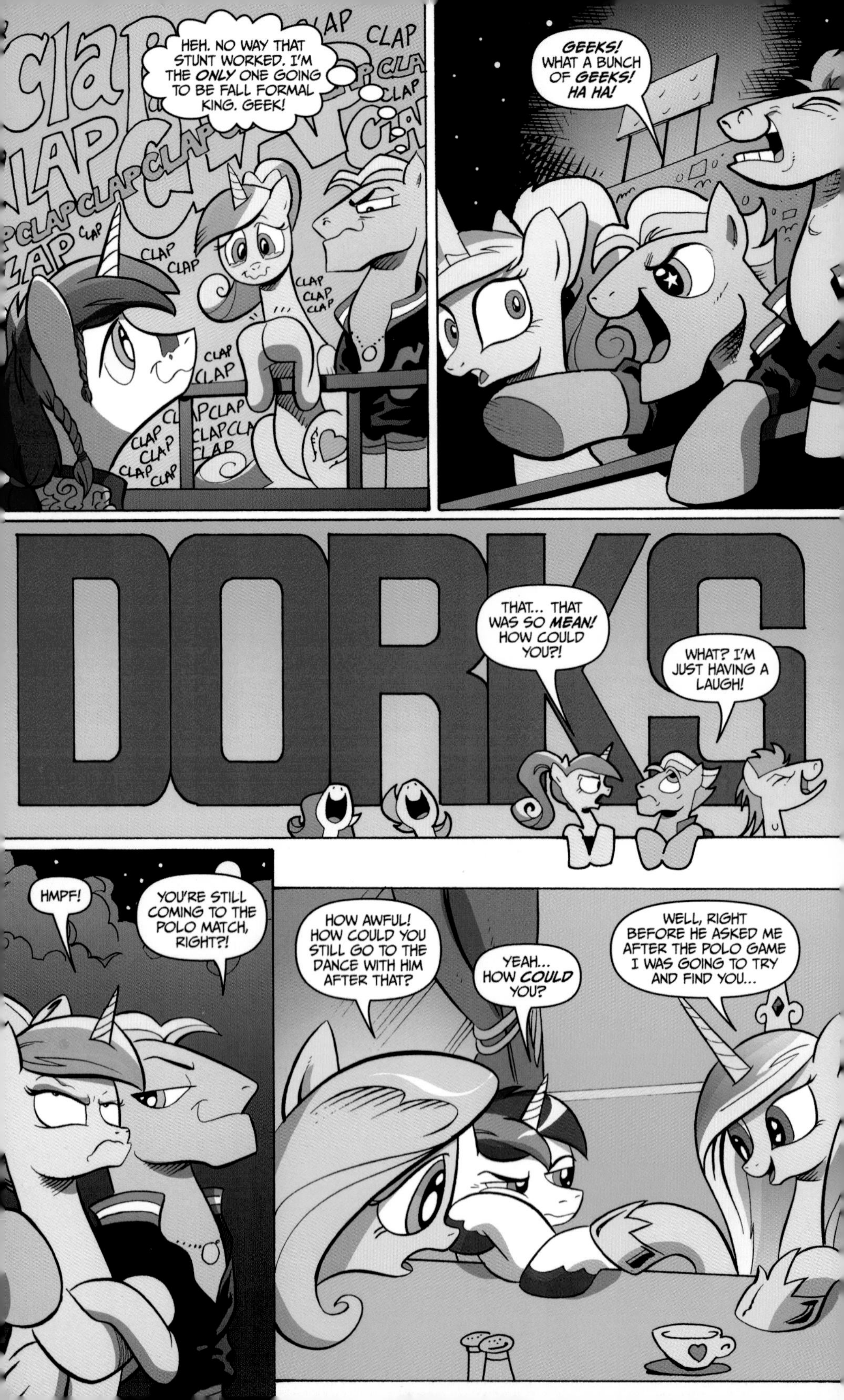

HEH. NO WAY THAT STUNT WORKED. I'M THE *ONLY* ONE GOING TO BE FALL FORMAL KING. GEEK!
CLAP CLAP CLAP CLAP CLAP
GEEKS! WHAT A BUNCH OF ***GEEKS!*** ***HA HA!***
DORKS
THAT... THAT WAS SO ***MEAN!*** HOW COULD YOU?!
WHAT? I'M JUST HAVING A LAUGH!
HMPF!
YOU'RE STILL COMING TO THE POLO MATCH, RIGHT?!
HOW AWFUL! HOW COULD YOU STILL GO TO THE DANCE WITH HIM AFTER THAT?
YEAH... HOW ***COULD*** YOU?
WELL, RIGHT BEFORE HE ASKED ME AFTER THE POLO GAME I WAS GOING TO TRY AND FIND YOU...

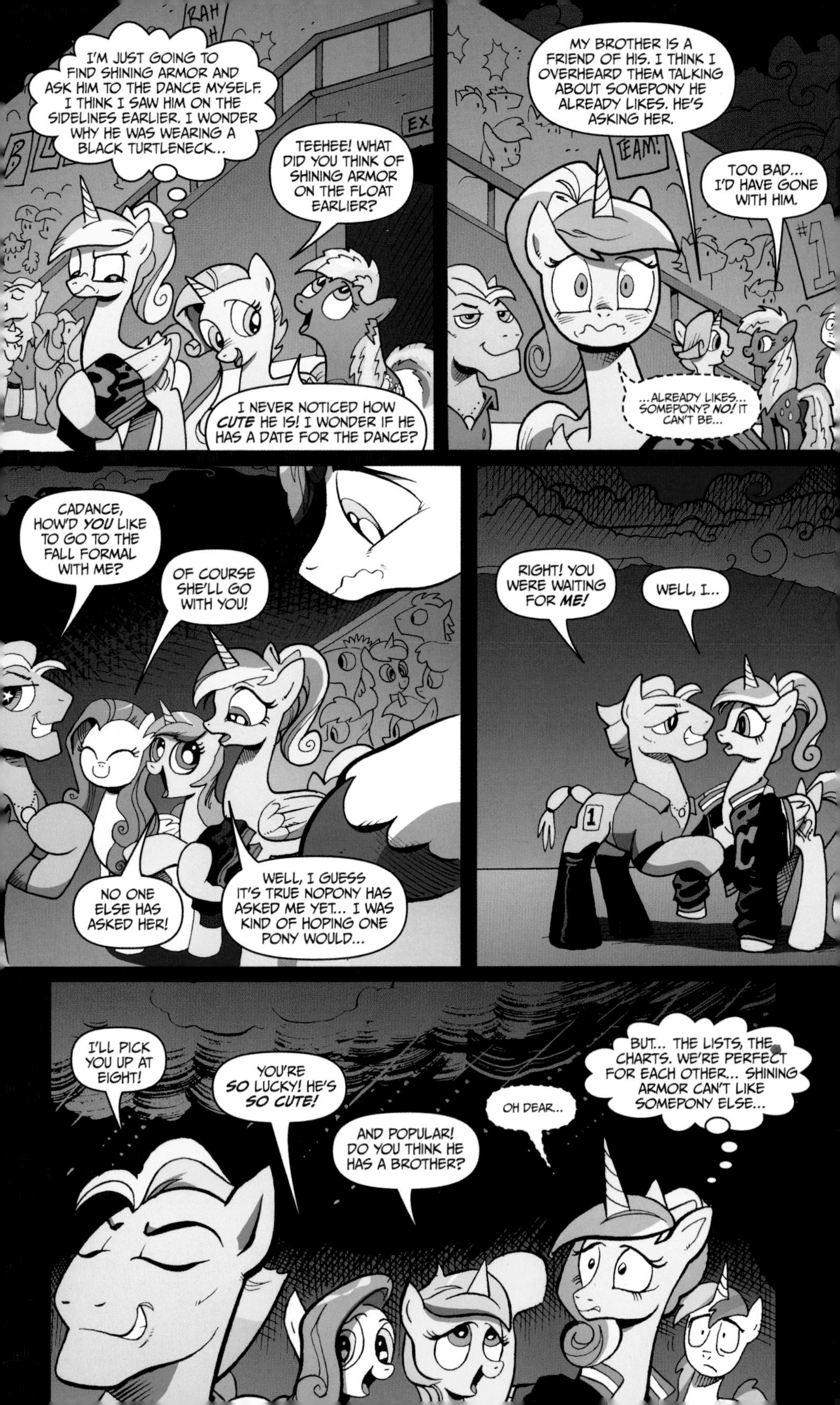
RAH
I'M JUST GOING TO FIND SHINING ARMOR AND ASK HIM TO THE DANCE MYSELF. I THINK I SAW HIM ON THE SIDELINES EARLIER. I WONDER WHY HE WAS WEARING A BLACK TURTLENECK...
TEEHEE! WHAT DID YOU THINK OF SHINING ARMOR ON THE FLOAT EARLIER?
I NEVER NOTICED HOW CUTE HE IS! I WONDER IF HE HAS A DATE FOR THE DANCE?
MY BROTHER IS A FRIEND OF HIS. I THINK I OVERHEARD THEM TALKING ABOUT SOMEPONY HE ALREADY LIKES. HE'S ASKING HER.
TEAM!
TOO BAD... I'D HAVE GONE WITH HIM.
...ALREADY LIKES... SOMEPONY? NO! IT CAN'T BE...
CADANCE, HOW'D YOU LIKE TO GO TO THE FALL FORMAL WITH ME?
OF COURSE SHE'LL GO WITH YOU!
NO ONE ELSE HAS ASKED HER!
WELL, I GUESS IT'S TRUE NOPONY HAS ASKED ME YET... I WAS KIND OF HOPING ONE PONY WOULD...
RIGHT! YOU WERE WAITING FOR ME!
WELL, I...
I'LL PICK YOU UP AT EIGHT!
YOU'RE SO LUCKY! HE'S SO CUTE!
AND POPULAR! DO YOU THINK HE HAS A BROTHER?
OH DEAR...
BUT... THE LISTS, THE CHARTS. WE'RE PERFECT FOR EACH OTHER... SHINING ARMOR CAN'T LIKE SOMEPONY ELSE...

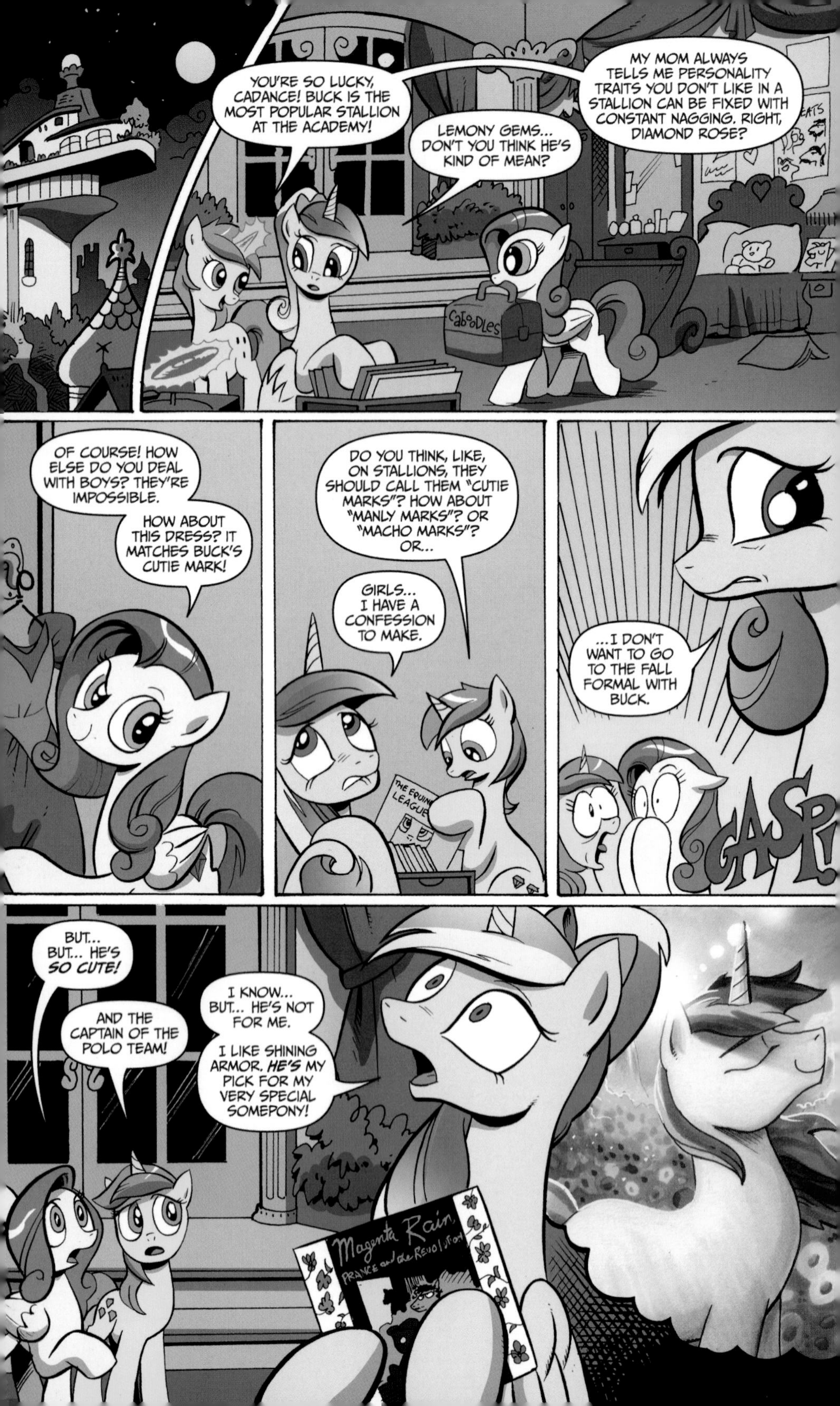
YOU'RE SO LUCKY, CADANCE! BUCK IS THE MOST POPULAR STALLION AT THE ACADEMY!
LEMONY GEMS... DON'T YOU THINK HE'S KIND OF MEAN?
MY MOM ALWAYS TELLS ME PERSONALITY TRAITS YOU DON'T LIKE IN A STALLION CAN BE FIXED WITH CONSTANT NAGGING. RIGHT, DIAMOND ROSE?
CABOODLES
OF COURSE! HOW ELSE DO YOU DEAL WITH BOYS? THEY'RE IMPOSSIBLE.
HOW ABOUT THIS DRESS? IT MATCHES BUCK'S CUTIE MARK!
DO YOU THINK, LIKE, ON STALLIONS, THEY SHOULD CALL THEM "CUTIE MARKS"? HOW ABOUT "MANLY MARKS"? OR "MACHO MARKS"? OR...
GIRLS... I HAVE A CONFESSION TO MAKE.
THE EQUINE LEAGUE
...I DON'T WANT TO GO TO THE FALL FORMAL WITH BUCK.
GASP!
BUT... BUT... HE'S *SO CUTE!*
AND THE CAPTAIN OF THE POLO TEAM!
I KNOW... BUT... HE'S NOT FOR ME.
I LIKE SHINING ARMOR. ***HE'S*** MY PICK FOR MY VERY SPECIAL SOMEPONY!
Magenta Rain
PRANCE and the REVOLUTION

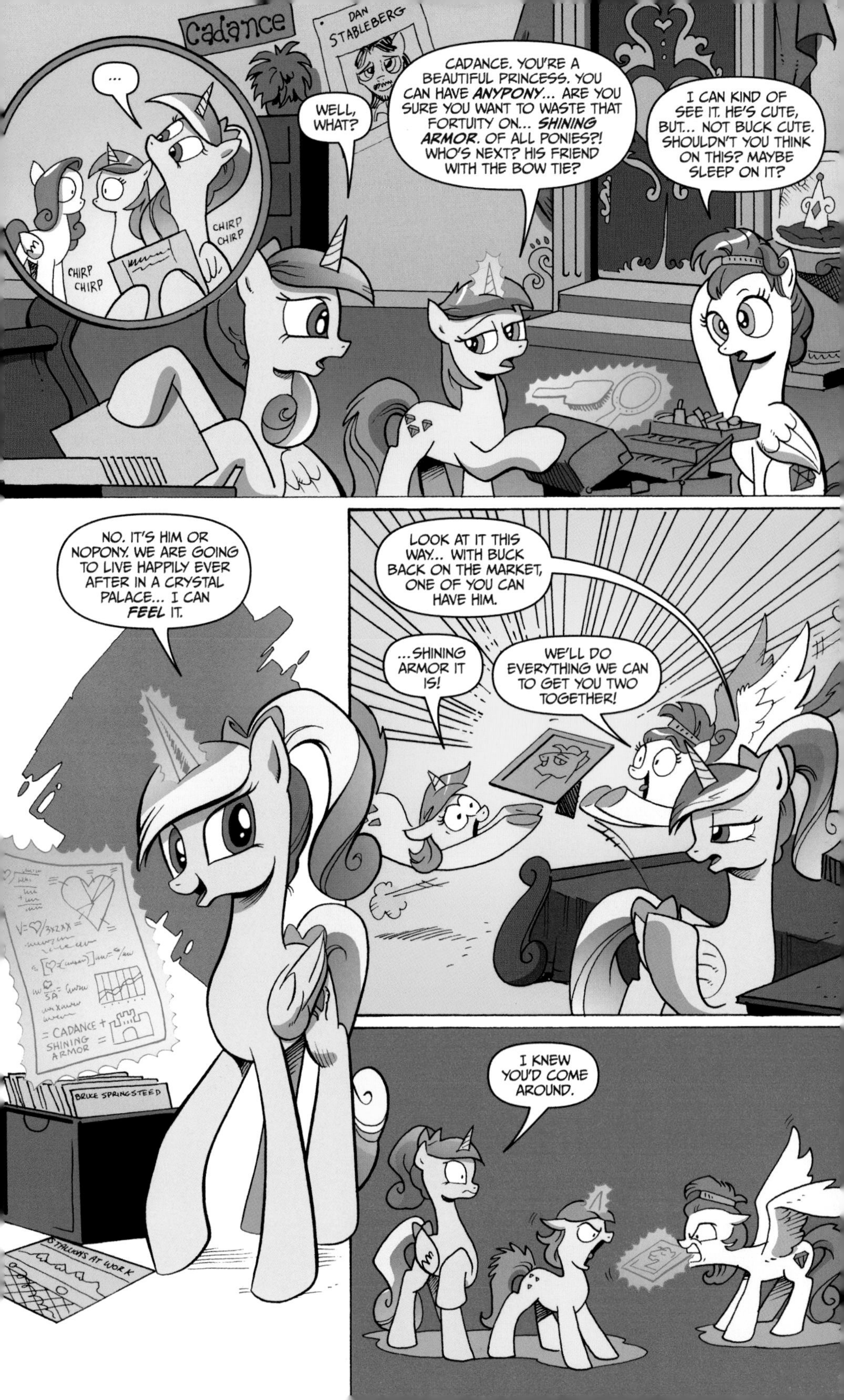

Cadance
DAN STABLEBERG
...
CHIRP CHIRP
CHIRP CHIRP
WELL, WHAT?
CADANCE. YOU'RE A BEAUTIFUL PRINCESS. YOU CAN HAVE ANYPONY... ARE YOU SURE YOU WANT TO WASTE THAT FORTUITY ON... SHINING ARMOR. OF ALL PONIES?! WHO'S NEXT? HIS FRIEND WITH THE BOW TIE?
I CAN KIND OF SEE IT. HE'S CUTE, BUT... NOT BUCK CUTE. SHOULDN'T YOU THINK ON THIS? MAYBE SLEEP ON IT?
NO. IT'S HIM OR NOPONY. WE ARE GOING TO LIVE HAPPILY EVER AFTER IN A CRYSTAL PALACE... I CAN FEEL IT.
= CADANCE + SHINING ARMOR =
BRUCE SPRINGSTEED
STALLIONS AT WORK
LOOK AT IT THIS WAY... WITH BUCK BACK ON THE MARKET, ONE OF YOU CAN HAVE HIM.
...SHINING ARMOR IT IS!
WE'LL DO EVERYTHING WE CAN TO GET YOU TWO TOGETHER!
I KNEW YOU'D COME AROUND.

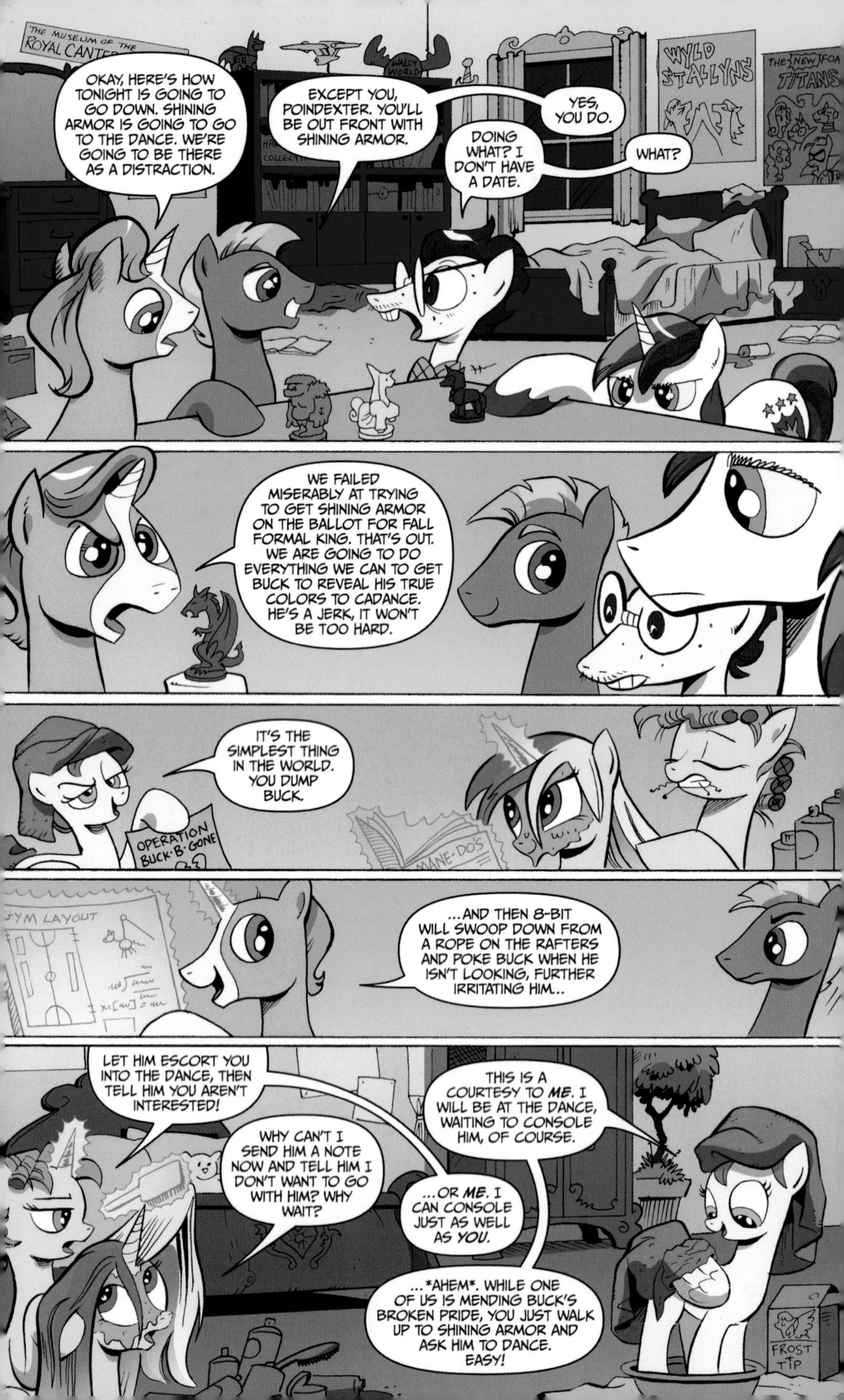
THE MUSEUM OF THE
WALLY WORLD
WYLD STALLYNS
OKAY, HERE'S HOW TONIGHT IS GOING TO GO DOWN. SHINING ARMOR IS GOING TO GO TO THE DANCE. WE'RE GOING TO BE THERE AS A DISTRACTION.
EXCEPT YOU, POINDEXTER. YOU'LL BE OUT FRONT WITH SHINING ARMOR.
WHAT?
DOING WHAT? I DON'T HAVE A DATE.
YES, YOU DO.
WE FAILED MISERABLY AT TRYING TO GET SHINING ARMOR ON THE BALLOT FOR FALL FORMAL KING. THAT'S OUT. WE ARE GOING TO DO EVERYTHING WE CAN TO GET BUCK TO REVEAL HIS TRUE COLORS TO CADANCE. HE'S A JERK, IT WON'T BE TOO HARD.
IT'S THE SIMPLEST THING IN THE WORLD. YOU DUMP BUCK.
OPERATION BUCK-B-GONE
MANE-DO'S
GYM LAYOUT
...AND THEN 8-BIT WILL SWOOP DOWN FROM A ROPE ON THE RAFTERS AND POKE BUCK WHEN HE ISN'T LOOKING, FURTHER IRRITATING HIM...
LET HIM ESCORT YOU INTO THE DANCE, THEN TELL HIM YOU AREN'T INTERESTED!
WHY CAN'T I SEND HIM A NOTE NOW AND TELL HIM I DON'T WANT TO GO WITH HIM? WHY WAIT?
THIS IS A COURTESY TO *ME*. I WILL BE AT THE DANCE, WAITING TO CONSOLE HIM, OF COURSE.
...OR *ME*. I CAN CONSOLE JUST AS WELL AS *YOU*.
...*AHEM*. WHILE ONE OF US IS MENDING BUCK'S BROKEN PRIDE, YOU JUST WALK UP TO SHINING ARMOR AND ASK HIM TO DANCE. EASY!
FROST TIP

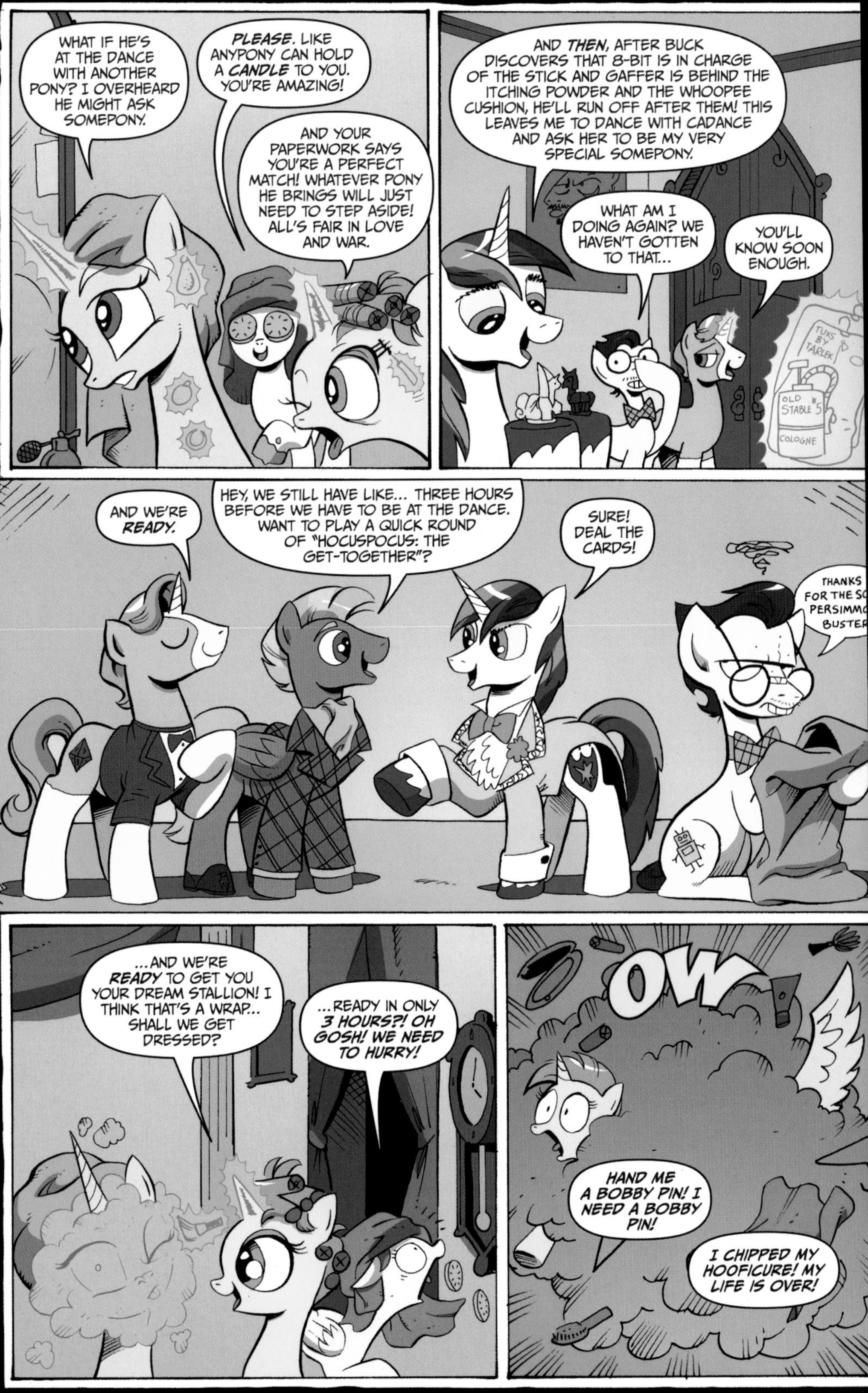
WHAT IF HE'S AT THE DANCE WITH ANOTHER PONY? I OVERHEARD HE MIGHT ASK SOMEPONY.
PLEASE. LIKE ANYPONY CAN HOLD A CANDLE TO YOU. YOU'RE AMAZING!
AND YOUR PAPERWORK SAYS YOU'RE A PERFECT MATCH! WHATEVER PONY HE BRINGS WILL JUST NEED TO STEP ASIDE! ALL'S FAIR IN LOVE AND WAR.
AND THEN, AFTER BUCK DISCOVERS THAT 8-BIT IS IN CHARGE OF THE STICK AND GAFFER IS BEHIND THE ITCHING POWDER AND THE WHOOPEE CUSHION, HE'LL RUN OFF AFTER THEM! THIS LEAVES ME TO DANCE WITH CADANCE AND ASK HER TO BE MY VERY SPECIAL SOMEPONY.
WHAT AM I DOING AGAIN? WE HAVEN'T GOTTEN TO THAT...
YOU'LL KNOW SOON ENOUGH.
TUXS BY TARLEK
OLD STABLE #5
COLOGNE
AND WE'RE READY.
HEY, WE STILL HAVE LIKE... THREE HOURS BEFORE WE HAVE TO BE AT THE DANCE. WANT TO PLAY A QUICK ROUND OF "HOCUSPOCUS: THE GET-TOGETHER"?
SURE! DEAL THE CARDS!
THANKS FOR THE
...AND WE'RE READY TO GET YOU YOUR DREAM STALLION! I THINK THAT'S A WRAP... SHALL WE GET DRESSED?
...READY IN ONLY 3 HOURS?! OH GOSH! WE NEED TO HURRY!
OW
HAND ME A BOBBY PIN! I NEED A BOBBY PIN!
I CHIPPED MY HOOFICURE! MY LIFE IS OVER!

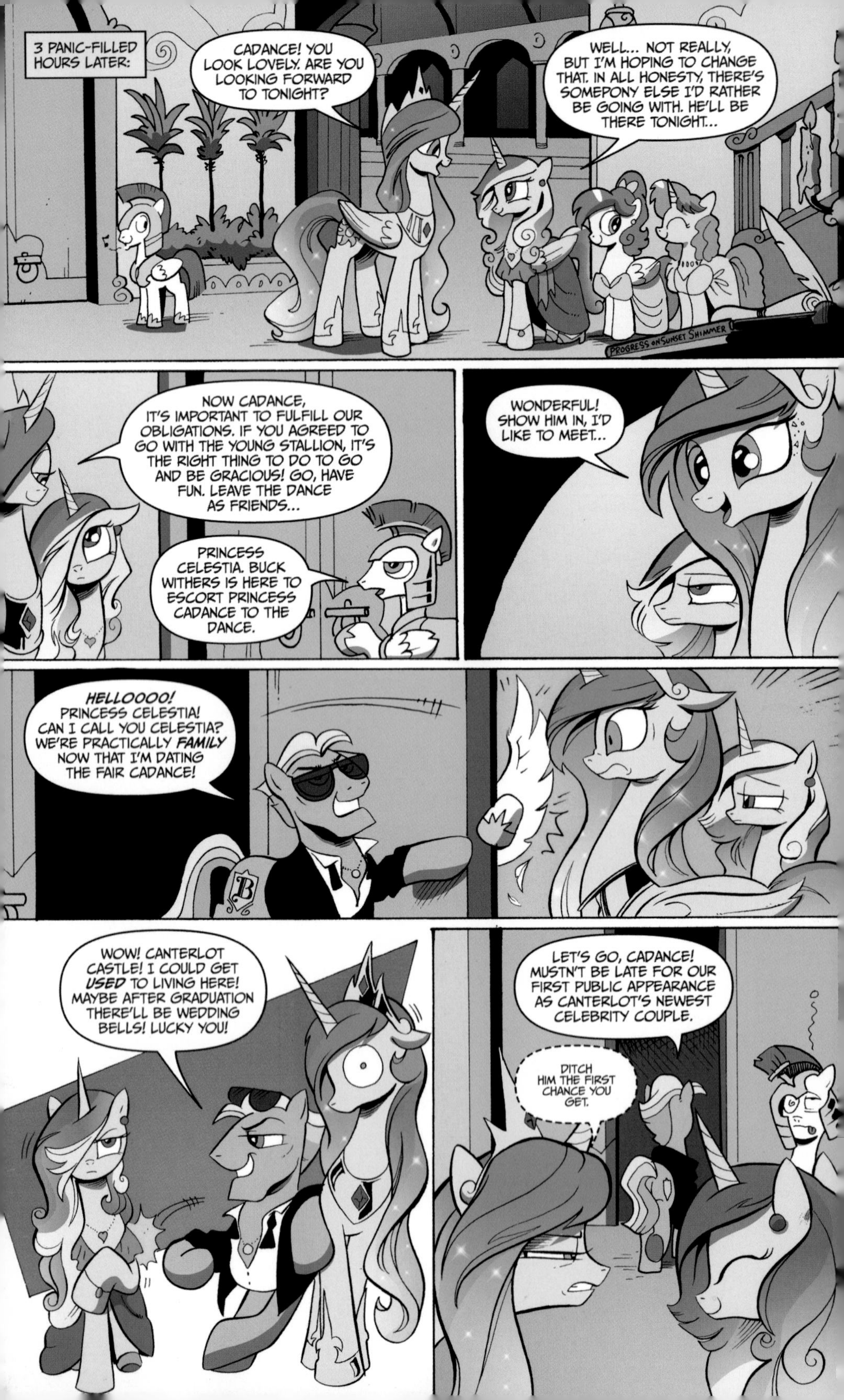
3 PANIC-FILLED HOURS LATER:
CADANCE! YOU LOOK LOVELY. ARE YOU LOOKING FORWARD TO TONIGHT?
WELL... NOT REALLY, BUT I'M HOPING TO CHANGE THAT. IN ALL HONESTY, THERE'S SOMEPONY ELSE I'D RATHER BE GOING WITH. HE'LL BE THERE TONIGHT...
PROGRESS ON SUNSET SHIMMER
NOW CADANCE, IT'S IMPORTANT TO FULFILL OUR OBLIGATIONS. IF YOU AGREED TO GO WITH THE YOUNG STALLION, IT'S THE RIGHT THING TO DO TO GO AND BE GRACIOUS! GO, HAVE FUN. LEAVE THE DANCE AS FRIENDS...
PRINCESS CELESTIA. BUCK WITHERS IS HERE TO ESCORT PRINCESS CADANCE TO THE DANCE.
WONDERFUL! SHOW HIM IN, I'D LIKE TO MEET...
HELLOOOO! PRINCESS CELESTIA! CAN I CALL YOU CELESTIA? WE'RE PRACTICALLY FAMILY NOW THAT I'M DATING THE FAIR CADANCE!
WOW! CANTERLOT CASTLE! I COULD GET USED TO LIVING HERE! MAYBE AFTER GRADUATION THERE'LL BE WEDDING BELLS! LUCKY YOU!
LET'S GO, CADANCE! MUSTN'T BE LATE FOR OUR FIRST PUBLIC APPEARANCE AS CANTERLOT'S NEWEST CELEBRITY COUPLE.
DITCH HIM THE FIRST CHANCE YOU GET.

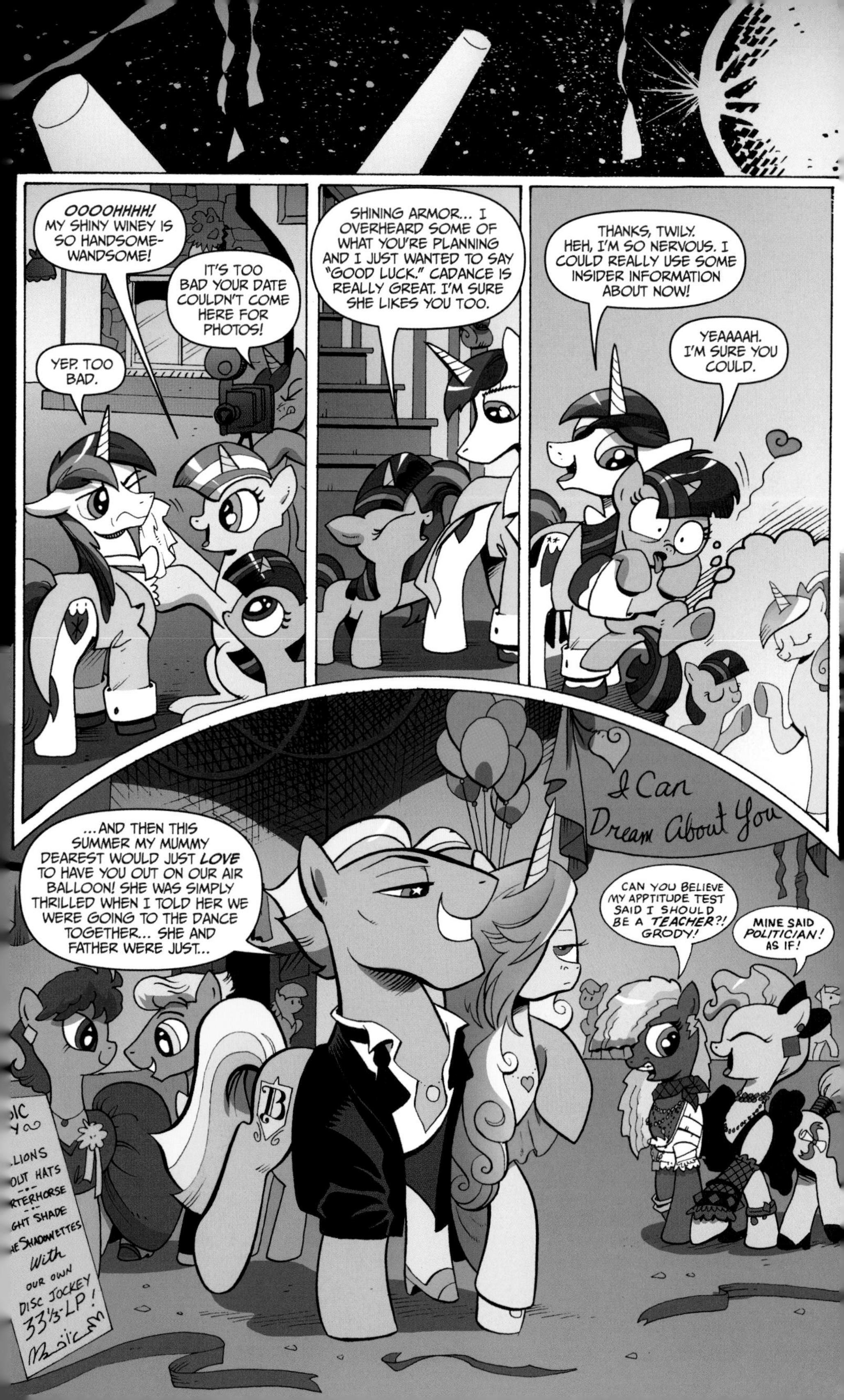
OOOOHHHH! MY SHINY WINEY IS SO HANDSOME-WANDSOME!
IT'S TOO BAD YOUR DATE COULDN'T COME HERE FOR PHOTOS!
YEP. TOO BAD.
SHINING ARMOR... I OVERHEARD SOME OF WHAT YOU'RE PLANNING AND I JUST WANTED TO SAY "GOOD LUCK." CADANCE IS REALLY GREAT. I'M SURE SHE LIKES YOU TOO.
THANKS, TWILY. HEH, I'M SO NERVOUS. I COULD REALLY USE SOME INSIDER INFORMATION ABOUT NOW!
YEAAAAH. I'M SURE YOU COULD.
I Can Dream About You
...AND THEN THIS SUMMER MY MUMMY DEAREST WOULD JUST LOVE TO HAVE YOU OUT ON OUR AIR BALLOON! SHE WAS SIMPLY THRILLED WHEN I TOLD HER WE WERE GOING TO THE DANCE TOGETHER... SHE AND FATHER WERE JUST...
CAN YOU BELIEVE MY APPTITUDE TEST SAID I SHOULD BE A TEACHER?! GRODY!
MINE SAID POLITICIAN! AS IF!
With
OUR OWN
DISC JOCKEY
33⅓-LP!

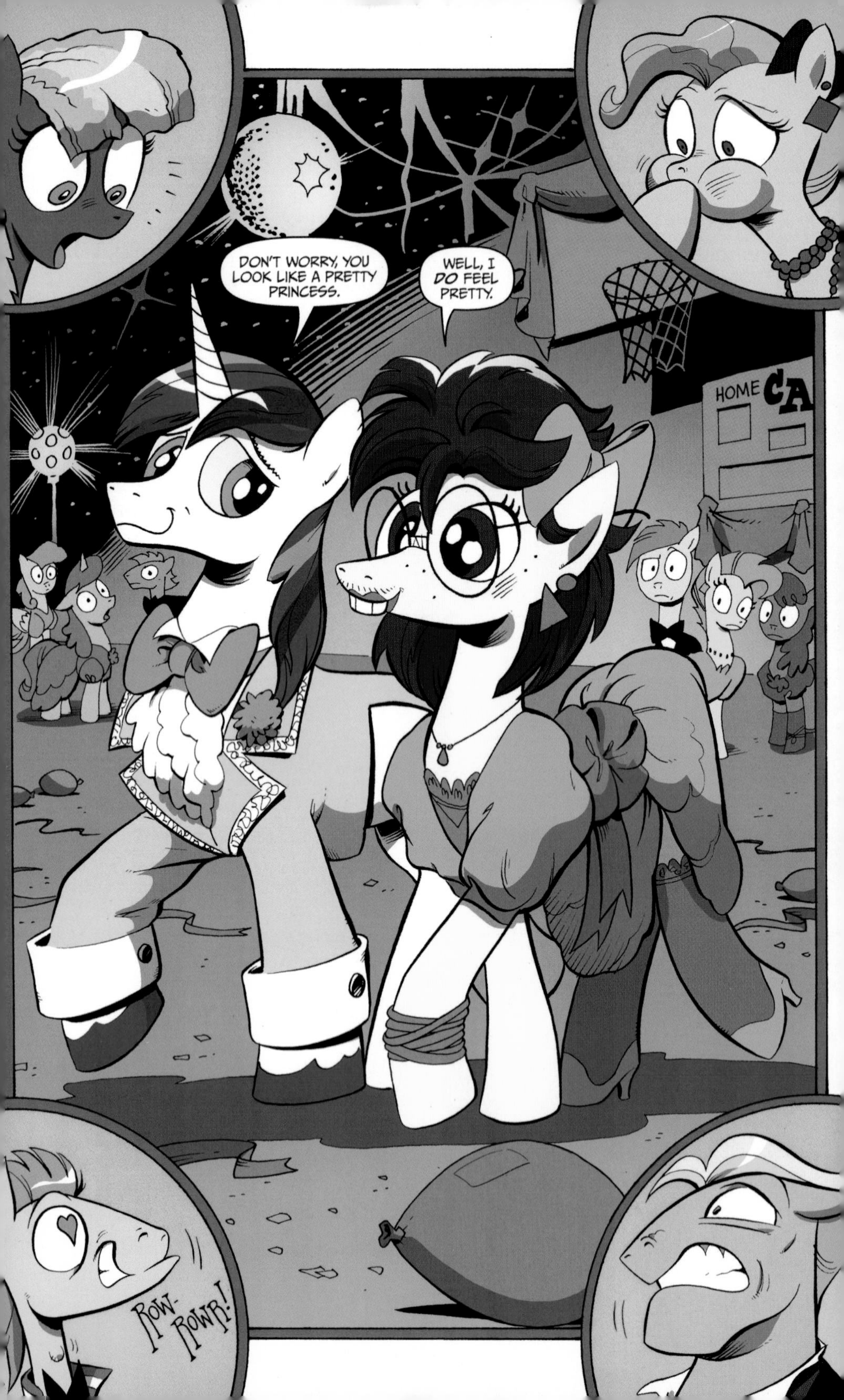
DON'T WORRY, YOU LOOK LIKE A PRETTY PRINCESS.
WELL, I DO FEEL PRETTY.
HOME CA
ROW-ROWR!

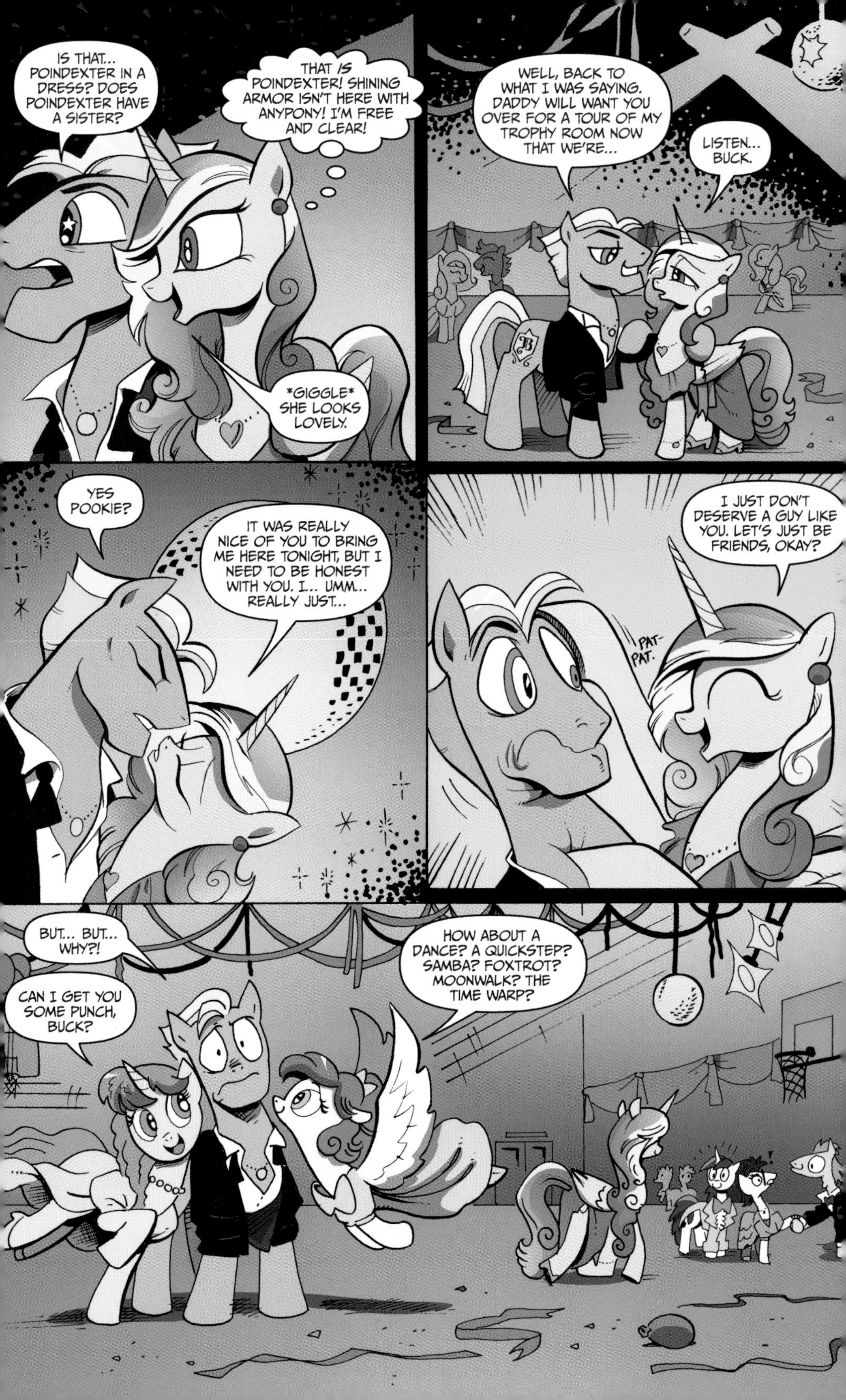
IS THAT... POINDEXTER IN A DRESS? DOES POINDEXTER HAVE A SISTER?
THAT IS POINDEXTER! SHINING ARMOR ISN'T HERE WITH ANYPONY! I'M FREE AND CLEAR!
GIGGLE SHE LOOKS LOVELY.
WELL, BACK TO WHAT I WAS SAYING. DADDY WILL WANT YOU OVER FOR A TOUR OF MY TROPHY ROOM NOW THAT WE'RE...
LISTEN... BUCK.
YES POOKIE?
IT WAS REALLY NICE OF YOU TO BRING ME HERE TONIGHT, BUT I NEED TO BE HONEST WITH YOU. I... UMM... REALLY JUST...
I JUST DON'T DESERVE A GUY LIKE YOU. LET'S JUST BE FRIENDS, OKAY?
PAT-PAT.
BUT... BUT... WHY?!
CAN I GET YOU SOME PUNCH, BUCK?
HOW ABOUT A DANCE? A QUICKSTEP? SAMBA? FOXTROT? MOONWALK? THE TIME WARP?

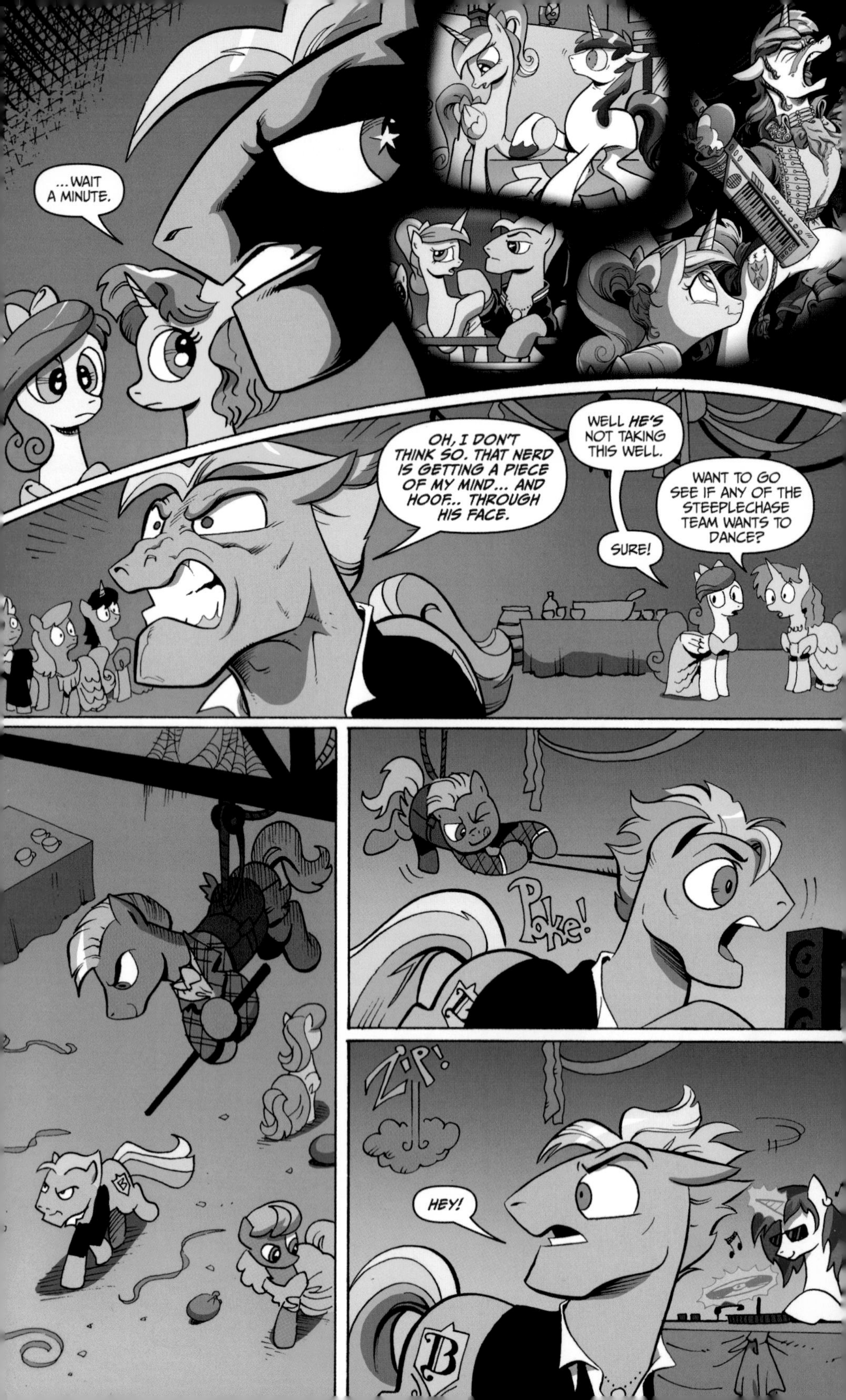
...WAIT A MINUTE.
OH, I DON'T THINK SO. THAT NERD IS GETTING A PIECE OF MY MIND... AND HOOF... THROUGH HIS FACE.
WELL HE'S NOT TAKING THIS WELL.
WANT TO GO SEE IF ANY OF THE STEEPLECHASE TEAM WANTS TO DANCE?
SURE!
Poke!
ZIP!
HEY!

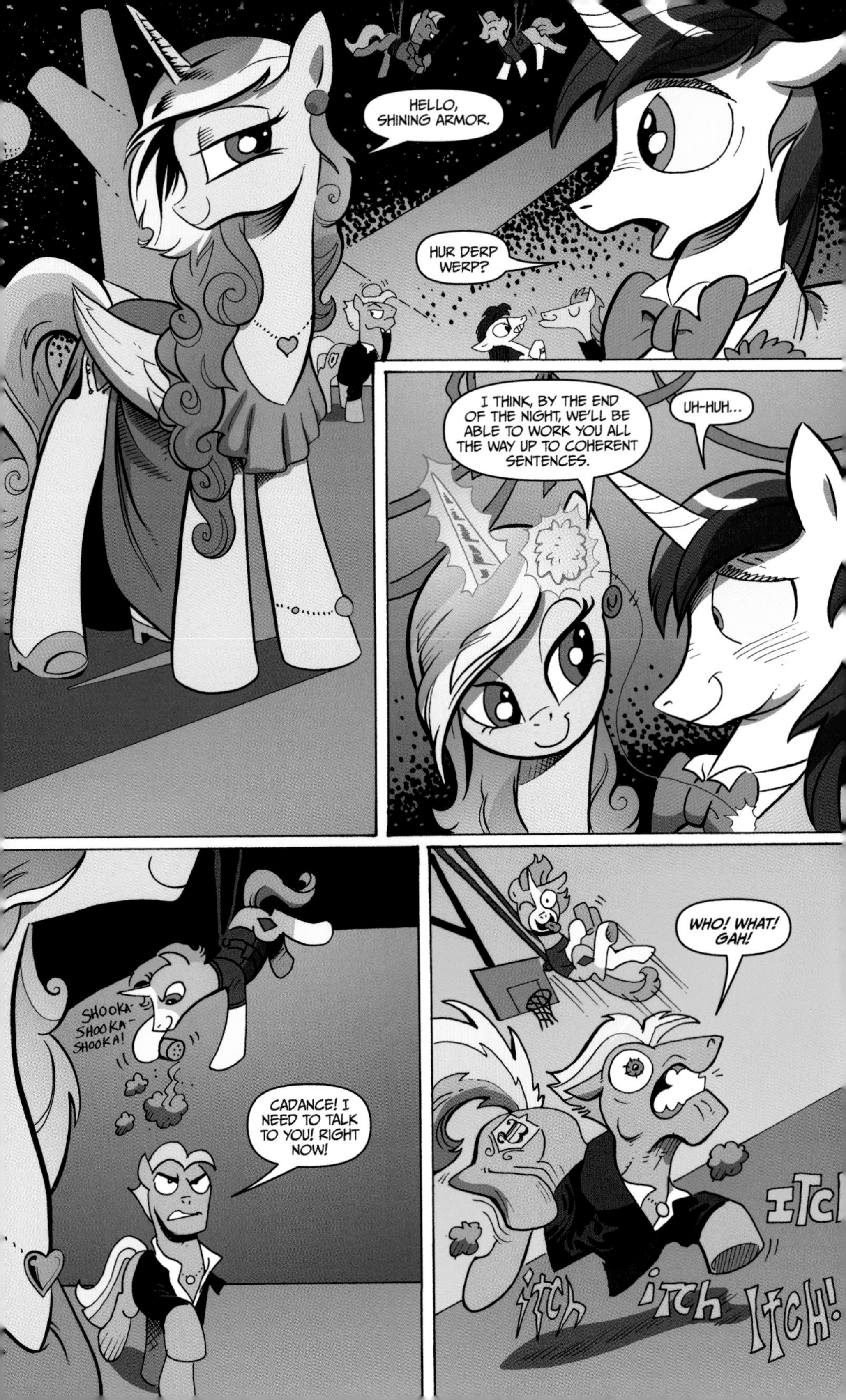
HELLO, SHINING ARMOR.
HUR DERP WERP?
I THINK, BY THE END OF THE NIGHT, WE'LL BE ABLE TO WORK YOU ALL THE WAY UP TO COHERENT SENTENCES.
UH-HUH...
SHOOKA-SHOOKA-SHOOKA!
CADANCE! I NEED TO TALK TO YOU! RIGHT NOW!
WHO! WHAT! GAH!
ITCH
ITCH
ITCH
ITCH!

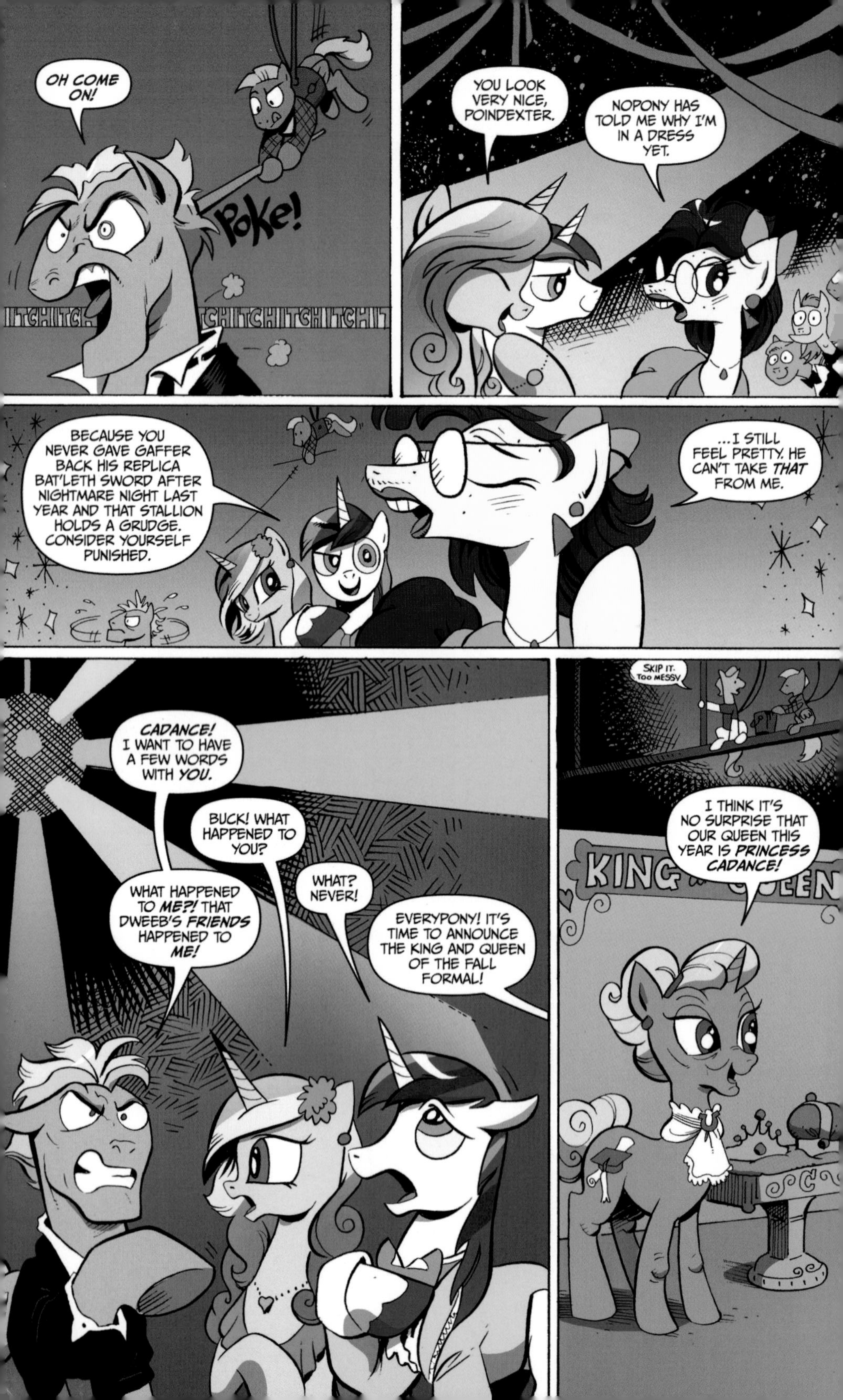

OH COME ON!
POKE!
ITCHITCH
CHITCHITCHITCHITCHIT
YOU LOOK VERY NICE, POINDEXTER.
NOPONY HAS TOLD ME WHY I'M IN A DRESS YET.
BECAUSE YOU NEVER GAVE GAFFER BACK HIS REPLICA BAT'LETH SWORD AFTER NIGHTMARE NIGHT LAST YEAR AND THAT STALLION HOLDS A GRUDGE. CONSIDER YOURSELF PUNISHED.
...I STILL FEEL PRETTY. HE CAN'T TAKE THAT FROM ME.
CADANCE! I WANT TO HAVE A FEW WORDS WITH YOU.
BUCK! WHAT HAPPENED TO YOU?
WHAT HAPPENED TO ME?! THAT DWEEB'S FRIENDS HAPPENED TO ME!
WHAT? NEVER!
EVERYPONY! IT'S TIME TO ANNOUNCE THE KING AND QUEEN OF THE FALL FORMAL!
SKIP IT. TOO MESSY
KING
I THINK IT'S NO SURPRISE THAT OUR QUEEN THIS YEAR IS PRINCESS CADANCE!

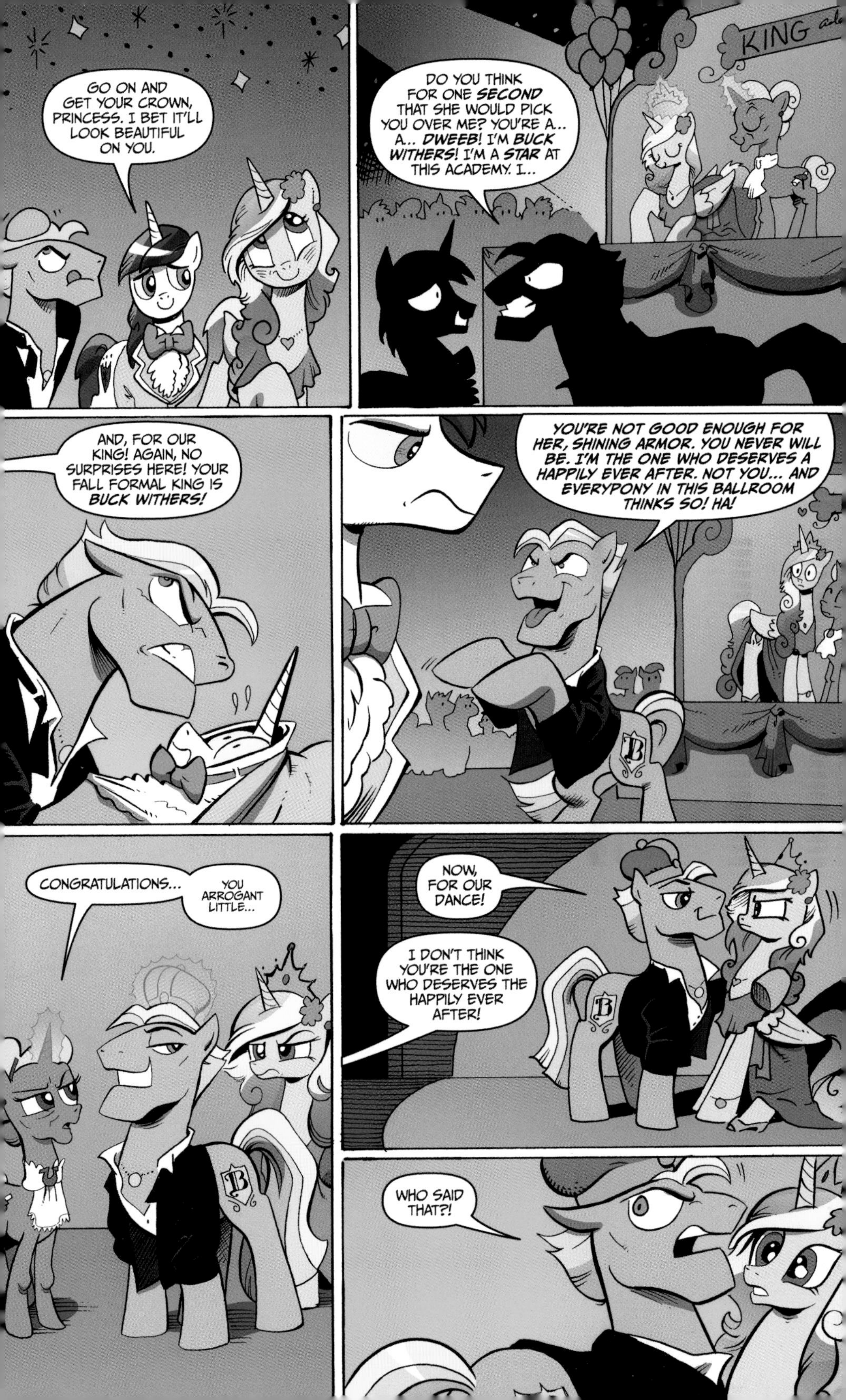
GO ON AND GET YOUR CROWN, PRINCESS. I BET IT'LL LOOK BEAUTIFUL ON YOU.
KING
DO YOU THINK FOR ONE SECOND THAT SHE WOULD PICK YOU OVER ME? YOU'RE A... A... DWEEB! I'M BUCK WITHERS! I'M A STAR AT THIS ACADEMY. I...
AND, FOR OUR KING! AGAIN, NO SURPRISES HERE! YOUR FALL FORMAL KING IS BUCK WITHERS!
YOU'RE NOT GOOD ENOUGH FOR HER, SHINING ARMOR. YOU NEVER WILL BE. I'M THE ONE WHO DESERVES A HAPPILY EVER AFTER. NOT YOU... AND EVERYPONY IN THIS BALLROOM THINKS SO! HA!
CONGRATULATIONS...
YOU ARROGANT LITTLE...
NOW, FOR OUR DANCE!
I DON'T THINK YOU'RE THE ONE WHO DESERVES THE HAPPILY EVER AFTER!
WHO SAID THAT?!

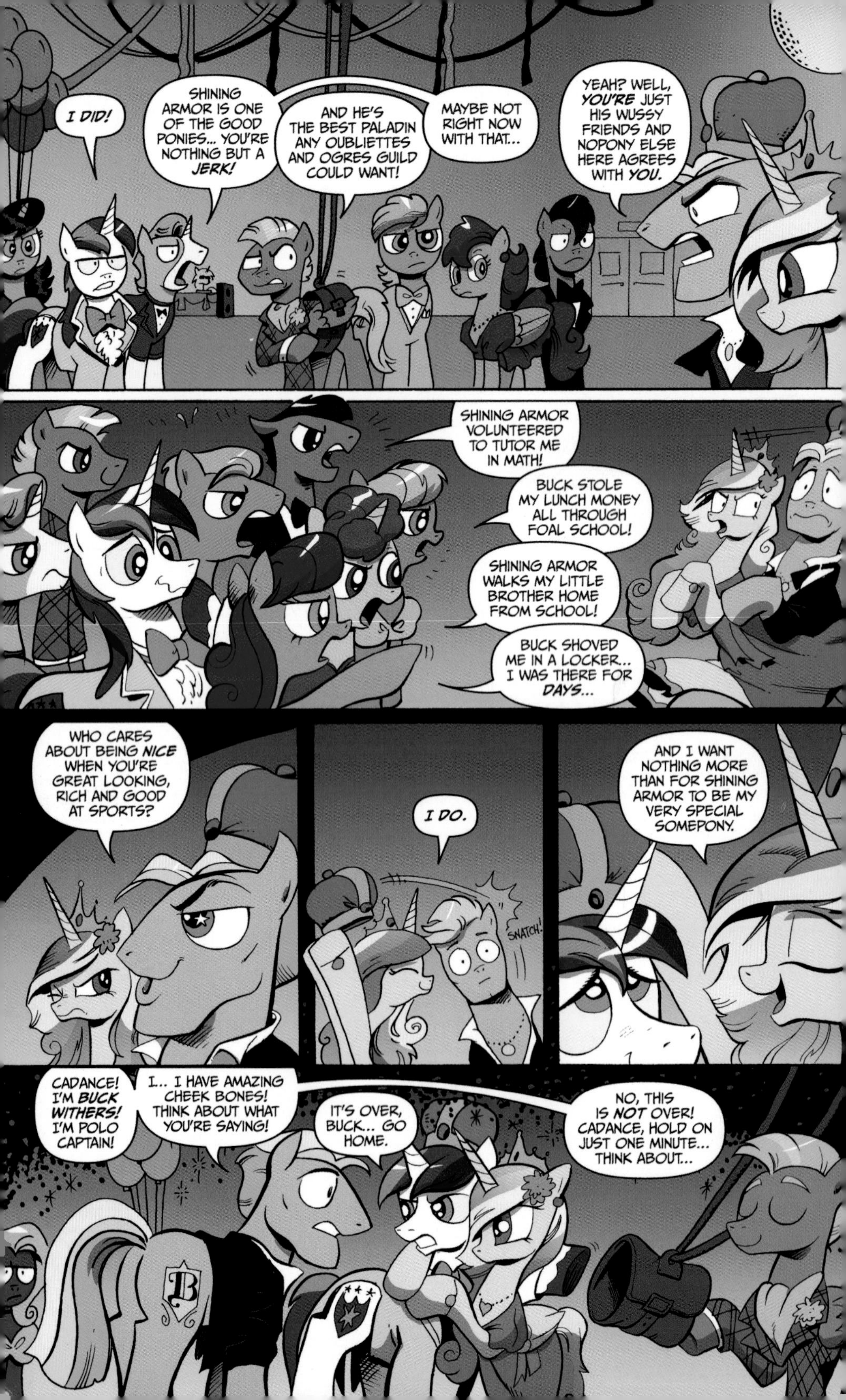
I DID!
SHINING ARMOR IS ONE OF THE GOOD PONIES... YOU'RE NOTHING BUT A JERK!
AND HE'S THE BEST PALADIN ANY OUBLIETTES AND OGRES GUILD COULD WANT!
MAYBE NOT RIGHT NOW WITH THAT...
YEAH? WELL, YOU'RE JUST HIS WUSSY FRIENDS AND NOPONY ELSE HERE AGREES WITH YOU.
SHINING ARMOR VOLUNTEERED TO TUTOR ME IN MATH!
BUCK STOLE MY LUNCH MONEY ALL THROUGH FOAL SCHOOL!
SHINING ARMOR WALKS MY LITTLE BROTHER HOME FROM SCHOOL!
BUCK SHOVED ME IN A LOCKER... I WAS THERE FOR DAYS...
WHO CARES ABOUT BEING NICE WHEN YOU'RE GREAT LOOKING, RICH AND GOOD AT SPORTS?
I DO.
SNATCH!
AND I WANT NOTHING MORE THAN FOR SHINING ARMOR TO BE MY VERY SPECIAL SOMEPONY.
CADANCE! I'M BUCK WITHERS! I'M POLO CAPTAIN!
I... I HAVE AMAZING CHEEK BONES! THINK ABOUT WHAT YOU'RE SAYING!
IT'S OVER, BUCK... GO HOME.
NO, THIS IS NOT OVER! CADANCE, HOLD ON JUST ONE MINUTE... THINK ABOUT...

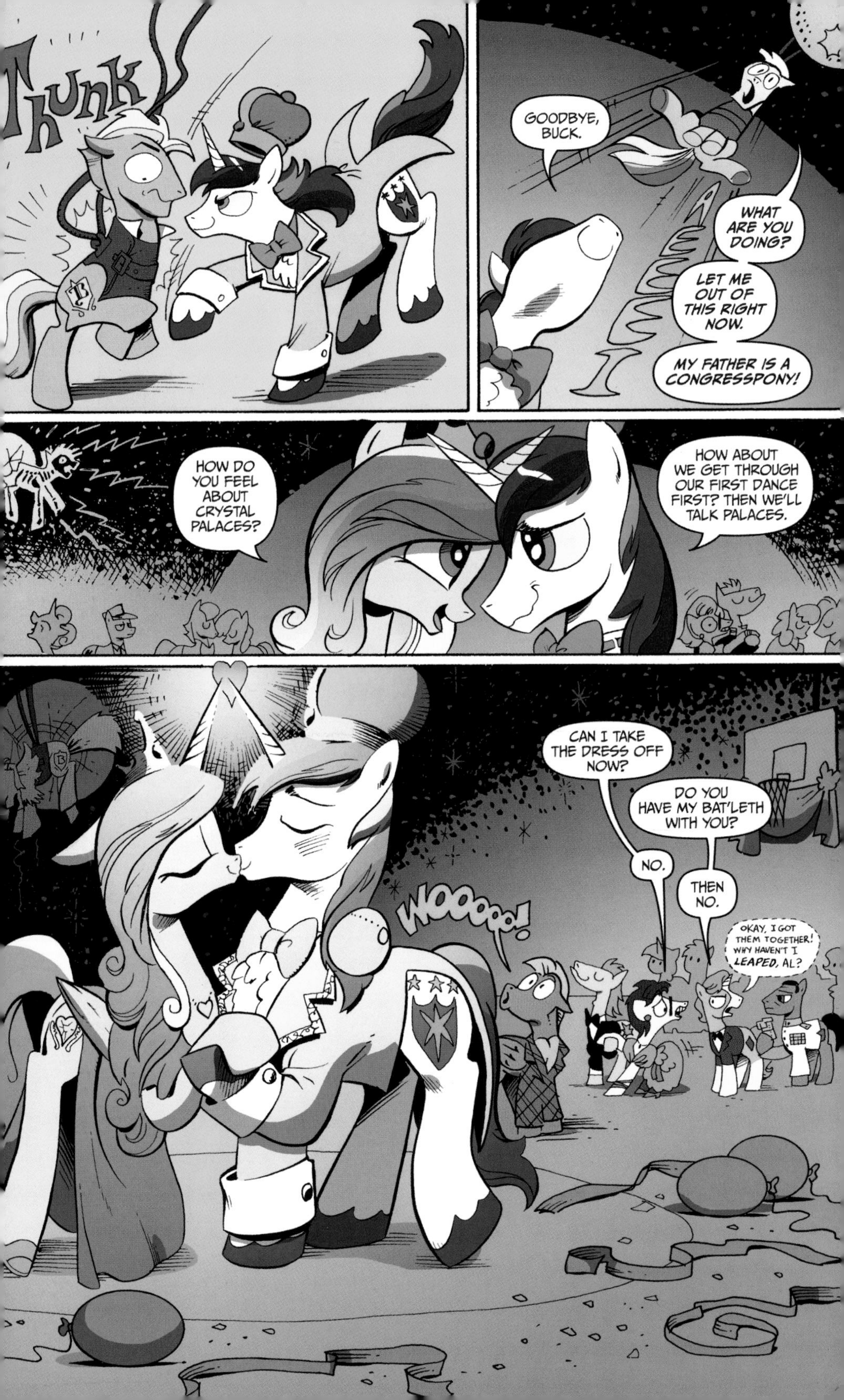
THUNK
GOODBYE, BUCK.
WHAT ARE YOU DOING?
LET ME OUT OF THIS RIGHT NOW.
MY FATHER IS A CONGRESSPONY!
HOW DO YOU FEEL ABOUT CRYSTAL PALACES?
HOW ABOUT WE GET THROUGH OUR FIRST DANCE FIRST? THEN WE'LL TALK PALACES.
CAN I TAKE THE DRESS OFF NOW?
DO YOU HAVE MY BAT'LETH WITH YOU?
NO.
THEN NO.
WOOOoo!
OKAY, I GOT THEM TOGETHER! WHY HAVEN'T I LEAPED, AL?

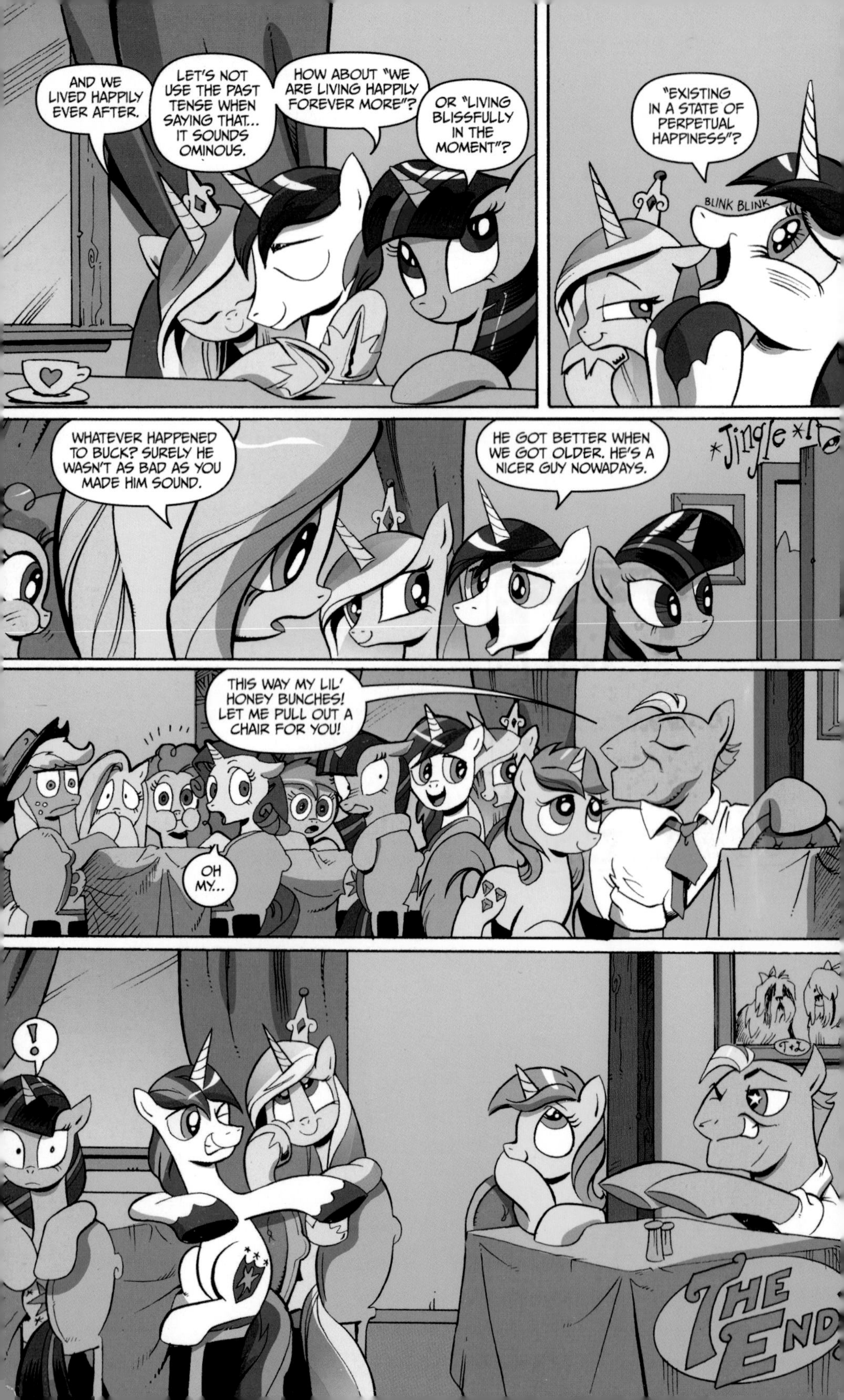
AND WE LIVED HAPPILY EVER AFTER.
LET'S NOT USE THE PAST TENSE WHEN SAYING THAT... IT SOUNDS OMINOUS.
HOW ABOUT "WE ARE LIVING HAPPILY FOREVER MORE"?
OR "LIVING BLISSFULLY IN THE MOMENT"?
"EXISTING IN A STATE OF PERPETUAL HAPPINESS"?
BLINK BLINK
WHATEVER HAPPENED TO BUCK? SURELY HE WASN'T AS BAD AS YOU MADE HIM SOUND.
HE GOT BETTER WHEN WE GOT OLDER. HE'S A NICER GUY NOWADAYS.
Jingle
THIS WAY MY LIL' HONEY BUNCHES! LET ME PULL OUT A CHAIR FOR YOU!
OH MY...
!
THE END